Secrets

Volumes 7 and 8

The Best in Women's Sensual Fiction

Volumes 7 and 8
The Best in Women's Sensual Fiction

Red Sage Publishing

SECRETS VOLUMES 7 AND 8
The Best in Women's Sensual Fiction

Red Sage Publishing, Inc.
P.O. Box 4844
Seminole, FL 33775
727-391-3847

SECRETS Volume 7
A Red Sage Publishing book
All Rights Reserved/December 2001
Copyright © 2001 by Red Sage Publishing, Inc.

SECRETS Volume 8

A Red Sage Publishing book
All Rights Reserved/December 2002
Copyright © 2002 by Red Sage Publishing, Inc.

ISBN 0-7394-3236-2

Contents

Secrets

Volume 7

The Best in Women's Sensual Fiction

Amelia's Innocence

by Julia Welles

To My Reader:
Step back in time with me to an age of tall ships and high adventure. Watch closely as a maiden boards a ship by dark of night—a maiden whose future was just bartered away in a reckless game of chance. Learn her fate as we set sail aboard the *Soul-Catcher*.

Chapter One

Still fully clothed despite the approach of dawn, Captain Quentin Hawke reclined on his bed and eased his pounding head onto the pillow. After a night of hard drinking and revelry, he was mortally glad to be back aboard the *Soul-Catcher*, where he could finally close his eyes and—

"Devil take you all, stan' aside or I'll run y'through!"

The bellowed threat, issuing from the far side of his closed door, was whiskey-slurred, making up in volume for what it lacked in clarity. With a groan, Hawke recognized the voice. It was that idiot from the tavern, the drunken blacksmith who'd lost game after game to him at cards. How had the sot managed to stagger as far as the docks? It was a mystery to Hawke, since the man had downed three gulps of whiskey for each one Hawke consumed.

The sounds of a tussle ensued, with much banging and swearing in the narrow companionway.

Hawke scowled. How could he sleep with such a set-to going on outside his door? "Henderson!" he shouted, never doubting that the first mate would be just outside, guarding his cabin with the loyal ferocity of a mastiff. "Get yourself in here!"

The door opened to admit the little man, wearing the tidy vest that had long since become his trademark aboard the ship. Closing the door, he stood with his back pressed to it, for good measure and said, "Sorry, Captain. There's a Mr. Fletcher outside, come from the town, demanding to see you."

"So I hear. How did he get aboard?"

"Slykin let him through, sir."

"Slykin. No surprise there. I should have dismissed him from the crew in Portland, when I had the chance."

"Aye, sir. But in the meantime, he's let Mr. Fletcher aboard, and Mr. Fletcher claims he owes you a gambling debt from tonight's gaming. He seems dead set on paying up."

At the memory, Hawke frowned. "It was nothing. A piece of drunken nonsense. Tell him to go home and forget the whole—"

In the corridor, a woman cried out sharply.

Hawke sat up with a jolt that hurt his head. "What the devil—?"

"He's brought a girl with him, sir."

"And the men assume that gives them license to behave like animals? No one harms a woman aboard a ship of mine. Get back out there, Henderson. Tell the crew—"

"Oh, it's not our men hurting her, sir. It's Mr. Fletcher."

The girl cried out again.

Hawke surged to his feet. "Then you'd damn well better bring her *and* Fletcher in here to me. Now. And I want you to stay, as well."

"Aye, Captain," came the calm reply, and Henderson slipped into the corridor.

The noise level outside the door dropped immediately. Wishing he had stuck to ale, Hawke took a seat behind the chart table and waited for Henderson to herd the newcomers inside.

They entered a moment later. Fletcher, a burly man still red-faced with drink, pulled out of Henderson's grip and staggered forward until he collided with the table's edge. "Eh, Cap'n, there y'are," he said with a lopsided grin. "I told those stupid louts you'd want t'see me. Brung my daughter to you like I promised, see if I didn'. Ain't she a treat, though? Innocent as the day is long, and twice as lovely."

Fletcher was a blacksmith, with a blacksmith's muscles. By contrast, the honey-haired girl he hauled along beside him was slender, built with the spare elegance of ship's rigging before the sails were hauled aloft.

Her father's features were coarse, but young Miss Fletcher had a dainty nose and a tidy chin, while her dove-gray eyes and rosebud mouth, to Hawke's pleasure, were constructed on a more generous scale. She was a pretty thing, neat as a ship's cat, and although her clothes were shabby, they were scrupulously clean. She looked fresh-scrubbed, as well, except for a smudge on her cheek and another just above the modest neckline of her gown.

Standing no taller than her father's sweaty armpit, she looked now from Fletcher to Hawke, her expression one of bewilderment. She opened her mouth as if to speak, then closed it again, her shapely lips thinning to a fine line of pain as her father tightened his grip on her wrist.

Sickened and angry, Hawk said, "Let go of her, Fletcher."

"Certainly, Cap'n." The man took his beefy hand away immediately, allowing the girl to stand free. "Whatever y'please. She's yours to direct. And when you've seen t'your business, Amelia and me'll be on our way." He managed an exaggerated wink. "I'll jus' wait out there." And he stumbled toward the door.

At a nod from Hawke, Henderson followed the blacksmith out, leaving the captain to deal with the girl alone.

"I'm very sorry for the intrusion, sir," she said, and smoothed the skirt of her gown with a jerky stroke of her palms. "If you could just tell me what this is about . . . ?"

Her voice was soft, and a faint scent of lavender whispered through the air that separated Hawke from where she stood. Her hands were clean but rough, her only adornment the bracelet of bruises imprinted on her right wrist by her father's punishing grip. Her waist was small enough for Hawke to span easily with his hands, while the generous curve of her gown's drab bodice hinted richly at hidden treasures.

When had he last enjoyed a woman's company? His inability to look away from the promising rise of the girl's modestly covered bosom told him that it had been entirely too long. Ah well. Three more days and the *Soul-Catcher* would reach home port, where any number of ladies would be glad of his favors, eager to shed their laces and lacings in order to ease a man's needs.

Lord knew, he had needs.

"My father drinks," the girl said bluntly, breaking into his heated reverie. "When he drinks, he gambles. And when he gambles, he loses. What was tonight's bet, Captain? Am I here to clean your cabin? Mend your shirts? Cook a meal for you?"

Hawke considered how best to reply.

"You're embarrassed," she continued. "I understand. He embarrasses me, as well. But I'm not afraid of work, and I'm stronger than I look. Tell me the terms of the wager and I'll make good on it, right now. I know the hour is late, but it's the only way he'll give me a moment's peace, with the drink still on him. Just tell me plainly, Captain. What service of mine did you win from my father?"

After careful deliberation, Hawke decided that no genteel answer to that question was possible. "I won the right to claim your maidenhead, Miss Fletcher."

The words hung between them like acrid smoke. As he watched, her calm façade fell away, leaving her looking white and shaken and very, very young. "Surely not," she said, but her voice had thinned to a whisper, and it was clear from her stark expression that she did not doubt his words.

Hawke let the silence ride, curious to see what she would propose now that she knew the stakes. Despite her brave talk of making good on her father's wager, she didn't look the type to fall back merrily on his bunk and lift her skirts for him to have his wicked way with her.

A pity, that.

Hawke studied her with new interest. Her daintiness appealed to him, as did her cleanliness. There'd be no pox to worry about with a maiden such as this. Moreover, a man would feel powerful, coupled with such a wisp of a thing. It stirred him to imagine unpinning that golden hair to tumble about her shoulders before stripping off her dowdy dress and freeing the generous breasts trapped within it. He thought about tight pink nipples and high, firm orbs of moon-white flesh filling his eager palms, and suddenly his trousers were too snug for comfort.

Despite her father's generally untrustworthy air, Hawke tended to believe that she truly was a virgin. Girls who knew their way about a man's bed tended to have a certain air about them, an air that this young woman clearly lacked. Generally speaking, he preferred the enthusiasm of a well-tempered lover to the timid skittishness of a maiden, but this girl's fragile beauty aroused his hunger for the unexplored territory beneath her skirts.

He had not claimed a maidenhead since the earliest days of his own green youth, and he smiled ruefully at the memory of his ignorant urgency the first time he had stretched himself between a pair of shapely legs and used his avid cock to force a passage to paradise.

As he recalled, it had been a less than glorious experience for his young partner. But he was no longer that fumbling boy. If another virgin made her way into his bed, he would see to it that they traded joy for joy. The women he bedded called him a generous lover, and it was a reputation he valued. There was enough pain in the world, by God. Why should any man take pride in adding to it?

At that thought, the marks of violence on young Miss Fletcher's wrist drew his eye again, affronting his sensibilities. Remembering the disregard her father had shown for her suffering, Hawke looked again to her neck and cheek, and saw that the dark marks he had noticed were not really 'smudges' at all.

A sick certainty filled him. "You're bruised," he stated.

She shrugged. "No matter."

"Why should it be no matter? Because you deserve to be treated in such a way? Or because you have known far worse at your father's hands? Tell me, Miss Fletcher, does he beat you often?"

She eyed Hawke warily. "I never said he beat me."

"Ah, but I know his kind. Let us be plain with one another. Do you deny that he beats you?"

He watched her struggle between caution and honesty. In the end, she said simply, "No. I do not deny it."

Hawke was not surprised, for he did indeed know Fletcher's kind all too well. A man like that was too sly to beat a woman with his fists, unless he was lost in a haze of liquor. More likely she had known a pinch here, a bruising grip there, building to the bite of a willow switch if her father found one handy, or his belt if he did not.

"So the village blacksmith is not only a drunk but a bully," Hawke observed with contempt. Driven by his own demons, he asked, "Where does he whip you, when he sets his belt to whistling?"

The girl eyed him coolly. "At home, mostly."

He was hard pressed not to smile in grim amusement at her intentional evasion. Still, he could not decide on a course of action until he had heard more of the truth from her.

Hawke sat forward in his chair. "I see a fading bruise on your cheek. Does he often strike your face?"

"No, sir. That would show, and people would talk. Not good for business, you know."

"Ah. A bully *and* a coward. Well, then, Miss Fletcher, how does he vent his wrath?"

"When I was young, he would strike the palms of my hands, but he has not done that in years."

"Likely it seems too tame to him. What does it take, now, to slake his fury? Does he whip you through your clothing?"

"No." Her mouth twisted as if she had bitten down on something sour. "He says he needs to see the stripes he's laid, to know he's done a proper job." She bridled, her color high. "And that is the last I have to say about the matter, sir. Indeed, I do not know why I have gone this far to satisfy your prying curiosity."

Touched by her defiance, Hawke steeled himself against the kinship he felt for her. "Nevertheless, I have one question more, Miss Fletcher. Has your father forced himself upon you and taken his pleasure in your body?"

"No!" she said, so fiercely that he knew it must be true. Then, in a scalded whisper, she added, "Not yet."

His heartbeats were heavy and slow, like the tolling of a bell. "But you fear he may, someday, when the drink is on him."

She winced from his statement as if he had struck her with a willow switch. Then, slowly, she nodded.

Her innocence, of body and of spirit, mattered more to Hawke in that moment than he could easily explain. As much as he burned to possess her, he yearned even more strongly to protect her.

Without regret, he resolved to sever her from her past.

"Understand clearly what you face, Miss Fletcher. Your father brought you here tonight expressly for the purpose of allowing me to deflower you. He thinks I am joining with you this very minute, forcing my body into yours regardless of your wishes. When he wakes tomorrow morning, will he be ashamed that he bartered his daughter's chastity as if it were a penny trifle?"

"He is always ashamed when he wakes," she answered, looking old beyond her years. "Then he rises, and drowns his shame in a bottle, and the nightmare begins again."

"That has been so in the past," Hawke persisted, "but perhaps you believe, this time, that his repentance will last."

"No, sir. I know that it will not. Tonight is a time for truths, however hard. And the truth is that I cannot change him."

"I agree," Hawke said, impressed by her courage. "Indeed, now that your father has wagered you once, I fear he will find it easier to silence his conscience the next time. In his heart he has already traded your purity away. If I excuse you from this debt and allow him to drag you from my ship, I predict that you will find yourself dealt into some other man's bed before the month is out. That thought does not please me in any way, and I doubt it pleases you, either."

"There is a way to prevent it, if you are willing," she said, hope animating her thin face. "You could take me with you when you sail, but leave me chaste."

Startled by the audacity of her proposal, Hawke laughed. "Have you money for your fare?"

"Not a penny," she confessed. "But there is such a thing in this world as Christian charity, is there not, Captain Hawke?"

He stretched slowly, aware that he had her full attention. "Unfortunately for you, Miss Fletcher, I am no Christian. Nor am I feeling quite that charitable."

"Then I could work my passage honorably," she offered, "by cooking for you."

"We already have an excellent cook aboard the *Soul-Catcher*."

"Then I could tend your cabin and care for your belongings."

"Those needs are already being quite well met. You would be surprised what a fine seam Henderson can sew."

"Then what?" she demanded, panic flaring in her eyes. "There has to be a way, for I tell you plainly that I must leave this place tonight."

"There is a way," he said, parroting her own words back at her, "if you are willing, for I have one mighty need that the crew cannot fill. Claim that position as your own and you shall have my fiercest protection."

Shock and distress had turned her cheeks ashen. "Warm your bed, you mean?" she demanded, as if the words choked her.

"Warm my body, and allow me to warm yours in a variety of delightful ways."

She swayed, and pressed her hand to the table's edge in order to steady herself. "Everyone would think I was your whore!"

"Who is 'everyone' and why should you concern yourself with their uninformed opinions? If you leave here with me, do you ever intend to return to this place?"

"No, of course not. How big a fool do you take me for? But that doesn't mean I have no morals or standards. What you are asking of me is a shameful thing!"

Hawke spread his hands. "I see no shame in it. But if you do, then by all means you should leave. You are entirely free to do so. I will not detain you."

Her eyes narrowed. "Do not mock me, Captain Hawke. You know full well that I would leave here if I could. But if I step into that corridor and you do not intervene on my behalf, my father will reclaim me."

"A truth," he acknowledged with an air of calm.

"So it is your advice that I should stay aboard and trade my former position of servitude for a new one?"

Hawke managed a wounded look, although he was beginning to thoroughly enjoy the turn this conversation had taken. "Indeed not. You insult me by suggesting it. Have I not just told you that I have crew aplenty to cook my meals and mend my clothes and scour the decks of this fine ship? What I offer to you is a position of privilege, not servitude. You need not scrub my sheets. You need only disport with me between them." He allowed himself a smile. "I promise you, you would find it no great hardship."

"Easily said."

"Easily proven."

"But if time proved you wrong, I would be left with no remedy. My virginal state, once lost, cannot be reclaimed."

"Well, then, I make you an offer. When I leave on the next tide,

Soul-Catcher faces a three-day journey to her home port. Sail with me, and for those three days be mine in all things . . . except the claiming of your maidenhead. In return, when we dock, I shall escort you ashore with money enough to buy a month's keep at a decent inn. A girl as hard-working as you claim to be can surely find a respectable position for herself within a month's time."

"I know that I could. But can I trust you, sir?"

"More than you can trust your father."

"You swear I will leave your ship unviolated?"

"You shall leave the *Soul-Catcher* with your maidenhead unbroken. But I intend to make free of your body in every other way that pleases me. If you refuse my attentions during the voyage, you will have broken our agreement and I will have the right to claim you fully."

Her brow furrowed prettily as she debated his offer. "So I must permit you to kiss me . . . ?"

He shook his head impatiently. "Understand me, Miss Fletcher. If you accept my offer, you must permit me to rid you of your clothing. To stroke your naked body. To kiss your mouth, and suckle your breasts and fondle you between your legs. There is no part of you that I will not be free to touch, and no part of me that you will refuse to caress at my command. I intend for these three days to teach you a great deal about the pleasure a man and woman can find together. By the time we reach port and you descend the *Soul-Catcher*'s gangplank, you will be a far better educated maiden than you are tonight. But a maiden you still shall be."

He could see that she was shocked anew by his plain speaking, nearly as shocked as she was desperate. His conscience winced, but it was a small wince. Her future husband—and Hawke had no doubt that there would be a husband in such a sweet morsel's future—would take a virgin bride to the marriage bed. That fortunate man should thank him for the tutoring she was about to receive, Hawke decided virtuously.

"And if I am not?" the girl asked, rallying with a visible effort. "What if you lose control and rob me of my virginity? What do you stand to lose in such a case, Captain? It is a poor wager where only one side sets anything at risk."

"True enough," he conceded, "although I have no intention of losing my control or this bet. Still, if your virginity should be taken, what penalty would you demand?"

Her chin lifted proudly. "That you then make an honest woman of me by wedding me in a proper church on the day we dock."

"Fegs, woman!" he exclaimed, startled by her courage. Shocked she might be, even desperate, but there was a good brain behind those limpid gray eyes, and the girl was negotiating the best possible terms for herself, even with her back to the wall. She was spirited, and would likely bring that same bold spirit to bed.

The thought tightened his crotch and made his palms itch.

She tilted her head, eyeing him warily, as if she sensed his appetite's increase. "Of course, you may already have a wife. Do you, Captain Hawke?"

"No, nor do I intend to acquire one."

"It seems to me, then, if you do not wish to marry, that you need only make certain that I leave your ship a virgin. Do we have an understanding?"

He admired her pluck . . . and a great deal else about her, as well. Allowing his gaze to caress her body while his imagination caught fire, Hawke savored the sight of her. There was a woman's ripe body hidden away beneath all that clothing, and he was eager for the sight of it. He longed to discard her drab dress and peel away her stays, to untie the modest pantalettes and send them tumbling to the floor. Thus revealed, her flesh would be pale and pearly, as untouched by the sun as it was by a lover's hands. He would be the first to explore her treasures, to woo her toward the brink of passionate surrender, to part her thighs and place his lips—

"Do we have an understanding?" she persisted.

Shaken from his fantasies, Hawke snatched a breath and met her gaze, allowing her a glimpse of the hunger her presence had ignited. "An odd one, to be sure. But yes. We have an understanding."

"Very well then. I am in your hands, good sir."

"No," he replied, smiling in heated anticipation, "but you soon will be."

Chapter Two

With the deal struck, Amelia was astonished by how quickly things progressed. The ship captain summoned his first mate and dispatched a series of orders, assigning men to remove her father from the ship, specifying that he was not to be harmed, directing the sailors to escort him home and stay with him until he was well-launched upon his drunken slumbers.

The first mate acknowledged the instructions and departed, leaving Amelia alone with the captain.

She eyed him nervously. He was a big man, not burly like her father but broad-shouldered in a way that bespoke strength and endurance. His hair was dark and somewhat longer than the fashion, while his eyes were smoky blue beneath raven brows. His hands, resting on the table before him, were the hands of a working seaman, not a pampered commander of men.

He stood up, and Amelia swallowed nervously, surprised by his towering height. His hair brushed the ceiling of the cabin, giving him the look of a wild creature confined within too small a cage. "That," he said, pointing, "is our bed."

She looked where he directed. The bed in question was wider than the meager cot on which she slept at home, but it was clearly meant to accommodate a single body.

"I do not wish to sleep on the floor," he said, "nor do I wish for you to do so. Two bodies provide more heat than one, even when their repose is chaste."

She nodded at this truth and started forward, marginally reassured by his reference to chastity.

"Undress first," he said.

She could feel her cheeks reddening. "I will be warmer in my clothes."

"I will keep you quite warm enough. Undress. To the skin."

It was beginning, the battle of wits and wills she had undertaken. She remembered his shocking words: *You must permit me to rid you of your clothing. To stroke your naked body. To kiss your mouth, and suckle your breasts and fondle you between your . . .*

His laugh cut through her thoughts. "Be at peace, woman. I've consumed a skinful of drink since sundown and my head feels larger than a melon. Your education can begin tomorrow. For tonight, my wants are simple—to sleep and to be warmed by you while I do so." As if to prove his point, he yawned cavernously, then said, "As I see it, your choices are three." He held up a single finger. "You can go and re-join your father, while he and my men are still near." A second finger joined the first. "You can undress yourself and climb between those sheets, which I assure you were laundered less than a week ago, thanks to Henderson's exaggerated penchant for cleanliness. Or—" He lofted a third finger. "—I can remove your clothing for you. If there is an-other choice open to you, it escapes me. I suggest you make your se-lection without further delay or I will choose for you."

Put like that, her course was clear. Turning her back to him, she undressed with swift efficiency and scuttled beneath the covers, breathless with embarrassment and anxiety. But Hawke only bent, blew out the lantern and, after a muted rustling that hinted at the re-moval of his own clothes, joined her.

It was impossible to keep her body separate from his. Even when she turned on her side at the far edge of the mattress, the warm flesh of his thigh grazed her bottom. She recoiled, and nearly fell out onto the floor.

At that, he hooked a lazy arm over her and drew her more securely onto the mattress, shifting his own position until they lay nested like spoons in a drawer, the length of him radiating a beguiling heat.

She was unused to the intimacy of sharing her bed with another human being. It made her inescapably aware of Hawke's size, of the subtle difference between the texture of his skin and her own, and of the presence of his long arm encircling her. Moreover, she could feel the press of his flesh, hot and hard, against the curve of her bare bot-tom, motionless but undeniable. Inescapable.

An hour ago, she had not even known this man existed. By any de-cent standards, her situation was beyond scandalous. She should have found her presence in Captain Hawke's bed terrifying, or at least op-pressive. Instead, slowly, despite herself, Amelia began to relax. Some might say she was sharing the devil's bed, in mortal danger of defilement, but for the first time all night, she was warm. And, oddly, for the first time in far too long a time, she felt safe.

She was nervous, of course, about what Hawke intended to do with her when the new day dawned, but she couldn't prevent an excited shiver of anticipation in that regard, as well. She was a passenger upon his ship, a resident of his cabin, a companion in his bed. Whatever liberties he took, she would have little choice but to accept his attentions.

Acceptance, however, suddenly did not seem so horrible a concept. She sensed already that he would not willingly frighten or harm her. Indeed, for tonight, he seemed content simply to sleep in this warm, dry bed, and to allow her to do the same, far away from the threatening presence of her father. And tomorrow. . . . She closed her eyes. She would deal with tomorrow when it dawned.

Hawke's encircling arm grew heavier, and his breathing slowed.

Amelia waited, long accustomed to her father's ear-splitting snores. But no such noisy assault issued from Hawke's mouth. Instead, he sank into sleep silently, like a broken ship slipping beneath the waves. And in time, exhausted, so did she.

Waking long past dawn, cozy in a cocoon of blankets, rocked by the gentle, rhythmic hand of the tide, Amelia came to a series of realizations.

She was hungry.

She was at sea.

She was entirely naked.

That final thought forced her eyelids apart. A quick glance assured her that she was alone in Captain Hawke's cabin; a slower one told her that the cabin, tidily kept and sparsely furnished, revealed no sight at all of her clothing. It also revealed a mug and a covered tray on the nearby table.

Amelia inhaled slowly, assessing the air, and detected a faint but savory aroma that caused her empty insides to stir.

Food and drink.

Unfortunately, the mug and tray were on the table, she was on the bed, and her clothes were precisely nowhere.

She didn't permit it to trouble her for long. Draped in a blanket, she hurried to the table and removed the cover from the tray, revealing a biscuit, two rashers of bacon, and a bowl of oatmeal from which steam still rose in a languid curl. The mug proved to hold apple cider.

Not just food and drink. Heaven.

* * *

Hawke leaned on the forward rail, watching the antics of the gulls while he contemplated the day ahead.

He had already made it clear to Henderson that the three-day voyage that lay before them was a perfect opportunity for the young seaman to show his mettle. Hawke would stand down unless a true emergency arose, allowing his first mate to try his hand at truly mastering the *Soul-Catcher* as she beat her way south along the coast. Henderson had received the news with gratitude, clearly eager for the test.

Hawke was eager, himself. It had been nothing short of extraordinary to wake this morning from a whiskey fog to find Miss Amelia Fletcher asleep in the curve of his body like a ship's cat in a rope coil. He had been sorely tempted to end his body's current plague of abstinence, then and there.

But that would mean he had to wed her, and he did not intend to wed. Not Amelia Fletcher. Not any woman. Not now. Not ever. Whatever else he might do for good or ill in his lifetime, he would not risk repeating his father's mistakes.

So resolved, he had risen from the bed and tucked the blankets snug about her instead, marveling when she slept on, undisturbed. Fletcher struck him as the kind of man who would not hesitate to demand a full day's work from his daughter. No doubt Amelia had earned her rest. Besides, Hawke liked his partners bright-eyed and alert.

With that in mind, he had waited another hour before securing a breakfast for her and returning to his cabin. When he opened the door, she was just as he had left her, her features still lax with slumber. Quietly, he entered. Quietly, he set the mug and tray on the chart table. Quietly, he returned to the companionway.

Then, with a firm hand, he'd closed the cabin door, relying on the thud to rouse her.

It had taken discipline to wait on deck for a long enough interval to allow her to dine in peace, but discipline was a necessary weapon in any captain's arsenal. Judiciously applied, it nearly always bore fruit.

He was ready to begin that harvest now.

Hawke looked about for Henderson, but the figure his gaze lit upon instead was Slykin, loitering idly by the mast. Hawke strode toward him, intent on exacting retribution for last night's dereliction of duty.

"Mister Slykin," he barked, with an edge to his voice that made every sailor in earshot straighten.

Slykin turned to stare at him insolently. "Cap'n?"

"Last night, you failed to bar that drunken blacksmith from boarding. Have you anything to say in your own defense?"

A shrug. "He was that big, he was. And sozzled, to boot."

"You are not a small man, yourself, and sobriety should have given you the advantage. You failed in your duty to me and to this ship, Slykin. If it happens again, you'll find yourself put ashore."

"Aye, sir," he acknowledged with an air of indifference, and started to turn away.

"I have not dismissed you."

He turned back, and Hawke found little to trust in the look that met his. "Goin' to have me flogged?" Slykin asked.

Hawke felt the muscles of his jaw knot. "I do not flog my crew, as you well know. Violence solves little on a ship, and you are of more use to me whole than marred. But that does not mean that I tolerate failures of duty, any more than I tolerate insolence."

Henderson, belatedly, arrived to stand at Hawke's elbow. "Is there aught amiss, Captain?"

"Indeed not, Mr. Henderson. I was just informing Slykin that he is to spend his morning polishing brass and recoiling the lines. Have him begin at the stern, and see that he gives full satisfaction. Am I understood?"

"Aye, sir." Henderson glared at the big sailor. "You heard the Captain, Slykin. Go aft and get started before you land yourself in any worse trouble. And don't expect to take another meal until you've finished to my satisfaction, d'you hear?"

Content that the matter was well in hand, Hawke said, "I'll be in my cabin, Mr. Henderson," and left him to it.

Turning his back on crisp sea air and sunshine, he walked down the shadowy companionway and opened the door to his cabin.

Amelia was in bed, the covers pulled to her chin, but the plate on his table was empty. "You're awake," he said, closing the door behind himself. "Did you enjoy your breakfast?"

He had thought she might try to pretend she was still asleep. Instead, she raised her head from the pillow and offered him a sweet smile. "It was wonderful," she said. "Thank you."

"My pleasure. You slept well?"

Her cheeks grew pink. "You know I did."

Hawke laughed. "Actually, I know fairly little about last night, since I passed out shortly after my head touched the pillow. But you appeared to be resting comfortably when I rose, this morning. You found the chamber pot without any difficulty?"

This time, her blush was more pronounced. "Yes. Thank you."

"So then, you've eaten and seen to the necessities of life. Is there anything more you require?"

Her gaze dropped. "My clothes seem to have vanished."

"Yes," he agreed. "I asked Henderson to give them a good cleaning."

"I see. I suppose I should thank you for that."

He shrugged. "I would have shut them away even if they hadn't needed washing. We'll have no need of them today." He walked to the end of the bed and sat down on it, careful to avoid her blanketed feet. "Let me tell you how things are going to go."

She watched him, wide-eyed, her smile a thing of the past.

"I shall call you Amelia. You may refer to me as 'sir' or 'captain.' Understood?"

She nodded.

"What do you know about men, Amelia?"

She shrank against the pillow. "I'm not certain what you mean."

"Have you ever seen a man without his clothes?"

"My father."

Hawke grinned at her expression of distaste. "Anyone else?"

"Timothy Hutchins."

"And who might he be? Your sweetheart?"

"No. He's the child of the family who run the inn."

"I see. And how old is Timothy?"

"Three."

Hawke was having a wonderful time. "So," he summarized, "you have seen your father's body and the body of a three-year-old child. Anyone else?"

"No, sir."

"Ever touched a man's body, Amelia?"

"No, sir. Not unless you count Timothy."

"I think we can discount Timothy, for the purposes of this discussion. Do you know how a man's body works?"

She blinked at him, beautiful in her bewilderment.

"If you've seen a naked man, even one who's only three, then you must have noticed what hangs between a man's legs. Am I right?"

She nodded.

"Do you have a name for it?"

"No, sir."

"Not even in your thoughts? Never heard your father speak of it? Never had a boy from the village tell you a dirty tale about one, and then snigger?"

"No, sir."

"Well, then, do you at least know what it is there for?"

Her cheeks were scarlet. "It's for making water, sir. In the chamber pot."

"Or over a ship's rail," he elaborated, for the pleasure of startling her, and chuckled when he saw that he had succeeded. "Aye. That's one use for it. But there's another, as well. Perhaps you've heard tell of it."

Her head bobbed obediently. "It . . . it makes girls have babies."

"Indeed. And how do you suppose it manages that?"

"I wouldn't know, sir. But my father said never to let a man open his trousers around me unless I was prepared to bear a babe."

Hawke nodded, amused. "So men have this mysterious, nameless object between their legs that makes water and babies. Do I have the right of it, Amelia?"

"Yes, sir."

"Well, I can only say that you have a great deal to learn. First, let us decide what to call it. It goes by many names, but I prefer to call it a cock."

"Like a rooster."

"More so than you may imagine. A man's cock is proud and powerful and vain. It loves to greet the dawn. And, like a rooster, it can't make babies until it pokes around inside a hen. You're a hen, Amelia, but our wager guarantees I won't go poking around inside you with my cock. No babies will come of this voyage."

She looked relieved.

"Still, there's plenty else we can do to enjoy ourselves. And we shall. But I'm the captain of this ship, and I intend to exercise my rights as senior officer and precede you. Today, you shall learn how to pleasure me. Tomorrow, I shall pleasure you. And the third day, before we dock, the two of us will enjoy all that you have learned."

"But—"

He waited for her question. "It's all right, lass. Ask."

"Well, sir, if I am to spend the day learning how to pleasure you, why can I not have my clothes?"

"Because," he said, laying hands on the covers, "the sight of you without them will bring me a great deal of pleasure, and my pleasure is what today is all about. Now, let us begin."

Chapter Three

When Amelia felt the top edge of the blanket slide slowly down her throat toward her shoulders, her first instinct was to clutch it with both fists and arrest its descent.

Instead, she hesitated.

Last night, she had stood at the branching of two paths. Faced with entrusting herself to her father or to Captain Hawke, she had chosen Hawke. Now, faced with resisting his attentions or cooperating with them, she chose cooperation.

It might well be that she would repent of her choice before nightfall. He might prove cruel. He might ignore the terms of their wager and force himself upon her. He was, after all, a stranger, and she was not an experienced judge of men.

But it was to his credit that he had spent the entire night beside her without incident. Perhaps that was due to whiskey when they first retired, as he had claimed, but he had risen before her and could have accosted her then, if he was of a mind to do so. Instead, he had allowed her to sleep peacefully and had provided her with a fine breakfast. If she needed a basis for trust beyond her own instincts, that seemed as good a set of reasons as any.

The covers slid over her skin.

The set of Hawke's mouth tightened as her breasts appeared. Amelia felt the tips gather in reaction to the cool morning air . . . or perhaps in reaction to Hawke's heated gaze. The blanket drifted lower, revealing ribs, belly, hips . . . and then the curls between her legs came into view.

Hawke's lips parted as if he wished to speak, but he made no sound.

Her thighs were revealed, then her knees. And all the while, Amelia kept her hands knotted at her sides, permitting it to happen. Hot embarrassment clashed with the chilly air, sending a dozen conflicting signals dancing through her. The teachings of a lifetime told her that what was happening was wrong, sinful, shameful, dangerous . . . but the light in Hawke's eyes told a different story.

When the covers came to rest in a bunch at her ankles, he nodded, as if agreeing with some unspoken comment, and said, "You are indeed a thing of beauty, Amelia Fletcher."

The praise flustered her and yet she was hungry for it, starved for a kindly word, grateful for the least sign of approval from him. She recalled her father's oft-repeated judgments: she was a runt, too small to be of use, hardly worth wasting a meal upon, a skinny stick of a girl when what he needed was a fine, strapping son who could learn the trade and follow in his father's footsteps. She was only good to cook and clean and keep the accounts and mend the clothes. . . .

You are indeed a thing of beauty, Amelia Fletcher.

Overwhelmed, she looked at the rugged man at the foot of the bed, and felt her heart unclench. "In truth," she said softly, "if you find the sight of me pleasing, I am glad of it."

"If?" Smiling, he cocked his head. "Did my words leave you in any doubt?" Standing up, he reached out to her. "Rise, lass. Rise and help dispose of these clothes that bind me. When you witness what the sight of you has done to this body of mine, there will be no more talk of 'if.' "

She placed her hand in his and felt the effortless strength with which he drew her to her feet. Her father was a strong man, too, with hands just as rough-palmed and callused, but there was a finely-judged control to Hawke's grip that won her admiration. As often as not, her father used his strength to intimidate and to inflict pain. Hawke used only the force necessary to help her to stand, then released her.

The deck moved gently beneath her bare feet, prompting her to shift her weight in compensation.

Hawke smiled. "Do a thing for me, if you will. Walk to the door and back."

It seemed a harmless request and yet her heart hammered as she turned her back on him and crossed the floor. Her bottom swayed with each step, try as she might to control it, and she knew that he was watching attentively, assessing her body, observing her nakedness.

Approving of it.

The thought gave her the confidence to turn and face him when she reached the far side of the room.

His face had taken on a ruddy hue, and his voice was husky when he spread his hands and said, "Come back to me now, lass. Slowly."

It seemed to take a million steps. When she finally stood before him, her eyes on a level with his chest, she was no longer cold at all. Her entire body glowed with warmth, as if Hawke's gaze had the power to heat the very blood in her veins.

Crooking his finger beneath her chin, he coaxed her gaze up to meet his own. "A kiss would be pleasant," he said, and bent his head, offering his mouth.

She pressed her lips briefly to his, then stepped back.

"What was that?" he asked, looking puzzled.

Uncertain what he meant, she said, "A kiss. You told me you wanted one and I obliged you."

He chuckled. "A kiss such as that might please young Timothy, but no man upward of the age of three would gladly settle for such a dry little peck. Come and try again."

She moved closer at once, but her thoughts were haring wildly about. 'A dry little peck,' that was his damning assessment of her first effort. Had her lips chafed him? She ran the tip of her tongue over them swiftly, then met his descending mouth with her own, prolonging the contact while she counted slowly to ten. Then she withdrew and looked to him for judgment.

He shook his head in sad negation. "A pitiful effort."

"Then tell me what you expect!"

He goggled at her as if he suspected her of some ill-timed jest. "Are you saying you've never even kissed a lad before?"

Amelia sighed. "My father wouldn't have it. If the village boys so much as looked my way, he threatened to thrash them, and everyone knew he would do it if they gave him an excuse. But what does it matter? I know what a kiss is. I've given you two. If they don't please you, then you must take pity on me and explain what you would have me do differently."

She was afraid her words might anger him, but his expression softened instead, and his hands came up to hold her shoulders in a grip that was nearly an embrace. "I'm sorry, little one. Having seen your father, I should have guessed. But no matter. Kissing of the sort I'm after is a fine thing, easily learned. I want you to yield and allow me to explore your mouth, just as you should explore mine."

"Explore . . . ?"

"Here. I will show you."

This time, when he pressed his mouth to hers, she felt the tip of his tongue trace along the seam between her upper and lower lip. The touch startled her, and she froze, but Hawke's hands rose from her shoulders to cradle her jaw, tilting her head and holding her still while his tongue tip slipped between her lips and glided over the surface of her teeth.

It was the oddest sensation, and it grew stranger still when his fingertips massaged the points of her jaw, relaxing the muscles there, so that his tongue could steal deeper yet, into the very cavern of her mouth.

She began to understand what he meant by the word 'explore' when his tongue swept over hers, touching it playfully, tickling at the hidden tissues of her mouth, teasing her to respond. It was an invasion of the sweetest sort, a tender game that stirred her pulse to new rhythms.

She whimpered when he pulled away, but he retreated only far enough to enable him to speak, his lips brushing against hers as he said, "That, lass, is a kiss. Have you one for me in return, do you suppose?"

In answer, before she could think better of it, she rose on tiptoe to press her mouth to his.

Hawke was tall, and she found it hard to reach high enough. Raising one hand, she slipped her fingers through the curls at his nape and drew him down so that she could meet his lips squarely.

He allowed it but did nothing more.

Eager to display what she had learned, she sent her tongue on a gentle foray, insinuating it between his lips.

Like a dragon resting in its lair, his tongue waited for her touch before it stirred. But it awoke and, as if to reward her for her efforts, slid around, then beneath, then over her own. She sensed a subtle provocation in its actions, and was not altogether surprised when Hawke reasserted his control, drawing on her tongue, pressing his lips more firmly to hers. His hands moved to her throat, then to her shoulders, then slid around to stroke her back, urging her closer within the circle of his arms.

She went willingly, dizzy with the need to breathe but loathe to lose the contact of his mouth on her own.

Hawke raised his head, breaking the kiss, but held her close when she would have stepped away. "Much better," he said. "I will enjoy the next one even more, after you have divested me of these unnecessary clothes."

He released her by degrees, giving her time to recapture her breath and stiffen her rubbery legs.

"First, the shirt," he directed. "Begin with the cuffs."

It should have taken only moments to free the buttons at his wrists, but her fingers were clumsy in their haste.

"Now pull the shirttail free."

She took fistfuls of the much-laundered fabric and tugged it slowly from his trousers.

"If I sit down on the edge of the bed, can you draw the shirt off, over my head?"

"Yes," she promised, and did so.

His chest was lean, the muscles of his abdomen clearly defined, unlike her father's barrel chest and belly which bore a graying, grizzled mat of hair. She stood between Hawke's muscled thighs, with the soft cambric of his shirt bundled in her hands, looking down at him in silent admiration, tingling with her awareness of his proximity. But he made no effort to take the shirt from her, nor did he attempt to touch her breasts. Instead, he leaned back on his elbows with a matter-of-fact air, and asked, "Think you can manage the boots?"

Their removal proved to be far less onerous a task than removing her father's boots. A man who spent long hours around horses inevitably stepped in his fair share of dung before the day was done. Hawke's boots were pristine by comparison, and smelled of nothing but leather.

The socks revealed beneath them, however, were in a sad state of disrepair. "I can darn these properly for you, if you like."

Hawke waved the offer away. "I've told you, I have better ways for you to spend your time." He grinned. "Unfastening my trouser buttons, for a start."

The buttons in question paraded down a pronounced bulge that distended the front of Hawke's trousers. Kneeling beside him, she set to work, freeing each button from its hole. Hawke held himself rigid as she worked, his breathing increasingly troubled, until at last the touch of her fingers against the fabric wrung a gasp from him.

"Have I hurt you?" Amelia asked anxiously, lifting her hands away.

"Wonderfully," he replied. "Hurt me again."

She had never felt so foolish in her life. "What sort of nonsense is that, sir? Pain is nothing to be courted. If I have hurt you, then I am sorry and I shall strive not to do so again."

The set of his jaw eased, and he offered her an indulgent, knowing smile. "We are not speaking of true pain. You have done me no harm. Have you never experienced a pleasure so intense that it almost seemed a pain to your beleaguered mind? You shall, before this voyage ends, I promise you."

"I do not think I wish to feel such a thing."

"You'll wish it, right enough," he promised. "Indeed, you shall beg me for it, before we dock. But for now, Amelia, satisfy yourself with knowing that I am pleased with you, not displeased, and that I wish you to finish ridding me of these blasted trousers with the least possible delay."

Reassured, Amelia returned to the task at hand, ending at last by kneeling on the floor, where she could grasp the bottoms of his pant legs, the better to draw them off.

By the time his trousers and underclothes finally lay scattered on the floor, she felt as if her eyes had grown stalks. Captain Hawke reclined across the mattress, as naked as the day he was born, with his swollen cock rising at a vigorous angle from its bed of dark curls. There was almost no resemblance between his organ and the innocent little wand of young Timothy Hutchins, and the difference between Hawke's proud organ and her father's seemed nearly as great.

In the few unpleasant glances she'd had, her father's cock had been plump and stubby, overshadowed by the shelf of his great belly, half-hidden in the hair that grew around it. Hawke's cock was a grand thing, sleek and tall, rising firm as a ship's mast from his groin. As she watched, it hitched upward smoothly from time to time for no reason she could discern.

"Sit beside me," Hawke said, turning to stretch full-length with his head settled comfortably on the pillow.

Amelia perched on the edge of the mattress.

"Learning a lot today, are you?" Hawke asked.

She nodded.

"And what do you think of what you see?"

She considered the question, her gaze fixed on his groin. "I don't see how you fit it into your trousers to begin with."

He laughed, not derisively but on a merry note of pleasure. "It is not always so large," he said.

She looked at him uncertainly. "Body parts that grow and shrink. Do I look gullible to you, then? A green girl who'll believe any tale, however outlandish?"

Hawke laughed again. "I swear to you, it is no jest."

"Then prove it to me. Make it smaller."

He was grinning now, looking almighty pleased with himself. "I can't. You're too beautiful."

"What has that to do with it?"

"Everything, Amelia. Absolutely everything. It has risen to such a size because it finds you so appealing."

"You speak of it as if it had a brain."

"If not a brain, then at least a mind of its own."

"More foolishness," she accused, not liking to be mocked.

"Not foolishness at all. What of your nipples? Can you command whether they are soft and smooth or tight and gathered?"

She looked down at her breasts, each wearing a crinkled cap of pink.

"Tell your nipples to relax," Hawke instructed. "Make them sink down."

She tried to will it so, but her body remained unchanged.

"And so it is with my cock," Hawke told her. "It knows its own weather, in a manner of speaking. If I closed my eyes and thought about charting a sea course, perhaps I could make it waver and come down, but it would rise again just as soon as I opened my eyes and saw you there, all pink and white like spun sugar. Touch it, Amelia. Allow your ardent admirer to introduce himself."

Reaching out, she pressed a single finger to its rosy tip.

It jerked in response, startling her.

"A kiss would be pleasant," Hawke said mildly, but there was nothing mild about the color flags adorning his cheekbones.

Amelia looked at him askance. "You want me to kiss your . . . ?"

"It has a name."

"You are asking me to kiss your cock?"

"That's right."

Determined to please him, and intrigued despite her wariness, she bowed her head and brushed her lips lightly over the peak of his cock. Nothing happened. Mindful of Hawke's earlier lesson about kisses, she bent her head to try again, this time offering a quick touch of her tongue to the glossy flesh.

Hawke made a little sound, low in his throat, and his cock nodded sharply.

Startled, Amelia looked up.

"Pleasure," Hawke assured her again, his voice thick. "Not pain."

"I see."

And she did see. She saw how the lids of Hawke's eyes had grown abruptly heavy, though not with drowsiness. She saw how the rise and fall of his chest quickened as his breathing grew shallow. She saw the pleasure flush paint his cheeks with fresh intensity.

It pleased her—more, it excited her—to know that she had wrought this change in him. Her father had used brute strength and the promise of pain to control others. But this was control of another kind, and no less compelling: a mastery achieved through the giving of pleasure.

Of her own accord, Amelia lowered her head and skated her tongue across the head of his cock in a firm stroke.

He tasted faintly of salt, and the skin at the tip of his cock was the smoothest thing she'd ever felt. A shiver raced through his limbs, and he lifted one hand to twine his fingers in her hair.

"Would that be a complaint?" she asked, and this time it was she who smiled.

"Complaint that you stopped, perhaps."

"Then I will go on." Gripping him gently with one hand, she licked again, laving him with her tongue as if she held a batter spoon, sweet from the mixing bowl.

In answer, his hips danced on the mattress, and his cock struggled in her grasp.

"Shall I stop?" she asked uncertainly, shaken by the intensity of his response.

"No. Please. More."

She resumed.

"Harder," he implored, and she tried to oblige, but he changed his request almost before she had begun. "Put your lips around it. Take me in your mouth."

Gingerly, she parted her lips and enfolded the stiffened cap of flesh.

Once, twice, three times he pumped his hips, thrusting up between her yielding lips. Then, so suddenly that it frightened her, he cried, "Fegs!" and wrenched away. Wrapping his fist around his rigid shaft, he gave several sharp yanks and then exclaimed aloud as arcs of milky fluid burst from the end of his cock, shooting high into the air to fall, spattering around them.

"Sweet mother of Neptune," Hawke whispered when it was finally over. He was shaking like a man with the ague, and another long minute passed before he gathered himself sufficiently to spare a look for her where she sat, sunk in shame and misery.

Meeting his gaze, she gathered her courage and said, "I'm so sorry. Tell me what it is that I did wrong and I'll do better by you the next time, I swear."

Chapter Four

Hawke hadn't the strength to laugh. "No, lass, it's me who's sorry for startling you so. You did a fine job. Indeed, you did such a fine job that things got away from me, a bit." Seeing that she didn't understand, he dabbed a bit of spunk off his belly and held it out for her inspection. "See that? It's baby juice."

Her look of confusion grew so much more pronounced that he laughed in spite of himself.

"You did nothing wrong," he assured her. "When a man's cock is happier than it can bear, this is what comes out. And if that cock happens to be up inside you at the time, well, that's how babies get made. So now you know." He wished she'd quit looking so solemn about it all. "Are you feeling any wiser yet, Amelia?"

"Beyond a doubt. You run a most unusual school, Captain." Then her gaze dropped lower, and she said, on a note of astonished discovery, "Oh look! It *has* gotten smaller."

If he were any less satisfied, he might have taken offense. As it was, her words amused him. Rising, he crossed the cabin to make use of the wash basin and sponge. "Aye. It's tired now. For that matter, I'm tired, as well. Do you fancy a nap?"

She looked scandalized by the suggestion, as if going back to bed in the middle of the morning was more shocking to her than their recent activities had been. But she yawned, as suddenly and inoffensively as a kitten, and offered him a shy nod. Shifting over, she made room for him when he returned, and nestled down against him as if it were the most natural thing in the world.

* * *

When she woke for the second time that morning, Amelia could scarcely credit her recollection of what had gone on since sunrise. Nevertheless, those memories were difficult to dismiss with Hawke still asleep beside her, taking up three-quarters of the mattress.

She was already teetering on the edge. From there, it was an easy matter to slide to the floor altogether. There she found Hawke's shirt. Pleased, she popped it over her head, then hauled at the lengthy sleeves until her hands emerged.

Donning his shirt wasn't meant as a mutiny, she reasoned, simply a legitimate safeguard for her modesty, in case some member of the crew came in search of their captain. She would return it to Hawke as soon as he woke to demand it. For now, however, the possession of an article of clothing, especially one that covered her nearly as well as a nightshirt, was heartening.

And it gave her an odd shiver of pleasure, somehow, to know that it had touched his skin, as well.

No promise of Heaven or threat of Hell could have induced her to leave the cabin unaccompanied. She trusted Hawke, but that trust did not extend to the men who toiled in his service, least of all when she was in such a spectacular state of undress. No, she would bide her time here and wait for Hawke to wake.

Her thought from a moment earlier returned to plague her: she trusted Hawke. Dear God, she must, to have allowed him the liberties he had taken. In less than a day, she had left behind the world of her childhood and traded it for . . . this.

She smiled wryly. In her experience, people talked sentimental twaddle about their childhoods. Since the death of her mother when she was nine, hers had been a thorny, difficult thing, a time of unremitting labor and will-sapping fear as she learned how to sidestep her father's drunken wrath and safeguard the little flame, deep within her heart, that was her secret self.

Let the gossips say what they would; she had known more kindness from Captain Hawke in the past twelve hours than her father had shown her in the past twelve years. Missish girls from fine families might wail and faint at the sight of a man's naked body. Let them. She was not prepared to condemn the captain for taking an honest joy in the bodies God had fashioned for them. And if that marked her out as a sinner as well, then she would at least have a good-hearted traveling companion on the road to perdition.

Hawke slept on, oblivious to her judgment of his character. Wandering to the table in search of quiet occupation, Amelia glanced idly at the chart weighted open there, its edges held down by a pair of leather-bound books.

Books. She touched the bindings with wistful reverence. Her mother had taught her to unravel the mystery of letters and numbers at a tender age, and had guided her studies to a point where Amelia had an unseemly ability to scan a bill of sale for accuracy or dispute a tradesman's biased arithmetic.

Pleased, she took a seat, pinned the corner of the chart in place with her elbow, and lifted the first of the leather-bound volumes for a closer inspection.

Hawke woke luxuriously, filled with a delicious, slack-muscled sense of ease that allowed him to drift in a languid haze for some timeless interval. He was warm enough; he was cool enough; the clean pillowcase beneath his cheek was soft and welcoming.

Finally, thought returned, in the form of memories.

Amelia, naked.

Amelia, learning how to kiss.

Amelia, wooing his cock with utterly innocent enthusiasm.

With his eyes still closed, he reached out a hand, but he knew even as he did so that she wasn't beside him. He would have felt her warmth, smelled her scent, heard her breathe.

Anxiety pinched at his heart, answered at once by his faith that Henderson would have herded her back to the cabin if she had strayed. Reassured, he opened his eyes.

She was sitting at the table, her little chin resting on her hand, his shirt covering her like a mainsail, and she appeared to be lost in contemplation of . . . what?

"What is it that you find so engrossing?" he asked.

She looked up with an air of eagerness, not guilt. "You're awake," she exclaimed, as if it pleased her. "I was looking at the ship's ledgers while I waited for you."

"I see. And why are you so far away, wearing so very many clothes?"

She thought for a moment, and he saw a dimple deepen in her cheek. "So that you might have the pleasure of reclaiming your shirt?" she suggested.

"Better yet, so that I might have the pleasure of watching you remove it."

She closed the ledger promptly and waited for his next command.

A part of his mind, the part that made him a captain whose men obeyed him, considered speaking harshly, just to keep his bluff in. But she had done nothing wrong, and he could not bear to banish the bright smile from her face. "Stand and deliver, my dear. I need that shirt if I am to secure a meal for us."

"Are you hungry, sir?" she asked, rising to her feet.

He sat up. "Hungry for the sight of you, at the moment. Remove the shirt and hand it to me."

She whipped it off with an alacrity that surprised him. Where was the blushing child who had cowered beneath the covers just this morning? But he knew the answer. That shy child still resided in Amelia's heart, and he would have the pleasure of watching her emerge again tomorrow, when the tables turned and he undertook the delightful task of teaching her body the multiple meanings of pleasure received, in contrast to pleasure given. And he would enjoy the lessons as thoroughly as she, of that he had no doubt, for rarely in his life had he felt as generously inclined toward anyone as he was feeling right now toward Amelia Fletcher.

Their noon meal was a sketchy affair of bread and cheese. "Tonight, we'll dine on finer fare," he promised her.

Amelia looked at him as if he had lost his mind. "The bread is fresh, and the cheese tastes as if it came from Angus McGregor's dairy, which is the finest for miles around. What fault do you find with a meal such as this? Many's the time I've made do with worse."

"And why was that?" Hawke asked, finishing off his ale. "A blacksmith worth his salt makes a good living, and your father had the look of a man who dined heartily and often."

She looked down, clearly regretting that she had spoken.

Reaching out, he covered her hand with his own. "Peace, Amelia. You've left that life behind you now. Let it trouble you no more. I'm sorry to have asked."

She shrugged his words away with a little lift of her shoulders but made no move to withdraw her hand. Instead, she asked, "Didn't it hurt when you pulled at it like that? I should have thought it would."

For a moment, lost in happy contemplation of Amelia's breasts, he had no idea what she was asking. Then he remembered how he had rolled aside and finished matters off for himself when her attentions grew too much for him to withstand. "When I pulled at my cock, you mean?"

"Yes." She lifted a moist crumb of bread from the tabletop and rolled it between her fingertips. "It looked painful. You swore, and you hauled on it as if you wanted to tear it away from your body. And then it . . . went off."

"That it did, most satisfactorily." Setting his empty tankard on the table, he stood up and drew her with him to sit on the edge of the mattress. "I'm sorry if I frightened you. I suppose it looked strange, but it's a grand sort of violence. Your nerves knot up, steam pours out your ears, your toes curl, your spine unravels, and then a miracle happens."

"You make it sound very grand."

"And you sound very skeptical. Am I to understand, then, that you take no pleasure from your body?"

"Well, I can't say I've ever noticed steam pouring from my ears."

"Believe me, Amelia, if it had happened, you'd have noticed. A woman's body is much neater about it than a man's, but I've seen many a spine unravel, in my day."

"Is that so?"

"It is. And tomorrow, I intend to unravel yours."

The skepticism in her eyes pleased him.

"Wait and see," he said. "Before sunset tomorrow, I'll make it happen."

"You're very sure of yourself."

"I am."

"So it's something one person can do for another, then?"

"Of course."

"I wondered, because you pulled away from me when the time came. Did you think I wouldn't manage it properly?"

"No. I simply thought I'd die if I didn't manage it in the next three heartbeats, and I knew I could get myself there in a hurry. It was selfish of me, I suppose, but you'll find that it's a feeling that makes you selfish, at least for those few moments. It's a thing that happens deep inside you, and once it starts, it shuts out everything else until it's over."

"You seem to know a great deal about it."

"I should. It's a gift I've been giving myself since I was a lad of fourteen. Sailors live a lonely life, and it can be a great comfort in a cold bunk when you haven't sighted land for the better part of a month." He grinned. "Or a week. Or a day, if the spirit's on you."

"And once you do such a thing, how long is it before you feel the need again?"

"That depends on the man and the mood, I suppose." He smiled down at her. "Are you asking how long it will be before the mood is on me again?"

"I did wonder."

"Well, wonder no more. I've had a rest and a meal, there's a pretty girl sitting beside me in her altogether, and I'm eager to carry on."

"Oh. Well. In that case. . . ."

"Out with it, girl. What do you want to say?"

"This time, sir, if you wouldn't mind too awfully, could you let me finish the matter for you?"

Hawke could feel a grin of anticipation spreading across his face. "Why, yes, Amelia. I certainly think that that could be arranged."

Chapter Five

By the time Amelia retired that night, she was filled with a glow of accomplishment and a cautious but growing excitement. All her life, she had been at the mercy of her father, ruled by him, controlled by him, the circumstances of her life dictated by him. From earliest memory, he had been the tyrant in her life, acting as he saw fit without reference to anyone else's needs or wishes; an implacable god who hurled thunderbolts at anyone who dared to thwart his will.

Today was the first day in her entire life that she had spent totally apart from him, and the relief was staggering.

It would have been compensation enough, that relief. It more than made up for the loss of all else that was familiar. But the rewards, unexpectedly, had proven to be greater still. And those rewards began and ended with the person of Captain Hawke.

He showed her kindness. He found her beautiful. More startling still, he told her so. He taught her how to please him, and abandoned himself to that pleasure as if his trust in her was absolute. This afternoon, and again tonight after an evening meal as generous as he had promised it would be, he'd stripped off his clothing and surrendered himself to her ministrations. And she had succeeded, both times, in building his pleasure, layer by layer, until she could call forth from him those fountaining spasms of delight that so intrigued her.

Fastidious Mr. Henderson would no doubt have been appalled by the state of the sheets.

It was on that thought, smiling, that Amelia fell asleep, safe and warm in the shelter of Hawke's embrace.

* * *

"So, Mr. Henderson," Hawke said soon after first light, "how fares the ship?"

"Well enough, sir. We're on course, and I expect to bring her to dock by late afternoon tomorrow."

"Very good. No difficulties in my absence?"

"None that haven't been resolved, sir."

"Excellent. And what of the errant Mr. Slykin?"

Henderson pulled a long face. "That one's a snake, Captain. I'd not care to turn my back on him, or trust him at the top end of a line if I were hanging from the end of it. His work yesterday was slapdash, at best, even under close supervision. He has the muscles for the job, sir, but not the temperament."

"I agree with your assessment, Mr. Henderson. When we reach port, pay him off and send him on his way, whether you can find a replacement for him or not. We'll run better short-handed than we will with a troublemaker on board. But I don't recommend spelling that out for him until we've docked. If he knows for a certainty that he's to be put ashore, we shall lose any small leverage we may yet have with him."

"Aye, sir. Just as you say."

"Any questions before I return to my cabin, Mr. Henderson?"

The young man fingered the buttons of his vest and blushed. "No, sir. That is to say, will you be needing anything, sir?"

"No, Mr. Henderson." Hawke smiled, filled with the benevolent confidence that comes to a man who has had his ashes hauled three times and fully expects more of the same to follow. "For the moment, my needs are being met quite satisfactorily, thank you."

Again, Amelia woke to find that Hawke had provided a breakfast for her, but there the similarities ceased.

Standing fully dressed beside the bed, looking aggressively wide awake, Hawke said, "I'll step out again for a moment or two while you set yourself to rights and put on the gown you'll find draped over the back of the chair. But don't touch the tray. I intend to feed you myself this morning."

And he left.

Amelia scrambled from beneath the covers and dealt with her body's needs, then hurried to the chair, her head abuzz with questions. Why did Hawke want her to dress? Yesterday, he had been most emphatic about depriving her of her clothing. Had he tired of the sight of her so soon?

The gown, she saw as she drew it over her head, was not her own.

She supposed it would have to be considered a nightdress; certainly it was wholly unsuitable to be worn in public. Made of some gossamer fabric, with a high neck, long sleeves and trailing length, it gave an initial appearance of propriety. It was, nevertheless, a scandalous garment. Despite its abundance of yardage, the filmy material clung to her, outlining every curve and allowing shadowed glimpses of color at the tips of her breasts and the juncture of her thighs. The opening at its front plunged nearly to her waist, and the only means of securing the two sides of the bodice to one another was a procession of ribbon laces, apparently intended to be joined in cunning little bows.

Losing no time, she set herself to tying them.

Despite her haste, Hawke returned before she was finished. From long habit, she clutched the neckline closed as he came in.

"Do you think my memory is so short?" he asked, a teasing light in his eyes.

Chagrined, she eased her desperate hold. "No. That is not what I was thinking."

He nodded as if she had said more, and Amelia had the oddest feeling that he understood the specter of uneasiness that had hovered over her for so long at home. The need for privacy. The need for modesty. The need for wary caution.

With Hawke, there was no need for caution and little point in modesty. And yet she blushed, feeling more exposed in that diaphanous gown than when she had worn nothing at all.

Hawke's unhurried gaze conveyed its own eloquent message.

Amelia groped for something to say, some gambit that might break the sensual tension building between them. "This seems an odd garment for a ship's captain to own."

"Not so very odd."

The answer flustered her. What did he mean by it? Did he often have need of such a gown? How many women before her had felt its airy folds embrace their limbs? For how many women had Hawke's clever fingers untied those little ribbons?

"You are the first."

Oh, how she wanted to believe that. "You read minds, do you, Captain?"

"I read faces, and I find yours particularly expressive. I purchased this gown as a present for my sister. My married sister."

Breathing became much easier. "And what will she say when she learns that you have squandered her present on a perfect stranger?"

"If she objects, I shall buy her another. But am I squandering it? I thought of it, rather, as an investment."

"In what, pray tell?"

He smiled. "Your education. We have important lessons to tackle, this morning, and it seemed to me that wearing this gown might help to put you in the proper frame of mind." He reached into his pocket. "I brought this along for you, as well."

'This' proved to be a long scarf of purest white.

"You want me to wear it?"

"I want to put it on you myself. May I?"

"If you wish."

"I wish," he said softly, and started toward her in a slow, purposeful manner that unnerved her a bit.

"What's the matter, Amelia?" he asked, still in that low, caressing voice.

"You move like a cat stalking pigeons," she accused.

"How very observant you are. That is precisely what I feel like right now. And what are you feeling, Amelia?"

"I feel as if it's me that you intend to eat for breakfast."

"Right again, and I find that I am very hungry indeed. Do you think you'll be enough to satisfy me?"

He was almost close enough to touch her now, and it took an effort of will not to skitter backwards and put the table between them. "You're frightening me, captain."

"Am I? Is it fear? Or have I awakened some other emotion in you, one you are not quite certain how to deal with?"

"I don't know."

"What do you think I intend to do with you?"

"I don't know."

"Are you afraid I'll harm you?"

"No," she said, and felt the edging of nervous dread recede a little. "But you seem an altogether different man this morning."

"In what way?"

"More serious. More . . . intent."

"Intent on you, Amelia. Is that a bad thing?"

"It can be, from some."

"Is it, from me?"

She looked into his eyes. They were magical eyes, dark and mysterious, filled with surprises enough to last a lifetime, each more delightful than the last. Amelia felt something within her shift, as if the ship had struck a cross-current and then resumed its true course. "No," she said. "From you, it is not a bad thing at all." She lowered her hands to her sides and relaxed them. "Do with me what you will."

He did not smile, but his mouth softened artlessly. "In that case, may I put the scarf on you now?" he asked, holding it up for her scrutiny.

Dangling, the heavy silk shimmered in the morning light with a glow all its own.

"Yes, you may."

"May I bind your eyes with it?"

Amelia hesitated. She did not like the dark, nor was it easy for her to willingly cede so much power to another. She looked again at the scarf, and then at Hawke, and tried not to tremble. "If that is your wish," she said at last, and stood firm while he circled behind her and stepped close.

"You are safe with me," he murmured in her ear, his breath stirring the unbound mass of her hair. Then the scarf settled, soft and impenetrable, over her eyes, extinguishing the sun.

His movements were deft as he tied it at the back of her head. *Sailors are good with knots*, she told herself, to keep the demons at bay.

"Come and sit with me," he said, and took her by the shoulders to guide her forward.

She thrust a hand in front of herself and felt her way cautiously, her bare toes searching the planked floor for obstacles where she knew none existed.

"Your body is cautious," Hawke said. "I don't think it trusts me yet."

"It's afraid of hurting itself," she said, taking refuge in speaking of her body as if it were a separate being.

"It is afraid of being hurt," said Hawke, "which is quite a different matter. Three steps more. I will stop you before we reach the table."

She made an effort to step forward more naturally, and felt approval in the way Hawke's grip changed on her upper arms. "Turn now," he prompted, drawing her backward and down. "Bend your knees, Amelia. Sit."

She was braced for the wooden seat of the chair, and found instead that she was perched upon Hawke's lap, his legs warm beneath her own. Despite the intervention of his trousers and her gown, she could feel the play of his muscles as he settled her more comfortably.

"And now," he said, "it is time for your breakfast."

She reached out blindly, her fingers questing for the plate and mug.

"No," said Hawke.

She dropped her hands back into her lap.

"I intend to feed you myself," Hawke said. "You need only part those pretty lips and accept what I place between them."

He spoke lightly, as if she should find it a pleasant game, but the inbred caution of years was not so easily overthrown. It was one thing to feel trust; it was quite another to translate that feeling into action.

"Taste this," he whispered, and Amelia felt something touch her lower lip. She had expected the cool metal of a spoon; instead, Hawke's fingertip slipped inside her mouth, coated with something sweet and viscous.

"Honey," he told her, "fresh from the comb."

Dazed by the luxury, she suckled his finger.

"You like that," he said, and she could hear his smile. His finger slid slowly from her mouth, and she felt him shift his weight. "You will need to open your mouth a little wider for your next morsel of nourishment."

Encouraged, she obeyed, and felt him place something warm and substantial on her tongue. Exploring, she found it to be a bite of warm biscuit, laced with more honey. The bite after that was ham, warm as well, its salty tang cutting pleasantly through the sweet aftertaste the honey had left behind.

"Does your crew dine half this well?" she asked.

He laughed. "Do they deserve to? Have they brought me half as much pleasure as you have?"

"It hardly seems fair to compare their honest labor to . . . what you and I have shared."

"My men eat heartily, and the food they are served is fresh and wholesome. I would be a sorry captain if it were not, on a trip such as this where we make landfall every third day. Do not waste your worry on my crew. Save it all for me."

"And why should I worry for you?"

His hand at her waist tightened. "Because a siren has found her way into my cabin and may yet lure me onto the rocks."

"I am no siren, sir."

"So you claim," he said. "But I am at a loss for how else to explain the hold you exert over me. Now hush and eat. No more questions for a time." And he fed her on ham and honeyed biscuits until she could hold no more.

"I am at my limit," she said at last. "Not another bite, I beg you."

"Indeed, you would do well to lie down and digest your meal in peace, while I find some way to occupy my time. Does that not sound like a wise and prudent course?"

"It might," she said as he guided her to her feet, "if it were not for the laughing tone I hear beneath your words. Somehow I do not think you intend to join your crew on deck."

"Ah, you begin to know me well." Ten paces brought them to the bed. "Recline and take your ease, Amelia." He helped her to do so. "And leave the scarf where it is. Does the knot trouble you when you rest your head? Let me move it to the side." When he had made her comfortable, he said, "I will leave you for a moment only, while I fetch a chair for myself. Be at peace."

His footsteps faded and returned, followed by a brief clatter of wood on wood as he settled himself beside the bed.

"Now put your hands behind your head. Pretend you are stretched upon the grass in a summer meadow, contemplating the clouds above you."

It was a pleasant conceit. She toyed with the fancy and felt her limbs relax.

Something stirred against her stomach, tickling just a bit.

"Hold very still," Hawke said, and the sensation came again, slightly higher this time. At the fourth occurrence, she realized what was happening: Hawke had begun untying, one by one, the dainty bows that secured her gown.

Chapter Six

"You seem as eager to remove this gown as you were to have me don it," Amelia said, trying to sound unconcerned.

"I am removing nothing. Just rearranging things for my greater convenience and your greater pleasure."

"My pleasure?"

"Have you forgotten so soon? Your pleasure is the focus of our day today."

It was a mystifying answer. Breakfast had pleased her; she could not dispute that. And it was pleasing to be the focus of Hawke's attention. But beyond that. . . .

"I can hear that busy brain of yours, ticking like a watch," Hawke chided. "Don't think. Today isn't about thinking. It's about feeling. For instance, tell me what you feel now."

Something light and insubstantial glided across the surface of her nipple, followed by a sudden touch of cooler air.

Amelia shivered in response. "You have drawn the gown aside."

"The entire gown?"

"No. Just the bodice."

"The entire bodice?"

"No. Just one side."

"To reveal what?"

"My bosom."

Hawke chuckled. "Elderly aunts attired in black bombazine have bosoms. What have I revealed, Amelia?"

"My breast."

"Yes, and a lovely one it is, I must say. Now, concentrate again and tell me what you feel."

Something moist spiraled onto her skin and clung.

"I don't know. What is that?"

"I have adorned your breast with honey."

"Don't stain your sister's gown!" she said in sharp alarm, trying to hold perfectly still.

"Very well, then," he said on a note of rich amusement. "If Cecily's gown is to be preserved, I had better deal with this."

She expected to feel the brisk scrub of a cloth. Instead, something warm and soft dragged gently across her nipple, sending a delicious shiver through her. "What is that?"

"My tongue," he answered, and licked her breast again.

Only her certainty that trickles of honey would slide down the curve of her breast and spoil the delicate fabric kept her motionless beneath the sweet assault of Hawke's attentions. Her nipple peaked as he laved it, and she found that his caresses woke an answering ache between her thighs. Her hips wanted to shift and twitch within the confines of the gown, and her other breast, untouched and decently covered, throbbed its discontent.

A whimper escaped her lips.

"Am I hurting you?" he asked, his lips brushing the slope of her breast as he spoke.

"No."

"You're quite certain?"

He was teasing her, the devil. "I don't understand," she confessed. "Why should the touch of your mouth on one part of my body make me ache in others, as well?"

"That depends. Where do you ache?"

She was too embarrassed to answer.

When she made no reply, Hawke licked her nipple again, then enclosed it in the warm haven of his mouth. He suckled her gently, then more insistently, and another cry escaped her at the strange new sensations elicited deep within her.

"Where do you ache, Amelia? Show me, if you cannot find the words."

"Here," she said, touching her hand lightly to the fabric that covered her other breast.

"Is that the only place?" he asked, and drew deeply on her nipple again.

Squirming, she gestured vaguely at her lower body. "And there."

He pressed the flat of his palm gently to her stomach. "Here?"

"Lower."

"Here?" he asked, placing his hand across her thighs.

"Higher."

His fingers curved to cup her mound, molding the fabric over her curls. "Here, Amelia?" The pressure of his hand increased, claiming the spot as his own. "Is this where you ache? I am captain of this ship and you are my passenger. If something ails you, I must do everything in my power to ease your suffering." His fingertips stirred, lightly massaging the curls between her legs. "Are you suffering, Amelia?"

Recklessness rose in her blood like a fever. "I do not know if you could rightly call it suffering, but something very strange is happening to me. I have never felt this way before."

His fingers rubbed and probed. "Never before?"

"Never. It is altogether a new thing."

"Well, then, perhaps we have caught it in time. Let me see if I can determine the cause of your . . . agitation."

She heard him rise from his chair, then felt the mattress sink as he sat down on the edge of the bed. A moment later, the hem of her gown stirred, and she felt his hand on her ankle. "Does my touch here cause you pain?"

"No, sir."

He stroked his way up her calf to her knee. "Here?"

"No."

His fingers traced a firm line up her thigh. "And now?"

"I feel . . . something," she answered truthfully.

"Then we may be nearing the source. Is the ache closer to where I sit or more toward the center of your body?"

"The center."

He slipped his hand between her thighs. "Lower or higher than this?"

"Higher."

Slowly, skating over the surface, he slid his fingertips up to rest just above her mound. "And now?"

She had forgotten to breathe. "Lower."

"Very good. It seems we are making progress. Part your legs for me, if you please, and I will investigate the matter more thoroughly."

Did she dare? Could she bear not to? Stealthily, as if hoping to avoid her own notice, she widened the space between her thighs.

"A bit more," Hawke requested.

She granted him—and herself—another inch, half convinced that some celestial retribution would strike her down if she went any farther. But there was only a quicksilver thrill between her legs when Hawke's hand reclaimed her mound and massaged it more firmly than before.

"Is this the spot?"

She nodded.

"I can't hear you, Amelia. Is this the spot?"

"Yes!" she said, on a gasp.

His fingertips continued their magic. "Odd. I feel nothing amiss here. Perhaps your problem lies deeper." The gentle rubbing ceased. She felt his fingers trace with maddening leisure along the line where her nether lips met, parting her curls as he descended, revealing her moist inner folds. . . .

"Don't!"

"Tell me why not, and perhaps I will stop."

"Because—" It was hard to speak, hard to think while his fingers delved with such exquisite care. "Because—"

He reached the secret wellspring of heated moisture that had been gathering under the influence of his caress, and she flinched, certain that he would recoil. Instead, he dipped his fingertip into it and said, on a note of pleasure, "Ah. More honey."

She understood, then, that he had known what he would find . . . which must mean that other women's bodies reacted as hers had done . . . which meant that she must not be so aberrantly made as she had supposed. Comforted, she relaxed fractionally, allowing herself to cherish the heat lightning which flickered through her loins as Hawke fondled her. As she eased, his finger pressed gently against her flesh, gliding forward by tiny increments, deepening the pleasurable assault on her senses.

"I think, perhaps," he murmured, "that I have found the cause of that ache which troubles you. Tell me, do you feel it still?"

A tension impossible to ignore built within her. "Yes."

His finger climbed. "Is it growing stronger?"

Prodded by pleasure, goaded by the knowing pressure of his fingertip, she squirmed beneath his touch. "Yes."

"Ah." Again, his touch ascended. "In that case, I deduce that the source of your agitation lies . . . here."

Sensation jolted through her. Stunned, she jerked from beneath his touch, breaking the fragile connection between his finger and her flesh. He pursued her and renewed the contact, causing an even stronger surge of pleasure, one that shook her to the bone. "Stop!" she cried in alarm.

"By no means," Hawke said, and began to stroke her in earnest.

She writhed beneath his determined assault, frightened and exhilarated by the rush of sensation his touch evoked. Deep within her, it was as if a wind were sharpening into a gale. Waves dashed themselves to death upon the rocks while seagulls shrieked a warning. But it was too late for warnings, too late to flee, too late to plead, too late to do anything but surrender to the harsh glory of the storm Hawke had unleashed. Overset, she struggled and sobbed as the mighty sea gathered and rose within her, welling up, surging high, cresting—

Amelia screamed.

"Fegs!" she heard Hawke exclaim, and his mouth descended to cover her own, stifling her outcry.

She clung to his broad shoulders, overcome.

Gradually, as the ecstasy ebbed, she felt her sanity return. With a twinge of guilt, she eased her frantic grip on his shoulders, still trembling from the intensity of what she had experienced. As if reassured, Hawke's mouth lifted from her own. "Lusty wench," he whispered against her cheek, his lips tickling her skin.

He was teasing again, sounding pleased and complacent.

When he pushed the blindfold down, allowing her to see again, she almost wished he had left it in place. "I'm sorry," she said, not meeting his gaze. "I didn't mean—" She took an unsteady breath. "I didn't know—"

Hawke smiled down at her, his eyes crinkling with tender humor. "I think we cured your ache."

She pressed her palms to her flaming cheeks.

"I gather you are new to such pleasures."

"Is that—?" She gestured helplessly.

He laughed. "Eventually, my dear Amelia, you will have to finish a sentence."

For the moment, words were nearly beyond her. Never had she imagined that her own body could produce such a maelstrom of sensation, such a depth of need and then such an explosion of need fulfilled. It astonished her, as if she had awakened one morning to find that she had sprouted wings. Were there other marvels within her, other abilities and possibilities of which she was equally unaware?

There was, at least, one sentence she could finish. Gazing into Hawke's eyes, she said, "Thank you."

"It was my pleasure. But I might well have employed that scarf as a gag rather than a blindfold if I had known how you were going to react to my attentions."

"I'm sorry. I should not have cried out. I didn't intend to. I didn't even realize I was going to, until it happened. If I caused you any difficulty—"

Hawke grinned. "If we had been on land, within earshot of others, it might have proved awkward. But we are at sea, on a ship I command. What difficulty could you cause me? Indeed, if any of my crew chanced to hear you, I imagine my reputation has been greatly enhanced."

"I don't understand."

"A jest, Amelia. I meant it as a jest . . . although it is true that men take a lively interest in bedroom matters and questions of prowess."

"And they would think more of you because I screamed?"

"Because you screamed from pleasure. A scream of pain would be quite a different matter, although there are some twisted souls who might find that arousing, as well."

Her head spun as she tried to assimilate all that had gone on. Without thinking, she said, "You called me . . ." But she could not bring herself to say the words.

"I called you a lusty wench," Hawke said for her. "Virgins are a skittish lot, by and large, and most are difficult to pleasure. The vigor of your response took me by surprise."

"Then you think me common," she said unhappily.

His eyes twinkled. "No, I find you very uncommon indeed."

"It is no laughing matter!"

"But no matter if I laugh. We are private, here. Therefore let us be honest. We both know that you have a fine mind and an honorable nature. Circumstance dealt harshly with you and so you took steps to protect yourself from the worst that might have befallen you. There are those who will say your choice was an improper one, but I find it admirable and brave."

"You do?"

"Yes. It took courage to cut the ties that bound you to your old life, never knowing what the future might hold. It was a dangerous course you set, and it could have landed you where you had no wish to be—sold into white slavery in New Orleans, or shared out roughly to some rowdy crew of sailors. Compared with that, the cost of your passage will be light. I intend to see you safely ashore tomorrow, burdened by nothing worse than a few incendiary memories and a tender conscience, perhaps. And now," he said, pressing a light kiss to her brow, "if you will pardon me, there is a ship's matter that requires my attention briefly. I shall be back before long."

Amelia watched him go, wishing she had the right to call him back. Her body craved the pleasure of his touch and the comfort of his warmth. And her heart . . .

Amelia sighed. Her heart—poor, silly thing that it was—wanted altogether more from Captain Hawke than it was ever likely to receive.

Chapter Seven

Hawke strode on deck and claimed the wheel from Henderson, desperate for a task that would distract him from dwelling on the intoxicating game in which he'd just taken part.

Despite her innocence, or perhaps because of it, Amelia Fletcher was becoming a serious problem. 'A siren,' he had called her at breakfast, and a siren she was. How else could he explain his sudden urge to chart a course for Barbados, rather than hold to tomorrow's scheduled docking?

Oh, he'd talked a fine act. *I intend to see you safely ashore tomorrow, burdened by nothing worse than a few incendiary memories and a tender conscience, perhaps.* But he would rest easier if his intentions and his desires were one and the same.

What was wrong with him? He had never felt particularly possessive about the women he bedded. . . .

Hell's bells, he hadn't even bedded Amelia, nor did he intend to! All he had done was beguile her to her first climax. And yet, somehow, he felt more entangled with her than if he'd claimed her maidenhead.

Her deflowering was a privilege and responsibility that would fall to some other man, just as it would fall to some other man to wed her, and to sire her first child. She would want a land-locked husband, that girl would, a man who would be there to lie beside her at night and rise with her in the morning to face each new day. She'd have no use for a ship rat like himself who plied his trade up and down the coast, rarely sleeping in the same town two nights running. And even if she were balmy enough to think otherwise, she deserved better than that.

She deserved better than him.

A pox on it! Why did he care what or who she deserved? It should be a matter of supreme indifference to him. He had no use for this woman. He had no use for *any* woman, beyond the universal need shared by all his gender. Physical gratification. That was what men sought, and that was the payment he'd negotiated in exchange for her passage. So why was he up here, wasting time on deck, when he had a half-naked maiden on board who was at his beck and call? Had he lost his mind?

"Henderson!"

"Captain?"

"Take the wheel."

"Aye, sir."

And Hawke strode back toward his cabin.

When she heard Hawke's footsteps in the corridor, Amelia could not prevent the thrill of sweet anticipation that filled her. Only the uncompromising numbers inked on the page she was examining tempered her excitement.

He opened the cabin door without knocking, as was his right, and she thought he appeared just a little disappointed when he saw her settled at the table, with the ledger book open before her.

"You seem to be taking quite an interest in my business affairs," Hawke said, his tone indulgent.

"Do you keep these ledgers yourself?" Amelia asked, but she suspected that she already knew the answer. Hawke was a man of action, not the sort who would find record-keeping much to his taste, unless she missed her guess.

"That's what I keep Henderson for," he said with a dismissive wave of his hand. "I make the profits and he tallies them."

Tracing her fingertip nervously down the column of numbers, she was shaken by the memory of Hawke's fingertip tracing the sensitive line between her nether lips. Snatching her thoughts away from that burning image, she asked, "Has he been with you long, Captain?"

"Henderson? A year or more."

"And his work has pleased you?"

Hawke was not a stupid man. His gaze sharpened, as did his voice. "Yes. I've found him most satisfactory. Is there some reason why I shouldn't?"

Amelia sighed. "Well, either his ciphering is careless or . . . "

"Or what? I have never known Henderson to be careless in any task he undertook. The man is meticulous to a fault. What is this ominous alternative that you imply?"

Intimidated by his fierce expression, Amelia said, "I leave such deductions to you. All I know for certain is that the individual amounts entered do not tally with the totals at the bottom of each page."

Hawke stood very still. "Are you accusing Henderson of cheating me?"

"I accuse no one. I only state that the figures do not tally . . . and that the errors are consistent in their nature."

"And what is that nature?"

"The page totals are always less than they should be. Never by much, mind you. A little here, a little there. But over the span of the pages I have examined, it begins to accumulate rather impressively."

"Take off your gown."

The suddenness of the demand shocked her. "What?"

"You heard me. These are matters for men to determine. I have better uses for my time with you. Now close the ledger, rise from the table, and take off your gown," he said, his words clipped, his expression forbidding.

She'd heard her father use that tone on many occasions. It had never boded well. "I'm sorry if I displeased you by looking at your ledgers," she said, and then shuddered, for she could hear the disgusting cringe that had crept into her tone, just as she could feel the submissive droop in the set of her shoulders. She knew the unspoken message it conveyed: *I am small and harmless, unworthy of your anger. Pay no attention to me. Don't cause me pain . . .* But that attitude belonged to her old life.

With conscious intent, Amelia straightened her spine and looked Hawke directly in the eye. "Someone is cheating you," she said. "Perhaps it is Henderson, perhaps someone else. But you are being cheated. The ledgers make that clear. Having informed you of it, my conscience is now clear and my involvement is at an end. If you wish to tolerate being swindled, that is your affair. I simply felt I owed it to you to tell you what I saw. If you prefer not to know, then pretend I never spoke. But my intention was only ever to act as your friend."

"It is not your friendship I crave. Close the ledger," Hawke repeated implacably, "rise from the table, and take off your gown. Or face the consequences of your refusal."

His words struck her like a slap. Seething, she closed the ledger and stood, defiantly untying bow after bow until the gown dropped to the floor to form a gauzy cloud around her ankles. Amelia stepped free of it. "There. I'm naked. Are you pleased?"

His eyes told her nothing, but she had learned enough to know that he was not indifferent, for the cloth at his groin was filled to bursting. "Lie down on the bed."

Fear tried to find a foothold within her, but stronger than the fear was her conviction that she knew this man. He was not a bully, nor was he a coward. Whatever might happen next, it would not be a beating or a rape. She could not be so wrong about him. If she was, it would break her heart.

She walked to the bed and reclined.

Hawke snatched up the ivory scarf and knotted the ends of it together, then twisted the soft cloth into a figure-eight. Approaching the bed, he hung both loops over his hand, then doubled and twisted the scarf again, reducing the size of the loops by half while increasing their thickness two-fold.

He thrust it toward her. "Put your hands through here."

She slipped a hand through each loop. It was a snug fit, but the material was whisper-soft against her skin. "An elegant imprisonment," she observed, looking up to where he towered over her. "What purpose does it serve?"

For answer, Hawke grasped the silken folds and lifted, raising her arms over her head, until he could hook the center of the silken binding over one of the brass hooks that protruded from the wall above the headboard.

Again the fear tried to assail her, and again she rejected it. This was a bondage she could easily escape, since her wrists were secured only by loops of slippery fabric.

"I want you to leave them there," Hawke said, and she realized that he knew full well that she could free herself without undue difficulty.

"For how long?"

His smile was a dark thing. "Until I have made you scream with pleasure again."

That silenced her. The thought of feeling those renegade sensations once more set her heart to racing, and the appearance of helplessness Hawke had fashioned for her started a tingling between her thighs. "I thought you were angry with me," she said.

"Perhaps I am. Let's find out."

She expected him to stroke her with his hands, as he had done before to such amazing effect. Instead, he kicked off his boots, climbed upon the bed, straddled her body and bent forward to press his lips briefly to hers, as if in some formal salute.

Then his kisses began to rove.

Smoothing her hair back, he tilted her head and trailed his lips down the outer curve of her ear, then nipped at the tender lobe. Startled by the unconventional caress, she turned her head to grant him greater access, gasping when the tip of his tongue launched a damp invasion.

It traced along her ear's whorled channels as if they were a maze, then plunged into the hollow, damming it, shutting out the sounds of the world as he licked and teased with increasing vigor.

It was only her ear. It should have meant nothing. But she recognized in that rapacious rhythm a distant twin of the motions that yesterday had preceded his own physical release. This was a claiming of sorts, and the strange nature of it did not prevent her senses from catching fire.

From there, his lips descended the column of her throat and explored the hollow between her breasts. Her nipples, untouched, were already straining skyward, crinkled with need, aching for the hot, wet touch of his mouth.

He made her wait while he strung a shivery line of kisses along the outer curves of her breasts. Only then, when he had completed the entire circuit, did he close his lips over one of her nipples and begin to suckle, while his fingers flicked and stroked the other.

She closed her eyes, the better to savor his attentions. And as she responded, his motions grew rougher, his mouth exerting a greater suction, his fingers pinching and squeezing. To her surprise, his roughness brought no pain, just sharper bursts of pleasure, until she groaned aloud from the sheer power of the hunger in her loins.

His mouth moved down to claim her navel, while his hands stayed behind to comfort her abandoned breasts. His knees gouged the mattress on either side of her legs, trapping them together when she would willingly have parted them. She could feel the fabric of his shirt brushing lightly against her thighs, while the rougher material of his trousers pressed the outer curves of her calves. And somewhere above loomed the hard heat of his cock, but he held it away from her, denying her any direct contact with it.

He moved lower still, and she felt him nuzzle at her groin. Then, to her astonishment, she felt his tongue insinuate itself, delving beneath the curls.

She stiffened in dazed delight, hardly daring to believe that the caress was intentional. His tongue moved farther, slipping between her plump outer lips and continuing inward to graze the uppermost slope of her inner folds, a frustrating inch above the spot where her hunger throbbed most ardently for his touch. She tried to widen the distance between her thighs, but the twin barriers of his legs defeated her.

As if his tongue sympathized with her need, it persisted in its efforts, coming close but never quite reaching the magical place that was begging to be stimulated.

Amelia writhed, lifting her hips in an attempt to grant him deeper access. For a single instant, the tip of his tongue reached its goal, and she cried out at the glorious sensation that resulted, but the contact was only momentary.

"Please," she whispered.

Hawke lifted his head and rested his chin lightly on her mound while his dark gaze challenged her. "Please? What do you mean? What is it that you desire?"

"I want . . ."

He waited.

"I want you to . . . kiss me. Down there."

It seemed a shameful request, and she would never have voiced it if he had not already shown his willingness to do so. But she longed for him to continue, and if he insisted on hearing the words before he would proceed, then she would do her best to meet his demands.

But a devilish mood seemed to be on him, for he took her response quite literally, tucking his chin to press a light kiss to the curls on her mound. "There. Are you satisfied?"

"You know I am not."

"Then tell me what it is you desire."

"Why? Why must I say it? You know what I hunger for."

"Then name it. You spoke boldly enough when you sat at my table and told me how to manage my business. Where is that boldness now? Tell me what you desire, or else forego it."

Amelia glared at him. Tomorrow he would escort her from his ship and be glad to see the back of her, or so he had implied. Well, then, why must she be shy about asking for what she wanted? They were words, only words. There was no one else to hear them. And her body ached and burned, begging her to pay Hawke's price. If she had to choose between pride and pleasure, would it be so very terrible, just this once, if pleasure won?

"I want you to part my legs," she said, her voice husky with need. "I want you to stroke me with your tongue as you stroked me with your fingers this morning. I want . . . I want to fly free again, as if I were shedding my body and soaring into the clouds."

She was braced for ridicule, or even refusal. Instead, his harsh expression melted and he smiled into her eyes with all the ardent tenderness her heart could desire. "Well, then," he said softly, raising up to reposition them both, "prepare to fly."

Spreading her legs, he nestled between them and offered her one last smile. Then he bent to his loving task.

His work-roughened thumbs slid between her outer lips and urged them apart, holding them there with a sure touch that made her pulse flutter. His tongue began its courtship skimming the frills of her inner lips, then plundering between them before rising to lick the little nub of flesh that housed her body's most volatile desires.

At first he teased at it, coaxing her higher and higher on the steep path of arousal. Then, when the restless rhythm of her hips made it impossible for her to hide her readiness, he suckled the nub as he had suckled her nipples, and Amelia felt a surge of pleasure fling her high, as if she were a gull rising effortlessly on a current of air.

Hawke's mouth grew more insistent. Panicking, she tried to squirm away from his shrewd demands, seeking a moment's respite in which to catch her breath and recapture her sanity, but he would not allow it. He held her fast and devoured her, driving her to the edge of sweetest madness. Drumming her heels, she twisted and bucked in desperation, calling his name, crying for mercy, throbbing, seeking—

And in the end, overwhelmed, she screamed out her pleasure, just as he had promised that she would.

Chapter Eight

In the aftermath of Amelia's climax, Hawke's own body clamored for relief, but he ignored it, refusing to ask Amelia to gratify him, just as he refused to take steps to gratify himself. What had begun as an idle plan was now a point of stiff-necked pride for him: yesterday had been consecrated to his physical pleasure, but today was solely for Amelia. Only tomorrow, on their final day together, would he permit them to pleasure one another.

He told himself that the structure of the schedule, hatched before he became enamored of her, would protect him now from his own wayward emotions. But he was beginning to have his doubts about that.

He was beginning to have his doubts about other things, as well. As soon as he unbound her wrists, he stretched out beside her on the bed and pulled her close against him, kissing her hair as he cradled her in his arms. She nestled willingly against him, not knowing how great a risk she had run, not dreaming that, half an hour past, when she made her accusations against Henderson's honesty, anger had filled him— anger fierce enough to test his control and threaten her well-being.

He'd been all too conscious of the belt at his waist, and of the dangerous little voice in his head reminding him that she'd felt the sting of a good strapping often enough at her father's hands; that perhaps it was all she respected; that perhaps her wild accusation was a twisted plea for just such a whipping.

But he had known it wasn't so. Dear God, who better than he to know such a thing? How many times had he and his sister felt the bite of a belt across their backsides? Far worse, how many times, as children, had they cowered in their beds, sobbing into their pillows, listening to the leather whistle and crack while their father punished their mother for some imagined trespass?

"It's no more than your grandfather did to me when I was growing up," his father would growl if they dared to complain. "Spare the rod and spoil the child. And women are in worse need of correction than children. Mark my words, boy, when you're old enough to take a wife you'll see the truth of it. And you, girl—" he had said, shaking his finger in Cecily's tiny face, "mind that you honor your husband in all things when you're a woman grown, or be prepared to pay the price of your folly."

Hawke recalled all too well how, in the end, their father's vile temper had been the family's undoing, and both children had been sent to live with their aunt and uncle. It must be twenty years or more since he had heard his father's grating voice or seen his muscles bulge as he vented his anger on the innocents around him. But Hawke remembered. He remembered, and he never ceased his own internal vigilance, monitoring himself and his temper, testing his control, fearing that he might yet prove to be his father's son.

Cecily, younger and braver, had found a kind man to marry, but Hawke had avoided taking a wife. Sea captains were often a solitary lot, and he always had a welcome place at the inn his sister and her husband ran. If he sometimes tired of paying for a woman's favors, or wished in a weak moment that he had someone special in his life who cared about him and him alone, that was his misfortune. The real tragedy would be to give his heart to some sweet girl and only then discover that he could not control his inner demons, after all.

Naked in his arms, Amelia drifted off, all innocence and trust. Cherishing the fleeting miracle of her presence, Hawke let her sleep.

It was clear to Amelia, as they ate their evening meal, that whatever had been troubling Hawke all day still had not left him in peace. She almost wished she had not mentioned Henderson's perfidy to him, but what kindness would that have been? If someone took advantage of her trust, she would want to know of it, and she could only assume that the same was true for Hawke. Perhaps he was contemplating the difficulties that would attend dismissing his first mate and finding a replacement for him.

Or perhaps he still did not believe her accusation. After all, she and the captain had scarcely known each other for two days. By society's standards, they were virtual strangers.

Indeed, by society's standards, there was no easy word at all for what they had become to one another.

"Tomorrow, when we dock," Hawke said into the silence, "I want you to wait here in my cabin until the initial arrangements have been made for the cargo. Then I'll be free to take you to the inn."

Clearly, he still had every intention of winning their wager and escorting her from his life. She could only imagine how astonished he would be if he knew how she longed to defeat his plan and stay by his side.

Perhaps he would relent. Perhaps there would yet be a chance to persuade him not to leave her behind.

Or perhaps, by this time tomorrow, her passage aboard the *Soul-Catcher* would be at an end and she would be faced with the cool indifference of a strange town, without a single friend to whom she could turn. "You are certain there will be room for me at the inn?"

She thought that the question might anger him, but he offered her a quick smile of reassurance. "The inn is run by my sister and brother-in-law. Don't worry. They'll make room for you."

Hawke's sister? The owner of the gown? Did she dare to hope, then, that she might have one friend, ready-made? If it was her fate to leave the ship, there was some crumb of comfort to be had from the thought that she'd be sleeping beneath Hawke's sister's roof.

But she had learned the taste of greed, these past two days, and she had always had a taste for honesty. Relieved though she might be by Hawke's news, it was not his sister's roof she longed to sleep beneath, nor was it his sister whose affection Amelia most craved.

She had made the wretched mistake of losing her heart to Hawke, and after he dumped her on his sister's doorstep tomorrow like an unwanted orphan, she would have an entire empty lifetime in which to repent of her foolishness.

Hawke couldn't sleep. The cabin was too warm; the bed was too small; Amelia was too desirable. For hours, he had lain upon the mattress as if he were a torture victim on the rack, trying not to disturb her by tossing and turning, all the while longing to disturb her with something far more potent than his restlessness.

He tried counting his breaths, but found himself counting Amelia's, instead. He tried to make his mind a blank, but found himself reviewing the past two days in such a wealth of sensual detail that sweat formed on his forehead. Finally, desperate, he tried consciously relaxing his muscles, starting at his toes and working upward . . . but the folly of that effort became painfully apparent when shins, knees and thighs lead the way inexorably to that particular muscle of his anatomy which seemed incapable of relaxing so long as Amelia was stretched beside him.

On deck, eight bells rang, announcing the midnight hour. Tomorrow night, he would sleep ashore. The night after that, he would sleep at sea, snug in this cabin, snug in this bed.

Alone.

Sadness filled him, a lost, woebegone feeling he had not experienced in years. He tried to exert control and steel himself against it, but the sadness seemed to have a life of its own. The need to gather Amelia into his arms became a physical pain, an aching in his chest that made him shudder.

"Hawke?" Her soft whisper broke the silence.

He lay motionless, holding his breath.

She turned toward him. "Hawke? Are you all right?"

If he stayed here, if she touched him, he would break. Instead, he sat up and slid from the bed, out of her reach.

A new thought struck him: the old day was done and the new one—his last with Amelia—had just begun. It was now 'tomorrow.' At the very least, he could win some physical release for them both.

"Get up," he entreated with sudden energy, reaching for his trousers. "Come with me."

"Come with you? Out of the cabin? You can't mean it. I'm naked!"

"Here. Put on Cecily's gown and take my cloak. That will suffice. It's the dead of night. No one will see."

And she came. Sweet and willing, she donned the gown and allowed him to fasten the heavy cape around her shoulders. It swallowed her whole, the dark fabric dragging on the floor, covering her bare feet. Within the cloak's hooded embrace, she was no more than a moon-pale face floating on air.

"Come with me," he said again, and they left the cabin together.

For two days, they had sailed steadily south, and the touch of tonight's air was noticeably warm, as if summer had been racing north to keep this rendezvous with them. With a nod to the sailor on night watch, who was patrolling near the stern, Hawke guided Amelia to the prow of the ship, urging her on until they stood at the forward rail.

The breeze, stiff and lively, pushed at the heavy fabric of the cloak, and Amelia grasped its edges anxiously, clutching it close.

Hawke positioned himself behind her, pressing his chest to her back, his groin to the pert swell of her bottom. Then he teased back the edge of the hood so that he could murmur in her ear. "The night watchman will not venture forward while we are here. And even if he did, he would see the back of me, nothing more. Enjoy the air, Amelia. Enjoy the night. Have you ever seen such stars?"

She leaned her head against him, the better to view them. "Beautiful," she whispered.

"Indeed. They are the night watch's bonus pay, the sprinkling of bright beauty that compensates a man for the hours he spends on deck, away from his warm bunk. And tonight, they are my gift to you."

"You are giving me the stars?"

"I am."

She relaxed against him. "Young girls are told to be wary of men who offer such extravagant gifts."

"Are you feeling wary, Amelia?"

"Of you? Never."

Her answer should have alarmed him. Instead, he felt a glow of pride. "They are no more than you deserve."

She made a little sound of contentment, deep in her throat. At the merest urging of his hand against her cheek, she turned her head and raised her chin, seeking his mouth with her own.

It was an eager kiss she offered him, generous and arousing. Hawke gloried in it, and when he slid his hand beneath the weighty fabric of the cloak to stroke her breast through the airy gauze that covered it, he found a ready welcome there, as well. In a trice, he loosed several of the little bows and slipped his hand within to touch her satin flesh.

For a minute, he was content, but the yearning of his cock redoubled, inciting him to seek a more intimate invasion. One by one, moving ever lower, he dispensed with the neatly tied ribbons, then stroked the flat of his hand over the sweet curve of her belly, down to the dainty thicket of curls.

And that was all the farther he could reach. She was such a tiny thing that even his long arms had their limit. With a little moan of arousal, she rose on tiptoe, trying to aid him in his quest, but he knew it was not a pose she could easily maintain. "Step up onto my boots," he urged.

"I'll hurt your feet!"

"Nonsense. You weigh next to nothing. Step up, I say."

And she did, light as a sparrow. His fingertips slid down to claim her pearl, and she gasped, arching against him.

With one hand at her breast and the other plundering the treasure between her nether lips, Hawke strove to delight her, and found that the effort fed his own delight as well. He and Amelia courted ecstasy, partnering one another in a dance as old as time, swept out of their separate selves and combined by means of a mysterious alchemy into something far grander than either of them could ever hope to be alone.

When Hawke sensed that Amelia's climax was nearly upon her, he allowed himself to thrust with increasing abandon against the sweet cushion of her bottom. Although his cock was imprisoned in his trousers and separated from her by layers of his clothing and her own, the excitement of the moment was enough to compensate. He felt his balls tighten and lift, felt the need and frustration of the past day evaporate, felt the heady pressure build . . .

Amelia's cry of completion merged with the surging hiss of the ocean waves, freeing Hawke to follow. Crushing her against him, he strained and bucked, groaning aloud, abandoning himself to his passion, his pleasure, his deliverance.

His love.

Chapter Nine

Afterwards, when Hawke swept her into his arms, Amelia clung to him, limp with pleasure, pressing kisses to his cheek, his jaw, his neck. "Must we go in?" she begged.

"You're chilled."

"No, I'm trembling from what you make me feel."

"In either event, we will be more comfortable in our bed."

Our bed. Whether he had spoken the words intentionally or not, Amelia thrilled to the thought. *Our bed. The bed we share. The bed where we belong together.*

As Hawke carried her across the deck, she let her head fall back, intent on capturing one last look at the stars he had gifted to her.

Instead, high above, she saw a dark form and a pale face, its gaze trained on her.

Fear tightened her arms around Hawke's neck.

He stopped. "What's wrong?"

"A man up there," she whispered, "looking down at us."

Hawke pivoted, his gaze searching the rigging. She knew when he spotted the man, for he stiffened, then called out, his voice low but sharp as a whip crack. "Slykin!"

"Cap'n," came the laconic reply.

"Why aren't you below?"

"Couldn't sleep. Thought I'd climb up here for a breath of air." His chuckle was a nasty thing. "Got a show instead."

She could feel fury pulsing through Hawke, but his voice remained steady. "When we reach port, collect your final pay packet, Slykin. I've no more use for you on a ship of mine."

"That's hardly fair, sir," the big man whined. "Not my fault now, was it, sir, me bein' here first and all? Can't very well blame a man for what he sees, can you?"

"You're off my ship tomorrow," Hawke repeated. "Now get back to your bunk." Then he turned and continued on his way. When he passed the sailor on watch, he said, "Slykin is under orders to go below immediately. If he loiters, get Williams and Dennison to tie him to the mast for the rest of the night. I've had all I intend to take from that man."

"Aye, sir. I'll see to it."

When Hawke and Amelia reached the privacy of their cabin, he stood her gently on her feet and divested her of the heavy cloak. "I am so sorry," he said, lighting a candle. "So very sorry—"

"For what?" she demanded. "From his vantage point, I doubt whether the man could see anything more than the tops of our heads. And as to what he may have heard, it's my own fault for not being able to curb my tongue when the moment is on me."

He cupped her cheek, frowning. "That's a generous attitude, but you can't deny that you found his presence alarming. I assured you that we would have a measure of privacy, and you took me at my word."

Touched by his distress, she said gently, "If it makes you feel better to apologize, then I accept, but I imagine the members of your crew have long since come to their own conclusions about why I am on this ship. In their view, my reputation is already lost. Why then should you fret yourself unduly about this incident?"

Hawke looked stricken. "I will assemble them all tomorrow, before we dock, and disabuse them of the notion that you . . . that I've . . . that we. . . ."

"They will not believe you, even if you do," she told him. "Don't dwell on it. They are sailors, not townsmen. I doubt they will linger long enough to soil my name very widely. So long as your family understands the truth of the matter, that is all I can fairly ask."

But it was not all she desired. *If you are so concerned about my well-being, you could wed me.* The words lurked, unspoken, in her mind. *I would be a good wife to you and love you faithfully for all our days.*

But there was no point in crying for the moon. She would have to be content with the stars.

The porthole was rosy with dawn when Amelia woke to face her final day aboard the *Soul-Catcher*. Snug beneath the blankets, with the man she loved sleeping soundly at her side, she wished the moment could last forever.

But the rolling motion of the cabin told its own tale. The ship was sailing inexorably toward its next destination. And when they reached it, her idyll with Hawke would be at an end.

The thought made her heart ache. Stricken, she gazed at the walls which had stood silent witness to the happiest moments of her life. She wanted to memorize every detail of her surroundings, storing it all away against the long, lonely famine that lay before her.

For the moment, safe as a nesting bird, she sheltered there, taking stock, savoring the cabin's clean confines and tidy furnishings. Here in Hawke's well-ordered haven, away from the abusive chaos of her father's house, she had begun to discover who she truly was and what she might yet become. When the *Soul-Catcher* reached port in a few short hours, how could she bear to leave this place?

Far worse, how could she bear to leave Hawke?

She felt as if she belonged here, tucked close against his side, but her presence was, in reality, an ephemeral thing. When she left, there would be nothing here to remind Hawke of the few magical days during which she had shared his cabin, his bed, his body. Even the lovely gown she had worn when he pleasured her belonged to someone else.

Amelia fought back tears, determined not to taint the little time that remained. Today, by Hawke's own decree, she and he were to enjoy what she had learned, sharing the pleasure between them. It would be foolish to allow the coming separation to overshadow that joy. Right now, in this moment, Hawke was here with her. That would have to be enough.

I thought you wanted to stay with him forever.

She spurned the little voice within. Of course she longed to stay, but no one was offering her that choice.

Persuade Hawke to offer it.

Heaven knew, she would if she could.

But you can. If you dare.

Amelia's pulse fluttered. Words would not sway Hawke from his decision. If she wanted to stay, she knew of only one way to accomplish it, and that was to use all she had learned to tempt him into claiming her virginity.

A rush of emotions flooded her at the very thought: hope, excitement, arousal and, truth be told, a shiver of apprehension at the thought of such a union. For the past two days, she had marveled at his glorious cock, proud thing that it was. But how her body could possibly accommodate something of that length and girth surpassed her understanding and tested her faith.

It must be one of nature's miracles, that was all she could tell herself. Hadn't her village been full of married women? Did she really imagine that each and every one of them possessed some special physical ability that she lacked?

No. Strange as it seemed, it must be how the world worked. Somehow, despite the disparity between them, men's bodies and women's bodies joined. It was as simple—and as mysterious—as that. When the time came, she would put herself in Hawke's hands, trusting him to show her the way.

She bent her gaze on his sleeping face. When he was awake, he exuded an impressive aura of command, of strength under tight control just beneath his smooth manners and surface civility. But she had also experienced the gentler side of his personality. Observing him now, she saw that the vulnerability of sleep revealed that softer facet of his nature in the sensual set of his mouth and the web of smile lines that gathered at the corners of his eyes.

This was a man worthy of her trust, deserving of her love.

Unbidden, she had already given him her heart. Now she was determined to give her body as well.

Amelia eyed the bedclothes, and saw that the blanket was already subtly tented at his groin. Despite the early hour, Hawke's cock was awake. And she knew just the salute with which to help it greet the morning.

In his dream, Hawke swam through a kelp forest far beneath the surface of the sea, chasing a mermaid with hair the color of pirate doubloons. She drifted just out of reach, and he followed after her, miraculously untroubled by the lack of air. Strands of seaweed whispered over his body as he passed, arousing against his skin but maddeningly insubstantial. His cock throbbed in vain, hungry and frustrated, and a soft groan escaped his lips.

As if finally moved to pity, the mermaid slowed and looked back over her shoulder at him, her dove-gray eyes wide with some unspoken emotion. Then she smiled and, lithe as a fish, darted back to him to take his cock between her warm and lovely lips.

Pleasure raced through him like a bolt of lightning, and Hawke woke to find himself in the midst of a reality as potent as his dream. He was in bed, the covers stripped away to reveal his rampant cock to the morning light, and Amelia was kneeling astride his legs, her yellow hair spread about her like sunshine as she lowered her mouth onto his shaft.

Hawke groped for control, finding his voice with difficulty. "What a very apt pupil you are proving to be!"

Instead of replying, she took him deeper, intensifying the suction of her mouth on his rigid flesh.

If she kept this up, he would spend in another minute. "Ease up there, lass, and let me sweeten your morning as you are sweetening mine."

At that, she raised up until only the cap of his cock remained between her satiny lips. Her gaze met his, her eyebrows lifted in puzzled inquiry.

"What you're doing to me feels marvelous, and I'm loathe to miss a moment of it, but there's no reason why only one of us should be pleasured. Come straddle my chest," Hawke encouraged, "so that I can reach to caress you as well, sweeting."

She hesitated, as if considering the invitation, and swirled her tongue over the head of his cock.

A surge of pleasure flooded his brain, drying his mouth and causing his heartbeat to quicken. With difficulty, Hawke fought the urge to pump his hips skyward, driving himself ever deeper into that luscious mouth. It would be wonderful to lay back and allow Amelia to excite his cock to the bursting point . . . but, to his own amazement, he wanted more from the moment than just that.

He wanted to explore her soft curves with the palms of his hands. He wanted to send his fingertips delving in the mysteries hidden between her legs. He wanted the scent of her to fill his head, and then he wanted to dine upon her, savoring the delicate love-dew that would gather in response to his worshiping touch. He wanted to listen to her moan as the pleasure built within her, and to hear her cry out with passion as he wooed her to the edge of endurance and beyond.

Naturally, he was eager for his own release as well, but he sensed, somehow, that her joy would enhance his own, transforming the moment into more than a fleeting ripple of physical pleasure.

"Come to me," he urged, and reached out to her with beseeching hands.

Allowing his cock to slip from between her lips, she smiled and obeyed, moving up the mattress on hands and knees, her breasts pendulous and perfect as she made her way toward him.

The sight enflamed him. With greedy hands, Hawke stroked her shoulders and reached for her breasts, plumping the generous flesh before saluting each nipple with the gentlest of pinches.

Amelia's cheeks glowed and her lips parted.

Gratified, Hawke smiled. "Faith, girl, you have the most magnificent breasts north of the equator. Come closer still and let me sample them."

Docile as a lamb, she placed her hands on either side of his head and lowered herself by small degrees until he could finally capture a taut, pink nipple between his eager lips. Nibbling and licking, he played with it, then settled happily to the task, delighting in her reactions as he suckled one breast rhythmically while toying with the other.

Soon she was squirming above him with beautiful abandon. What a little firebrand she was, when the mood was on her! Hawke reveled in her responsiveness, proud to know that it was he who had taught her the pleasure her body could bring to them both. Sliding his hand lower, he used his fingertips to draw a line from breast to belly, and from there reached to stroke between her parted thighs.

A fresh thrill of arousal rocked him when he discovered that her crisp curls were already damp with desire. Giddy with power, he pressed a single finger between her nether lips and traced the honeyed slit from her pearl to the heated core of her entrance.

Amelia bore down instinctively at his touch, and the first inch of his finger entered her.

Hawke froze.

Above him, in a hoarse whisper, she asked, "Is that where it would go into me, that fine cock of yours?"

The thought was incendiary. For answer, he drew more deeply on her nipple and slid his finger a careful inch deeper.

It was like sinking into the heart of a molten flame. Her flesh closed around him, grasping in vain at the slender invader whose passage was eased by the generous honey she exuded.

"More," she pleaded, her untutored hips moving as she tried to take him deeper. Instead, Hawke withdrew his finger from her core and used it to tantalize her avid pearl. His efforts soon won a convulsive shudder from her, followed by a sweet whimper of need that set his cock on fire.

He quickened his efforts, intending to stroke her to completion, but she retreated and edged back to kneel upright at his groin, her knees far-spread by the width of his body. With a winsome blush that raced from her cheeks down to her breasts, she pressed her own hand briefly between her thighs, then lowered her glistening fingers to stroke his cock.

He nearly came up off the bed, the sensation was so grand.

"Yes," he huffed as she massaged the length of his shaft, down and then up again, her coated fingers gliding effortlessly.

He closed his eyes, the better to relish the sensation, and groaned aloud as her fingers tightened and the pleasure intensified. The head of his cock was suddenly drowning in liquid delight, pressed against something hot and sleek. Opening his eyes with difficulty, he saw that Amelia was teasing him with the ball of her thumb, rubbing her juices into the tip of his ravenous cock, then pausing while she slipped her thumb between her legs again before returning to rub him in quick little circles that made his brain seize and his pulse redouble.

Giving himself up to the ecstasy she created, he let his heavy eyelids slide back down, concentrating on delaying the inevitable moment when the pleasure would overwhelm him. He needed to focus his attention on something else, anything else, in order to blunt his exquisite awareness of her touch. He tried to think about the long candle-lit hours he had spent the night before, poring laboriously over the columns in his ledger, while Amelia slept a few scant feet away as tempting as Eve. He tried to think about the stubborn figures that would not resolve themselves as they ought, figures that supported Amelia's claims of Henderson's perfidy. He tried to think—

He abandoned all thought, certain that he would die of delight, as Amelia shifted her hold on him and found a way to nestle the cap of his cock in an embrace that was hotter, wetter, tighter than anything she had yet managed. Spurred by this escalation, Hawke felt his control slipping as his pulse began to thunder and his balls tightened. It was too good, too rich, too sweet . . . and yet he needed it to be better, richer, sweeter still.

Delirious with need, he bucked upward and was rewarded by the very sensations he sought. He panted, and heard Amelia's breath catch as well. He bucked again, close to the moment, frantic to achieve the pinnacle.

Her grip on him now was a velvet vise, capturing more and more of his cock, leaving it nowhere to go but upward, where it longed to be, but requiring him to work for it, making him push and strain in order to progress even fractionally. Nearly overcome, Hawke opened his eyes, wanting the sight of his cock in her hands to fill his brain as she overmastered his body.

What he saw instead was his stout shaft rising between Amelia's thighs, the head of it already well lodged within her entrance.

She wriggled. His cock slid a little deeper, and a fresh wave of pleasure crashed through him.

There was still time to thwart her, if he had the will to do so. As proof of that, Amelia's next effort brought his cock-head up against a new resistance, one that stopped his progress even as it stoked his ravenous need of her.

If he thought the barrier would daunt her, he was quickly disabused of the notion. Her nipples were pebble-hard, her cheeks flaming, her breath a raw stutter in her throat. The long lashes that veiled her eyes lifted, and she snared him with an ardent look. "Please," she gasped, and he knew he had never seen a greater look of certainty and passion on any woman's face.

The temptation was more than he could withstand. Reaching out, he gripped her tiny waist and guided her higher before urging her to descend again.

Instead of resisting, she bore down with a will, and he matched her with an upward thrust of his own, repeating the motion once, twice, then a vigorous third time before he felt the fragile membrane give way beneath his assault.

With a roar, Hawke pressed fully into her, his cock burying itself to the hilt. At his hands' urging, Amelia continued to rise and fall, rise and fall, rise and fall, finding the rhythm of it, taking in all that he had to offer, riding him like a ship in a gale, until he could bear it no more. His cock went mad, thundering into her as if it could bury itself forever in the sweet depths of her body, spewing its essence in long, urgent spasms. And at the end, just as the demands of his own deliverance began to fade, he felt Amelia's body quicken of its own accord, pressing down onto him in tiny, desperate pulses that came more and more quickly until, at last, she cried out as if her heart had been pierced, and crumpled forward, still impaled on his dwindling cock.

And only then, with his heart still thudding and Amelia's dear, sweet body cradled against his chest, did Hawke begin to face the full import of what he had done.

Chapter Ten

One moment, Hawke was warm and lax beneath her, his heartbeat a strong, comforting rhythm in her ear. The next, his muscles grew rigid and the beating of his heart became as erratic as a bird trapped in a hunter's net.

He had not said a word, nor had she, since the momentous joining of their bodies changed her world forever. Dazzled by the experience, she had even dared to hope that, when Hawke did speak, it would be to voice his happiness over what had transpired. But the sudden tensing of his body warned her that those dreams were vain ones.

Taking the burden on herself, she braced her hands on the mattress and slid free of him, wincing as his cock slid from within her. "I'm all sticky," she said by way of excuse, and tried to banish the quaver from her voice. "Do you suppose I might have some fresh water for the basin?"

"Lie down," Hawke directed brusquely. "You've had a shock. If it's water you want, I'll fetch it."

"And I'll be needing my clothes," she continued, as if he hadn't spoken. "My own clothes, that is." She moved stiffly toward the edge of the bed, but Hawke put a hand on her arm as if to detain her. Amelia pulled away and moved beyond his reach. "Have we long until we reach port?"

"Long enough. Look here, I'll get your clothes for you and I'll fetch some water. But not yet. Face me, Amelia."

She would not weep, for it would squander what little pride remained to her. Sternly, she willed her tears to recede unshed, and then turned back to confront his wrath . . . only to find, to her surprise, that she could detect no anger in his eyes, only distress. Cast adrift by this, she waited in silence, taking in the sight of his once mighty cock, which now lay draped upon his thigh, limp and spent and streaked here and there with red.

He must have followed her gaze, for he said more gently, "Blood from your maidenhead. Are you in pain?"

She felt sore and stretched, nothing worse. "No."

Hawke said, "Good," but his forehead was pleated with worry. "Still, I did what I swore I would not, Amelia. I took your virginity."

"I gave it," she said, her voice still unsteady.

"Nevertheless, you made it quite clear when you undertook this voyage that you intended to remain a maiden. Indeed, you offered me a wager, one which I accepted and had no intention of losing. But I have lost. Indeed, we have both lost."

What could she possibly say to that? She held her tongue, waiting to see where his words would lead.

"I consider myself to be an honorable man," Hawke said, "and yet I must now choose between reneging on a bet and breaking a solemn vow." Sitting up, he stretched out his hand and touched her cheek with disarming gentleness. "Amelia, as much as it pains me to say so, I cannot marry you."

This was pain, this sudden thrust as if her soul had been ripped from her body. It left her gasping in response to its cruel intensity, and she could tell that Hawke had read her emotions, for his own face looked tortured, as well.

"What was the vow?" she asked, trembling. "Was it a marriage pledge? Did you lie when you said you had no wife?"

"No. I have never had a wife and never will."

"Then what was this solemn vow you claim you gave? What is so important that it excuses you from your promise to me?"

The skin around his eyes looked bruised, as if he had lain awake all night while she slept. "It is a vow I made on the day we buried my mother, after my father beat her to death."

Amelia stared at him, stunned to silence by his answer.

"I swore on her grave that I would never risk harming a woman I loved, the way my father had harmed my mother for all the years they were together. Never." He rose abruptly from the bed. "I won't risk breaking that oath, not even to preserve my honor. For your sake, I do not dare."

"But you would never—"

He turned away, picking up his pants. "Stay with my sister," he instructed as his feet slid into the pantlegs. "I will pay for your keep for two months, not the single month we agreed upon. Stay with her until you are certain you are not with child as a result of my recklessness today. If you are, I will pay for your keep and the child's for the rest of your lives, and that is a promise that I would die before breaking." Looking around wildly, he snatched his shirt from the back of the desk chair and pulled it over his head, emerging a moment later to say, "But if we are spared that fate, then make a new life for yourself. A happy life. Cecily is bound to know some fine young men in search of a wife, men who will cherish you as you deserve to be cherished. Trust her. She has a good heart."

"As do you," Amelia said stubbornly.

Hawke was already grabbing up his boots and striding barefoot toward the door. "I wish that it were true," he said, his voice laced with longing. "You will never know how dearly I wish it."

"Wait! If you'd only listen to reason—"

But he shook his head in brisk denial. "I will have your clothes and a pitcher of warm water brought down. You will have the cabin to yourself until we dock. Wait here for me. I will come as soon after that as I can get free, to escort you to my sister's inn." A vein throbbed at his temple. "It is not enough. I know that. At the inn, you and I will speak of this matter again, and lay plans for how best I can atone for all you have been through. But for now, I think it is wisest that we stay separate."

And he walked out of the cabin, leaving Amelia to surrender in solitary anguish to her tears.

The wind was brisk, the sails were taut, and the *Soul-Catcher* was making fine time as she beat her way down the coastline toward her home port. Standing alone on the foredeck where he and Amelia had played out their passion under the wide night sky, Hawke acknowledged his heavy heart.

He was usually glad enough to see a voyage end, since he enjoyed negotiating the sale of his cargo almost as much as he enjoyed the sea itself. But the end of this journey promised enough difficulties to daunt any man.

First of all, Slykin would have to be paid off and dismissed, and while Hawke looked forward to the man's departure, he loathed the prospect of a final encounter with him. Still, he had been fool enough to hire the man, and now it was his duty to rid the ship of Slykin's disagreeable presence.

The second difficulty was the problem of Henderson. In his heart, Hawke had known all along that Amelia was not the sort of person to lay an accusation that was groundless. He knew, as well, that he himself had been guilty of delegating far too much responsibility to Henderson. But the man excelled at all the shipboard tasks that were the least appealing, and it had been all too easy to turn more and more matters over to Henderson that were properly his own to manage.

He hated being proven foolish by Amelia, just as he hated to think that Henderson would abuse his trust. But neither of those unpleasant emotions solved a thing. Being captain meant taking responsibility for his own actions and those of his crew. Late last night, while Amelia slept, he had lighted a candle and worked his way laboriously down seven different pages of the recent ledger, reckoning the numbers on paper when he could, counting on his fingers when he had to, and the result had been the same in each case: Henderson's neat columns of figures came up short, every time. And the money in the cash box, to which only Hawke and the first mate had access, tallied precisely with what Henderson's figures said should be there.

Perhaps the overage lay hidden in Henderson's tiny cabin. Or perhaps the man had found a better hiding place for it, elsewhere on the ship. In either event, Hawke faced the need for ordering a second dismissal, one that would cause him far more inconvenience and distress than Slykin ever could.

And then, Hawke thought with a pang, there was the matter of Amelia herself.

If he had suspected, when he claimed a chair at that hapless card game, where a night's drunken wagering might lead, he would have turned tail and run for the lonely safety of his ship. Instead, he had stayed, and played, and won. And the result of that caprice was the presence of this dainty, spirited woman in his cabin, in his life, in his heart . . . where she could not, for her own sake, be permitted to stay, even though he had now marred her future as surely as her abusive father had marred her past.

"Captain?"

It was Henderson, looking as fresh-scrubbed and efficient as ever, his vest buttoned neatly over a crisp, white shirt.

"Yes?"

"The young woman's clothes are ready whenever you require them, sir. And you'll be pleased to know that the wind has enabled us to make excellent time. We should dock by midday, several hours ahead of our initial expectation."

"Very good, Mr. Henderson." But it wasn't good. It wasn't good at all.

"Shall I take the clothing to your cabin, sir?"

"No, bring it to me here on deck. But first take a bucket of warm water from the galley to my cabin."

"Aye, sir," came the prompt reply, in the first mate's unfailingly efficient manner.

Suddenly, the duplicity of it all was more than Hawke could stomach. "And as soon as we dock, Henderson, I'd like a word with you in my cabin."

"Aye, sir," Henderson replied with a bright smile.

No doubt he thought Hawke intended to deliver a private message of commendation for the manner in which he'd handled the voyage. Well, let him think what he liked. He'd know the truth of the matter shortly.

Hawke gave a nod. "That will be all, Mr. Henderson."

"Aye, sir," said Henderson, and Hawke watched grimly as his first mate headed off to fetch Amelia's clothes.

It had never been Amelia's way to cry for long. In her experience, tears solved nothing, and she needed to think. Something in what Hawke had said before he walked out was nagging at her memory, something important that had flown by in the heat of the instant. Something she needed to recall.

Wiping her eyes with the heel of her hand, she decided to tidy the bed, and then to tidy herself. Routine. Routine would bring calm and, with it, the best chance for her mind to cast about for whatever it was that she was trying to remember.

Smoothing the rumpled sheets, she found two small smears of blood upon the bottom one. So, she reflected wryly, Hawke would have a visible reminder of her, after all—at least until Henderson did the laundry.

When the blankets had been smoothed as well, and the pillows plumped and placed, Amelia made her ablutions as best she could with the scant inch of chilly water left in the pitcher. Then she donned Cecily's gown for a final time, rather than huddle naked while she waited for her clothes to be brought. That accomplished, she plaited her hair, then looked for some further occupation that might force the time to pass.

As her gaze traveled the familiar room, she was surprised to see that the ledger stood open on Hawke's desk, accompanied by a much-bitten stub of pencil, a crumpled sheaf of loose pages, and a burned-down candle stub that had not been there before. Puzzled, Amelia stepped closer to examine her find.

Large, uneven lines of figures covered the papers, printed in a rough hand far different from Henderson's delicate penmanship on the official ledger pages. Hawke's writing? But why would he undertake such a task? And when had he found the leisure to do so?

She could think of only one explanation: despite his growls to the contrary, it seemed that Hawke had not totally dismissed her warnings about Henderson's manipulation of the accounts. And she could only suppose that he had set to work on double-checking the totals late last night, after she and he had returned from their midnight assignation on deck, under the stars.

Under the stars he had given to her.

She stopped still, remembering the moment . . . and suddenly she knew what it was that Hawke had said, just a short while ago.

I swore on her grave that I would never risk harming a woman I loved.

Those had been his very words. *A woman I loved.*

Hawke . . . loved her?

A sharp rap on the door made her jump. Warm water, no doubt, and a welcome addition it would be. She waited long enough for the sailor who had delivered it to be on about his other duties. Then, still adorned in Cecily's pretty gown, she opened the door and bent quickly to claim the bucket.

To her shock, a beefy hand shoved her back into the room, and a booted foot kicked the cabin door farther open, knocking over the pail and spilling its contents. She cried out in startled protest as a massive man thrust his way inside and closed the door behind himself.

Amelia looked into his face, and her heart pounded as she recognized him as the man who had spied on them from the rigging.

He leered at her. "Edward Slykin, at your service, missy. And I know just who you are. You're the captain's poppet."

Chapter Eleven

Slykin offered her a leering smile. "Well, here's a fine turn of events. I spent all last night thinking up ways to get a moment alone with you before we land. And now, with the crew preparing to dock and that little clerk of the captain's too proud to tote a bucket, look where I was ordered to come!"

Refusing to reveal her terror, Amelia drew herself up proudly. "You've spilled the water all over the hallway. If you're wise, you'll fetch another bucket immediately."

"I've a better idea," he said, and made a grab for her, his thick fingers snagging on the bodice of the gown.

Amelia screamed as the delicate fabric tore. Wrenching free, she scrambled to put the desk between herself and Slykin.

Grinning, the big man simply shoved the table toward her with careless strength, trapping Amelia painfully between its edge and the wall. Unfastening his trousers, he let them drop, leaving nothing but the tail of his filthy shirt to cover his groin. "Come along now, puss," he coaxed in an oily voice. "Don't make me hurt you. We can both have a bit of fun here if you stop your screeching. A good tupping is what you—"

Before he could finish the threat, the cabin door flew open, and Amelia heard a sound she knew as well as her own name: the crack of leather against flesh.

Slykin jumped and looked over his shoulder at his attacker. The leather cracked again, and he howled with pain.

"Come along now, sir," said Hawke, his voice a knife blade of menace. "We can both have a bit of fun here if you stop screeching."

Hobbled by his trousers, Slykin turned awkwardly to face Hawke.

Presented with a rear view, Amelia could see a livid weal marring the backs of his thighs, just below the tattered hem of his shirt.

When the leather cracked for a third time, it seemed to find an exquisitely sensitive target, for the big man let out a high-pitched shriek and toppled like a felled oak, his hands clasped to his groin.

Hawke's gaze was murderous, his face damp with sweat. He stood over his fallen adversary for a frozen moment, fingering the belt in his hands. Then, with a shudder, he knelt and used it to bind Slykin's ankles.

With the big man immobilized, Hawke dragged the table away and came to frame Amelia's face between his hands. "Are you hurt?" he asked in a voice so strained she scarcely recognized it.

His unexpected gentleness nearly caused her control to break. Summoning the dregs of her courage, she answered, "Bruised and frightened, nothing more."

"You're certain?"

"I swear."

"Thank God." Hawke kissed her forehead, then her cheek. "Can you bear to wait a few more minutes then, while I drag this garbage out of your presence?"

She nodded, no longer trusting her voice.

Stepping back around the table, Hawke seized the writhing man beneath the armpits, hauled him out into the corridor and pulled the door firmly shut behind himself, leaving Amelia alone in the cabin once again.

Shivering with reaction, she listened to the muted sounds of his voice as he shouted for assistance and issued crisp, angry orders concerning Slykin's fate. Only when the tramp of booted feet had faded to silence did he open the door and return.

This time, he came to her immediately and gathered her into his embrace, wrapping his arms around her so tightly that she found it difficult to breathe. "Dear God," she heard him say against her hair. "Dear God."

She realized that he was shivering now, just as she was. Stirring against him, she said in apology, "Cecily's new gown. . . ." And with that, sobs escaped her for the second time that morning, hurting her chest with the force of their passage.

He let her cry for a time, then said softly in her ear, "My dear Amelia, gowns can be mended, or new ones bought. Don't distress yourself over it. And don't worry any further about Slykin. He's under guard, and he'll be turned over to the authorities as soon as we reach port. You're certain he didn't harm you?"

That won a shaky laugh from her. "Yes," she reassured him for the third time. "Give me a moment or two and I'll be right as rain."

His embrace eased slightly, although he kept her tucked snugly against him. "I must admit, I'm relieved to hear it, for I need you to be calm and clear-headed now."

"And why is that?"

"Because there is one last difficulty that needs to be resolved, and I cannot accomplish that without you."

Intrigued in spite of herself, Amelia dried her tears. "What could you possibly need from me?"

His blue eyes widened in surprise. "What do I need from you? A million things," Hawke assured her tenderly, "for you are a woman of many talents and graces. Just now, however, I am in sore need of one talent in particular. Come and sit beside me while I explain."

Shortly after the *Soul-Catcher* docked, the expected knock sounded on the cabin door. Amelia looked to Hawke, who was seated behind his desk, looking every inch the fine captain, master of all he surveyed.

He nodded gravely. "You're certain you don't mind acting as a distraction, to allay his suspicions?"

Amelia felt a thrill of excitement at the role she was about to play. "I don't mind a bit," she said, and crossed the room to open the door.

Revealed on the threshold, Mr. Henderson blinked at her in surprise—perhaps startled by her presence or perhaps by the fact that she still wore Cecily's gossamer gown. "I've come at the captain's orders, Miss Fletcher," he said stiffly, his face going red. "But if this is an inconvenient time. . . ."

She giggled and raised an negligent hand to toy with the bodice of her gown, which gaped immodestly as a result of Slykin's rough handling. "We're through," she said, "at least for now. Come in. He's been waiting for you, Mr. Henderson."

Standing aside, she allowed Henderson to enter, then peeked out into the companionway, where she was relieved to see two muscular sailors taking up their positions outside the cabin, just as Hawke had ordered.

Satisfied, she closed the door and strolled to a spot just behind Hawke's chair, where she could rub his shoulders while watching Henderson.

Hawke leaned into her touch like a cat willing to be stroked. "You know, Henderson, I've been thinking about your situation."

Amelia saw Henderson's spine stiffen. "Yes, sir?"

"Yes, and I'm no longer confident that I've dealt fairly with you."

"In what way, sir?"

"Well, you and I both know that your duties as first mate are heavy, and that your attention to them has always been above reproach. And yet, instead of valuing you for that and rewarding the degree of your effort, I assigned you the additional burden of tallying the ship's ledger. Most unfair of me, wouldn't you say?"

"Unfair to me? Not at all," the first mate asserted. "Indeed, Captain, you do yourself an injustice. If you think back, you will recall that it was I who volunteered to shoulder the task."

"Why, so it was," Hawke said slowly. "I am much relieved." Taking Amelia's hand, he drew her around the chair and down onto his lap before addressing Henderson further. "Since you are not feeling ill-used, perhaps you would be willing to use your skill with numbers to render me one additional service this morning. I've made a list of my various winnings at the card tables over these past few voyages. Might you tot it up for me?"

The little man smoothed his vest and smiled. "It would be my pleasure, sir."

Reaching around Amelia, Hawke pawed through the loose papers on his desk, finally claiming a creased half-sheet. "Here we are," he said, handing it across the table. "Have at it, Henderson. I'm eager to see how well I've done."

Henderson drew a stub of pencil from the watch pocket of his vest and examined the list for a moment, then wrote a figure at the bottom of the column. "There you are, sir," he said, and handed the paper back.

Hawke pretended to consult it, careful to hold it where Amelia had a clear view of the numbers in the column and Henderson's total. She ran her tongue along the curve of Hawke's ear, then pressed a kiss to his temple and murmured, "Perfect."

Raising his eyebrows, Hawke looked at Henderson. "As much as all this? And here I was nearly certain it came to less." He dropped the list onto the desktop again and gave Amelia a squeeze. "No insult intended, Henderson, but would you mind reviewing your work?"

"Certainly, sir." If Henderson's answering look held a trace of smug superiority, Amelia could hardly fault him for it. Hawke sounded for all the world like a man too distracted by the woman in his arms to add two and two reliably.

Enjoying her role as an empty-headed wanton, she slipped her hand through the open neck of Hawke's shirt and ran her fingertips over his chest, teasing his nipples. As they hardened, she felt his cock swell against her, trapped though it was inside his trousers. Withdrawing her hand from his shirt, she reached down and offered it a brief salute, scratching her nails lightly against the rough material of Hawke's clothing, knowing that the table's bulk and her own body shielded the action from Henderson's view.

In answer, Hawke laid a trail of nuzzling kisses from her chin down to the pale rise of her breast where the gown was torn away.

Amelia's breath caught in her throat, and her pearl throbbed in envy.

Delicately, Henderson cleared his throat.

Flushed and panting, Hawke and Amelia disentangled themselves.

"Same total again," the first mate said cheerfully. "I had no idea you wagered to such a degree, Captain, and so successfully. You're far richer than I thought."

Hawke shook his head. "On the contrary, Mr. Henderson. It appears that I am much the poorer as a result of entrusting my books to you. The numbers you just tallied are a decimal of the profits we have earned so far on this voyage. With the addition of a final zero, they should match your ledger entry exactly . . . and yet the total you derived and confirmed just now is substantially more generous than what our ledger shows. Why do you suppose that is?"

Henderson went pale.

"Well? What do you have to say for yourself, man?"

The man stood speechless, looking ill, as if the ceiling had tumbled down upon him without warning.

"No justifications to offer?" Hawke asked coldly. "No story to tell of a dying mother who requires more care than a mere first mate can afford to procure? No sweetheart whose unbending father will only allow her to wed you if your bank balance increases? No bitter tale of how I have misused you, thereby forcing you to steal from me? Come now, man. Surely you can find *something* to say in your own defense."

"I . . . didn't think you'd notice."

Hawke allowed the silence to stretch on for a long minute. Then he sighed and passed judgment on the man before him. "You will wait under guard in the galley while your cabin and belongings are searched, after which you will be escorted off this ship, never to return. Is that understood?"

"Yes, sir," Henderson replied, and turned as if to leave.

It struck Amelia that he looked remarkably unconcerned for a man who was about to be parted from the monetary spoils of his crime. In the next instant, something Hawke had said to her on her first night aboard stirred to life in Amelia's memory. She had offered to look after his belongings in return for her passage, and he had replied, 'Those needs are already being quite well met. You would be surprised what a fine seam Henderson can sew.'

"Wait," Amelia said, rising from Hawke's lap.

Henderson could hardly have looked more surprised if the desk itself had spoken. Hawke, too, appeared startled but he made no move to stop her as she rounded the table and approached the first mate. When she reached out, Henderson recoiled, but she pursued him and placed her hand against his neat, black vest.

Everywhere her questing fingers pressed, they met rock-hard resistance.

She turned toward Hawke. "I believe I have found—" she began, but Henderson, snarling, shoved her violently aside and bolted for the cabin door. Wrenching it open, he tried to run, only to find two bulky sailors barring his way.

"—your missing profits," Amelia concluded a bit breathlessly from her position on the floor. "Sewn into the lining of his vest," she elaborated as Hawke arrived to kneel beside her.

"Are you hurt?"

She twined her arms around his neck. "You seem to be asking that quite often, today. No, I am fine. Why don't you finish dealing with this man so that we can see the last of him?"

Hawke cast a look over his shoulder at the sailors who were holding the struggling first mate. "For starters, leave the vest here," he said.

They wrestled Henderson out of his vest and tossed it to Hawke.

He prodded it briefly and nodded in satisfaction. "Fine. Now I want you to take him to the galley, strip him to the waist, and make certain he isn't wearing a money belt. Then tie him to a chair while his quarters and his baggage are searched. If you find nothing more . . . let him go. Put him off the ship."

"You don't want us to summon—"

"I don't want you to summon anyone. I have plans for the rest of my day that don't include pressing charges against this piece of flotsam. But feel free to spread an account of his dismissal around the docks. I doubt he'll find another ship willing to take a chance on him. And you," he said sternly, pointing a finger at Henderson, "be glad that I'm not a flogging man, for you've earned a few stripes with your devious ways."

The big sailors started to drag Henderson from the room, but he fought against them long enough to say, "Perhaps that's true, Captain, but I think you'll find me very hard to replace."

"Hard? Not a bit," Hawke said calmly, "for I don't intend to hire a replacement. I intend to marry one." And he waved his hand in brisk dismissal.

Amelia sat, stunned, as the sailors retreated down the companion-way, dragging Henderson between them. She continued to sit while Hawke rose and closed the cabin door. She was still sitting, thunder-struck, when he returned to her side. "Wh-what you just said . . ." she stammered.

With a loving smile, Hawke dropped the vest into her lap and said, "Here is your dowry—or a windfall with which to start your new life, if you decide you do not wish to wed me."

"But your oath! Your sacred vow!"

He gathered her hands in his. "My vow was that I would never risk harming a woman I love. Nor shall I. But this day has taught me many things. I used to believe that taking a woman to wife would put her at risk from me, because I feared my temper might yet prove ungovern-able. But if I did not lose control when I found Slykin here, half-naked, threatening you, or when Henderson threw you to the floor, then I am willing to gamble that no provocation you offer could ever induce me to lift a hand to you . . . except in this way." Raising their joined hands, he kissed her fingers. "If you are prepared to chance it, then so am I. After all, I am a gambling man, as you may recall."

"And a lucky thing for me that you are." She searched his gaze. "But are you certain that you wish a wife?"

"Yes."

"And that you wish that wife to be me?"

He grinned. "After all the care I've invested in training you? Who else could possibly take your place? But you should consider the mat-ter carefully. I make my living at sea. If your heart is set on a house and a little plot of garden, then I may not be the man to make you happiest. And I do want you to be happy, Amelia, for I love you with all my heart."

Her own heart was singing. "Ever since I was a young girl," she said, "I labored to tend my father's house, and weed his garden, and cook his meals, and wash his clothes, and empty his chamber pots. And now, if I understand what you said to Henderson, you are offering me the chance to live by your side aboard the *Soul-Catcher*, with a ship's cook and a willing crew to keep me like a queen. And in return, I will happily keep the books and see to any other trifling needs the captain may have from time to time."

"Trifling?" Hawke echoed, feigning indignation. "From time to time? Fegs, woman, let us be clear about this before we present our-selves at the church. If you accept my offer, you must permit me to rid you of your clothing. To stroke your naked body. To kiss your mouth, and suckle your breasts and fondle you between your legs. There is no part of you that I will not be free to touch, and no part of me that—"

"Oh, hush," Amelia said in delight, and silenced his precious nonsense with a lusty kiss.

About the Author:

Julia Welles, who also writes for Harlequin Books as Julie Meyers, lives on the West Coast and is a past recipient of Romance Writers of America's Golden Heart award. Her thanks go out to Kathy, for vetting the earliest draft of this novella; to Cat, for offering friendship and encouragement; and to Megan, for laughing—and blushing—in all the right places. You can reach Julie by email at Juliawelles@aol.com.

The Woman of His Dreams

by Jade Lawless

To my reader:
I hope you enjoy my fantasy tale of two lovers parted by death and reunited again in the present. Although they exist in my heart, the characters are in reality fictional and are not based on anyone living or dead. In my story I made a creative choice not to use birth control. In real life I strongly advocate safe sex.

Chapter One

He came to her again.

A myriad of stars lit the sky and moonlight shone through the French doors into her bedroom. Then, as before, he silently stepped with his bare feet through the doors from the balcony and onto the plush rug. A soft breeze carried his musky scent to her and she breathed it in, her body flooding with desire. The billowing white curtains surrounding the doors blew around him, gliding against his copper-brown skin. Reaching behind him, he pulled the doors closed. She watched the play of muscles on his wide chest as they rippled and flexed with each movement.

He was beautiful. His jet black hair lay flipped back away from his forehead, falling down past his neck and below his shoulders. High cheekbones and an aquiline nose wider at the top than the bottom spoke of his Native American heritage. A muscle clenched along his square jaw, drawing her heavy lidded gaze to his lips. They were firm and sensual and she wanted to touch them, to have them open for her, to feel their moist heat against her mouth.

Like a sleek hungry panther stalking his prey, he moved toward the bed where she lay waiting for him. His jeans—the only piece of clothing he wore—rested low on his slim hips, the button undone. Her gaze lowered and followed the darkened line of hair on his taut abdomen until it disappeared beneath partially unzipped pants.

He was already hard, hard and bulging under the tight jeans cupping his sex like a second skin. The sight sent her heart skipping faster, her breathing short and rapid. His mahogany eyes narrowed when her tongue slipped out to wet her parted lips. Then he smiled and slowly pulled the zipper down. The head of his manhood peeked out, and she noticed pearls of moisture at the tip. As she watched, a small drop slid down his shaft and disappeared into the dark, curly tufts of hair at the base.

God, how she wanted him. She flung the cotton sheet off her heated body and reached for him.

Stay, he ordered in a low husky voice. She lay back down, remaining still. His gaze burned down the length of her body. *Take off your gown.*

Slipping off the thin straps, she tugged the short nightie over her hips and tossed it away. Her nipples tingled in the warm sultry air, waiting and aching for his touch.

He pushed the jeans down his muscled legs and stepped out of them. *Close your eyes.*

But—

Close your eyes, he demanded. Then his tone softened. *Trust me, Little Bird.*

Without further question she let her eyelids drop. Silence. She could hear only her own breathing and then . . .

His warm callused hands closed around her breasts. *Yes.* She moaned in pure bliss. Sliding, rubbing, stroking, they massaged her sensitized skin. When he lightly pinched her nipples, she cried out loud with delight, her fists clenching the bunched sheet beneath her.

His strong fingers spread out against her ribs, then smoothed downward along her side and slipped around to her belly. Her legs moved apart, her hips jerked up from the bed and her back bowed in anticipation. She felt light headed, as if she could float away or die of pleasure at any moment. Her ears began to ring.

The ringing grew louder.

No. Not now! She groaned in dismay.

". . . awake?" A voice broke through her dream. "Come on, Jo, pick up the phone. I know you're there."

Joanna jackknifed up in bed, her breathing ragged. Her unfocused gaze searched the room. The bright moonlight lit her bedroom enough for her to see she was alone.

"Joanna!" The insistent voice called from her answering machine.

Confused and not certain what was dream or reality, she groped for the cordless telephone on the bed stand. "H-hello?"

"It's about time! When did you start sleeping so soundly?" her sister complained.

Joanna spied her nightgown at the foot of her bed and bit back a gasp. Wrapping the bed sheet around herself, she stumbled to the French doors. The latch rested in the "locked" position. She pulled the sheer curtain back, still clutching the phone to her ear. The old Victorian house next door lay steeped in darkness.

Fool, she berated herself. *Did you really think he'd been here, making love to you?*

"Jo?" Her sister's tone changed from irritation to concern. "What's going on? Are you all right?"

"I'm fine." She dropped the curtain and glanced at the clock radio. "Kelly? What are you doing calling me at two in the morning?"

"I'm on my way to Florida for a shoot and I thought I'd stop for a visit. I took a late flight from Boston."

"You're here?" Joanna snapped on the night stand lamp then sat back on the bed, her eyebrows drawing together. "At the airport?"

"No, I'm talking to you on my cellular phone. I rented a car and I'm in your driveway. If I knock on your door, are you going to let me in?"

"Do I have a choice?" Joanna's voice rang dry with sarcasm. She hung up the phone then pulled an oversized T-shirt out of her dresser and yanked it over her head.

Hurrying through the small gate house, she made her way to the front door just in time to hear her sister's impatient pounding. Flipping the locks, she pulled the door open and Kelly breezed in, carrying a shoulder bag and her camera case.

"God, this place is still like the set of a horror flick." She glanced around at the dark wood and heavy floral wallpaper in the entryway. "When will you lighten it up a little?"

"When I get the money." Joanna slammed the door and followed her sister through the living room to the kitchen in the back of the house.

"I'm starving." Kelly opened up the refrigerator and started rummaging through. "Jesus, don't you have anything besides rabbit food and low fat yogurt?"

"No," Joanna answered with some satisfaction. Kelly had always been a junk food eater. Not that it showed. With her slim and darkly exotic looks she could have been a model, had she not decided she liked it better on the other side of the camera. "So what are you shooting in Florida? Bathing suits? Beefcake calendar?"

"Very funny. Actually, it will be a very tastefully done condom ad. Ahha!" she exclaimed, pulling out the package Joanna had hidden under a head of lettuce. "I knew it. Godiva chocolates."

Joanna shrugged. "I was saving them for a special occasion."

"What's more special than a visit from your loving sister?" She grinned and opened the box, stuffing a morsel into her mouth. "Mmm . . . these are almost as good as sex."

Kelly raised an eyebrow at the dark look on Joanna's face. "Relax Jo, I'll replace them. I sent you this box, didn't I?"

It wasn't the fact that Kelly was devouring her favorite chocolates that irritated Joanna. It was the fact that her sister's sex life didn't consist of erotic dreams about a neighbor the way Joanna's did. If Kelly wanted a man, she went out and got him. Men seemed to crawl out of the woodwork when she was around.

Suddenly depressed, Joanna held her hand out. "Don't hog them all, give me a couple."

✻❀⟨♡⟩❀✻

Joanna tried to move around quietly the next day while getting ready for work but her sister shuffled into the kitchen while she brewed coffee.

"What are you doing?" Kelly asked. "You aren't going to work, are you?"

"I have to. I need to inform the bank at least a week ahead to take a vacation day."

"Call in sick." Kelly leaned back against the counter, her arms crossed petulantly. "Let somebody else turn down loan applications today. Come on, Jo. I can only stay one day. I don't know when I'll be free again until the Christmas holidays. That's another three months away."

"I can't call in sick," Joanna told her. "I have appointments this morning. But I can probably arrange to take off this afternoon."

Kelly sighed. "I suppose that's better than nothing."

Joanna took two mugs from her cabinet and poured coffee, leaving one black and one with extra cream and sugar for her sister.

"Oh my. Look at the gorgeous view from this window." Kelly leaned over the kitchen sink, her gaze glued to the back yard.

What view? Joanna wondered. It's not as if Kelly hadn't seen her back yard during the two years she'd lived in the gate house. And she'd certainly never raved about it. Joanna carried the mug over, setting it on the counter. Craning her neck, she looked over Kelly's shoulder. Her stomach clenched tightly at the sight.

Her neighbor stood in his backyard bent over a table made of wood boards and two saw horses. He wore his usual work clothes, the tight jeans of her dreams and a white tank shirt that exposed his raw and sinewy physique. His long raven hair was gathered and tied at the neck, but a piece had loosened, falling across his dark brow. Her body immediately reacted to him, her nipples hardening and heat forming between her legs. Suddenly she had a vision of herself in the yard, wearing her nightgown and no panties. Her back lay stretched over his table, the nightgown pulled above her breasts. His hands gripped each widespread leg, his dark thighs sinking between them . . .

"Who *is* he?" her sister asked, startling her out of the daydream.

"I don't know his name." Joanna cleared her throat to dislodge the lump that had manifested itself there. "He moved in a few months ago."

Her sister looked at her with disbelief. "A few months and you don't know his name? Is he married?"

Joanna shrugged. "I've never seen anyone but an older woman come and go. But I don't stare out the window and spy on him." She prayed she wouldn't be struck by lightning at the outright lie.

"Do you need your eyes examined? This guy's a babe." Kelly went back to ogling him through the window.

As they watched, he straightened up, pushing the hair out of his eyes in an almost graceful movement, his biceps flexing. The motion brought his head up until he looked directly into the window they stood behind. He stared back for a moment before lifting a hand in greeting. Joanna jerked away from the window but Kelly smiled and returned his wave.

"I'm going to be late," Joanna said, eager to leave before her sister saw signs of the strange obsession she held for her neighbor.

"Don't worry about me," Kelly waved her hand without turning from the window. "I'll find something to amuse myself with."

Joanna sighed. "That's what I'm afraid of," she muttered to herself.

Chapter Two

Tired and annoyed, Joanna opened her front door and stepped into the entryway. The bank manager had called "an important meeting" in the early afternoon and droned on for three hours about new IRS forms and proper procedure. By now Kelly was probably climbing the walls with boredom. Joanna would have to spend the rest of the evening making it up to her.

At the sound of her sister's laughter mixed with the low husky rumble of a man's, she stopped abruptly. She deliberately slammed the door behind her and then dropped her briefcase to the hardwood floor with a loud crash.

"Jo?" Kelly called out. "We're in the kitchen."

A sense of foreboding enveloped her as she advanced down the hall, her worst fears confirmed when she saw who sat with her sister at the kitchen table. As she walked in, her neighbor stood, and she noticed he had added a plaid flannel shirt to the clothing he'd worn earlier that morning.

"Gray, this is my sister, Joanna Morgan. Jo, this is Gray Avonaco, your neighbor."

He held out his hand. Joanna hesitated before placing hers inside his, regretting her decision the instant they touched. His rough palm seared her skin. A hot jolt of electricity zapped up her arm, exploding in heated ripples through her body. Her first instinct was to yank away, but his fingers clasped hers tightly.

A slow smile spread across his face, and his thumb rubbed softly against the back of her hand. "I'm very happy to finally meet you."

That's strange, she thought. His deep-timbered voice sounded the same in her dreams. And she'd never heard him speak before now.

"He's an artist. Isn't that exciting?" her sister said, interrupting her reflection.

"Y-yes, it is." Joanna drew her hand free and reached up to push a strand of hair from her eyes. She looked like hell. Her mousy brown hair was falling out of its bun as a result of her drive home with the car top down. She wore her oldest and most conservative gray skirt suit with an equally plain white blouse underneath. Next to Kelly's form-fitting black leather outfit, sheer stockings and chic stiletto heels, she probably reminded him of somebody's grandmother.

The telephone rang suddenly and Kelly stopped her before she could answer it. "That's for me. I've been expecting a call from my agent. I'll take it in the living room." She smiled at Gray. "Don't run off yet, this will only take a minute."

Joanna stood in uncomfortable silence after Kelly left to take the telephone call. Her nervous gaze fluttered around the room before meeting Gray's deep, enigmatic eyes. She thought vaguely that no man should be that handsome. It made him too dangerous.

She searched for something to say, blurting out the first thing that came to mind. "What do you paint?"

He gave her a quizzical look. "Paint?"

"Landscapes? Portraits?"

Comprehension replaced the puzzled expression on his face. "I'm a sculptor."

"I'm sorry." Her cheeks flushed. "It was stupid of me to assume all artists are painters."

He shrugged. "I did some painting while I was attending art school, but I never really liked it."

"What kind of sculptures do you do?" she asked, knowing she had probably shown her total ignorance of the art by the amused glint in his eyes.

"I work with clay and stone, but my real love is wood." His voice lowered as his gaze held hers. "I like the feel of wood in my hands. The different textures and colors . . . and the smell."

Portions of last night's dream flashed through her head in quick succession. The sight of him next to her bed, the feel of his hands on her breasts, the husky tone of his voice as he told her to trust him. Her mouth went dry, her breathing accelerated. She forced herself to glance away and coughed to clear her throat.

"Would you . . . like another cup of coffee?" she asked. Grasping the empty mug from the table, she clutched it in her trembling hands like a drowning person latched onto a life preserver.

"Yes, thank you, that would be nice." He smiled that devastating smile again. She felt the effect of it from the top of her head all the way down to her toes. Gray Avonaco was not just dangerous, he was deadly.

Joanna walked with shaky legs to the counter. *Get a grip, you idiot*, she told herself. She poured coffee from the carafe, using the time to collect herself. She took a deep calming breath before plastering a composed smile on her face and turning back to him. "Cream and sugar?"

"Just cream."

She fixed the coffee and he held out his hand to take it from her. Unwilling to let her fingers touch his again, she jerked them back and let out a gasp when some coffee sloshed over her hand. He gripped the cup and put it on the table, his eyebrows drawn together with concern. "Are you hurt?"

Joanna shook her head. "No, it's—"

"You've burnt yourself."

Before she could answer that she was fine, he grasped her wrist and pulled her over to the sink. He turned on the tap, holding her hand under the cold running water. "Does that feel better?"

Feel better? Even if the coffee cup had been filled with flesh eating acid, the only thing she would have felt at that moment was the hard length of his body pressed against her back. Not trusting her voice, she nodded her head.

"Good." He rubbed her fingers under the flowing water and her heart raced. His warm breath tickled the top of her head, sending delightful shivers through her body. He smelled of wood shavings mixed with sweat and a light scent of musk. Just as he did in her dreams. She closed her eyes. If she turned her head she could nuzzle her lips into his neck and taste the salty heat of his skin—

"What happened?" Her sister's voice brought her back to earth with a bang. She pulled her hand from Gray's, snatching a dish towel off the counter to dry it.

He shifted from behind her and turned off the water before answering Kelly. "Joanna burned herself."

"You all right?" Kelly hurried over to view the damage.

"It's nothing." She held her hand up for Kelly to see the two small red patches. "Really. It doesn't even hurt."

Kelly looked at Joanna, then glanced at Gray, a curious expression on her face. "Did Gray tell you he invited us to dinner? He wants to show us some of his work and what he's done with the house."

"Dinner?" Joanna tried to stop the look of dismay that threatened to erupt on her face. "But—"

"I know you've always lusted after the house, so I accepted for both of us."

Gray Avonaco's curious gaze shifted to Joanna. "Lusted?"

Joanna felt the heat rush to her cheeks. *I'll kill her. Put a gun in my hand right now and my sister is history.*

"When we were kids, Jo used to tell my Mom and Dad she was going to live there someday with her handsome warrior prince. What was his name, Jo? Tonkala or Talaka?"

"I don't remember," she answered through gritted teeth.

"Well, when the gatekeeper's cottage, which originally belonged to the same estate as yours, went up for sale, she went into debt to buy it." Kelly rambled on, "If she could afford it—"

"Kelly! I really don't think Mr. Avonaco wants to hear the sad story of my finances." Joanna glanced at him, startled for a moment at the odd look on his face. She gave him a strained smile. "I guess I am a bit in love with your house. It has so much character and history. You must have felt it, too. You bought it."

His gaze held hers, his eyes darkening with some strong emotion she couldn't read. "Yes, I felt it."

"About dinner . . . I'm not sure—"

He quickly raised his hand and interrupted her. "Don't worry, I'm not doing the cooking. I have someone who cooks for me three nights a week. It's three less times I'm forced to eat out." His wry smile sent her heart skittering again. "Tonight she's making a roast, and she always cooks enough to feed an army."

"Mmm . . ." Kelly licked her lips provocatively and smiled up at Gray. "I adore red meat. All I've had to eat today is low fat yogurt. Jo lives on the stuff."

A gun would be too quick, Joanna thought, her eyes narrowed at Kelly. A slower, more painful death would be much, much better.

"Great, it's settled. If that's agreeable to you?" he asked, watching Joanna.

"Sure," Joanna answered before looking pointedly at Kelly. "I wouldn't want my sister to fade away from hunger."

Kelly leaned toward Gray and said in a low, conspiring voice, "Don't mind her. She's still mad at me for eating her stash of chocolate last night."

"What time would you like us to be there?" Joanna asked, ignoring her sister's comment.

"Give me a few minutes to shower and change," he said. "Anytime after that is fine."

Joanna's gaze dropped from his face and trailed down his work-clothed body. The light above her began to dim and the room took on a surreal appearance until fading completely into nothingness.

"Tokala," she called over the sound of soft rushing water. She watched as water coursed over his ebony hair, plastering it to his head and neck before flowing over his shoulders. Rivulets formed and streamed against his smooth chest, then ran down the firm lines of his stomach and abdomen to his manhood.

"Come here, wife."

She laughed as he took her arm and pulled her under the waterfall with him. The water flowed warm against her skin, the smooth stone hard beneath her feet. He threaded his fingers through her drenched hair, dragging her lips to his and turning her laughter to a groan of pleasure.

Her hands slithered down his back to cup his buttocks, and the muscles tightened under her palms, his hard heat pushing against her belly. Moving around his hips, she traced a teasing finger along the scar on his thigh before clasping him in her hands and running her palms up and down the length of him.

He thrust himself into them, his head lifting from her lips until his eyes met hers. "You must stop or I will spill into your hands."

She smiled wickedly, refusing to stop until with a loud curse he jerked her up, poising her over his length. With a wild thrust he was inside her and she let out a scream of pleasure that echoed off the stones and spurred him to pull out and thrust again. She tightly wrapped her legs around him as he buried his head between her breasts, suckling and licking them as the water cascaded over them both.

"Yes, oh please . . ." she cried, begging him to take her over the edge. But he held his pulsing thickness deeply within her, his grip on her buttocks keeping her from moving. She glanced down to see the knowing grin on his own face.

"You devil." She dug desperate hands into his back. "Finish before I die."

His answer was half groan and half laughter. "You seek to tease me and yet now beg for mercy?"

"Please . . ." she cried, half angry at the desperate mewling sound in her voice.

He pulled out and thrust again. Her head flew back as the tight throbbing began within her and the climax flashed like lightning through her body. She felt him empty himself inside her as her loud screams of pleasure echoed on and on . . .

"Jo?" Kelly said, her voice full of amusement.

Joanna's eyes flew open, her face suffusing with color. "I-I'm

sorry, I was thinking about—about something I forgot to do at work."
She glanced at Gray, who stared back, his dark and compelling eyes
boring into hers. For a moment she thought she saw an answering
flame in their depths before he turned to follow Kelly, who walked him
to the back door.

The sound of her sister's laughter spurred her into movement.
She hurried up the stairs to her bathroom where she turned on the
faucet and leaned over the sink to splash cold water across her heated
face.

That had to be just about the most humiliating experience of her
life. She straightened up and stared at herself in the oval mirror, propping her hands on the sides of the sink. Okay, maybe not the most humiliating, she conceded. Walking in on her fiancé in bed with another
woman still held that rank. It wasn't just the sight of Wilson cheating
on her that made it the most humiliating experience, it was when he'd
proceeded to tell her, in front of his voluptuous consort, that it was all
her fault because she wasn't good enough in bed to satisfy him. Joanna
could still see his thin lip curled back in a sneer as he gave her the final
parting shot; "Going to bed with you was like screwing a cadaver."

She grimaced at her reflection. It was funny, really. Her erotic
dreams were a hundred times more exciting than her actual sexual experiences. Wilson's idea of making love had been to grope her breasts
a little, then just plunge in, pumping away until he came. Never worrying whether or not she was satisfied before taking his pleasure. He'd
certainly never taken the time to stroke her or nuzzle her skin or taste
her with warm hungry lips—

"Stop it!" she admonished her mirror image. "It's not real!"

"What's not real?" Kelly leaned against the bathroom doorjamb,
her arms crossed and a curious look on her face.

"Do you have to sneak up on me? I nearly had a heart attack."
Joanna scowled at her sister before jerking a fluffy peach towel off the
brass towel bar and swiping it across her wet face.

"If you weren't so busy talking to yourself, you might have
heard me."

Not bothering to reply, Joanna draped the towel back over the bar
and slid by Kelly, stalking through her bedroom to the small closet.
With jerky motions she searched her conservative clothing for something to wear.

Kelly shifted to lounge on the canopy bed, watching her. "This is
all very fascinating," she said, purring like a cat that had just discovered a bowl full of cream.

Joanna's movements faltered for a moment before she deliberately went back to her wardrobe. "What's fascinating?" she asked, striving to sound casual.

"You and your new neighbor."

Her hand trembled slightly as she pulled out a beige dress and pretended to study it, then hooked it back on the clothes rack. She glanced over her shoulder at Kelly. "Am I supposed to know what you're talking about?"

"I think you do," Kelly told her in a singsong voice.

"Well, I don't," Joanna parroted her sister's tone.

A wide grin broke over Kelly's face and she sat up, her eyes sparkling with excitement. "Come on, Jo, you have something going on with that stud next door. I thought you said you'd never met him?"

"I haven't. Not until today."

"Yeah, right," Kelly said with disbelief. "Normally people don't look at other people like they're starving and you're their favorite dessert. Especially when they've just met."

Joanna spun around, her cheeks flaming. "I did not look at him like that!"

Kelly's eyebrows rose at Joanna's distress. "I'm not talking about you, silly. I'm talking about him."

"*Him?*"

"Yes, him. He never took his eyes off you." Kelly looked genuinely surprised at Joanna's disbelief. "You can't be that blind."

"I'm not blind. *You* are delusional," she snapped back, annoyed at her sister's teasing.

"Hey, I'm not the one who stood in a trance for a good sixty seconds." Kelly's forehead creased thoughtfully before she continued, "It was so bizarre. You both went into this weird altered-state kind of thing." Her smile was wicked. "Whatever happened there must have been really good. You could have carved the heavy atmosphere with a knife."

"You're imagining things." Joanna dismissed her and turned back to rummaging in the closet.

"I could be. But sometimes it's very obvious what's on a man's mind. And—mmm hmm—I saw some pretty hard evidence that Gray Avonaco's attracted to you."

"You have a fixation with sex." Joanna yanked out one of her many navy trouser suits and tossed it on the bed. "It's unnatural."

"Sex is as natural as breathing." Kelly waggled a sculptured brow. "Let's just say I have a larger lung capacity than most." Her gaze dropped to the suit, and she picked it up with a look of distaste. "You're *not* going to wear this, are you?"

Joanna looked down at the outfit. "What's wrong with it?"

"Nothing, if you're closing a deal on Wall Street. Everything, if you're having dinner with a man who's got the hots for you. Come on, Jo! You must have something that's sexier than this." Kelly thrust it aside before striding to the closet and foraging through the clothes. "Not this. No. No. Good God, no." She punctuated every discarded piece with a shake of her head.

Joanna sat on the edge of the bed and watched her with growing irritation. "Did it ever occur to you that the attraction you felt was directed at you, not me?"

Kelly twisted to look at Joanna, rolling her eyes. "Give me enough credit to know when a man's not interested in me that way. It's not like it's a common occurrence, you know." She turned back to the closet. "Where's that red dress I bought you for your birthday last year?"

"All right," Joanna said, after taking a deep breath. "Let's say for the sake of argument that he is attracted. What makes you think I want to get involved with a man again? I don't have very good luck with them."

"There it is." Kelly pulled out the dress, still in its original covering. "You've never even worn it, have you?" she accused.

Joanna grabbed the dress out of her sister's hand, and tossed it on the bed beside her. "Did you hear what I said?"

"You said you didn't have good luck with men." Kelly's eyes narrowed. "I hope you're not sticking Wilson Banning III into the category of 'man.' Weasel, yes. Man, no." She shivered theatrically. "Hell, if he were a typical example of the species, I'd be the first in line to join a convent."

Joanna smiled at the thought of her bohemian sister trading in her leather and lace for a nun's habit.

"I never knew what you saw in him." Kelly plopped down on the bed next to her. "He was a sleazy, slimy—"

"I get the point." Joanna rubbed her eyes before letting her hands drop into her lap in a weary motion.

"I don't think you do." After picking up Joanna's loose palm, Kelly squeezed it, her expression sober. "I saw that bastard take your self-confidence and grind it into the dirt. He hurt you. Are you going to let him keep hurting you by being afraid to have another relationship?"

Lifting the dress off the bed, Joanna sighed. "I've gained five pounds since you gave me this. I'll look like a beached whale. That is, if it fits at all."

"You'll look beautiful." Her sister grinned. "And when I get through with you, Gray Avonaco is never going to know what hit him."

Chapter Three

"This was a bad idea," Joanna said, as they walked up Gray's cement walk toward his front door. She tugged at the short and tight dress, groaning when the material snapped back into figure-hugging place. "I feel ridiculous." She swore when she almost twisted her ankle for the third time. "How the hell do you walk in these without breaking your neck?"

Kelly laughed. "Very slowly and with a pronounced wiggle. You're gorgeous. Relax."

"How can I relax? I don't have a bra on!"

"If you wore a bra, your straps would have shown," Kelly told her logically while they mounted the wide wooden steps. "Then you'd *look* ridiculous."

"At least it would match my mood." Joanna halted abruptly on the top step. "I can't do this."

Kelly clutched her arm and dragged her forward, then gave the door bell a quick jab. "Too late." Joanna heard the muffled tinkle of chimes sounding in the house. If it weren't for the deadly high-heel shoes and Kelly's grip on her arm, she would have turned and ran. The heavy door creaked open and her chance for escape was lost.

It wasn't Gray behind the door, but a small older woman with a welcoming smile on her round face. "Good evening," she said, her voice soft and lyrical. "Please come in." She motioned them inside, and Kelly gave Joanna an inconspicuous push between the shoulder blades.

"Come. Come." The woman waved them into a parlor off the impressive entryway floored with Italian tile. Joanna glanced at Kelly, who shrugged and followed the woman. A single braid of blue-gray hair fell down the woman's back tied by a beautiful turquoise clasp shaped like a turtle. After entering the double oak doors, Joanna froze in silent surprise. The room was pure Victorian romance. The walls were painted a muted rose, and the rest of the room decorated in a blending of mauve with green tones. White, frothing curtains draped the open floor-to-ceiling windows and floated gently in the early September breeze. Stepping further into the room, her feet sank into the pale jade Oriental carpet. She inhaled the scent of roses, and her eyes searched and found a dozen red blossoms held in a Waterford crystal vase.

Joanna had expected to see leather and dark wood—a typical choice of bachelor men—not this incredible mixture of antique and expensive reproductions. It contained everything she desired, from the claw-foot couch and wing chairs, all the way down to the silver tea set spread out on a small mahogany tray table. Maybe it was sexist, but she couldn't imagine a man as potently male as Gray Avonaco using such a feminine room.

"Now which of you is it?" The small woman looked into Kelly's eyes, then shifted her gaze to Joanna and smiled with satisfaction. "Yes, yes . . . it's you. Do you like your room?"

"Excuse me?" Joanna thought she'd heard incorrectly.

"Your room." The woman made a waving motion with her hand. "Does it please you?"

Joanna looked over the woman's head at Kelly, who raised her hand and made a circular motion next to her ear, mouthing the words, "out to lunch."

Joanna gave the woman a strained smile. "It—it's very lovely. But I'm not sure—"

"Mrs. Ohako." Gray stood in the parlor doorway, a frown on his handsome face. Joanna's heart began to beat in double time, her skin tingling with electrical reaction. Gone was the rugged workman. In his place stood a man who could have stepped off the pages of GQ. His raven hair lay sleeked back and held at the nape by a thin ornate gold clasp. His charcoal gray suit possessed an expensive designer label, of that she had no doubt, and most likely, so did the light blue silk shirt and dark tie underneath.

"*Eoti' anay moh'ato. Yasi'?*" The dialect he spoke contained a rough and guttural edge.

"*Yasi'.*" Mrs. Ohako answered, then mumbled unintelligibly as she shuffled to where he stood by the door. She glanced back at Joanna, before looking up at Gray. "*Cheota nosoch.*"

Gray's gaze moved to Joanna, slowly traveling down her low-cut dress and lingering on her legs before raising to meet hers. Her breathing nearly stopped at the fierce look of raw desire in his eyes. The look vanished so quickly she wondered if she imagined it.

"*Cheota i'nchedanosoch.*" He smiled and leaned down to kiss the old woman's cheek. "*Ni'chan.*"

After she left the room, Gray turned to Joanna and Kelly. "I apologize for our rudeness. She told me what a lucky man I am to be having dinner alone with two beautiful women. I agreed."

"Why, thank you, sir," Kelly teased, blinking her eyelashes with mock flirtatiousness.

Joanna raised a brow in disbelief. Somehow the reproach in his tone hadn't matched his version of the conversation with Mrs. Ohako.

"I would offer you a glass of wine and the tour before dinner but I don't want to keep Mrs. Ohako late," he told them. "I thought we could have the wine with dinner and save the tour until after. I hope you don't mind?"

"That would be lovely," Kelly said and looked pointedly at Joanna. "Wouldn't it, Jo?"

"Lovely," Joanna echoed Kelly with a trace of sarcasm.

Gray swept his arm in a courteous gesture for them to precede him out of the parlor. Joanna followed her sister, propelled by the darkly critical look Kelly threw her way as she passed.

※ ❧(♥)❧ ※

The wine tasted more delicious with every glass she drank. Joanna raised the delicate long-stemmed glass and tipped it against her lips. The fruity flavor purled against her tongue before sliding down her throat and ending as liquid heat in her belly. She stared across the French provincial table at Gray, who listened intently while Kelly talked about her last photo shoot in Jamaica.

Her eyes narrowed and she struggled to keep them focused. God, he looked handsome. Not handsome in a classical way, but in a more earthy, sensual way. His suave and sophisticated clothing didn't completely mask the savage masculinity he exuded.

Setting the empty glass down, she breathed deeply. The spicy scent of his after-shave had driven her crazy for the last hour. She kept imagining what it would be like to shove everything off the table and make wild reckless love to him on top of it. No thinking, no regrets.

". . . more wine, Joanna?"

The sound of her name on his lips sent shafts of desire spiraling through her. She closed her eyes and tried to concentrate. What had he asked her? Do you want me, Joanna? Do you need me, Joanna?

She slowly opened her eyes and looked into his. *"Yes."* Her voice came out in a husky slur. His movements seemed to be in slow motion as he raised the bottle of wine and poured the ruby nectar into her glass. She watched the liquid whorl and bubble against the sides until he pulled back just as the goblet threatened to overflow.

"Oh, damn!"

Startled, they both looked at Kelly. Her wine glass lay tipped over on the table, wine spilling into her lap. Gray moved quickly, reaching over to stand the goblet upright. Most of the liquid had already slopped onto Kelly's leather skirt.

She picked up a linen napkin and dabbed at the mess. "What a clumsy idiot I am. This is my favorite outfit! I'm going to have to take it back to Jo's, and see if I can repair the damage."

A mixture of relief and regret washed over Joanna at the thought of the evening coming to an early end. She started to rise.

Kelly stood, waving Joanna back in her seat. "Oh no, stay. Let Gray show you the house."

Joanna frowned. The look on her sister's face suggested some kind of plot. She left before Joanna's clouded mind could figure out what.

After a moment of silence Joanna picked the soiled white napkin up from the table and examined it. "You should probably soak this. And the table cloth. Red wine is hard to get out, once it sets in."

When he didn't answer, her gaze lifted to meet his. He made no attempt to hide the fact that he watched her. His dark amber eyes gleamed almost black and her heart thundered in response. They stared at each other until his hooded gaze lowered to rest on her mouth.

The look flustered her. With a trembling hand she grasped the wine glass, the liquid sloshing precariously as she picked it up then swallowed half of the contents in one gulp.

He rose, walking around the table until he stood directly behind her chair. "Mrs. Ohako will take care of it." She felt his warm fingers against her bare shoulders as he gripped the chair, helping her move it back. "Shall we take your sister's advice and start the tour?"

Joanna pushed from the chair and stood. Her head reeled at the sudden movement, the effects of the wine fully hitting her. When her legs began to falter, she quickly grabbed hold of his arm. For some reason it struck her as funny, and she laughed. Her laughter ceased abruptly at the look of concern on his face.

"Kelly's shoes," she said, with a foolish grin, as if that explained everything.

He inspected the shoes, his dark eyebrows drawn together. "You'd probably be more comfortable if you took them off," he said, then before she could react, he crouched down, his palm sliding along her calf until he encircled the heel of her shoe. When he began to pull the high-heel off, she lifted her leg, clutching his shoulders to keep her balance. His muscles stirred beneath her grip, and she felt his warm breath against her knee as he shifted to remove the other shoe, his hand slightly squeezing her calf. Disappointment speared her when he released her leg, sliding the shoes into his suit coat pockets. "Better?" he asked, then straightened, steadying her when she loosened her hold on his shoulders.

"Yes." She reluctantly dropped her hands to her side.

"Before we start, I need to speak to Mrs. Ohako for a moment. Would you mind waiting for me in the parlor?"

"No, I don't mind." She stopped him as he turned toward the kitchen. "Umm—Gray?"

"Yes?" He looked back at her, an eyebrow raised in question.

A strange tingling sensation swept over Joanna. Like being zapped by a low current of electricity, it made the tiny hairs on her neck stand on end. Time seemed to grind to a halt as Gray's face altered before her eyes. It was his face and yet it wasn't. His features became harder with sharp angles and dark savage brows. A thin beaded headband wrapped around his forehead and held back a mane of wild black hair. In the next instant the image disappeared and his face reverted to normal.

She let out the breath she didn't know she'd been holding and swallowed the fear that had landed like a lump in her throat. A few glasses of wine and she was seeing things. Forcing a smile, she hoped he didn't notice her reaction to the hallucination. "W-would you please thank Mrs. Ohako for me and tell her that dinner was delicious?"

He nodded. "She'll be pleased that you enjoyed it."

Joanna padded across the tile foyer and into the parlor. She felt strange, as if there were something she knew she should remember but couldn't. The wine from dinner wasn't helping. If he hadn't had her shoes, she may have been tempted to keep going out the door and back home.

Chapter Four

Even the cozy and welcoming room couldn't dispel the layer of goose flesh that covered Joanna's body. Glancing around the parlor, her gaze was caught and held by the beautiful wooden carving of a young woman displayed on the fireplace mantle. *That's strange*, she thought to herself. She could have sworn that the carving hadn't been there when she was in the room earlier. A curious sense of unreality swept over her again as she drew closer and studied the carving. The woman rested in a half reclining pose, her hair flowing down to cover her breasts, her knee slightly bent and her arm stretched out along her bare waist and thigh. Something about it tugged at the back of her mind. Did she know this woman? No. She would have remembered meeting her. And she wouldn't have forgotten the carving if she'd seen it before, either. The odd feeling intensified and Joanna rubbed her hands up and down her arms, shivering.

"You're cold."

Gray's voice startled her and she spun around, her hand splayed across her heart. "You scared me. I-I didn't hear you coming."

"Sorry. I'll get you a sweater—"

"No," she gave a nervous laugh, "I'm fine. Really."

He strode over and bent down, opening a cabinet under a built-in bookcase. She watched him curiously as he pulled out two small brandy snifters and a bottle.

"At least let me do this for you." He poured two glasses of the amber liquid, setting the bottle on the small tea table before handing her one.

"Thank you." She took a sip of the brandy, then walked over to the fireplace. "Is this your work?" she asked, pointing toward the carving.

"Yes." Gray moved next to her and lifted the figurine from the mantle, studying it for a moment. "It was my first attempt at a human subject," he said, smiling down at the piece before looking at Joanna. "Up until then I only carved animal figures. I did it about twenty years ago." He held it out to her and she took it.

Still warm from his touch, the small figurine felt alive in the cradle of her palm. "Twenty years ago? But you were only about . . . what— twelve years old?" she guessed.

"Sixteen. My grandfather taught me to carve when I was five years old, so I'd already been selling my animal pieces at the tourist places in town. We lived on a small farm on the New York-Canadian border near the St. Lawrence Seaway."

Her thumb followed the smooth lines carved into the wood with meticulous care. "It's breathtaking." Joanna marveled at the awe-inspiring talent he'd possessed even at such an early age.

"I call it, 'The Maiden.'"

She looked up to find him watching her closely. "It's so vivid and lifelike." She carefully handed it back to him. "Is she someone you knew very well?"

Gray put the figurine back on the mantle, an odd smile on his face. "She came to me in a *Chi'toki'* or vision. You might call it a dream."

A pretty erotic dream for a sixteen year old, Joanna thought, taking another drink. She'd learned from Kelly that Gray had lost both his parents in a car crash and that his grandfather had raised him off the reservation. She tried to imagine him at the age of sixteen. Even then he'd probably had a devastating effect on the opposite sex.

Lifting the glass, she drank the remainder of the brandy in one swallow.

"Can I pour you another?" he asked, motioning at her empty glass.

"No, thank you. I feel like I should be helping Mrs. Ohako clean up. I hate to think of her doing it alone."

With deliberate motions, Gray set his unfinished drink on the tea table, his steady gaze on her. "You don't have to worry about that. I sent her home. I told her I'd take care of it myself. Tomorrow morning."

They were in his house alone. Joanna twisted the glass in her hands, suddenly nervous. "Maybe I should go."

"Is that what you want?" He sounded skeptical.

"I didn't expect . . . my sister to abandon me." Her eyes avoided his. Did he think she and Kelly had set this up between them? *Oh Kelly, I'm really going to kill you this time,* she pledged to herself.

"Your sister is a very perceptive woman."

Perceptive? No. Manipulative, scheming—

"She sees things you're afraid to." Her stomach stirred uneasily, her eyes widening when he took the glass from her trembling hands and set it next to his.

"It's getting late . . ." If she didn't leave now she might end up doing something she'd regret. "Perhaps we can finish the tour another time? I need my shoes," she ended lamely.

He silently took the shoes out of his pockets and handed them to her.

"Thank you." Propping a hand on the back of the sofa for balance, she put one heel on, then the other, before facing him. "Dinner was lovely." She edged toward the parlor doors and he followed. "And . . . well . . . thank you again."

Joanna turned abruptly and her heel caught on the fringe of the Oriental carpet. Her body lurched forward. With nothing to grab onto, she extended her hands, preparing herself for impact with the floor. Gray seized her around the waist and pulled her back against him before she tumbled. Surprise held her still for a moment, then she relaxed and closed her eyes, savoring the press of his solid length against her.

"Are you all right?" His warm breath tickled the back of her neck, rustling tendrils of hair escaping her silver clip. She sighed, shivers of delight passing through her. His grasp on her waist tightened for an instant then eased and shifted, his fingers spreading. Slowly, as if giving her time to object, he moved his palms in a caressing motion down over her hips then trailed them up her stomach. The movements ceased when his hands came to rest beneath her breasts. His labored breath whispered in her ear.

It vaguely occurred to Joanna that the situation was escalating beyond her power to stop it, but she pushed the thought away. She didn't want to stop. He felt too good. Too right.

"Joanna?" His voice, hoarse and low, questioning.

She didn't want him to ask permission because then she'd have to think. And she didn't want to think. She just wanted to feel. Gripping his large hands in hers, she moved them up to cup her breasts.

"*Ti' amota chi'*," he groaned, the guttural tones thick with passion. The heat of his palms burned through her dress while his lips lowered and nuzzled the pulse throbbing in her neck. She tilted her head back, blindly searching for his lips. His mouth finally covered hers and a burst of liquid fire surged into her bloodstream.

Turning her within his arms, he thrust his tongue between her lips and explored the inside of her mouth with feverish intensity. His taste flooded her senses. Brandy mixed with a musky primitive flavor that belonged solely to Gray. Straining against him, she groaned when his erection prodded her thigh.

He pushed the dress straps off her shoulders and shoved the material to her waist with impatient hands, his lips tracing a hot wet path over her cheek and down her neck. His mouth closed over her taut nipple and she cried out, her head slumping back in pleasure. Cupping the breast, he laved it with his tongue before gently sucking and nipping with his teeth, then repeated the torturous play with the other breast.

Her legs may as well have been made of rubber because they no longer seemed capable of holding her up. Only his grip on her waist kept her from falling into a boneless mass on the floor. Pulling at the clasp that held his hair, she let it drop before entwining her fingers into the long dark strands.

"*Please.*" She tugged at his hair, wanting the feel and taste of his lips on hers again.

He lifted his head and she tried drawing his mouth to hers but he held back, his eyes smoldering with scarcely controlled hunger. "Are you certain this is what you want?" he asked, a muscle in his jaw twitching. Fascinated, she traced it with her fingers before splaying them softly along the side of his face. His nostrils flared and his eyes closed. Chanting something under his breath, he gripped her hand tightly in his, halting her exploring fingers. He brought her hand to his mouth, kissing the tender skin of her palm. Then he opened his eyes, his gaze boring into hers. "Be sure *Naki'ti,* because in a few minutes I don't think I'll be able to stop."

He wanted her. Maybe almost as much as she wanted him. The realization grew along with the sense of power she felt at the knowledge. Perhaps it was partially due to the effects of the brandy and wine, but she'd never felt more desirable in her life.

"I don't want you to stop." The pent-up yearning of the past weeks exploded inside her. Clutching the lapels of his coat, she pulled him down to meet her lips halfway. He moaned beneath her onslaught, his hands biting into her buttocks as he lifted her and nudged his hardness between her legs. Her arms raised to encircle his neck, her legs curled around his hips. One of her heels dropped with a thud to the floor and she kicked off the other one.

Wanting to feel his bare chest against her, she pushed his coat aside, yanking the silk shirt from his pants. She struggled to unbutton the shirt and some of the buttons popped off in her fingers. Finally his skin lay bare beneath her touch. She ran her hands over the warm, hard expanse of his chest and along his rigid stomach.

With a low growl, he broke his mouth away from hers, his breath as jerky and uneven as hers. He moved her until she felt her back against the wall, then reached between their bodies and pushed her dress further up. He pulled at her stockings, then lost his patience and ripped them apart at the seam from crotch to waist, her panties quickly following suit. The fierceness of his actions should have frightened her, instead it fueled her hunger. Her hips jerked forward against him, heightening the growing pressure that coiled between her thighs.

He held her with one hand, while the other unzipped his pants, quickly adjusting himself until his erection burst free. Grasping her buttocks with both hands, he entered her in one furious thrust, filling her completely and pushing her over the edge of reason. She locked her legs together around his hips, enwrapping him tightly, her hips rocking against him.

"Joanna . . . no—damn it—don't move," he ordered desperately, his hands tightening on her, trying to hold her still while he fought to keep control. But her writhing body refused to obey him in its search for release. Cursing violently, he pulled out and plunged into her again. Her eyes flew open in astonishment as she climaxed, the pulsating contractions tearing through her body. She cried out, her nails digging into his shoulders. He answered by silently driving into her again and again, until she thought she would die from the prolonged pleasure. With one final thrust he came, his head whipping back, the cords of muscle standing out in his neck. Keeping his thick shaft embedded deep within her, she felt the explosive spurts of his orgasm. Aftershocks rippled over her and she clung to him while he emptied himself. It seemed as though his very life force jetted into her body, invading her heart, penetrating her soul.

Gray leaned against her, his panting breath, like hers, slowly returning to normal. She unhooked her legs from around him, sliding down until she stood and felt a sense of loss as their bodies pulled apart.

Cupping her chin with his palm, he raised her head. Dismay crossed his face at the silent tears running down her cheeks. "Joanna? Oh God, I'm sorry. Did I hurt you?"

"No!" She shook her head vehemently. "You didn't hurt me."

His thumbs wiped at the moisture on her face. "Then why are you crying?"

"It's silly really. I've never . . ." she sniffled, her face burning with embarrassment. "I've never . . . you know—had *that* happen before."

Absently, his fingers tucked a tendril of her escaping hair behind her ear. Then understanding dawned on his features. "You've never—"

"No," she cut him off, then glanced away, struggling to find the words to describe her joy. "It was so . . . incredible. I felt so . . ." Her eyes met his again and she gave up the struggle.

"Incredible?" he teased her, with a smile.

"You're making fun of me," Joanna accused, too happy to take any real offense.

He shook his head, his face suddenly serious. "No, Joanna. I feel honored I was the first one to give you that pleasure. If anyone deserves to be made fun of, it's me. Usually I have more control." He frowned. "I've never resorted to tearing a woman's clothing before."

"Then I feel honored I was the first one to give you that pleasure." Running her hands up his wide chest she grinned suggestively. "Shall we do it again?"

Gray laughed, then gave her a long and lingering kiss. "Yes, again," he promised, kissing her eyelids. "And again . . ." he kissed her cheeks, her nose. "And again . . ."

When he pulled away from her, she moaned in objection. She pulled the straps up on her dress while he fixed his pants, then he picked her up, an arm under her knees. "In my bed this time, *Naki'ti*. I've waited a long time to see your chestnut hair spread out on my pillows."

"A long time? But we've only—"

Leaning his head down, he silenced her with a blistering kiss. When they finally broke apart, she couldn't remember what she'd been about to say. The man need only kiss her and her mind went blank, her body enveloped by sensations she never thought possible.

He carried her up the stairs and into an open door to the left, where a bedside lamp bathed the room in a soft glow of light. Pushing the door closed behind them with his foot, he stopped to kiss her before moving over to lay her down on the bed. Her gaze vaguely registered the southwestern decor and roughhewn furniture before he bent down to kiss her again.

"When I saw you tonight standing in my parlor, I wanted you so badly it took my breath away." He gently tugged at her dress, dragging the elastic material down. "If it weren't for Mrs. Ohako and your sister, I'm not sure that I wouldn't have taken you right then." Joanna lifted her hips and he drew her dress the rest of the way off.

"Maybe I should tell you what I wanted to do during dinner." She playfully nibbled his square chin, slipping her hands under his shirt and pushing it, along with his suit coat, off his shoulders. "On top of the table."

He pulled away and stood, shrugging the clothing from his arms. "Tell me."

Rising to her knees on the edge of the bed, she pressed kisses onto his chest, her hands unbuttoning his pants. "I'd rather show you." She shoved the loose pants from his hips and they fell to the floor. Her fingers dipped beneath his jockey shorts and he moaned as she stroked the velvet tip of his shaft.

Grasping her hand, he held it tightly against him, halting her movements. "No. This time is for you."

After removing the rest of his clothing, he quickly rid her of her torn pantyhose and underwear. Then he set her on the bed before carefully unclipping her hair, watching it cascade over her shoulders.

Weaving his fingers into her tangled mane, he gathered some and brought it to his rough cheek before drawing it across his lips. "Your hair is like silk. Beautiful, shining silk. Why do you wear it bound so tightly?"

The compliment warmed her already fluttering heart. "I have to look professional at work and—I guess it's just easier to take care of that way."

Sliding her back against the pillows, his lips caressed her cheek and nuzzled into her neck. "Will you wear it loose for me?" His mouth traveled down and tasted her breasts, gently suckling the tips.

She melted beneath his lips, the molten fire once more gathering in white-hot force between her legs. "Yes," she told him, already breathless. His long hair brushed over her hardened nipples. She wanted him so badly she would have shaved her head if he'd asked.

He moved on, his tongue whirling and licking as his mouth journeyed downwards. Pausing at her navel, he dipped into the shallow divot with a rhythm that caused her hips to undulate restlessly beneath him. When his lips shifted farther down to the triangle of hair between her legs, she stiffened in a mixture of pleasure and shock.

"What—what are you doing?"

His darkened gaze lifted to meet hers. "Making love to you." The heat of his breath blew against her.

"But—no . . . I can't . . ." She squirmed under his foraging mouth and he clamped her hips and buttocks under him.

"You can, *Naki'ti*. Let me love you." His tongue worried the nub of her desire before delving inside her. Her heels dug into the bed, her hands clutching the bedspread. Then she was lost. She cried out as pleasure crashed over her like a tidal wave, drowning her body in pure sensation. When the last few spasms faded away, he withdrew, planting a kiss on her moist nest one last time.

"Look at me," he ordered, sounding so rough and strained that she obeyed without question. His eyes were dark and fierce, reminding her of the image she had seen transposed on his face.

"Spread your legs wider and bend your knees," he told her. A flurry of alarm mixed with excitement rushed through her. She bent her knees, allowing her legs to go slack. He ran his hands along the underside of her calves and up the inside of her thighs.

"You're so beautiful. So soft." His hands gripped her hips on either side and he ground his erection against her still sensitive sex. "I'm going to bury myself deep inside of you. Until you feel nothing but me."

Dark flames of desire shot back through her. "Yes," she breathed.

Gently, his fingers stretched apart her folds, the tip of his manhood pressing into her. His face was taut with desire, but no longer held the strange savage quality. "Tilt your hips, *Naki'ti*. Like that . . ." He slowly sank into her body until he completely filled her. "Oh, God . . . you're perfect . . . so hot and wet."

She wrapped her arms around him, moving her hands down his back until they settled on the firm muscles of his buttocks. The muscles clenched and unclenched under her palms as he slipped in and out of her again and again.

Should she tell him he'd gotten what he wanted? That all she could feel was him inside her? Dear Lord, she felt him. So big, so hard within her. Every thrust, every short teasing stab. Nothing else mattered but reaching the top again and this time tumbling over together.

He kissed her and she tasted herself on him, the musky scent of sex filling her nostrils. With a sobbing moan, she felt the tremors start and tried to put them off, wanting it to last longer. "Come with me, *Naki'ti*," he rasped in her ear. "Come with me."

"No . . . oh—" Her hands flailed against him. Pushing him away, pulling him to her.

"*Yes*." He reached down between them, stroking her swollen nub with his thumb as he plunged deep inside her. Her hips bucked wildly, matching him thrust for thrust. Then he stiffened and cried out in his native language, letting her contracting muscles milk him, drawing his male juice into her body.

Exhausted, Joanna slumped back into the bed. Her eyes closed and she felt Gray pull the comforter over them.

"Gray?" she whispered, half asleep. "What does '*Naki'ti*' mean?"

He looped his arm around her waist and pulled her back against him, spoon-style. "Little Bird."

Little Bird. There was something in the back of her mind . . . but she was too tired to think about it now. She cuddled into his warmth and immediately descended into sleep. And dreamed.

Chapter Five

Kai balanced on a jutting rock and looked with anticipation into the pool of water, the full moon reflecting on its smooth, glassy surface. Twisting, she jumped from the rock back to the grassy bank. She smiled, pretending not to hear the quiet tread of feet behind her. Excitement stirred her blood and caused her heartbeat to race. Raising her hands, she slowly untied her elk-skin dress, imagining how good it would feel when the water cooled her heated skin. She let the top of her dress fall around her hips and groaned with pleasure as her breasts sprang free, the soft breeze caressing them. Lifting her arms, she stretched her hands toward the moon in homage, shifting her hips until the dress slid down to pool at her feet.

She felt his burning presence close behind her and her smile widened at the sound of his quickening breath. Soon he would be inside her, taking her to unsurpassed heights of pleasure, but first she would toy with him and make him wait.

Before he could touch her, she leapt onto the rock and dived into the chilled water. Immediately she felt relief from the sultry heat. Surfacing where the water was chin deep, she laughed out loud, pushing her long black hair away from her face.

The light of the moon outlined his firm body. His hair hung loose to his shoulders, held back from his dark eyes by a headband around his forehead. He was so big! The muscles on his chest and arms bulged with strength. Beneath the breechcloth he wore, were legs as solid and sturdy as the oak tree that towered over her family's tipi.

A thrill of love and desire rippled through her as he vaulted, graceful and sure, despite his size, to the large rock she had dived from moments ago. He sat on his haunches, his elbows resting on his knees.

"Why do you run, Little Bird? Surely you do not fear me?" he said, his tone low and teasing.

She smothered a laugh. *"I fear no man, great beast,"* she told him with fake disdain. *"Especially one who favors the back end of a buffalo."*

He raised an eyebrow and stood, reaching for the fastenings on his breechcloth. *"You mock me, Little Bird. Now you must pay."*

Kai watched as he unlaced the ties and let the cloth drop to the rock, catching sight of his swollen maleness before he plunged into the water. When he disappeared beneath the surface, she yelped, splashing and clawing her way toward the bank, intent on evading him once more. Her hands gripped the dirt of the shore when she was caught about the waist and pulled back into the water. She struggled to escape him but his arm whipped around her, pulling her firmly against him and tightening on her shoulders, his hardened manhood pressing against her buttocks.

"Be still," he commanded, his breath hot in her ear. *"It's time for you to use your sharp tongue for pleasure."*

She stopped struggling and went limp in his arms. When his grip on her shoulders slackened, she opened her mouth, sinking her teeth into the flesh of his solid arm. He cursed in surprise, his arms dropping away from her. Suddenly free, she lunged through the water, swimming furiously toward the other side of the pool.

"Now you know it is not only my tongue that is sharp," she taunted, nearly out of breath. *"Come to me, Kai,"* his deep voice ordered. *"You do not want my anger."*

Did he think because she loved him that she would obey his every command? His arrogance strengthened her resolve to make him wait. *"No."*

His eyes narrowed. *"So, you would play the game to the end?"*

It no longer seemed a game, but more a battle of wills. *"What game? Perhaps I no longer want you."*

The frigid smile on his face gave her second thoughts. *"I will make you regret the words you say in jest. And then beg my forgiveness."*

A sliver of foreboding mixed with dangerous excitement danced through her stomach. *"Beg your forgiveness? Never."* Her gaze locked with his. *"I was mistaken. I think you favor more of the buffalo than just his back end."*

Too late, she realized her mistake in provoking him. She'd never seen such fierce determination in anyone before. Certainly not in the man she loved above all others. He swam with the swiftness of an eel, *catching her by the hair as she fled. Winding the long wet strands around his fist, his other arm clutched her kicking legs. "You need cooling off, Little Bird. The summer heat has addled you." He dunked her.*

When he pulled her up, she sputtered, "You—you devil—"

"Still you fail to curb your tongue." He shifted to dunk her again, hesitating when she screeched and clutched at his shoulders. "Do you wish to beg my forgiveness?"

"No—yes," she cried, when he tipped her head back toward the water.

"Say it," he demanded.

She lowered her eyelashes to hide her seething anger. "Forgive me."

He untangled his hand from her hair and gripped her chin, raising her head until she glared into his searching gaze. "You are like a wild and untamed mare. To master such a magnificent animal," his finger traced down her breast, "one must ride them long and hard."

She slapped his hand away and pulled from his hold. "Dare to touch me and I will—"

"I grow tired of your foolishness," his harsh voice interrupted her. "I have been mistaken treating a child as a woman. And why? There are many more comely maidens that would spread their legs for me."

Surprise held her motionless as she watched him wade to the shore and pull himself out of the water. He told the truth. Many of the women in their tribe desired him. Glaring at his naked dripping form, she slowly followed him to the bank, recalling how long it had taken for him to see her as a woman. There were other young men whose hungry eyes had begun to follow her. But Kai did not want them. She wanted Tokala. A man born eighteen winters before her own ten and seven, who had already buried a wife and child.

She imagined him making love to another woman and pain speared her. "Go then! You are not the only brave who seeks my hand. Nayati has offered my father ten ponies."

"He is a fool," Tokala's dismissive gaze raked her as she rose from the pool, "for I find nothing to equal your worth to ten ponies."

"Perhaps he measures it by my skill as a lover," she lied, feeling spiteful delight when she noticed his fists clench and unclench.

His sudden bark of laughter startled her. "Then he is as unskilled as you are."

Black dots of rage covered her eyes as she flew at him, her nails curved in eagle-like talons. Tokala caught her wrists before she could scratch his face, but the force of her impact sent them sprawling to the ground. He took her slight weight with a grunt and whoosh before deftly twisting until she lay beneath him. For a moment she remained still, her treacherous body reacting to the hard and naked length of him against her. Then she silently struggled to tug her hands free, the slick wetness of their skin working in her favor.

Her knee struck his groin and a gasp hissed through his clenched teeth, his hands loosening. Easily slipping from his hold, she scrabbled for the pile of clothing. Her knife would keep him from pursuit. Sweeping the knife in her hand, she swung around, yelping in surprise when the tip of the knife slashed his thigh. He cursed in outrage and lurched back. With shocked horror, she watched the blood seep from the small wound and trail down his leg.

The knife fell from her slack fingers and her gaze lifted to see the look of hurt fury on his face. Not hurt from the wound, but from her rejection of him. Unable to face him, she turned and began to run, tears flooding her eyes, blocking her vision. Her scream rent the air as she stumbled over a small rock and the ground rushed up to meet her. The impact tore the breath from her body and the world turned gray . . .

She jackknifed up, gasping for breath. Someone was chasing her! A large hand lay lightly clamped around her waist and she lurched away, falling off something and landing on her hands and knees. Her lungs worked furiously to take in air as she scrambled in the dark, coming up hard against a wall. Following the length of it, she felt her way with her hands until she ran into another wall. She crouched into the corner, her eyes darting around the dark and unfamiliar place.

"*Naki'ti?*" A husky voice came out of the shadows and she pressed further into the corner. "Where are you?"

A light flared and she blinked and squinted, unable to make out the face of the large naked form that suddenly stepped forward. He reached out a hand toward her and she sobbed, shrinking away. "*Nukpana helki'!*"

She heard the sharp intake of breath as his hand jerked back and he sank slowly to his knees. "*Kai.*" The name he spoke came out in no more than a shocked whisper but reverberated like a shout through her brain. Shaking her head, she clamped her hands over her ears to try and stop the tumultuous din.

No. Not Kai. Joanna. My name is Joanna.

The deafening noise in her head began to recede and her eyes slowly adjusted to the light. She lowered her trembling hands and hugged them around her bare breasts. Still disoriented, her tearful gaze focused with confusion on the man kneeling before her. "Gray?"

Silently he pulled her quivering body tight against his, rubbing his hands in a soothing motion beneath her long hair and across her back. "I dreamed someone was chasing me."

Crooning softly in her ear, he promised her that she was safe and no one would harm her. He picked her up and carried her back to the bed, carefully laying her on the sheets before sliding next to her. Bunching the quilt around them, he gathered her to him and she snuggled into his arms, letting the fear drain out of her. The shaking gradually subsided as his warmth seeped into her body.

Her heavy lids were almost closed when her thigh encountered his rigid shaft. For a moment she lay still, slight wonder at his stamina running through her. She didn't know if she had enough strength to make love one more time. But she did know she wanted to please him as he had pleased her earlier. She ran her hand down his chest and gently stroked his steel hardness. "Do you want to . . . ?"

He groaned softly. "Yes, I want to. But I want us both to be ready for it." He stilled her hand and settled his lips lightly on hers for a short kiss. "It's enough for now just to hold you, *Naki'ti*." His voice lowered to a whisper, "Let me hold you."

She sighed and nestled back against him, instantly falling into a deep and dreamless sleep.

Chapter Six

Joanna came slowly awake, a nagging pain drumming a slow beat in the back of her head. Moaning, she tried to turn over but a heavy weight across her stomach kept her immobile.

"What . . . ?" She lifted her head, struggling to figure out why there would be a heavy weight on her stomach. Then her foggy mind cleared and comprehension hit. Her slumberous eyes flew wide open and she stared down at the muscular arm draped around her bare mid-drift.

Oh God, what have I done? she thought. Cocking her head slightly, she looked directly into the watchful eyes of her new lover.

"Good morning." He smiled at her, revealing his even white teeth. A dark shadow of stubble covered his square jaw. An inherited trait from his French-Canadian mother's side of the family, she was sure.

When he leaned down to kiss her, she quickly turned her head and his lips landed against her cheek. She swallowed and clamped her mouth shut. If the awful taste in her mouth was anything to go by, her breath smelled like rotting apples. Scampering from beneath his arm, she slid off the bed and scooped up her dress from the floor, holding it in front of her.

He's even more beautiful in broad daylight, she thought. He raised up on his elbow, his muscles rippling and tightening across his chest. Her gaze moved down his Adonis-like body, trying not to remember how warm and hard he felt beneath her hands. His generous manhood lay in semi-erect repose across his thigh and she noticed the small scar below it.

Her head pounded. The scar . . . there was something about it, but she couldn't remember. She pointed a shaky finger at his thigh. "Where did you get that scar?"

Gray looked surprised at her question. "I'm not sure. I've always had it. Probably a childhood accident. Why? Does it bother you?"

She shook her head. "No ... I'm—" Realizing where she had been staring the last few minutes, she yanked her gaze away in embarrassment. "I need to ... um ... Could I use your bathroom?" She shifted the minuscule bit of material around, trying to cover more of her bare skin.

His smile broadened as he watched her futile attempt at modesty. "Right in there." He pointed to a door behind her.

"Thank you." Carrying her dress like a shield, she backed up to the door, only lowering the piece of clothing when she was safely inside the bathroom. After closing the door quietly, she leaned her head against it. He probably thought she was a half-wit, but she'd never spent the night with a man before. Wilson had always wanted to sleep in his own bed, alone. She often wondered if he would have insisted on twin beds after they were married.

Pulling away from the door, she turned, her eyes widening in delight. A huge skylight in the roof hung centered over a sunken tile tub big enough to hold two people. Gathered around it lay dozens of plants, ferns, and even two small trees. It gave the effect of a small pool in the middle of an exotic jungle. On the other side of the room— which looked as large as her bedroom at home—stood a shower stall, commode and a double sink area.

She padded across the tiled mosaic floor to one of the sinks and frowned at her reflection in the large mirror. Her mascara lay smudged beneath her slightly bloodshot eyes. "Well, what do you expect after an evening of drinking and debauchery?" she murmured. Her headache seemed to magnify as she remembered her behavior the night before. Not only had she thrown herself at him, but then she'd asked if they could do it again.

After draping her dress over a towel bar, she opened his medicine cabinet and searched through the shaving equipment for an aspirin. Nothing. He didn't even have the old prescription bottles that people usually collected with one or two forgotten pills still inside.

She reached up and pulled out a tube of toothpaste, opened it and squeezed some onto her finger. Using her finger as a toothbrush, she scrubbed her teeth, then rinsed her mouth. Curious, her hand wavered in front of a bottle of his aftershave. She finally grabbed it, twisting the top off and bringing it to her nose. Musky spice. Closing her eyes, she sniffed his scent and a dozen remembered sensations drifted through her.

"Joanna?" He knocked on the door and her hand jerked in guilty surprise, sending the liquid sloshing over her fingers. She replaced the cap with clumsy hands.

"Yes?" she answered, pushing the aftershave back into the cabinet before closing it.

"The towels are in the closet next to the sink. Help yourself to a shower." His voice lowered suggestively, "Or you're welcome to take a leisurely bath if you want."

Eyeing the bathtub with longing, she mentally chastened herself for even considering his offer. Having spent the night with Gray was a crazy mistake. The sooner she rectified the situation and left, the better. She moaned and rubbed her aching temples. How could she have made love with a man she barely knew? She'd dated Wilson five months before sleeping with him. With Gray it had only been a matter of hours.

As she stood under the steaming spray, scenes from the strange fantasy she'd had about the Indian warrior floated back. The water flowing down his dark hair . . . rolling off his muscular flesh . . . She quickly pushed the thoughts away and lathered Gray's soap over her body. It's funny how Gray's bare torso matched her fantasy almost perfectly. Right down to the— Joanna's fingers went lax and the bar of soap fell to the floor with a loud thud.

The scar on his thigh.

She shivered. *It's just a strange coincidence.* Squatting under the streaming hot water, she grasped the soap. Maybe she was still spooked from the bizarre dream she'd had. A dream that seemed so real that she had awakened confused, still believing someone was chasing her. Another thing to blame on the wine and brandy.

Joanna rinsed and dried off with one of Gray's thick white towels before pulling the dress on. Running her fingers through her wet hair, she tried to untangle it, then gave up, deciding to fix it when she got home. After all, Gray had already seen her at her worst.

She slowly opened the door, relieved to find him nowhere in sight. Striding into the room, she stopped at the bed and leaned down to pick up her ruined underwear and stockings strewn over the floor. She rolled them into a tight ball, digging her fingers into the nylon cloth as her gaze settled on the rumpled sheets and comforter.

Vivid memories of the night before came racing back. Memories of him caressing and kissing her body, murmuring his encouragement as she drowned in pleasure. She'd never forget the deeply erotic sight of him kneeling between her legs—his mouth and tongue sending her to a skyrocketing climax.

"I'm going to bury myself deep inside of you." Closing her eyes, she recalled his fierce pledge. *"Until you feel nothing but me . . ."*

The depth of his sensuality and passion excited her. And scared her to death.

Moving quietly, she peered outside into the hall and, after seeing no one, proceeded to tiptoe down the stairs. The sound of dishes clattering and the smell of brewing coffee floated from the kitchen area as she made her way to the parlor. Kelly's shoes were where she'd left them when she kicked them off last night. A blush spread over her face as she recalled how she'd wrapped her legs around Gray to keep him within her. She'd never behaved so aggressively and with such abandon in her life. Certainly not with Wilson. After quickly sweeping up the shoes, she turned to make her escape, skidding to a stop when Gray suddenly appeared in the doorway carrying a tray. The shoes fell out of her arms and she made no attempt to retrieve them.

He wore only a pair of jeans hanging low on his hips, and he noted the guilty expression on her face with a puzzled smile. She glanced down at the bundle still clutched in her hands. Anything was better than staring at his naked chest and remembering how his heated skin tasted and felt against her lips.

He advanced into the room and set the tray on the couch before moving to stand in front of her, his silent scrutiny causing her even more discomfort.

"I'm not sure . . ." She twisted the ball of cloth tighter between her fists.

He reached his hand out, tilting her chin and forcing her to look at him. His amber eyes searched hers and whatever he found in them seemed to assure him, because he smiled.

"I don't usually—" The awkward speech died in her throat as he lowered his head and covered her lips with his. The wad of clothing dropped from her hands, following the shoes to the floor. Shoving them out of the way with his foot, he pulled her closer, molding her body to his, while slanting his mouth and deepening the kiss.

Her body reacted to his like a lit match tossed at a highly volatile chemical. She exploded into flames. His tongue searched along the edge of her lips and she opened her mouth wider, letting him in. He delved inside her moist heat with deep, velvet licks and she wrapped her arms around his neck, yielding to the sleek invasion. Why did it seem so new and yet so familiar to be in his arms? His taste, his smell, his touch were indelibly etched into her senses.

"No," she murmured, weakly pushing on his shoulders and attempting to pull her lips from his. His hands stroked her bare buttocks, grasping her cheeks and locking her against him. She almost succumbed completely when his aroused manhood, outlined by the rough material of his jeans, nudged between her legs.

"No!" She panicked, shoving at his shoulders until he let her go. Yanking down her dress, she stumbled around a wing-back chair until it stood between them. At the look of distress on her face, he started to skirt the chair and she stepped back, holding her palm up. "Don't."

He halted. "Joanna." He ran a jerky hand through his hair, his face creased with concern. "I wouldn't—you know I wouldn't do anything to hurt you, don't you?"

She swallowed and nodded, striving to regain control of her labored breathing.

"Then what's wrong?"

"What's wrong?" A laugh bubbled out of her, containing a definite hysterical pitch. "I just woke up in bed with someone that I've only known for a matter of hours. I'm not even sure how it happened!"

He crossed his arms over his chest and stared at her thoughtfully. "All right," he conceded, his tone low and calm. "Maybe we skipped a few steps in between. Is that so terrible?"

"Yes!" A frown tightened his jaw and she babbled on, "I mean, I don't know." She bent her head and massaged her temples, her headache having resumed in full force. "I don't know what to think. And when you touch me, I can't think at all."

"Are you sorry we made love?"

She opened her mouth to answer "Yes" but the word stuck in her throat. No man had ever made her feel so beautiful and desirable in her life. Certainly not Wilson. If she said she was sorry that last night happened, it would be a lie.

Suddenly the front doorbell rang and Joanna breathed a sigh of relief at the timely interruption.

"Damn," he uttered, a look of uncertainty on his face. For a moment, Joanna thought he was going to ignore it, but then he seemed to make up his mind about something and turned to her. "Please, don't go anywhere. I'll handle whoever it is and then we can talk."

She reluctantly heeded his request, trying to sort out what she'd say when he returned. At the sound of her sister's voice moving through the entryway, she scurried over and snatched the ruined clothing from the floor, quickly stuffing it under a pillow on his claw foot settee.

Kelly flounced into the parlor, dressed in a short orange skirt and tight matching suit coat with diamond shaped gold buttons. On anyone else the outfit would have appeared ridiculous. On her it looked terrific.

"Good morning, Jo." She raised an amused eyebrow. "I do hope I'm not interrupting anything?"

"No," Joanna said, edging toward the door. "Actually, I was just leaving."

Kelly ignored her, stepping around her and further into the parlor. "Is that coffee I smell?" she asked, lifting her nose in the air like a well-pedigreed bloodhound.

Gray grinned and motioned toward the tray. "Would you like a cup?"

"If I can have it to go." Kelly sighed and glanced at her watch. "Unfortunately I have to catch a plane in forty-five minutes."

"I'll fix some in a travel mug." He started toward the kitchen, pausing at the parlor door. "Would you like to try some of Mrs. Ohako's fruit danish?"

"Apple?" her sister asked hopefully.

He nodded, then smiled when Kelly's eyes lit up like a child being offered her favorite candy. "Oh, yes! Please."

As soon as he left, Kelly turned to Joanna. "Well?"

"I'm going to kill you."

She waved her hand dismissively. "Sure you are. But first tell your little sister everything and don't leave out any of the lovely details."

"I'm not going to tell you a darn thing. How could you leave me here like that?"

"I don't know what you're complaining about," Kelly said, matter-of-factly. "You both looked ready to jump each other's bones throughout dinner. All I did was clear the way, so to speak. And don't tell me the sex wasn't good, because I won't buy it."

"Would you lower your voice?" Joanna hissed, feeling her face flush in embarrassment. "You know, sometimes it's hard to believe our veins carry the same blood. I blame this whole fiasco on you." She poked an accusing finger at Kelly's chest.

"*Puh-leeze.*" Her sister rolled her eyes. "I might have thrown you the ball, but you picked it up and ran with it."

Joanna looked at her in disbelief. "Now you're reducing your behavior down to a simple football analogy?"

"Why do you have to make everything so damn complicat—" Kelly suddenly broke off, her gaze riveted to the other side of the parlor. "Oh my God. That's really beautiful!"

Joanna watched with annoyance as her sister went to the fireplace and picked up the wooden figurine from the mantel. Studying it a moment, Kelly turned it around in her hand before looking up at Joanna, a wide smile on her face. "He must have done this last night."

"He told me he carved that piece when he was sixteen." She glared at Kelly. "Are you trying to change the subject? Because it's not going to work. I'm still angry as hell."

Kelly shook her head, staring at the carving, her brows drawn together in confusion. "That can't be true."

"Oh yes it is! Did you expect me to thank you for—"

"I'm talking about this," Kelly interrupted, holding the carving up. Joanna eyed the figurine, then shrugged. "What about it?"

"Don't you see?"

"All right, I give up," she said with frustration. "What am I supposed to see?"

"This is you."

Chapter Seven

"What?" Joanna took the figurine from Kelly's hand. She glanced down at it and then looked at Kelly. "You're crazy. This doesn't look like me. First of all it's obviously a native American woman."

"Did you forget that Great Grandma Taylor was a full-blooded Cherokee Indian? Mom commented more than once that you looked just like her." She smiled. "Remember all those stories you used to tell me about the Indian village? As if you'd really lived there. Dad said you had such a vivid imagination you were probably going to be a writer."

"I don't remember." Joanna smoothed her thumb along the wood of the figurine, pain tightening her chest. The time before her parents' death and directly after was something she hadn't allowed herself to think about in ages.

"Well I do. I remember everything before the plane crash and then having to go live with Aunt Claire. That's when you stopped telling the stories. She made your life miserable, the repressed old bitch, and if you hadn't run interference, she would have done the same thing to me."

Joanna put the carving back on the mantel, feeling suddenly drained. "It was a long time ago."

"But she's still doing it, isn't she? I think it's the reason you became engaged to Wilson. Maybe you don't even realize it, but you're still trying to win her approval, even now after she's dead."

Joanna gave a short, hollow laugh. "You make me sound like an emotional cripple."

"I don't mean to." Kelly put her arms around Joanna and gave her a hug. "I love you and I just want you to be happy. You've always taken care of everything, including working at the bank to put me through school. I don't know why you won't let me do the same for you."

She opened her mouth to argue, but closed it again when she noticed Gray standing in the doorway holding the coffee and a paper bag. How long had he been there? The idea that he may have overheard Kelly dredging up the past made her uncomfortable.

Kelly turned and followed her gaze, smiling at Gray. "I guess it's time for me to go."

"I'm coming with you," Joanna said quickly.

Her sister gave her a puzzled look. "Why would—"

"I want to see you off," she told her, with a tone set to prevent any argument.

"All right." Kelly shrugged. "But have you forgotten that I have a rental car? How are you going to get home?"

"I'll take a taxi."

Her gaze avoided Gray. She knew she was behaving like a coward, but she needed time to think before she could talk to him.

Kelly put a finger to her cheek and tapped it, giving him an assessing stare. "You would be just perfect for this shoot I'm doing in the Bahamas. I don't suppose you'd ever consider doing an advertisement for cond—"

"Kelly!" Joanna interrupted her sister before Kelly could embarrass her further. "We'd better get going."

Gray grinned at Kelly, handing her the coffee and bag. *"Anahuac ce'iba mictlan dahpike."*

"What does that mean?" Kelly asked.

"Safe journey, sister of my heart."

"Thank you," she told him, then to Joanna's irritation, reached up and gave him a kiss on the cheek before saying, with what sounded like regret, "hmmm . . . lucky Jo."

※⟪⟫※

The airport bustled with weekend travelers. Joanna stood staring out the huge glass window of the airport lounge, watching the 747 as it gathered speed and lifted off the ground. When the airplane was just a dot in the sky, she turned, ready to make her way to the front entrance to hail a cab.

"Joanna?"

Her stomach plummeted. She knew that voice. Just the sound of it made her want to find the nearest hole and crawl into it. She twisted around to see her ex-fiancé striding toward her, his face incredulous.

"Hello, Wilson," she said in a flat voice. "What are you doing here?"

"Returning from a conference. Good God, Joanna, what have you been doing to yourself? You look like hell." His disapproving gaze took in her snarled hair, bare legs and tight dress. And the fact that she didn't have a bra on. She wondered what he'd think if he knew she wasn't wearing panties either.

"Thank you. I could always count on you for a compliment," she said sarcastically.

He tucked a well-manicured hand into his impeccable gray suit, striking a pose that she had no doubt he practiced in front of a mirror. "Would you prefer that I lie?"

"Why not?" Joanna straightened her slumping shoulders, her jaw tightening. "You did it for two months while you boffed your dental hygienist."

Wilson's thin eyebrows drew together with displeasure. "Perhaps if you'd been less of a frigid icicle, I wouldn't have been tempted by another woman."

His well-aimed arrow hit the mark. The anger and hurt welled up and her eyes began to sting.

Suddenly a pair of hands gripped her shoulders, turning her around.

"Gray?" There was a moment of astonishment before Gray's mouth descended on hers, kissing her into silence. His palms framed her face, then smoothed along her cheeks, his fingers burrowing into her thick hair. She opened up to him like a flower unfolded to the morning sun, his heat melting away the hurt and anger until all that remained was pure, raw pleasure.

Her arms slid up his shoulders, encircling his neck. She tilted her head, deepening the kiss, leaning into him and molding her body against his. It wasn't until she heard a voice over the loudspeaker announcing a flight arrival that she remembered where she was.

He pulled slightly away to smile down at her. "I know it's only been an hour, but I've missed you."

Her head spun and she worked hard to make sense of what he was saying. *He missed her.* He had followed her to the airport and kissed her in front of anyone and everyone even though he must have been angry with her. She couldn't help smiling back. Wilson would never have kissed her in a public place. *Wilson.* His gaze moved past her and

she realized that Wilson had been standing behind them the whole
time. Watching her cling and wrap herself around Gray.

She turned around to see Wilson staring at her as if he'd never seen
her before. The thought that she had shocked him filled her with im-
mense satisfaction. All the things Gray had said and done to make her
feel desirable the night before returned, seeping through her body like
warm honey. He'd told her she was beautiful, yes, but it was the way
he'd made her *feel* beautiful that made all the difference. Desirable,
beautiful, sexy. What Wilson had gradually taken away while they
were engaged, Gray had given her back tenfold in just one night of
glorious lovemaking.

Next to Gray, Wilson's skin looked flaccid and white, his chin
rounded and weak where Gray's was square and strong. Why had she
never noticed how close Wilson's eyes were together or how he
combed his hair over to the side to hide a growing bald spot?

"Wilson, this is Gray Avonaco, my . . . neighbor." Joanna glanced
up at Gray and said matter-of-factly, "Wilson was my fiancé until I
caught him in bed with his dental hygienist." If she surprised Gray
with her less than tactful revelation, he hid it well.

"Really?" Gray held out his hand and Wilson automatically took
it, a dull red tint of embarrassed anger on his face.

"Yes. He was just kind enough to explain his reasons for cheating
on me. Apparently, I'm a frigid icicle." Joanna's eyebrows rose in
question. "What do you think, Gray?"

Gray put his forefinger and thumb under her chin to tilt her head
back, his dark gaze searching hers. "I think . . ." he paused to lightly
kiss the corner of her jaw. "that you're about as frigid as . . ." he
brushed his lips across her cheek and nibbled at the edge of her parted
lips. "an active volcano." She couldn't prevent the moan of pleasure
that escaped her as his teasing mouth finally covered hers. The kiss
only lasted a moment before Gray pulled back and smiled at Wilson.
"Your loss is my gain."

"Yes, well," Wilson raised his arm and looked pointedly at his
watch, the stain of embarrassment still coloring his face, "if you'll excuse me, I have an appointment." He nodded at them and quickly disappeared out of the lounge and into the moving crowd of travelers.

Some of Joanna's newly found confidence went out the door with
her ex-fiancé. She looked at Gray through her eyelashes, wondering
what he was thinking. The expression on his face was impossible to
read.

"My car's double parked out front," he said, taking her hand. He
didn't give her time to argue and started toward the exit with her trail-

ing blindly after him. As they made their way through the crowd, she tried to come up with the right words to say in apology. Even though he had played along with her game of revenge, he couldn't be happy with the way she'd used him to get back at Wilson.

He opened the passenger door to his black Chevy Blazer and she climbed in. Before slipping behind the wheel, he pulled out a traffic violation ticket that lay tucked under the windshield wiper, shoving it into his jeans pocket.

Neither one of them spoke as he maneuvered the car into traffic and headed home. She kept her gaze glued out the window during the twenty-minute ride, looking, but not really seeing anything. When he stopped the car in her driveway, she pushed the door open and stepped out before he could open the door for her.

He stood quietly while she unlocked her front door with shaking fingers. The longer he remained silent, the worse the sick clench in her stomach felt.

"Please come in," she said, moving aside so he could enter. She closed the door behind them, then stood with her hands gripped together, avoiding his gaze. "Would you like a cup of coffee?"

"No, thank you," he said in a clipped tone.

She finally glanced up at his frowning face. His resemblance to the stern warrior in her dream was astonishing. And he seemed almost as angry. The thought that she may have carelessly ruined any chance of a growing relationship with him filled her with dismay. "Gray, I'm so sor—"

"Do you still love him?"

Surprise left her speechless. Whatever she expected him to say, it certainly wasn't that. "Do I love Wilson?" She shook her head. "No." Her eyebrows drew together as she added with dawning realization, "I don't think I ever really did."

Relief rushed through her when he smiled, her answer obviously pleasing him.

"Kelly told me this morning that I was only engaged to him because my aunt would have approved. I'm starting to think she may have been right."

"I am so sorry about what happened at the airport. I can't believe I said those things. Then I practically flaunted in his face that I . . . that we—"

"Joanna," Gray put his finger over her lips, effectively silencing her. "Don't apologize. I don't care if the whole world knows we've made love."

"You don't?"

He shook his head, letting his finger slide across her lips before taking it away. "No. I don't."

"I'm not sorry we made love last night." She smiled at him and his searing gaze lowered to her lips a moment before lifting to meet her eyes again.

He raised a dark eyebrow. "But?"

"It happened so fast. I just—I need some time."

"For us to get to know each other?" he said, with a wry smile.

She felt herself blush as the previous night's memories came back to haunt her once again. "That sounds pretty foolish, doesn't it? Considering we know each other in the most intimate way there is." Would she ever figure out what made her act out of character and do things with this man that she'd never even thought of doing with Wilson?

"There's a reception for me tonight at an art gallery a friend of mine owns. Will you come with me?"

"I don't know. I—"

"It will be completely platonic. I promise." Although he looked solemn, his eyes held a teasing light. "I won't even hold your hand."

Fear of his behavior didn't worry her, but her own weakness where he was concerned scared her to death. Kelly's words echoed in her head. *"Maybe you don't even realize it, but you're still trying to get Aunt Claire's approval, even though she's dead."* No, Aunt Claire wouldn't have approved of Gray. It made Joanna furious to think she was still letting her aunt influence her life. "Yes." She smiled up at him. "I'd love to go."

Chapter Eight

Kai fought the gray mist of horror threatening to engulf her. She had not meant to stab him. Surely he knew she would never purposely hurt him?

The rough grass scratched her bare skin and small stones dug into her back and buttocks. Tokala's hand held her wrists clamped to the ground above her head, though she didn't struggle against his hold. His other hand raised her knife so she could see the blood clinging to the tip. She shut her eyes against the sight.

"Look at me!" he demanded. Lifting her lids, she flinched at the savageness in his features. "Only great warriors have drawn the blood of Tokala." He brushed the knife across her cheek, trailing the bloody point down her chin to rest at her throat. "None have lived to tell the tale of their feat."

Had she angered him so much that he would kill her? A whimper escaped her lips. His eyes darkened at the sound and he skimmed the blade down her throat to her breast. Laying the flat end lightly against her nipple, he slowly brushed it over the beaded tip. She bit her lip, trying to quell the tears that spilled from her eyes. He watched the knife as he grazed it down her belly and lower, to the curly tufts of dark hair between her legs.

"You have lain with Nayati?" His accusing gaze searched hers.

"No." She shook her head, her body trembling when he rubbed the knife against her inner thigh.

"You lie to me."

She stared into his furious black eyes. He truly believed she would betray him with another. "Kill me, then," she whispered, too full of grief and sorrow to remain afraid. "Kill me. For I will love you into death."

Tokala cursed and jerked the knife away from her, plunging it with great force into the ground. "I would sooner kill myself, Little Bird," he told her, his voice bitter. "This is the fate I live with."

His head swooped down, his lips plundering hers. She let the tears flow freely, opening her mouth to his thrusting tongue. If he sought retribution, she would accept her due. Loosening the hold on her wrists, his hands moved over her breasts and down, finally resting on her thighs and pushing her legs apart. His fingers separated her folds and without pausing, he drove his hardened manhood inside her. She held in a gasp of pain.

"You unman me," he rasped, pulling out and plunging into her again. His words confused her, but his tone made her raise her hand and caress the side of his clenched jaw in a soothing motion.

"And your touch weakens me like a disease." His eyes closed tightly, the wretchedness of his confession apparent. She lifted her legs and wrapped them around him, tilting her hips to take him deep into her. He groaned, his hard, rhythmic thrusts becoming wild and hurried. Her hands wandered up and down his taut body urging him on, holding him close against her. With one final thrust, his face tightened and the pulsing rush of his seed flowed into her.

When the glaze of passion began to clear from his eyes, she thought she read regret in them before he turned away, lifting his body from hers and standing. Without saying a word, he paced to the edge of the pool and dived in.

Kai rose from the ground, shame for her careless game overwhelming her. How could she have played with him so? Tokala was a strong brave, abhorring any sign of weakness in himself. And that is how he saw his love for her, as a weakness. Knowing this, she had used it against him, like the child he accused her of being.

She watched him swim through the water, his anger still clearly visible. He would not glance her way. Finally he swam to the edge of the pool, pulled himself out of the water and dropped onto his back, his breath coming in ragged pants.

His dark gaze followed her as she came to him, kneeling on the ground by his side. The gash on his muscled thigh no longer bled. Leaning over him, she softly put her lips to the wound. "Forgive me." She rested her head against his heaving chest. "Please say I have not lost your love."

For a moment he stiffened beneath her. Then he laughed harshly as his arms slowly encircled her, his hands rubbing along her back with calming strokes while his breathing slowed. "If only it were so simple, Little Bird." He pulled her up until she lay on top of him. "I thought having you once would be enough. Instead I desire you more." Pushing her damp hair away from her face, his thumbs brushed the tear drops from her cheeks. "Every time we lay together, the fire burning inside me grows only hotter for you."

"This is bad?" She curled her fingers into his hair, her lips nuzzling his neck.

He laughed, this time with genuine humor. "No. This is good." His hand caressed her breast before pulling her up until he could take one burnished globe in his mouth, gently sucking the tip and grazing it with his tongue. She moaned with pleasure as he switched his attention to the other breast, his hands kneading her buttocks.

"Then you will offer for me?"

His palms shifted, cupping her chin and forcing her gaze to meet his. "I am too old for you. If my son had lived, he would be younger than you by one winter. Perhaps he would even have offered for you as Nayati has."

"I would not have him. As I would not have Nayati. I want only you." She pressed desperate kisses against his wide chest. "If you were as old as Kitowa, my great-grandfather, I would still want you."

He chuckled. "If I were so old, how could I please you so well?"

Kai raised her head and slowly smiled at him. "I would please us both."

Leaning over, she brushed the tips of her breasts along his stomach, moving down his body until her mouth lay even with his swollen manhood. She heard his startled grunt when her tongue flicked out, licking the drops of moisture off the tip. The taste of his essence was salty and warm on her lips as she closed them around the head of his staff. Sliding her hands under his buttocks, she squeezed the flexing muscles, taking him further into her mouth. He rewarded her with a low groan, rumbling from deep in his throat. His manhood throbbed against her tongue and she lapped it along its hard length, then caressed him with her lips, copying the motions he made within her body. Moving her hands from his buttocks, she fondled the two tightly drawn sacs below his staff before closing her fist around him and stroking the pulsing length that could not fit into her mouth.

He cursed, his fingers gripping and pulling her away from him. "Stop," he told her breathlessly. "Or you will finish me." Instead of pulling her beneath him, his hands clamped around her buttocks, setting her astride his body and lowering her onto his manhood.

"Ride me," he told her hoarsely. His nostrils flared as she rocked *against him, his eyes once again darkening in fierce passion. Sliding his hands up her belly, he cupped her breasts, his thumbs worrying the firm buds at their peak. She braced her hands on his hard chest, lifting herself up until only the tip of his staff penetrated her heat. Their gaze locked as she slowly sank down upon him. He groaned his approval and she did it again, pulling up, then with torturous unhurried movements, sinking down to take his hardness within her.*

His muscles stood out beneath her hands, his skin stretched tight across his face. She suddenly realized the power she possessed. Not to master him as she'd tried and failed, but to please him. To bring him to heights of ecstasy and delight that no other could. It was her power and it was her joy.

"Kai . . ." he groaned as she began to move her hips with short pumping thrusts. The turgid heat of him stroked against her core and she whimpered her pleasure as they traveled closer to the edge of paradise. "Ahhh . . ." His chest heaved as he tried and lost the struggle to hold his release. He grasped her hips and thrust deep into her, holding her tight as his manhood swelled and erupted, spilling himself into her womb . . .

Joanna rolled over in bed and moaned, her thighs squeezed tightly together as the climax washed over her. Her breath came in gasps as it died away and a feeling of emptiness took its place. Even after a fulfilling night with Gray, why was she still having erotic dreams about someone who didn't exist?

The doorbell rang out and she gasped, looking at the time on her watch. It was Gray and she wasn't even dressed yet. She jumped out of bed and threw on her robe, tying the belt around her waist as she hurried down the stairs. Checking the hall mirror, she paused to inspect her image, not surprised to see her wild, unruly hair and overly bright eyes.

She pulled open the door, her eyes widening at the sight of Gray in a black tuxedo. He looked devastatingly handsome. And he also looked as rich and successful as he truly was. There seemed to be so many sides to this man she barely knew. The debonair bachelor of last night, who without much effort, seduced her into bed after only knowing him a matter of hours. The talented artist, that created such awe-inspiring beauty from his bare hands, it made her want to weep. Then there was the common laborer who wore torn jeans and built his own cabinets. And now this sophisticated version that espoused pure money and power. Who was he truly?

His eyebrow rose in question at her and she suddenly remembered that she wasn't dressed.

"I'm sorry." She smoothed a nervous hand down the front of her robe and he followed her movements with darkening eyes. "I fell asleep."

He stepped into the entryway and closed the door behind him, his gaze never leaving hers. "And what did you dream?"

Joanna's mouth opened a bit in surprise at his question and she took a step back. "I-I don't really remember."

"Liar," he said softly and moved forward, his arm reaching out to touch a slightly callused hand to her cheek. "Your face is flushed." His thumb brushed her lips. "Your mouth soft and wet." Her eyes fluttered shut when he moved closer and his mouth came down to lightly touch her lips. "You taste delicious." He lightly nipped her bottom lip, drawing it into his mouth for a moment before letting go. "The same earthy flavor of last night, when we made love."

She sighed in pleasure when his warm palm slipped her robe aside and cupped her bare breast. "Your nipples are as taut and hard as I am." Sliding his heated lips to the corner of her mouth, he moved them in a slow, blazing trail across her cheek to her ear. "Did you dream about us, Joanna? Together, making love?" She felt the soft rustle of air as he breathed in her scent and his voice said hoarsely, "I smell it on you, as if we just lay together, as if I were just inside you—"

"*Gray.*" His name burst from her as a sob. Whether it was a plea for him to stop or to go on, she wasn't certain. He took mercy on her and dropped his hands, backing away.

"I'm sorry. I know I promised I wouldn't touch you."

She was sorry too, because all she wanted was for him to yank her up in his arms and just carry her back to bed. But she was too afraid. And she wasn't even sure what she was so afraid of.

He gave her a wry smile. "My only excuse is that you look so damn tempting in that robe, and I'm almost certain you have nothing on underneath it. Am I right?"

She pulled the gaping lapels tight together. "I-I have to go get dressed," she stuttered and heard his low chuckle as she scurried away up the stairs like a frightened mouse.

Chapter Nine

The small exclusive gallery was filled wall to wall with people when they entered. Most of the men were dressed like Gray, in a tuxedo. The women wore long or short gowns, none of which came off the rack like Joanna's. And there were more diamonds in the room than she'd ever seen in her life. A burst of anxiety hit her. What if she embarrassed him? She was horrible at making small talk and usually babbled like a fool when she was nervous. Glancing down at her plain black dress, she wondered why she'd decided to wear it. What she thought was conservative and classic now seemed frumpy and out of date. Kelly would have told her to stop being so insecure and have a good time. She was with Gray, wasn't she? She smiled up at him as he linked their hands together and walked further into the gallery.

"Would you like a glass of champagne?" a man in a catering uniform asked and she smiled, taking the elegant flute that he held out. She gulped half of it down in an effort to calm her nerves, wondering vaguely if spending time with Gray was going to turn her into a lush. She stood silently at his side as Gray smoothly led them through the crowd, only speaking when he introduced her to a friend or client.

"You're very quiet," he said, pulling her off to the side for a moment. "Are you all right?"

"Yes, I'm wonderful. It's really . . . wonderful," she said, snatching another glass of champagne from a passing waiter.

He gave her a crooked smile and looked about to say something when an older woman dressed in a flowing silver gown came up to them. "Welcome, Graywolf." She smiled at Gray and kissed him on the cheek before turning to Joanna. The woman's eyes widened in recognition. Had Joanna met her before? No. She would have remembered her exotic dark eyes and the lone streak of gray that flowed in a thin band through her blue-black hair.

"*Nitehya eyota tama?*" She glanced with question at Gray.

"Yasi."

Gray turned to Joanna. "This is Nita Tolkan, my mentor and also the owner of the gallery. Nita, this is Joanna Morgan."

Nita took her hand and held it between her own, a smile of real pleasure on her face. "I'm so happy to meet you, Joanna. Gray has told me—" She suddenly broke off as she glanced at Gray. "Well, any friend of Gray's is certainly welcome here."

"Thank you," Joanna said, before looking from Gray's face to Nita's. There appeared to have been some kind of unspoken communication between them.

"I have a buyer for your 'Maiden' carving. But he wants to meet you first." Joanna remembered it as the one that he had on his mantle the night before.

Gray frowned. "I don't want to sell that one."

"I know. But sometimes you need to replenish the well, Graywolf. The man has offered enough to keep you and your students in supplies for quite some time."

"Students?" Joanna looked at him with surprise.

"He probably didn't tell you that he funds the art program on the *Chioti'* reservation. Or that he gives a college scholarship every year to the most promising student." Nita laughed at the annoyance on his face. "He's very modest, your Graywolf."

"A very nice diversionary tactic, Nita. I still won't sell the piece."

"Now that you have the real thing, I thought perhaps you would change your mind." She raised an eyebrow at his terse silence. "No? Well, then I'll have to insist you do damage control." Nita pointed to a short stocky man who stood in conversation with a beautiful tall blond woman. "His name is Helmut Jenner. Take care not to upset him, he's gotten very rich investing in garbage. And for God's sake don't charm his fiancée too much. I hear he's very jealous."

She took Joanna's hand. "While you're busy, I'll give Joanna a personal tour of the gallery."

Gray didn't look very happy as Nita led her away. She winked at Joanna. "You'd think I was carrying you off forever the way he's frowning at me."

"He doesn't seem very happy to have to talk to your client. That's probably the reason he was frowning at you."

"Maybe." Her smile was enigmatic. "Or maybe he's afraid I'll say too much."

"Say too much? To me?" Joanna glanced back at Gray who watched them like a hawk, barely listening to what the little man beside him was saying. "About what?"

"His past. And other things." Nita took her hand and pulled her through the crowd, all the while nodding and calling greetings out as she passed several people.

"Ah, there's an important client. Pots and pots of money. But you must be careful, Javier Vega has a craving to collect all beauty, not just in the art form."

"Then there's nothing to worry about," Joanna said wryly. "I'm not beautiful."

"Are you calling me a liar?" Nita lifted a haughty dark eyebrow.

"N-no." Oh God, now she'd insulted Gray's best friend. "I'm sorry. I just meant . . ."

Nita stopped and put her hand under Joanna's chin. "Silly woman. You don't even know, do you? Your beauty is not harsh and cold, like that woman over there." She pointed to Helmut Jenner's fiancée. "It's soft and spiritual. It's in every sensual movement of your body, especially when Graywolf looks at you."

A blush rose to cover Joanna's face and to hide it she took another gulp of champagne. All the sexual attraction she felt for Gray was there for everyone to see.

Nita smiled again. "No wonder Graywolf is so protective of you. You have no idea of your power." She sighed wistfully. "I'm still waiting for my soul mate. A love to surpass all time. Do you know how lucky you are, Joanna?"

Before she could reply, Javier Vega approached them. Joanna automatically smiled politely when she was introduced, but remained quiet during the teasing repartee between Nita and the handsome Spaniard.

What had Nita been talking about? Did she think Gray was her "soul mate"? Joanna never believed in that kind of new age mumbo jumbo.

". . . promised Joanna that I would take her back to see 'The Waterfall'."

The sound of her name brought her back to attention.

"This is something I haven't seen yet?" he asked, his smile coaxing. "Perhaps I could view it with you?"

Nita shook her head. "No, this is not ready for sale yet. I'm afraid you'll have to wait to see this one."

If the man was disappointed, he hid it well. "Then of course I will

excuse you." Javier took Joanna's free hand in his. "It was a true pleasure to meet you, Joanna. Perhaps we—"

"Don't miss the 'Wild Stallion' piece, Javier. I think you'll find it
delightful." Nita cut him off effortlessly and managed to pull Joanna
free from his grasp. She led her to the back of the gallery where it was
less crowded. "Your silent indifference seemed to attract him even
more. He's not used to being ignored."

"I didn't offend him, did I?" Joanna clasped her hands together. "I
just feel so out of place. I don't know why Gray brought me."

"Don't be silly. You can't offend a man with skin as thick as a rhi-
noceros. And you're no more out of place than I am. I want to show
you something."

Joanna followed as Nita led her to a door in the back of the gallery.
She unlocked it and motioned Joanna in before her. After flipping on
the light switch, she closed the door behind them, shutting out the dull
noise of the crowd. The small room held stacks of boxes like a storage
area but also seemed to double as an office with a desk and two file
cabinets in a corner.

"Here." Nita smiled as she pointed to a carving that stood on a
large table against an empty wall.

Joanna's breath caught in her throat.

It was them. The two lovers in her dreams. In a very erotic pose.
The brave's head lay buried between the woman's breasts, his hair
plastered against her thrusting nipples. The woman's head was thrown
back in what could only be described as pure ecstasy, her legs twined
around the brave's back, her arms wound in his hair. The brave held
the woman's buttocks cupped in his hand. They both stood under
what looked like a waterfall, though it gave only the image of water
through their slick flattened hair and the glistening rocks behind
them.

It was just like the scene she had dreamed only a day earlier, when
she'd met Gray.

Nita smiled and shook her head. "I thought you might like it. Of
course, Gray didn't want it shown to the world. He was afraid that it
might embarrass you."

"I don't understand." It wasn't her. It couldn't be. It was the same
woman as he had carved in the 'Maiden.' But it wasn't her. Dizziness
assailed her and the room began to spin.

"Joanna, are you all right?"

"I don't feel very well." She swallowed and put a hand to her spinning head.

She heard the sound of the door opening behind them and turned away from the disturbing carving to see Gray standing in the doorway.

His eyes darkened as he noted her distress. "What have you done?" he asked Nita.

"Nothing, I—"

"She hasn't done anything. I'm sorry. I don't feel well." Joanna's shaking hand automatically reached out to him and he quickly took it. "I have to go home."

Pulling her against him, he wrapped steadying arms around her. "Have Gerard bring my jeep around to the back, Nita." His arms lay gentle against her, but his voice was laced with fury.

"No." Joanna felt his controlled anger, and wondered if it was directed at her or Nita. "I can take a taxi." She turned to Nita with pleading eyes. "Could I use your phone to call please?"

Nita's gaze was on Gray and Joanna vaguely registered the look of concern on her face. "I'm so sorry, Graywolf. How could I have known—"

"Just have the car brought around, Nita." His terse voice cut her off. "We'll speak later."

Nita disappeared through the office door and back into the crowd. Joanna kept her eyes on his chest, too afraid to look up and see the displeasure on his face. "I'd really rather take a taxi. I don't want to take you away from your reception."

"I'll take you home," Gray told her in a tone that brooked no argument. It wasn't long before the young man who had parked the car opened the back exit out of the storage area. Before she knew it, Gray had whisked her out the door and tucked her into his jeep.

She noted his terse silence and the dark brooding expression on his face. With each passing mile, the roiling motion in her stomach worsened until she finally blurted out, "I'm going to be sick."

He stopped the car on the side of the road and jumped out, opening the door for her just in time. Then he held her head as she threw up all four glasses of champagne and whatever hors d'oeuvres she had nibbled on the past two hours, all over the bottom side of his car and his shoes.

When she was through, he silently took his handkerchief and gently rubbed her mouth with it. She groaned in embarrassment. Would she forever be humiliating herself in front of this man? He helped her sit back and closed the door.

Leaning her head back against the leather seat, she closed her eyes, only opening them when she felt the weight and warmth of his jacket draping over her. He bent down to remove his shoes and wrapped them in an old tattered towel before putting them in the back of the Jeep.

"I'm so sorry. I ruined your shoes. I'll buy you a new pair—and your poor car. I'll have it washed—"

"Joanna, stop," he ordered as he slid into the front seat. Then his voice softened when he turned to her and asked, "How do you feel?"

"Like crawling into a hole and never coming out," she told him, lifting a hand to rub her aching forehead. "I've ruined the whole evening and took you away from your own reception. I understand why you're angry at me—"

"I'm not angry with you." He reached for her other hand from beneath the coat and brought it to his lips for a quick kiss. "Don't think that, not even for a moment."

She shook her head, not believing him. "I took you away and you were having such a good time."

"I hate it. I've always hated this part of my work. How could I be angry when you gave me an excuse to leave early? The only thing nice about this evening was when you were at my side."

"But . . . you seemed to be so at ease and happy."

"I learned a long time ago that you have to do some things you don't like in order to achieve the things that matter most."

"You mean the money for the program?"

"Yes. And don't worry that you've hurt that. I'd made over half a million before we left the gallery." He grinned when her mouth dropped open.

"Half a million?"

He restarted the car and pulled out into traffic. "It won't be quite that after taxes, but I'll have enough for the students."

Half a million dollars, she pondered as they drove up to her door. He was so blasé about money. She would have to work thirty years to accumulate that amount, if then. What did she have in common with this man? And what could he possibly see in her?

He turned off the car and glanced at her. "We need to talk, but I know tonight isn't the time. Can I see you tomorrow?"

Joanna took a deep breath before answering hesitantly, "I don't know, Gray. I—"

He put a finger across her lips. "Don't give me an answer now. You don't feel well and I . . . need to think some things over myself. Please just let me call you in the morning and we'll go from there?"

She reached up to touch his hand, gently pulling it away from her lips. "All right."

Depression settled over her when she closed the door to her house.

He hadn't even tried to kiss her when he'd walked her to the door. Why would he after she'd vomited all over him? What a horrible night. She headed up the stairs just longing for a warm shower and bed.

When she got into her bedroom, the phone began to ring.

"Hey, where were you all night?" Kelly asked, after Joanna picked it up and said hello.

"I had a date with Gray and before you ask how it went, I'll give you a little clue. I puked all over his shoes."

"What?"

Joanna kicked off her high heels. "It was a total disaster. I'm sure he'll never want to see me again."

"I'm sure you're exaggerating. Gray isn't the type to be put off by a little vomit. What the hell did you do, eat something that didn't agree with you?"

"No. I saw something that didn't agree with me." She pulled the dress over her head and tossed it on the floor. "You're never going to believe me if I try to explain it."

Kelly sighed. "Try anyway."

"It's these damn dreams I've been having." She walked over to the window and pulled back the drape. The only light shining from the Victorian was in Gray's bedroom. "Ever since Gray moved next door. They all seem so real. Now . . . "

"Now?" Kelly prodded, beginning to sound impatient.

Joanna let the curtain drop from her hand. "Remember the Indian warrior I always talked about when I was growing up?"

"The one who was going to—"

"Yes, marry me and live happily ever after in Gray's house. Well, he's the one I've been dreaming about." She moved over to the bed and lay back on the cotton comforter. "Not just dreaming, Kel. They seem so real. Like memories of another life. Very erotic memories, I might add. Sometimes I think it's Gray. But a more . . . I don't know—savage Gray."

"Every woman has erotic fantasies. It doesn't make you crazy."

"Does it make me crazy when my new lover carves a scene directly from my fantasy?" She stared up at the ceiling, the sight of the carving etched deep in her memory. "I mean, just exactly the way I dreamed it. I certainly never told him about the dream. So how could he know?"

"How could he make a carving of you fifteen years ago? Maybe your dreams are real and you did live a life together before. Who's to say?"

"Come on, Kelly. Don't tell me you believe in reincarnation?"

"I'm keeping an open mind, which is what you should be doing instead of freaking out all over the place." Kelly paused for a second, then asked point blank, "What are you so scared of?"

"I'm not sure. I just have a really bad feeling. Like I'm on a fast moving train that's hurtling toward disaster and I can't stop it."

"Would it be so horrible to live happily ever after with Gray?"

Joanna closed her eyes and shook her head. "I can't imagine 'happily ever after.' It's just a childish dream."

"Think about life without him, Jo. Maybe that's your disaster. And it'll be one of your own making. Sweet dreams." Joanna heard the soft click as Kelly hung up on her.

"Thanks for nothing," she said out loud and hung up the phone. After taking a short shower, then brushing her teeth, she flopped back into bed, exhausted. The last thing she imagined before falling asleep was a long lonely life without Gray.

Chapter Ten

Kai gazed across the blazing fire at her new husband as he lay on his side in the grass, gloriously naked and wonderful to her sight. The village Koyoka had married them today and the drumming feast had lasted long after the sun left the sky and the full moon rose.

Tokala swore and rolled over to remove a small stone from under his muscled thigh. "Why do I lie here when I could have a soft pallet in the marriage lodge?"

Moonlight shimmered across the small pool and the soft rush of water from the hidden falls murmured in the distance. She moved around the fire and knelt beside him, slowly untying her ceremonial gown as he watched with darkening eyes. "Would you consummate our marriage in any other place?"

"I would have you anywhere." Rising to his knees, he pulled her close, lifting her by the buttocks and pressing her tight against his hardening body. "Have I not earned the right, wife?"

A thrill of pure happiness flowed through her. Wife. They were well and truly one, in the eyes of the Great Spirit and the villagers.

Still, she could not resist the urge to tease him. "Certainly, husband, you have more than earned the right, since you offered twenty ponies, though I'm not worthy of ten," she said, her head downcast.

Lightly clasping her chin, he raised it to meet his look, concern on his face. The concern turned into chagrin at the teasing light in her eyes. "My wife's memory is as long as the cold winter." His palm spread across her cheek, his eyes full of regret. "Can you forgive the words I spoke in anger? What I did to you—"

"With love," she said, her fingers across his lips. "With love. Always."

"Yes." Taking a finger in his mouth, he nibbled at the tip. "Always."

He shifted his hands, pushing apart the ties of her gown and she groaned as his palms gently covered her breasts. She tilted her head back so his lips could more easily nuzzle her neck. "Do you remember that it was also the day I begged you to offer for me?"

"Yes," he confided next to her ear, laughter in his tone. "Two moons after I had already offered your father twenty ponies for you."

Gasping in surprise, she pulled away from him, her eyebrows drawn together in indignation. "You had already offered for me? Yet you let me beg—"

Covering her mouth with his, he swiftly quelled her rising ire and sent her heart pounding. "What would you have me do with twenty ponies? It will take all my strength taming you."

"I will be a good wife," she said, smiling up at him. "As tame as Koyoka's trained hawk."

His laughter carried across the pool, echoing against the surrounding rocks. "Then must I tether you to my wrist, lest you flee from my side?"

"No." She grasped his hand, placing the palm across her breast. "My heart ties and binds me to your side, Tokala. If you ever leave me, it will surely stop beating and I will die."

A strange looked crossed his face before he pulled her close against his warmth. "I will be with you always. This I promise."

Her lips nestled into his neck as she whispered, "I will make you keep your promise, my love." Her hand slid down his side to his thigh and she ran her finger along the small scar there. "I'm sorry I hurt you."

"You have marked me yours forever," he moaned, as she slid her palm over his hardness. For a moment he put his hand over hers, pressing it firmer against him. "Perhaps that is your punishment."

"Or perhaps . . ." Suddenly he scooped her up in his arms and strode to the edge of the pool. She gave a startled shriek as he tossed her into the cool water. "**that** is your punishment," he finished, when she rose to the surface sputtering.

She pushed sodden hair out of her eyes and glared at him. He tossed his head back and laughed at the expression on her face and she could not stay angry with him. Love poured from every corner of her being. Such feelings used to frighten her, but now she clung to them and basked in them.

"I have taken your punishment, husband," she said, affecting a submissive tone, "but must I be kept in the water on our wedding night?"

He looked at her skeptically, one eyebrow raised as if he expected her to retaliate. She smiled innocently at him, reaching her arm out for his help. Hunkering down, he held his hand out to her. She took it and for a moment made as if to climb out of the pool. Then, using all her strength, she yanked as hard as she could. Caught off guard, he faltered, lost his footing on the dew dampened grass and fell into the water beside her.

He laughed, and drew her up against him. "Vixen."

Kai wound her arms around his neck and pulled his mouth to hers. The heat of his body warmed her chilled skin and she felt his hardness against her jutting into her stomach. He groaned against her mouth when her hands reached down between them and stroked him. Before she could do anything more, he picked her up and set her on the grass, leaving her legs dangling in the water. Spreading her knees apart, he leaned down, nuzzling her. Weaving her hands into his hair, she moaned in delight at his attentions.

He breathed her in. "I need only smell you and I harden like a rutting stag." The movement of his breath sent shivering darts of pleasure that traveled to the tips of her breasts. "When I'm away from you, my only thoughts are when I will be inside you again."

She gasped as his tongue thrust inside her and pulled out, the tip flickering against the nub of her desire. He took the nub lightly between his teeth, drawing it in between his lips with a sucking motion until she thought she would simply die. Her scream of release echoed around the rocks again and again.

"Stop, please . . ." she begged him, her hips undulating against his mouth, her hands still clasped tightly in his hair.

He laughed and continued to please her with his mouth until she once more fell over the edge of paradise. Her body throbbed with sensual heat, every nerve alive and humming so that even the blades of grass rubbing against her buttocks heightened her pleasure.

Picking her up in his arms, he carried her over to where furs were lined up beside the fire and gently lay her down. She clasped her hand around him, feeling the end slick with his juices and rubbed them around the tip. "When you are away, you truly think only of being inside me again?"

"Truly." He lay down beside her and smoothed his hand across her sensitive nipples.

"When I could not have you—I would dream of you. I would pretend you were with me and . . ." she broke off as he pulled her closer and began to nibble and lick her arched neck.

"And what?" Tokala asked her, his breath warm against her cheek.

"Do things to myself."

His arms loosened from around her and he leaned up on one elbow, a curious look on his face. "What things?"

She pulled away, hiding a secret smile. Laying back against the soft bear rug, she glided her hands up her moist skin. "Shall I show you?"

"Yes." Tokala's hoarse voice told her.

"I would pretend you were with me. Your warm hands caressing me, like this." She heard the hiss of his breath as her hands slid up to touch her own breasts, lightly pinching the tips as he had done. She was surprised at how good it felt, to touch herself, but more importantly to see how he was affected by her play. Through slitted eyes, she watched his face as she spread her legs, her hands slowly traveling down her belly to her swollen and moist apex. "As if you were inside me." Her eyes met his as she delved a finger inside herself and bit her lip in pleasure. "Hard and deep between my legs." She felt him throbbing against her leg, yet he made no move to take her, his gaze fixed on the hand that stroked her essence and her other hand as it wandered back to her breasts. Her breathing became as short and labored as his. How much more could he endure before pleasuring himself in her?

"When I finish, I can feel my inside gripping my finger as I would grip you." She slid her hand down to clasp his hardness. "Like this . . ." She tightened her grip and then loosened it repeatedly, her fingers gliding up and down his slick manhood. He grunted his pleasure and thrust further into her hand, then a burst of warm liquid spurted from him and drenched her leg. With a sensual smile, she reached down and dipped her fingers into his seed, then began to rub it between her legs. "You mustn't waste yourself, Tokala. I would have your baby."

She gasped in surprise as he quickly rolled over and pulled her on top of him. He pushed himself against her, his hips thrusting up and down, until his still swollen manhood hardened and slid in to fill her once again. "And I would give you my baby." Reaching down, he swiped his hand over her leg, then rubbed the spilled seed he had gathered against her breasts, kneading it into her taut nipples. She whimpered, her back arching so he could more easily stroke his hands over her breasts as her hips moved against him, matching the slow rhythm of his hard thrusts into her body.

Then, as suddenly as before, he shifted, rolling them both over until he was once more on top of her.

*"Look, Little Bird." He reared back. "See how we fit together?"
She rose on her elbows, staring as he pulled out and slowly slid into
her again. Her legs fell further apart, a keening wail rising from deep
inside her. "Joined as one." He drove into her with increased motion.
"Feel me. Only me. There will never . . ." His thrusting became
harder, his face fierce in its intensity, "**never** be another for you.
Never . . ."*

A loud crash of thunder shook the house. Joanna's eyes flew open
and she rolled over in bed squeezing her throbbing thighs together. Her
body shook with unsatisfied desire. "Oh God," she moaned out loud,
trying to calm her rapid breathing. Another dream. It seemed so real.
Real enough to bring her frustratingly close to the point of climax.
Real enough to make her feel a sense of loss because he wasn't still inside of her. She glanced at the illuminated clock. Two A.M. A blinding
streak of lightning flashed, followed by a crack of thunder that shook
the glass panes in her windows. She kicked the cotton sheet off and
slid from the bed, then walked to the French doors and yanked them
open, letting the racing wind blow into her room to cool her heated
body. Another jagged bolt of lightning lit the sky and it was then that
she saw him, standing in the yard beneath her maple tree, staring up at
her.

Her heart pounded as if she'd just finished running a marathon. He
was there and she wanted him. It didn't matter anymore how or why.

Heedless of the thunderstorm, she moved onto the balcony, her
silk nightgown flapping against her legs and her long hair whipping
around her head. The first drops of rain began to fall. Big, fat raindrops
carried by the wind that slapped against her, saturating the nightgown
and plastering it to her body. He stood motionless, his dark outline re-
sembling a stone statue.

"Gray." She didn't know whether she shouted or whispered his
name, or just chanted it in her head. Somehow he knew what she
wanted. He gripped the wide limb of the tree and pulled himself up,
climbing two more branches before swinging over the wrought iron
railing and onto her small balcony.

Lightning flashed above them, creating an eerie light and shadow
effect on his face, once more giving him the same savage appearance
of the Indian brave in her dreams. He wore only his jeans and his hair
hung loose around his bare shoulders and chest. Without saying a
word, he came to her, took her face between his hands and lowered his
mouth to hers. The kiss was smooth and wet. She basked in its gentle
warmth, the perfect antithesis of the storm that raged around them.
Water sluiced over their bodies and thunder shook the floor they stood

on, but she felt safe in his arms, the heat of his body tight against her as if they were already naked.

She broke off the kiss, her hands sliding up his rain-slicked chest to clasp around his neck. "Make love to me," she said, her voice barely loud enough to be heard above the din. He swept her up in his arms and carried her through the doors.

The storm lay directly overhead. Lightning flashed, illuminating the room like a strobe light, wild crashes of thunder instantly following. It seemed like part of the fantasy. As if she was still asleep and dreaming that it was Tokala who set her feet down on the floor and held her up as he suckled her breasts through the drenched silk of her nightgown. It was Tokala she saw through the flickering bursts of light and it was him she pressed against, cupping her palm along the hard ridge outlined by his jeans. With a low groan, his mouth moved back to hers, this time kissing her with the same rough and savage passion as he did in her dreams.

She wanted him. Now.

Joanna tried to undo the metal clasp of his jeans, her trembling fingers struggling with the wet material. He kept their mouths joined together while his hands shifted and released the fastener for her. She unzipped his fly, feeling the sound of pleasure he uttered against her lips when she dipped her hands into his briefs, stroking his velvet heat. He strained against her hand and her fingers curled around him, easily sliding up and down as she slicked the length of him with the drops of his own desire.

He took a step toward the bed but she stopped him. The urgent need to have him inside her, right then, consumed her. "Now. Please. I want you inside me now." She sank down to the floor, pulling him with her so frantically that he stumbled a bit before righting himself and bracing his arms on either side of her. A soft mist of rain blew over them through the open doors as her desperate hands shoved his pants down below his buttocks then yanked her nightgown up around her waist. Flexing her hips against him, she clasped her palms on his lower back, tugging him to her. The burning throb between her legs intensified as he easily glided into her moist flesh.

It was almost more than she could bear. She felt as if they were both inside her. Gray. Tokala. Both of them, together, making love to her. The smell, the touch, the taste of them blended and circulated through her senses until their differences blurred into obscurity. She cried out his name, feeling him stiffen and hesitate a moment before pulling back and sinking into her once more.

His hand slid up to caress her breast, lightly pinching the erect tip as he began a slow, rhythmic thrusting. When she tried to increase the pace, he held her hips. "Easy, *Niki'ti*. I'll bring you there. Just let it happen."

Her nails lightly raked across his shoulders and he shuddered against her. "Please," she begged him, her breath coming in gasps. "I can't . . . stand it. I can't . . ."

"You can," his husky voice told her. "Because I won't stop." He drove into her again, filling her to the hilt. "Not until you come for me."

Her back arched off the floor as she climaxed, seized by rapture so great that her breath caught in her throat and her lips parted in a silent cry. His hands left her hips to cup her buttocks, tilting them and plunging deeper into her heat as he groaned with his own release. The spasms of pleasure seemed to go on forever and yet not long enough.

"Olathe taima na'hele," he whispered, nibbling at her ear. She didn't have the strength left to ask him what it meant.

Her hands slid down from around his back to spread along the rigid muscles of his chest, her lips burrowing into the hard chords of his neck. A sense of well being settled over her as she lay in his arms, her heartbeat returning to normal. It was right to be here with him. Because—

Because she loved him.

She *loved* him.

Her breath caught in her throat as she realized it was true. She had been tossed irrevocably, inconceivably in love with a man she hardly knew. And why? Because he saw her mousy brown hair as shining silk? Because he could bring her to orgasm? A banners flying, rockets shooting, I-could-die-right-now-because-I've-experienced-an-epiphany, kind of climax. With Gray it wasn't just a pleasurable melding of bodies. It was something more, something she couldn't even put into words if someone were to ask her. As if her love for him had always been there, dormant inside her and waiting to be released the moment he entered her life. That's what was so frightening. She'd never felt this way about anyone, even Wilson, who, when she thought about it, had really only wounded her pride. Gray held the power to wound her down to the very depths of her soul. He pulled back, his dark gaze searching her face. "How long have you known?"

"Known . . . known what?" she asked haltingly, wondering how he could have read her newly discovered feelings so quickly.

"That I'm Tokala."

Chapter Eleven

She lay passive when he picked her up from the floor, then carried her to the bed, as her brain struggled to process what he had said. He leaned down to kiss her and she stopped him, pressing her hand against his chest before sitting up. "What did you say?"

He kneeled next to the bed and took her hand, bringing the palm to his lips for a moment before answering. "You called out Tokala's name."

Her eyes widened in dismay. "Oh God, I'm sorry. I was having this dream earlier . . . ," she trailed off, the heat of embarrassment flooding her face. She didn't want him to know what she'd been dreaming. Or that she'd been fantasizing that both he and the dream man—who didn't exist—were making love to her.

"There's no need to apologize, *Niki'ti*." He helped her pull the soaked nightgown over her head, then tossed it to the floor. "The name doesn't matter. Then or now. It's still me."

Joanna felt light-headed and a buzzing noise started in her ears. "But it's just a dream."

"No." His solemn gaze met hers. "We've been together before. Your dreams of Tokala are memories of that time."

"Together before? What do you mean?" She gave a nervous laugh, tugging her hand from his. "Reincarnation?"

He smiled at her. "Is the concept so hard to accept?"

"I've never really thought about it, but yes, I think I find it hard to accept."

"Then explain the dreams I've had of you since I was a child. The same dreams I know you've been having. The first night we made love you woke from a nightmare and spoke to me in my native tongue. Do you remember?"

She sat up, pulling the sheet up to cover her breasts. "I thought it was part of the dream."

"You said, *'Nukpna helki.'*"

"What does it mean?"

He ran a hand through his damp hair, pushing it back away from his face before answering, "Loosely translated it means, 'Please forgive me.'"

"How could I say something in a language I've never spoken, let alone heard, before I met you?"

"Exactly. How could you?"

"No." She shook her head. "I just can't believe it."

"Then believe this. The minute I saw you at the Fremont Auction I knew you were the woman of my dreams."

"The Fremont Auction?" She looked at him in confusion. "That was six months ago. I didn't see you there; I would have remembered."

"I didn't let you see me." He sighed deeply before continuing, "I wasn't sure how you would react. I bought everything you looked at. The tea table, the couch . . . everything I knew would please you. Then I followed you home. Having found you, I wasn't going to let you walk out of my life, so I offered the Langly's twice what the house was worth. I would have paid any price to be near you. Why do you think they moved so quickly?"

The furniture in the parlor. That's why Mrs. Ohako had asked her how she liked her room. Oh God. This was all so bizarre. She closed her eyes. "I wasn't going to go to that auction. I didn't even have any money to spend."

"Yet you felt compelled to go anyway, didn't you? I know because it was the same with me. I saw the advertisement. Someone had left a flyer on my Jeep and I couldn't throw it away. I felt as if someone had handed me a map to my destiny, so I followed it. And I found you."

She opened her eyes to look at him. Was he telling the truth or was he just some kind of deranged stalker? The man she loved could be as crazy as a loon. She felt tears form in her eyes. "Why?"

"Because I love you. And I made a promise to you."

"What promise could you have made? You didn't even know me. We never met until a week ago." The tears began to trail down her face and he watched them, a look of self-derision on his face.

"Please don't cry, *Naki'ti*. I'm sorry. You weren't ready yet. I just thought . . ."

He reached out his hand and she jerked away. The hurt on his face sent a shaft of pain through Joanna. "You're afraid of me now."

"I don't know." She wiped the tears from her face. "I just . . . I'm so confused. I don't understand any of this. I'm tired and I can't think."

"Go to sleep, then." His troubled gaze rested on her. "We'll talk in the morning."

He stood from his kneeling position to leave.

"Wait." She stopped him. Suddenly it seemed more frightening to her that he leave rather than stay. "I don't understand all of this, but . . ." Crazy or not, she was completely in love with him. She knew he would never hurt her, it was the only thing she knew with any certainty. He said he loved her and she believed him.

Gray stared at her, waiting for her to finish.

"I don't want you to leave." She wiped her eyes again and looked up at him. "Please don't go."

He reached out to take her hand and this time she let him. "Are you sure?"

"Yes." Maybe she was crazy, too. But if he left her she felt as if her life would be over.

He unzipped his pants and pulled them off, but left his briefs on, as he crawled into bed with her. He'd called her "the woman of his dreams" she thought, snuggling up to him as he put his arms around her. She'd worry about it all tomorrow, tonight she was just going to bask in the warmth of his love. She fell asleep.

Kai knelt next to the bearskin pallet where her husband lay. She wanted to cover her ears, to try and drown out the drumbeats and chanting of his mourning family. He could not die! There was no life for her without him.

His skin was pale, his eyes closed, and his breathing slow and shallow. She had tended the wound to his chest with acorn meal after the other braves had carried him home, while the village medicine man looked on, only shaking his head. Now the Kyaklo built a fire in their hearth and prepared his powders for the death rite.

She spun to glare at him, anguish and fear swelling inside her. If she allowed him to perform the death rite, the Great Spirit would surely take her husband from her.

"No!" she cried. The chanting ceased. Kai pulled her knife from

*its sheath and gripped it tightly in her hand. "Leave my home!"
Tokala's family looked at her with confusion, the Kyaklo, with anger,
for no one had ever dared to dismiss him.*

*"Grief has unbalanced her," Tokala's brother whispered to his
plump wife. Kai leapt up, swinging the knife in a threatening arc. The
group slowly filed out of the lodge until only she and Tokala remained.*

*There would be no death rite, she would make sure of it. She
quickly sank to her knees, small sobs escaping her as she frantically
dug into the hard ground with the knife and her fingers. The fire hissed
and smoked as she tossed handfuls of dirt on it, dousing the flame.*

"Kai."

*She stopped her manic digging and twisted to see Tokala's gaze on
her, his eyes dark with pain. She scampered to his side, taking his hand
in hers and bringing it to her cheek. "My husband."*

"You cannot change . . . what is to be. I am dying."

*"No!" She shook her head, denying her worst fear. "I can make
you well. I will pray to the Great Spirit—"*

*"Kai, hear me." She went silent, closing her eyes and burying her
lips into the palm of his hand. He sighed, wiping a finger over the trail
of tears on her cheek. "I have seen this day. I knew our time together
would be short."*

"Please, no," she begged him. "If you leave me, I will die, too."

*His hand moved to her stomach, his fingers spreading across the
small mound growing there. "Your time has not come yet. You will
raise our son and make certain he is a strong warrior. Promise me this,
Kai."*

*She shook her head. "I cannot." Anguish pierced her heart at the
knowledge that her husband would not live to see his child. Would
never hold him or play with him or teach him the ways of their people.*

*"You will raise him well," he said softly. "Long ago, in a vision, I
saw this day. I also saw something . . . ," He began to cough and she
cradled his head, wiping the bloody spittle from his mouth with softened deer hide.*

"Don't speak, it will only weaken you more."

*He gripped her hand tightly. "We will be together again. When
you see me . . . you'll dream of our life together and I will find you. I
will . . ." His eyes closed and the hand that held hers in a tight clasp,
went slack.*

*"Nooo . . ." The mournful wail rose from the depths of her soul.
She clutched him tightly to her, rocking back and forth as the world
spun in a cold, dark whirl around her . . .*

"Nooo . . ."

"Joanna. Wake up."

"It hurts so much." She kept her eyes closed, not even attempting to fight the overwhelming pain that held her in its grip. Dead. Her husband was dead. He would never hold her again or make love to her. "Oh God, please. I don't want to live."

"Stop it." Rough hands grasped her shoulders and shook her. "Joanna, you have to wake up."

Her eyes opened and she stared at the man she loved through a haze of tears. "You left me!" she accused him, weakly beating her clenched fists against his chest. "Why? Why did you leave me? You promised."

"I'm here." His palm stroked the side of her wet cheek and she burrowed against it, seeking solace in his warm touch. "I'm not going to leave you." His voice was hoarse with emotion as he pulled her against him, enclosing her in a protective embrace. "Do you understand? Never. You don't have to be afraid."

She looked up at him, the tears trailing down her face. "I saw you die."

"Feel this." He brought her hand to the pulse throbbing in his neck, letting her feel the steady beat of his heart beneath her fingers. "You see? I'm alive."

"Yes." She threw her arms around him, clutching him tightly. He was very much alive, his lips branding her with a heated kiss on her forehead.

"You told me we'd be together again. I remember it. I can't understand—is this crazy, Gray?" Pulling back, she stared into his dark eyes. "I don't know how, but I remember it all. Living in the village and growing up, loving you even as a child. I pursued you shamelessly. You thought I was too young."

"Do you remember the first time we made love?" He smiled. "You followed me to the hidden pool and watched me swim."

She grinned sheepishly back at him. "Yes. Your naked body was so strong and big. And I wanted you so badly. I seduced you."

"Not a difficult feat since I wanted you just as badly." He slid a warm hand up the curve of her hip and around to cup her breast. "Just as I want you now."

A moan rose from her throat as he leaned down to kiss her breasts. Nothing seemed to matter anymore, but that he was alive and making love to her. She could still feel the grief she had felt as the young maiden, Kai. It made her cling to Gray and gave a desperate edge to their lovemaking.

She held his head taut to her breasts, her fingers clasped tightly in his hair. "You'll never leave me again. You won't."

"No."

She pushed him back against the bed, her hands holding down his chest. "I need to feel you. Please . . . I have to touch you, every inch of you." Just to know that he was alive. He seemed to realize the desperation in her voice and easily complied. He lay still as she ran her anxious hands up and down his torso, feeling the heated skin, resting for long moments against his pulsing heart before moving down to cover his hardness.

He pushed himself against her hand, the sound of his breathing becoming labored as she stroked the throbbing shaft and cupped the tight sacs underneath with her palm.

"Joanna . . ." he groaned, as she leaned down and took him in her mouth. He tasted so good. She pulled back and lapped up the male juice that pearled at the tip with her tongue. Watching him closely, she spread the drop of his essence around the rim of her mouth. His eyes darkened and more juice seeped under her stroking hand from the tip. She felt her own orgasm grow close, just by watching his reaction to her ministrations. She wanted him to come in her mouth, to spurt his heat into her and make him feel as out of control as he made her feel. But more than that, she needed to feel him hard and alive inside of her.

"Joanna . . . Joanna," his voice rasped, his hips undulating under her hands. "I can't take much more. You have to stop."

She quickly pulled her hands away. His eyes closed and his chest heaved as he struggled to control himself. Sliding her leg over his hips, she straddled him, easily sliding his rigid length inside of her to the hilt. She immediately came, crying out his name as he gripped her buttocks and bucked underneath her. He thrust into her again and again until she came once more, this time feeling the pulse of his seed as it spurted into her. "Oh God, I can feel you inside me . . ." Her back arched as the orgasm continued and she rode him until he was done.

He pulled her down next to him, kissing her lips and wrapping his arms tightly around her sated body. She put her hand in between them and ran a finger along the scar there. "I remember stabbing you by mistake. Is this the scar?"

"I don't remember how I got that scar, it just seemed to be there one day." He shrugged his shoulders. "I know it doesn't make sense."

"None of this does." Moving her hand up, she ran a finger along his square jaw. "It doesn't matter to me anymore."

He kissed the tip of her finger. "I'm glad."

Snuggling up to him, she draped her arm across his chest. "I had your son." She smiled softly at the memory. "He was like his father. Handsome, stubborn, strong." Her smile faltered. "But I also remember how lonely I was without you." She buried her head into the crook of his arm. "I missed you *so much*, every single day of my life."

"I'm sorry, *Naki'ti*." He raised his palm and tilted her head back, then lowered his mouth to gently kiss her lips. "If I could have stayed, I would have. It was just meant to be."

"Gray," she pulled back, tears gathering in her eyes again. "I love you. I couldn't bear losing you again. I couldn't."

"You won't lose me. I promise."

"How can you be so sure?"

"I've seen our future in a vision, just as I saw it as Tokala. But this time I see a long life with us together. And many children."

Joanna's eyes widened. "How many?"

Gray laughed. "Enough to keep both of us very busy, *Niki'ti*. I think we should start making them right now."

"Isn't that what we were doing a few minutes ago?"

"Yes." He pulled her underneath him. "We did it so well I think it bears repeating."

She laughed and wrapped her legs around him, her arms around his neck.

"You're the woman of my dreams." He cupped her cheek, his expression fierce, yet tender. "I've loved you forever. In the past and now." Sliding into her, he joined them in body as well as soul. "And into eternity."

About the author:

Jade Lawless spent most of her spare time during high school and college, writing poetry and reading romance. She lives in upstate New York with her husband, son, dog and cat. When she is not sitting at her computer writing, she works as a bookkeeper, hangs out with her grown daughter, or reads her favorite paranormal romances. She plans to someday live in a small cottage near the ocean in the home of her heart, Maine, where she will continue to dazzle readers with wickedly sexy, and outrageous heroes.

Surrender

by Kathryn Anne Dubois

To my reader:
In this complex, faced paced world, what a delight it is to escape into delicious fantasy. No less delicious is the writing of it. I hope you adore Nicholas as much as I do. And I hope you'd like to be Johanna . . . for just one night, by embracing the story. As a debut writer with Red Sage, I would love to hear from you!

Chapter One

Johanna brought Olympia to an abrupt halt and dismounted, tying her to a large oak. The heat of the sun, coupled with her strenuous ride, made the brook a tempting invitation. Like a mantra, the gentle trickle of water over smooth stone beckoned her. She stripped off her day dress and unlaced her corset, dropping them and her stockings onto the grassy bank, leaving only her thin underslip in place. The dewy blades tickled her soles, and her chemise pressed to her bosom in the moist, hot air of dawn. As she lowered herself into the cool water, she felt her nipples tighten against the cold.

She took delight twirling in the icy ripples, enjoying her freedom, yet careful not to wet her hair and alert her mother to her antics. Her mother had been particularly piqued with her unladylike behavior of late. Any further transgressions and Johanna would suffer her due.

This was her last thought as she sprawled out on the spongy bed of moss to dry, her beloved Olympia keeping watch as her mistress drifted off into sleep.

The sound of unfamiliar voices woke her much later, the sun that of mid-morning. She blinked up into the faces of three men on horseback, one with the tip of his saber hooked into the hem of her shift. All three were smiling.

"By all heavenly delight, are we dreaming?" one asked, his deep voice rumbling with laughter as they peered down at the soft tuft of black hair nestled between her thighs.

She gasped and scooted back from the sword. When their horses surrounded her, she jumped up. The strap of her slip fell and revealed the coral tip of her breast.

"Lovely," one man murmured, his expression dangerously close to a leer.

"You, sir, move back," she reprimanded with a haughty glare while another rider advanced and teased her hem up over her bottom.

"Splendor of God," the blond man said with a chuckle as she slapped at her hem. It was then she noticed the ornate crest on their saddles. All three men were dressed in the finery of the court. She was appalled. Only the younger one seemed discomforted by the taunting.

Johanna riffled with anger as they continued to rake their eyes over her. When a sound came through the clearing of trees, all three men turned to the approaching stallion and the tall rider atop it. Johanna scurried to retrieve her clothes. Clutching them before her, she watched as the trio of riders stepped their horses aside so he could pass, and then he drew up before her.

"Look what we found, Nicholas," one tormenter told him.

"Can we keep her?" another jested.

The silent stranger pressed closer, and they grew quiet as he gazed down at her. He was too male to be truly handsome. His dark eyes were threatening and his thick brows were knit together in a scowl. He boldly studied her, sweeping a glance over her scantily clad figure. His stallion whinnied, and he gave an impatient jerk on the rein.

"Are you hurt?" The deep timbre of his voice was quiet and curiously gentle coming from such a powerful body, and in sharp contrast to his expression of agitation.

She hesitated for the briefest of seconds as she weighed her response. The man's gaze, darkly fierce, scorched her as it settled on her throat. Instinctively she fanned her palm over her breast, but then dropped her hand to her side and returned his gaze with a bold stare of her own.

With her long tresses atumble, she eyed him defiantly. "These . . . brutes have offended my honor and I am shocked to find these are men of our King's Court." She flashed them a murderous look before turning her attention back to the dark man.

The others raised a cry of protest. "We didn't touch her—"

The leader lifted a hand, his gaze still fixed on her, and the three ruffians fell silent. He looked to her gelding and back at her. "Young lady, you are fortunate these men are honorable. Highway thieves would not have hesitated to take their pleasure with you. Dress and my knights will escort you back to the village."

She didn't like the arrogant set of his jaw. With a subtle motion, he directed his men to turn their backs, but before he could lead his own horse around, she squared her shoulders and tipped up her chin, no longer too concerned that she stood before him in just a sheer under-dress with her nipples poking against the soft linen.

"You, sir, are on *my* land and I order you to leave."

The trace of amusement in his eyes fled and his mouth straightened. "What is your name?" He raised his voice for the first time, his eyes flaring with intensity.

For a fleeting moment she was almost afraid, so powerful was his demeanor. But she would not let him see her falter. She straightened and lifted her slim nose. "I am Lady Johanna and you—"

He jerked at his bridle. "Damnation!"

In one fluid motion he whipped off his cloak and swooped down, his muscled arms catching her up easily before he settled her deftly onto his lap.

"What are you doing?" she screeched, alarmed by the swiftness with which he snatched her up. She grabbed at his thick forearm locked around her waist. "Let go of me," she hissed, sinking her nails into his skin.

"Blasted!" He clamped one large hand around both her wrists. He ordered his men to take her horse and ride ahead and then, with an irritated burst of energy, he urged his horse into a gallop. She twisted and jabbed her shoulder against the hard wall of his chest, but still he raced on, muttering something unintelligible and then ignoring her, his riding flawlessly smooth. The massive feel of him surrounding her was disquieting, and his scent disturbingly masculine. She had never been this close to a man. She was too curious now to be frightened, but still he unsettled her.

"Where are you taking me?" His only response was to crush her harder against his alarmingly solid body. "I demand an answer!" Her elbows connected ineffectually with his muscled width. Without warning, he released her wrists. Suddenly, she found herself with no anchor, dangerously bouncing along at a rapid speed. She screamed and leaned back into him, burrowing into his chest and clutching the thick strength of his arms. His deep chuckle vibrated in her ear as he wrapped his arm around her torso and pinned her arms to her side. With sinking dread she saw he was heading toward the manor house and her mother. Lady Carlton would never forgive *this*.

She watched with increasing distress as his men mounted the stone steps and spoke to their steward. Her mother and stepfather appeared within the moment, and one look at her mother's wide eyes and her stepfather's blustering exclamations, and Johanna knew she was in trouble. Well, she thought with mild trepidation, this won't be the first time.

Her mother hurried gracefully down the steps, trailing her long skirts behind her and curtsied low, as the dark brute handling her reined in his horse and stopped abruptly.

"My Lady." He nodded curtly.

"Your Grace," her mother responded in a breathless tone and then straightened. Johanna smiled to herself at her mother's stricken expression. Then she realized her mother had referred to him as a Duke.

She sighed in dismay. They would confine her to her chambers for weeks.

The Duke dismounted and hauled Johanna into his arms. She pounded at him with her fists. "Release me!" Her pointed boot connected with his shin.

"By all the saints!" he ground out viciously as he swept her into his arms and took the stairs two at a time, sailing arrogantly past her stepfather without acknowledging the man as he waited on the landing. He marched past a string of servants who were all in a titter and headed straight to the drawing room with an ease that told her he had been to Havenford before. Her mother trailed behind, issuing orders to the staff.

With a commanding thrust, he pushed against the heavy mahogany door and swung her into the room. "Put . . . me . . . down!" she demanded in a tone that challenged his disgraceful manhandling.

He stopped and peered into her face, his eyes black and fiery. She noticed for the first time the shadow that traveled along his neck and disappeared into the thick mat of dark hair under his neckline. His skin looked rough and his chin held a deep cleft. He was too close. "Unhand me!"

He dropped her on her bottom. She yelped when she landed in a heap atop his cloak. When her mother sucked in her breath, Johanna looked down to see the straps of her chemise falling down her arms and the filmy lace trim of the neckline hanging off the tips of her nipples. Her stepfather sputtered something nonsensical and spun away, slamming the drawing room door against the crowd of gathering servants.

"Johanna!" her mother wailed. "What have you done?"

The cool stranger stared down at Johanna, his eyes glittering with tension and perhaps a touch of satisfaction as her mother dropped to her knees to gather the cloak around her. Poor mother. Lady Carlton's blue eyes, so like her own, were bright with fear as she looked from Johanna to the dark Duke. "The servants have been searching the countryside for you. Are you hurt?"

The Duke gave a snort, his lips curling at the corners. The black orbs of his eyes were like polished stone.

Johanna leaped to her feet, still wrapped in his cloak, and scoffed. "I was riding, Mother." She shot the Duke a defiant glare. "And I stopped to cool off."

The Duke's brow lifted, and he scrutinized her with a scowl. She could smell him on the cloak. A purely male scent of musk and leather and . . . something else. When she met his gaze, an imperceptible gleam sparked in his eyes.

Her stepfather advanced, his own composure sorely tested. "Would you care for a brandy, your Grace?" he interjected, no doubt trying to distract the two women from yet another altercation.

Much to her relief, the Duke dragged his gaze from Johanna and nodded to her stepfather. The intensity of the man unnerved her and she drew a steadying breath before she also replied. "Thank you, Sir Carlton, I'd like a brandy, too."

"Johanna!" her mother gasped, clutching her by the shoulders and shuffling her to a nearby chair. "Sit down, for heaven's sake." She tucked the cloak under her chin.

"Indeed, Mother. I desire my chambers so I may change," Johanna replied blithely, attempting to rise despite her mother's frantic pushing on her shoulders. The Duke had settled into the chair opposite her and Sir Carlton handed him his brandy. When Johanna grabbed at her mother's hands, she heard a deep growl come from the Duke's throat.

"You will sit there," he ordered, his eyes boring into hers. He leaned forward menacingly, the masculine power of him releasing an energy that startled her.

She tipped her chin and raised a brow. "I think not, your Grace."

His eyes flickered with astonishment and then flashed with fury. His shoulders bunched with raw tension. *Well, so be it*! Johanna was appalled that he thought he could order her about. She smoothed her skirt and with a practiced air of dignity started to rise when he spoke again.

His eyes glimmered and his voice was softly dangerous. "You defy me, young lady, and I will lift your skirt, take you over my knee, and spank your bare bottom."

She blanched inwardly at the image, but then her eyes dropped involuntarily to his large hands resting on his thighs. He flexed them subtly and the thought of that raw strength on her tender bottom sent blood coursing through her veins. But she gave no sign of alarm. His eyes were like burning coals, challenging her. A silky lock of raven hair fell over his forehead. He looked the devil incarnate. She decided not to test him.

Her mother was holding her breath. Good God, the woman was afraid of this beast. The thought gave Johanna unquestionable pleasure.

"Very well," Johanna replied with a stiff toss of her head. "I will stay for my mother's sake. She looks fairly ready to swoon. But make no mistake, I am not the least afraid of you." She met his gaze levelly. He was an intriguing specimen of male strength although his confidence was infuriating, but it confirmed her thought that it was best not to tangle with him for now.

A tick jumped in his jaw and repressed power flickered from every pore. But then that bedeviled gleam surfaced, and the faint twitch of his lips told her he arrogantly assumed he had won. Johanna resolutely held his stare.

"Bloody hell," the devil himself muttered. He jerked his head toward her mother. Victoria Carlton had finally released an audible breath and her stepfather sank into the nearest chair.

The Duke's tone was calm, but his eyes flashed a fiery challenge. "This . . . this little Madame has had far too much freedom."

Her mother attempted a protest, but the blackguard cut her off. Johanna fumed at being referred to as a child. She would be eighteen next week. Who was this tyrant?

"Is she still a maid?" He looked to Lady Carlton.

She sputtered a response. "Of course, your Grace. My daughter is untouch—"

Johanna cast her mother a horrified glance as the reason for this visit became all too apparent. She gathered her wits and rallied quickly, this time succeeding in escaping the chair. "Nay, Mother." She dropped the cloak and stood before him, her chemise dipping dangerously low to reveal the full cleft of her bosom. She knew her nipples were clearly visible through the transparent slip as was the dark hair shielding her womanhood.

Her mother's mouth dropped and her stepfather made clucking noises and fled the room.

Johanna moved closer to the black demon. Sitting as he was, his eyes were level with hers. She expected outrage, but his cool gaze swept over her, his eyes faintly lit with interest.

Undaunted, she fingered the dark waves of her long hair. "The truth, your Grace, is that I am ungovernable and my mother would admit nothing so she can wash her hands of me." Although it was difficult, she held his steady gaze.

Her mother came out of her stupor in time to interfere. "Your Grace," she started, her panic evidently rising to zenith heights, but he stopped her with a harsh command.

"Leave us," he breathed, never taking his eyes off Johanna. He moved closer so that their breaths mingled. The light scent of mint reached her, and she found her gaze dropping to his lips. They were too lustful to be decent. Johanna heard the door close behind him. Had her mother lost her senses . . . leaving her alone with this man who was old enough to be her father and with her scarcely dressed? Sudden fright lodged in her throat.

He settled back, ankle atop his knee with his elbows propped on the chair's arms and his fingers laced across his lap. His voice was low and controlled as his eyes drifted down the length of her. "Boys have had you?" he asked her, his tone matter-of-fact, confusing her.

Although he appeared to withhold judgment, she didn't like that he implied she was a child. Yet, she needed him to reject her. She'd worry about the consequences later.

"Yes." She stiffened under his blatant stare. She hated his relaxed attitude while she stood before him tense with uncertainty . . . and practically naked.

He steepled his fingers, touching them to his lips. "It matters not," he said simply, his gaze settling on the tips of her breasts. She shifted uncomfortably and then stopped for fear her breasts would simply slip out with the subtle movement. She flushed to the tips of her toes before she realized his meaning. He didn't care that she was not a virgin?

Incredulously, she lifted her eyes to his. Surely he couldn't mean it. His gaze was melting and a warmth flooded her limbs, disturbing her. His male scent stirred her senses.

"I . . ." she faltered. "I've done . . . wicked things—unspeakable things." She willed herself not to cross her arms across her breasts in an attempt to cover herself. She would not retreat.

"I see." His voice held the hint of smile. "Tell me," he softly demanded.

"Tell you?" She searched his expression, unsure of his meaning.

"Tell me the details." A tiny sparkle lit the center of his irises. She wanted to murder him. How dare he use her quandary for his amusement while she struggled to keep her freedom? A man like him, most men, knew nothing of such terror. Marriage was simply a necessary inconvenience for them, its reward the attendant pleasures, while the women became no more than property at the disposal of their masters.

She tossed her hair, giving him a dismissive look, and attempted to whirl away from him. But he caught her waist roughly with both hands and held her, locking his strong fingers around her. She drew in a sharp breath, clutching at him as her eyes riveted on his face. Surely he wouldn't raise a hand to her for her insolence?

Her heart thundered as she watched him. His eyes grew soft as he studied her quietly. Her breath stopped as he drew out the moment.

And then his lips were on her, warm and lightly brushing hers, his eyes half-lidded and watching her, like a cat toying with its prey. Even in her inexperience, she recognized the arousal in the darkening of his eyes and the tension of his hands clutching her waist. Her pulse began to pound in her ears.

Before she could draw a breath, he pressed her between his muscular thighs. "What are you doing?" she whispered. Her head was spinning, the experience too foreign, and her thoughts sweeping irreverently to the hard strength of him that sent quivers racing down her spine. She pushed at him half-heartedly, thrilling unexpectedly at the feel of his muscles under the coarse linen of his shirt. His lips were soft, his scent so male and pleasing . . . she grew dizzy.

His lips tasted of brandy and mint, exciting her as he brushed lazily along her mouth. She felt herself melting. At his gentle urging, her chemise slipped down and her breasts spilled into his palms. She grabbed onto his wrists in a moment of fright before the warmth of his hands on her bare skin heated her deliciously. Distant protests surfaced and then disappeared with the feel of his lightly calloused thumbs tingling her nipples. She softened into him, clutching his wrists for support as her body swam in a titillating pool of sensation, threatening to drown her. Then he boldly licked her lips with his wet tongue, and her body ignited.

It was too much. She startled and pushed forcefully at him. He finally released her.

She stumbled back. "You, sir," she sputtered, "are no gentleman!" She yanked her slip up modestly while he relaxed back, studying her quietly, allowing his eyes to travel insolently over her body. How could such an ill-bred brute cause her to behave so wantonly?

She glared at him. "You betray my mother's trust and are no longer welcome in this house!"

He graced her with a bemused expression. "Surely what I did is not as 'unspeakable' as what you have done?" He arched a brow.

She raised her hand to smack the confident grin off his face, and a flash of excitement glinted in his eyes before he caught her wrists and pulled her toward him. He held her tight against him, his massive body vibrating with tension. Her imagination scrambled to think what he would do next when he captured her mouth in a kiss so carnal she thought he would devour her in one large gulp. She managed a strangled cry. He growled against her lips and then released her as quickly as he had grabbed her up.

He muttered incoherently and walked with swift purpose to the door and yanked it open. With just an inclination of his head, the servants came running and her mother appeared in seconds. Lady Carlton frantically scooped his cloak off the floor. Johanna was still too stunned to protest when her mother covered her and dragged her to the davenport to sit beside her. How could one man storm into her life and within minutes throw the household into turmoil? She would not have it!

"Lady Carlton," the Duke spoke evenly, pulling a bit at the cuffs of his shirt. "I have been misled. Your daughter is willful and unprepared to serve a husband."

"Your Grace—"

"He's right, Mother—"

"Hush up, Johanna! For once in your life be quiet."

"I will not sit here while—"

The Duke stepped forward. "My Lady," he interrupted, his tone brooking no argument, "your daughter should please her husband, not exhaust him," he drawled. "For that reason I am leaving—"

"But—" Her mother jumped up, no doubt attempting to dissuade him, but Johanna heaved a sigh of relief. Even Johanna knew this was not a man susceptible to persuasion, but still her mother persisted. "You promised my late husband—"

He held up a silencing hand. "That I did," he responded blandly. "When I return within the week I expect Lady Johanna to be properly subdued and awaiting the pleasure of her betrothed."

Johanna's mouth dropped and her eyes flittered between the two . . . lunatics. Even though her mother looked as stunned as she, Lady Carlton managed to respond first. "Oh, of course . . . subdued you say?"

Johanna watched in stupefaction as the Duke took her mother's hand and bowed graciously. "Lady Carlton, you will handle your daughter." He gazed back at Johanna, his eyes challenging. Her mother curtsied before slipping out of the room.

Fury, like she had never experienced, rose in Johanna at her mother's cowardice and this beast's arrogance, but she would not allow him to strip her further of her dignity with his childlike treatment of her. He thought she was difficult *now?*

Johanna stood proudly before him, hardly mindful that he towered over her. His eyes blazed as he looked down at her, but she returned a hard gaze of her own. He bent closer and leaned in, nose to nose now, and waited.

She took a silent breath. "Don't think you will have me now or ever," she bit out. "Neither you nor my mother hold lord over me." She lifted her chin a notch, never breaking her gaze. His head tilted almost imperceptibly and his nostrils flared. Without warning, he slipped his hand under her cloak and pinched her nipple. The jolt of sensation brought a startled cry to her lips. She snatched indignantly at his hand.

He released a throaty chuckle before he turned on his heels and sailed out the door, leaving his rich dark laughter to taunt her.

Chapter Two

Havenford was a flurry of activity as Earl and Lady Carlton prepared for the visit the following week of the Duke of Chandlemare, Nicholas Kentridge. The Duke would arrive with a party of five knights and three squires and the stables were made ready and grooms on stand-by to attend the horses.

Victoria Carlton rushed through an order of fine gowns, determined that her daughter would snare the Duke. Johanna whirled on her mother as she suffered through yet another torturous fitting.

"Mother, I will rip this gown off me if you don't stop fussing." Johanna yanked the bodice up over her breasts just to have her mother yank it down again. Her breasts spilled dangerously over the gilded edge of the ivory satin. One movement and her nipples would peak out. "This gown is indecent and I won't wear it."

"You professed yourself a fallen woman. What does it matter?" Lady Victoria snorted.

"I'll run away!"

"You've already tried that," her mother shot back, "and if you try again, I'll have you locked in your bedchambers until Nicholas returns."

"How can you do this?" Johanna wailed.

"Stop it, you silly child. Nicholas Kentridge is a powerful man. He will not put up with your spoiled tantrums. And if you run him off, there will be hell to pay."

"Why are you set on my marrying him?" Johanna raced across the room and flung herself onto the bed, burying her face in the soft down pillows.

Her mother's delicate hand patted her back. Her soft touch soothed Johanna and softened her anger.

"Oh, Johanna," she murmured softly. "Have you not eyes? The man is the epitome of male grace and virility. Common knowledge holds that he keeps many mistresses." Her mother ran her fingers through the thick tumble of Johanna's hair. "You'll be fortunate if he turns his eye to you for more than producing his heirs. Yet, that aside, his name and his wealth will reward you and your children with protection and security all your life."

Johanna flopped onto her back in a whoosh of crinoline and satin, suddenly overcome with the enormity of marriage to the Duke. "But Mother," she pleaded with genuine sincerity, "have you watched him?" Johanna's eyes widened. "He's . . . wicked."

Lady Victoria sighed wistfully and smoothed the front of her daughter's frock. "Yes, my dear. In that way, he reminds me of your father."

※⁓ৡৢৣ৶ৠ⁓※

With the week of activity finally behind her, Johanna brushed her hair idly before the large etched mirror in no hurry to apply the new paint to her eyes and cheeks that her mother had so painstakingly laid out.

Charlotte pulled and tugged at Johanna's corset in exasperation. "We'll never be ready for the Duke, and your mother will have my head if we keep him waiting."

"Nonsense," Johanna scoffed. "I have no intention of being at his beck and call. If he wishes to see me, he can wait . . . perhaps even until tomorrow."

"By my Lord and all the saints, you can't mean it," the young attendant whimpered. "I don't think the Duke is a man to be toyed with." The corset was so tight now, Johanna could barely breathe and with each shallow inhalation, her breasts rose and fell against the silky top of her chemise. Charlotte pulled down the neckline so that her nipples were barely covered and then began catching up large sweeps of thick dark hair to pin atop Johanna's head, but Johanna slapped at her hands.

At that moment they heard the hooves scuffling outside the high turret window of her chamber, and she knew he had arrived at the lower courtyard. The scurry of footfalls below alerted her the servants had lined up to receive him and distant voices traveled up the long stairwell, signaling that he had entered with his entourage.

Johanna's skin was naturally white, so she told herself that her color had not drained a shade. She pinched her cheeks for assurance and gave a futile tug on her slip from under the restraints of her corset. She smiled an encouragement to herself in the mirror and then frowned. By the saints! He was only a man.

The swish of fabric and soft quick steps warned her that Lady Victoria was about to burst in. She braced herself. Her mother entered amidst a swirl of petticoats, beautiful pale skin glowing against her raven hair. Her thick-lashed blue eyes were bright with anticipation. People often told Johanna she was the image of her mother, but she didn't believe it. Victoria Carlton was very tiny, while Johanna was too tall and lanky. And although Johanna's breasts had finally developed, she was still waiting on the rest of her curves. Her stepfather, Sir Richard, told her if she would stop riding Olympia like a wild banshee, she'd be more rounded, but Johanna was not about to give up riding.

Victoria's beautiful smile faded. "Why aren't you dressed?" her mother gaped, hesitating for an alarmed moment before she flung open the armoire and began riffling through it.

Johanna graced her with an expression of implacable boredom.

For once her mother did not become hysterical but simply fixed her with a knowing look. "Very well, Johanna. I'll simply tell His Grace you will be down shortly." Without another word, her mother exited gracefully, a gesture Johanna found mildly disturbing.

While Charlotte twittered around for some time cajoling Johanna to hurry, the housemaid, Mona, appeared with the announcement that His Grace was awaiting her and trusted she was now ready to receive him.

"Please tell him, Mona, that I am not."

"When shall I tell him ye be ready, Milady?"

"Don't tell him anything," Johanna smiled mischievously.

Charlotte expelled a nervous sigh and began pacing. Johanna smiled with pleasure, imagining his fury while she sat before her dressing mirror, plucking idly at unruly tendrils. Within minutes they heard heavy footfalls gaining quickly on the stairs. Charlotte stopped her pacing and sucked in her breath.

"Bolt the door!" Johanna screeched.

Too late. Nicholas Kentridge wrenched open the door, his large frame filling the archway. His seething brows knit together in a dark scowl as he impaled her with his eyes.

Johanna froze.

To her relief, her mother appeared within seconds and slipped past him and into the room. But her relief was short-lived as she watched in horror as Lady Victoria grabbed Charlotte's hand and dragged her out.

"Mother," Johanna screamed. "Don't leave me here with him."

He kicked the door closed with the heavy heel of his boot, his eyes like black orbs, primitive, and flicking over her like flames banking to a rising inferno. She drew in her breath and for the first time in her life, her hands trembled.

His voice came out in a low growl. "I told you what I would do if you defied me." He slipped off one leather glove and then the other, his pace slow and deliberate as he approached. Her mind raced. What was it he had said? And then she blushed fully as the memory came flooding of his warning that he would smack her bare bottom. The air left her lungs in a moment of panic. He wouldn't dare!

But looking at him now, she wasn't sure.

She edged back, meeting his narrowed glittering gaze with an intensity of her own. This barbarian would be sorry if he touched her. She reached behind her back and curled her fingers around the handle of the heavy brush laying on her vanity. He lunged and she brought it down upon him with the full force of her weight, hitting him dead center in the chest with a sharp whack. The tortoise shell handle snapped in half like a small twig and then deflected off him, dropping to the floor between their feet. She looked at it, stunned, and then back at him. His eyes shone bright. There was nowhere to flee.

She would try to talk him out of this.

"Your Grace . . ." She dipped into a deferential curtsy.

He snorted and gave her a merciless leer. Then he swooped down of a sudden and hauled her up with one muscled arm and marched to the bed.

He dropped her unceremoniously over his knee. "I'm going to enjoy this!" he growled.

Before she could gather her wits, he clamped his one leg over her two, trapping her between his hard thighs. When he lifted her chemise to her waist and she felt the cool air hit her skin, she gasped on a strangled cry.

"Abominable beast!" she screamed and then sank her teeth into his forearm with a vengeance.

"Almighty God!" he roared, and followed it up with a shock of oaths for which her virgin ears had never heard, then he grabbed her wrists with one large hand and anchored them in front of her. She tried biting his thigh, but couldn't reach him. And then the sting of his hand landed once, full and flat across her bare bottom, and then several times. She couldn't allow this to happen, horrified more at the thought of what she must look like with her naked buttocks wriggling beneath his hot gaze than anger by any real pain she was suffering. Another slap, short and quick, sent her pushing and struggling against him.

"You are wicked, truly wicked!" she railed at him, feeling the heat emanating from her rounded flesh with the next slap. "A miserable bastard," she spat, kicking like the wild banshee her stepfather claimed her to be and caring not a whit that her language would shock him and invite another spanking.

He anchored her tighter as she struggled. "God's teeth," he muttered. His hand felt huge against her burning flesh, tender now from more stinging slaps. Tears of shame threatened traitorously on the brink.

This devil would get his comeuppance!

The next shock of spanks sent her gasping in surprise as the heat traveled over her skin in waves, centering in the soft cleft between her legs. She stopped struggling. Another spank and she moaned with the answering throb.

"God's teeth," he murmured, resting his hand against her burning skin and smoothing his palm over the gentle curves. In the heat of her struggle, it took her more than a moment to realize he had stopped spanking her. She felt his palm skimming over her plumpened mounds. His hand slid lower, the tips of his fingers stroking the sensitive flesh of her thighs and then up again over her hot heated globes.

She muffled a cry. She knew she should protest, but when he traced his fingers between the soft crease of her bottom, her delicate folds swelled and tingled. His manhood reared up to nudge her, hard and powerful, separated from her core by just a thin layer of fabric. A deep blush suffused her body and her blood turned to liquid heat.

"Nicholas," she breathed before she could stop herself, having had no intention of addressing him so intimately. When she felt his lips against her bare bottom, warm and caressing, and then his palm cup and squeeze the plump underswell of her flesh where buttock met thigh, she nearly expired.

"What are you doing?" she choked, ashamed by the throbbing he'd started. His tongue ran deliciously along the small of her back and down again over the two rounded orbs. His hands were everywhere, burning a path down her thighs and nudging them apart.

"Spread your legs," he murmured, his voice thick and vibrating against her heated skin.

"No, Nicholas," she said, but her body turned mutinous. She parted her thighs instinctively, and without her consent her buttocks thrust up shamelessly, seeking, reaching . . . for what, she didn't know.

"Ah, yes," he murmured.

She moaned when he brushed his fingertips between her legs and trailed them gently along her swollen folds, teasing her, and sending little shock waves through her sensitized lips. An embarrassing wetness followed and sinful thoughts flooded her. "Oh, noooo . . . Nicholas," she breathed. "Please."

"My pleasure, Johanna," he murmured, his voice husky with desire. "You're delectable." The sound of his voice, deep with arousal, caused her to arch into his hand wantonly. He eased one long finger up into the heat of her, and she whimpered at the pleasurable shock. Furious with herself that she no longer struggled against him, she nonetheless couldn't protest.

His breathing grew ragged. "Ah, Johanna . . ." He nipped her young flesh with his teeth and then thrust his finger deeper. Her answering moan and the wetness that coated his fingers as he slipped and slid along her ripened cleft seemed to incite him. She meant to stop him, but she didn't want to stop the fire raging between her thighs.

He groaned and thrust up against her belly with his rigid shaft. She could feel him through the rough cloth of his breeches, and she had a sudden urge to feel him. She shuddered at her wicked thoughts. What was he doing to her?

My God! She was right. He was the devil himself!

With a surge of indignation, she hauled herself up quickly, breaking his hold easily now that he had freed her wrists, and struggled to aright herself as she stood before him, panting breathlessly and making a dignified effort to smooth the skirt of her chemise and pull it down over her thighs. He watched her quietly, his eyes glazed and the tip of his manhood, red and swollen, peeking out above the waist of his breeches. She shouldn't look at him, but she was awestruck. He unlaced his breeches silently and lifted himself out. She was rendered breathless . . . the sheer size of him daunting. He pulsed lightly, the large knob at the top red and eager. She choked on the horrified thought that she wanted to touch him, but she didn't dare.

He chuckled softly and her eyes flew up to him. "You've never seen a man before, have you, Johanna?"

The rough timbre of his voice excited her further. But she couldn't tell if he was taunting her because his eyes were soft, confusing her. "Of course I have," she said, swallowing lightly, her eyes returning involuntarily to his unbelievable manhood.

"I see," he gentled and then offered her his hand. "Come here and lift your slip."

Disbelieving of his scandalous invitation, she backed up a pace. "What?" she stuttered, still unable to take her eyes off his engorged rod.

He stroked himself idly and a hot flash of desire settled between her legs. "Come here and I will pleasure you. Do all the wicked things you're so familiar with." She gulped down a swallow of air and looked back up at him, trying to ignore the warm sting of her bottom and the intimate ache he had ignited. His eyes twinkled. "I'm sure I know them all and then some," he toyed with her.

The warm huskiness of his voice almost seduced her, but she managed to return a haughty reprimand. "That's very amusing." She gave her hair a disdainful toss. "You are impossibly lewd and distasteful," she said, as she walked briskly to her chamber door. Turning primly, she lifted her chin and ordered him to leave.

He had the nerve to respond with soft laughter that so unnerved her it was difficult for her to divert her gaze from watching him relace his breeches. How did it ever fit back in? A delicious shudder captured her as she thought of his pulsing sword of power.

He sauntered over and stopped before her. "I trust you will be ready shortly?" His tone was soft and provocative as his eyes melted rudely over her body.

"We'll see." She stood ramrod straight.

"Ah." He lifted his chin, a trace of suppressed laughter edging his voice. Without warning he dragged her against him, slipping his hand under her chemise and cupping her bottom boldly. He claimed her mouth in a brutally tender kiss, his tongue pressing insistently to gain entrance. Her heart raced, but she clamped her lips shut and braced her hands between them.

He released her abruptly and she stumbled back. He was like a tidal wave braced to crash onto shore and consume her in its wake. She girded herself against his next attack, but he reached up tentatively and traced his fingers gently along the line of her jaw. "Don't be long," he whispered, cupping her chin and stroking along her cheek with the pad of his thumb.

She was too stunned to respond.

It was only after she closed the door behind him, insuring that it was fully bolted, that she expelled an audible breath.

Chapter Three

Nicholas Mooreland Kentridge IV had thought the betrothal would be easily settled when he first sent word he was coming to discuss his commitment to his late friend, the Baron de Chilton.

During their last battle in the King's army, Nicholas had assured Chilton that he would consider his friend's then baby daughter when she came of age. Nicholas had no desire to marry anymore now than he did then.

But Nicholas hadn't counted on the stirrings for heirs that now, at the age of thirty-six, pressed upon him. His thoughts had returned to his pledge. Having known the baby's parents he knew she would be a beautiful girl, cultured and trained for her future role as mistress of a large estate and no doubt instructed on the virtues of a devoted wife.

He had not expected Johanna.

She was a hellion . . . and she was exquisite.

As he waited in the drawing room, he grew bone hard at the thought of her tender bottom, warm and firm under his palm just minutes ago. He glanced toward the double doors, impatient for her arrival. Surely she wouldn't test him again.

A smile tempted him as he remembered the way his blood heated when he first set eyes on the graceful nymph tousled among the wild flowers of the meadow, eyes fiery beneath the sooty lashes, the pearl luster of her skin flushed with frustration over the antics of his knights. Her ripe young body caused his bullocks to pull up in arousal. The powerful response had surprised him. But then he was furious over discovering her personage and had to restrain himself from paddling her then, too. When he'd snatched her up, his anger had turned carnal as she slid and squirmed against him, causing his loins to ache dangerously in response. The temptation to lift her skirt and take her tortured him . . . her scent was intoxicating.

She would not be easy to tame and mold to his ways. Yet she would, for he intended to marry her. She was young and healthy—he'd have many heirs—and producing them would be pleasurable. He would bring her to heel in time.

He watched with pride when she finally joined them, her ivory satin gown glowing against her raven hair. Her delicately boned face with startling blue eyes and lustrous lashes bespoke of fragile femininity so deceptive in light of her boldness and obstinacy. Gold thread braided around her gently rounded hips. She was a study in feminine grace with the will of a tigress. He wondered what she'd be like to bed. Despite her claims of fallen virtue, his gentle examination proved her a virgin, maidenhood intact. He suppressed a chuckle over the way she had responded to his sex play . . . to the extent of showing an interest in his anatomy. He grinned smugly, thinking of her stricken look. Despite her shock, he would initiate her further tonight. By the time he took her, she would be warm, willing.

When his little hellion finally joined them, Earl Carlton rose to greet her and inquired solicitously after her rest while her mother shot her a look of reproof. The Earl had been assuring him that Johanna was simply spirited and would adjust to marriage in time—a bright girl, full of energy and enthusiasm for life. Nicholas had agreed with all but the adjusting theory but had held his tongue. The Earl was also quick to remind him that she came with a handsome dowry, but Nicholas had no need of money.

He noticed with irritation that both adults danced around the girl as though avoiding stepping on eggs. He would not do the same. And the sooner she realized it the better.

She was still in a snit, but to her credit, she extended her hand regally. He bent low to kiss it under the watchful eye of the Carltons. When he pressed his lips fully against her succulent translucent skin, he lingered, drinking in her scent, and wanting to taste her. He gave her an imperceptible bite along the vein. She startled slightly and jerked her hand away. When he met her gaze, she frowned at him, her expression one of guarded caution. She was perceptive indeed.

Between courses of roast game bird and buttered shrimp, Lady Carlton discussed the details of the wedding scheduled just two weeks hence. Nicholas chuckled to himself. She probably feared a delay would risk the loss of the betrothal . . . or was she afraid Johanna would bolt again? It mattered not. Nicholas had no intention of waiting longer than two weeks to consummate his union with Johanna.

He tipped the frosted decanter and filled her glass with more wine. He wanted her relaxed—if that were possible—and wondered if she felt the crackling sexual tension between them as he did. Her breasts swelled and gleamed like satin, their rosy buds disappearing just fractions of an inch inside her gown. He was finding it hard to concentrate on the endless details of the betrothal as visions of her high-tipped breasts loomed unbidden, stirring his loins. He chided himself for his utter lack of control with this girl.

The banns had been posted and preparations were underway, so her mother talked to him of Johanna's love of horses. Johanna remained conspicuously silent. He was pleased that she evidently realized the error of her ways.

After an endless discussion of his trading business and his polite devouring of the rich candied fruits, Nicholas begged off, expressing his wishes to get to know his future bride. At his suggestion of a walk in the gardens, her parents exchanged apprehensive glances, while the idea drew an annoyed frown from Johanna. He was anxious to discover what else he didn't know about this tempestuous vixen.

✣❧✤❀✥

"You have horses?" Johanna turned to Nicholas suddenly, stopping midstep along the stone path, the moonlight dancing through her shining hair, a thick silky curtain of midnight that he wanted to run his hands through. She eyed him keenly. He could tell that she would weigh his answer.

"I breed them, Johanna."

"Arabians?" she probed, her eyes widening ever so slightly.

He was unable to hide the small smile forming along his lips in response to her obvious attempt to hide her enthusiasm.

"If you like horses, Johanna, you could have your pick and supervise the grooms."

Her eyes lit up at the suggestion, and he felt inordinate pleasure at her response. And then she surprised him. She smiled . . . a small teasing smile that set a fire under him. "I'd ride like a banshee all over your lands."

His lips twitched. "Now why doesn't that surprise me?"

She gazed at him guardedly for a lingering moment, but then her eyes softened when she saw he was teasing her. *God, she was beautiful.*

"Come here," he commanded her gently, his eyes traveling over the slender column of her throat. She stiffened. But rather than the gesture annoying him, it reminded him how young she was. An untried girl with a man she considered a rogue. She knew nothing about a man's powerful desires.

She tipped her head. "Why?" she questioned, bravely struggling with her apprehension.

He leaned back against the low rock wall of the orchard and studied her, choosing his words carefully. "Soon you will be my wife, Johanna. I need to know you."

Her eyes blinked a bit, before she drew in a fresh breath, although this time she didn't claim to be a woman of the world. "How well?" she asked, her voice gaining strength as a beautiful light flush crept up her neck.

He folded his arms and lifted his brow in question.

"How well do you plan on getting to know me?" She folded her own arms under her breasts and set her chin in a sudden show of impatience. "A gentleman would keep his distance until our wedding night."

His response was a bark of laughter. "I see." He smiled at her wickedly, enjoying the full blush spreading suggestively across her cleavage. Her nipples hardened under the smooth satin and his bulge jumped to attention. *Lord, she was delightful.* "Now, Johanna. We both know I am no gentleman."

She dropped her arms and stepped back. Her eyes flashed before she stammered. "You are . . . the devil himself and I . . . I will scream if you set one hand on me."

His eyes lingered on her full mouth and over the shadow between her barely concealed breasts. He chuckled softly. "I don't think so, because you like me touching you as much as I like doing it."

Her hands flew to her hips, thrusting up those lovely twin peaks, begging him to tweak the pebbled tips. She scoffed. "That's nothing but your arrogant imaginings. I grow tired of you. I give you my leave, sir."

He laughed richly. "Oh, no, you won't."

She turned in haste, but he caught her waist and whirled her around, pressing her against the full length of him. He was already hard and aching, and he knew she could feel his sex as he trapped her against the low stone wall.

"Nicholas," she gasped.

His face was inches from hers. "I like it when you say my name, Johanna." He gave a small tug on her bodice and her breasts spilled out.

"Oh!" She sucked in a breath, her expression a mixture of panic and arousal. His hands swept over the firm velvety mounds and his thumbs teased the peaks. "I beg of you, Nicholas," she breathed, clutching at his wrists.

"But of course, Madame." He dipped and licked her nipples, pleased with the feel of her rosy buds raising and hardening under his gentle ministrations. He pinched her sensitive flesh lightly between his thumb and forefinger and smiled when she arched her hips, knowing she was feeling the answering tug in her loins. He liked that her nipples were so responsive.

"Nicholas," she murmured, squirming seductively beneath him. "You are truly—," she yelped as he nipped her with his teeth. Then she moaned with pleasure, ". . . wicked."

"Yes," he breathed between succulent nibbles. "But you like it."

She started to protest, but he lifted her onto the rock wall and held her from him, gazing at her nakedness.

"Ah, such a vision of loveliness, Johanna." He stroked along the soft swells, feeling their fullness and flicking his thumbs over her erect tips. She blushed profusely but didn't stop him and his cock lengthened another inch.

"Nicholas, surely you don't plan to have me on this rock wall," she gasped, and for the first time, he sensed real fear in her.

He cradled her chin in one hand and tipped her lovely face to his. "Nay, that pleasure will await our wedding night. But I'll prepare you so you don't swoon with fright when I take you as my wife."

She slapped his hand down and yanked up her bodice. "I have never swooned with fright in my life and I don't plan to, just because . . . ," she paused, and he could see her uncertainty, "because your monstrous weapon will . . ." For all her bravery, she blushed considerably, unable to continue.

He smiled as he moved closer, resting his hands along the wall on either side of her, trapping her.

"Now let me go," she ordered.

He wanted to slide his hand beneath those endless ruffles of petticoat and feel how wet he'd made her, but he cautioned himself to slow or she would surely run from him.

"I don't know if I will," he teased, leaning in closer and brushing his lips against hers.

Her only resistance was to push with delicate hands against his chest, and her mouth softened. She was waging a war within herself, he was sure. There was little doubt of the passion lurking just below her proud surface, and he ached to sample some. He bit her lip gently. "I want to eat you up, Johanna."

She startled and clutched at his shirt, but continued to offer him her full ripened lips. The gesture of trust awakened within him something tender that surprised him. With protective fingers he traced along her throat and could feel her pulse racing. Her hands relaxed and her palms rested on his chest. His muscles twitched under her teasing touch.

"Johanna . . ." He ran his tongue along her bottom lip. She parted her lips tentatively. He dipped in and stroked his tongue restlessly along hers.

With clever agility, he teased her hem up and slipped his hand under her skirt.

When he palmed the smooth skin of her thighs above her stockings, she cried against his lips. "Nicholas." He was throbbing now and could feel his seed fill him like a young squire unschooled in the delights of women . . . so little control.

"Part your thighs for me."

"No, Nicholas. Stop that." She pulled and grabbed at him, frantically searching for his hand buried under the billowy satin. They tussled with the voluminous layers, she snatching them down as fast as he tossed them up, kicking and jumping with each contact of his burning palm on her skin and crying out as his fingers teased smoothly along her silky nest of hair. As much as he enjoyed their skirmish, he longed to feel her. He nudged her knees apart with his leg and slipped one long finger into her honeyed sweetness. She stifled a long moan. She was so wet.

"You like me touching you."

"Nicholas . . . this is indecent."

"Yes." He ran his tongue back to her ear and nipped lightly on her thin lobe, feeling her womanhood swell and soften as he thrust gently.

When he slid his finger out and then up through her sensitive folds, she jumped at his finding the small bud that was the center of her pleasure. He sighed with satisfaction. She moaned aloud as he cradled the tiny hardened nub, his fingers slippery and gentle.

"What are you doing?" she cried, her virginal confusion igniting him further. The urgency to bury inside her and claim her rose up unexpectedly.

He tamped down his own desires and leaned her back against the sloping grass. "Pleasuring you, my sweet." He nibbled her neck while his fingers explored her plump lips. While he had always prided his skills in bringing a woman to pleasure, he was touched by her untutored response. She writhed restlessly beneath him as he kept her gently in his control.

"Nicholas . . . I feel strange." He cradled her protectively as she arched to his hand, her breathing coming in ragged gasps. He spread her thighs further. "Please, Nicholas . . . Oh, no, oh." She clutched at his shirt. He knew she had no idea what was happening. "I don't think—"

"Don't think," he growled against her neck and then clamped his teeth onto the edge of her bodice, stripping the satin top off her to get at her nipples again. He sucked greedily while he played with her and teased. Her sex lips throbbed against his hand, hot and full.

"Wait, Nicholas!" She gasped and writhed under his skillful fingers. And then she convulsed gently in his arms, little sobs punctuating her moans. The feel of her burning skin vibrating under his fingers and lips unbearably pleasured him. The scent of her arousal was almost too much to resist. She was so wet and soft now, hot. He could slip so easily into her despite her tight barrier of virtue.

She collapsed against the grass, her hair fanned out around her face, her breasts flushed and heaving. He wanted to take her and soothe his rod, hard and aching for release. But he had schooled himself in patience.

"What happened, Nicholas?" she murmured, still catching her breath and clutching his shirt with fragile fingers, her eyes wide with wonder. "That was wonderful."

He eased her skirt up and stood between her silken thighs. She was too dazed to protest. Her ripened lips peeked out through the wet crinkly hairs. He gazed at her. God, he wanted to lick and taste her.

But he held himself in check and, lying himself instead along the length of her, he kissed her chastely, delighting in the warm glow that filled her sapphire eyes. He dropped kisses over her cheeks, her lips, her delicately winged brows while he took himself in hand and ran the head of his cock through her full wet lips. She moaned languidly and stroked the straining cords of his neck. All it took was for him to rub his heavily veined underskin along her clit for him to explode, coming in one long shuddering groan, his seed spilling over her soft mound and down her thighs. Her eyes widened at the feel of the wet warmth.

She was so innocent in her surprise. "Will you do that again? I want to see you," she whispered.

He groaned against her neck and chuckled.

Chapter Four

Johanna flushed at the thought of how Nicholas made her behave and wondered if all men did those things or if he was just particularly wicked. Then, to her horror, she found herself wondering what else he had in store. She wanted to ask her mother about the intimacies of marriage. Common lore spoke of a man's pleasure but never a woman's. Was she improper in that way? As she was in everything else?

As she gazed out her chamber window to the gardens below, her mind wandered to the figure he cut this morning when he was called back to his castle. To look at him caused naughty feelings to stir in places they shouldn't.

His fawn colored hose had clearly showed his manly bulge, and to her consternation, she'd been caught staring. He had smiled darkly, causing her blood to heat. There was a danger about the man that attracted her as much as it panicked her. But she'd not be so foolish as to let him know and give him the power to consume her. He was far too male to be trusted.

Her mother led her to the dressing mirror and Johanna blushed profusely as Lady Victoria tucked and nipped a sheer bedding gown to accentuate Johanna's feminine curves in the most alluring way. She swelled indecently at the thought of the Duke looking at her clad only in a thin cloud of ivory.

"Johanna," her mother spoke to her reflection, "I trust you got to know the Duke a bit on your walk and you feel more comfortable with the man?" Her mother smiled.

"Comfortable?" Johanna gaped. "I don't think he's a man one feels comfortable with, Mother."

Her mother shifted the cloth, allowing it to fall to the floor in delicate gathers that caressed Johanna's thighs. Each fold shimmered and moved, playing hide and seek with her body, revealing her nakedness and then covering her seconds later as the fabric swirled and settled. "This is lovely," Victoria murmured. The gown fastened at each shoulder by ribbons. A tiny pull would have it cascading to the floor. Johanna was mesmerized.

Her mother's expression was gentle. "What I mean is, you needn't be afraid of intimacy with a man like him."

Johanna blushed crimson, her nipples tightening at the suggestion. "Afraid?" she quipped. "Why would I be afraid?"

Her mother's lips curved into a thoughtful frown. "The Duke is a man with . . . developed appetites. But you are a lovely woman, Johanna . . . innocent, yet with a fire a man like that can cultivate. And then he would have no need to seek other women."

Johanna's temper flared at the thought of other women. At the same time she acknowledged that a man of his "appetites" would choose her for her breeding abilities and nothing more.

"Johanna, are you listening?"

"Yes, Mother. I will run his home, bear his children, honor his name. And I will do so with grace and pride. Anything else will be negotiated."

Her mother heaved a sigh of exasperation. "Johanna, you are truly an impossible child." She turned Johanna abruptly to face the mirror square. "And one who certainly doesn't deserve to wear this lusciously seductive gown. But I am through trying to handle you. You are the Duke's problem. He thinks he can tame you? Fine!" Her mother turned and stormed out the door.

❦⬥❧

Johanna luxuriated in the tub of scented oils, her hair tangling over the high rim and her skin flushed. At the sound of the door she turned, expecting to see Charlotte, only to see the commanding figure of Nicholas close and bolt the door. Her heart hammered in her chest. It was one thing to be half naked in the moonlight and another to be naked as a babe in daylight. Knowing he'd just arrived, she concluded the man hadn't an ounce of patience.

"Enjoying your bath?" he said, his voice provocative as he removed his wine colored doublet and tossed it over her vanity chair.

Her pulse tripped another beat. His fine linen shirt opened at the neck, and her eyes dropped involuntarily to the curly mat of hair.

She opened her mouth as he stepped further into the room, but nothing came out. The air bristled with tension as she tried to avert her eyes from the bulge in his breeches. Were all men so large?

"Shall I join you?" With an adept hand, he stripped off his tunic and dropped it to the floor. His bronze chest was a study in muscle . . . so much hard flesh. As she watched the supple chords of his arms flex with each subtle movement, her eyes traced the thick line of hair rippling down his stomach and disappearing into his breeches. But then she realized he was unlacing the ties. She gave a start. When his bulge seemed to swell right before her eyes, her gaze flew to his face. He grinned lasciviously.

"You wouldn't dare," she gasped. But the last time she'd thought that, he had dared. She realized he considered their betrothal license for him to do what he wished with her. "You have no claim on me yet."

"Don't I?" He followed his words with a soft chuckle, giving her a long sweep with his eyes as he approached. He loomed above her. "I'm not a man to wait for my pleasure."

He dropped down deftly beside her, huge and threatening in his strength and rational thought fled as the pure male scent of him taunted her. Before she could succumb to his skillful seduction, she drew back against the opposite side of the tub and sank lower to cover her swelling breasts.

"Let me soap you," he suggested, his voice low and his eyes glittering with anticipation.

Her breath left her as she watched his hand dip into the water and disappear. "Your Grace, please," she whispered.

"What? No, Nicholas?" He moved closer and pressed his lips gently against hers and held them, sucking lightly on her lower lip and then running his wet tongue deliciously along it.

She reveled in the feel of his rough skin skimming along her smooth cheek. "Oh . . ." she murmured with the honeyed warmth that filled her. He smelled of leather and fresh air, and she loved the hard strength of his jaw as he ran his lips along the line of her chin and then down her throat, slowly, as though savoring every inch of her. He breathed deep and a low growl rumbled up from his throat.

She gave a quiet sigh and felt herself dissolving. He seemed so gentle as he stroked his hand along her ankle, his fingers encircling her and caressing smoothly, patiently, his pace languid as he smoothed a path up her leg and behind her knee. He kneaded muscles sore from her ride today on Olympia, and she relaxed into his touch, while his lips lazily nibbled on a sensitive spot at the base of her throat. He had said he wanted to eat her up the last time he did those wicked things. She wanted him to, she realized, half horrified—the other half feeling a frightening thrill.

"Your pulse is soft and quick under my tongue." He nicked her lightly with his teeth, drawing her skin between his lips and sucking gently, his hands still kneading tenderly. He leaned in closer. She flattened her hands against the hard planes of his chest, the ridges vibrating with tension, and she couldn't stop herself from smoothing her palms over the muscled contours, defining them with her fingertips. He moaned softly and ran his hand up her leg. She knew she should push him away, but a warm liquid burned through her, then ignited when he palmed her thigh and stroked with a silky touch. She parted her thighs instinctively, shocking herself with her licentious behavior, but this desire, so new to her, sucked her under. Surely he was Satan and had cast a spell too strong for her to resist.

He began to caress her, gently separating the folds of her womanhood with deft fingers. He stopped nibbling and drew back to look at her, capturing her in a gaze that was so tender she lay back and opened wider for him, her heart pounding in her chest. His gaze dropped to her nipples just above the water line, and she could see how they stoked his arousal. She was drowning in him, and he was devouring her bit by bit. Soon she would be nothing but a toy to play with when it suited him.

Abruptly, she struggled to sit up, but he stroked her teasingly, running one finger up through her layers to that tiny spot he'd found last time that drove her to distraction. She pulsed achingly under his skilled hand, grabbing his arms.

His dark eyes, smoldering like black hot coals, watched as her breath caught. He slid his finger into her silky depths then stroked her cleverly with his thumb. A small cry broke from her lips.

Dizzying pleasure consumed her. Soon she would shamelessly beg to see him spill his seed and lose all sense of control. Like a drowning person struggling for air, her common sense rose to the surface, and she sprang up and moved swiftly to the foot of the iron tub. To her horror she now stood before him while he knelt, his face just inches from her burning center. She was dripping suds from the tips of her nipples and down over her thighs. In one quick movement, he clutched her hips and buried his face in her womanly folds, licking along the swollen petals.

"Nicholas," she gasped, shocked by his wanton possession of her, his tongue warm and wet and now sliding into the heat of her. She collapsed, splashing into the full tub of water and overflowing its sides, soaking him. She slipped under and then sat up sputtering, her hair drenched and falling over her face.

"You . . ." She threw water at him, furious that he'd made her look foolish. But he just fell back on his heels, soaked through and laughed in that deep dark way that sent shivers through her.

She leaped out of the tub, tugging a wrapper around her of material so thin it molded against her wet body. She glared at him. "What gives you leave to enter my chambers at your whim?"

His gaze was like flames licking over her, and the shudder capturing her body sent her breasts quivering in the silky fabric. She expected him to lick his lips at any moment.

"We are betrothed, Johanna," he reminded her smoothly, the lust in his voice dangerously uninhibited and his erection full and hard, clearly outlined against his soaked breeches. "And I don't think I can resist you now."

He closed the distance between them in one long stride and before she could back up, he pulled her hard against him, slipping his hand inside her robe and stroking her breast. His nostrils flared, breathing her in.

"I'm not a patient man," he growled, bent swiftly, and nipped her breast. "I can be uncontrollable when I don't get what I want." He grazed her nipple with his teeth, making her jump from the pleasure and pain of it. Then he suckled with his arms tight around her, his expert fondling turning her to mush.

"Let go of me," she hissed, furious for weakening.

He released her abruptly, dropping her carelessly onto the vanity chair. "Lord, you try my patience."

He widened his stance and folded his arms across his massive chest. He spoke to her as though she were a child. "Whenever I choose, I will kiss you senseless. Is that clear?"

"You were doing more than kissing me!" she snapped.

"Yes . . ." He smiled with satisfaction. "And that too." He released a soft chuckle. "Get dressed. Your mother is expecting us for dinner or I would have finished this. I *could* have, if not for your stubbornness."

"Finished it?" she sniffed. "You said you would not take me until our wedding night. Would you breach your promise?"

He held her chin with one long finger. "Ah, such an innocent. In many ways does a man pleasure a woman, even a virgin."

She flicked off his finger and picked up a brush, tugging it through her tangled hair. "You might as well know that I've decided that I will not be handled until our wedding night."

He leaned down and spoke to her reflection in the mirror, pressing his lips against her hair. "I'll 'handle' you whenever I choose."

She shrugged away, carefully avoiding his gaze. *Lord, the man was difficult.* Had no one refused him? It annoyed her that his declaration was titillating, tempting her. She wanted to believe his arrogant desire was for her alone.

He lifted a silky strand of her hair with one long finger and slid it through his teeth. When he turned and swept toward the door, she stifled her disappointment and on impulse flung her brass-handled brush after him. It bounced off the dark wood panels of the door that he had slammed with a vengeance.

Chapter Five

News of the wedding had spread throughout most of England and all were eager to see the woman who had captured the dark Duke. Well after the bride and groom retreated to their lush chambers in the West Wing, the evening wedding would continue—indeed probably into the next morning.

Johanna stood before the large gilded mirror as a league of sewing maids fit her into the delicately beaded gown. They pinched her waist and lifted her breasts so they swelled above the low scalloped neckline. The skirt erupted in myriad layers of tulle and taffeta that ended in a long flowing train.

"You look like an angel," one maid murmured to Johanna's reflection in the mirror.

Johanna smiled weakly. She didn't feel like an angel. She felt like a witch. And she wondered if her future husband would even look at her once they were secluded in their chambers. Would he sleep in the adjoining room after he took her for the purpose of consummation?

She fought back tears, thinking how evil she'd been all week. While at first it seemed like a game of wits that served to heat her blood further, now she worried. After their last altercation, he had waved his hand in the manner that befitted a man who had reached the end of his patience, but she was powerless to reverse the course she had set. Now she regretted her haste.

While she had been anxious about her wedding night, it was now her own fault that she was upset. She'd driven him away. While she was sure he would be polite and attentive during the festivities, she fretted now that he had lost his spark for her.

Well, she would not disgrace herself or her husband and, regardless of his displeasure, would take her place by his side—if only as the bearer of his children . . . their children. A vision sprang of his holding a tiny baby in his strong arms.

✳᷽ৈ৲ৈ৲

Nicholas shifted his weight and pulled on his black velvet surcoat, reaching in stiffly to straighten the cuffs. He resisted the urge to run his finger under his neck collar as he awaited Johanna's entrance to the chapel.

Wheylan, his groomsman, grinned in enjoyment. "Unless my eyes betray me, my friend, you are nervous. Or is it that a host of mistresses, both former and present, await to greet you at your wedding reception?"

"I have no mistresses now, Wheylan," Nicholas said, making no attempt to cover his impatience. His comrades had refused to believe that he would settle into marriage, and handsome bets were waged against it. Weeks ago he would have joined in the wagering. But that was before he'd met Johanna.

She had a way of snaking under his skin and slipping into his dreams. And not all his dreams were of him ravishing her. She came to him with her bewitching smile, riding free and reckless on a stallion, and then later full with his child.

Wheylan chuckled softly. "I'm not sure your mistresses know. And with half of London here—"

"All of London," Nicholas drawled.

The organ struck a chord and both men turned their attention to the stained glass entrance. "I suppose if she were mine, I'd feel the same," Wheylan murmured.

Nicholas breathed in quiet admiration as he caught sight of her floating regally toward him on the arm of the Earl. Even shrouded by a veil, her beauty stood undiminished. For the hundredth time he was overcome by his desire for her.

Then he smiled to himself, wondering what awaited him this time. She had driven him to near damnation all week, but he'd wager she now suffered as much as he. Nothing seemed to make her as furious as being ignored.

But tonight he had no intention of ignoring her. She would be his.

As she approached, he offered his arm, and she lay a slim hand delicately along his cuffed sleeve. With eyes demurely downcast, a less perceptive person would think her almost tame. Yet, hardly fooled, he kept himself braced.

Throughout the ceremony he frowned at the feel of her trembling under his gaze. He was thoughtless to think she wouldn't be nervous. She was barely eighteen and had learned just weeks ago she would marry a stranger twice her age. And she was innocent to the ways of men.

When he slipped his ring on her, her small hand shook. He had an irrational urge to take her in his arms and protect her from all she feared until he realized, grimly, that Johanna *had* no fears—other than of him.

"You may kiss the bride."

Wheylan nudged him out of his reverie. When he lifted Johanna's veil, her lush mouth quivered with uncertainty. She was soft now and he found himself responding to her silent plea.

He cradled her face in his hands. "You're mine now, Johanna." Then he took her in a soul wrenching kiss, drawing his arms around her and bending her back to accept his passion.

A thunder of cheers arose from the throng of guests. She was warm and supple in his arms, but he forced himself to release her. Breathless, she took his hand as he led her back down the aisle through the host of well-wishers.

If Johanna was subdued during the ceremony, she came alive during the reception, and he'd stake its cause that she suspected his former relationships with women who greeted them. He liked that she was jealous.

He watched as her gaze followed the retreating figure of the Baroness de Compe.

"Another conquest?" She slid him a disparaging glance.

He gave her a look of mock innocence.

"Oh, please," she retorted.

Seated to the right of her on the flowered dais were Earl and Lady Carlton looking pleasantly relieved while Wheylan sat to Nicholas' left, eyeing the inebriated maidens with illicit expectation. The guests ate their fill of roasted wild bird and pig while decanters of wine were replenished as everyone from distinguished royalty to squires and knights danced to the jovial beat of the music and drank yet again.

The frenzy heightened with each new course and the music grew louder. By the time the toasts began, Nicholas feared for his wife's delicate ears.

He poured her another glass of wine. "You may need this," he murmured, acutely aware of her every move and sigh as she sat by his side. He leaned in close and once again pressed his lips against her hair, drinking in her scent.

She eyed him suspiciously. "Trying to get me drunk so you can do what you will with me?"

He smiled at her through half-lidded eyes. "On the contrary. I want you alert and focused tonight. But yes, I *will* do what I want with you."

The crimson blush that stained her cheeks drew his immediate remorse. "Don't worry." He breathed into her hair. "I'll not devour you. I prefer to eat you up in delectable morsels." He nipped her earlobe delicately, sending a visible shudder through her; he wished its cause due to lustful anticipation, but her trembling hands belied that indulgent thought. He longed to slide his hand up to her breast and sweep his thumb across the rise of her nipple that pointed temptingly against the smooth cloth stretched across her bosom. He wanted to feel her grow warm and languid in his arms, melting drip by drip, begging for him to taste the sweet honey that was her.

"'Tis time for a toast from the groomsman," shouted Wheylan, his words conspicuously slurred as he tottered to his feet, his wine sloshing precariously over the goblet's rim. He swept a hand through his thicket of tawny hair and let out a large belch. The crowd groaned and then pounded their fists on the heavy table tops, impatient for the toasts to begin.

Wheylan thrust an unsteady arm into the air and bellowed out, "Cheers to the dark Duke and his lady love. May he taste of her sweetness and drink of her passion, and in wonderful consummation sire a houseful of heirs."

"Here! Here!" The horde roared and stomped.

Nicholas grinned and, raising his fluted glass, turned to Johanna. "To my fairy princess with the sting of a bee, my gentle tigress, my delicate hellion." He wrapped a possessive finger around her silken tresses and brushed it along her cheek. "I'll delight in your spirit and your lush beauty until the last breath I take. Even if it is you who takes that breath from me!"

He swooped down and caught her in a punishing kiss, sinking his fingers into her thick mane and pulling a few dark tendrils free. The guests clapped and shouted while his lovely wife scowled.

It was Johanna's turn. She raised her jeweled goblet in imitation of him and then tossed her head haughtily. "If ever a rogue be found, or tale of a rake be told, this scoundrel I thee wed, has won his prize in gold!"

The crowd laughed in merriment and Nicholas dragged her face up to his once again and claimed her for all to see. But this time when he dipped into her soft mouth and stroked his tongue with hers, he sprang to life.

"Let us retire to our chambers, Johanna," he murmured thickly against her lips. A flicker of anxiety passed through her expression. He kissed her softly. "I'll guide you through the throng. Let's hope no plans were hatched for a royal bedding."

"A bedding?" Her eyes widened in fright.

"Did no one tell you of such things?" he asked with concern. She shook her head and swallowed visibly, her eyes darting from him and then back to the crowd, her vulnerability tugging on his heart. He stroked along her cheek. "I trust the crowd is too drunk to carry it out, my love. Come, stay close to me."

He ushered her through the inebriated singing of verse that grew more lewd by every turn. As he drew her up the back stairwell, the bawdy refrain hung in the air. His innocent wife shuddered lightly as they rounded the corridor. When he swung open the heavy carved doors to their chambers, they were greeted by Johanna's maids, awaiting to attend the virgin. A filmy nightgown lay across the vanity dressing chair and warm flames banked in the fireplace. Taking up one table was a silver tray holding a brandy flask and two etched glasses.

He nodded to the maids. "You may leave."

They looked at each other quizzically. "We are to help our lady with her toilette."

He smiled. "Of course you are. But the pleasure of undressing my wife is mine tonight." Johanna gasped while the maids attempted without success to stifle giggles. As they scurried to leave, the doors burst open and a lecherous crowd, led by Wheylan, surrounded them.

Nicholas whirled on him. "God's blood," he hissed. "You couldn't keep them at bay?"

Wheylan bent close and whispered, "They're too far gone to dissuade. Just give them something, Nicholas, and they'll leave satisfied." Wheylan nudged him and motioned to Nicholas' dressing robe laid out on the four poster bed. While the men dragged off Nicholas' doublet, Nicholas watched Wheylan stuff a wine blotched napkin into one pocket.

Nicholas growled as a circle of maids surrounded his wife, and her eyes grew wide with fright.

The mob chanted for a royal bedding, and knowing they would not let up, Nicholas planned to make haste.

The women peeled off Johanna's dress, their skirts shielding her from the male onlookers who were working on him, tugging off his shirt and then stripping him of his breeches. The women demurely diverted their eyes from his naked form while the men ogled Johanna, hoping for a glance of the untouched maiden as each layer of petticoat fell to the floor. Glimpses of her snowy globes and rosy tits teased and taunted them as they peeked out and then disappeared behind the wall of women.

As Johanna's hair fell free, the women draped it over her body, chastely concealing her from the hungry eyes of the men. Only her shoulders, velvety soft in their luster, could be viewed before her dressers draped the silky robe over her nakedness. Nicholas grabbed his own robe off the bedpost and belted it.

The women and the men drew aside, leaving the bride and groom to face each other just a few feet away. Her look of fear and hatred made him want to commit murder on the nearest person, but he forced himself to concentrate on getting the job done.

He strode forward. She jumped back.

"Take her," they cheered. "Bed her and make her your wife."

Nicholas swept an arm under her knees and scooped her up.

She pounded against him. "How could you?" she cried, her eyes burning with betrayal.

The frenzy of the party escalated. "She'd not be the first reluctant maid to turn wanton in your arms," they laughed and jeered. "Time to take that great sword and sheath the virgin," one bellowed.

Johanna began lightly sobbing.

"Trust me," Nicholas whispered as he lay her down on the large bed and pulled the catches on the white organza so that the bed was curtained in a veil from the voyeurs.

"Listen to me," he coaxed her. Before he stripped off his robe, he dipped into his pocket and fisted his hand around the stained napkin. She lay before him shaking and beautiful and, despite the raucous audience, he was hard and pounding. He let his robe fall. Her visible distress reached a new height.

He climbed onto the bed. "I'll not hurt you," he said, kneeling at her feet. She lay rigid, her hands balled tight at her sides in a gesture of resigned fury, her legs locked together. Her limbs shook as he clasped her knees through the shimmering fabric and drew up her legs. The shock of it made her jump up and struggle back towards the headboard, but he gripped her ankles and held her still. "Johanna," he murmured as he pulled himself on top of her, forcing her knees apart with his legs and settling between her thighs.

"I hate you," she sobbed against his neck.

He cradled her in his arms. "It'll be over in a minute. If I don't take charge, they'll climb in with us to prepare you, a man on either side, rubbing oil between your legs so that I may enter you easily while the other guides my cock. Barbarian, yes, but tradition for shy grooms."

"You can't mean it," she choked, her nails scoring him.

"Swive her!" The crowd began to chant as if in answer.

Nicholas lifted her wrapper and bucked against her.

She screamed in his ear and proceeded to scratch at him and bite his shoulder. He genuinely groaned having no need to pretend, but then he added a loud grunt for good measure.

An uproarious cheer went up. "It is done! It is done!"

Nicholas grumbled as he dragged himself from his trembling and enraged wife and off the bed. She clutched her robe about her. When he swept aside the curtain he was still fully erect and waved the red stained napkin like a banner declaring her virginity taken—a tribute to his conquest.

"Now leave us and let me finish this, spill my seed and produce my heirs."

"Here! Here!" they boasted in manly camaraderie and filed out at Wheylan's urging. Nicholas donned his robe and heaved a sigh of relief.

Chapter Six

Peaceful silence cloaked the room. Nicholas watched how the fire's glow caused soft light to flicker along the walls and draperies. Candles scented the room with subtle fragrance and fresh flowers adorned every corner and surface.

A place of seduction. Yet, how to woo his wife?

He lifted the filmy nightgown from the dressing chair and held it up between his hands. It was ivory and sheer, completely so, and tied at the sides with small blue ribbons. He wanted to see her in it. But from the looks of her now, it would take some work.

She sat against the ornate headboard, knees drawn up to her chin, hugging her legs and scowling. He chuckled softly as he poured them each a snifter of brandy.

Easing down beside her, he offered her the glass. She turned her head.

"Oh, come now," he cajoled. "You'll not let that mob of ruffians get the better of you."

She turned her whole body from him.

"You surprise me," he commented smoothly. "I thought you of sterner stuff."

Her head snapped around and her eyes burned into his. "Sterner stuff? I'd have to be made of iron to withstand that, you dolt."

He made no attempt to hide his amusement. "Yes, I suspect so." His mouth twitched into a smile as he reached forward and pressed a glass to her lips, urging her to drink.

She covered his hands and drank large gulping drafts.

"Easy now." He smiled, but, nevertheless, allowed her the cup in the hope it might assuage her nerves. As he ran his fingers lazily through her silky strands of hair, he sipped from his own cup, watching her over the rim.

Her breasts shimmered against the thin wrapper, her nipples pouting prettily underneath. He longed to slip his hand inside, but he restrained himself, knowing it wise to coax her to him. He twirled a strand of hair around his fingers.

Her lips were red and wet from the brandy, mimicking what her sex would look like before long. He intended to drink from both swollen lips tonight. He hardened and lengthened at the thought.

She drew in her breath. When he followed her gaze, he smiled with pride to see her fixated on his erection jutting through the opening in his robe.

He chuckled playfully. "I think it's time, Johanna . . . to consummate our marriage." He slipped his hand inside her robe and claimed a breast. Her thick lashes closed and fanned across her cheek and then she delicately arched her neck and writhed softly under his gentle touch. He stroked along the smooth underswells and then lingered at the peak, drawing her nipple between his fingers and squeezing.

She moaned lightly.

He took their glasses and placed them on the side table and then climbed up beside her. "And time to produce those wonderful heirs," he teased, laying himself alongside her and drawing her against the length of him. He bent to kiss her glistening lips.

She yanked his hand off and sat up, stiffening. "Of course. Then when you're done you can seek your pleasure from a host of guests in the east wing."

His brows shot up in amusement. His little hellion was most possessive and it made him inordinately pleased.

"I won't deny I've tasted the delights of more than one of your mother's guests, Johanna. Other than my close male friends, I had no hand in the invitations," he assured her calmly.

"Humph!" She lifted her chin. "I suppose my mother would have had to bar half the females in London in order to avoid inviting a former mistress."

"Probably . . ." He smiled easily. She tossed her head in disdain.

So, she would make it a battle. He grinned to himself. More the fun.

"Johanna," he spoke briskly. "Do you deny me my conjugal rights?" He knit his brows and watched her lovely face turn slowly in surprise. She was probably wondering if she could do that.

"I . . ." she faltered. "Yes!"

He chuckled wickedly and rolled onto her, placing his knee between her legs. "I see . . ."

She arched back, laying her hands against his chest, pushing. Her palms burned through the cloth of his robe. He wanted them all over him. "Then, my dear, I shall get out my velvet rope and tie you to the bedpost." His lips quirked.

She choked on a breath. "You wouldn't dare."

"Oh, but you know I would. I'm wicked, remember?" He snatched her around her waist and dragged her down to him. She pushed harder against him. "I'm the devil, you said so yourself."

"No, I didn't mean it." He delighted in her squirming before letting her slip free from under him, enjoying the chase. She slid across the sheets until she reached the bedpost. He leered at her and began slowly unbelting his robe.

"Nicholas . . ." Her eyes dropped to his throbbing erection and then skittered away only to return again with heightened interest. He dropped his robe over the side of the bed. She jumped up onto her knees and wrapped one arm around the post, clutching the inanimate lifeline as though it alone could rescue her from the rapturous hunger of her husband.

"You know I'll catch you, Johanna," he whispered silkily. A shudder fluttered the length of her, her breasts quivering delectably with the movement. In one quick motion he lunged and caught the hem of her wrapper.

"Let go, Nicholas!" She gave a desperate yank but the more she pulled, the farther her robe drew up until he was gazing at her firm lush derriere. He wanted to take a bite out of the tempting globes.

"Stop it, you bastard!" She twisted, giving him a tantalizing glimpse of her nakedness.

"Tsk! Tsk! Such language on a virgin," he chastised her, swelling thicker at the sight of her rosebud nipples peeking out from the front opening.

He pulled harder, slowly dragging her back to the bed, and then to his pleasure, she slipped out of her robe and stood frozen before him in all her naked glory. He stopped, transfixed, as candlelight flickered over every curve. Her feeble attempts to cover herself modestly with palms too small to cover all that female flesh, ignited his rampant lust.

He groaned audibly and grew another inch.

"Nicholas, this is not the way to do this," she breathed, her eyes wide with bewilderment. He swallowed thickly. Was she actually trying to reason with him? He chuckled to himself while his gaze raked over her silken body, settling finally on the soft dark triangle between her milky thighs.

"Then show me, Johanna," he offered reasonably, propping his hand under his head. He stretched out as though intending to leisurely converse instead of struggling to control his raging arousal.

She bent seductively to snatch up her wrapper, her breasts like pendulums, liquid with movement. "First," she instructed, cinching the belt, "I need more time." She pivoted with purpose and walked casually to the mantle as though they had all evening. They did, but he would not use the hours for conversation. He smiled to himself as she relaxed into the cozy circle of chairs, settling herself onto a thickly cushioned settee. She thought she had the upper hand.

"How much time?" he asked conversationally, still languishing on the bed and stiff with arousal.

She avoided looking at him and concentrated her attention on the banking fire, thoughtful. "A couple of weeks."

A raw chuckle erupted from his throat. He climbed stealthily off the bed. "I don't think so," he growled, playfully stalking her.

She flew off the chair in a frenetic panic and attempted to run, but he laughed richly and plucked her up easily despite her flailing and kicking limbs. He tossed her lightly onto the soft cool linen. Her raven locks fanned out against the feather pillows. She was temptingly beautiful and he would take her, hard and fast, but not before she begged him.

"You had better not touch me, Nicholas," she said sternly, lifting up on her elbows.

He chuckled darkly at her attempted intimidation. "I'll do more than that my virgin princess. I'll kiss every inch of your body and lick along your velvety skin."

She scampered on her knees across the bed but he intercepted her. "I'll devour you, Johanna, bit by delicious bit." His body tensed with anticipation. He knew she could see the aggressive gleam in his eye.

He began his climb over the foot of the bed. A terrified exhilaration glittered in her eyes. He smiled inwardly. Her gaze traveled suggestively over his supple chest and sculpted arms as he crawled to her on all fours, his erection full and hard. In one quick motion, he grabbed up her ankle and nipped at her heel. She jumped. "Mm . . ." he growled and slid his hand over her calf and stroked seductively. "Delicious . . ."

His tongue traveled up her leg. She wrestled against him, struggling to scoot back, but he held her ankle firmly with one hand and, with the other, he slipped under her robe and found her soft folds already swollen.

"Nicholas . . . wait."

He sank a finger into her cleft and she moaned.

"Why should I wait, my love, you're already wet." He crawled farther up her body, anchoring her with his weight and bit her thighs gently. He wanted to taste her. But when he lifted her robe, she tugged it down, tucking it furiously between her thighs, a look of genuine shock gracing her lovely features.

"I want to look at you, Johanna," he explained calmly. "The way you like to look at me."

"No, I don't," she denied.

"I think you do." He knelt back on his heels, his shaft stiff, pointing at her and watched as her eyes dropped to take in the sight of him. "See?" He reached for her hand. "Touch me, Johanna." She slipped out of his reach, still staring at him. He chuckled softly. "You'll get used to the size of me."

"No, Nicholas." Her eyes searched his. "You're too big. It will never work." Her breathless voice warned him that she was truly overwhelmed. He softened measurably at her innocence.

"Ah . . . I see." He stretched himself leisurely alongside her, resting his chin on her shoulder. "'Tis true." He smiled, reaching up to play with her hair and sliding idle strands between two fingers. She relaxed into the pillows and instinctually snuggled into him.

"So, you understand, Nicholas? And you are not the brute purported to be?" she pouted.

He weighed his words. "I understand you're hesitant—"

"I'm terrified—" she blurted.

He stroked along her throat with gentle fingertips. "A little hesitant, yes," he murmured, running his nose in back of her ear and taking in her scent. "'Tis natural . . ." His lips grazed along the line of her jaw. "'Tis all natural. But if we are to join, you must surrender to me."

It was the wrong choice of words. She stiffened perceptibly, her delicate brows drawing together in a thoughtful frown. The war within her surfaced. It pleased him that she found him difficult to resist, settling into his caress one moment and then withdrawing the next.

He sifted through the folds of her robe so that the smooth skin of his cock lay against her thigh. Taking her hand, he laid it tentatively on him. This time she didn't pull away. He jumped in her hand. She gasped, but continued to play her fingertips lightly along him, feeling the raised veins and swollen head. He moaned lightly in her ear. She turned into him, growing bolder, reaching lower to cradle his sack, drawn up tightly against his aching body. He filled with seed and moaned as he brought her hand to feel the small pearly drop with her fingertips. She stroked around the tip, feeling his strength, but still not looking at him.

"Is that what you spilled that night?" she asked in wonder. He was enchanted by her virgin curiosity.

He smiled against her skin, wanting to consume her but fighting the impulse. "Yes. And I will spill into your hand if you don't stop now," he chastised her, teasingly. When he set her firmly from him, he could see the pleasure in her eyes. And although she obeyed him for the moment, she insisted on leaning closer for a look at him. Her eyes widened in awe, the nearness of her lips torturing him. She smoothed his seed over him with one delicate finger. He groaned aloud and grabbed her wrist.

"Now it's my turn," he ordered, his voice tight with arousal.

Her look of pleasure turned to panic. With his body tense with repressed desire, he hoped she wouldn't resist him now, because he'd scarce be able to stop himself.

But like a child who understands fair play, she lay back against the plush pillows, willingly, and lifted her wrapper for him—albeit with her legs locked together. He throbbed at the sight of the tight curls nestled between her smooth thighs. He nudged his hand between her legs, urging her to spread her thighs for him. She did. He groaned audibly and knelt between her legs, reaching for her petaled softness and separating her lips gently with his fingers.

She watched him, blushing profusely. He drew up her knees, and then slipped two thick fingers through her folds. When he stroked his thumb along her pebbled bud, teasing it out, she cried out his name and her body shuddered with pleasure. "Nicholas." Her voice held on a whisper and her eyes glazed over.

He wanted her to climax, to ease the moment when he would tear through her innocence.

He drew his finger out and licked her sweetness off greedily. As aroused as she was, she startled in shock and pulled her robe between her thighs once more.

"Oh, no, you don't," he growled, pushing the silk up to her waist despite her frantic attempts to stop him. He dipped his head between her legs. His mouth was on her, licking deliciously as she dug her fingers into his hair, tugging at him as he drank in her taste. "Nicholas . . . you can't." Her words drowned on a sigh and her fingers finally relaxed. She spread her thighs wider and sifted her slim fingers through his hair. A low guttural moan escaped from deep in her throat as he ran the tip of his tongue along her swollen lips, teasing and flicking lightly on her clit and then retreating. She moaned and arched her hips, melting against him as he dipped his tongue and massaged temptingly. She rocked shamelessly against him.

It was when he sucked gently on the center of her pleasure that he felt her explode around his fingers buried deep inside her. She cried out before she dissolved into waves of pure heat, her body imprisoned by her sweet flames.

Her sex lips were a deep red, wet and throbbing, and they looked delicious. He could enter her now.

He opened her robe and laid himself atop her, skin to skin. She was dazed and the telltale flush spread enticingly over her breasts and her engorged nipples, ripe from her climax.

"Nicholas," she said dreamily as her small hands ran along his arms and up over his shoulders. He propped himself on his elbows. She was so trusting. He hated to take her pleasure away.

He guided the tip of his cock to her entrance and nudged her. Her eyes widened with childlike naiveté and she spread her legs, opening for him sweetly.

"Draw up your knees, love."

She obeyed him, inviting him into her body. A touch of regret surfaced within him as he eased into her plush softness. He groaned as he felt her silken folds caress him. He withdrew quickly, on the brink of taking her too swiftly.

She blinked with disappointment. "Nicholas, please." She stroked down his back and settled her small hands on his buttocks, pushing gently.

He slipped between her folds, stopping just short of her maidenhood, and pressing gently against the fragile barrier. She rocked sinuously with an inborn need of which she could have no conscious knowledge. "This feels wonderful, Nicholas."

He grimaced at the short shallow thrusts, the need to take her building. She bucked against him. "Please, Nicholas." He knew she didn't understand what she was asking . . . she only knew intuitively of more.

She was too swollen and too wet and too tight . . . and she wanted him. He thrust deep, tearing through her virginity and burying himself in her liquid softness. She tensed and cried out, her nails digging into his back as she dragged them along his skin. The unbearable pleasure of her drove him to greater heights, but he clung desperately to his last vestiges of control.

He held her close, unmoving. "It is done," he whispered, burying his lips against her hair.

She sobbed and clutched at him. "I don't like this, Nicholas. You're going to rip me in two. Get off of me."

"Shh . . ." He held her still with the weight of his body as she struggled ineffectually. He kissed her tears. "It's all right," he crooned, barely touching her lips to his and then brushing lightly along her chin. He willed himself to control his need to rock into her, to thrust into her over and over again. He smoothed her hair back off her face. His cock swelled thicker and he throbbed, so close to the edge.

"Nicholas?" Her eyes widened in amazement. "How big will you get?"

He chuckled, thankful for the release of tension. "Any thicker and I will spill into you."

"I want to feel that," she breathed and stroked his buttocks.

He closed his eyes against the feel of her. Before he spilled his seed, he wanted to take her with a violence that matched his need for her and bring her to greater heights of ecstasy. "I thought you wanted me to get off of you," he teased, allowing himself time to control his ache for her.

She frowned impatiently. "I changed my mind."

"I see . . ." He smiled gently and withdrew slowly from her silken sheath.

"No," she clutched his buttocks, trying to push him back into her.

"Do you want me, Johanna?" He impaled her with his gaze, suddenly wanting her complete surrender.

Her expression was guarded. "You are my husband," she replied with caution. "I will submit to you."

He threw back his head and laughed. "Submit?" He gave her a wicked smile. "You'll do more than that."

She writhed under him while his cock remained poised at her entrance. She nudged him in encouragement, but he held back, ignoring his rampant ache for her.

He slid the throbbing head along her wet folds and then slipped over her clit with tantalizing gentleness. She moaned and arched, her fingers digging into his backside.

"Say it, Johanna," he breathed, perched on the edge, his hands on her thighs, spreading her wide. He was rock hard and the driving need to bury himself inside her tortured him. Why didn't he just take her? Why did he want more? "Say you'll surrender to me," he murmured, slipping along her folds.

She thrashed and sobbed, bucking against him, her own need consuming her, but still she fought him.

He grabbed her wrists and stretched her arms up over her head, threading his fingers with hers, trapping her. He settled between her burning thighs, throbbing and waiting.

"Nicholas," she pleaded and drew her knees up far, lifting frantically for him to fill her. Her eyes were liquid fire. He thrust his tongue into the soft depths of her mouth, mimicking the mating he longed to do with their bodies. She slid her tongue along his and he sucked gently. She was desperate now, sliding her body along his, her nipples teasing the wiry hairs of his chest. He licked the pointed tips and sucked hard, tugging brutally with his lips and grazing her with his teeth.

"Beg me," he growled, pulling up his head and daring her to defy him.

"No," she screamed, her eyes blazing. He claimed her mouth in a punishing kiss and she bit him, drawing blood from his lips. He couldn't hold back.

He plunged into her with a reckless fury, his cock thick and hard, spreading her and plundering her with abandon.

"Oh, my God," she moaned, her hips jumping beneath him, her teeth sinking into his shoulder. She rocked against him, meeting his every thrust with a fury of her own.

He fucked her mindlessly, as though every thrust would be his last and trying to stave off his awaiting ecstasy while at the same time wanting to fill her with his seed.

He was home.

The moment he thought it, she clutched him violently within her hot depths, pulling him deeper within her. Her cries of pleasure shattered his control. His cock erupted explosively as he spilled into her in long shuddering groans and buried himself as deep as he could. He held her fiercely to him.

He had no intention of ever letting her go.

Chapter Seven

Johanna sobbed quietly against his chest, her humiliation complete. He'd done it again. Caused her to behave wickedly and with total abandon. Her cheeks burned at the thought of how she begged him with her eyes, her body, her cries . . . even if she had held her tongue when he fiercely demanded her surrender—commanding her to obey.

She pushed at him, hard, and felt his massive manhood slip out and his weight lift. The emptiness that followed echoed her feelings. "Are you satisfied?" she clipped, giving him another shove.

He rolled off her and moaned. "I'll never be satisfied, Johanna."

She slipped out from under him, grabbed up her robe and dragged herself off the bed. Clutching the silk around her, she sank before the fire, feeling his seed drip down her thighs. She swelled in response. Damn him! Despite his having ravished her, she still wanted him, wanted him stroking and petting her . . . wanted to feel her body splinter into little pieces of burning fire under his skillful touch. She wanted to lick him like he licked her. The thought caused what little composure she had left to shatter.

"I hate you," she screamed at the long licking flames dancing before her, mocking her. She picked up the brandy flask and tossed it into the fire. Bursts of flame shot out and then retreated and then flared up again; that's how she felt in his arms.

She could sense him ease down behind her and could feel his warmth . . . smell him, that disturbingly masculine scent. If she turned now, she would see a wall of chest, acres of muscle and dark hair filling her vision. She didn't dare look.

"Johanna?" She felt his lips against her hair before she felt the soothing warmth of his hands gentle on her shoulders drawing her back against him. She twisted away from him. "Did I hurt you?" His voice was soft.

She whirled on him and leaped up, wrapping her robe tightly around her. He knelt back on his heels, completely naked, his sex thick and resting against his thigh. His gaze held hers in a look of tenderness that confused her.

"Of course you hurt me," she bit out. "I was a virgin and you knew it. But you took no care when you plunged yourself into me." She re-lived that moment in an instant. His thick shaft filling her, stretching her; she wanted to feel him inside of her again . . . wanted to walk over and sit in his lap and feel him ease up into her.

She shivered against her lascivious thoughts. She was allowing him to consume her. Soon she would be merely his plaything—one among many—until she carried his heir. Then he would leave her until the next time he required a namesake.

She wanted more. The realization frightened her. Theirs was a simple agreement: his name and protection in exchange for providing an heir. She was foolish to expect more when he had at his disposal any woman he desired. Why would he want her?

"Come here, Johanna."

She was startled out of her misery.

He was sitting back, gazing at her. The soft flickering lights from the fireplace played over the tight mat of black hair trailing over the sculpted ridges of his chest. His member was hard again, pointing up at her, thick and swollen. She stifled a whimper and tried to drag her eyes away.

"Sit here, Johanna." He motioned to his lap.

Her eyes flew to his face, dark with passion, his lips full and sen-sual. His hair glistened with moisture, its inky blackness shining in the warm glow of the fire. She noticed for the first time the scar that ran just above his left brow and then disappeared under the thicket of hair falling over his forehead. She wanted to run her fingers along the ten-der skin, kiss its line. But her good sense overrode her conflicting emo-tions.

"Haven't you had enough?" she quipped, turning from him and heading briskly towards the door of the adjoining suite.

"Come now," he ordered calmly, not even bothering to rise, an-noyingly confidant of his power over her.

She would show him!

"I'll be sleeping in the other chamber. I ache from your attentions and need time to recover. Only a thoughtless brute would take a virgin again so soon."

"Johanna," he said, his voice still low but with an unmistakable edge. When she didn't stop, his voice rose an octave. "Johanna, come back here."

When she heard him rise behind her, she quickened her pace. At the sound of his footfalls, she fairly flew across the room and then raced through the door.

"Johanna!" He stormed after her.

She slammed and bolted it without a moment to spare and collapsed against the solid mahogany.

"Young lady, open this door before I break it down."

"No, Nicholas. I won't. And you won't break it down for it is not your home and you would be hard pressed to explain it in the morning. Are you unable to control your young bride? Or are you simply a brute?" She held her breath and waited.

After a prolonged silence his voice, male and powerful, traveled through the thick panels. "I'll not spar, Johanna, and make no mistake, you'll not want this settled in the morning. Now open this door."

She held her breath and gave no answer.

"Did you hear me . . . little Madame?" he growled.

The deep timbre of his voice resonated through the door. Muttering a long string of oaths, he paced with heavy steps on his side of the door.

And then his pacing ceased. She could hear his heavy breathing.

"I'll give you one last chance. Now open this door," he warned her, his voice low and threatening.

She remained silent, her heart in her throat.

"God's teeth, you are a hellion!" he ground out viciously. "Did you hear me? A little hellion!"

After a fresh string of oaths, she heard him bound back across the room.

She breathed a sigh a relief laced with a sense of triumph . . . until she spied the empty bed. So devoid of him and his large male warmth.

Suddenly she wondered if she *had* won . . . this time.

Or if she really wanted to win at all.

Chapter Eight

The carriage rocked and swayed it seemed for hours, although Johanna knew it had only been a short time since she had been imprisoned with Nicholas in his luxurious coach. He was annoyingly polite as he sat across from her and explained what she should expect upon their arrival at his castle. He described the servants, their names, their duties, all of whom she would be in charge, and he spoke of several feasts and tournaments the vassals had planned in their honor. While he spoke to her formally, as one would with a business partner, behind those dark irises she saw a smoldering fire.

She sat pensively, waiting for his eruption over her locking him out last night. The longer it took, the more anxious she became.

"Are you still interested in the horses, Johanna?" His eyes grazed over her body and then returned to her face. Her nipples hardened traitorously. When his eyes dropped a moment to her breasts, she saw the flicker of recognition. She wanted to blast him. But intent on playing his little game of casual repartee, she nodded with decorum.

"Then I shall introduce the stableman to you in the morning and you will pick out an Arabian."

She smiled spontaneously, so excited at the thought of a purebred.

His speculative gaze turned warm and melted over her. She felt a tingling arousal snake under her skin. "Johanna . . ." His eyes turned a soft coal. "Come sit next to me."

She hesitated, but then felt silly. What could he do to her in the coach?

She glanced out the window and saw the endless expanse of trees and noted the silence of all but the sound of the wheels over crushed stone and the beat of the horse's hooves. It would be more than an hour before they reached his stronghold.

"Come here," he repeated, his tone commanding. His eyes glittered.

"Nicholas," she breathed. "I'm not certain I should." Why must he be so unsettling? Were all men like this? She was sure they weren't.

He chuckled softly, a rich sensuous laugh. "You needn't wonder whether you should. I am your husband."

Her eyes flashed in defiance, but she struggled to swallow a lump of sheer terror. "Then I was right. You *are* planning to have your way with me . . . right here in the carriage."

His brows shot up in ill-feigned innocence. "Since you suggest it," he smiled easily, "it *is* a tempting idea."

"No." She lifted her chin.

He leaned in and slanted his brows. "Yes, Johanna."

"I will not let you take me here like a rutting hog."

"You *will* and I *will*. You are my wife and you will lift your skirts when I desire you and spread your luscious thighs—"

"Don't be vulgar, Nicholas."

"Yes, let's Johanna."

"I'll scream—"

"No one will pay heed. They are used to my ways." His lips quirked.

"Nicholas, you can't mean it." She appealed to his sense of chivalry, if he had any.

His eyes softened. Her momentary relief turned to horror when he eased slowly off the bench and came to her, large and forbidding; she knew that he considered he had rights, and she also doubted she could stop him. He dropped to his knees and braced his hands beside her on the bench, his face level with hers. His eyes were confusingly gentle, his lips relaxed.

She squirmed back from the hard wall of his chest, and away from his warm scent surrounding her. She could almost taste his skin. Lewd thoughts of his member, hard and glistening in her hand, loomed, turning her veins to liquid.

He brushed his lips along hers, leisurely, his body so powerful and commanding, yet gentle, his maleness infuriating in the way it made her dizzy and unable to think. Her body heated instantly. A few kisses couldn't hurt. She surrendered on a soft sigh.

When he ran his warm, wet tongue over her bottom lip, her mouth opened of its own accord. He groaned audibly. Any thinking vanished as she gave herself over to the familiar sensations warring within her. His tongue stroked deliciously along hers, alarmingly alive. The faint touch of mint teased her, his warmth a drugging aphrodisiac.

A cool breeze brushed over her skin and she realized that he had unlaced her bodice. Her nipples peaked under her chemise, sending a rush of blood to wicked places, the throbbing ache a torment of pleasure. "Nicholas, but—"

"Yes, Johanna. Such a tasty idea," he growled, biting along her jaw line and sliding his hands into her slip to cover her breasts with his palms, feeling their weight. She clutched his wrists, but his skillful fondling was unbearably stimulating. "Nicholas, have you no shame?" she whimpered.

"None whatsoever."

"What if the driver stops?"

"He better not," he breathed, pulling and plucking. She moaned into his mouth.

At the feel of his tongue trailing down her throat, she gave up. He licked first one nipple and then the other, but the restless ache wouldn't cease, the wet friction of his tongue drove the spiraling sensation deeper. He tore through her crinolines, fussing impatiently through the layers of slip and ruffles to get to her skin. Her heart pounded at the thought of his hands on her thighs, stroking and petting her secret places.

He tangled in the silk, lost in a profusion of crinoline and tulle. "Blast it," he grumbled. Then he pulled down her chemise, stripping her to the waist. He sat back on his heels and devoured her with his eyes.

When she reached to cover herself, he grabbed her wrists, imprisoning her arms at her side as his gaze whipped over every bare inch of her. A crimson blush burned her breasts while she struggled feebly.

Her eyes darted to the windows. "Someone will see us."

He sprang up and jerked the heavy curtains closed, throwing the coach into a dusky twilight.

He fingered her nipples. She couldn't stop herself from watching as he pinched and teased them into hardened buds. "These rosy nipples were my undoing that day in the meadow," he grumbled as he palmed her again.

"Nicholas, must you be so— Oh!" she gasped and then spread her thighs in answering response.

She had no will left when he inched her bottom to the edge of the bench, and then tossed up her skirts, every last layer, until she lay before him, exposed for all but her boots and long silk stockings. "Christ," he mumbled.

She could feel how wet and swollen she was and although her secret folds were fully exposed to him she felt no shame, only an urgent longing for him to fill her.

He moved between her legs and unlaced his breeches with urgent hands while he reached with one finger and stroked her gently along her swollen lips. Pleasure stripped through her. When he eased a finger up her, she cried out, arching into his hand. His thumb stroked her sensitive bud and she jumped with the shock of it.

"By my life, you're a temptress, Johanna." His eyes were aflame as he drew his large shaft out and guided the head toward her throbbing lips.

But she scooted back from him. The pearly drop glistened and she wanted to lick him. She didn't understand her own lewd thoughts but she couldn't stop herself. With the tip of her finger she stroked him. He jerked from her touch.

"By Christ! You're a vixen."

Then she swooped down spontaneously and licked him, once, quickly, and then retreated.

He growled, the chords of his neck bulging while she lay back watching his reaction and shocked by her own abandon. Was that ever done?

"Johanna," he rasped. "Place your lips on me, again."

She bent, tentatively, looking at the heavy veins and fascinated by the pulsing of his blood. The tip of her tongue traced around his silky head, so smooth over such hardness. His strength took her breath away.

She felt his hand slip into her hair, gently urging her forward. Her lips encircled him and he slipped the tip of his shaft between her lips and into her mouth. She gasped and withdrew, her eyes wide and questioning him.

His raw chuckle aroused her, emboldening her. She slipped him down her throat and felt the velvety softness of his skin and the manly taste of him. He groaned, a loud, torturous animal sound, and then he cupped her chin as she slid her lips up his shaft and then down again, feeling his length.

"Faster," he groaned, and she obliged.

He was rock hard and thick when he grabbed her chin with both hands and quickly lifted her off him.

"That's enough, my love," he whispered, his voice rough. "You're going to kill me." He descended toward her once again.

His eyes burned, like a highly polished glaze that gently caressed her with warmth. "Watch me," he said as he balanced himself above her with one arm and stroked his rod along her tiny nub. She moaned and whimpered, drawing her legs up wider. When their eyes met, she knew he wanted her as desperately as she wanted him.

She closed her eyes in anticipation while he positioned himself at her entrance. "Open your eyes, Johanna." His voice vibrated with arousal.

She watched as his thickness eased into her, red and hard and smooth, slowly, tortuously. Every nerve awakened and centered on their joining. The full feel of him stretching her assuaged the burning ache for him she only half understood. He groaned aloud and withdrew, slipping out of her folds and titillating her tender flesh. The chords of his neck strained. He shuddered like a man fighting for control.

"I want you, Johanna." His eyes bore into hers in desperate agony. "And I won't give up until you surrender to me."

He thrust hard. She arched to meet him, grabbing onto his shoulders, her body captured by his massive shaft.

He withdrew just as fast, leaving her bereft and wanting.

Oh, God! He wasn't going to torture her again?

His jaw clenched. "Give yourself to me, Johanna." She spread her legs wider and arched her hips to him.

He grabbed her thighs and stretched her wide. "I have your body, now I want your—"

The carriage tipped and swayed in the aftermath of a crashing sound and they were sent sprawling to the floor.

His legs tangled in her skirts as they tried to steady themselves against the jostling. "Blasted! The road must be pitted from the rains."

She lay beneath him as he reared up and slipped his hand under her skirts, flinging up layers of tulle and lace in a frantic attempt to uncover her.

"The carriage is stopping," she gasped, tugging down her skirts as fast as he shoved them up.

"Johanna," he growled. She heard the rip of fabric as she tussled with him and grabbed at his wrists. She was still stripped to the waist and now he was ripping at her skirts. Her clothes would be in shreds by the time they arrived.

She kicked at him to listen and caught the heel of her boot in the waist of his breeches and then leapt up.

"Wife!" He grabbed the hem of her skirts and yanked. She fell, tumbling back on top of him.

"Will you listen to me, Nicholas!" He crushed her against the length of him. Her skirts flew up and she felt the cool air caressing her bottom and then his hands. "The carriage is slowing." She pushed herself up on her arms, trying to ignore the feel of his palms smoothing a hot path over her bare backside.

He grabbed a nipple between his lips.

"Milord . . ." A voice called to them from the front of the carriage.

Nicholas groaned. "What is it, Fenworth?" he shouted over the grinding wheels.

"We need to stop, sir."

"Not now," Nicholas bit out.

He was lifting her hips now, trying to impale her. She pushed against him, but he held her firm, sliding himself, rock hard and wet, through her folds, searching.

"Nicholas, we must stop."

He slipped his hand between them and cradled her little bud between the tips of his fingers and stroked. "Oh . . ." The burning jolt of fire that shot through her caused her to shudder and rock wantonly as waves of pure bliss threw caution back into the recesses of her mind.

Fenworth's disturbed entreaty was dimming. "I'm sorry sir, but—"

"Keep driving," Nicholas shouted at the poor man loud enough to rock Johanna back to her senses. She rolled off him and scrambled to the other side of the coach.

Nicholas let out a pained moan and started crawling to her, fully erect. He snatched for her ankle while she tugged frantically for him to release her.

The coach rocked dangerously.

Nicholas rasped, "If I have to wrestle you to the ground, I will."

"Nicholas, listen to yourself, you've got to stop this."

"I can't, Johanna." His voice was a tortured groan.

"Sir," Fenworth shouted louder as the crank of the wheels rang out and the horses whinnied in resistance. "The road is getting worse and we're still a good distance from your estate. There's a clearing up ahead where I should look at the front wheel. Just a few yards or so."

"Fine," Nicholas grunted loudly.

Johanna was backed into a corner as Nicholas struggled to stand, fighting with his breeches and then finally flinging them off. His erection tented the soft linen of his shirt. He was coming toward her.

"Didn't you hear the man? He'll be stopping in just moments," Johanna said, agog.

"That's all we need." His pupils dilated with tension. She turned her back on him and pulled up her bodice, lacing it hurriedly.

"No, Nicholas," she reprimanded him over her shoulder. "Just get control of your—"

She was pulled back against him. He locked his arms around her waist and buried his lips in her hair. "Bend over," he breathed.

She gasped on a horrified breath. "Nicholas, you can't mean to—"

He leaned her forward and threw up her skirts. The smooth head of his shaft slid over the sensitive mounds of her bottom.

He growled deep in his throat. His hands rested on her buttocks, stroking her. "Johanna, what a sight you are."

"This is . . . obscene." She shivered at the feel of him rubbing against her, poised to take her like an animal.

As though reading her thoughts, he responded huskily. "God's blood, I can't resist you."

He stroked between her lips and then plunged his thumb deep within her. The swift bolt of pleasure, ignited every nerve. But it wasn't enough. She tilted her bottom up wantonly, wriggling and begging for him to fill her. Then he thrust himself into her, deep and thick, powerful, sinking into the very heart of her, and the raw delight of it shocked her. She could no more stop now than he could.

He grunted with the effort. Her body tightened into a torture of sensation as he thrust with a steady quickening rhythm, building the pressure unbearably. His thumb stroked between her bottom, probing entrance. He growled.

"Nicholas," she choked. "What are you doing?"

He murmured in her ear, "Are you going to come for me, Johanna?" Then he eased his slick thumb, so wet from her, into her most private of entrances. The full shocking feel of it coupled with his erotic plea sent her tumulting into an abyss of unbridled ecstasy. Her body shattered out of control as his thumb sank up to its full depth. He groaned in delight and pumped into her, hot thick spurts exploding deep inside her womb and warming her, consuming them both with hot vibrating pleasure.

The slower, thick throbbing of his member soothed her and his warm seed spilling down her thighs made her sigh with contentment. She didn't want him to pull out.

He held her close, and then pivoted to fall onto the padded bench, taking her with him onto his lap, still impaled. They sat silent, sucking in drafts of air while their bodies slowly settled. With a soothing stroke, his fingers petted where they joined, languidly easing her tension. She leaned into him and sighed. He sank his lips into her hair and held her protectively.

It was then that they noticed the silence . . . all around them.

The carriage had stopped.

Chapter Nine

Johanna drew in a shocking breath, mentally envisioning what awaited her outside the carriage. "Nicholas!" She pushed at him, but he burrowed his lips in her neck. "The carriage, it's stopped."

With a panicked shriek, she slid off his lap, frantically righting her skirts. Running an impatient hand through her hair, she looked to see him languished back, his linen shirt down to his bare thighs and smiling like a stuffed pig.

"Nicholas, you brute," she hissed, careful not to raise her voice lest the servants hear. "Do something!" She flung his breeches and boots at him.

And then to her consternation, she burst into tears. He was at her side in an instant.

"Johanna," he murmured, gathering her up. "What is it?"

She choked on a sob and railed against him, her fists beating into the solid sinew of his chest. "Ouch!" she wailed.

He held her close and ran his lips over her forehead, murmuring useless reassurances that, nonetheless, soothed her. "What is it, my love?" His voice was achingly tender for a man who had just taken her like a beast.

It took every bit of her strength not to dissolve in his arms the way she longed to, for she had to rectify their appalling circumstances.

"Are you such a dolt?" she whispered, swiping at her tears, her gaze flickering to the carriage doors. She pictured the small entourage of servants who had traveled with Nicholas to escort the newly married couple back to his estate all lined up now ready to help her alight for this brief interruption in their trip, their faces expressionless while they had heard everything—or had they? How long had they been stopped?

He drew her to him. "There, there, you needn't care, the—"

"Needn't care?" She balled up her fists and wrenched herself from him. "I'm the new mistress of Chandlemare and still a child in most eyes. And now I'm a whore, unworthy of respect—"

He gripped her arms and shook her. "Who says these things?"

"No one," she howled. "But they will and they'll have a tale to tell the others when we arrive." Tears welled up unbidden. "You've got to do something."

His eyes darkened, and then he donned his pants and boots quickly and bounded out of the carriage.

She heard voices rise and feet scurrying. Her husband's rich baritone thundered for all to hear. "The Duchess is ill, her breathing suffers . . . the blasted dust is causing her to gasp for breath. Get that wheel fixed and make haste!"

Johanna remained hidden inside as he rang out commands. She fussed at her hair and clothes, trying to pin and tuck herself into respectability. Finally composed, she took a deep breath and readied herself just as her husband swooped in and captured her in his arms, sweeping her out.

"Come, my dear." He cradled her to his chest. "Ladies, bring the cloths and water . . . over here, near the shade."

"Yes sir, aye," the frightened voices murmured. When he set her gently upon a soft bed of moss, myriad skirts encircled her. He pressed the water to her lips and winked so only she could see. If she hadn't fallen in love with him already, she would now.

He lifted her easily onto his lap. "I rescued you well, better than slaying a dragon. Do I get your sweet lips as my reward?"

"You do," she responded.

His surprise at her acquiescence made her laugh and then her heart skipped a beat at the tenderness in his eyes.

"Johanna . . ." His voice was like rough velvet.

"Yes, Nicholas?" she breathed, instinctively feeling on the precipice of something she couldn't name.

His black orbs burned into her, but gently this time, caressing her with a vulnerability she'd never seen, so at odds with the raw power of him.

His lips brushed hers in a tender dance. "Johanna, I—"

"Your Grace," a voice called out, "can we speak with you a moment, sir?"

"Aye," he nodded in acknowledgment, and then gave an impatient sigh as he turned to her and pecked her cheek before leaving. But she tugged on his shirt.

"Nicholas, what was it you wanted to say?"

"It can wait." His voice was gruff. Then he barked out orders to the maids to come watch over her before he left to join the men.

By the time they arrived at his massive stone estate, she was calmer and did her best to behave as befitted a duchess. She was inordinately pleased when she caught Nicholas watching her with pride as she greeted the servants, knowing their names before they spoke, having memorized his descriptions.

The next month disappeared in a flurry of activity as she settled into her role and assumed her responsibilities. She continually admonished Nicholas to take care with his cavalier behavior of grabbing and stroking her at will in front of the servants, at least until she established her authority. But at night she turned to him eagerly and was astounded by his passion. It was impossible not to dissolve into him, become consumed by his strength. And his ardor was fierce. At times she convinced herself he was in love with her, foolish though it be.

During the week Nicholas was in London, she missed him terribly. When she was informed that her brunch with Lady Byron was canceled, Johanna was pleased to receive the news. She happily donned her riding skirt and boots and hurried out, scurrying to the stable, anticipating a brisk ride on Hellion, her new Arabian that her husband had insisted on naming. Only Hellion could stave her loneliness.

An hour later she walked into the foyer to the sound of feminine laughter. She froze.

"We knew this time would come, darling," the woman crooned, her soft whisper slicing through Johanna like a sword. "I'm sure she's a lovely child, but when she herself is with child, you will come to me and we'll make up for so many lost nights."

"Your sultry persuasion is legendary for shattering a man's resolve, Camellia."

She chuckled delightedly. "Please, introduce me to the young Johanna. I feel terrible I was away on the continent and missed your wedding. But word holds she'll serve as an excellent breeder. I'm happy for you, darling."

Johanna's cheeks burned. She flew up the stairs and into their chamber. Once her heart was safely ensconced from their treacherous confidences, she paced before the large windows, fighting to control the edges of panic. She would not allow herself to think the past month meant nothing to Nicholas.

A shuffle of horses' hooves drew her to the curtained window overlooking the front court. Nicholas was helping a fair-haired beauty onto her mount. Before she galloped away on the gentle mare, she swooped down and planted a full kiss on his mouth.

Johanna clutched her stomach and, in a mad dash across the room, heaved, spilling her breakfast into the chamber pot. Then she collapsed into a faint.

❧❀❧

Nicholas dipped the cloth into the cool water and pressed it again to Johanna's forehead, and then stroked along her neck and between her breasts as she slept fitfully. His maid, Bridie, fluttered about like a nervous bird, setting his teeth on edge.

"She's suffered a stroke," Bridie bemoaned, glaring at him with a vengeance. "'Tis no wonder with what yiv put her through."

Nicholas had no idea what the woman was talking about but had no patience for it.

Johanna lay nauseous and faint for days, unable to keep down any food but dry bread. He waited impatiently for the doctor as he ran his hand over her flushed skin.

"Go see to that doctor again," he ordered brusquely. "What could be keeping the man?" he muttered. Bridie had wasted no time in chasing off to find out, leaving him mercifully alone. The faithful servant had warmed to Johanna immediately as did all the servants. Nicholas hardly recognized the spoiled young girl he met just two months ago. She had blossomed under the freedom he allowed her and carried her responsibilities with the grace of a true duchess.

He opened her dressing gown down to her waist and drew it aside to cool her. She shifted and moaned, exhausted from dry heaving for hours.

He tried not to react to the sight of her ripe nipples, but they looked different against her translucent skin. It had been days since he had taken her, and he craved the communion with her that he had come to expect and need. He fought down his fear that her illness was something serious as he drew the cooling cloth over her throat and over her breasts that rose and fell in light sleep.

Her nipples were browner, less pink. He traced a finger along a swollen nipple and as it hardened and lengthened, his groin swelled.

The outer edge of the areola was less defined. He bent for a lick . . . tasted the same—delicious. She moaned.

He pinched her nipple lightly.

She moaned again, but this time a frown creased her brow as though he'd hurt her.

He cupped her breasts in his palms and considered them, feeling their weight. Beautiful and lush and somehow heavier, he was sure of it.

The doctor burst into the room and Nicholas covered his wife and stepped aside. After the physician's cursory examination, he turned to Nicholas. "When was her last monthly flow?"

Nicholas looked at him blankly.

"Your Grace?" The doctor waited.

Nicholas blinked. "She . . . she hasn't had one."

"Well then . . ." The doctor smiled. "You've been married a month? I expect with a man like yourself . . ." His voice trailed off into a soft chuckle.

⁂🜚☙⁂

"Are you sure you want to do this, Milady?" Bridie's excitable flapping had lit Johanna's nerves to a fever pitch.

"Hush Bridie, and finish before he returns." Johanna wanted her things set up in her new chamber so she could retire there tonight. She had promised herself that the first day she was up and about she would move, before Nicholas had to tell her. Although separate rooms were customary with the upper class, she and Nicholas had never discussed any future arrangements so Johanna had foolishly thought she'd continue to share his bed. At least that was what she had hoped until she saw him with the blond Countess.

It hurt that he would take his pleasure elsewhere until he required another heir. Indeed, at this moment, he was visiting Lady Hamilton, the vivacious blond who he had assisted in mounting her horse . . . Johanna grew furious. He was no doubt mounting *her* now.

Johanna flung the brush and shattered the mirror. Bridie jumped. Then Johanna burst into tears.

"Ah, now there," Bridie murmured, leading her to the cushioned divan by the fire. "You've gotten yourself in a state and all for nothing. His Grace will be moving yer things back as soon as he sees this foolishness."

"He's with her now, Bridie," Johanna sobbed.

"Aye, and yiv let yer imagination get away with ya. The lady needed talkin' to, privately, what with the way she hounds him."

As Bridie rose at the sound of heavy footfalls, Johanna swiped a soft hanky to her tear-strained eyes. If she wasn't strong, Nicholas would forever have the upper hand and this could represent an important turning point in their marriage.

He swept into the room, dark and dangerous, and as always vibrating with energy.

Johanna dabbed her eyes before facing him and watched as he strode confidently toward her, having yet to notice the rearrangement of the chambers. Bridie slipped out.

When he looked at her, his eyes were warm coals, the light from the candles reflecting their intensity. "You're better I see," he murmured, gathering her up. As he kissed along her eyebrows, she drank in the leathery outdoor scent of him, fresh from his ride. She ran her forehead against the rough feel of his chin. He felt so warm and safe, she wanted to cry.

Then he stiffened. His head jerked up, and when she looked at him, he set her from him and then turned in a quick arc around the center of the room, taking in the shattered mirror.

He flung open the armoire.

She tensed at the sight of his massive shoulders bunching under his linen shirt. She knew how powerful he was and, although he'd never hurt her, she was awed by his virility.

He took a cautious step toward her, his face impassive. "Where are your things?" Although his voice was controlled, his eyes were on fire.

She stumbled back, the raw power of him like a gale of wind pushing at her. "I . . . my things are in my chamber adjoining yours."

A muscle jumped in his jaw. "You will move them back."

He began pulling his shirttails out of his breeches. The chords of his biceps flexed and jumped with the movement, and then he stripped the cloth off, carelessly flinging it over the chair rest. She swallowed down her immediate response to his muscled torso as he sat to unlace his boots. Then she realized he had tossed the order over his shoulder as though the matter was settled.

She began a slow boil. "I will not," she answered him quietly.

He raised his head. She awaited his explosion, clutching the slippery satin ribbons of her sheer tulle nightgown with nervous fingers. The air hummed with vibrancy, and the flickering candles jumped anxiously along the walls.

Then he heaved a sigh and dragged a hand slowly through the top of his scalp. Her heart clenched, he seemed so weary of a sudden. She wanted to press his tousled head to her breast and comfort him.

"Nicholas?" She beckoned with her heart for him to say what she longed to hear, yet for which she dared not hope.

"Johanna," he said quietly. "You will sleep with me." He walked to the mantle and picked up a fluted glass and then reached for the flask of brandy.

"Why?"

He stopped midpour, the amber liquid sloshing the sides in pregnant pause before he resumed, but the width of his shoulders drooped in resignation. "You are my wife, it is enough."

"I think not, your Grace," she clipped, turning on her heels and padding over to her connecting suite.

"Johanna!" he growled.

She continued on through the door into a sea of lace and flowers, so lovely, yet with not a hint of his strong presence. Her heart sank. She almost turned and ran into his arms, begging him to love her, but her sense of pride stopped her along with her determination to force him to acknowledge the strength of his feelings for her . . . if indeed he did love her.

The long mirror on the dressing table reflected his image at her back, looming in the doorway, half naked and male. The lines along his forehead deepened as he took in the contents of the room. She picked up her brush and stood before the mirror watching him as she idly ran the soft bristles down her scalp to the tips of her curls, the wedding nightgown that he loved draping her body.

He drew up in back of her and the gentleness in his eyes made her heart ache.

His large hands came around her waist as he settled his chin on her shoulder and stroked down the length of her belly and then up again. "I won't press myself upon you while you're with child, our child, if that is what concerns you." He met her gaze in the mirror and tenderly ran one fingertip down the length of her throat, languidly taking in its curve.

Hope sprang in her heart. He wanted her, not just her body or her abilities to breed. Now she needed to hear him say it. Her body was already surrendering to him, but she held firm.

"Then why should I share your bed?"

Her unwavering gaze pierced his black orbs and set them on fire.

He dropped his hands, fisting them. "You will do as you are told."

He walked briskly to her wardrobe and gathered up an impressive pile of lacy undergarments and stomped to his room, making a show of it.

She smiled inwardly but didn't budge.

"We'll move the rest in the morning, now come to bed."

"No."

"Johanna," he growled, marching toward her, about to pick her up but then he stopped. She knew he was worried about her delicate condition. "Don't make me haul you in there."

"I *won't* and you *won't*, Nicholas," she echoed back to him his arrogant commands the day he ravished her in the coach. Her stomach did a somersault at the memory.

He was pacing furiously now, dragging his hand through his scalp in earnest. "By the sword," he grumbled, "you are the most unbiddable female. And I have the gross misfortune . . ."

Her heart stopped while her mind finished his words—*the misfortune of being your husband.*

"Of all the stupid, inept things," he railed, shaking his head. "By the saints, I'll be a laughing stock," he grumbled more to himself than to her. "From the moment I laid eyes on you I should have known."

In a fury, he swung wide the connecting door to their suites. "'Tis no greater curse than for a man to have fallen in love with his own wife. Now get in here, Johanna!"

The room began to spin as she stared at his reflection filling the archway, his massive chest heaving and his rock hard stomach glistening with sweat. He was frighteningly beautiful, a barbarian, and he had just confessed that he was in love with her.

She turned as though in a dream. "What did you say?" she breathed.

"I said get in—"

"Before that," she said, her voice strained as she walked with deliberate steadiness toward his tall towering height. His warmth penetrated her as she drew closer. "The first part," she questioned him, her heart in her eyes as she continued to float toward him.

"I said you were a curse." He feigned unbridled annoyance and motioned her through the door. But his eyes betrayed him . . . his dark, tender eyes.

She stopped before him and placed a tentative hand on his chest. The hard warmth of him vibrated under her silky touch. His muscles jumped in response.

"Say it again," she pleaded, her voice soft and unsure, already worried she had misunderstood.

The naked emotion in his expression as he covered her hand with his and drew her closer vanished any lingering doubt.

"By all the heavenly saints, you'll be the downfall of me, Johanna, but I love you." He gathered her up into the strong warmth of his arms and laid her cheek against the dark fur of his chest. The steady drum of his heart echoed straight to her own and lingered and mixed until they beat as one.

"I love you, Nicholas," she breathed, sinking into his roughened skin, drinking in his scent that was so distinctly his and wanting to get closer.

He kissed the top of her head and whispered again that he loved her. "I want only you, Johanna . . . all of you. To share my bed, my life . . . to share my heart." He pulled at one delicate ribbon and let the filmy fabric whisper off her breast. He stroked her gently. "Surrender to me, Johanna, and let me love you."

"Yes, Nicholas. I surrender only to you, my love, my husband."

He lifted her into his arms in one large sweep and nuzzled her neck as he whispered once again the words of love she had so longed to hear. And she thought of only the days and *nights* they would spend together . . . in surrender . . . to each other.

About the author:

Kathryn Anne Dubois is a pseudonym for a public school teacher, a mother of five, and a wife of twenty-eight years who lives the life of a soccer mom in New Jersey. When she is not tending to her family and writing, she is enjoying her other passions—gardening, reading, sewing, and downhill skiing.

Kissing the Hunter

by Angela Knight

Chapter One

The binoculars felt slick in Logan McLean's hands, and sweat beaded his forehead. His thighs cramped from crouching in the notch of the tree, while mosquitos for miles raided every inch of hot male skin they could reach. Still, Logan resisted the urge to wipe, stretch or swat. He knew the smallest movement could draw the attention of his target and blow the whole thing.

A professional could take a little discomfort.

And in fact, the sweat, ache and bugs didn't really bother him; discomfort—and worse—was part of his job. As a Navy SEAL, Logan had endured gunshot wounds, bad parachute jumps, and the general stupidity of the military's top brass. After ten years as a special forces warrior, very little could shake his concentration.

But having a hard-on for a woman he'd come to kill—now, *that* bothered him.

He focused the binoculars past the lace curtains as Virginia Hart licked her way up her date's naked torso. *Wrong direction, lady*, Logan thought; the path of tiny kisses and nibbles she pressed to the guy's belly led away from his straining cock. Her date evidently agreed: he twisted in the sheets like a man in torment, though the expression on his face did not suggest pain of any kind.

Virginia lifted her head and gave Loverboy a look of wicked teasing with those big, dark eyes, her pretty chocolate curls cascading over his naked thighs in a silken waterfall. Logan set his teeth and tried to ignore the way his own erection rasped against his fly.

He didn't like this job one damn bit.

Killing Ivanov had been different. Shooting an arrow into that bastard's heart had been an act of justice and revenge, but it had also saved countless women from the brutal death Gwen had suffered.

And no one but Logan could have done it. The cops had certainly been helpless.

But killing a woman didn't sit that easily. Yeah, he'd shot that female terrorist in Lebanon a couple of years ago, but she'd been drawing a bead on him at the time. Besides, the little bitch had just blown up a busload of kids to make a point, and she and her psychotic buddies planned to bomb a school next. That she still starred in his nightmares proved conclusively that he had an overactive conscience.

Oh, God. Virginia had stopped to lick the guy's belly button. His cock thrust through her curtain of curls as he writhed and laughed. She just went right on nibbling, her gorgeous, heart-shaped butt in the air.

Logan focused his binoculars and felt his mouth go dry. No doubt about it, Virginia had a truly world-class ass, the kind any man would love to get his hands on. And since she wore nothing but a black lace garter belt and a pair of silk stockings, he had an excellent view of those taut curves and the plump rose lips between them. Not to mention her long, amazing legs with their muscled thighs and slender calves.

Her breasts tempted him even more. Round and pink-tipped, they swayed seductively with every wiggle, nipples hard as cherry pits as they brushed the guy's chest. Logan had no idea how her partner kept his hands off them. If he'd been in the guy's place, he sure as hell wouldn't be lying in the sheets like a limp mackerel.

Okay, so maybe "limp" wasn't exactly the word.

He grinned behind his binoculars as the guy wrapped both hands in Virginia's hair and began moaning something. Probably pleas for mercy . . .

Logan's grin faded. Gwen had pleaded for mercy. They all had.

Shit.

What the fuck was he thinking? He wasn't here to stare at Virginia's ass and fantasize about making love to her. He'd come to kill her, and he damn well couldn't let himself forget it. *She may look like a woman,* Logan thought, *but she's not. And if she is just a woman, I'm not going to touch a hair on her pretty little head.*

Which was why Virginia was still alive. He could have finished this an hour ago, but he had to make sure she deserved it. He had no intention of murdering an innocent by mistake.

The guy squirmed. Virginia threw back her head and laughed, her tight brunette curls spilling over his belly like a dark waterfall. Reaching up, she traced a circle around his navel with a long, delicate finger and watched as he pumped his hips pleadingly.

Logan refocused his binoculars, feeling like a pervert.

Ivanov could be wrong. Hell, he'd been stark, staring crazy; Logan had known that the first time he'd read those journals. The bastard's gloating descriptions of torture and murder had haunted Logan for months. And the video tapes . . .

When he'd stuck the tape labeled "Brandy Martin" in Ivanov's VCR the night he'd broken in, he reasoned he had to be sure those journals weren't just a sick fantasy. Now he wished he'd just killed the bastard on the spot instead of infecting himself with the kind of nightmares that ate a man's soul.

Even on fast forward, it had taken Brandy so damn long to die under Ivanov's knife. Until finally the blade had flashed across her throat and finished it. That last, choked scream still rang in Logan's nightmares.

Unable to take anymore, he'd finally hit the stop button. Looking up, he'd seen another tape on the shelf above the VCR. Its neatly written label read "Gwen McLean." He'd vomited right between the toes of his boots.

Logan had killed Ivanov an hour later. Too late to save Gwen.

He'd loved her, married her, taken her to his bed. But he'd been in the middle of the Pacific Ocean the one time she'd needed him. Even if the marriage had been something less than he'd hoped, knowing she'd died the way she did ate at him. He'd had so many screaming nightmares in the past year his bunkmates thought he was cracking up.

He saw a way out eight days ago, when he'd found the last journal in the trunk of his car. He thought he'd destroyed them all, but it must have slipped under the floor mat when he'd disposed of Ivanov's body and the rest of those nasty little trophies.

Logan had been about to burn the thing when he'd glimpsed the passage about Virginia. Reading it, he'd realized there was another Ivanov out there. And he'd known he had to do something about it. If nothing else, maybe killing the monster would lay his own demons to rest.

Twenty-four hours and one leave request later, he was on a plane for Georgia.

For all the good it had done him. He'd had Virginia under surveillance for the past week, and until tonight, she'd never even set foot out the door of her neat little Victorian house. If she had any friends, let alone lovers, they never visited. Even the phone tap he'd planted the morning after his arrival had come up empty.

There'd been no physical evidence either. Unlike Ivanov, Virginia evidently didn't have a trophy collection—and Logan had looked pretty damn thoroughly when he'd broken in to install the tap. His search turned up nothing but a houseful of pretty, female stuff; flowers and antiques and all those paintings she did. Hell, the only thing she owned that looked even remotely suggestive was the portrait of the naked guy hanging over her couch.

Big and blond, he was built like an athlete, with a narrow, handsome face and a Roman nose. And judging from the heat in those painted green eyes, he'd really, really liked Virginia.

Logan saw why when he'd walked into her bedroom and gotten his first good look at the artist herself. She was curled on her side asleep in her big brass bed, one pink nipple of her full breasts peeking over the V neckline of her peach negligee. Her sleeping profile seemed as innocent as the Virgin Mary's framed against all those wild curls.

She didn't look like a monster. She looked . . . familiar. Yet he'd never seen her before.

Logan had gotten out of there in a hurry, feeling as if somebody should shoot him as a public service.

When Virginia had sauntered out of her house earlier this evening in that little black dress, Logan had thought he'd finally hit pay dirt. Yet three hours had gone by since she'd picked Loverboy up in that bar, and the only torturing she'd done involved her tongue. And her hands. And the way she wiggled that tempting little butt.

What if she was just as innocent as she seemed?

Maybe he should pack up his bow and vanish before the neighbors called the police. One look at Logan playing peeping Tarzan in the tree outside Loverboy's bedroom, and the cops would haul his ass to jail.

But if he bailed on this God-awful job and Ivanov was right, the guy currently begging Virginia to put his dick in her mouth would be dead in an hour. And if he died anything like Gwen . . .

Oh, hell.

Logan watched Virginia lap the guy's nipples, her tongue a long pink curve, her lips smiling. She slipped a slender hand down and closed it over Loverboy's cock. Subjected him to a few long strokes. Then, just when he trembled on the verge of losing it, she dropped her hand down to his balls for a gentle, lingering caress. Logan shifted and almost fell out of his tree.

OK, Virginia, he thought, irritated and aroused, *fuck him, already. Or whatever it is you're going to do.*

Instead she turned around, opened her sweet lips, and slid them down over the dark rose head of Loverboy's dick. He arched his back, his mouth opening in a yell that was audible right through the closed window.

Logan started to grab for his bow, but relaxed when he saw the guy's expression. That had definitely not been a cry of pain. Remembering what he'd thought she'd done, Logan shuddered. *Damn, there's an image to make a man swear off blow jobs.*

Then he took another look. *On second thought . . .*

Virginia suckled Loverboy slowly, savoring every inch of his cock. Gwen had given head like somebody doing a duty, something she did to get Logan off even though she considered it physically tiresome and uncomfortable. He'd always ended up stopping her and going on to something else.

Yet Virginia wore an expression of erotic delight even though the guy was too lost in his own pleasure to notice. And she took him deep, with a skill that impressed Logan as much as it turned him on, sucking and bobbing until Loverboy writhed in ecstasy.

By the time the blond grabbed the back of her head and started pleading again, Logan felt like doing some begging himself. It took an effort to keep his hands off his zipper.

He damn well wasn't going to jerk off watching a woman he might have to kill.

⁂

It bothered Virginia, the sheer sensual delight she felt at Gary's silken length stroking her tongue, her lips. She could accept this only if she didn't take too much pleasure in it.

Time to wrap it up. She reached out and brushed his thoughts, looking for the proper incoherent jumble of late-stage lust.

Hot slut bitch, God, her mouth . . . The predatory contempt in Gary's mind steadied her. He was a cad, of course—she never took anyone she liked as a lover, since she didn't want to feel too much. She was definitely safe from this one, who was using her as surely as she was using him.

Virginia gently stroked a hand between his legs, testing the drum tautness of his sac. He was almost ready. She wanted him to come almost as soon as she mounted him. Though she needed Gary's orgasm, she had no intention of riding him long enough to reach her own peak. The only man Virginia had ever climaxed with was her husband, and she meant to keep it that way.

Still, at times the temptation tormented her. Thirty-two years was a long, long time, even for one of her kind.

Sometimes Virginia thought she should give up. John wouldn't return, no matter what he'd promised. How could he, after what Ivanov had done to him?

She should look for some handsome Kith and turn him. It could never be the same, but at least she wouldn't be forced into this empty, endless game of pleasuring blackguards to survive. Unfortunately, until she found one of her own kind, she had very little choice. Besides, John had made her promise to wait for him.

Yet every time she crept from a man's bed before the sun rose, Virginia felt a wave of crushing loneliness and guilt. She knew her husband wouldn't have blamed her for what she had to do to survive, but the guilt had never faded.

The first one had been the worst. It had been only two weeks after John's murder, and she'd never have taken the man at all if the Hunger hadn't driven her to it. She'd been so far gone she remembered nothing about it except the shame afterward—and the relief she hadn't hurt her partner in her need.

"I'm coming!" Gary gasped, jolting her out of her thoughts.

Virginia studied his face appraisingly. Not yet. But soon. Another minute, maybe two, and it would be safe to mount him.

❦

God, she was the most erotic thing Logan had ever seen. Her body formed a lush, curving line as she bent over Loverboy, her lips tight around his shaft, her breasts so full and round Logan ached to get his hands on them. Other women looked lewd and clumsy sucking a man off, but Virginia somehow managed to do it with the slow, sensuous grace of a geisha performing a tea ceremony.

Face it, McLean, Logan thought, *Ivanov was crazy.* The passage about Virginia in that journal was nothing more than the delusion of a sick mind with dreams of torturing a woman who couldn't die. Embedding an arrow in his heart had been far less than the psychotic fuck deserved.

Remembering Ivanov's agonized writhing, Logan prayed Virginia wouldn't give him a reason to kill her. It was one thing to put a bullet through a female terrorist's skull, but to drive an arrow between those perfect breasts and watch Virginia suffer the same way . . .

Suddenly she lifted her full lips from the guy's erection and sat up.

Murmuring something, she threw a long leg over his hips and strad-dled him. He lunged up and grabbed for her, looking wild around the eyes.

She caught his reaching hands and pushed him back down, pin-ning him until she could impale herself on his cock. The muscles in his powerful arms flexed, but she just laughed and held him still as she be-gan to pump.

Logan stiffened. The guy easily outweighed her by seventy pounds, but tiny little Virginia had just overpowered him.

He felt his heart sink. Ivanov was right.

Maybe not, Logan cautioned himself as she rose and fell, back arched until her breasts thrust out in tempting invitation. Maybe the guy hadn't really tried to grab her. Maybe . . .

She rolled her hips, grinding down hard. Her partner clenched his eyes shut and opened his mouth to bellow out his orgasm.

Virginia's pretty lips peeled back from her teeth. As Logan watched, two needle-sharp fangs descended from her upper jaw.

Ah, hell.

No way he could make a heart shot at this angle. He had to get closer.

The window was five feet away. An easy jump.

Virginia was bending to taste the big vein under her lover's chin when the window exploded in a shower of glass. Something black shot through it with a roar of male fury that sounded a lot like . . . Betrayal?

Superhuman reflexes catapulted her off Gary's body and halfway across the room. *No!* Virginia jolted to a stop inches from the door. She was the vampire, the strong one, and she had a duty to defend her lover. She'd sworn she'd never let another man die. Straightening her shoulders, she forced herself to face the intruder.

He wore something black and military, and he towered as he moved toward her, all muscular menace. She wondered how he'd even maneuvered those broad, bull shoulders through the window.

A knit mask covered his face, except for a slit across the eyes. He'd blackened the skin that showed through the opening, and his nar-rowed blue gaze glittered like ice against the dark paint. In his gloved hands he held a compound bow, an arrow nocked and pointed at her heart. Taking a closer look, Virginia felt ice chill her veins. The wooden shaft lacked the usual steel tip; it had simply been whittled to a lethal point. Making it a very serviceable stake.

Oh, God. He knew what she was.

"What the fuck is this!" Gary roared, coming off the bed.

Stop! Virginia thought, reaching into her lover's mind with a psychic command that froze him in his tracks. She didn't dare let him jar the assassin's elbow; if those big hands slipped on that arrow, she'd be impaled like a butterfly on a hatpin.

Don't panic, Virginia, she told herself. *Just use the power.*

She made herself meet the stranger's cold blue eyes and reached for the mind behind them. "Put it down," she ordered, hating the breathless note in her own voice. "You don't want to hurt me."

With an easy flex of those powerful shoulders, the assassin drew the bow to its full extension. "Actually, I do."

Virginia froze in shock as her telepathic command failed to penetrate the shield of his thoughts. He should have been as helpless to disobey as Gary—as helpless as any other man she'd ever turned her power on. Instead it failed to even touch him. She knew what that meant.

He was one of the Kith—the very few who could become vampires.

Virginia swallowed a panicky laugh. She'd finally met the man she'd been searching for, and he was about to shoot a yard-long piece of wood through her heart.

Just her luck.

☙⟨ೞ⟩❧

Goddamn it, Logan, shoot.

But as Virginia looked at him with wide brown eyes and pink lips parted in terror, he couldn't seem to send the arrow on its way.

Funny. Ivanov had said the exact same thing she had a minute ago—"Put it down!" As if the command alone would be enough to stop a man intent on killing. When Logan hadn't immediately dropped his bow, there'd been a split second when Ivanov had worn the same expression of amazed comprehension Virginia wore now.

But that night Logan hadn't hesitated. His arrow thudded home in Ivanov's chest, and the vampire died snarling and growling like a wolf.

He hadn't turned into a neat pile of dust the way they did in the movies. For a moment, Logan had wondered if the vampirism Ivanov had claimed in his journals was just another of the sick fuck's fantasies. But a look at those fangs proved otherwise.

Evidently the movies were wrong about a lot of things.

"Why are you doing this?" Virginia asked, a quaver in her voice, her lovely breasts trembling with each panting breath. He would not, dammit, think how obscene the arrow would look buried between them.

"You know why." Logan flexed his hands on the bow. "And you know why you have to be stopped." So what if she weighed maybe a hundred pounds soaking wet, and had the prettiest tits he'd ever seen in his life? He couldn't let her go on killing people.

She shrank back, crossing her arms protectively across those sweet breasts and the heart beneath them. The gesture struck him as pitiful, and he fought to harden his resolve.

Her dark eyes were focused on the arrow. "I don't know what you think I've done, but I haven't hurt anyone."

"Don't give me that," he snapped. "I saw the fangs, lady."

She'd gone as pale as fresh snow, and Logan felt like a monster. Stupid, stupid; *she* was the monster. Why did everything in him rebel at what he had to do? He should have killed her by now. *You know your duty*, he told himself savagely. *Do it.*

He thought of the tape Ivanov had made of that poor girl, her screams and pleas as the vampire murdered her. He made himself remember Gwen's body in the morgue, tiny and bloodless and dead.

Cleansing, blessed rage roared through him. Logan clenched his teeth and drew in a breath, about to send the arrow on its way . . .

"Put it up," a male voice roared, "or I'll blow your fucking head off!"

Startled, Logan looked over at Virginia's partner—and down the muzzle of the nine-millimeter Smith & Wesson in his hand.

Oh, hell. He'd been so caught up in the vampire he'd forgotten to make sure her would-be victim didn't go for a gun. Unfortunately, Loverboy kept one right by the bed, judging from the open drawer in the night stand.

"Drop the bow, Robin Hood!" the man barked again. Though naked, he was almost as tall as Logan, and he held the pistol like a man who knew what to do with it.

Logan looked back at Virginia, who stared from him to her partner in shock. If he let himself be captured, he'd end up in jail on attempted murder charges. And Loverboy wouldn't live out the night.

Virginia's stud took two cocky steps toward him. Seeing his chance, Logan let up the tension on the bow and ducked into a spinning kick. The toe of his combat boot slammed into Loverboy's hand, and the gun went flying. As the stud watched his weapon skid under the bed, Logan gave him an uppercut that folded his knees and put him out for the count. Logan reached for him, meaning to make sure he stayed down until this was finished . . .

"Leave him alone," a feminine voice cried. "You came for me. So come and get me!"

Logan whirled as Virginia scooped up her little black dress, shrugged it over her head, and lunged for the window. The fabric barely made it over her magnificent ass by the time she leaped through the broken glass like a gazelle.

Stunned, he took one long stride and looked through the shattered glass after her, the bow in his hand. She'd already hit the ground and was running hard. He nocked the arrow and drew a bead on her slim, fleeing body.

Shit. Vampire or not, Logan couldn't shoot a woman in the back.

Cursing his own misplaced chivalry, he tucked the bow and arrow under one arm and plunged after her. He hit the ground with his knees bent to absorb the shock, just as he had on countless parachute jumps. But as he landed, Logan heard an ominous rattle—arrows falling from the quiver he wore across his back. No time to collect them. Cursing, he shot off in hot pursuit of the vampire through the moonlit night.

Which had to be, hands down, the stupidest thing he'd ever done in his life.

She was headed straight for the woods behind Loverboy's house. Logan would have done the same in her shoes, if he could see in the dark. He couldn't, which begged the question what the hell he thought he was doing following her.

She was going to eat his ass, and it would serve him right.

Virginia ran hard, increasing the lead she had on the assassin as her heart pounded in desperate lunges in her chest. She hadn't felt such terror since John's murder.

When she'd looked down that arrow into those ice pale eyes, she'd thought she was finished. She'd watched the assassin's fingers flex, about to send the arrow on its way. And she'd seen her death in his eyes.

If Gary hadn't stopped him . . .

The question was, what should she do now? Yes, she could outrun the assassin, but what if he knew where she lived? He'd been prepared for her; that arrow indicated he knew exactly what he hunted, and knew no bullet would do the job. If he was as knowledgeable about where she lived as what she was, she wouldn't be safe even if she escaped. He could come for her in the morning while she slept the deep sleep of her kind. And she'd never wake up.

She had to do something about him, and she had to do it now. Now, while she had the advantage in the darkness. While she could become the hunter.

Virginia halted her headlong plunge and turned. She felt such terror her stomach pitched like a ship in a gale, but she had no choice. *He's only human,* she told herself. *I've got five times his strength and speed.*

Too bad she'd never thrown a punch in her life. She could almost hear her mother now: *"Ladies do not fight, Virginia."* A lady maintained her dignity, used her tongue and her wits as weapons. But somehow she doubted a ringing set-down would stop an assassin bent on vampire slaying.

Well, she would just have to manage. She would try talking first. And if that didn't work . . .

How much skill could it take to break a man's neck?

Logan moved through the woods, wishing he had a pair of night vision goggles. He couldn't think of anything more brainless than chasing a vampire in the dark.

Too bad. He had to do it anyway.

Logan had been a Navy SEAL since he was twenty—planting underwater explosives; jumping out of airplanes; hunting terrorists through the Mideast. The whole Sea, Air, and Land thing that gave the SEALs their name. They were the best special forces warriors in the world, and he'd earned a place among them.

He could do this too, even though he could see no possible victory in it. If he won, Logan knew killing lush little Virginia would haunt him the rest of his life. And he had enough women haunting him as it was. On the other hand, if he lost, she'd rip out his throat.

Hell with it. He just wouldn't lose. This wasn't the first time doing his duty had turned his stomach.

As he'd been taught, Logan blanked his mind and focused himself, stretching his senses for the least sound, the least scent, that might reveal where she was. And heard nothing. No crunch and scuff of running feet through the leaves, no faint whiff of perfume. Nothing.

She'd stopped. But where?

Chapter Two

Virginia stood in the deep night shadows of the trees and watched the assassin slip through patches of moonlight like a ghost. He was so big, so broad, yet he moved like a predator, with a silent, liquid skill that spoke of years of training. Despite her superhuman strength and speed, despite the vampire vision that allowed her to see in the dark, his feral grace made her feel clumsy.

He frightened her, but something about him perversely attracted her as well. She'd become a connoisseur of masculinity over one hundred and seventy-two years as a vampire, and this man intrigued her as no one had in three decades.

No one since John, the vampire who'd made and married her.

The assassin reminded her a little of her husband, though she had no idea why. He was even bigger than John had been, with deadly menace rather than gentle compassion in those ice-pale eyes. And her love would never have turned his strength against a woman.

Yet something in her called to him. Because he was Kith? Did her instincts see him as a potential mate simply because he could become a vampire?

Not that it mattered. She still had to convince him to leave her alone—or do whatever she had to do if the attempt failed.

"You know," Virginia said as he glided past, "I'm not a killer. I take no more than a pint at most."

The assassin rumbled triumphantly in his throat as he whirled toward her like a hungry wolf. Alarmed, Virginia retreated. He followed her, tracking the scuff of her feet in the leaves.

Terror sent her heart lunging in her chest. She might be far stronger than he, but his height and brawn intimidated her. And staring into that black mask and those cold blue eyes was coldly unnerving.

Virginia licked her dry lips and tried again to reach him. "If you asked my lovers, they'd consider the pleasure I give them a fair exchange for a little blood."

"Oh, I don't doubt they die smiling." He slipped the bow off his shoulder and nocked an arrow. "But they still die."

"Other than my teeth and whatever bad movies you've seen, what makes you so certain I'm a killer?" She slipped silently to one side. Not realizing she'd moved, he lifted the bow and pointed his arrow in the direction her voice had come from. Virginia smiled in relief. He might be a skilled warrior, but he couldn't see in the dark. She did have that advantage.

"I've dealt with somebody like you before," he said, blue eyes narrowing even more with an expression that sent a chill up her spine. But she also recognized the undercurrent of pain beneath the rage. She'd seen it in her own mirror often enough.

"And he hurt someone you love." *Oh, wonderful.* "Most of us wouldn't dream of killing—there's no reason for it. But there are psychotics among us, just as there are among mortals." Her mouth twisted bitterly. "One of them murdered my husband."

His blue eyes flickered, then steadied as he turned to direct the arrow toward her voice. She ducked aside again. "Sorry, the grieving widow act doesn't play. I saw you with Loverboy's dick down your throat, remember?"

His words struck deep into her wounded soul. "How *dare* you judge me? I have grieved for John Hart every day for the past thirty-two years!"

"But I'll bet there were always plenty of men around to comfort you." His eyes crinkled with the cynical smile his mask hid as the arrow pivoted toward her again.

"So you mean to kill me because you find my morals dubious?"

"It's not the blow jobs that bother me. It's the other things you do with that hot little mouth."

"I told you, I don't kill my lovers," Virginia gritted, stepping from side to side as he tried to get a fix on her. "Ask them. I'll give you names."

He snorted. "Who are you trying to kid? You could make them say anything you wanted."

"But they're alive to say it."

"Unless they're strangers you picked off the street and ordered to lie for you."

She'd hoped to reason with him, but it was obvious he'd never listen. "Doesn't it bother you that I might be telling the truth? Is it that easy to kill just on suspicion?"

He laughed shortly. "It's evidently a lot harder for me to kill than it is for you."

"Let's find out." She stepped directly into a pool of moonlight shooting through the trees.

Virginia watched his eyes widen behind the mask as he saw her. Before he could react, she snatched the bow out of his hands and snapped it in two.

Damn, she was as strong and quick as he'd feared.

He struck out at her in sheer reflex, a hard right cross. Surprisingly, the punch actually landed on her elegant little nose. Logan winced at her feminine cry of pain as she staggered. His chivalrous instincts protested, but not enough to keep him from ducking her return swing. She was incredibly fast; he dodged her blurring fist more by training and instinct than sight. Good thing he'd been taking martial arts since childhood, or that blow would have snapped his head off his neck.

Her attack left her wide open for a gut punch, but as Logan looked at her slender torso with its pretty breasts and curvy hips, he found he couldn't bury his big fist in it. *Idiot*, he thought. *She's going to break you in two.*

Virginia threw another lightning blow straight at his jaw, and he swung an arm up to deflect it. The impact jarred his teeth and sent pain bolting all the way to his shoulder. Hell. One punch from that dainty fist would put him down like a slaughtered ox.

Yet when her big dark eyes met his in the moonlight, they were wide with fear and desperation. Not exactly the confident gaze of a supernatural monster. She looked more like a tiny female trying to fight someone a foot taller and a hundred pounds heavier.

She's playing you, dumbass. Logan forced himself to circle her, looking for an opening. And he saw several; she made no effort to guard her head and torso. Virginia fought like somebody without any training whatsoever, not even the kind of skills most children picked up on the playground.

Which won't stop her from putting a fist through your skull, you stupid bastard. Logan hit her, punching straight out from the shoulder in a quick, hard jab.

Virginia stumbled back a pace and reached up to wipe at her mouth. She looked down at the smear of blood on her fingers and shot him a look of such betrayal he almost apologized.

Then she tried to cave in his head with another one of those clumsy, incredibly fast punches. He jerked back just in time.

Pulled off-balance by the power of her own swing, Virginia lost her balance. Logan stepped in, hooked a foot between her ankles and tripped her. As she yelped and tumbled, he pounced, smashing her into the ground with his greater weight. He grabbed one delicate wrist and jerked it up between her shoulder blades.

"What are you doing?" Her voice was pitched high with pain, and she froze under him, as if to keep him from hurting her any worse. "Let me go!"

"I don't think so," he growled back. But still, he hesitated.

She's a vampire, dammit. She rips out people's throats. Hell, she'd rip out my throat. Gritting his teeth, he drove his full weight against her, applying force to the shoulder joint. No matter how supernaturally strong she was, no matter how dense her bones, a joint was a joint, and it wouldn't take much pressure at all to dislocate her shoulder.

Virginia screamed and began to struggle. He forced himself to clamp down. She surged against him, her body small and lush and deceptively delicate against his, her round little butt pressing up against his belly.

Yet it was all he could do to hang on. With her vampire strength, wrestling with her felt like a ride on a pissed-off Brahma bull. Only there would be no rodeo clown to save his ass if he let her throw him. "Quit struggling or I'll break it."

"Don't!" she gasped. "Please, let me go! I'll just leave, I swear."

"Yeah, off to bite some other poor bastard." Clinging to her bucking body, Logan reached back for the quiver that hung between his shoulder blades. One last arrow rattled around back there. He'd have to drive it into her like a stake, but it wasn't as if he had a hell of a lot of choice.

"I haven't hurt anybody!" Virginia cried out. "Why won't you believe me?"

"Because I've seen your kind at work." His fingers found the arrow, and he pulled it free.

"Don't kill me!" She surged upward against his weight, lifting his two hundred pounds easily despite the agonizing grip that made her shriek in pain. Logan felt the bone start to give under his hand.

And realized he couldn't bring himself to break it. Something in him, some instinct deeper even than chivalry, could not bear to hurt Virginia Hart. Not because she was a woman. Because she was *her*. It didn't make sense—he didn't even know her—but it was true. Even the knowledge that she would kill him didn't seem to matter to his gut instinct against hurting her.

She screamed again. Because there didn't seem to be anything else he could do, Logan let go. Virginia exploded out of his hold, her elbow slamming into his jaw. Light burst like a bomb in his skull.

He wasn't surprised.

The man fell over her like a big, heavy blanket, completely limp. For a panicked instant, Virginia thought she'd killed him. Until she heard the beat of his heart and realized she'd knocked him cold by sheer, dumb luck.

For a moment she just lay there, her arms wrapped loosely around his broad back, savoring her relief. It had been far too close.

Then she saw the arrow in his lax fingers and wanted to run for her life. She might be a vampire, but he knew all those deadly oriental combat techniques. Human or not, he could actually kill her. But if she just left him here, he'd come after her when he came to.

So what was she going to do?

Virginia pushed him off her and sat up, swiping the hair out of her face. A leaf in her curls rasped against her fingers, and she picked it out of her hair while studying her attacker's masked face.

True, she could run. But even assuming he didn't know where she lived now, he could probably find out. And next time, he might ignore the chivalric qualms that had made him hesitate tonight.

She should kill him. It wouldn't even be that hard. His own arrow . . .

Virginia shuddered with revulsion. No. She'd never taken a life, not even when love and revenge cried out for it. True, this man had tried to kill her, but only because he thought she was some kind of supernatural serial murderer who had to be stopped.

Which, when she stopped to think about it, had been a rather heroic thing to do.

Impulsively, Virginia wrapped a fist in the soft wool of the hunter's mask and pulled it off. And instantly realized she should have left it alone.

Even with that stripe of black paint across his eyes, the assassin was so handsome he took her breath. His dark hair was cut short, close to his head, but a lone curl fell across his broad forehead. His face was all interesting angles and sensuous curves—high cheekbones with deep hollows sculpted beneath them, a narrow nose, a broad, square jaw, an arrogant chin cut with a shallow cleft. And he had the most beautiful mouth she'd ever seen. His upper lip was full with a deep bow, and his lower lip looked so lush and soft she'd love to suck on it.

He looked like the kind of hero who'd face a vampire armed with nothing more than a bow and acid sarcasm.

Oh, drat. What a time for her romantic streak to surface. Virginia sighed in disgust. Well, killing him had never really been an option anyway, even if he'd been ugly as a mud fence. She just wasn't a killer.

She frowned, studying his face again. There was something about him. Something she couldn't put her finger on . . . Virginia pushed the thought away. Romanticism again.

Maybe she could try reasoning with him one more time. She had a way with men. They'd never been able to resist her, even a hundred and seventy-one years ago when she'd been mortal herself.

A twinge of pain zinged up her arm, and Virginia frowned, massaging her abused shoulder. If she meant to talk to him, she'd better make sure he couldn't get those big hands on her while she did it.

Sighing, she reached down and scooped his massive body into her arms, then got to her feet. The movement hurt, but she ignored the ache and draped him over her uninjured shoulder. He was so broad most of him hung unsupported, and she had to brace him there with both hands.

Turning, she trudged back toward Gary's house and the car she'd left parked out front. She just hoped she'd be able to get the assassin to see reason. For both their sakes.

She was loading the hunter into her car when Gary burst through the front door, his eyes wide, his broad chest bare, a gun in his hand. He looked like the hero of a cop show. And knew it.

Virginia sighed again. She did not need this.

"Baby, what happened?" he demanded. She saw in his mind that he called her "baby" because he couldn't remember her name. "I came to and you were gone!"

"Don't worry about it, Gary," she told him, reaching across the hunter's waist to pull the seat belt across and buckle him in. The strap barely spanned the full width of his chest. "Go to bed and forget me."

"But . . ."

She looked up and caught his eyes in the moonlight. "Go to bed, Gary."

He straightened as her mind caught his, his eyes going blank. Without another word, he turned and headed back inside. With a tired sigh, Virginia walked around to the driver's seat and got into the car.

For a moment she slumped behind the wheel, feeling battered and exhausted. What was worse, she hadn't even managed to feed.

※(۞)ఞ

Logan woke to a headache that throbbed in time to his heartbeat. Never a good sign. With a groan, he tried to lift both hands to his aching skull. Pressure at his wrists kept his hands from moving more than a few inches.

His eyes flew open. An unfamiliar ceiling stretched above him, washed in soft, pale light.

The last thing he remembered, he'd been in the woods trying to subdue a vampire bare-handed. Obviously, it hadn't gone well.

And it was about to get even worse, Logan realized as he looked around. He lay in the middle of a king-sized brass bed with both wrists crossed and bound to the headboard with thick white rope. The fibers felt slick and soft against his skin, not scratchy like hemp or nylon. Silk? He gave an experimental tug and grimaced. Silk or not, that rope could have held a bull.

He tried to draw up his feet, but his ankles were bound too. "Oh, shit!"

"You do have such a way with words," a familiar voice said, sounding prim.

Logan swore again as Virginia Hart stepped through the bedroom door, dressed in a long robe with bell sleeves and a skirt so full it trailed on the ground. Belted snugly, the red velvet fabric did amazing things for a figure already too damn tempting for his peace of mind. A white silk gown showed between its red lapels, its V-neckline displaying enough cleavage to make his mouth go dry—and worry the hell out of him. A woman just didn't dress like that for a man who'd tried to kill her.

Unless she was a vampire, and he'd interrupted dinner . . .

Virginia studied him as he tried to gather his scattered thoughts. "Though obviously you know my name—among other things—I don't believe we've been introduced." She tilted her delicate little chin like Queen Victoria addressing a peasant. "My name is Virginia Hart. And you would be?"

"Logan McLean." He eyed her, reluctantly admiring the curls tumbling around her pretty oval face, the nervous glint in her brown eyes—and all that luscious cleavage. God, Virginia had breasts. "You look like Scarlett O'Hara waiting to be carried up the stairs," he said, then jerked at the rope around his wrists. "But I don't remember Scarlett tying Rhett to the bed."

"Maybe if she had, he *would* have given a damn."

Logan lifted a brow and tried to look as arrogant as he could with a desperately pounding heart. "Should I be concerned for my virtue or my blood supply?"

Virginia twisted the ornate rings on her left hand. "I just want to talk."

"Most people don't find it necessary to tie me up when they 'just want to talk.'"

"They might if you made a habit of trying to kill them."

He noticed she'd pulled off his mask, so he tried out his best charming grin. "What's a little attempted homicide between friends? Particularly given your eating habits."

"I told you, I don't kill. You've been watching too much television."

He remembered Ivanov's nasty little video collection. "Well, that's the God's honest truth."

She took a step back from his snarl. "What do you mean?"

"I'm referring," Logan gritted between clenched teeth, "to your boyfriend's collection of snuff tapes."

Virginia blinked, obviously bewildered. Her fingers worried at those rings again. Taking a closer look, he realized one was a heavy, elaborately engraved gold band, the other a wedding ring mounted with a very impressive emerald. Her dead husband's tastes had been expensive. "Boyfriend?" she asked, frowning. "You mean Gary?"

Logan frowned back. "Gary?"

"Gary Jennings. The man I was with tonight."

"I mean Vladik Ivanov."

She recoiled, disgust curling her full lips. "Ivanov? I assure you, Mr. McLean, that murdering pig is *not* my boyfriend."

He snorted. "Not since I put an arrow through his heart, anyway."

"An arrow through . . . ?" Big doe eyes widened in astonishment. "You killed Ivanov?"

"Oh, yeah." He felt a bloodthirsty grin twist his mouth.

"And you saw the body? You're sure?"

"Since I cremated his ass, yeah." He'd burned the corpse on a pyre built from Ivanov's own journals, tapes and souvenirs, using so damn much gasoline he almost incinerated himself in the process.

Virginia lit up like a Christmas tree with a startling, savage joy. She swept over to the side of the bed and grinned down at him in delight. "Oh, thank God! You don't know what this means to me!"

He blinked. "What?"

"I would have killed him myself thirty years ago, but my husband . . ." She shook her head. "You're even more courageous than I thought. *I* wouldn't have gone after that monster with a bow and arrow." She wrapped both arms around herself and shuddered. "He was . . . terrifying."

Logan remembered the flat, soulless eyes, the fanged snarl, the Bowie knife he'd used to make those cuts on Brandy as she writhed in her chains. She'd screamed like a damned soul as Ivanov licked at the slices with his obscenely long tongue. Every cut had been deeper than the last, until . . .

"Yeah," Logan said, his voice rough and cracked. "He butchered my wife."

Virginia's big, brown eyes filled, and she reached a hand down toward him as if to offer comfort. "You poor man."

The sympathy on that lovely face warmed something cold in him. He instantly fought to chill it again. *She's trying to sucker you. She's got you tied to the fucking bed, you moron.* "Save it, lady," he snapped, glaring up at her. "What—you lost your chance at Gary, and now you think you can con me into taking his place? Flash a little cleavage, cry big, pretty tears, give the vampire hunter a hard-on? Then fang me after I . . ." He rolled his hips in a deliberately obscene upward thrust. "Bet you think it'd be funny to suck me dry."

She stiffened. "I told you. . . ."

". . . 'I never drink more than a pint.' Save it, *vampire*. Come on, I know you want it." Logan tilted his chin up and twisted his head, offering his neck. "I know how you like to use that mouth. Drop the act, baby. The only difference between you and Ivanov is tits and a dick."

"Do you think you're the only one who's suffered?" Virginia flared, a single huge tear spilling over. "Ivanov cut out my husband's heart in front of me!"

She whirled away from him as her shoulders started to shake. Shocked out of his rage, he stared at her slender back, remembering the painting of the naked guy he'd seen downstairs when he'd broken in to install the tap. Had to be the husband.

Ivanov cut my husband's heart out in front of me! Logan found himself believing her. He was too familiar with that kind of agony not to recognize it in somebody else's voice.

Vampire or not, he realized Virginia had loved her dead husband as Gwen had never loved him. Thirty years, and she still grieved for him. Gwen had barely waited for Logan to take off on his last mission before picking up Ivanov in that bar. He forced his mind away from the sick, guilty rage that thought triggered.

In a low, quiet voice, Virginia said, "If you value your life, never compare me to that animal again. I'm grateful to you for killing him, but that will only take you so far." Without another word, she swept from the room.

Chapter Three

How could lips that spewed such venom be so sexy?

Resentfully, Virginia studied her captive from the doorway. It had taken her half an hour to stop crying, and yet here she was, back for another round.

Idiot.

It was the contrast that got to her, she decided. The assassin's blue eyes were hard and narrow as he stared defiantly at her, deep-set under thick, dark brows. Yet his lips looked soft and seductive, as though they knew all kinds of wicked things to do if only he'd let them. He had a killer's eyes and a lover's mouth, and she wanted to kiss him more than she'd ever wanted to kiss anybody in her life.

She should have left the mask on. And the rest of his clothes, too. True, if she hadn't searched him, she wouldn't have found the two guns, one in a shoulder holster, the other strapped to his ankle. The combat knife on his belt looked every bit as deadly, with its razor-sharp black blade and serrated edge.

The rest of his collection was just as sinister. In the other pouches of his fatigues, she'd found ammunition clips for the two guns, twenty-five feet of nylon cord . . . and a set of titanium manacles. They looked thick and strong enough to restrain even someone with a vampire's strength. She would have used them on him, but they were too small for those thick male wrists. Though just the right size for hers . . . *Don't think about that.*

So yes, searching Logan had been wise. But she hadn't had to strip him.

With her captive still out cold, Virginia had pulled off his body armor, the long-sleeve shirt he'd worn under it, and his combat boots, leaving him in his black T-shirt and fatigue pants. She'd left his black gloves on as well, to protect his wrists when she bound him.

Yes, he'd be more comfortable without all that bulky gear. And yes, she was safer now that she'd taken his weapons away. But neither rationale had motivated her decision to take off his clothes.

She'd just wanted to discover whether Logan's big body matched that gorgeous face. And God help her, it did. He had the build of an Olympic gymnast—broad shoulders, powerful arms, and a deep, strong chest. When she'd searched his pants, she'd felt long, heavy muscle in his thighs and calves. She'd been strongly tempted to unzip him and find out if other parts of his body matched those legs.

She winced in shame at the memory. Not only had she tied the poor man to the bed, now she was ogling him.

The *ton* would have been scandalized that Virginia Grayson had sunk to such depths. Then again, every last soul who'd been at her 1831 come-out was dust in his or her grave. Including John Alexander Hart, rakehell, vampire, and the love of her life.

Thinking of John, Virginia twisted her wedding rings back and forth on her finger. She had no business lusting after Logan. True, he was Kith—though he obviously didn't know it—and she hadn't encountered another male of her own kind in all the years since John's death. But wanting him felt disloyal. Besides, he had a venomous tongue and the vocabulary of a dock worker, and she really didn't like him at all. Even if he was handsome and insanely brave.

It didn't help that Logan had stopped her before she'd drunk from Gary. Since she always put off hunting until she was driven to it by raw need, the Hunger burned with such intensity now her blood practically boiled with it. The taste she'd had of Gary had only sharpened its edge.

And now she had to deal with her homicidal captive, in his black undershirt that showed off those gorgeous biceps and muscled torso, his kiss-me mouth and killer's eyes. Keeping her hands off him would be difficult, but Virginia had no choice. She would not stoop to rape.

The lush mouth she'd been staring at curled into a wry smile. "You're making me nervous, Virginia. The last time I saw somebody wearing that look, it was a Marine visiting a strip club after a six-month deployment. I have this urge to tell you I'm not that kind of guy."

Heat flooded her cheekbones, and she jerked her eyes away from him, mortified. "Oh! Oh, I'm sorry!"

"Are you *blushing*?" He sounded amused.

Virginia pressed her palms against her hot cheeks. "I apologize if I . . ." She swallowed and made herself meet his cool blue eyes, ". . . gave any offense."

"I didn't say I was offended. Worried maybe, but not offended." Cynicism glinted in his eyes. "You do that well. You're a hell of an actress."

She frowned. "I don't know what you mean."

"That flustered Victorian virgin thing. If I hadn't seen you pick up Gary in that bar and fuck his brains out, I'd think it was genuine."

Virginia stiffened at the amused contempt on his face. "That again? Can't you come up with something more original than insulting my honor?"

"But it seems to work so well." A corner of his lip lifted in a mocking half-smile. "And it has such a ring of truth."

Just once, she'd like to slap him. But the only other time she'd given in to that temptation, she'd given the man a concussion. Anyway, one did not hit a bound man.

But oh, she was tempted.

Instead she gave him her best acid smile. "I'm sure I'd be mortally wounded—if I really cared what you think."

Despite her flippant words, Logan knew he'd hurt the vampire's feelings again. And idiot that he was, he felt guilty about it.

He couldn't figure her at all. After Ivanov, Logan had expected a cold-blooded demonic slut who lured men to bed so she could drain the life out of them. Instead she'd made love to that Gary character with such tender skill that just thinking about it threatened to give Logan a hard-on. Again.

Okay, so she'd also been about to bite Loverboy when he interrupted. Yet after she'd knocked Logan out, did she do the logical thing for a demonic slut? Nope. He's regained consciousness with his throat intact.

True, she'd trussed him like a Thanksgiving turkey, so he figured she'd spared him so he could take Gary's place on the menu. And the blatant hunger in her eyes a few minutes ago had seemed to confirm that idea. But when Logan had commented on her erotic stare—mostly because it was perversely giving him an erection—she'd blushed. What kind of demonic slut blushed?

Dammit, he was not going to apologize to a vampire for implying she was easy. She intended to munch on him like a crouton. Calling her easy was the least she deserved.

Her eyes slid away from his, and she blinked hard. Was her chin trembling?

"Ah, hell. Look, I'm sorry, all right?"

"Can't you find some other way of expressing yourself than by swearing like a sailor? It's very rude." She dipped into a pocket of her robe and came out with a lace handkerchief. And wiped surreptitiously at her eyes. Dammit.

"I am a sailor." He would *not* be guilted out by an undead creature of the night. "Look, lady, cut the shit. We both know you plan to eat me . . ."

Her head whipped around. "I beg your pardon?"

His face went hot. Damn, now she had him blushing. "If you're going to kill me, do it."

Virginia whirled to face him, stuffing the handkerchief away again as she glared at him. "How many times do I have to tell you, I'm not a murderer! If I was, you'd already be dead. You're the one who tried to drive that arrow through my heart, remember?"

"Don't give me that innocent act. I saw the fangs. I saw you bend over Gary. I know what you were going to do."

"You don't know anything," she snapped. "The fact that you think I'm a killer proves it."

"You're a vampire, lady. Of course you're a killer."

Virginia let the rage roll over her, let the Hunger rise until her fangs punched down from her jaw. Then she bared them at him. "Yes, I am a vampire."

He froze, staring at her mouth, his face going as blank as a mask. She scented a tang of fear in the air, but saw not even a hint of it in his eyes.

Slowly, Virginia stalked toward him. If words didn't convince him, she'd try something else. Maybe, she decided recklessly, she'd just scare the living daylights out of him. Maybe she'd just scare him so bad he'd stay away from her.

"I am a vampire," Virginia repeated, lowering her voice to a purr. "But I don't just drink blood. My kind feeds on emotion, too. Desire. Fear." She licked her fangs. "But the sweetest of all is orgasm. I can drink a man's climax out of his mind and feed it back to him until it's so hot and hard he's never felt anything like it. Then it spills back to me, even greater than before. That's what I really want, what we really feed on. Blood's only the medium."

His blue eyes flickered, but he didn't answer.

"You want me, Logan. I can sense your desire just as strongly as your fear." Slowly, Virginia reached up and unbelted her robe, let it slide down her shoulders. She watched his gaze slip down to the plunging V-neckline of her negligee and the round curves of her breasts. "Wouldn't you like me to do to you what I did to Gary?"

Logan's eyes hardened. "Not if it means dying for it."

"You watched me make love to him," Virginia said, gliding closer to the bed until she stood over her prisoner's body. "Did it excite you to see me take him so deep into my mouth?" She reached down, drew a finger down the length of his zipper, then lower, between his thighs. Cupped him. He felt so full, so thick, even soft. Against her palm, his organ stirred and began to harden. "Would you like me to do that to you?"

His mask of chill disinterest dropped, revealing rage. She wondered if all that fury was directed at her or his own unruly body. "That depends. Do you plan to bite it off?"

"What a revolting idea." She smiled tauntingly into his eyes. "I'd never, ever do anything like that. But you probably don't believe me. And that might make it more delicious—sucking you, making you come. While you wonder . . ."

He laughed scornfully. "Lady, if you think you can bring me off with that hanging over my head . . ."

"Perhaps not." She reached for his belt buckle. "But it would be such fun to try."

She shouldn't be doing this, Virginia thought as she unbuckled his belt under his simmering blue glare. She knew the Hunger drove her now as much as her need to frighten him away. She had to be careful not to go too far; she could lose control.

So what if she did, a small, reckless voice demanded. If she took him, he'd realize she didn't kill her lovers as he imagined. Still, it would be rape, and rape was wrong. But not as wrong as killing him. And not as stupid as letting him kill her.

She'd play it out, Virginia decided wildly. Let the chips fall where they would.

What the hell am I doing? Logan thought. He was hard as a fence post, even knowing what she could do to him.

He kept remembering the way she'd looked with Gary's cock sliding slowly between her pouting lips. Remembering her wicked smile as she'd tilted her head to look up at him through her curls.

Remembering how deeply she'd taken him.

With a soft purr of pleasure, Virginia slowly unzipped his pants. She reached into the opening of his fatigues to stroke her fingers along the underside of his swollen shaft. Logan bit back a moan at the lush sensation.

In his arousal, the tip of his cock thrust over the waistband of his briefs. She brushed her tapered fingertips over the sensitive head, coming away with a drop of pre-come. Lifting her hand to her lips, she licked her fingers with that little pink tongue. He managed not to writhe. Barely.

"You're very . . ." Virginia stopped and swallowed. "Big."

He gave her a deliberately insulting look. "I'm sure you've had bigger."

Her eyes flashed. "Probably."

She caught the waistband of his briefs and pulled them down, catching them under his balls. His cock pushed from the opening in his fatigues, hard and eager.

Virginia stroked him again, her fingers sliding over his skin. "You're beautiful here." She looked up at him through the curtain of her curls. Her brown eyes looked as hot as molten chocolate. "Everywhere."

Damn. He could feel an answering heat spinning into his groin, pulsing as it built. Involuntarily, he looked at the neckline of her gown, at the full swells of her round breasts.

She knelt beside the bed and lowered her head. Her lips parted. Her fangs had retracted, thank God, but that didn't mean they'd stay that way.

"Look, Mistress Virginia, I'm really not into pain." Even as he said it, he knew the rough rumble of desire in his voice revealed he didn't really expect it to hurt. At least not until he'd climaxed inside that hot little body. And in his present mood, a quart or two of A positive seemed a small price to pay for the chance to shoot Virginia full of his come.

She looked at him from the corner of her eye. "If it hurts, let me know."

Her long pink tongue curled out and touched the head of his cock. He'd have come off the bed, if not for the soft, silken ropes around his wrists and ankles.

The forcible reminder that he was bound hit Logan like a shot of ice water to the face. *I'm tied up*, he thought desperately. *Just like Gwen. Just like Brandy.* He let the memories that haunted him pour over his mind like acid. Brandy's screams as Ivanov murdered her. Gwen's blank, empty face as she lay on that morgue table.

And for the first time in his life, Logan McLean disappointed a woman with a disappearing hard-on. He gave her a taunting grin as his erection wilted. "I'm not going to cooperate in whatever sick games you like to play."

Virginia frowned at his softening cock. "I'm not going to do anything you don't like."

"That's just what Ivanov said to my wife." He clenched his fists. "Just before he tortured her to death."

* * *

Virginia looked up at him, lying there on the bed, his muscled arms bound over his head. His blue eyes blazed like a gas jet.

"I know," Logan said, "because I read the journal entry he made after he butchered her."

Oh, the poor man. "You . . . you read that?" The Hunger drained away as fast as his erection had.

"Oh yeah. And others." His beautiful mouth took on a bitter twist. "There were hundreds of tapes and films and photos going back decades. All women he'd murdered. I watched one of them. Watched him cut her and drink from the cuts while she screamed and begged. He played in her blood like finger paint while he raped her." Blue eyes hardened and chilled, cold with contempt. "So forgive me if I fuckin' don't want to play."

Virginia's stomach heaved as the memory of John's death roared over her like a train. His deep, tearing screams. The sadistic pleasure in Ivanov's eyes as he used the knife.

Fighting for control, she looked down at Logan's softly curled cock. Shame scalded her. Clumsily, she pulled his briefs up and zipped his pants with shaking hands. "I didn't know." She fumbled with the buckle of his fatigues. "Please, you've got to believe me. I didn't know he was killing mortals. What . . . what was her name?"

"Gwendolyn Marie McLean." His handsome face set like granite, he said, "She died last year. They called me back from a mission to identify the body. They'd found her ID in her handbag, but they needed me to verify it." He laughed shortly, a hollow, awful sound. "After what he'd done, I didn't even know her. I was relieved. Thought for a minute they had to be wrong. But she had a little tattoo of a butterfly on her shoulder. It was sliced up some, but I recognized it."

Virginia backed off his body to sit on the bed, her mind painting stark, ugly images of Logan standing over his wife's butchered body, his strength and his skills useless. As useless as her own had been. She remembered looking down at the gaping hole where John's heart should be. And swallowed hard, forcing her mind away from the unbearable memory. "I'm sorry."

He didn't seem to hear, his eyes focused on some little slice of hell inside his mind. "I couldn't figure it out. The cops weren't getting anywhere with the case, and they didn't really seem to care. But when I started investigating, I found a dozen witnesses that saw her leave that bar with a man. Ivanov. They knew him, they knew his name. The police must have talked to the same people, yet they'd done nothing."

"He wouldn't *let* them do anything," she said softly, feeling the bitter weight of her helplessness. "They probably did come after him, but he just ordered them to forget their suspicions. And they did."

Just as John had ordered her to stay away from Ivanov as he lay dying. She'd been equally helpless to break that compulsion.

Logan laughed again. Virginia wished he'd stop; if a corpse could laugh, it would sound like that—hollow, tortured and hopeless. "I guess that's why he was so incredibly arrogant. He never used a false name, even when he picked up women he planned to murder. Hell, he didn't even have an unlisted number. That's how I found him. I got his address from the fuckin' phone book, and I broke into his house. And I found it all."

She didn't know how much longer she could stand to listen to this. "Logan . . ."

"But he came back too soon; I barely had time to grab a couple of the journals and get out. I had to be sure before I confronted him." He stared at the ceiling. A muscle in his jaw flexed as he fought to control the horror, grief and rage that boiled off him like steam. "When I read them, I was sure. I called the detective working on Gwen's case, and that's when I really knew something was screwy. Because he wouldn't look at any of it. He wouldn't come. I even called the damn police chief, and neither would he. I figured Ivanov'd bought them all off, so I thought, 'Fuck 'em, I'll call the FBI. This guy is a serial killer.'"

"I couldn't do anything, Logan," Virginia whispered. "John wouldn't let me."

He didn't appear to hear. "But before I could waste my time doing that, I read some more. Figured I needed to know what to tell the Feds. When he claimed to be a vampire in one passage, I thought he was crazy. But then he described going to the chief and his detectives, using his power on them, and I started to wonder. So I didn't call the FBI. I went back to his apartment instead—brought a bow along, just in case. And I watched the tape. When I saw what he did . . . I wondered. A human couldn't drink that much blood, not even a psycho. He'd vomit; it's an involuntary reaction. Like drinking seawater."

"We're not human," she said, feeling battered.

"That's for fucking sure. When he walked in the door, I shot him six times, and he didn't go down."

"You can't kill one of us with a gun." Her skin felt so cold, like she'd never be warm again.

"No. Hell, I double tapped the fucker in the heart. You hit a man there, he'll drop no matter how tough he is, because the heart just stops. But Ivanov lunged for me. That's when I knew for sure he was exactly what he claimed to be. I jumped back and grabbed the bow off my shoulder. He ordered me to put it down, but the command didn't work. I shot him. I don't know how I was able to resist." He shook his head. "I guess it was because I was so pissed off."

"No," Virginia said. *You resisted because you're Kith.* But she didn't say it. He wouldn't want to know he was kith and kin to vampires.

She shuddered. If he hadn't taken Ivanov off-guard, he'd have been killed. "I'm so sorry. I wish to God I could have kept all this from happening. But as he died, John ordered me to stay away from Ivanov, and I've never been able to break the compulsion. Besides . . ." Her voice dropped to a whisper. ". . . I was so *afraid.* Maybe . . . Maybe I couldn't break it because I didn't want to. I don't know."

Yet this mortal had killed the vampire she'd so feared.

"Yeah, well, you had good reason to be frightened," Logan said. "He'd been stalking you for months. That's how I knew where you lived."

She stared at him, jolted by the implications. "He knew my address? He'd found me?"

"He planned to torture you the way he had the others," he said, his tone cool now, his blue eyes glittering and hot. "But you wouldn't have died. That's why he wanted you. Whatever he did, you could heal."

Lord, she owed Logan even more than she'd thought. "But you killed him first."

"Yeah, I'm a humanitarian. So how many people have *you* killed?"

Jolted out of her stunned gratitude, Virginia gave him a frustrated glare. "Why do you keep classifying me with that monster? I may have fangs, but I am not a sadistic animal."

He said nothing, but his biceps flexed, drawing her attention to his bound wrists.

The reminder stung. "I only tied you because you tried to kill me."

"I also saved you from being tortured. We're even. Turn me loose."

Virginia stared into those chilly blue eyes. Maybe if she did, it would prove to him that she wasn't a monster. "Do you swear to leave me alone?"

"You can't keep me tied up indefinitely. You're either going to have to free me or kill me."

"I'll free you once I have your promise." She knew in her bones that Logan, despite his hatred of her kind, would keep any vow he made.

He gave her a cynical smile. "I won't hurt a hair on your head. Scout's honor."

On the other hand . . . "Somehow I'm not convinced."

"Hey, you're as safe with me as I am with you."

"Which, since you think I'm going to kill you, is not very safe at all." She tilted up her chin. "But ask yourself this: if I was the monster you think, wouldn't you already be dead?"

"Maybe." He was wearing his expressionless mask again, as if he wasn't really interested in the topic at all. "Maybe not. Ivanov liked to play with his victims a long time."

Agitated, Virginia stood up and began to pace. "How can I prove I'm innocent? If you'd waited before jumping through that window, you'd have seen me take only a pint or so from Gary. But now even if I took someone else in front of you, you'd think I was holding back because you're watching."

"Probably."

She thought of something and whirled to face him. "Where are the bodies?"

"What?"

"If I'm killing all these men, where's the trail of drained corpses? You'd think that kind of thing would be in the news."

"Ivanov's victims weren't."

"And I'll bet he moved around a lot. I've lived in Farmington for five years. There are only about ten thousand people in the whole town. Wouldn't the police have noticed if I was killing any of them?"

"Maybe they have. I haven't checked. Why don't we call a cop and ask?" Logan smiled mockingly. "Of course, you might have a little trouble explaining me . . ." His eyes hardened, and she knew he remembered what Ivanov had done to the San Diego cops. "Or not."

She frowned and began to pace again. "You're putting me in a very difficult position."

Logan snorted. "Not as difficult as the one you've put me in."

"I can't free you because you'll kill me, but I can't hurt you because I owe you." Torn, Virginia dragged both hands through her hair.

He smiled bitterly. "I'm humbled by your gratitude."

"Good. Fine." She gave her hair a tug in sheer frustration. "Why don't you concentrate on being humble tied to that bed the rest of the day, and we'll see if you're more reasonable by nightfall." Turning, Virginia stalked out of the room.

"Where are you going?" he called after her.

"To sleep. It's almost dawn."

"Oh, come on. Wouldn't you like to watch the sunrise with me?"

She poked her head around the corner and glared at him. "I wouldn't turn to dust, if that's what you're hoping. That's one of the myths about us—along with the part about crosses, holy water, and draining people like Coke cans. And I am *not* a dead body possessed by a demon, no matter what you may have seen on *Buffy the Vampire Slayer*."

"Sure, whatever. Look, before you head to your coffin . . ." She snarled at him, and he grinned. ". . . your prisoner is hearing the call of nature. And it's calling real loud. How about untying me so I can take care of business?"

Virginia stopped dead. There were practical aspects to this she hadn't considered. Her face began to heat. "I'll . . . uh . . . get you a chamber pot."

"I'm not pissing in a bucket, lady. And in case you don't know, it's not the kind of thing a guy can do with his hands tied." He gave her a razored grin. "Unless you want to do the honors?"

"Better that than have you dislocate my arm again," she snapped, wondering frantically what to use for a bed pan.

"I didn't dislocate it the first time." Logan sighed and dropped the hostility. "Look, you've got my gun. You can point it at me if it makes you feel better."

"Do you promise you won't attack me?"

"I swear on my bulging bladder."

Virginia hesitated, thinking frantically. In theory, she was faster and stronger than Logan, but that didn't necessarily mean much. At least if she had the gun, he'd be less inclined to try anything. Besides, it was really the only dignified solution. Otherwise she'd have to find a bed pan, and then hold his organ while he . . . Oh, no. You didn't do that kind of thing to a man. Any chance of a civilized resolution would be gone.

Quickly, Virginia headed downstairs for the living room and the coffee table where she'd arranged that intimidating weapons collection of his. She chose the largest pistol, though the grip was literally too big for her hands, and carried it back upstairs.

Logan eyed the gun with amusement as she walked in with it. "Do you really think you're strong enough to pull the trigger on that . . ." She lifted an eyebrow at him. He grimaced. "I keep forgetting. Not only could you pull the trigger, you could tie the barrel into a pretzel."

"Not quite." She gave him her best menacing look. "But I could tie *you* into a pretzel, so don't give me any trouble." Ignoring his snort, she crossed to the night stand beside the bed, pulled open a drawer and removed the knife and coil of soft silk rope she'd used to bind him. She put them in easy reach and trained the gun on him.

Sidling to his closest foot, Virginia snapped the rope binding his ankle with one hand. She ducked back quickly. When he didn't try to kick her, she freed his other ankle as well. Logan watched impatiently as she stepped to the head of the bed and leaned over to stretch an arm toward his bound wrists. The minute the loop gave, she jumped back and aimed the gun at him.

"Somehow all this caution is rather flattering from a woman who can bench press farm equipment." One corner of that handsome mouth quirked, and he slid out of bed, rubbing his wrists.

"I may be stronger than you are, but I don't know karate or Kung Fu or any of that lethal weapon stuff you do." Virginia watched carefully as he padded toward the bathroom.

"Wrong on all counts." McLean laughed shortly. "I'm a black belt in Aikido."

"Whatever," she said, and stepped into the bathroom after him before he could close the door in her face.

Logan glowered down at her. "I do not need an audience."

Her eyes were level with his broad, muscular chest. My, there was a lot of him. Trying to project tough confidence, Virginia waved the gun at him. "Well, you've got one anyway. I'm not going to leave you alone in here to make poison gas out of my cleaning supplies. Go . . . you know."

Radiating offended dignity, he stripped off his gloves, stalked to the toilet and turned his back on her. Virginia heard his belt buckle rattle, then the hiss of a zipper sliding down. Feeling herself redden, she directed her gaze elsewhere and tried to ignore any other revealing sounds.

When he finished, Logan moved to the sink to wash up, his handsome profile set and angry. Against her will, Virginia noticed the size of his hands, the long, tapered length of his fingers. She wondered if he was as good at giving pleasure as he was at inflicting pain.

He turned toward her and silently loomed. Intimidated despite herself, she backed hastily out of the way. He stalked stiff-legged to the bed, lay down and crossed his wrists over his head, his face rigid.

She'd better do this fast. Virginia put the gun down on the night stand, grabbed the rope and the knife, and pounced, landing astride him on her knees.

McLean let out a startled woof of air at the impact of her hundred pounds hitting his lean belly. Before he could recover, she whipped several coils of rope around his crossed wrists, then passed the rope around one of the brass bars of the headboard and leaned over to knot it as tightly as she could.

"You do realize you had the safety on the whole time," he said, once he'd regained his breath. "If you'd tried to fire that gun, it wouldn't have gone off. I could have jumped you any time I wanted— but I didn't."

Virginia stopped dead, realizing he had indeed kept his promise. "I . . . You . . ." She looked down at him, fumbling for an apology.

And caught him staring at the plunging V of her dressing gown and the full curves it revealed. Stark male desire heated his eyes. As she watched, stunned, his seductive lips parted slightly.

She was abruptly aware of his warm, muscled strength between her thighs, the beat of his heart in her ears, the slow, tempting throb of the vein in his neck. And remembered how his organ looked in full erection. Thick, powerful, flushed with blood and sensual power.

The Hunger ambushed her, so dark and molten it snatched her breath.

His blue eyes finally left her breasts and met hers. Virginia shuddered at the combination of wariness and lust she saw in them.

Her attention flicked to that ridiculously tempting mouth. With a helpless moan, she lowered her head and took his lips. At first he lay rigid under her, almost vibrating with tension. Fighting the need to kiss her back with such ferocity she could almost sense the battle. She closed her eyes, concentrating on seducing his mouth. Licking, tasting, sucking his delicious lower lip, until he opened for her. She slipped her tongue inside his mouth in a slow, smooth stroke.

His control broke. He kissed her back, hungry, passionate, and just as skilled as she'd expected.

She had to touch him. Catching his face between her hands, Virginia explored its angular male contours with her fingertips, savoring the warm skin, the prickle of his five o'clock shadow. He raised his head, deepening the kiss, swirling his slick, wicked tongue around hers. She moaned into his mouth.

Virginia pressed closer until her breasts mashed into the hard muscle of his chest. Her breath caught in a broken sigh. She lowered her hands from his face to trace the broad planes of his pectoral muscles through the thin-ribbed fabric of his black undershirt. Blindly, she followed the shapes of the muscles to his massive shoulders, then up to the bunch of his powerful biceps, held flexed by the position of his bound wrists.

With another little sigh, she bent to nibble his lower lip. He made a needy sound and pumped his hips, letting her feel the contours of his stone-hard erection. Imagining it buried in her to the hilt, Virginia gasped.

Hungrily she left his seductive mouth to catch his earlobe between her teeth. She bit gently, then followed the thick cord of his neck down the line of his throat, kissing and licking. Until she reached his pulse. Closing her eyes, she let it throb against her lips as the Hunger rolled over her in a hot, tormenting wave.

His body went rigid between her thighs. "Get off me."

Chapter Four

Virginia blinked, realizing her mouth was pressed to his throat. Quickly, she lifted her head. "I wasn't . . ."

"Sure you weren't." He stared up at her, the heat in his eyes anger now instead of passion. "Get the hell off me, lady. I'm not the entree."

"Logan . . ."

"I said, get off! I don't want to play any more of your sick little games."

Stung, Virginia sat back on her heels. Feeling his demanding erection under her buttocks, she taunted him with a smile. "Don't you?"

"Yeah, well, I can fix that. All I have to do is think of my wife."

Virginia stopped dead, remembering John. Despite all the sex she'd had over three decades since his death, she'd still maintained a distance between herself and her lovers, remaining faithful to her husband in the only way she could.

Until now. Because when she'd started making love to Logan, she hadn't done it for survival. She'd done it to feed the lust she felt for him. Him, not the blood in his veins.

It made no sense. She'd had men with bodies as good as Logan's, faces as handsome, hands as skilled, but she'd never felt this vivid, helpless desire.

She looked down at him, at the stubborn jut of his shadowed jaw, the lock of dark hair brushing his broad forehead. His full, angry lips. Yet despite the rage in those blue eyes, his erection felt so thick and hot under her bottom she found herself leaning forward, hungry to taste that beautiful mouth. It curled into a snarl.

Oh, God.

She jerked back. What was she doing? She had to get away from him. Now, before she took it further than he wanted to go.

Virginia leaped off him and ran from the room, stopping only long enough to grab her robe and drag it on over her hungry, frustrated body.

❦

Breathing hard, trying to convince his stubborn hard-on it wouldn't be getting any Virginia, Logan stared at the ceiling. Damn, he couldn't believe he'd gone off like that. Just fucking lost it. And with a vampire, for God's sake. If he wasn't damn careful, his cock was going to write a check his blood supply couldn't cash.

He took a deep breath, blew it out. *Cool it, McLean*, he thought. *Just wait.*

Dawn was coming; he could sense it building behind the lace curtains. Soon the vampire would be asleep, and then he could get down to the business of escaping. Any knot she could tie, he could untie.

And then she'd be at *his* mercy.

❦

Logan listened to Virginia getting ready for bed. Water running, vigorous tooth brushing in the master bathroom, the squeak of bedsprings as she settled in across the hall. Then silence, tense and thrumming with a kind of resentful lust. He had the feeling Virginia didn't like this thing between them any more than he did.

She'd take a while to drift off, wound tight like that. He had time for a combat nap before he got down to business.

Like all successful SEALs, Logan had learned to sleep in fifteen minute stretches, then wake reasonably refreshed and ready for the task at hand. Which at the moment was getting out of Virginia's bondage job, sneaking into her bedroom and . . .

What?

He hadn't been able to kill her before, when he'd had her pinned before she'd knocked him out. What made him think he'd have any better luck attacking her in her sleep?

But that had been different, Logan told himself stubbornly. He'd been hurting her then.

And driving an arrow into her heart wouldn't hurt?

But goddamn it, she was a vampire. She killed people. She . . . No. He had to stop thinking about this. He needed to grab that nap and get to work.

Determined, Logan blanked his mind and went to work forcing each of his tight, coiled muscles to relax. His toes, his calves, his thighs, his . . .

In the first moments of the dream, he didn't recognize anything but a swirl of color illuminated by a golden glow. Then the world snapped into place, and he realized he stood in a ballroom filled with men in colorful frock coats and women in high-waisted gowns. A string quartet played something lively he didn't recognize, and a group of dancers romped in the middle of the room under a huge chandelier that blazed with candlelight.

Logan reached out with his mind. Scanning the throng, skimming the alien thoughts. Looking for the mind he couldn't read. He didn't expect to find anything; in all his long life, he rarely had, and even on those rare occasions, it had never worked out. Looking was simply automatic.

So when he actually found what he'd been searching for all these years, he wondered at first what the hell it was. To Logan's psychic senses, the shielded mind seemed to glow, standing out from the crowd of minds around it like fire opal lying in black gravel. For a moment he thought he had to be mistaken, but when he scanned again he got the same results. He simply couldn't probe beyond that shield. It protected the thoughts of its owner completely.

His heart leaped. After all these years of looking, he'd found . . . someone. One of his own kind. Male, female, he couldn't tell, couldn't see anything but the marvelous possibility.

Eagerly Logan moved through the crowd, searching with his mind, trying to pin down which face that bright mental shield belonged to.

Then a man stepped aside and he saw her. Logan's eyes locked instinctively on her cameo-perfect profile with its straight nose and round little chin and wide brown eyes. And he knew at once the shield belonged to her. Who was she? Pray God, not someone's young bride, for he didn't trust himself not to simply steal her away; he'd been alone for far too long. Besides, no mere husband could value her as he would, give her what he could.

Though Logan could not read her mind, those around her were not immune. The minds of her friends told him everything he needed to know—and what he discovered only added to his delight.

A debutante. In the midst of her first season, and yet unattached, though Logan knew from the thoughts around her that she interested plenty of young bucks. Too bloody bad. They weren't going to get her. Logan was.

The plan unfolded in his mind, quick and cunning. He knew he'd have to handle this delicately to avoid tipping his hand or frightening her. And with his rather dark reputation, her parents would distrust his motives. Marriageable virgins had never been an interest of his; only neglected married women and lonely widows. He would have to give every appearance of reforming, and be damned convincing at it.

Logan winced. He'd never had to do the pretty for anybody's mama, and he wasn't altogether sure how to go about it. Then he looked at that perfect face and slim, lithe body, and knew the rewards would be worth every earnest lie he had to tell.

And he'd best not waste any time while he was about it, or some silly young fop would steal a march on him. He couldn't allow that. He knew he'd do whatever he must to have her, and he would rather not be forced into true ruthlessness.

Logan started toward her, sending a wave of command ahead of him that made those blocking his way step aside without knowing why. His eyes never wavered from her.

She sensed him coming. Perhaps she felt the predatory heat of his stare. She turned toward him and looked up. A dimple flashed in her cheek before she turned away with a shy little duck of her head. Of course. She didn't know him. She didn't dare speak to him for fear of tarnishing her reputation. Pretty young debutantes did not talk to rakes.

An introduction. He needed an introduction. Logan grabbed a friend's shoulder and whispered in his ear.

The man looked toward her. "Her?" His friend glanced back at him dubiously. "Hardly your style, old man. Virginia Grayson is no lightskirt you can flirt with and dance away."

"I know," Logan said, unable to pull his eyes away from her. An end to his loneliness, his constant hunger. "But she's exactly what I want."

Logan jolted awake, his heart pounding in his chest. A familiar cold sweat beaded his forehead, but this time he hadn't been dreaming of Ivanov and the murders. It had been one of the other dreams, the ones he'd been having for years, though he never quite remembered them once he woke up.

There'd been . . . a ballroom, and people in costumes. And Virginia, dressed in an old-fashioned gown. Nothing menacing about the dream, just a sense of . . . need. A feeling he had something to do. Something urgent and important.

Why did such a harmless dream fill him with this cold, instinctive horror?

Logan spent most of the morning trying to escape, but Virginia had either known her business or gotten lucky. She'd positioned the knots behind one of the bars at the head of the bed, and he couldn't reach them with his feet tied.

Finally he gave up. He decided his best strategy was to make sure the next time she bound him, she didn't do such a good job. Which meant it was time to try charm and distraction. He was good at that— among other things. Sooner or later, something would work and he'd escape.

His mind drifted back to the dream, worrying at it compulsively. He thought about the way Virginia had looked in it, innocent and lovely, with feathers waving in her hair. More fairy princess than wanton killer. Maybe his subconscious was trying to tell him something.

Virginia argued passionately that she wasn't the monster Ivanov had been, and she had a point. Somebody that psychotic wouldn't have been able to resist killing Logan even if she'd wanted to; sexual murder had been a compulsion with Ivanov. And she'd had every reason to kill him last night. After all, he'd tried to kill *her*. Yet she hadn't. Maybe she was trying to lull him, but why bother?

He needed to know. He damn well didn't want to make a mistake about Virginia one way or the other.

Logan spent the next few hours making and discarding escape plans, all of which involved Virginia and varying degrees of risky seduction. By the time night fell and she bustled in with a tray, he was ready to begin.

She wore a gray sweater and a pair of blue jeans snug enough to remind him what an amazing ass she had. Her long, slender feet were bare.
Seduction was beginning to sound better all the time.

Virginia gave him a determined smile as she put the tray down on
the night stand, obviously intent on winning him over. "I thought
you'd be hungry."

"You thought right," he said, in no mood to quibble as his stomach
rumbled.

Delicious scents wafted to his nose from the small pile of biscuits
on the plate. Each was thick and flaky, stuffed with bacon and egg—
and almost as tempting as Virginia in that sweater. Logan swallowed
and lifted his eyes to her. "You going to turn me loose to eat?"

She fidgeted. "Actually, I'm going to feed you."

He started to growl his opinion of that idea, then remembered his
decision to charm his captor. He summoned his best smile instead. "If
you don't mind."

Virginia looked a little wary at that, but settled a slim hip next to
him on the bed and picked up a biscuit. When she presented it to his
mouth, Logan took a bite, keeping his eyes locked on her face the
whole time. Charm. He could do charm.

He could also juggle chainsaws. Tempting a vampire was probably
about that safe.

Virginia watched as Logan's lush mouth opened and his white
teeth took a slow bite of the biscuit. His blue eyes focused on hers,
looking heavy-lidded and hungry for something more than bacon.
Beard stubble darkened his cheeks, giving him a rakish look that com-
plemented that sexy male stare. The cords on his throat worked as he
swallowed.

"This is good," he told her. "Your cooking?"

Virginia licked her lips, not sure quite what to think of a mellow
Logan McLean. "Uh, yes. I like to keep a full cupboard, in case of . . .
guests."

He lifted his head off the pillow and took another bite, then settled
back to chew. There was a crumb on his lips, and his tongue flicked out
to lick it away.

Oh, my.

He lifted his blue eyes to her and gave her an innocent blink. "Coffee?"

She licked her lips and picked up the cup, then carefully brought it
to his mouth as he lifted his head. He sipped it, watching her over the
delicate china lip.

Over the next half hour, Logan worked his way through three biscuits and two cups of coffee. Half-hypnotized, Virginia watched him eat. She could picture him tasting her like that, his mobile mouth tight around her nipples, sucking fiercely, his clever tongue licking. Every time he closed his eyes and made those little appreciation moans, she pictured her mouth on him. On his lips, on that luscious erection he'd displayed for her last night.

On his throat.

God, he was so seductive, it had to be deliberate. Didn't he realize he played with fire? It had been too long since she'd fed, and the Hunger badly wanted a taste of him.

Evidently blind to the risk he was running, Logan gave her a wry smile flavored with an irresistible hint of little boy. "I wonder if I could take a shower? I've been wearing this sweat a little too long."

She gulped. "Certainly. Let me just clear away these things . . ."

Getting away from him long enough to carry the dishes downstairs helped cool the fire he'd built so skillfully. As she washed the plates in the sink, Virginia realized he was trying to set her up for an escape attempt. Of course. Why else would he try to seduce a vampire? *Idiot*, she told herself fiercely. *Do you think he'd want you otherwise?*

To Logan McLean, she was a killer, an undead creature of the night. And she couldn't afford to forget it, or the charming, seductive man upstairs would plant an arrow in her heart quicker than she could kiss him.

Grimly, Virginia walked into the living room and got the gun again, careful to take the safety off this time as she went upstairs and freed her captive for his shower.

If he noticed her icy wariness, Logan gave no sign, ignoring both it and the weapon she kept trained on him as he sauntered into the bathroom. His lack of protest when she slipped in after him made her feel doubly paranoid.

"I really appreciate the shower," he told her over her shoulder, strolling to the toilet to relieve himself. "SEALs get pretty damn grungy in the field, but I don't like being ripe if I can help it."

Finished, he casually reached for the hem of his shirt and pulled it off over his head.

With a gasp, Virginia jerked her head away and focused her eyes on the door. Too late. The sight of that broad muscled back had seared itself into her memory. Her nipples hardened.

"That's the thing I hated about Hell Week back in SEAL training," Logan continued, oblivious to her tension. "Not humping that damn rubber boat all over the place until every muscle ached." Rustles and rattles teased her—the jingle of his belt, the whisper of a zipper, the soft thump of his trousers hitting the ground. "What I really hated was being covered in sand. Sand everywhere—down my shirt, down my pants . . ." Helplessly, she remembered the silky rose length of his cock when she'd unzipped him last night. "The friction was murder. I just wanted to get naked and wash it all off. I actually welcomed being ordered into the ocean just to get rid of it. But once the sand was gone, the water was so damn cold it would literally turn your balls blue . . ."

Desperately, Virginia wished he'd stop talking about his privates. Logan was hung like a stallion, and she'd always found heavily endowed men wickedly tempting. She ached to turn and watch him step naked into that shower, muscle shifting in that big, animal body as he moved.

But she didn't dare. The Hunger howled in her blood, and she'd never be able to keep her hands off him if she let herself get a good look at him. She was just too close to the edge.

When Virginia heard the shower hiss, she told herself it was safe to turn around.

Wrong.

The bubble glass of the shower stall door made his body look dreamlike, but what she could make out of his broad torso, long legs and muscled rump turned her mouth to cotton. Virginia wanted to touch him so bad her hands shook.

"Shampoo's out," Logan called cheerfully over the sound of the water. "Got anymore?"

"Uh, yes. Certainly." She'd bought a new bottle last Wednesday.

Virginia dropped to one knee by the cabinet under the sink and got out the bottle, then stood and walked across the bathroom on shaking legs.

A bare, brawny arm reached over the shower door, and she put the shampoo into his dripping hand. She didn't get into the shower with him, but she thought about it. Hard.

Scurrying back across the bathroom, Virginia turned her back. Somehow she kept from looking around again even when she heard the shower cut off and the door open.

But she couldn't stop listening.

She heard the ringing whisper as Logan pulled the towel from its rack on the wall. Her sensitive vampire ears picked up the rasp of terrycloth over his skin as he dried himself briskly, humming under his breath. His bare feet padded across the floor toward her.

She pictured his strong hands reaching for her, catching her by the shoulders, turning her for another mind-searing kiss . . .

Virginia whirled, the Hunger clamoring.

"I don't suppose I could wash these too?" Logan held out his bundled clothing. "If they don't get hit with some detergent soon, they'll develop a separate consciousness."

His chest was broad and brown and sculpted with all sorts of fascinating ripples that were covered with a silky ruff of hair. With one tanned hand, he held the towel closed around his hips. Virginia watched a drop of water work its way down the topography of his belly toward the towel and gave serious thought to licking it off.

You can't do that, she told herself wildly, thrusting away the hot, wicked image of pushing him down and taking him, right on the bathroom floor. *It'd be rape. And he's not willing.*

I could make him willing, the Hunger whispered.

"Virginia?" Logan lifted a dark brow.

It took her a moment to remember what he'd asked about. "I'll . . ." She swallowed. "I'll take care of them. I think I have something you can wear while they wash."

He gave her that boyish grin again. She thought about kissing it off his face. "I doubt anything of yours will fit."

"It's a man's robe," she said.

"Oh." He didn't say anything else, but Virginia blushed. She wished she could stop doing that. She wasn't a slut. She did no more than she had to in order to survive.

Still holding the gun, Virginia backed out of the bathroom and turned toward the closet. Acutely conscious that he'd followed, she reached inside and fumbled until she managed to grab the thick white terrycloth robe. He took it from her and turned his back.

And let the towel drop.

Chapter Five

Virginia bit back a gasp and looked away, but once again the sight of his long, strong back and tight male buttocks set the Hunger roaring.

God, she wanted to touch him, see if he was as hard and firm as he looked.

When she dared look back again, he was belted into the robe. She squared her shoulders and braced for another battle. "I'll have to tie you up again while I wash these."

He shrugged and went to lie down on the bed. She followed, trying desperately not to think about the magnificently naked body under that robe.

Settling back on the mattress, Logan crossed his wrists over his head and looked at her, a half-smile on his handsome lips.

Oh, God. The bed was too wide; she couldn't reach his hands standing on the floor. She'd have to straddle him again.

She did it as quickly as she could, trying not to touch him this time. As she crawled off the bed, she felt the seam of her jeans rubbing her own swollen, hot flesh as her bra abraded erect nipples. Her upper jaw ached, and her fangs raked against her bottom teeth.

She knew better than to even try to tie his ankles.

Grabbing his clothes, Virginia escaped the bedroom with something like relief.

Well, Logan thought, watching her flee, *the plan to distract her is certainly going well*. He looked down at the thick bulge under his robe. Unfortunately, it seemed to be working equally well on him.

The trick, of course, was to play the game without losing control and winding up in bed with Virginia.

Oh, yeah, a little voice in his head whispered. *We sure wouldn't want to have that.*

He told it to shut up.

❧⟦ᏻᎾ⟧❧

Virginia knew she had to stay away from Logan until she regained control. She'd paint while his clothes washed. With her Atlanta museum show coming up, she needed to get back to work anyway. She still had a couple of pieces to finish.

Trying to ignore the warmth of his body that lingered in the fabric, Virginia carried his fatigues to her laundry room, tossed them into the washer with a scoop of detergent, and turned it on.

As the washer began to hum, she escaped upstairs to the bedroom she'd converted into a studio. No matter how bad things got in her life—and at times they'd been pretty bad—she could always find peace with a brush in her hand. But tonight the scent of wet oil paint and turpentine didn't have their usual soothing effect. Virginia quickly realized that if she wasn't careful, she'd ruin the painting of the street kid she was working on. Her concentration was shot.

She backed away from the easel and picked up a sketch pad. Doing a few charcoals was about the most she was up to tonight.

Which was when her mind ambushed her with an image—Logan, sprawled across the bed upstairs with that robe open to reveal his impressive cock at full erection, his wrists tied over his head.

I don't do porn, she told herself firmly.

Unfortunately, the image refused to go away. She gritted her teeth and began to draw. Anything. Circles, cubes, cylinders . . .

Long, hard cylinders.

Oh, God.

❧⟦ᏻᎾ⟧❧

Without Virginia to distract him, Logan's lack of sleep began to catch up with him. And since there didn't seem to be much else to do, he let it.

He rode a massive horse. Weight dragged at him, and for a second, Logan thought it was his SEAL combat gear. Then he looked down at his sleeve and saw chain mail. He wore full armor, from the great helm on his head to the mail leggings that covered his thighs.

Of course. He was, after all, a knight.

A female scream slashed through the night, its tone more furious than frightened. Logan's head snapped up and he kicked his stallion into a hard gallop. He'd taken an oath to protect women, children and the Church when he'd won his spurs, and it sounded as though his sword was needed.

Hearing the clash of combat off through the trees, Logan sent his mount plunging in that direction. It was dangerous to ride at such a clip with no more light than the moon, but he had little choice.

Man and horse burst into a wide, grassy clearing. As the scene before him registered, Logan's gloved hands tightened on the reins in astonishment. His stallion skidded to a well-trained halt.

Two knights battled in the moonlight, hacking at one another with great swords. Though both wore mail, they danced and leaped as if the armor weighed no more than a shirt and hose.

Nearby a lone woman with a sword held off six men-at-arms. Logan gaped at her, unable to believe his own eyes. She swung the massive weapon one-handed, though such a delicate lady should be unable to even lift it. With her free hand, she held her heavy skirts bunched at the thigh to free her long legs as she leaped and parried with a knight's skill.

She'd used her blade to good effect. One man lay at her feet, obviously dying from a massive chest wound. The other curs surrounded her, snarling and hacking, though none of them could get through her guard.

The knight with the wolf on his shield turned and tried to reach her, but the black knight he fought screamed a curse and slashed at him so fiercely he was forced to defend himself again.

Disgust curled Logan's mouth. Six men against a single woman— and from the look of her, a high-born one at that. Regardless of her unwomanly skill, such an attack reeked of cowardice.

Well, if the wolf knight could not go to her aid, Logan could. Spurring his horse, he charged, howling his battle cry.

The brigands weren't expecting a rescuer, and he hacked one to the ground before the others could turn. Alarm flooded their grimy faces as they realized they'd drawn the rage of yet another armored knight.

And their terror was justified. Logan cut down two more of them while the mysterious lady beheaded another with astonishing strength. The survivor took to his heels.

By then Logan's blood was up, and he wheeled his horse toward the fighting knights. He meant to deal with that treacherous black warrior. He reared his destrier and drew back his sword, preparing to take the head of the man who'd dared lead an attack on a noblewoman.

The black knight threw a hard look up at him, eyes glinting contempt through the slits in his great helm. "Get you gone, sirrah!" he roared, parrying the wolf knight's flashing blade. "This is no fight of yours."

Logan sneered at him. "I think it is, whoreson."

He chopped down with his sword. The black knight spun with a howl and swung up his kite-shaped shield, slamming it into Logan's blade so hard it spun from his hand.

Logan's eyes automatically tracked his weapon's glittering flight into the trees, his right arm gone numb to the shoulder from the impact.

The lady screamed, "NO!" Something struck his hip so hard it tore him from the saddle. Logan hit the ground with a jar that rattled his teeth. Dazed, he stared at the stars.

Glimpsing a long silhouette protruding upward, he looked down his body.

The black knight's sword was buried in his belly, right beside his hipbone. Oddly, Logan felt no pain, only a wave of ice that rolled from the injury, chilling him to the marrow.

As if from far away he could hear weapons clashing, and knew the knights fought again. Listening to his ears ring, he hoped for the lady's sake the wolf knight won.

A narrow hand wrapped around the hilt of the sword and jerked it free. Warmth instantly covered his abdomen. He would have been grateful for the relief from the icy chill, but he knew it was his blood. He was bleeding to death.

The lady's face hovered above his, glowing white and pure in the moonlight as she looked down at him, concern in her dark eyes. Slender hands caught his great helm and dragged it from his head with an ease that surprised him even through his growing numbness.

"You have one chance, lad," she said quickly. "It will take courage, but then, you have that."

As he watched, she reached up and tore the neck of her gown, baring most of one lovely white breast. Pressing a thumbnail to her own flesh, she cut herself deeply. Blood beaded and rolled down the slope of her breast.

"No," he murmured, "Don't hurt yourself . . ." It seemed a sin to mar that beautiful soft skin.

Despite the weight of his armor, the lady lifted him and drew his head to her breast. Astonished, he inhaled, smelling her rich female scent mingled with the sharp copper of blood.

"Drink!" she ordered fiercely.

"But . . . ," he whispered, confused, wondering if his spinning brain was playing tricks on him.

"If you want to live, drink! My blood is all that can save you."

Logan looked up into her demanding eyes and let her press his face to her soft skin. Her blood ran into his mouth. Dreamily, he licked at her breast, not entirely sure what he was doing.

She tasted hot, delicious. He closed his mouth over the cut and began to drink.

"Well, Ivanov's taken to his heels, the coward," said a man's voice, approaching. The lady's knight? "Since he'd lost his sword in our young friend, I suppose he decided he didn't want you that badly after all."

Then the man's voice changed. "What in the name of Our Lady are you doing, Alys?"

"Well, I couldn't let him die now, could I?"

Flustered, Logan tried to pull back from her, but somehow she tasted so delicious he couldn't drag his mouth away.

"I suppose not," said the knight at last, sounding irate. "But couldn't you have let him take from someplace else? Those are mine, dammit."

Her laughter rose up like bells. Logan smiled dreamily against her pretty breast, feeling surprisingly good for one who lay dying. There were worse ways to go, he supposed, than sipping at a lady's beauty.

Finally she drew back. "That's enough now, lad. Sleep now. When you awake, you will be a different man."

Helplessly obedient, he closed his eyes, expecting that the next face he saw would belong to Saint Peter. Instead, when he woke three days later, the lady and her knight were waiting.

Everything else had changed.

Virginia found Logan sleeping and woke him up for his meal. He ate without incident and dressed, then allowed himself to be tied again without a murmur of protest. All that cooperation struck her as suspicious, but she couldn't seem to concentrate well enough to decide what he was up to.

The Hunger kept showing her memories of his naked body and the feel of his shaft in her hands.

Keep him, it hissed now, as she tried to sketch a white clapboard church in her studio. *He's Kith.*

No, she told it. *He doesn't want to be one of us. He thinks we're monsters.*

Does it matter? He's tied. You could change him, and he would forget his objections.

No. It's not right.

Is being alone forever right? Is it right to take an endless series of men instead of having one of your own?

I love John. I won't betray him.

John has been dead thirty-two years. He would not want you to be alone forever.

He said he'd come back.

Not with the heart hacked out of his chest.

Virginia shoved the thought away and tried to pursue a less inflammatory mental path. Maybe she should try a religious painting. The Virgin and Child. Working on that particular composition would be uplifting. . . .

"Virginia?" Logan called from across the hall.

"Yes?"

"That tea you gave me wants to abandon ship."

She sighed and put down her sketch pad. If he started teasing her again, she was going to bite him.

Luckily, Logan behaved himself, not even raising a mocking eyebrow when she didn't try to accompany him into the bathroom. Maybe he sensed if she had to watch him drop his pants one more time, her control would snap like a guitar string.

Her foresight bitterly disappointed the Hunger, which retaliated by sending her a memory of a male throat against her lips, the hot liquor of blood in her mouth.

Virginia knew then she had to free him. And soon. If she kept him any longer . . .

No!

. . . she'd lose control of her need and take him before she knew what she was about.

If you free him, fool, he could come back some bright morning and drive a stake through your heart.

He wouldn't do that, her heart insisted. But dawn approached, and she decided not to test him after all.

When he came out again and lay down, Virginia realized she'd have to be doubly sure of the knots, or he'd untie himself before night-fall. With a sigh, she crawled up onto the bed and straddled him again.

And instantly realized she couldn't hold on any longer.

His broad, muscular chest felt hot and solid between her thighs. She remembered the way it looked beaded with water after his shower. And bit back a moan.

Logan's hot blue eyes didn't help as they focused on her face, heavy-lidded and seductive. "You can't keep me here much longer, Virginia," he rumbled. His chest rose and fell between her legs as he spoke. "You know that."

"I'll let you go tomorrow." He shifted under her, and his ridged abdominal muscles pressed against her sex through her jeans. Trying to ignore the sensation, Virginia stretched forward to reach behind the headboard with the ends of the rope. She didn't want to stick her crotch in his face again.

Unfortunately, the position put her breasts directly over his mouth. She tried very hard not to think about the deep V-neck of her sweater and the opportunities it gave him as she doggedly knotted and tied.

"I'm not going to hurt you," he murmured. "Hell, hurting you is the last thing on my mind now."

Now. She tried to seize on that "now." She didn't dare trust him, didn't dare give him the chance to . . .

Warm lips pressed against the upper curves of her breasts.

Virginia jolted. The Hunger leaped like an eager thing. "Don't do that." Breathlessly, she fought to tie the cords so she could get as far away from him as possible.

His teeth scraped against her flesh in an erotic caress. She tied off the last knot hurriedly and scooted back, looking down at his face.

Her bottom slid over something hot and thick. He smiled slowly.

"Oh, God," Virginia moaned. She had to kiss him. Or die.

She almost fell into his mouth. His lips opened under hers, hot and welcoming.

And she lost her mind.

Well, it worked, Logan thought. In her haste, she'd tied the knot where he could get to it.

But Virginia's small, soft hands were stroking him now, dancing over the muscles of his chest as she kissed him as though she could eat him alive. And she probably could.

And he'd probably enjoy it.

She straddled his erection, grinding deliciously as she licked and suckled his lips. He flashed on an image of Virginia making love to

Gary with her mouth. Heat flooded him. His dick hardened and lengthened until it felt huge behind his fly.

This, Logan thought, *is a really bad idea.*

Virginia sat up and rose on her knees to jerk her sweater off over her head. With a flex of her shoulders, she tossed it aside, then unsnapped her jeans with a flick of her tapered fingers.

He watched dry-mouthed as she slid off him just long enough to squirm those tight jeans off her hips and down her long legs. Her breasts quivered temptingly as she moved, barely covered by a black lace bra that matched the tiny panties she wore under the jeans.

Virginia twisted her arms back so she could get at the hooks of her bra. Freeing herself, she tossed the bra aside. Logan looked at her round, perfect breasts and forgot all the reasons he really shouldn't do this. He started to reach for her and growled in frustration at his bound hands. "Untie me," he ordered. "I want to touch you."

For a minute he thought she was going to do it, then caution flickered in her hot brown eyes. "I don't dare."

"Virginia . . ."

She crawled onto him again and caught his T-shirt in both hands, then shredded it like wrapping paper with one startling pull. For a minute her eyes roamed over his chest before she lowered her head to one tight male nipple. Her wet mouth made Logan close his eyes in delight. Her nipples brushed over his chest as she began to lick and nibble, and he shuddered.

He wanted to touch those hard little points, drive his fingers into her creamy sex. He burned for it. "Dammit, Virginia, let me taste you," Logan growled.

"Oh, yes," she gasped, and reared off him long enough to scoot her way up his torso. As she moved, he realized the fabric of her panties was already damp. Lust burned along his nerves in a singeing wave.

She lowered herself until Logan could reach one rose point with his mouth. But it wasn't enough. He wanted her breasts in his hands, wanted her silken skin yielding to his fingers. And she wouldn't let him have them.

So he exacted a delicious revenge, trapping the pink tip between his tongue and his teeth, licking and biting. Sucking. Teasing until she began to whimper. And he loved it. Loved making her squirm, this woman whose very life depended on driving men crazy. "Why don't you take off those pretty little panties," Logan whispered. "And we'll see how much I can do without using my hands."

Virginia looked down at him, her taut, creamy breasts rising and falling as she breathed hard and rapidly. With a moan, she lifted off him, hooked her thumbs in the thin silk over her sex, and ripped it in two before flinging the scraps aside. Logan stared hungrily at the soft brown curls between her long thighs, then looked up into her hot, dazed eyes.

Tempting a vampire might be suicide—but God, what a way to go.

Virginia knew she was doing this all wrong.

She should be driving *him* crazy, building his pleasure, drinking it like the blood, feeding the Hunger. Instead she'd given up all control to her captive, to his mouth and his hands and his hard, delicious erection. She burned for Logan McLean as she hadn't burned for a man since John died.

Virginia looked down into those taunting blue eyes and couldn't read a single thought behind them. A tiny, sane voice whispered, *He's dangerous. He thinks you're a killer and he wants to kill you.*

She ignored it.

"Ride my mouth," Logan ordered with those beautiful, wicked lips.

Closing her eyes, she shuddered. And wasn't sure she'd ever been this hot, not even with John. Not in one hundred and seventy-two years.

Knowing she shouldn't—shouldn't let herself get so far out of control, shouldn't give him this much power, *shouldn't*—she crawled up his body to grab the brass headboard and kneel astride his handsome head. Breathing hard, almost panting with need, she waited. He let her wait, damn him, let her tension build while his breath gusted over her wet, delicate flesh.

Then she felt his tongue. And had to fight a scream.

Logan tasted her with one slow lick. Deliciously creamy, strong and a little astringent, like a ripe persimmon. His cock hardened, a galvanized pipe in his fatigues as he thought about making her even hotter. Slowly, gently, he swirled his tongue through and around her wet folds. Crouching across his bound arms spread Virginia's legs wide, giving him access to every millimeter of her sex. He took ruthless advantage of it, licking and flicking and bathing in her as she whimpered in helpless need.

Finally she began to plead in a soft, broken voice that made him even harder. Logan smiled against her creamy flesh. He might be tied up, but just then he held *her* prisoner. Captive to his mouth. He decided he liked the idea of a captive Virginia.

A tempting image slid through his mind of what he could do after he escaped. And listening to her moan, he thought, *I wonder just how deeply you sleep . . .*

Logan's delicately skillful tongue was slowly driving Virginia insane. For the first time in decades, she trembled on the verge of a climax with a lover—if he'd let her come.

But she shouldn't. Holding herself aloof from her partners had always been her way of keeping her vows. She had to have sex to survive, but she didn't have to come. She shouldn't. She . . .

Couldn't stand it any more.

She shifted her hips, trying to concentrate his tongue where she wanted it. But he stubbornly swirled it around her clit, refusing to give her the direct touch that would send her up and over.

"Please, please Logan, let me come!" Virginia whimpered, past pride, past morality.

"God, I love to hear you beg," he said, sounding muffled against her body.

"Logaaaan!"

He closed his mouth around the tiny bud and sucked ruthlessly. She convulsed as pleasure seared up her spine in a hot, throbbing wave. Tormenting her with liquid skill, Logan drove her to a mindless, screaming orgasm that left her limp.

At last she pulled away to slump astride his powerful chest, tremors rolling through her thighs.

Until Logan purred, "Hey, vampire. Your stake is ready."

Alarmed, she opened her eyes, then relaxed at the heat and humor in his. His mouth shone slick with her cream. She leaned down and kissed him, tasting herself. "What kind of stake?" Virginia licked his full lips and smiled wickedly.

"A very long, hard stake." He grinned at her. "More of a baseball bat, really."

"Sounds frightening. Maybe I'd better check it out." She reached back and cupped him. Or tried to. Her eyes widened. "My, that is a very long stake. And you want to slide it into poor little me?"

"Every last inch," he growled, rolling his hips.

"What a nasty vampire hunter you are." She unbuckled his belt and slid his zipper down, then slipped a hand into the opening of his fatigues. His briefs strained to contain him. She worked her way into his waistband to wrap her fingers around the erotic, heated satin of his shaft. The thought of all that thick power sliding inside her sent the Hunger searing straight to her skull.

With a shudder of need, Virginia sat up and grabbed the waistbands of his briefs and fatigues. Pulled, stripping them down his narrow hips until his sex jerked free, rigid and eager and dark red. She jerked the pants the rest of the way off and threw them across the room, then turned to look at him.

Naked, he was even more impressive—long, strong legs, powerfully muscled torso as hard and chiseled as a Greek statue, arms bulging as they bent, bound over his head. She wished she dared cut him loose, but she knew better than to trust him.

Logan cocked a dark brow at her, a lock of black hair tumbling over his eyes. "I think I'll skip any more stake jokes—they're beginning to get a little creepy."

She licked her lips. "A little bit."

"Particularly since what I've got in mind won't hurt at all."

"No," Virginia whispered. "It's definitely not going to hurt."

She swung a leg over his thighs and directed his long shaft upward. And sank slowly, inch by inch, down on top of him. Until he filled her, her sex straining around his width.

She'd had lovers before, Virginia thought, in one brief, self-aware moment. Why did making love to Logan feel so utterly overwhelming? Was it because he was Kith? Was it the danger of taking a man who'd tried to kill her? Or was it just some wicked magic he had?

Then he made his first slow thrust, and every last thought vanished from her head.

She surrounded him in slick, wet satin, so incredibly tight he almost came on the spot. And the look on her face stole his breath—intense, blind pleasure, eyes closed, lush mouth slightly parted.

Virginia arched her back, and his eyes fell to the single lock of her hair that curled over one taut pink nipple. The contrast between her dark hair and white breast was intensely erotic.

With a growl of lust, Logan thrust himself upward, spearing even more deeply into her hot grip. She gasped and fell forward, not so much riding him as letting him impale her.

Half-crazed from the slick heat, Logan began to shaft her ruthlessly, driving as deep as he could go as hard as he could thrust. She braced herself against his chest, her dazed eyes meeting his. Surrendering to him, to his cock, to his strength.

Her submission spurred him on, until he could feel the pleasure gathering in his balls as a fierce pressure on the verge of explosion. Virginia gasped. And he saw her canine teeth lengthen into fangs.

Shit. She was going to betray him. Like Gwen.

He slammed up into her savagely with a growl of defiance. She fell forward against him, her breasts pressing into his chest, her face against his throat. He felt a hot sting of pain as her fangs slid into his skin . . .

"Bitch!"

Virginia winced as he snarled the word in her ear and drove up into her so hard he lifted both of them off the mattress. She reached for his mind, desperate to establish the connection. Even the Kith's mental shields dropped in such deep pleasure, and she should be able to create a psychic link between them as she fed that would prove to him she wasn't evil, wasn't a killer.

But though his orgasm rolled over him with such intensity she could feel it shaking his body, his fury was so hot she couldn't reach him. She could only writhe, trying to build his pleasure, trying to touch him, to draw him in even as she drank his blood.

"Bitch, bitch, bitch," he growled in time to each long, powerful stroke.

God, he felt so good, so hard, and he tasted so hot, and the Hunger demanded everything he gave so ruthlessly. She lost her concentration as her pleasure crested. Long, powerful spasms gripped her, rocking her in time to each surge of his thick length. Helpless, overwhelmed, she clung to him.

And drank.

He had never fucked a woman so tight, so lush and slick. Even her mouth working against his throat felt perversely erotic, the ache of her teeth acting as a spur to his lust. He reamed her without mercy, holding nothing back.

It wasn't as if he could hurt her, Logan thought viciously.

And why the hell should he care, anyway? She was killing him.

But she also gripped his shaft in juicy tight heat, her tiny muscles rippling around it with her climax. He slammed upward to his full length, and his own orgasm exploded down his shaft with a pounding intensity he'd never felt before. He roared in defiance and lust, his cock in her cunt, her teeth in his throat.

Possessing and possessed.

Chapter Six

Logan's muscles quivered, his skin slick with sweat as his chest rose and fell in hard, spent pants. Virginia lay draped over him like a delicious female blanket.

She'd stopped drinking from him. Now she tenderly licked the side of his neck where her teeth had punctured his skin, her hands stroking up and down his ribs, her sex still gripping his softened cock. Her gentle touch felt so warm, so comforting . . .

And he didn't want to be comforted. "If you're not going to kill me," Logan growled, "get the fuck off."

She sat up and looked down at him, a flicker of hurt in her brown eyes. "I told you, I don't kill people."

"So get off my dick." He realized he'd killed the mood, and he didn't care. He wanted it killed. He wanted the distance back. This intimacy between them was dangerous.

Her eyes hardened. "You were eager enough to have me on it a moment ago."

"That was before you decided to fucking *feed* on me, lady. I'm not the breakfast bar at Shoney's. Get off."

Virginia leaned forward until they were nose to nose. "News flash, sailor. You had sex with a vampire. You got bit. As the twenty-year-olds would say, 'Duh.' You needn't get all offended now."

"I suppose you think I should be grateful you didn't rip out my throat," Logan snapped, perversely delighted at the chance to fight. "Okay. Thanks. But I'd really appreciate it if you didn't go back for seconds."

She smiled tauntingly and leaned back on her heels, drawing his eyes to her sweet breasts with their hard pink nipples. "What's the matter, Logan? Afraid you won't be able to resist?"

"Considering you've got me tied to the bed, yeah."

Her mouth tightened. "Don't flatter yourself. I've had my midnight snack, so I think it's time I get some sleep." She rose from him, magnificent and haughty in her rage.

"I hope you don't think it'll be with me." Logan fought to ignore the regret he felt as his organ slid from her.

Virginia tossed her mane of curls and gave him a cool look. "Hardly. I've got a very sensitive nose, and you smell like sweat and sex. In fact, I feel the need for a shower."

She turned and strolled out. Logan watched her delicious ass roll with her walk and ground his teeth.

※※(♡)※※

Virginia slammed the bedroom door behind her and stalked across the hall to her own room and the bathroom adjoining it. "Why do men feel compelled to spoil everything they possibly can?" she growled to herself as she stepped naked into the shower stall.

With a vicious twist of her wrists, she turned on the taps. The hot, stinging water struck breasts still sensitive from Logan's clever mouth. Virginia gasped and turned her back, fumbling for the soap.

Damn it, it had been perfect until he ruined it.

Or she had. She should have known how he'd react when she bit him. But none of her partners had ever been Kith, and she always had them so dazzled by sex they never really noticed the bite. And if they did, she erased the memory. But this time she'd been the one dazzled. She'd never experienced anything like this, even with her husband.

Virginia froze in place at the realization, eyes widening. *She'd come with him!* She hadn't come with a partner in thirty years, but it had never even occurred to her to hold back with Logan.

Guilt sliced her in a hard, stinging stroke. How could she let herself forget John that way? Yes, it had been incredible, a ferocious assault on her senses that had left her mind blank of anything but the need to have him, *now*—but that was no excuse.

Virginia looked down at her emerald wedding ring and felt tears of shame start to her eyes. It was the exact same shade of green as her husband's eyes.

Oh, God. I've betrayed him.

Maybe she'd just responded to the danger Logan represented, she told herself desperately. She'd read somewhere that danger created a powerful sexual kick in some situations, and he had threatened to kill her. Had almost succeeded more than once. Given the chance, he'd try again.

She'd never felt threatened by John, even as a mortal debutante discovering that the handsome beau who'd offered for her hand was something more than human. He had always been so careful not to frighten her. Even the very first time, he'd taken her with such gentleness, explaining what he did, what it would do to her, and how it would feel. Her transformation had been as loving and kind as he could make it.

Even after Virginia had become a vampire, John had continued to treat her like the delicate upper-class miss she'd been as a mortal. And she'd loved him with everything she had, heart, soul and body. She'd continued to love him even after he died.

Yet she'd forgotten him in Logan's brawny arms. How could she sink so low?

It couldn't just be the danger he represented. She certainly hadn't responded that way to Ivanov, and he'd been far more of a menace to her.

She shuddered in revulsion, remembering her fear when the mad vampire had appeared on the doorstep of their Texas ranch house that night in 1970. She and John had sensed his insanity in the evil psychic wash from his mind, and they'd known he had to die.

Then Ivanov challenged John for her, showing her husband a psychic image of what he planned for Virginia. And for only the second time in their long romance, Virginia saw her husband's dark side.

John lunged at the Russian right there on the steps, snarling like a wolf. As she watched in horror, the two vampires tumbled onto the lawn in the moonlight, ripping and tearing at each other with fangs and hands. After a vicious, animalistic struggle, John ended up on top, pounding Ivanov's face with pile-driver blows of his big fists as blood spattered the grass.

Virginia ran forward and grabbed her husband's powerful shoulder, shouting at him to stop. She hadn't wanted him to murder for her. She'd spent the three decades since damning herself for not letting him finish.

Because as John turned to deal with her, Ivanov called out a command, the sound mangled by his broken jaw.

They looked up to see five men armed with machine guns step from the woods. Virginia would never forget all those black muzzles blazing fire with a sound like God's rage.

John leaped off Ivanov and grabbed her, spinning to put his body between her and the gunmen, but the bullets cut right through him. She went down in his arms, her body tangled with his in a knot of pain and blood.

Yet even that wouldn't have killed either of them. Virginia could remember her bewilderment—why was Ivanov doing this? He knew nothing kills a vampire but beheading, a stake, or removing the heart.

Then, as the echoes died, Ivanov reeled to his feet and drew a dagger. Virginia screamed a protest as he crouched over them and drove the knife into her husband's broad chest.

That moment had haunted her nightmares ever since—her own shrieks ringing over John's deeper screams as Ivanov began to cut the heart from his body. Even with a dozen bullets riddling her, Virginia lunged at the madman, desperate to save John.

Ivanov hit her like a cat batting a mouse, with such power she flew fifteen feet. When she slammed into the ground, everything went black.

As she lay senseless, John's spirit left his dying body and entered her mind. Because he'd made her a vampire, her husband had always possessed the ability to implant commands she could not disobey. Yet he'd never used that power. Until that night.

Don't avenge me. Stay away from him. Hide. He'll kill you—and worse. I will come back, and I will protect you.

But how . . . ? she'd demanded, grieving and desperate.

Before he could answer, John's spirit spun away as though pulled out of her mind by some alien force. Virginia screamed out to him with all the power in her soul, begging him to return.

Instead it seemed her own mind winked out like a candle. When she regained consciousness, Ivanov was gone. Remembering the Russian's mangled face, Virginia had realized John had hurt him badly, and he'd needed to heal.

The vampire's men could still have captured her, but he evidently gave them no such order. Knowing Ivanov, he'd wanted to hunt her himself at his leisure.

But Virginia made sure he never found her. She'd left Texas, erased her tracks, and gone to ground. She'd thought herself safe.

She'd been wrong. Ivanov had found out where she was. Eventually he'd have come for her—if Logan hadn't killed him first.

Vampire hunter or not, Virginia owed Logan a debt of gratitude. But how could she repay it without giving him another opportunity to kill her?

Ironic to fear a man who'd given her such pleasure. Could he drive a stake through her heart after making love to her? Remembering the rage on his face after she'd fed, she suspected he could.

But if the last hour meant nothing to him, to Virginia it had been everything. She felt a connection to him now, a sense that they were deeply bound in a way she'd never known with anyone but John. She didn't understand why, but she recognized the elemental power of the link. She just didn't know what to do about it.

❦

Logan listened to the shower run and tried not to imagine Virginia with water pounding her lithe, little body and high, round breasts. He had other things to concentrate on, dammit.

Like that carelessly tied knot. Frowning, he tried to force his nails into the rope. She'd tied it tight, but he thought if he dug at it long enough, he could pull it loose.

But as he worked, images flashed through his mind—beaded water clinging to the end of one pointed rose nipple, a thin stream running into the soft, thick curls between strong thighs, finding its way across the furls of Virginia's sex . . .

Her teeth sinking into your neck, you dumb son of a bitch.

So she hadn't killed him. Yet. Maybe she just liked to work slower than Ivanov. Anyway, if he didn't get his head out of her cunt, she'd suck him dry a pint at a time.

Doggedly, Logan twisted his head around so he could get a better view of the knot. He gave serious thought to gnawing at it. The rope might be thick, but it was also soft, even tied in knots the size of ping pong balls. If it had been made of hemp or even good old nylon, he'd have a hell of a time getting loose, besides having wrists abraded to hamburger. Luckily Virginia hadn't wanted him hurt . . .

How do you know that? Logan thought, bringing himself up short. *Why should she care whether you get rope burns? She probably used silk because she didn't have anything else.*

And why the hell did it matter to him whether she cared or not?

That's what came of letting your dick think for you, Logan told himself in disgust. His cock thought that just because a woman felt sweet and creamy, he could trust her. His head damn well knew better.

Look at Gwen. The minute Logan's plane had taken off, wifey had gone bar hopping, hunting a little cooperative cock. And she'd been doing it for most of the five years they'd been married. Would have gone right on doing it, if she hadn't picked up Mr. Goodfang.

Logan couldn't even get properly pissed off about her adultery. Even as hurt and betrayed as he'd felt when he'd found out, he couldn't forget the sight of her small, butchered body lying in the morgue.

And in the final analysis, Logan knew he was to blame for the whole mess. While he'd been saving the world with the Navy SEALs, his marriage had been dying, and he'd done nothing to save it.

Gwen had thought being married to a SEAL would be romantic. She hadn't counted on the long separations, on the beeper that called him away from dinners for two and rare quiet nights at home. Logan couldn't even claim ignorance. He'd seen the signs—her coolness and indifference when he'd roll in from a mission, eager to make up for weeks of celibacy.

In retrospect, Logan even knew the exact moment he'd lost her: the night that beeper had gone off when they were making love, and he'd answered it.

He'd turned from the phone to start getting ready to go to Serbia, and the look in her eyes was so cold he'd stopped in his tracks. He'd wanted to explain about the hostages, but it was against the regs to talk about missions, even with your wife. Besides, when it came right down to it, Gwen wouldn't have given a shit.

They'd been married eight months.

Their union had staggered on another four years. She'd wanted a divorce, but he'd always talked her into staying. If he'd let her go then, she'd still be alive now.

Had he ever really loved her, or had she simply been convenient?

All his life he'd felt such a gnawing sense of something missing. When they first met, he'd thought Gwen was that missing something. He'd been wrong.

If he'd loved her as he should have if he'd made more of an effort, would she have strayed anyway?

Fuck it.

Logan set his jaw and narrowed his eyes, pushing away his regrets. Rehashing this again was pointless. He hadn't given her what she'd needed, and she'd gone out looking for it. And found Ivanov. She'd died screaming while Logan was hundreds of miles away. Nothing he did could ever change that.

But goddamn it, he could save the others.

Under his fingers, the first knot gave. Unfortunately, the damn rope had more knots than macramé. How had Virginia concentrated on tying those suckers sitting on his hard-on? He must be losing his touch.

It took him another hour to escape.

He slid out of bed and stopped long enough to pull on his black fatigue pants. He grinned bitterly at the sun he could see rising just beyond Virginia's lace curtains, then padded warily out into the hall.

The master bedroom door was open. Heart in his throat, Logan stepped inside. Virginia lay curled in a ball under the sheets. Naked, judging from the curve of her bare back and the long, slim length of one arm flung across the pillow. Her dark hair surrounded her head in a tumble of corkscrew curls, and her soft rose lips were parted in sleep.

Logan set his jaw and turned his back. She'd gone downstairs to get his gun; the rest of his stuff must be down there, too.

He found it all lying on a coffee table in that intensely feminine living room of hers. Logan cocked a brow and looked around, taking in the flowered prints and antiques, inhaling the scent of the rose potpourri she'd put in a crystal bowl. His attention fell on her husband's portrait over the couch, captured staring at his artist wife with eyes as hot and green as a cat's. Logan turned away from the painting and picked up the last arrow. A grandfather clock ticked out in the hall, the sound loud in the utter silence of the house.

Barefoot, Logan moved silently into Virginia's bedroom. She'd rolled onto her back while he'd been gone. The sheet hooked over her shoulder and under the opposite hip, leaving one breast bare. He stopped in his tracks and looked down at the delicate white globe with its rose tip.

Swallowing, Logan dragged his eyes away from it, his fingers tightening on the arrow. Her face looked relaxed in sleep, her eyelashes long, silken fans against the pure curves of her cheeks, her full lips parted as she breathed softly in her sleep. A curl looped across her nose, and he leaned forward and tenderly brushed it back.

And straightened. "Fuck, McLean. Who are you trying to kid?"

There was no way in hell he could hurt this girl. There hadn't been since he'd watched her stroll out of her house the night before last, looking like somebody's virgin kid sister all dressed up in her bad sister's black dress.

Liquid diet notwithstanding, Virginia was about as evil as a Sunday school teacher. His body had known that even before the message had penetrated his thick skull. Otherwise he couldn't have made love to her. Sadism had never turned him on.

Ivanov had been evil, but that had more to do with his being a sick son of a bitch than his vampirism. If Virginia had been anything like that, she'd have ripped out Logan's throat back at Gary's house instead of knocking him cold.

True, she had tied him up and fucked his brains out without letting him touch her, but that wasn't exactly evil. Fun, but not evil.

Not, he thought, eyeing that bare pink nipple, that he was too noble for a little revenge . . .

※☽(♋☾☽⚹

When Virginia woke up, she lay on her back with both hands trapped under her body. She groaned and rolled on her side, meaning to pull them free. Instead, she heard only a musical rattle. Her eyes flew open. Somebody had chained her wrists together. And she had a very good idea who that somebody was.

"Has anybody ever mentioned you sleep like the dead?"

Virginia jerked her head up and stared wildly around. Logan sprawled in the rose arm chair beside her bed, playing with an arrow. A wave of cold slid across her skin. She jerked her wrists with all her strength. The titanium manacles rattled but didn't break.

"Didn't I leave you tied up?" she gritted, increasing the force of her pull. The chains didn't even creak.

He smiled. "I'm a sailor. I'm good with knots."

Virginia tried to kick out from under the sheets, only to realize he'd chained her ankles together too. Feeling panicky, she subsided to stare at him, wide-eyed.

"I'm not going to hurt you." He rolled the arrow between his palms and grinned. "See how unconvincing that sounds when you're tied up?"

"If you're trying to teach me a lesson, I'm a quick study. You can unlock the chains now."

His grin took on a downright demonic cast. "But we haven't gotten to the good part yet." Logan tossed the arrow aside and rolled out of the chair. Broad bands of muscle rippled in his chest and powerful arms as he crawled onto the mattress toward her. "Payback's hell," he said, looming over her, a thick, dark curl falling over one eye, his handsome face intent.

"What are you going to do?" Virginia's mouth went dry with something much closer to excitement than fear. "Bite me?"

"Among other things." He rocked back on his heels to smile wickedly down at her. His eyes lingered on her bare breasts, thrust upward by the position of her bound hands under her back. "Many other things."

He reached out to capture both her nipples in his strong fingers for a long, gentle squeeze. Virginia gasped as hot, quivering sensation rolled down her spine to pool between her thighs.

"You know, the bondage isn't really necessary." She had to stop to swallow. "I'm more than willing."

"True, but you also like to bite." He pinched ever so gently. "And I think it's my turn to feast on you."

She looked at him and licked her dry lips. "That's fair."

This time Logan intended to make good use of his hands. Her breasts filled them, warm satin skin and sweet pink nipples, deliciously round and pert. He stroked his fingers dreamily over their taut contours, then caught them in both hands and bent so he could suck first one hard tip, then the other.

"You know, I think . . ." Virginia stopped to gasp. "I think I like your revenge."

"Do you?" He looked up into her face as her eyes closed in pleasure. "How much?" Wickedly, he released one breast to slip a hand between her thighs. He brushed a finger through the damp curls, found her opening and slowly slid inside. She was slick and creamy, and her soft cry of pleasure made him smile. "*That* much, huh?"

Logan added a second finger, began to slowly pump. She gave a helpless little roll of her hips. Lowering his head, he went back to licking her utterly gorgeous breasts, still pumping, turning his wrist back and forth until his fingers screwed in and out of her buttery heat.

When he saw the flush of approaching orgasm spread across her pretty breasts, he slowed the pace of his stroking fingers.

"Don't stop!" Virginia gasped, sounding lusciously desperate.

"There's something I want," he told her, lifting his head. She looked tousled and dazed.

"Anything." That moan alone would have given him a hard-on, if his dick hadn't been rock solid already.

Logan smiled slowly. "It's what I've wanted since I saw you with Gary." He unzipped his fatigues and jerked them off to liberate his straining erection, then tossed them across the room. "Put your mouth on me."

Virginia sat up as he lay back, her dark eyes focusing on his hard, rosy length. She looked down at him. "Uncuff me."

"Hey, I did you tied."

She licked her lips. "Aren't you afraid I'll bite?"

"That'd be kind of like cutting off your nose to spite your face. Why do you think I didn't let you come first?"

"You are not a nice man." Virginia leaned across his thighs. Her breasts pressed against him, warm and silken.

"I never claimed to be."

Twisting her head, she ran her tongue up the underside of his rigid shaft. He sucked in a breath. Her dark eyes slid to meet his, and she gave him a wicked grin. "Like that?"

"Oh, yeah. Do it some more."

"Guess I don't have a choice." She flicked her tongue over the head of his cock. "You're the big, bad vampire hunter with the keys to the manacles."

Feeling very big and very bad, Logan watched her nibble and lick, both delicate wrists cuffed behind her back. His cock was so hard it was difficult for her to get it positioned without the use of her hands. Finally she straddled him, head-down along his body, and took him deep.

At the sensation of her hot mouth engulfing him, Logan thought his balls would detonate on the spot. To distract himself, he busied his hands with her luscious ass while her mouth did amazing things to his cock. Hungering for a taste of her, he lifted his head and buried his face against her wet, spread sex, plunging his stiffened tongue inside. She jerked and gasped, sounding muffled. "Like that?" he asked wickedly.

She made an incoherent sound, her mouth too full of cock to speak.

"I'll take that as a yes," he said, and began to nibble.

As if in a wicked echo, a hot, female mouth did the same.

God, the man knew how to use his tongue. Virginia closed her eyes in delight as Logan licked and suckled, her own mouth completely stuffed with his shaft. There was so much of him she could barely manage, especially with her hands bound. She was surprised at how erotic it was, draped across his powerful body in chains, straining to take his hot erection down her throat. With her other lovers, she'd always been in control; this submissive streak surprised her. Though John . . .

She shouldn't be doing this, Virginia thought, stung by the memory of her husband. John . . .

He inserted two fingers of one big hand into her body, gave her a single slow pump.

John . . .

He added a third. She froze, her mouth wrapped around the delicious width of him, her body clamoring to take him deep as her heart struggled with guilt and loyalty.

He rotated those fingers now, screwing her slowly. Reaching his free hand around her hips, he found one breast and began to toy with her nipple, squeezing it, rolling the hard nub, tugging. His right hand pumped at her opening, his thumb flicking her clit.

Oh, God.

John isn't coming back, the Hunger whispered, seductive as Satan. *And Logan is here. Now. You can torture yourself about it later.*

Virginia pulled off his cock slowly, feeling the slick skin slide past her lips. With a little whimper, she surrendered to her need.

And took him deep again.

Logan watched her in the bureau mirror, enjoying the way she looked with her hands chained and her mouth full of him. Her cunt felt so deliciously tight and creamy around his fingers, he knew he wasn't the only one getting off on the raw, hot kink of the situation.

Poor little vampire. He could do any damn thing he wanted with her.

That was not a nice thought, he told himself sternly. Just because Virginia had knocked him cold and tied him up, he shouldn't be taking such evil delight in turning the tables. Even if she was so deliciously willing to atone . . .

Damn, he wasn't going to be able to take any more of this, he thought, feeling her mouth sliding around his cock again. He had to stop her, or he'd never be able to finish this in that tight, creamy body of hers . . .

He should have known she'd know. She pulled away and began gently tonguing his testicles, drawing out the pleasure just as she had with Gary.

But she wasn't in control this time, dammit. Logan surged up under her, grabbed her lovely hips and rolled her off him, despite her startled cry of protest. "Logan, I wasn't finished!"

"Neither am I." He threw a pile of pillows in the middle of the bed, picked her up again and draped her belly down across them.

Angling her hips upward to make the best possible target of her wet opening, Logan reared over her and spread the delicate pink folds that had been driving him crazy. He positioned the crown of his cock at her opening.

"Now," he gritted, feeling insanely possessive. "Now I've got you like I want you."

He rammed her, hard and full in one stroke. Virginia cried out helplessly. She could see him in the mirror, his profile set and predatory as he braced his hands beside her head and covered her small body with his. In this position, with her on her knees with her rump lifted, he could take her as deep and hard as he wanted.

"How does that feel?" he purred in her ear.

"It's . . . it's too much . . . ," she gasped. He felt so big, so thick as he rode her. Overwhelming.

"But does it hurt?" Grinding against her, he circled his hips in a screwing motion, the strong, hard muscle of his thighs pinning hers.

"No! It feels . . ." She stopped to whimper, her eyes sliding closed. "Hot . . ."

"Good." And he plunged even harder.

He was inside her as deeply as he could get, thrusting in short digs of his cock. And she felt utterly helpless, unable to control her partner for the first time in decades. She couldn't make him stop, couldn't even slow him down. And she didn't want to.

The Hunger rolled over her, triggered by her lust and his, and her fangs slid to their full length. But she couldn't reach him, and she realized that was exactly why he'd taken her in this position. He was in control, and he wanted her to know it. But then, he'd been in control even when she'd had him tied.

"My clit," she pleaded.

He shifted just enough that he could reach her button with his thumb. That stimulation, combined with his powerful strokes, shot her toward her peak.

But the Hunger wanted more—wanted his pleasure, wanted his climax. Instinctively she reached out for his mind. And this time, without his rage to block her, they merged.

She felt the hot pressure of his pleasure gathering maddeningly in his balls, felt her own slick walls gripping his cock, so tight and creamy as he tunneled in and out of her. And felt his astonishment as he felt what *she* felt—his width filling her, his powerful thrusts. And the Hunger that burned for him so desperately.

No, he thought, even as their shared ecstasy rolled and crested, each driven higher by the other. *I'm not going to be just food to you.*

You're so much more than that, she thought.

And then the crest hit, and the sheer, ferocious intensity of it spun them apart and blanked everything else in a silent white explosion.

Chapter Seven

Logan collapsed beside her, dazed, and lay there gasping as he listened to her shallow pants. She seemed too far away, so he scooped her onto his chest.

Virginia made a little sighing sound of contentment and relaxed. He stroked her, her head, her shoulders, the slim line of her arms. Their awkward position reminded him of the manacles. Groaning, he rolled out from under her to go in search of his pants. She grumbled a protest. "I'm trying to find the key to the damn chains," he told her.

"God, don't tell me you've lost it," she said, in a tone halfway between a groan and a giggle.

He found the fatigues in a corner and delved in the pockets until his fingers closed on something cool and slim. "Nope. Here it is."

Virginia yawned as he unlocked the chains, pulled them off, and tossed them, rattling, into a corner. "Sorry about that," he told her, feeling guilty, as he sat down to rub the fine muscles in her arms. "I went a little nuts."

She turned her head to smile lazily at him. "No harm done." The smile broadened into a grin. "In fact, just the reverse."

Without thinking, he slid into bed next to her and gathered her against his chest. She felt warm, a little damp, and she sighed as she settled against him.

"Lord, I'm tired," she said, with another jaw-cracking yawn.

"You didn't get enough sleep." He stroked a hand down her arm, enjoying the texture of her skin. "It's barely noon. Which reminds me, I gather the thing about vampires not being able to wake up before sunset . . ."

"Is a myth. We sleep deeply, but we can wake during the day. We just don't like to. Especially after some hulking vampire hunter exhausts us by forcing us to serve his insatiable lusts." She sounded smug.

"Then we'll take a little nap, and I'll exhaust you some more." Logan reached out and snagged the pillows he'd piled in the middle of the bed and tossed them against the headboard. Settling back against them, he wrapped his arms around her slender body and held her.

I'm cuddling a vampire, some sane fragment whispered. He ignored it. She felt right in his arms, right in a way even Gwen never had. He felt as if he'd come home.

Resting his chin on top of her head, Logan smiled as her tight curls tickled his chin. Odd how familiar that felt, as if they'd lain this way a thousand times.

For the first time in months, he felt his rage and tension drain away. He smiled as he slipped into sleep.

Virginia listened to the beat of his heart slow as he drifted off. She felt . . . stunned. The touch of his mind as they made love . . .

She knew him now. She'd felt his heroism, his strength, his deep sense of honor. Despite his anger and grief for his wife, she realized she was safe with him. Probably always had been.

He was a warrior, yes. He could—and would—do what he thought was right, no matter what it cost him. But he felt something for her, something she suspected even he was unaware of. Something deep and inexplicable and instinctive. That instinct, whatever it was, had saved her every time she'd been at his mercy.

She didn't understand it any more than he did. Why would he feel such strong emotion for a woman he'd only just met, a woman he'd had reason to suspect of brutal crimes? Yet he'd felt the connection anyway.

And so did she. From the first, there had been something about him that reached into her and grabbed on tight, despite her deep loyalty to John. Love at first sight? No. This was no simple hormonal reaction to good bone structure. It had too much depth for that.

She'd even come with him. Twice. No, more than that . . .

What was more, given the chance she'd do it again. And she wanted even more. She wanted to be with him, stay with him. It made no sense, but she couldn't deny the strength of her own reaction.

Frowning, Virginia looked at her wedding rings, staring into the deep green emerald clasped by diamonds. Humans married again after the death of a mate. In fact, most would have remarried long since. And she was immortal. Failing a fatal encounter with another psychotic vampire or misguided vampire hunter, she could survive for hundreds of years. She did not want to live them alone.

For the past three decades, Virginia had told herself that she believed John's promise that he would return. But he hadn't. And he couldn't. Deep inside, she'd known that when she'd buried him with that gaping hole in his chest.

Though a part of her heart cried out in protest because it still belonged to him, she knew he wouldn't want her to remain forever alone. And John would have approved of Logan, despite his sailor's vocabulary and ruthless determination to do the right thing whatever the cost.

Too, Logan was Kith, the first Kith male she'd met since John's death. That meant it was physically possible for him to become a vampire if he chose to. Unfortunately, given what had happened with Ivanov, he might not want to.

Yes, she thought he'd soon be willing to admit the strength of the passion between them. Perhaps he'd even stay with her. But whether he'd agree to become a vampire was another question altogether.

Yet if he didn't choose to change, could she endure watching him grow old and die? Could she bear being left alone again?

God, she was so tired of being alone. Since John's death, she'd existed in a kind of empty limbo, faking life more than living it. She made good wages as an artist, had even gotten some recognition for it. She'd learned how to disappear into her work for days at a time, coming out only when the Hunger became more than she could tolerate.

Yet she could never form a connection with her lovers, despite her psychic powers. Whether it was the kind of men she chose or her determination to keep her vows, she always left them feeling empty and apart. They'd been no match for John, for the hot moments of completion when her mind had blended with her husband's. With him, she'd felt no hunger for anyone else.

Yes, she and John had needed the blood of others. More than once they'd scared the living daylights out of muggers who'd thought to hold them up, only to end up dinner. Many a reformed thief around the world couldn't quite explain his compulsion to go straight, except it had something to do with a handsome couple and one dark night.

Despite such amusements, when it came to sex, there'd been no one else for either of them. Even after John had died, that hadn't changed.

Until now.

No, Virginia thought, with the sudden fierce strength of conviction, she didn't want to go back to being alone. Didn't want to spend her days pining not only for John, but for Logan now as well. And she wouldn't, she decided. Somehow she'd persuade him to stay with her. As a vampire. No matter what it took.

Biting her lip, she took her rings between her thumb and forefinger and slowly pulled them off. A part of her cried out in grief, but she silenced it. John was the past.

Logan was her life now.

Logan could hear a strange rumbling sound, a rhythmic clopping as he sat inside the dark, swaying box. Looking out the window, he saw a passing street lamp. A flame danced behind its glass shield, and for a moment that struck him as odd.

Then the rumbling became the sound of coach wheels on cobblestones, and the clopping resolved itself into the sound of his team of matched bays driven at a trot by his coachman.

He was hurrying to Virginia.

He wondered if he should stay away. With the wedding yet a month off, resisting the temptation of her sweet, silken little body had become sheer torture. But the compulsion to see her overwhelmed his doubts.

He had to make sure she didn't change her mind. Had to keep her too enthralled to question why she never saw her handsome fiancé in daylight.

Logan had been alone since he'd left Alys and Richard all those centuries ago, and his loneliness had become unbearable. Virginia lit his darkness with her wit and set a match to his desire with her beauty. So young still, but he could see the strength and fire under the prim mask of demure debutante. She made him feel protective and predatory all at once.

The coach drew up in front of the red brick walls of her father's townhouse. Opening the door, he started to step down . . . just as he heard the shriek of rage and fear.

Logan had never heard Virginia scream, but somehow he knew the voice was hers. He grabbed the pistol and sword he kept in the coach and leaped out. Where the hell was she?

Another scream, this one coming from behind the townhouse. He raced in that direction with a speed no mortal man could match.

A high brick wall surrounded the house, and he snarled at it in frustration. He thought about vaulting the wall, but just as he gathered himself, he heard the sharp crack of a hand hitting flesh.

"Stop your howling, bitch," a rough male voice spat. "You're coming with me, and that's the end of it. You're mine now."

"I don't even know you!" Virginia cried. "Papa! Help me!"

Logan shot around the corner just as the back gate opened in the wall and a man hauled Virginia out into the street. The side of her face was flushed red in the shape of a hand print. The sight sent hot rage roaring through Logan's soul.

The kidnapper turned on Virginia, baring teeth that were inhumanly long and sharp. Logan recognized him. Reynard, an arrogant little prick of a vampire who had, by God, just overstepped his bounds. "Your papa won't save you—he'll do what I tell him, and I've told him you're mine."

"Not bloody likely, Reynard." Logan shoved the useless pistol into his waistband and drew the sword with a hiss of steel.

The vampire turned and saw the blade glinting in the moonlight. In a move almost too fast to follow, he jerked Virginia in front of him and fisted a hand in her hair, dragging her head back. "Stay back or I'll rip her open."

Logan coiled into a crouch. "If you so much as nibble, I'll slice off your dick and shove it so far down your throat I'll cut it in two when I hack off your head."

Reynard's eyes flickered with the knowledge that he meant every word. He gave Virginia a vicious shove that sent her sprawling to the pavement. And leaped.

Logan met the vampire's lunge with a shining arc of his sword, a single stroke born of centuries' practice. He stepped aside as Reynard's body toppled. The vampire's severed head hit the cobblestones and bounced. Logan gave it a contemptuous snarl, then glanced up. And felt his blood run cold.

Virginia was staring at him in shock, her huge brown eyes focused on his mouth. On the fangs he knew had descended in his rage.

"Whatever else I am," he said roughly, his heart in his throat, "I love you."

She met his eyes at last, and he saw trust in hers. "I know."

He reached for her. She ran into his arms.

❧⟨✦⟩❧

Logan shot upright in bed, his heart pounding. His stomach rebelled. He rolled out of bed and reeled into the bathroom.

At the sink, he twisted the taps and began splashing handfuls of water over his sweating face, fighting for control. At last his stomach settled, and he lifted his head to look in the mirror.

The eyes that stared back at him were green, not the blue they'd been all his life. His hair was all wrong too, blond instead of dark brown, and the face—it wasn't his at all. More narrow than his own, with a Roman nose and a wide mouth.

A stranger's face.

Who the hell am I?

"Logan?" He turned to see Virginia rubbing her eyes as she stood in the bathroom doorway.

Logan heard himself say in a voice he didn't even recognize, "I told you I'd come back."

All the blood drained from Virginia's face. She stared into his eyes as hers widened with fear—and a slowly dawning joy. "John?"

No! He shook himself, shaking off the alien presence, the remnants of the dream that couldn't possibly be memory. When he looked at the mirror again, the reflection was his own.

"John?" Virginia reached out a trembling hand toward his bare shoulder. "You promised you'd come back, but I never thought you meant like . . ."

"I don't know what the fuck you're talking about," Logan told her savagely. "My name is Logan McLean, and it always has been."

Virginia stared at him, at his cold, closed expression, wondering if she'd imagined the . . . presence in his eyes. *John?* It couldn't be . . .

And yet, he was about the right age. "What day were you born?"

He turned on her and loomed. He was taller than John had been by a good three inches, and his long body was even more heavily muscled than her husband's. And yet . . . "What difference does it make?"

"Please, Logan." She was begging, and she didn't care. "What day were you born? And where?"

"December 21, 1970. In Beverly, Texas."

Her heart leaped. "My husband died at our ranch just outside Beverly. On April 20, 1970. Nine months before you were born."

He clenched his big fists, but she knew he wouldn't use them on her. "Which means what, exactly? You think I'm the reincarnation of an eight-hundred-year-old vampire?"

"I never told you how old John was."

Unease flickered in his eyes. "I had a dream. Something about knights in chain mail. Looked like maybe 1200." He straightened his shoulders. "Coincidence." His expression hardened. "Too fucking much coincidence. The vampire who killed your husband thirty years ago just happens to murder my wife, and he just happens to have your address, sending me on a hunt for you, my wife from my last life? I don't think so."

"Maybe it wasn't a coincidence." Virginia watched as he shouldered past her and stalked into the bedroom to snatch up his fatigue pants. "What if Ivanov . . . recognized you somehow? He hated John. What if that's why he targeted Gwen?"

Logan froze, the fatigues in his hands. She could almost see his mind working desperately. Finally he looked up at her. "He said something . . . it didn't make any sense." He stopped. "No. That's bullshit. Even assuming there is such a thing as reincarnation, how would he have recognized my . . . soul? Particularly when you didn't."

"Maybe I just don't have the power. I've barely been a vampire two centuries, Logan. Ivanov was even older than John, and he was enormously powerful. You could feel it radiating from him as strongly as the evil." She studied his tight face. "What did he say to you?"

He lifted one shoulder. "I don't know. Something like, 'I've killed you twice now; I'll do it again.'"

A sensation of cold rolled over her. "John told me once that Ivanov had given him a killing blow as a mortal. That's why Alys changed him."

"Coincidence again." Logan set his jaw and stared fiercely at her, silently daring her to contradict him.

"You're afraid."

"No, I'm not. I just don't believe it." He turned and shoved one long leg into his fatigue pants. "Look, I realize you want your dead husband back, but lady, I ain't him. I'm a Navy SEAL, I was Gwen McLean's husband, *and I am not a vampire*."

She couldn't think, didn't know what to do. Could only stand there watching numbly as he finished jerking on his pants, then zipped them with quick, angry movements of his big hands. "Where are you going?"

"Home. To California. I've had enough of this *X-Files* shit."

"But what about me?" Virginia took a panicked step forward. "What am I supposed to do?"

"You don't have to do a goddamn thing."

"*But you came back.*"

"No. I didn't." He pushed past her and headed for the stairs. "That would mean I'd been here before." He shot her a glittering look over his shoulder. "And I've never met you until this week."

"I'm just supposed to forget this happened?" Virginia snatched up her robe and hurried after him, shrugging into it. "I'm supposed to pretend you're still dead? Do you have any idea how empty my life has been for the past thirty-two years?"

"I'm not dead, lady. And I'm not your husband."

"Okay." Frantically, she knotted the belt at her waist, her mind working faster than it ever had. "But you're Kith. Do you know how rare that is? You're the only Kith I've ever met."

Logan stopped on the stairs and frowned, looking back at her. "What the hell are you talking about now?"

"Kith," Virginia said rapidly, pausing on the step just above him so she was almost at his eye level. "As in 'kith and kin.' Have you wondered why there are so few vampires? It's because very few people can survive the transformation to become one. We call those who can the Kith."

"And this relates to me how, exactly?" He lifted a skeptical brow.

"Logan, that's why Ivanov's compulsion didn't work on you. Anger alone wouldn't have protected you. But the Kith have latent psychic abilities, so they develop natural mental shields to protect themselves, shields even we can't breach. That's how John knew I could become a vampire all those years ago. It's why he wanted me."

Logan's cold stare softened. "It wasn't the only reason." Turning, he continued down the stairs.

Something in his voice when he'd said those words warmed the chill in her. "How much do you remember?" Virginia asked softly. "About . . . before?"

"I don't remember a damn thing, because it didn't happen to me." He strode into the living room.

Trailing him, she took a breath and tried another tack. "What about me? I can never be anything but alone, Logan. The men . . . I can't be with them for more than one night, because if I did, I'd take too much blood from them." She rubbed her bare ring finger. "I'm always alone."

He looked up from the coffee table, where he'd begun packing his weapons away in the small rucksack he'd carried across his shoulders. Muscle rippled in his powerful chest as he moved. "I'm sorry for that, but I don't know what you think I can do about it. I wouldn't survive it either."

"But you could become one of us."

"And watch you fuck everything that moves?" He laughed, sounding so bitter Virginia flinched. "No thanks. I already had one unfaithful wife."

"A vampire couple doesn't need to sleep around," she said, desperate with the knowledge she was losing him. "Whatever we normally get from our sex partners, the bond gives. True, we need to take blood from others, but it doesn't have to be as . . . intimate."

"Yeah, well, whatever." He scooped up his long sleeved shirt and shrugged into it. "No offense, but I'm still not interested in a permanent liquid diet." His eyes lifted and flicked up and down her body. "No matter what . . . compensations there are."

She watched as he buckled on his shoulder holster, fighting desperately to think of something that would make him stay. "What you said about being an unfaithful wife . . . I was never that. I only took other men after John died because I would have starved otherwise."

He looked up at her, and compassion flickered in his blue eyes. She wondered if he'd heard the guilt in her voice. "He wouldn't have blamed you. He wouldn't have wanted you to suffer any more than you have."

"My point is . . . if I'm right, and John's soul lives on in you, it would be adultery to go on as I have. I can't do that."

Logan leaned over the coffee table toward her, bracing both arms on its surface. "John is dead, Virginia. Whether he got reincarnated or went to heaven, death did you part. You're not bound by those vows any more. It's been thirty years. Give him up."

She scrubbed at her bare ring finger again, trying to come up with a way to make him see. "How am I supposed to do that? You were half of me, John! When you died, it felt like . . ." Her lower lip quivered, and she bit it to hold it still. ". . . It felt like Ivanov had ripped out the core of my soul. *You promised me you'd come back, damn you!*"

"I'm not John," Logan said, his voice low and intensely controlled. "He was a desperate man dying with a hole in his chest, and he was afraid you'd be tortured to death. He deluded himself, and he deluded you."

"Logan, please!"

He looked away and swung the rucksack over his shoulder. "I'm sorry," he said stiffly. "I can't help you."

She drew herself up, feeling fierce and lost. "I can stop you. I can keep you, whether you like it or not."

His blue eyes swung to hers and narrowed. Then, reluctantly, softened. "But you won't. You wouldn't do that to me."

That last burst of energy drained away, leaving her feeling empty and ashen. "No. No, I wouldn't."

Without another word, he turned and headed for the door.

And she didn't stop him.

Chapter Eight

Logan had seen a convenience store when he'd first staked out her house. He hiked the mile or so it took to get there and used a pay phone to call a cab. Somehow he didn't feel he should test Virginia's shaky self-control by making the call from her home.

While he waited for the cab, he bought a Coke and a stale prepackaged sandwich and tried to ignore the nervous stare of the clerk. He couldn't really blame her. When a man dressed like Rambo walked into a convenience store at three in the morning, he usually had armed robbery in mind. Good thing all Logan's weapons were out of sight, or she'd be calling the cops. To spare her nerves, he went outside to wait.

Logan's looks didn't exactly thrill the cab driver either, but he was evidently desperate enough for a fare to take the chance. The cab dropped Logan off in Gary's neighborhood, where, wonder of wonders, his rental car still waited in the wooded lot where he'd hidden it.

He drove back to his hotel, called the airline he'd flown in on, and booked a flight home. He hadn't bought a round trip ticket to begin with because he hadn't been sure when—or even if—he'd return.

With several hours to kill before his flight, Logan took a shower and began to feel marginally more human. Dressed in a pair of briefs, he sprawled across the bed and turned on the television. He could have used the sleep he'd lost when the nightmare woke him, but he didn't want to chance it. He suspected he'd dream about Virginia again, and he damn well didn't want to dream about John.

Not that he believed her cockeyed reincarnation theory. Yeah, he'd been having the dreams for years, but they didn't mean anything. He didn't even remember them half the time anyway.

He'd probably just seen a Dracula movie when he was a little kid, and it had embedded itself in his subconscious. All the rest of it was nothing but coincidence and imagination.

He sure as hell didn't remember the taste of Virginia's blood in his mouth, hot and sweet and . . .

Thrusting that thought away, Logan checked out the hotel movie menu. The adult movies were definitely out—he didn't want to watch blowsy actresses fake interest in sex acts Virginia had loved—and the rest of the selections were just as poor. Chick flicks, something with "vampire" in the title—he didn't *think* so—and a slasher movie. All of which hit a little too close to home. Disgusted, he turned on CNN and tried to get interested in the latest doings in Washington.

When he caught his eyes sliding closed for the second time, Logan started channel surfing, trying to keep himself awake. Spotting a black and white close-up of John Wayne in a World War II uniform, he tossed the remote aside and settled in to watch the Duke kill Nazis.

He slid into sleep so seamlessly he didn't even notice.

Even after Virginia had seen John for what he was, she'd said she loved him. But it hadn't been enough. He'd wanted to put his mark on her so deeply she'd never think of calling off the wedding.

And he could think of only one way to do it. He'd taken her home with him, not even stopping to dispose of the other vampire's remains.

Even as innocent as she was, Virginia had known what he intended, but she hadn't demurred. He wondered if she, too, wanted to make sure she couldn't go back.

She had, of course, never seen his bedroom, and she made a great to-do of exploring it, commenting on the furnishings in a voice that quavered.

He'd be amused, if he wasn't just as nervous.

It amazed him. He'd taken so many women to bed over the past six hundred years that he should be far beyond a bridegroom's nerves. Hell, if it wasn't for the Hunger, he'd be bored with the whole business by now.

But Virginia wasn't one of his bon-bon women, sweet on the tongue, forgotten an hour later. He'd searched for her all his long life, needed her to end the endless, empty pursuit of sex for survival's sake. To end the loneliness of never having someone he could confide in, share his dreams with. He didn't want to bungle it.

Now, watching her walk quickly around the room, he thought of a little bird fluttering around a cat. "Are you afraid of me?" he asked. Not that he could blame her, after what she'd seen him do to the vampire who'd tried to kidnap her.

Virginia looked up, startled. "No. Not of you. You'd never hurt me." She said it with a quiet confidence all the more remarkable for a woman who'd seen his fangs.

"But you know what I am."

She looked at him, trust glowing in her brown eyes. "Yes. I do." Virginia folded her hands in that neat, quiet gesture he'd seen her make so many times before. "You have courted me a year now, John. In all that time, you have never acted less than a gentleman."

He studied her. "Then why are you so nervous?"

Her gaze slid away from him. "It's not you."

"Then what is it?"

"Abigail St. James . . . Well, you know, young ladies will talk, and she's the biggest chatterbox of any of my circle. She said she'd talked to her mother about . . . it . . . and her mother told her . . . it . . . was terribly painful, but she must endure for the sake of having children, and if she was fortunate the gentleman would be through quickly, and . . ."

"Abigail's father isn't doing something right."

She stopped in mid-babble. "I beg your pardon?"

He moved toward her slowly. "If Abigail's mother thinks the best thing about sex is that it's over quickly, her husband must be a wretched lover." Reaching out, John took her gently into his arms. "I am not a wretched lover."

He swept her up and stretched her out on the bed, then undressed her slowly, unveiling her lush round breasts and her slim hips and long legs, kissing and tasting every inch of her even as he pulled her clothing away.

She was a virgin, and he knew there would be some pain for her—he couldn't avoid it, given his size. But as the hours passed, he made sure the pain was not what she would remember.

He brought her to climax twice, first with his fingers, then with his mouth as she twisted under him in a combination of shyness and desire.

When he finally mounted her, she was slick and wet, and there was no fear at all in her eyes. As her desire crested, he spun a link between them and shared his pleasure through it as he thrust into her. She barely even felt her virgin's pain.

Then, as he climaxed deep within her, drawing out her third or-

gasm of the night, John lowered his head to the slim column of her throat.

Logan jolted upright with the taste of Virginia's blood in his mouth.

The television blared out an infomercial for some kind of thigh cream, and he stared at it with wild eyes. She had tasted so sweet.

It was just a dream, dammit, he told himself fiercely.

A dream, not a memory. He was not John Hart, and he wasn't a vampire. He didn't know what it felt like to sink his teeth into a woman's throat and feel her blood flooding hot and sweet over his tongue, tasting of pleasure and sex and life. He hadn't felt Virginia's hymen break around his cock, hadn't felt her slim body jolt against his with a virgin's surprise.

He just had a very good imagination.

Thank God it was dawn. He got up and dressed, wanting only to get away from Virginia and her tempting body and the memories— dreams!—of another man's life.

Then he drove to the airport, turned the car in, and flew back to Coronado, carefully not thinking of anything.

Virginia sat in front of her easel, the brush limp in her hand. She had to snap out of this. She had a show in a couple of months, and she'd promised to have at least two more paintings ready for it.

He'd been gone a week.

She kept hoping he'd call her, though she knew better. To call her was to admit she'd been something more to him than a one-night stand, and he'd never do that. It would be too much like admitting he remembered John's life, remembered what they'd been to one another.

Even she found it hard to think of him as John. In movies, reincarnated people always looked exactly the way they had in past lives, but Logan didn't resemble her husband in the slightest. They were both muscular men, yes, but John had been a product of the thirteenth century, when even the rich ate poorly compared to those in the twenty-first. Though his body had gained power from years of swinging a sword from horseback, he'd never had Logan's sheer size.

Mentally the two were quite different. Logan seemed a harder man than her husband, more focused, more ruthless. Or perhaps John had simply been better at hiding it.

Yet there'd also been something in Logan's eyes she recognized. As if, despite everything, the soul was the same.

It was confusing. And heartbreaking. And dangerous. Because though she felt her loneliness with an intensity she hadn't known in years, she hadn't been able to take another man since he'd left.

And God help her, the Hunger was driving her mad.

Alice Kendall had gorgeous breasts, mile-long legs and blow job lips, and she seemed cheerfully willing to let Logan take her home. All in all, the perfect cure for everything that ailed him.

He'd come to this particular bar just outside the Navy base hoping to find somebody just like her. A night between those long legs should neatly erase Virginia from his memory.

Good plan. So why couldn't he work up any interest at all in putting it into practice? And why did his attention keep drifting to the big pulse in Alice's neck? Especially given the spectacular cleavage the round neckline of her top put on display?

It had been ten days, and the dreams about John hadn't gone away. Not even putting the latest class of would-be commandos through their paces could distract him. And serving as an instructor for BUD/S—the Basic Underwater Demolition/SEAL training course—was normally exhausting enough to wipe every other thought out of his head.

Logan found himself wishing for a few trigger-happy terrorists to fight, but no such luck. The brass had rotated him into the instructor's slot after Gwen's death, feeling he needed to stay out of the line of fire for a while. And given the looks he'd been getting lately, they hadn't changed their minds.

At least Logan no longer dreamed about Gwen, though the new dreams were almost as troubling. Even worse, they'd started to bleed into his waking hours.

To kill time last night, Logan had turned on a History Channel special on the Duke of Wellington, Arthur Wellesley. As a portrait of the British hero appeared on the screen, he'd thought, *That's a lousy likeness.* And an image of the man's face had flashed through his mind.

Logan didn't remember how John knew the man who'd defeated Napoleon, or anything else about Wellington except how he looked.

But somehow he couldn't just dismiss the whole thing as simple imagination.

At first such flashes had scared the shit out of him, but in the last day or so he'd begun to adjust. For one thing, he'd always had moments of *déjà vu*, even before he'd met Virginia. He'd just dismissed them as the kind of mental short-circuit everybody experiences periodically. Now he was beginning to wonder.

Hell, he was actually coming to welcome those weird little flashes. If nothing else, they took his mind off Virginia.

She'd become an obsession. Memories of her, laughing up at him with wicked humor in her brown eyes, gasping in passion as he sucked her little pink nipples. Her husky voice begging him to take her. The grief in her eyes when she'd pleaded with him to stay.

Virginia was driving him crazy.

Suddenly he became aware that Alice had stopped talking. She eyed him, leaning back in her chair. "Am I interrupting?"

Logan blinked at her. "I'm sorry, what?"

"Who is she? Wife, girlfriend, ex-? Or is it a he?"

Caught. He sighed. "It sure as hell isn't a he."

"Didn't think so. So are you cheating, or did she?"

He shrugged and moved his beer around in a circle on the small table. "My wife picked up the wrong guy in a bar. He murdered her."

Alice winced. "Tough break. I can see why you're not in the mood to be sparkling company."

"Maybe you'd better save the sympathy. My wife is not the obsession." Logan tipped back his beer and drank deeply.

She lifted a brow. "No?"

He shook his head. "No. Gwen's been dead a year, and we'd been having problems for a long time before that—guess she wouldn't have been in that bar if we hadn't."

"And?"

"And I met this woman two weeks ago. We were only together three days, but I find myself missing Virginia a lot more than Gwen. Doesn't seem right."

"The heart doesn't have a sense of justice." Alice shrugged and sipped her own drink. "Sounds to me like you ought to be with her instead of here, raising the hopes of unsuspecting women."

He winced a little at the gentle barb. "Sorry about that. I just thought I'd try to find something a little less complicated."

"It's never uncomplicated." She met his eyes and peeled back her lips from her teeth.

Alice had fangs.

"Go back to Virginia, John—or Logan, or whoever you think you are," she said in the rippling Norman French of the twelfth century. Which Logan should not be able to understand.

Icy shock washed over his skin. "Alys?"

A man sitting at the next table rose, walked over, and dropped into the booth beside her. "Quit staring at my wife's pulse, John. It's rude."

The newcomer was dressed in a leather jacket and jeans, but in Logan's dreams, he'd always worn chain mail. Richard's familiar narrow, bony face was now framed by a hundred-dollar twenty-first century haircut instead of the shaggy mane he'd worn as a knight. He looked no more than twenty-five—until Logan met his eyes and saw the ancient power in them.

"You've shrunk," Logan said, then winced at the sheer witlessness of the comment.

Richard smiled. "No, you're just three inches taller."

Alys leaned across the table and laid her soft little palm over one of his white-knuckled fists. "It broke our hearts to hear what happened to you, John."

"I hunted the son of a bitch Ivanov for years afterward, but I could never find him," Richard said. "I understand you took care of him yourself. Impressive, particularly given your handicap."

He felt dazed, as if someone had hit him in the head one too many times. "Handicap?"

Richard smiled. "Mortality. Took guts, what you did. But then, you've never lacked for that."

"How did you know I was here? Did Virginia . . . ?"

Alys shook her head. "I happened to call her a couple of days ago, and forced her to tell the whole story. I've been checking up on her periodically, since . . . what happened to you. It's been very hard on her."

"And worse since you walked out," Richard said. "It's been ten days, John. You need to get back to her."

"I'm not John." He shook his head. "How did you know I'd be here?"

"We didn't." Richard leaned back in the booth, sliding an arm around his wife's shoulders. "It just stood to reason that sooner or later you'd show up in one of the bars around the base, looking for either a woman or a beer."

Logan looked at Alys. "But why the charade? Why pretend to pick me up?"

"We wanted to see if you'd recognize me." She shrugged. "And we wanted to talk to you first, make sure Virginia was right. She's always believed you'd come back, and I feared the strain . . . But she was right. So much is different, but your soul's the same."

"Yeah, well, she didn't recognize me. Not at first."

"She didn't make you a vampire," Richard told him. "And she doesn't have the power that comes with age."

Logan wanted to laugh. Between one hundred and seventy years as a vampire and another twenty as a mortal, Virginia was almost two centuries old. Yet these people considered her a child.

He met Richard's ancient eyes. His heart was pounding hard in his chest, and he wondered if the two vampires could hear it. "Has anyone ever come back . . . before?"

The other man hesitated, considering the question. "There's a theory I heard once. I never really believed it until now. But some think that's what the Kith are—the souls of our kind reborn as mortal. Few of us remember our other lives, but when the vampire lived as long as you did . . . that's a great weight of experience, enough even to punch through the barriers that normally protect a soul from its past."

After the last few days, Logan could easily imagine how disruptive it would be to remember an endless series of lives. "So I've always been a vampire?"

"No, but you've always been Kith. Remember, Kith don't change unless they encounter a vampire willing to change them."

He frowned. "Isn't that a chicken and egg thing? I mean, if vampires come from Kith, and Kith come from vampires, where did the first vampires come from?"

Richard smiled. "God."

Logan snorted and drained his beer. "This is . . . creepy, being another man."

Alys shook her head. "Love, you're the same man you've always been. You've just got a very old soul." She gave his hand a motherly pat. "Now, hadn't you better be getting back to Virginia? I think she's been alone long enough."

Logan drew himself up straight. "I think you're right." He wouldn't be able to go tonight, not without permission from his commanding officer. But first thing tomorrow, he'd have a long talk with his CO. It was time to resign his commission.

A vampire could hardly be a Navy SEAL.

He called the waitress over to pay the tab, said his goodbyes, and strode toward the door.

The two vampires watched him go. "It's good to have you back, lad," Alys said softly.

Richard turned to look at her. "By the way, I noticed he wasn't the only one staring at someone's pulse."

She smiled wickedly and quirked an eyebrow at him. "Well, that new body of his is rather handsome, don't you think?"

"What I think," he growled, "is that you need a spanking."

Alys purred out a laugh. "Only if you can catch me."

And she was off with him at her heels so fast the mortals didn't even see them go.

※≈(⊙⊙)≈※

Virginia paced the bedroom, the Hunger a dark, raging thing. She was running out of time. She'd hoped Logan would return and she wouldn't be forced to this, but now she had to face facts. It had been eleven days. He wasn't coming back. And if she didn't feed soon, the Hunger would drive her to attack some poor man in the dark like something out of a horror movie.

She glanced over at her mirror and winced at her own reflection. She felt weak and sick, and her skin was as pale as milk. She wasn't even sure she could attract a man in her current condition. He'd probably take one look at her haggard face and think she was a cancer victim out for one last night on the town.

No, she couldn't wait any longer.

Virginia showered and changed into her best come-take-me dress—the one with the deep cleavage and the skirt that barely covered her bottom. She'd need all the help she could get.

Her makeup was a bit more tricky, because her hands shook so badly she could barely hold her makeup brush. She had to redo her lipstick three times because it looked so ragged.

God, she hated this. It was worse than when John died. The guilt had eaten at her then, but she'd known she wasn't really cheating, just as she'd known he wouldn't have wanted her to starve. Not that the Hunger would have given her that option.

Virginia had heard of mortals who literally starved themselves to death. She could only assume that either her Hunger was much more intense than theirs, or her willpower was much weaker.

God, if only Logan would come back. Then she wouldn't have to do this. But he wouldn't, and that was that. She had to get on with her life.

We aren't married, she told herself fiercely. *This isn't really cheating.*

But her distaste for the idea of looking for another man was more than just her morality talking, and she knew it. The idea of touching someone else seemed . . . unsatisfying. Not enough. She wanted Logan.

But you're not going to get him, Virginia, she told herself sternly. *So you might as well just quit pining for the moon.*

One day there'd be another Kith male. True, she couldn't imagine ever loving him, not the way she did Logan/John. At least the loneliness would be over. In the meantime, she'd just have to take what she could get.

But what would happen to Logan? He was a Navy SEAL, a special forces warrior. He could be killed, and she'd never know. The thought that he could die again brought tears to her eyes.

You could find him, the Hunger whispered. *Force him.*

No. She squared her shoulders. She'd already faced that temptation, and she wouldn't yield to it now. It was Logan's decision, and she would not make it for him.

But God, how it hurt.

✺⦅✿⦆✺

When Logan arrived at Virginia's place after the flight from California, the house was dark and still. He knew immediately she was out hunting, and he felt a flare of startling jealousy. He snuffed it ruthlessly. *You know better than that, moron. With vampires, celibacy equals starvation.* He'd left eleven days ago. By now she had no choice except to look for a lover, if she hadn't already.

Fortunately, this early in the evening he had a good chance of catching her before she found someone. He knew she often went out to surrounding towns to hunt, but he had a hunch she wouldn't be up to a long trip today. He headed for the bar he'd found her in last time.

Knowing Virginia the way he did now, it surprised Logan she'd even be caught dead in Boot Scoot. A long, low roadhouse, it was the sort of joint the cops got called to twice a night on Saturdays. The walls and floors were dark brown planks, and most of the illumination came from neon beer signs. Peanut shells crunched underfoot, and a voice from the jukebox sang about cheating and beer.

When he walked in, Virginia was the first thing he saw.

She sat at a little round table, and that son of a bitch Gary had one muscled arm looped over her shoulder as he spoke to her earnestly. A wave of possessive fury took Logan by surprise, and he crunched across the peanut shells toward them before his common sense had time to remind him that none of this was her fault.

". . . still don't understand why I didn't come after you. I could kick myself," the blond was saying. "You sure that big bastard didn't hurt you?"

"I'm fine, Gary. It was just a misunderstanding." Her voice sounded weak, and Logan frowned.

Studying her as he approached, he saw that she looked drawn, though it wasn't obvious between her expert makeup and the dim lighting. Had she waited the whole eleven days to hunt?

"I should have called the cops," Gary said, still fretting. "I don't know why I didn't . . ." He looked up as Logan stopped in front of the table. "Hey, buddy, do you mind? This is a private conversation."

"Not anymore." He pulled out a chair and sat down, then leaned across to take Virginia's hands.

She looked up, and her eyes lit with desperate hope. "Logan?"

"Who the fuck are you?" Gary growled, starting up out of his chair. "I said . . ."

"Gary, this is my . . . husband," Virginia cut him off. "Logan McLean."

The blond stiffened. "You little . . ."

She looked up at him, and he broke off and blinked hard. He opened his mouth again, then shook his head and wandered off, visibly confused.

"Handy talent to have," Logan said. "I thought I'd have to deck him again." He frowned. Her hands felt like ice. "You shouldn't have waited this long, Virginia."

Her eyes filled. "I'm glad I did. I hoped you'd come back." She went still. "You are back?"

"Yeah." He looked up at the single light that illuminated the table, then stood up. "Come on. I think we need a little more privacy."

Virginia rose and slipped her hand into his. His frown deepened at the way it felt, chill and too delicate, like bird bones. He led her quickly through the crowd, wanting only to get outside.

As they stepped out onto the cement porch of the building, Virginia stumbled against him. Logan turned and smoothly picked her up. She looped her arms around his neck and curled against him like a cat. He carried her around the corner of the building, looking for a dim, quiet spot. A sense of urgency pounded in his blood.

"Logan?" she asked, in a too-breathy voice. "Why did you come back?"

"I couldn't stay away." He spotted a stand of trees across the street and made for it. "I ran into Richard and Alys last night . . ."

"I told them not to interfere!" Anger lit two spots of red over her too-pale cheeks.

"They only accelerated the process, darlin'," he told her. "I couldn't have stayed away much longer anyway. It feels like I've got a piece missing, and you're it. As if I've been looking for you for a long time."

"I know what you mean," she said softly.

"I never loved Gwen. That's the hell of it. I married her looking for . . . Hell, I guess it was you. And she knew it. Maybe that's why she cheated." He smiled bitterly. "She knew I was cheating her."

"Haven't you blamed yourself for that long enough?" Virginia asked as they reached the shadows of the trees at last. "I realize you're a compulsive hero, but there's only so much you can do."

He smiled and let her slide down the length of his body, then pushed her against a tree trunk. A fever rose in him, a need to slide into her, feel her breasts filling his hands. "Why don't we just see how much I'm up to?"

Her slender arms slipped around his back, and she pulled him to her with that astonishing strength. He cupped the back of her head with his hand and tried to guide her face to his neck, but she couldn't quite reach him. She made a sound halfway between a groan and a laugh. "I'm too short."

"I'll take care of that." Catching her bottom in one hand, Logan lifted her. She wrapped both long legs around his waist, but when he guided her to his throat, she only kissed him.

"No, Virginia," Logan said. "Take what you need."

"But . . ."

"You're too weak." He smiled wickedly. "And you're going to need all the strength you can get."

"Cocky man."

He rolled his hips in the cradle of her thighs and flexed his fingers against the cleft of her peach-shaped ass. Her short skirt had ridden up, and only her panties kept his hands from her sex. "Which is exactly why you need your strength."

She laughed, a husky sound that made her breath puff warmly against his skin. Then he felt the cool brush of her lips as she kissed his throat—and the press of her teeth.

Chapter Nine

The sting of Virginia's fangs felt deliciously erotic. Her mouth began to work against his skin, sucking gently, and she moaned in need. Logan gasped and hardened against his fly as his hands tightened convulsively on her ass.

She flexed her hips as she drank from him, grinding against his ravenous erection. He growled and grabbed a handful of her panties. Jerked. The thin silk shredded. Hungrily, he slipped a hand down under her ass and between her legs. His fingers could just brush the lips of her wet, pouting sex. It wasn't enough.

Logan shifted his grip on her butt and pulled back just far enough to worm his hand down between their bodies. He entered her with one finger. She felt like hot butter around him, and he moaned in lust as she squirmed.

Without breaking her grip on his throat, he unzipped his jeans and freed his aching cock. With a twist of his hips, he impaled her.

Sliding into her wet cream heat sent such searing pleasure up Logan's spine he wanted to bellow in pleasure. Slowly, gently, he rocked in and out of her as her mouth worked at his throat. He hadn't realized how erotic it would be to deliberately feed her like this as he took her. Before, he'd always seen her bite as an invasion, not the delicious mutual possession it was.

Finally, Virginia's fangs slid from his throat, and she gasped in his ear.

"God, Logan, you feel so . . ."

He growled back at her and gathered her close, then began to hunch with short, strong digs of his cock. She writhed. He closed his eyes and fought not to come, lost in her silken heat.

* * *

God, Virginia thought, dazed. Logan felt so good inside her, so long and thick and hot. She hadn't known how cold she'd been until he'd shoved his heat into her. With his powerful arms wrapped around her and his big body stretching and surging between her legs, she felt overwhelmed and helpless.

The bark of the tree behind her scraped against her back as he took her, but she didn't care. Logan was back, and she didn't give a damn about anything else. "I love you," Virginia gasped. And she realized suddenly she wasn't just talking about John.

"And . . . I . . . love . . . *you*," he rumbled, punctuating each word with a deep, breath-stealing thrust that claimed and overwhelmed.

Every stroke ground against her clit, and she could feel herself going over. She surrendered to the rise of her orgasm, tightening her grip with her thighs and her arms, wanting only to be as close to him as she could.

The climax detonated in a white hot flash up her spine. Virginia convulsed helplessly. And reached for his mind. She felt his hot triumph as she came for him, and showed him how it felt—the skull-searing sensation of his width buried in her to the balls, of the purely female pleasure of his body wrapped around hers.

Her pleasure tipped him over into his. She shuddered at the great, pulsing wave rolling up from his balls and down his shaft to burst hot inside her. It was hardly the first time she'd experienced a man's orgasm since John's death, but she'd never felt such a shattering sense of *rightness*. As if he was all she needed and everything she'd ever been denied.

The pleasure built and built and built, her mind reflecting it into his, which reflected it back. Until everything went sharply white in a hot, silent explosion.

The next thing Virginia knew, she lay across his chest. Blearily she lifted her head. They were sprawled on the ground. "How'd we get here?"

Logan made a sound halfway between a groan and a laugh. "I think I passed out." He shook his head. "Man. First time that's ever happened."

Virginia yawned, then hastily covered her mouth with her hand. His body felt delicious under hers, all long, heated muscle, magnificently relaxed. A thought struck her, and she reared up and looked down at him anxiously. "You didn't hurt anything, did you?"

"Nope." He gave her a wicked smile. "In fact, I'm more than ready for round two."

She smiled back. "So am I."

But even as she said it, Virginia frowned. Yes, he was here, he'd made love to her. But still, nothing was settled.

Where would they go from here?

⁂ༀ☙☙⁂

They decided that round two was best conducted in her bed at home. Logan followed her in his rental car, his eyes locked on the taillights of her Saturn.

Everything would change after he became a vampire, he thought, as he trailed the red glow through the dark. He regretted leaving the SEALs, but he really had no choice. He supposed he could use the psychic influence vampires had and stay in the service that way, but that idea didn't feel right. Besides, there were too many people along the chain of command who'd ask questions about the SEAL who never went out in daylight. Even though he wouldn't have to sleep during the day, he knew from Ivanov's journals that sunlight could cause deep, ugly burns on a vampire's skin with very little exposure.

So resigning his commission was the only logical choice. He'd miss the SEALs, and he had no damn idea what he'd do instead, but a choice between the Navy and Virginia was no choice at all.

If nothing else, he couldn't let her go on starving herself out of a sense of loyalty to John. He felt a bitter surge of jealousy and fought to control it. He *was* John, dammit. Besides, Logan knew once he got a ring on Virginia's finger, she'd be committed to him. Even when she realized he wasn't quite the man her dead husband had been.

But the soul was the same. Alys and Richard had demonstrated that sheer, inescapable truth. Besides, there was no other explanation for his knowledge of the twelfth century French spoken in the court of King Henry II, particularly given that he'd studied Spanish in high school.

So it seemed Virginia would be marrying John for the second time.

Absently, Logan reached and picked up the small velvet box that sat beside him. And grinned at a sudden thought.

It was definitely going to be an evening ceremony.

Virginia got out of the car and watched as Logan's rental rolled up the driveway toward her. Her stomach felt as if a colony of Monarch butterflies had taken up residence. Yes, he was here, and he'd said he loved her. But what did that mean? Would he agree to become a vampire? Surely he knew he'd have to. They couldn't remain together with him as a mortal. She would have to hunt elsewhere or risk taking too much from him, and she knew Logan wouldn't tolerate that.

He parked the car behind hers in the drive, blocking her in, and got out with a duffle bag in his hand. She watched him walk toward her, admiring the breadth of his shoulders and the length of his legs. When he reached her, he didn't pause—his head just swooped down to claim her mouth in a long, hard kiss. She melted against him as he dropped the bag and wrapped his arms around her, surrounding her with his body.

God, he felt good, so big and warm and hard against her. His hands wrapped possessively around her bottom, lifting her until she could feel the thick ridge of his erection.

Finally she squirmed free, gasping and giggling. "If we don't get inside, I'm going to rape you on the lawn and shock the neighbors."

Logan's answering smile looked a little tight, but she didn't take time to puzzle about it. She simply pulled out of his arms and dashed off with a giggle, listening to his heavier footsteps running after her.

Virginia got the door unlocked and ran into the living room before he could grab her again. Still laughing, she turned to throw herself into his arms. He caught her, chuckling, as she wrapped herself around him, curling her legs across his hips to grip him close.

"God," she said, "I'm so glad you came back."

His eyes slid to the side, and his hands tightened on her bottom. "I couldn't stay away. I'm addicted."

Frowning, she turned her head to see what he was looking at. And saw John's portrait hanging over the couch. "Logan . . ."

But before Virginia could say anything more, he let her slide down his body, then dropped to one knee. As she stared down at him, bewildered, he pulled a blue velvet box out of his pocket and flipped it open with his thumb. Inside was a ring—a ruby flanked by two diamonds, set in a heavily worked gold band. She could tell at a glance it was more than a century old.

"My great-grandfather bought this ring for my great-grandmother,"

Logan said. "It's been passed down in my family ever since." Utter vulnerability darkened his eyes. "Will you marry me?"

Virginia swayed on her feet in shock. "Yes, Logan. God, yes." Holding out a shaking hand, she watched while he slid the heavy band onto her finger.

"You've probably got more valuable stuff—hell, that emerald of John's was probably somebody's crown jewels once—but this is a nice ring," he said.

She frowned at the tension in his voice. "It's beautiful. I'm honored."

Still down on one knee, he wrapped her hand in his. "And I want you to make me a vampire. Tonight."

Virginia stared at him. "Are you sure? Your career . . ."

"You said it yourself—it's the only way we can be together." He stood and took her into his arms again. "And I've learned in the last eleven days that living without you isn't living at all."

She hesitated, looking into his narrow, determined eyes. "It's not an easy process, Logan. Vampirism is caused by a virus, and the transformation takes days. And it's painful."

He looked down at her. "I'm used to pain."

But at least at first, there was damn little suffering. Logan took her in every conceivable position, determined to erase every other man from her memory. Including John.

But by the next day sex grew more difficult as she fed from him, taking far more than she ever would have normally. Drinking from her in turn wasn't easy; as he'd said himself, mortals can't ingest much blood without becoming sick.

Yet soon the taste began to change from the familiar copper he knew, taking on a hot, intoxicating flavor that burned the tongue like cognac. And there was something darkly erotic about pressing his mouth to the cuts she made against her pretty breast and feeling the blood flood his mouth.

It's happening, Logan thought, resting his spinning head against her. *I'm becoming a vampire.*

On the fourth night, Virginia walked into the bedroom with a tall glass of the sports drink she'd been giving him to soothe his tormenting thirst.

He lay sprawled across the bed, his eyes closed, dark beard stubble shadowing his jaw. He scarcely seemed to be breathing, and Virginia frowned.

"Logan?" She put the glass down and crawled onto the bed. The minute she touched him, she knew he'd fallen into the deep coma of the Change. Now his body would begin to restructure itself, its very cells altering to accommodate his new nature.

Frantically, Virginia put a hand against his cheek and reached for his mind with hers. Unconscious like this, the shields that had protected his consciousness were gone. She had to link with him, guide his mind through the process, or he might sink so deep he'd never wake up.

But as she entered his mind, all she saw was a deep, endless black, so thick it seemed she swam in it. The emptiness felt almost tactile, a cold that penetrated to the bone.

He was gone.

Fighting panic, Virginia shot off through the chill darkness, searching. At last she sensed a faint warmth. She swam toward it until she could see a glimmer of white against the utter psychic night.

As she came closer, the glimmer became a huge pearl floating in the darkness like some kind of space ship—iridescent white and easily the size of a house. Reaching it, she touched it warily. It was smooth and slick, like the pearl it resembled, but a living heat radiated from it. Looking closer, Virginia saw shadows moving beneath its translucent surface. She instinctively spread herself against it. Slowly, she sank inside. And found him.

He floated in tangled memories—chasing terrorists one minute with SEAL Team Seven, fighting a mace-swinging knight the next. Virginia could tell whether the experiences were Logan's or John's only by the time period; he seemed to make no distinction himself, seemed unaware of any.

She could only watch, breath caught in fear. She'd had no idea he'd come so close to death, so many times.

Then she began to notice images that made no sense. In one memory, he wore what seemed to be skins as he worked with a group of other men to stalk a huge, furry animal. Catching a glimpse of it, Virginia saw it had enormous tusks. A mastodon? That wasn't John, she realized—even his memories didn't go that far back.

In yet another memory, he wore the armor of a Roman centurion, hacking with a sword at a man wearing little more than blue paint and a homicidal expression.

How many times had he lived?

As she studied the shifting images, Virginia realized they all had a common theme. He'd always been a warrior. And he'd always been a man who fought to protect others, motivated by a strong inner sense of duty.

Yet most of the memories she saw seemed to be either Logan's—probably because they were the most recent—or John's. Because John's was the last life he lived, or because John had lived for such a long time? Was that why Logan kept remembering John's experiences?

As a vampire, her husband's mind had been enormously powerful, able to reach even beyond the psychic shell that protected Logan's modern mind from his deepest memories. Could she push those memories out of the shell so that Logan could remember John's life more clearly? Could he love her as John had?

But if she did, would he be overwhelmed by the sheer weight of John's experiences? Would Logan even exist at all?

Did it matter? a small voice whispered. The spirit was the same, after all.

Yet, it did matter. This life was Logan's, and he had a right to it. John had lived his life, just as the mastodon hunter had, just as the Roman centurion had. Just as all the others had. And she loved Logan, not just that piece of him that was John. It was Logan that she'd live the rest of her life with.

In that moment, inside herself, Virginia finally let go of the man who had been her husband.

She reached into the tangle of memories and grabbed the glowing thread she recognized as Logan. Pressing against the wall of the pearl, she sank through it and began to swim through the darkness, drawing him with her.

Toward life.

In the dream, Logan flew through the night, his ears filled with a rapid flapping sound. He wheeled past a tree, blinking in astonishment at the size of the massive branches that were as thick as his entire body.

Next to the tree stood a house built on the same outrageous scale. As he studied his surroundings, he realized that everything appeared to be outsized. Somehow he'd shrunk.

Suddenly Logan recognized the flapping sound. Wings. He was a bat. A vampire bat.

Dropping on the tree limb, he began to grow. Grow until he was the size he should be, and a man again. Glancing down at himself, Logan saw he wore the black fatigues and SEAL gear he'd worn to hunt Virginia.

When he looked up again, he found himself staring into the window of the house. Inside, Virginia lay naked in the arms of a blond man. At first Logan thought it was Gary, but then he looked more closely.

John.

Logan snarled. Coiling his body, he leaped, smashing through the glass to hit the floor beside their bed. Glaring at them, he bared his teeth. Fangs descended from his jaw. "Get away from her!"

John's familiar green eyes met his calmly. "Why?"

Logan clenched his fists and coiled to spring. "She's mine now."

"Is she?" He smiled slowly. "Perhaps we should ask her."

John rose naked and backed away from the bed. Virginia crouched in the center of the mattress, watching him go. Looking closely, Logan thought he saw a sheen of tears in her eyes. Gracefully, she slid off the bed and stood. He tensed.

But she walked to Logan and slid her arms around him. The warmth of her slim body penetrated the chill in his as her eyes met his. "I choose you."

Triumphantly, Logan turned to look at his rival. John smiled a slight, sad smile. "I knew she would." His eyes met Logan's. "After all, I'm dead."

As Logan watched, John turned toward the wall and began to crawl up it like a spider, moving toward a huge painting that hung over the bed. It was a duplicate of the one downstairs, but the blue settee John had sprawled across was empty.

The vampire slid onto the canvas surface and slowly sank into it, his outline flattening, his skin taking on the pattern of brush strokes. Until he turned to look out at them with painted green eyes.

Unable to leave it like this, Logan stepped closer to the painting. "You're not dead, John. You're still here."

John grinned suddenly. "I know. I just wasn't sure you did. Take care of her, or I'll haunt your ass."

❊❧(ℭ❂)ℰ❊

Logan jolted awake. Nausea hit him like a sledgehammer. He rolled off the bed and staggered into the bathroom to collapse in front of the toilet. As he convulsed in dry heaves, he felt his incisors loosen. He spat them out and watched dully as the teeth sank to the bottom of the toilet.

Where the hell was Virginia?

He felt strange—so hungry he shook, yet stronger than he'd ever been in his life. And he wanted Virginia. God, he hungered for her. He remembered all her rich female textures, her delicate taste, her heady scent, and he ached for her.

Logan took a deep breath and grimaced as he caught scent of his own stink. Considering Virginia's sensitive vampire nose, he'd better get a shower if he meant to have her when she returned.

And he did mean to have her. Had to have her. God, where was she?

He got to his feet, barely managing to avoid falling on his face. Opening the shower stall door, he reeled inside to turn on the taps full force. As the water struck him, Logan realized he was desperately thirsty. Opening his mouth, he tried to drink the water that pounded his face. But it didn't help. God, his mouth was so dry . . .

Suddenly his upper jaw began to hurt, building rapidly to a stabbing pain so intense he clamped a hand over his mouth. Two long, sharp teeth slid against his palm from the empty sockets left by his missing incisors.

He slammed open the shower stall door and staggered to the bathroom sink and the mirror that hung over it. Staring at his reflection, Logan opened his mouth. He had fangs.

Shit, it worked, he thought numbly. *I'm a vampire.*

Taking a deep breath, Logan grimaced. A vampire who stank.

Retreating back into the shower, he scrubbed his skin and tried not to think about his new nature.

Where the hell is Virginia?

❊❧(ℭ❂)ℰ❊

Virginia opened the front door and slipped inside, so full she felt gorged. Logan would regain consciousness any moment, and when he did, he'd need to drink far more than their kind normally did. Enough to kill a mortal. Which meant he'd have to feed on her.

Anticipating that, and the need to survive it, Virginia had gone out trolling for the type of men who'd prey on a lone woman in the dark. And she'd found them—a nasty little gang of five who'd thought beating and raping her a fine idea.

She'd left them dazed and thoroughly disinclined to ever attack another woman. Or anyone else. Ever again.

Now she had Logan to deal with. Which might be a real challenge. Virginia remembered nothing of her own first time—just a blur of sex and need. Alys had told her once that a male vampire's first hunger was even more intense than a female's, more overtly sexual.

"It's a wild, hot rut," Alys told her in a tone that simultaneously suggested longing and a relief she'd survived it. "And let me tell you, Richard Kendall was not a happy man when John woke wanting me. He allowed it only because the lad had gotten killed trying to save us both. And he stayed with us the whole time to keep an . . . eye on things."

Her smile had been so smug Virginia had been tempted to smack her.

Now Virginia didn't know whether to feel eagerness or fear. She just hoped Logan hadn't regained consciousness while she was gone.

Half wary, half hopeful, she climbed the stairs to her room. But even before she opened the bedroom door, Virginia heard the sounds of him moving around in the bathroom. She froze, her heart in her throat, feeling intensely vulnerable, intensely female.

A wild, hot rut.

I can handle it. Maybe.

She tugged at the short red dress she wore, pulling it down further on her stockinged thighs. Then, straightening her shoulders, she pushed open the door.

Logan heard her come in and stepped out of the bathroom, both powerful arms lifted to towel off his wet black hair. His blue eyes snapped to hers and ignited into a gas-jet blaze of lust.

He didn't say a word. And Virginia found she was incapable of speech under that hot, predatory stare. Logan's burning eyes left her face and slowly tracked down her body, lingering at the cleavage showcased by the deep neckline of her dress, then wandering slowly downward, dwelling on her hips a moment before sliding like a hand down the length of her legs.

A bead of water trickled slowly through the thick hair on his chest, toward the sculpted ridges of his abdomen. His cock thickened between his brawny thighs, tilting slowly upward as it grew longer. She watched it distend, hypnotized.

His changed body had regenerated enough blood for a truly impressive erection.

When Virginia looked up, his eyes were locked on her face again. His carnal lips were parted. And between them, she saw the tips of his fangs. Her nipples began to ache, and she felt her own fangs slide down from her jaw.

Logan started toward her. The sense of erotic menace radiating from him was so intense she barely fought down the urge to run. Virginia managed to hold her ground even when he loomed over her, so damn big she felt tiny. And he was a vampire now, which meant the strength advantage she'd always enjoyed was gone, despite the power her greater age had given her.

He could rape her now if he chose. And in his present mood, Virginia wasn't sure he wouldn't.

No, she reminded herself. She'd made him a vampire, and the process had given her power over him. She could stop him. But looking up into his hard, intent face, Virginia knew she didn't want to.

He said nothing—probably wasn't capable of speech in the extremity of his lust. Instead he dropped to one knee in front of her. She took a half-step back, but he reached out and grabbed her hips, then smoothed his big hands down to her thighs. And up, pushing up under her short, full skirt. Until the fabric bunched over his wrists, and her sex was bared in the thin, red lace panties.

Logan extended his head, pushing his face close to her. And slowly inhaled. Breathing in the scent of her need. She felt his long fingers flex as they gripped her hips. A hot trickle of cream worked its way through her sex, and she set her high-heeled feet apart.

His fingers caught in the waistband of her panties, pulling them down. Not off, not all the way. Just down, until he could see her dark curls, the pout of her sex. Virginia watched his eyes close until his lashes were dark fans against his cheek. Then he slowly put out his tongue and tasted her in a single lick.

Her knees buckled. She forced them to straighten again.

He looked up at her, his blue eyes glittering. And spoke, his voice a rasp. "Mine."

She licked her dry lips. "Yours."

Logan tightened his grip and pulled, tumbling her down on the carpeting. She scarcely felt her shoulders hit the floor.

He locked his fingers in the thin lace and pulled, shredding it. Greedily, he pressed his face against her and began to plunder her with his tongue and his lips and his teeth, both hands wrapping around her thighs to spread her wide.

Between strokes he rumbled, "You taste so . . . rich. Different than before." His blue eyes flashed up to meet hers over her body. "I want your tits."

Sitting up, he grabbed her dress and jerked, ripping it in impatient pulls, stripping it away until she wore nothing but her thigh-high stockings and a bra.

The bra didn't have a prayer against his big hands. Its lace cups flew in opposite directions as he came down on top of her. His mouth began to ravish one hard nipple while his long fingers simultaneously impaled her sex.

Deliciously rough, Logan alternately bit and sucked both her distended pink peaks. She tried to fist her hands in the silk of his hair, but his military haircut was so short she had to shift her grip to his shoulders. Digging her fingers in helplessly, she held on as he devoured her.

He buried three fingers in her sex, screwing them deep while he thumbed her clit. That sensation, combined with the feeling of his mouth on her breasts, was far too much. With a breathless scream, she tumbled into an orgasm.

Before she'd even finished coming, he covered her completely, lifting off her just enough to take his meaty cock in his hand and aim it for her wet opening. She managed to draw in a breath just as he rammed it to the hilt.

"Now," he rasped in her ear. "Now I'm going to feast on you."

"Yes." Virginia closed her eyes in surrender and hooked her legs over his hips. And threw back her head.

She felt his lips on her throat. It had taken her time to learn how to bite, where to place her fangs, how to make the tiny openings. But he bit her as if he'd had centuries of practice.

John's.

The sting of his fangs penetrating made her gasp out, but she didn't have the attention to give to the sensation. He'd begun to drive into her, his powerful hips working between her thighs. She wrapped her arms around his broad back and surrendered.

Logan rode her hard, in long, savage strokes, even as he drank greedily from her throat. *Mine. Mine. Mine*, his mind chanted in a primitive chorus of masculine possession as he fucked and fed on her.

And this time no one would damn well take her away. He'd kill anybody who tried.

He felt her orgasm building, sensed it in the shivers racking her delicate body. Without even knowing how he did it, he reached out and claimed her mind, felt her pleasure roll over her in long, glorious waves. Felt his cock buried deep in her, felt his teeth in her throat.

Mine, he thought at her fiercely.

Yours, she agreed.

I love you, Logan told her, mind to mind.

And I love you, she answered.

Forever.

Neither could tell who'd thought it. And it didn't matter, because it was equally true for them both.

Secrets

Volume 8

The Best in Women's Sensual Fiction

Taming Kate

by Jeanie Cesarini

To My Reader:
I was in the mood for a cowboy and since ***this*** cowboy would be my very first . . . ***Secrets*** provides the perfect place to explore my mood, a place where stories indulge sensual fantasies and deep dark desires. So, dearest reader, hop on and let's go for a red-hot ride west, to a town called Love where just about anything can happen . . . and does.

Her Family Tree was a Shrub

Kathryn Roman stared at the telephone receiver, then brought it back to her ear with a chuckle. She'd been on this phone so much while launching the new ad campaign for Simply Seductive fragrances she was beginning to hear things. "Forgive me. Could you please repeat that? Kitty left me what? I thought you said *brothel*."

"I did," the masculine voice confirmed over the line. "The late Ms. Romanov left you sole ownership of Katia's Palace, a brothel in Love, Nevada. I'll make the records of material assets available when you come to town. We have some issues involving the inheritance taxes to discuss . . ."

The lawyer, whose name had flown right out of Kathryn's head, droned on, his words forming a western-edged buzz that echoed in her ear without making a bit of sense.

Kitty had owned a brothel?

A brothel?

Kitty Romanov, bless her soul, had been a little old lady who'd kept a condo in the same Central Park West hi-rise where Kathryn had lived all her life. For the past seven years, ever since Kathryn's mother had died in fact, Kitty had become a late-night-ice-cream-and-sigh-at-old-movies buddy. Someone Kathryn had considered a friend.

Not a full-time friend, by any means. Kitty hadn't been around long enough to be a full-time anything. She'd only stayed one week a month in New York. The rest of her time she'd spent playing one-armed bandits and soaking up the dry Nevada air. Or at least that's what she'd led Kathryn to believe.

"A brothel, Mr.—" What was the man's name? "Sir. Obviously there's some mistake. This isn't the Old West."

"There are legalized brothels in the state of Nevada, I assure you, Miss Roman, and Kitty Romanov was the proprietor of one of the most renowned."

Kitty had been a *madam*?

The idea alone seemed absurd, even more so when coupled with the image that sprang to mind of Kitty, swirls of coiffed white hair piled high on top of her head, juggling a poopie-scooper in one hand while fighting to get her trio of fluffy Maltese dogs into their twelfth floor elevator.

Kitty had been a character to be sure, and Kathryn had been genuinely sorry when she'd passed on not long after celebrating her eightieth birthday. But a *madam*?

"If Kitty did own a brothel . . ." Even the words sounded stupid. "Why would she leave it to me?"

"Ownership of Katia's Palace passes to the oldest female of the Romanov family."

Kathryn sank back in her leather chair and issued a sigh of relief that sounded shakier than it should have. "There has definitely been a mistake, Mr. . . . *Carter.*" That was his name. "You've confused me with someone else. My name is Roman, not Romanov."

"No mistake, Miss Roman. I'm aware of the circumstances surrounding your name." She heard no emotion in the lawyer's voice, not even a hint of censure, yet Kathryn felt the hairs on the back of her neck tingle.

"If you know that I go by my mother's maiden name, then you should also know I have no living family."

The silence on the other end of the line turned those few tingling nape hairs into fully-fledged raised hackles.

"Miss Roman." His voice held a note of caution, as though he held an open can of worms and was prepared to dump them right onto the lap of her lined silk skirt. Kathryn knew the tone and braced herself. "I'm aware that you and your mother reverted to her maiden name after her divorce from your father. Apparently you weren't aware she also legally changed her name from Romanov to Roman at that time. The records are on file with the court."

Kathryn inhaled sharply. Her thoughts spun wildly out of her grasp, like a box of puzzle pieces dropped on the floor. Her mother had legally changed her name? Why? So she wouldn't be connected with the family business?

It fit. It *definitely* fit. Kathryn's high society mother would never have tolerated a legalized prostitution skeleton in her closet without slamming the door tight and sealing it in with the safest security system money could buy.

Kathryn's mother had been a respectable matron of New York's elite, hosting charity functions for all the right causes, never stepping an elegant toe out of line. She'd educated her only child at all the best schools, debuted her to society with the finest parties, had done everything by the letter—everything except open her heart and allow her daughter to get close.

"You're telling me I was related to Kitty?"

"She was your great aunt. Your grandmother's sister."

Great aunt? Grandmother? Kathryn's fingers tightened around the receiver until her knuckles grew white. She'd never had a clue these people had existed—the ultimate irony, given how often she'd longed for a family during those lonely years of her youth. Having a great aunt like Kitty visit her boarding school just once would have done wonders.

"I surmise that my news has come as something of a shock," Mr. Carter said.

Something of a shock? That was *something* of a mild understatement. Shaking her head, Kathryn forced her attention back to the matter at hand. "I'm sorry. You were saying?"

"I'll fax the preliminary information to your office today for you to review. When can you make it to Love, Miss Roman? Business decisions need to be made immediately—"

"I can't leave New York right now. I'm in the middle of launching an ad campaign that requires my undivided attention. But I readily admit you've taken me by surprise. Why don't you just fax me that information? I'll bring myself up to speed, confirm the details of my mother's name change and get back with you."

"Fine, Miss Roman, but certain decisions regarding the business require immediate—"

"I'll get back with you, Mr. Carter. Good day."

Kathryn's hand shook as she settled the receiver back in the cradle. Unable to sit still any longer, she launched to her feet, found her favorite spot in front of the floor-to-ceiling windows that cornered her office.

"Kitty, why didn't you ever tell me?" she asked aloud, her voice echoing emptily above the drone of the air conditioning.

Folding her arms across her chest, she willed the heat of the midday June sun that baked the city outside to ease her sudden chill.

How she'd longed for a family, a sister, a brother, an aunt . . . someone she could feel connected to, someone to giggle with, commiserate with or even cry with. Someone other than her mother, who'd always done her best in rearing Kathryn, but who'd never allowed a drop of emotion to crack through her veneer of proper deportment.

A smile tugged at her lips at the incongruity of caftan-loving Kitty sporting the same bloodlines as Kathryn's own designer silk suit mother. Imagine them running into each other in the hallway. Kathryn's mother would have fainted, before she uprooted every last stake and relocated to Boston.

Nevertheless, Kathryn had liked Kitty. They'd had fun together, had feasted on pints of Haagen-Dazs wrapped in dishtowels and had laughed themselves silly watching old comedies. They'd even remarked upon the similarities of their last names, yet Kitty had never told her the truth.

She'd had a great aunt, and she'd never even known it.

Now she had a brothel. The trade off seemed lopsided in the extreme. What on earth was she going to do with a brothel?

Kathryn gazed around her office, fashionably decorated with corner windows that overlooked the city, where she created multi-million dollar advertising campaigns that sent businesses spiraling off in new and exciting directions. She was a new partner in one of the most respected advertising firms in the country. Imagine, her running a brothel.

Her smile faded. Like her mother, she'd obviously missed whatever gene had made the women in their family capable of running a business that involved sex and men. Her track record with the gender was beyond abysmal. Her fiancé's words when he'd broken their engagement were chiseled in her head.

I need a woman with fire, Kathryn.

Those genes must skip a generation. Or in her case two.

What on earth was she going to do with Kitty's brothel?

Kathryn would have to do something, simply out of respect for Kitty. Unfortunately, she didn't have the time or the brain cells to hash through the problem at the moment. The Simply Seductive campaign demanded all of her attention, and if that wasn't enough, she'd have to track down the documents confirming her mother's name change . . . and work through her feelings about having discovered and lost a great aunt all in one phone call.

She'd had family. For a little while at least.

Turning away from the window, Kathryn returned to her desk, doing exactly what she always did when life got too complicated to deal with—work.

Life's as Crazy as Popcorn on a Hot Skillet

Six Weeks Later

"Belt up, city girl." On-the-Wing Joe shot the command over his shoulder in a crusty voice. "We're heading down."

Belt up? Kathryn wasn't only belted; she white-knuckled the seat to stay attached during this hour-long ride from hell.

Squeezing her eyes shut, she staved off one more round of queasiness as the engines whirred and the plane jerkily dropped another dozen feet. What insanity had possessed her to fly into Love on a commuter plane that typically hauled copper miners into the area?

Here was a classic example of how trying to save time would wind up costing her some. If she could walk straight once this plane—*hopefully*—landed, she wouldn't be up for much except hiding in a dark room with a washcloth on her pounding head.

Forget about blowing into town, meeting with the mayor and lawyer, and blowing out again by Friday. She'd lose even more time traveling back to the city and a real airport, because she would *not* be making the return flight with On-the-Wing Joe.

Chancing a glance as the plane jerkily descended another twenty feet, Kathryn caught the pilot squinting myopically and suspected he couldn't see the terrain through the windscreen, let alone read the numbers and dials on the instrument panel.

No problem, Kathryn told herself, taking a deep breath. She could handle anything. This would be the first and only time she'd have to act on behalf of her family, and she planned to act with dignity.

Dignity did *not* mean arriving in Love and beelining straight for the nearest bathroom to lose the remains of the bagel she'd eaten back in the Big Apple.

"Looks like the posse's here to welcome you, city girl."

"Posse?" she croaked out, loosening her grip on the seat to lean into the aisle and peek through the windscreen. "Don't posses hang people?"

On-the-Wing Joe gave a rusty chuckle. "Don't think the folks down there are gonna be inviting the Palace's new owner to a necktie social. Every man in this county and the next, and his daddy and granddaddy, has lost his virginity to one of the princesses. They'll want to stay on friendly-like terms, if you know what I mean."

Kathryn did indeed and swallowed back a curt retort. What business was it of his if she planned to turn over management of Katia's Palace to the town as soon as she could sign the papers?

"Are we landing in that field, Joe?" she asked incredulously as the plane's gears gnashed louder than the noisy engines on the snowplows back home. "There are people down there. It looks like a riot."

"Naw, city girl. They're here to welcome you. We Nevadans are friendly folk."

Kathryn leaned back and gazed out over the wingspan as they approached, confirming with one glance what she'd suspected since first boarding this deathtrap—On-the-Wing Joe's eyesight wasn't nearly what it should be.

A large group circled the field, following the path of the plane as if sucked into its air stream. Some held signs high. Welcome signs? Kathryn didn't think so. As a "city girl," she'd developed the ability to spot trouble in large crowds.

"They don't look very friendly."

"Aw, pshaw. They're giving you a special Love welcome."

If a special Love welcome involved a crowd that looked about as happy as fans at Shea Stadium the last time an ump had called Mike Piazza out, Kathryn would have to agree. But she didn't get a chance to comment as the plane touched down with a bump and a thud and the gears whined shrilly.

Whispering a mental prayer of thanks to be in one piece, Kathryn popped the clasp on her seatbelt, stretched her legs, and caught sight of one of the "welcome" signs.

Historic landmarks need to be preserved, not closed.

Closed? Who was planning to close a historic landmark?

Katia's Palace is part of Love's History.

Uh oh.

"Don't open that door, Joe!"

He swung a puzzled glance her way, his grizzled brows drawn tight in a frown. "What's the trouble, city girl?"

This cornpone still didn't realize the mob was here to lynch her. She pointed out at the sea of bobbing cowboy hats and handmade signs swarming the plane. "Look out there."

Joe obliged, and she saw surprise, then understanding dawn on his craggy face. "Well, now, would you look at that? Your arrival sure did stir up a hornet's nest. What'dya do, city girl? Put the princesses on vacation?"

Kathryn assumed the princesses were Kitty's . . . *employees.* "I didn't put anyone on vacation. In fact, I haven't spoken with anyone except the mayor—"

Joe's bristly brow shot clear up to his hairline. "Now why would you be talking to Mayor Barclay? Aren't you fixing to step into Miss Kitty's place and run the Palace?"

"Of course not," she snapped.

Joe shot a nervous glance out the window. While the crowd wasn't eye level with the cockpit, the picket signs were.

Don't leave the princesses homeless!

Joe gave a decided shake of his head. "You sure are stepping into a pile of dung."

Kathryn didn't intend to step anywhere, least of all into that angry mob, but options were limited. Did she tempt fate by heading back into the sky with a pilot who couldn't see?

"Can you get us back in the air, Joe?"

"Not unless you want me to run down a few of these folks."

She sank back into the seat with a huff, avoiding another sign that popped into the window's view and read *The Royal Fraud!* feeling as though the confines of the plane were shrinking as the grumbling and catcalls outside grew louder.

"What's this all about?" she asked rhetorically, but Joe obliged her anyway.

"Don't know, city girl. Except if you've been talking to Mayor Barclay then you might have headed down the wrong mine shaft. The Mayor sold his saddle to get elected and his ideas about what's best for Love have got most folks gritting their teeth like they could bite the sights off a six gun."

Kathryn could only stare, brain cells churning to comprehend the man's language. She recognized Mayor Barclay's name and could only surmise that selling saddles to finance his mayoral campaign was *not* a good thing.

"Well, here comes Trey Holliday. He'll see you through."

"Trey Holliday?"

"He's the ranching vet, the Palace's overseer, too."

Overseer? Now that Kathryn thought about it, she remembered seeing a signature on some paperwork Kitty's lawyer had faxed to her. She couldn't remember the name. One thing was clear, though, Trey Holliday commanded a great deal of respect with Love's townspeople. The crowd parted like the Red Sea had for Charlton Heston in her favorite Easter film.

And out strode a real live, honest-to-goodness cowboy.

Kathryn's mouth popped open. Trey Holliday looked as if he'd emerged straight off the silver screen. One of those old Westerns that always left her sighing and wishing they made real men like that nowadays.

Tall and broad-shouldered, he strode along with a sort of loose-limbed grace that lent him an aura of authority. He nodded politely and responded to what she assumed were greetings, and faces that had worn expressions reminding her of snarling street dogs now wore relieved, even pleased smiles.

The cowboy *was* pleasing to look at.

His jeans slung low on trim hips, and his boots kicked up little puffs of dust with each step. With his checked cotton shirt and plain leather vest, Trey Holliday was as different from the men in Kathryn's world as if he'd just appeared from a different century.

Even Joe seemed relieved to see him, and before she could object, he flung open the cockpit window. "Well, hey there, Trey. I'm right glad to see you."

"The lady in there with you?" asked a deep male voice, a strange combination of Western twang and throaty richness.

"Sure is. Get those folks back and I'll let you in."

"Joe, don't—"

Before Kathryn cleared her seat, a metallic lock clicked and the cowboy pulled open the door. While he lowered the steps, Kathryn could only see the top of his Stetson. The breath seemed stuck in her throat as he propped one booted foot on a rung and tipped his head back to gaze up at her.

He couldn't have been much older than she was, maybe thirty-two or three, but his face was all hard lines to match his hard, outdoorsy body, a study of character in every inch of weathered skin the color of freshly tanned leather, or at least what Kathryn imagined freshly tanned leather would look like if she'd ever seen any. Crinkles fanned outward from his eyes when he grinned, which appeared to be a familiar expression, given the depth of the grooves.

As his gaze moved over her, assessed her with a glance that made her feel the caress of his deep brown eyes like a warm breeze, Kathryn stood riveted to the spot, felt the breath dislodge in her throat when his smile widened.

"Trey Holliday, ma'am." He touched the brim of his hat politely. "See you're in a spot of trouble here."

She forced a tight smile. "A pleasure, Mr. Holliday. But I don't understand what's happening here. These people must have been misinformed. I don't plan on closing Katia's Palace."

"Call me Trey," he said genially. "Are you planning to turn over management?"

"I am, but I'm turning it over to the town. Katia's Palace is part of Love's history."

"Yes, ma'am, it is. And most folks around here believe it needs to be preserved. Others, though, think it's standing in the way of Love's future."

A chill zipped along her spine, whether from the niggling suspicion that much more was going on around here than she knew or the intense way this cowboy kept staring at her, Kathryn couldn't say. Instead she asked, "How's that?"

"The brothel zoning ordinance limits the town's population. The mayor and his supporters want the brothel closed down to attract developers into the area so they can build a mega-mall."

"With a twenty-four screen cinema," Joe piped in.

Kathryn ignored him and faced the cowboy. "Are you telling me if I turn over management of Katia's Palace to the town, the mayor will close the doors?"

The cowboy nodded.

She sank down to the edge of the seat. "I've walked into a turf war, haven't I?"

That quirky half-smile never wavered. "You have, ma'am."

Kathryn let her face flop into her hands, a gesture of despair that had the bonus of blocking out sight of the cowboy.

What had Kitty been thinking to bequeath a brothel to a New York City ad exec? An ad exec who didn't know the first thing about romance? Kathryn couldn't seriously entertain the idea that Kitty thought she'd run the place. They may have only known each other for the past seven of Kathryn's twenty-eight years, but Kitty had known work took precedence in Kathryn's life. She'd remarked upon it often enough.

Was that what Kitty had been counting on, that somehow Kathryn's business experience might ensure the brothel's future?

Quite simply, Kathryn didn't have enough information to formulate an opinion. The opinion she'd already formulated, though, was if all families were this much trouble, she understood why her mother had run far away from hers.

"Ma'am?"

Inhaling deeply, Kathryn forced herself to meet his gaze. "Are those the . . . *princesses* out there?"

The cowboy shook his head. "The townsfolk. The princesses can't leave the Palace while they're on duty, except to visit the doctor for their medical exams."

"How long is 'on duty'?" she asked.

"Three weeks."

Something of her horror must have shown on her face, because the cowboy frowned and changed the subject.

"I can get you to the Palace safely."

"Those people want to roast me alive, Mr. Holliday."

"Trey."

"Trey. I'm not leaving this plane." She glanced at the myopic cornpone and placed her fate in God's hands. "Joe, take me back to the airport."

"Now?" Joe asked, none too cheerfully. "I was heading for Sadie's. It's Wednesday and she's fixing meatloaf."

"I'll buy you your own cow," Kathryn said. "Just get me out of here."

The ensuing silence spiked her heartrate, then her temper when On-the-Wing Joe said, "If Trey says it's okay."

"You won't be needing your own cow tonight, Joe. If you get a move on to Sadie's, you'll miss the dinner crowd." The cowboy flipped the brim of his hat back to reveal a thatch of wheat blonde hair in such contrast with his tanned skin that his brown eyes seemed to melt into warm molasses. "The way I see it, ma'am, you've only got two choices. I can carry you to my truck, so the first glimpse this town gets of their new madam will be of her backside propped over my shoulder, or you can walk on your own two feet. Lady's choice."

"Excuse me? How . . . dare you," she sputtered, unable to form a coherent reply, but outraged enough to try.

The cowboy smiled, a full-fledged smile that drove two pencil-point dimples into his cheeks and made his eyes twinkle. "You're no bigger than a nubbin'. I'd be pleased to carry you."

A nubbin? Kathryn didn't have time to ponder this new and strange land where people spoke an incomprehensible language before the cowboy stepped up another rung on the ladder.

Leaping from her seat, she backed away. "I don't need you to carry me, cowboy."

His smile faded, but that stupid grin replaced it, playing at the corners of his mouth, and making her feel as though she'd just purchased a twenty-dollar Rolex from a street vendor.

"You'll walk then?"

Slinging her purse over her shoulder, Kathryn fixed a stony expression on her face. "I'm not going anywhere until I see the sheriff. Surely this town has a sheriff."

Trey Holliday nodded casually, inclined his head toward the window. "He's right over there. His deputy, too."

Before Kathryn had a chance to register that the sheriff and his deputy appeared to be chatting with the protesters rather than making any attempt to disperse them, the cowboy shot forward and whipcord arms threaded around her.

Kathryn gasped as he brought her hard against him and then hoisted her up over his shoulder, as easily as though she were no bigger than—what had he said?—a *nubbin'*.

Her bottom bumped the plane's ceiling and she found herself imprisoned by strong arms as he carried her down the steps to the sound of Joe's laughter.

Enter the Tenderfoot

The reluctant new madam of Katia's Palace had better sense than to create a fuss by kicking her legs and throwing him off balance. Though judging by the way the townsfolk hooted and hollered, Trey guessed they would've enjoyed the show.

Some made some rather promising suggestions for what he might do with this pretty lady once he got her back to the Palace. Trey couldn't see the lady's face to know what she thought of their ideas, but reckoned the way her body went all stiff was a pretty good indication.

Figuring he'd made his point that he wouldn't help her turn tail and run from town, he planned to set her back on her feet once they reached the edge of the crowd. A plan that changed quick enough when her teeth sank into his ribs.

"Damn." He instinctively slid her off his shoulder and blessedly, every curvy inch of her body rode down his, distracting him from the pain.

Looked like he wasn't the only one with a point to make.

"You got a pootin' pony there, Trey," Chester McGee, owner of the Bar M commented. "She'll have you cinched by the last hole if you ain't careful."

Trey didn't get a chance to reply before the lady took a few unsteady paces away from him and yelled, "Sheriff."

Rubbing the tender spot below his ribs, Trey smiled at the lady, greeted Sheriff Luke and his son, the town's deputy.

"Yes, ma'am," Luke said.

"I demand protection from this man until I can secure a restraining order."

Luke rocked back on his heels, stroked his chin and regarded the lady thoughtfully. "From Trey, ma'am? Why would you be needing protection from him?"

"He assaulted me."

"I didn't see any assault." He turned to his son. "Did you, Jess?"

Jess only shook his head and Trey bit back a smile at the lady's obvious outrage. Her pretty eyes flashed blue fire, just like a lightning bolt.

"You have an easy two hundred witnesses here, Sheriff." She swept a hand around in a gesture that was no less elegant for its impatience. "If you and your deputy were temporarily blinded, I'm sure any of these people can tell you what happened."

Luke cupped his hands around his mouth and yelled, "Any of ya'll see Trey assault this lady?"

With every denial issued in his defense, the lady became more stoic, more remote. Old Minnie Crocker said, "I saw the lady assault Trey," before turning to him and advising, "Better give yourself a tetanus shot. Wouldn't want you catching anything." Trey reckoned the lady just might explode.

"Let's go to the Palace," he said. "We'll work out everything there."

She fixed him with that lightning blue stare. "I'm not going anywhere with you."

"Trey here's your overseer, ma'am," Luke said. "I suggest you go talk things out with him. He knows best what Kitty wanted for you and the Palace. You have my word that Trey'll treat you with respect."

Kate scowled, clearly disbelieving that she could take Luke's word on anything.

"My truck's this way." Trey motioned to a field beyond the edge of the crowd.

A war raged in those blue eyes. Kissable lips narrowed into a line straight with displeasure. But Trey sensed the instant she made her decision, the slight flare to her nostrils, the lift of her dainty chin. She spun on her heels and swept into the crowd as regally as a queen.

Trey followed up the rear, far enough to stay clear of the lady's claws, yet close enough to step in if more trouble brewed. To the townsfolk's credit, though, most just gawked, and Trey right along with them.

Lady Kate, as he'd dubbed her the instant his eyes fixed on her pretty face with those big eyes and shiny black hair, was something of a sight. In her sleek blue suit, she stuck out like a mustang in a herd of muleys, a city girl lifted right off the shiny cover of a magazine and plunked smack dab into a crowd of rumpled denim and dirt-scuffed boots.

He liked the contrast. Her sleek suit hugged her slim curves in a way rumpled denim never could. And she did have the sweetest little body.

More petite than he'd pegged her from Kitty's accountings, he'd somehow imagined that a woman who dealt in the multi-million dollar advertising business should have been taller, more aggressive. While Lady Kate might have thorns, the top of her head didn't quite reach his shoulder. Even in high heels that made the going over the dusty summer ground a mite slow.

But the lady didn't let that trouble her in the least. Sweeping along with her head held high, she measured each step as if she was walking along a satin runner in some fancy hotel.

Trey liked her spunk.

He got her to his truck without further incident, but no sooner had he slammed the door behind her than folk started firing off questions faster than grease jumped on a hot plate.

"You'll set her straight, Trey, won't you?"

"You won't let her toss out the princesses, will you?"

"Tell her what'll happen if she closes the Palace."

Trey wound his way around the front of the truck. "You've got my word I'll explain the situation to the lady," he assured them. "In the meanwhile, calm down. We'll work something out."

Judging by the doubt on their faces—and he'd known most of these people his whole life—they didn't believe him. After meeting the lady who controlled the Palace's fate, Trey wasn't so sure he blamed them.

"Keep the faith, Cody." Kicking in the clutch, he shifted into first. "And let me know how Tilly's doing with the colic."

Gunning the engine, he sped off toward town, watching the crowd recede in the rearview mirror. He had a good ten minutes to start over again with this stubborn lady, but as luck would have it, she took the initiative and saved him the trouble.

"I won't talk about anything with you, cowboy, unless you promise to keep your hands off me."

"Agreed. You talk and I'll keep my hands off you."

She eyed him doubtfully, as though gauging whether he was a man who made promises he didn't intend to keep. Then she nodded, clearly deciding to take him at his word. "Those people put a lot of faith in your abilities. How long have you been overseer for Katia's Palace?"

"Since my father died. The job came along with the Tex's Sweet and has passed from owner to owner ever since Tex Justice brought himself a real Russian Princess to run the brothel back in 1916. My father bought the place when I was two."

"The Tex's Sweet? If memory serves, that's the ranch that leases the property to the brothel."

"Memory serves." Though he couldn't help noticing how the new owner of said brothel didn't look happy about sitting across from the man who held her lease. "It's an honorary post. Lending a hand to the madam, keeping an eye on the princesses, making an appearance when customers get out of hand."

"A bouncer?"

"When someone needs bouncing."

She fixed her gaze on the view through the windshield, a vista that encompassed summer green valley and snow-capped mountaintops with miles of bright blue sky in between. What did a woman raised around buildings so tall she could barely see the sky think about all this nature?

Trey couldn't guess from her expression. Her delicate profile might have been whittled from white pine. Whatever else Lady Kate might be, she was surely in control of her emotions. He'd bet his last biscuit after a day in the saddle that she didn't let her hair down nearly enough.

Not that she had much hair to let down. That shiny black mass only fell to the middle of her neck, but it was cut full in one of those kicky styles that waved around her face and swung whenever she moved her head, surely as slick as spring water to the touch.

"No chance you'll run the Palace like Kitty wanted you to?"

"Not a chance, cowboy."

Well, he'd agreed not to touch the lady for her promise to talk. But raking another appreciative gaze over silky black hair and full red lips made just for kissing and Trey reckoned he wasn't much in the mood for talk, anyway.

The Stampede

When the cowboy wheeled off Love's main road and pointed to a road sign, Kathryn sat up in her seat and assumed her best boardroom expression. She wasn't going to let him know he'd rattled her the tiniest bit.

She could handle him and she could handle Katia's Palace. She'd listen to what he had to say about turf wars as a courtesy and then come up with a viable alternative. No problem. She may have to extend her trip a few days, but she'd manage.

"Are you ready, pretty lady? The Palace is at the end of this road."

Her breath slowed expectantly as he wound along a narrow forest path, cut off from the rest of the world before opening onto a bright valley, where a Spanish-style villa sprawled in the shadow of a towering ridge.

"Well, what do you think?" he asked. "It's a Russian princess's Western palace."

The place did have a palatial presence. Perhaps the sheer size of the sprawling villa lent to its splendor. Or the way it nestled between the valley and the ridge as if springing from the ground in a burst of quirky grandeur.

The cowboy drove around the building and wheeled into a parking space with a laugh. "And it's your family home."

"I can see Kitty here," she grudgingly admitted.

But Kathryn couldn't ever see her mother stepping foot inside. Krystal Roman had been a woman much more at home with the high-ceilinged condos of Manhattan and the Mid-Atlantic summer homes on Long Island Sound. And sex? To Kathryn's knowledge, her mother had never even had sex after doing the deed that had conceived her. At least, Kathryn had never met any love interests on trips home from school.

"Tex Justice built this place for the Princess Katia."

"Was he the princess's pimp?"

The cowboy winced. "Legal prostitutes are a whole different breed from streetwalkers, Kate."

"The name's Kathryn," she said abruptly when a blush crept into her cheeks. "So what makes them different? They have a physical address? Or their rates?"

The cowboy circled the car, opened her door and stared down at her with a hard-edged expression. "Respect."

His answer cut straight to the point, and his steely tone left her no doubt he wouldn't tolerate any confusion on the issue. She stepped out of the truck and immediately put distance between them, squelching the ridiculous feeling of embarrassment that she hadn't made the distinction herself. Romanov blood might run in her veins, but she'd been reared a Roman through and through. Neither *streetwalker* nor *legal prostitute* had been words ever spoken in her home.

The cowboy led her toward the ornate double-doored entry, looking so stoic she wondered if he'd finally accepted what she'd known since Kitty's lawyer had first called—this world was not hers and never could be.

Steeling herself mentally when he held the door wide, Kathryn swept past the cowboy. One step inside and the open expanse of the sunny outdoors gave way to carved woodwork, tiled floors, and ornate gold stenciling that made her feel as if she'd stepped inside a world of wealthy Spanish grandees from another century.

Elegant, expensive and beyond extravagant, the entrance room of Katia's Palace reminded her of a mansion on the Cape rather than any brothel she might have imagined. Two arched doorways with fanned windows splintered sunlight across the room and flanked a full-length portrait of a very beautiful woman, dressed in what Kathryn recognized as an early-last-century gown. The woman welcomed visitors with an enigmatic smile.

"That's the lady herself. You resemble her a lot."

The cowboy's observation wasn't lost on Kathryn. Staring up at her ancestor's portrait, she forced herself to ignore the heat of his gaze and the sensation of being crowded by his big-bodied nearness. He hovered somewhere above her right shoulder, invading her personal space.

Kathryn didn't like the feeling one bit. With every breath she inhaled his man/leather/outdoorsy scent, an unfamiliar combination she found rather unique, and . . . well, *male*.

The men she'd known all her life would never have dreamed of leaving their clubs without first showering and making themselves presentable for polite society. By comparison, the cowboy was so much more earthy, real . . . *neanderthal*, if she judged by his manner of getting her off the plane.

"Your eyes." He touched a rough fingertip to her temple.

Surprised, she could only stare as he traced the line of her cheek to her jaw, riveted by his melting gaze and the appreciation in his expression. She got the distinct impression that he couldn't resist touching her, and her breath hitched, a funny little fluttering sound that emphasized their closeness.

"Your delicate features, too." His finger trailed upwards along her chin and brushed her parted lips. "You're a very beautiful woman, Kate."

Kathryn.

The name shrieked in her mind, but she couldn't force the correction to her lips. Not when the slightly salty flavor of his skin created such an unfamiliar intimacy between them that Kathryn only managed to respond by staggering back a full step, desperate to break the connection.

"You agreed to keep your hands off me."

"I agreed to keep my hands off you if you agreed to talk. I don't care much about talking anymore."

Surely he didn't mean . . . Clutching her purse like she did when awaiting a taxi late at night, she held it close, an anchor, a shield, or a weapon if necessary. But when that crazy half-grin kicked up the corners of the cowboy's mouth, Kathryn felt annoyed she'd provided him an easy source of amusement.

"Katia was a tiny woman, too." His deep voice bridged the distance she'd placed between them with its rich timbre. "Just like you, Kate. Like a china doll."

"The name's Kathryn, and size notwithstanding, I can't think of anyone less china doll-like than me."

She'd earned the reputation as a competent businesswoman in her world, and better he know that up front, especially if he planned on sneaking touches to catch her off guard. He should also know she wasn't stupid. She wasn't falling for his gentle-the-wild-horse routine, either.

Before she had a chance to tell him a shrill screech had her pivoting in the direction of the sound.

"Trey, why didn't you come in? We've been waiting—"

A very pretty blonde skidded to a halt in the middle of the room, eyes growing wide when she noticed Kathryn. "Ohmigosh, you're *her*." With that, she spun around and shot from the room like a bolt, yelling, "She's here. She's here."

The cowboy folded his arms over his chest and watched the blonde's retreat with a smile. "Take a deep breath, pretty lady, because we're about to be rodeoed. Ready to meet your staff?"

Kathryn opened her mouth to correct him—the princesses were not her staff, nor would they be—but the thought flew out of her head entirely, when the blonde's reaction to seeing the cowboy suddenly struck her.

Every man in this county and the next, and his daddy and grand-daddy, has lost his virginity to one of the princesses.

Trey Holliday had been raised in the shadow of Katia's Palace. He kept an eye out for the place and had probably sampled each and every princess who'd ever worked here. He may have been Kitty's taste tester, for all Kathryn knew, which would certainly explain the fond smile driving pinprick dimples into his cheeks at the moment.

Kathryn didn't have time to dwell on what she thought about that, or why the observation had even popped into her head, before a racket the decibel level of an elevated train—or a stampede of wild bulls, if she wanted to get into the spirit of things—erupted down the hallway.

Drawing herself up to full height, Kathryn adopted her best walking-into-a-boardroom-full-of-men expression and refused to flinch when women stampeded into the room.

She barely had time to take in the remarkable collection of blondes, brunettes, and redheads, when a tall black woman, who resembled the striking Grace Jones, demanded, "Why aren't you letting us work?"

"Excuse me?" Kathryn edged near the cowboy, recognizing the woman's battle stance and not sure whether a special Love welcome might also include pummeling the accidental madam.

"Gwendolyn," the cowboy said. "Didn't anyone ever tell you you'll catch more flies with honey than vinegar?"

"I'm not interested in catching flies. I impose order around here remember? And right now we need a good dose."

Kathryn wasn't quite sure what to make of that remark, but every-one else in the room seemed to understand, and her gaze slipped to the riding quirt the woman tapped agitatedly against the palm of one ta-pered hand.

"You really going to shut us down for good?" a pixie-haired brunette asked.

"Now let's all just calm down and give Lady Kate a chance to catch her breath. I haven't explained the trouble yet."

Lady Kate?

Kathryn wasn't inclined to correct him as he took her arm and led her through the crowd and down the hallway into a formal dining room, furnished with antiques as exquisite as those she'd seen on her last trip to Christie's.

Over the next hour, and several cups of coffee to which the cowboy had added draughts of something called "bottled courage," Kathryn was brought up to speed.

In a nutshell, the trouble involved varying viewpoints about the town of Love's future. The cowboy had been right when he said the brothel's zoning ordinance forced the town to stay within a certain population. Mayor Barclay and his ilk wanted the brothel closed to attract developers to the area, while the cowboy, most ranchers and the rest of the townsfolk opposed the mayor's plan.

The lease with the Tex's Sweet Ranch meant land usage was restricted. Katia's Palace could only be run as a brothel. If Kathryn agreed to let the town manage the Palace, Mayor Barclay and his council could and would cease operation, which meant the land would revert back to the cowboy.

Like On-the-Wing Joe had said, she'd stepped right into a pile of dung.

But Joe hadn't counted on Kathryn's business experience. "Cowboy, you've got to run this place."

"No can do, pretty lady. Running a ranch takes up most of my time."

The cowboy couldn't give up the ranch to run the brothel, because he owned the land the brothel sat on. What a mess. "You can hire someone like Tex Justice did. I don't know if you can manage a princess, but . . ."

"I already got me a lady to run it." He stared at her meaningfully.

Damn, the cowboy was going to be stubborn. A suffocating sort of alarm constricted her throat as she stared around the table, where a host of pretty faces looked to her for answers. Hopping to her feet, Kathryn paced, brainstorming alternatives before panic got the better of her.

She didn't feel obligated to these women. Not really. But she couldn't just ignore the fact that Kitty had cared for them. She'd cared for Kitty. And she couldn't deny a certain sense of sadness that she'd been so cut off from the Romanovs, echoes of the little girl who'd desperately wanted a family no matter how unsuitable their trade.

"I'll just have to find someone to manage this place, then," she finally said. "Someone who wants to run the Palace."

"You won't find anyone, ma'am," the fresh-faced blonde princess said. "The mayor will make sure of that. He's got most of the town council in his pocket."

"Dale Barclay is mean enough to eat off the same plate with a snake," the pixyish princess said. "Most people don't want to cross him."

"Yet you want me to take him on?"

"I'll protect you, pretty lady." The cowboy smiled.

Kathryn scowled.

"The mayor won't mess with Trey," the sultry brunette said. "That's why he's been doing all his dirty work behind the scenes. Kitty told us you could handle him."

Kathryn exhaled sharply, collecting her racing thoughts to find some way to translate into words what these people didn't seem to understand. "Forgive me, but you all are missing the point. I have no desire to take on Mayor Barclay. This isn't my fight, my town or my home, and it never will be. All I can do is promise not to turn over management to the mayor and attempt to find another manager."

"But Kitty wanted you to run the place," the blonde said.

"Not an option." She spread her hands in entreaty, ignoring a pinprick of guilt for going against Kitty's wishes so completely. "Kitty knew that, which is why she sprung this on me *after* she died."

"You are one heartless bitch, Lady Kate," the tall black woman said. "I'm glad Kitty's not here to find out she put her faith in someone who can't live up to her expectations."

"Here, here." The glamour queen saluted with bottled spring water.

Kathryn stared around the table of accusing faces, shocked by their animosity, relieved to be standing so she could lock her knees against the weakness that made them tremble.

Who were these women to judge her? She didn't even know them. She hadn't asked to be left in charge of their futures, and she'd offered as much help as she could. Worst of all was the cowboy's dark eyes, staring through her as if wondering what Kitty had seen that he was missing.

Why did she even care?

Swallowing past the tightness in her throat, Kathryn faced them all with her best I-will-not-back-down boardroom stare, refusing to be intimidated because everyone in this room obviously knew a great deal more about her than she knew about them. "Kitty had no right to tell you to expect miracles from me. I wish you all the best of luck."

Turning on her heel, she strode across the room, hoping she could find her way to the door, because she had every intention of walking straight to town. She'd meet with the lawyer and then hole up in a dark hotel room. One glorious migraine echoed in her head, and she'd forgotten her medication. Surely there was a pharmacy in this hick town.

Kathryn hadn't even passed beneath the arch of the dining room doorway before another accusation brought her to a halt.

"You're just going to walk out that door and let Trey keep footing the bills?" one of the women—Kathryn wasn't sure which one—said, sounding astonished.

That got her attention and she spun back around to recognize the glamour queen sliding her chair back from the table.

"Gwen's right," she said. "You're not half the woman Kitty thought you were."

A chorus of agreements erupted only to be stifled just as quickly by the cowboy. "Pull in the claws, ladies."

His warning worked on every woman in that room. Except Kathryn. "What are they talking about? What bills?"

Sliding his chair back, he rose to his feet in a leisurely motion of fluid strength that drew lots of appreciative gazes.

Kathryn's included, before she realized she gawked right along with the rest of them and fixed her gaze on the Gothic iron chandelier overhead.

"The princesses split their earnings with the Palace fifty/fifty," he explained. "When they don't work, they don't get paid. I've been covering their lost wages."

Kathryn rubbed her temples to stimulate her memory and dull the ache throbbing there. "I just didn't realize this was a problem. Do I need to sign something to reopen? What was that paper you faxed me, cowboy?"

The paper she obviously hadn't paid close enough attention to. And she couldn't even blame her lawyer—he'd tried to tell her to get out here and reopen the place, but she'd flat out refused, not wanting to be forced into operating the business even temporarily.

"A letter about the reopening. Nevada law requires the manager— the madam—to be on-site while we're open for business."

He didn't smirk, but several of the princesses did, and Kathryn got her first taste of swallowing a bitter pill.

"Mayor Barclay is looking very tempting about now," she admitted, wondering if she could turn the place over and still live with herself. Maybe if she sold her condo and moved into another building where she wouldn't see Kitty's face every time she stepped into the hallway?

"Well, now that we're down to it, there's a problem with that, Kate." The cowboy braced his hands on the back of his chair and faced her with a mildly apologetic grimace. "Legally you can't do anything with the Palace when it's not in the black. A provision of the property lease with the Tex's Sweet."

"So I owe you money?"

The cowboy nodded.

"A lot?"

"Reckon it might be to some folks."

The pixyish princess shook her head. "He's paid me almost three thousand in lost wages already."

The ensuing chorus of numbers had Kathryn totaling a sum that had her drawing deep breaths to stave off hyperventilation. She'd had no idea *princesses* earned so much. And remembering Julia Roberts in *Pretty Woman* only called to mind the cowboy's definition of the differences between legal prostitutes and streetwalkers.

Surely there'd been other expenses, as well. A place this size must cost a bundle to operate, Kathryn knew. But the amount she owed him really didn't matter. Anything over the few thousand she kept in a conventional savings account for emergencies was an amount she couldn't pay.

The money her mother had left her would be tied up in trust until she was thirty, which wouldn't help her put Love, Nevada and Katia's Palace behind her for another two years.

Letting her eyes flutter shut for the briefest moment, she rallied the courage to admit the truth. "The exact amount doesn't matter. My money's tied up at the moment."

The cowboy smiled a smile that made Kathryn's heartbeat slow to a crawl while she waited for him to make his move.

She didn't wait long.

"I don't want your money anyway, pretty lady. I promised Miss Kitty I'd encourage you to take over."

"You go, Trey," the glamour queen said, raising her hand for a ringing high-five with the blonde.

This time the sultry brunette raised her spring water and clinked bottles with the pixie-haired beauty in salute.

The cowboy shrugged, plainly unfazed by their approval. He just locked that intense gaze on Kathryn until her heartbeat stopped crawling and halted altogether.

"You mean *coerce*, don't you?"

"*Encourage*," he repeated, and the warmth in those molasses-dark eyes promised he'd encourage her in ways she'd never dreamed of. "I just need a chance to convince you."

"Where's the phone?" Panic expelled the words right through her suddenly dry mouth. "I need to talk to my lawyer."

The cowboy nodded obligingly. "Bring the lady a phone."

One of the princesses complied, Kathryn wasn't sure which, because she was too busy forcing her rattled brain to remember her own calling card number. Then she began the battle of making her shaking hands press the right buttons.

Damn, damn and double damn, she mentally cursed while dragging the telephone through the doorway to hide from the chattering princesses, all of whom had rushed into the cowboy's corner as though he were a prizefighter contending for a belt.

There had to be some way out of this mess. But the conference call with Kathryn and Kitty's respective lawyers quickly proved that Kitty had backed her into a neat little corner with her legal agreements, restrictions on long-term leases, and high-handed overseers. Had Kathryn not signed the agreement six weeks ago . . . but she'd decided to see the transfer of Katia's Palace through.

Kitty had known her well enough to guess she'd feel obligated. Or had she simply counted on her being interested enough in her family to get involved? Either way, Kitty had set her up, big-time.

Why? Surely eating the last of the macadamia nut during *Breakfast at Tiffanys* didn't warrant this sort of retribution. Then something Kitty said not long before her death echoed in Kathryn's memory.

You need to make time in your life to relax and have fun.

That's what her legacy was all about. From beyond the grave, Kitty was forcing Kathryn to leave the high-powered lifestyle she'd never approved.

Slamming the receiver down onto the cradle, Kathryn dragged the phone cord back into the dining room.

"Well, Trey Holliday," she said in a voice a cross between hysterical laughter and growl, "I don't have the money to pay you back, so what do you want?"

"For you to run the place."

"I can't do that." Had she been in her right mind, Kathryn would have been mortified that she'd stamped her foot to emphasize her point. "I have to be in my office on Monday."

"Then go."

"But I'm legally responsible for this place now. I'm liable for any expenses you incur and if the princesses can't work. . . ."

The cowboy rocked back on his heels, clearly amused by her panic and untroubled by the sea of bright gazes around the table, bouncing between them like spectators at a tennis match.

He flashed her a smile that was the embodiment of all those bad boy grins she'd ever seen on the silver screen. "Seems to me you only have one choice then. Work off your debt."

A silence fell as complete as a blackout in Manhattan. Everyone stared at her, waiting, and Kathryn's worsening migraine had to be dulling her senses because a good minute passed before she realized they were all awaiting *her* reaction.

"Work off my debt?" Kathryn noticed the meaningful glance he slanted at the table and the amusement of those seated there. The Amazonian princess handed her a brochure. In slowly dawning horror, Kathryn scanned the page.

Princesses' Menu

Straight
In-dates
Three-way
Half-and-half
Fetishes
Bondage
Submission
Role-playing
Dominance

Exciting Extras

French	Meal-in-bed
Striptease	Erotic Videos
Water Play	Manual Stimulation
Massage	Lingerie Modeling

$200.00 House Minimum

By all rights the bagel she'd eaten for breakfast should have been long gone, but it roiled uneasily in her stomach. She sank back against the wall, not wanting to show any weakness to these bullies, but the ache in her temples grew ferocious.

"Are you insane, cowboy?" she finally choked out. "You expect me to become a . . . a—" His molasses gaze warned her to choose her word very carefully— "*Princess*?"

"You can service the clients, or you can service me," he said in that rough silk voice. "Lady's choice."

Kathryn had barely strung all his words together in her aching head before the room receded from view.

Code of the West

A sadist fired a blowtorch inside Kathryn's head, and she dared not move while her stomach churned, unsure whether its contents wanted to come up or stay where they were.

The moist cloth on her head appeared like a cool breath from heaven and a sigh escaped her, a pathetically grateful sound that resembled more of a whimper.

"You feeling okay, Kate?"

The cowboy.

No, she wasn't okay. Not with her head aching like a train had run through it, the memory of her whole sorry situation crashing along at a hundred miles per hour.

"What . . . wha—?" The words didn't resemble any sounds she recognized, but the cowboy must have understood what she was asking because he said, "You fainted."

Fainted? She'd never fainted in her life. Had he hit her on the head? She tried to sit up and face her enemy.

Unfortunately, sitting wasn't in the game plan. Neither was opening her eyes. Someone had left the drapes open, and the sunlight streaming through the windows seared through her eyelids like a laser. She could barely lift her head off the pillow. She was at this man's mercy.

"Should I have Jed call the doctor?"

Who was Jed? Did she even care? No. Not when she heard worry in his voice. She sighed deeply, gratified he sounded genuinely concerned. As much as she wanted to blame the cowboy for this blinding ache in her head, she recognized a migraine. The mother of all migraines, apparently, and she'd had enough bad ones to compare it to.

"No." A croak.

She'd be fine if she could just rest for a bit. Though she wasn't sure where she was, she was definitely horizontal. She wouldn't try to open her eyes, just lay here and not move . . .

The next time Kathryn approached awareness, the migraine had abated enough to make some sense of her surroundings and the first thing that struck her was that she was lying someplace soft and comfortable—a bed?—and she was naked. *Naked*? Yes, definitely and completely without a stitch of clothing.

Disbelief drove her to sit up, or try to, as a blast of pain hindered her best effort. Then the bed sank as though someone sat beside her.

Kathryn's stomach pitched with the motion, but before she could demand directions to the bathroom or question whether or not she might actually make it there, strong hands slipped beneath her shoulders and lifted her.

Suddenly she was cradled between hard thighs, could even feel a suspicious bump beneath the seam of jeans pressing lightly between her bare shoulder blades.

The cowboy.

She tried to pull away, but he held her firmly, which given her current state, didn't require much effort.

"Shhh. Relax. You're still as white as biscuit dough."

He guided her head back against his tight stomach, and Kathryn was too weak and too nauseous to fight. She lay as limp as a rag doll against him, moaned when he massaged her temples.

Relax?

"My . . . clothes," she croaked out.

"You don't need them. I wanted you to be comfortable."

She'd be more comfortable *in* her clothes, but she couldn't rally the strength to tell him that.

"Migraine?" he asked.

Who was this man? And, better yet, when had she time-traveled into another century, a time when it was okay for a man to strip a woman without her permission?

She almost refused to answer him out of pure defiance but couldn't quite see what defiance would accomplish, except letting him know he'd rattled her. Letting him think she was used to lounging around in the buff between strange men's legs, might level the playing field a bit.

"I get them sometimes." Rather, she got them often, but Kathryn wouldn't admit that.

"Kitty told me. Stress."

The assurance in his voice irked her. "Not stress."

"I may be a vet, pretty lady, but I still had to go through med school. You move quicker than a road agent on the dodge. Trust me, stress."

In her current state, Kathryn couldn't even contemplate translating that remark. "In English, please?"

He chuckled, a warm rich sound that should have driven a spike through her brain, but surprisingly didn't, which meant she was definitely on the mend.

"You don't relax enough."

"No time."

His warm fingertips stroked her head with just the right amount of pressure to soothe, not hurt. "Make the time."

Easily said by a man who'd only known her two hours, but arrogance aside, she did have to admit he had a magic touch.

The black clouds in her brain slowly receded, freeing up enough brains cells to wonder why he'd undressed her. Was he trying to shake her confidence so he could bully her into his ridiculous proposition? If he was, he had another thing coming.

"Just tell me what you want." Good, she sounded stronger.

"I want to prove Kitty was right about you, that you belong running the Palace."

"And you expect to prove that by forcing me to have sex with you?"

"Not exactly." His throaty chuckle made her bristle. "I want to make love because I'm attracted to you. I'm asking you to work off your debt because I can't see another way to keep you here long enough to seduce you."

Kathryn wavered violently between being more offended than she'd ever been in her life to being absurdly excited that this cowboy wanted her. The conflict made her head pound all over again.

"As long as you're in the Palace, the princesses can return to work and you won't run up any more debt. As far as paying off what you owe me goes, I'll tell you what I like and pay fair market price. You have my word."

The word of a cowboy. Wasn't that sacred? The code of the West or some such nonsense she'd seen in a movie once?

He sounded so reasonable, so civilized, and a strange voice inside urged her to go for it, to drop everything and tempt fate once in her life. A few days of sex the likes of which she'd never had before, she'd pay off her debt, sell Katia's Palace, and head home with her reputation no less for the wear.

Beneath the Western drawl and corny similes, the cowboy was attractive in a Marlboro-man sort of way. How hard could it possibly be to please him? He said he'd tell her what he liked . . . and he'd know because he was a man who'd had an entire brothel at his disposal since the day he'd lost his virginity. Maybe even before.

Kathryn gulped and the brunette's earlier accusation echoed in memory.

You're not half the woman Kitty thought you were.

"Forget it, cowboy."

Leading a Filly to Water

Taming Kate wouldn't be easy, but Trey looked forward to the challenge.

"Why don't we get you feeling better before we lock horns, pretty lady?" He knew an ailing woman when he saw one, and though she put on a brave show, he figured she still hurt.

"I'm on a time limit. We've got to come up with some sort of resolution and fast." That pretty mouth of hers thinned, a sure sign of stress.

This wasn't where he wanted her to go. "Let's not deal with tomorrow just yet. You don't want to rush right to the end of your visit and miss all the fun of getting there."

"The fun?" Her eyes closed, her lashes forming silky half moons on her pale cheeks. "Fun isn't part of this equation."

"It will be. I plan to surprise you."

"I hate surprises."

He supposed she would. Surprises meant veering down unexpected trails. That'd surely mess with her schedule.

"You may hate them, but you've been handling them pretty well, I'd say. Especially being attracted to me. I'll bet you never expected that when you hopped on Joe's plane."

"Whatever gave you the idea I'm attracted to you?" she scoffed. "We just met."

"And we're already in bed. First surprise." He traced the curve of her clenched jaw, rewarded by the goosebumps spraying up her arms. She might hiss like a rattler, but her body told the only tale worth listening to.

"I'm beginning to wonder if any of your lovers ever took the time to woo you right." When she jerked her face away indignantly, he caught her chin between his thumb and forefinger and urged her back. "I know when a woman's attracted to me."

"All that training with the princesses?"

So his friendliness with the princesses bothered her. Trey had moved farther down the trail than he'd reckoned. "I might have an edge."

"Not with me you don't. Now why don't you answer my question? How are we going to fix this? I don't want to leave the princesses in a bind, but you're not leaving me a choice."

"You have no choices, Kate. Even if you're willing to abandon the princesses and turn over the Palace to Barclay, you can't until you're square with me. You already said you don't have the money to pay."

A fact that plainly outraged her, judging by the way she tried to leap off the bed. But Trey had anticipated her move and countered by wrapping both his legs and arms around hers.

"Let me go."

"No." The games were over. "Kitty believed you belonged here, and she asked me to show you why. I gave my word."

"Damn it, cowboy," she hissed, squirming like a hog-tied calf and in the process touching every inch of him with her creamy skin. "This isn't the wild west. This is assault."

"Not if you stop fighting."

"I'll have you arrested."

"Not if I don't let you up."

That got her attention, because she sucked in a sharp breath and stopped fighting. Trey used the opportunity to drive home his point by thumbing the undersides of her satiny breasts. "You won't be sorry."

"You're, you're . . . *molesting* me. This will be rape."

"Trust me, Kate." He couldn't swallow back a chuckle, which started her struggling all over again. "Rape won't enter the picture. I'm not much for fetish sex and I promise you'll want me as much as I want you before we make love." He grazed his thumbs over rosy nipples that had already hardened into greedy little points. "I know when a woman's wanting."

She struggled. He only held her tighter until she gave up.

"Give Kitty a chance," he murmured in a tone he used on scared critters. "Give me a chance."

Her chest heaved, driving those pebbled tips right into his hands. He obliged with another caress that made her suck in more air. No matter how hard Kate fought, she couldn't deny her body's response.

"Why was Kitty so convinced I'd be happier being a madam than I am in New York with my own career?"

Beneath her resentful words, Trey heard the question she didn't ask: *didn't she approve of what I'm doing with my life?*

To reassure her, he loosened the vice grip he had around her upper body, smoothed his thumb along the stubborn curve of her jaw as he pondered his answer.

There were any number of ways to bridge the distance with her, but only one he thought she'd respect. The truth.

"Kitty told me all about you, Kate. *Kathryn and I* did this. *Kathryn and I* did that. She thought you were the strongest Romanov woman yet, a fireball who accomplished anything you set your mind to. She admired and respected you. But she worried about you, too."

Trey watched a tiny frown play between her brows. A certain vulnerability shone through Kate's prickly hide like a sunbeam on a cloudy day, and he found that he liked feeling warm.

"Don't you want to know why Kitty worried about you?"

When she stubbornly refused to answer, he scooted farther down on the bed, hauling her up until his erection sat squarely between her sweet cheeks and he could rest his chin on the top of her silky head.

"She thought you were too comfortable being alone, that you worked too much and didn't live enough. She wasn't sure if you'd been taught how."

"So she wants you and the princesses to teach me?"

Her tone was pure resentment, but at least she'd stopped fighting. "Something like that."

Her black silk hair felt as cool as spring water against his cheek, and he breathed deeply, liking the taste of her fresh scent in his nose and mouth. "She didn't want you living your whole life without love."

When she stiffened slightly, Trey knew he'd made the right choice, allowing her to face away from him and keep her expressions, and her pride, to herself. She resisted showing him any sign of what she perceived as weakness, and not having love in her life was clearly a sticking point. He had to show her that sharing her emotions wasn't weak, and to do that she had to trust him.

But getting Kate to trust him might be a problem, if he couldn't control his own emotions. Right now lust topped the list. The warm curves of her breasts taunted him, just a hairsbreadth below a hand that itched to touch, to roll those tight peaks between his thumb and forefinger until they speared toward his hand again, eager.

He wanted to hear this pretty lady moan softly with pleasure and the power of that want stiffened his erection.

"When you say that Kitty wanted me to have love in my life," she whispered into a silence that had grown thick and charged with sex. "Are you talking about companionship love or romantic love?"

If he was reading her right, she didn't want to fall in love, with him or anyone else. "There are all kinds of love and Kitty wanted you to know them all. She didn't want you going through life thinking no man could satisfy you better than your vibrator could."

"Damn Kitty. Damn *you*, cowboy." She tried to jerk away, but Trey held her firm.

"Don't judge Kitty too hard for betraying your confidences, Kate. She was only giving me ammunition to work with."

"Now you're telling me what to think, too," she hissed.

"You're a woman who deserves to know pleasure." He pressed his erection against her backside. "You've got me aching with want, pretty lady. I'm ready to pleasure you."

She shot her head back, catching him in the chin hard enough to make his teeth thunk together. "I won't be coerced into sleeping with you."

But that breathy quality to her voice suggested the idea wasn't as offensive as she'd have him believe. And that was exactly the response Trey had been hoping for. He skimmed his palm down her smooth belly, was rewarded when her muscles twitched.

"I'm not giving you a choice, Kate."

"This is ridiculous."

"What's ridiculous? That I want to make love to you? Or that Kitty thought you needed love in your life? What's the worst that would happen here?"

"All I'm doing is proving to you and everyone else I'm not cut out to be a madam."

Trey heard the note of despair beneath her frustration and realized there was more to Kate's refusal than met the eye. "Why are you so convinced you can't take Kitty's place?"

"The passion genes skipped a few generations in the Romanov family, all right, cowboy? Trust me on this."

"Trust you on what? Are you telling me you're not a passionate woman?"

"As a matter of fact, I'm not. No passion. No fire. Not a spark."

Trey blinked. He heard her expressionless tone, felt her tension in every curve that had gone rigid against him, but he still couldn't believe what he was hearing. Her beautiful breasts had stretched taut, her nipples puckering into needy rosebuds that aimed for his hands. Where in all creation had she gotten this notion?

One glance at the set to her dainty jaw told Trey she wasn't about to answer that question even if he asked politely. In fact, she was so stubborn; he didn't think she'd hear a word he had to say, even if he spoke the gospel truth.

Kitty had told him all about her ex-fiancé but Trey had never imagined she would take the idiot's criticism to heart. Kitty had flat-out said the man had been blaming his own bedroom deficiencies on Kate and Kitty had been a madam long enough to spot a sidewinder from a mile off.

But what could he possibly say to Kate to convince her?

Nothing, plain and simple. Kate wouldn't listen to him, but she might listen to her own body. Might not have much of a choice, if he played his hand right. And right now his hand wanted to play . . . he speared his fingers into the silky hair between her legs.

"Don't," she cried, but her protest cut off in mid-gasp when he found that silky little nubbin peeping through the folds of her soft skin.

"I can't imagine why you don't think you're a passionate woman, but I aim to show you different."

She was either struck speechless or feeling a good bit of something that twisted her tongue into a knot, because she didn't reply. He took her silence as another step toward consent and stoked her soft woman's skin until she shivered.

"I suggest we start with an in-date," he said quietly. "It's a long party that costs a bundle, but we'll have time to get to know each other. I want to know all about you."

He ran a hand slowly down the length of her bare arm. "You're not shying from me now. You might enjoy letting me touch you like this."

His answer was a slight arching of her hips, so slight, he wondered if she even guessed he'd noticed. He did, and he continued to stroke her, slow and steady, a touch designed to gentle, to reassure. To drive him crazy with trying to control himself. Trey usually scratched his itch when the need arose, and with the way he ached right now, denial might not be his best event.

But taming Kate would make the wait worth his best efforts. Her slender legs stretched out between his, shapely and pale, her creamy curves all begging to be touched and her breasts . . . rosy-tipped and full, he knew this woman would be worth rallying every ounce of patience and skill he could muster.

She was passion in the flesh, though she may not have discovered that about herself yet. But she would soon. She hadn't broken away, though he held her only with one hand resting lightly on her belly, while the other entertained itself—and her, he thought—between her thighs.

He enjoyed the feel of her response, the way her sex grew moist beneath his fingers. He sank the tip of his finger into her heat, just enough to make her shiver and to feel her hot, wet walls clench greedily.

"Feel that?" he whispered against her ear, was rewarded with another shiver. "You may think you're not passionate, but your body's singing a different tune. Are you so sure you want me to stop?"

She was silent so long, he'd have thought she'd fallen back asleep if not for the thready rise and fall of those beautiful breasts. Finally she said, "I don't know if I can do this."

"Why?"

"I've never made much time for this sort of thing."

"You don't have to *do* anything. I'll be in charge."

"So basically I'm just supposed to lie here and let you do as you please."

"Basically." He prodded his erection into her backside again, sank his finger a little deeper. She sucked in a broken breath, a gratifying sound that told him he'd shocked her, that he had her. She was going to give in. "All you have to do is stop fighting. I'll tell you what I want. All you have to do is obey my commands and enjoy yourself."

Taking the First Sip

Obey his commands?

Was this man insane? And just what would happen if she disobeyed? Was disobeying even an option, sandwiched as she was between his erection and the hand he worked his magic with? Disobeying would mean finding the energy to break away and Kathryn wasn't so eager to disturb the unfamiliar languor that made her melt back against the cowboy like her body had dissolved into a hot puddle.

She'd pleasured herself before, but that pleasure had only been the barest fraction of this intense sensation, a sensation that perhaps should have frightened her given her nudity and the fact that this cowboy was a stranger.

Kathryn didn't feel frightened, though. She didn't feel much beyond amazed that *a stranger* could coax such a red-hot response from her usually tepid body.

Did she really want to disobey him? Or did she want to take the chance that Kitty had been right about her? If she'd never learned how to relax and have fun, wasn't it possible she hadn't learned how to experience pleasure either, that a spark of fire smoldered inside her, waiting to be stoked into a flame?

The cowboy certainly seemed to think so. But the cowboy also claimed he wasn't much for fetish sex, yet here he was suggesting she *obey his commands*, which smacked of serious fetish sex in her estimation.

Once Kathryn had accidentally surfed across a pornographic website that had literally taken possession of her computer, windows popping up of men and women in black leather and studs engaged in all sorts of shockingly dominant and submissive acts.

When all else had failed to stop the images from popping up on her screen, she'd freaked, finally shut off the power without backing out of the operating system. She'd begged the network administrator from work to erase all remnants of those sites from her hard drive, on the off chance she died and someone happened upon them while packing up her things for charity. Was that kind of graphic role-playing what the cowboy wanted?

Tipping her head back, she gazed up at him, saw no hint of a threat, or any other strange obsession in his sun-weathered face. He looked relaxed, easy, as though he'd asked her nothing more out of the ordinary than to pass the salt. His lack of emotion when she felt so shaky and vulnerable annoyed her. "You're crossing the line."

"What line is that?"

"The socially acceptable line."

He contemplated her intently, a frown wrinkling his blonde brow. "I don't believe I am. You're a strong woman who has already made up her mind about the Palace and what we do here. I'm just asking you to come at it from another angle."

"You're asking me to trust you."

"Is trust a problem for you?"

"You're a stranger."

"I'd like to change that." His fingers moved over her sex in sleek swirls, an intimacy she shouldn't have allowed him, yet couldn't seem to deny. That realization irritated her, too.

"Would it help if I promised to respect you?" He flashed that quicksilver grin, and those dimples peeked at her from his tanned cheeks. "But I think you already know I do, otherwise you wouldn't be lying here letting me touch you like this."

His finger probed a little deeper, just to make sure she noticed exactly how intimately he touched her. Her sex yielded up one slow, aching throb.

She'd *never* felt anything like this before, an incredible ache as though her insides begged for his touch. The cowboy was right. If she'd questioned her safety, she would still be screaming. While he might have Kitty's reference to vouch for his character, he'd asked her to step into uncharted territory.

What if he was wrong about her?

I need a woman with fire, Kathryn.

She'd admitted the truth about her broken engagement to Kitty late one night while they'd been sobbing over the movie *Camille*. Kitty had said something about men who weren't fit to shoot when you wanted to unload and clean your gun.

While remembering that statement in reference to her ex still made her smile, Kathryn remembered more vividly what Kitty had told her afterward. She'd said that some women just needed the right man to get them in the mood.

Kathryn had scoffed, but deep down, in a barely-acknowledged place, she'd nursed the hope that some day the right man would come along and she'd know what it meant to . . . *want*.

Could the cowboy be that man?

Just hearing him talk about her submission had started a fluttering deep inside, like a thousand butterflies that had munched their way through a pound of espresso beans. Not exactly a flame, but she couldn't deny the situation excited her. His touch made her achy and needy in a way she'd never felt before, not from her own sexual explorations, which had been her only orgasms to date—hardly worth the name compared to what she was building toward right now.

If the possibility of a real orgasm wasn't enough reason to take a chance, the cowboy's impressive erection was. He had a physical reaction to *her*, a compliment to a woman who'd been accused of having no fire. This man had a bevy of beauties who made love for a living at his disposal, yet he wanted *her*.

And like he'd already pointed out, what was the worst that could happened? If Kathryn turned out to be a disaster in bed, she'd just hop on a plane and head home, leaving the cowboy to convalesce in the willing arms of the princesses. She'd be off the hook and no one would be the wiser. Except for her. She hadn't realized how much she didn't want to be a disaster.

Perhaps her headache placed her in the pitifully desperate category. Or maybe the cowboy's touch had just bewitched her, but either way, lying sandwiched between his thighs seemed as natural as his fingers caressing her skin. She wanted to trust him. She wanted him to be right.

"I shouldn't be surprised that Kitty charged you to get me to take over this place," she murmured in a thick voice. "Only Kitty would try to manipulate me from the grave. But what's your deal, cowboy? What do you get out of all this?"

"Besides making love with a beautiful woman?"

She sighed. "If you only knew who you were talking to, you might not be so eager to take on the job. *Fire*. To date, my personal reserve only flares in the boardroom."

His laughter rumbled deep in his chest. "I think we can find something that sparks your kindling, pretty lady."

"Do you really think so?" she asked a bit hysterically. "Until right now, I didn't even know I had kindling."

"Enough to start a forest fire, I'd say." Another rough-velvet chuckle burst hotly against her ear.

Grinding his erection into her bottom, the cowboy found that tiny bundle at her core and applied a slow, steady pressure, so exquisite her sex clenched in reply.

"Looks like we found a hot spot." His deep drawling voice reflected his satisfaction.

He had indeed. This ache, while unexpected, held such promise, a natural sort of potential that prompted her to spread her legs a bit wider to savor the sensation, so intense, Kathryn thought she might be content to lie in this man's arms forever.

An outrageous thought, to match this outrageous situation.

"I want to make you feel good," the cowboy whispered against her skin, a breathy declaration that made her shiver in reply. "Let me."

Let him? she thought wildly. Could she stop him? Kathryn could barely think beyond the need to arch into his touch, to foster this desire he'd ignited in her.

"I'll fulfill my promise to Kitty." His finger sank deeper inside her, a slow, wet stroke that made her ache. "And I'll help you discover who you are. Trust me, Kate."

He sounded as though he had no greater aspiration. Kathryn couldn't deny him, or herself in that moment, not while he caressed her most intimate place, a slow, knowing rhythm that made her sex gather in long, exquisite pulls.

Yet she couldn't seem to speak the words that would give him so much power over her, either. She simply closed her eyes, spread her legs wider and hoped he understood her silent invitation.

"I'll take that as a yes."

Yes.

With his chin resting on top of her head, he took control, using his palm to ride that sensitive gathering of nerves in exactly the right place, coiling the tension inside her tighter. She gave way to the sensation, eager to follow where it led and soon found herself rocking against his hand to meet his strokes, needing, *wanting* to increase the pressure.

Had Kitty been right all along? Had she just needed the right man to help her find her own sexuality?

Kathryn couldn't say, but she hoped, *desperately* hoped, that Kitty had been right. Yet she couldn't dwell on whether the cowboy was the right man or not. Not now. Not with him touching her so intimately. Not unless she wanted to freak out all over again and wind up in bankruptcy court with her name splashed all over the tabloids as *The Madam Who Wasn't*.

She breathed deeply to clear her thoughts and focused on the cowboy instead, noticed all sorts of little things about him. The quiet whisper of his breathing when he inhaled, the soft, slow release. She followed the rise and fall of his chest, an expanse of muscle that created a warm cushion beneath her. His hard thighs flanked hers, his strong torso and broad shoulders sheltering her body in a way that made her feel strangely protected, possessed.

When he drove his finger deeper, starting a hot thrusting that wound her insides tight and demonstrated he could make good on his erotic promise, Kathryn began to hope.

Her heart raced. Her skin grew flushed. She tried not to think about lying naked in this stranger's arms, her bottom swaying against his tanned hand, her breasts jiggling with her shallow breaths.

Whatever sight she presented seemed to arouse the cowboy. His chest heaved. His erection prodded her bottom like a length of hot steel. And somewhere beneath the restless stirrings of her body, the knowledge that she affected him so physically fueled her hope, made her eager to experience this passion he offered.

And the cowboy knew, oh, he knew better than she knew herself, exactly how to build the pressure, increasing the friction of his palm, using his fingertip against that magic spot deep inside until the sounds of her body's response smacked wetly with his every thrust. And when the work-rough fingers of his other hand cupped her breast, plucked at her nipple, Kathryn almost came off the bed.

He held her down.

Sensation coiled through her with a blinding intensity, wound her so tight inside, she squeezed her eyes shut hard and barely dared to breath. She was on the edge, a place she only recognized from the climaxes she'd had before, vague echoes of what she felt right now, a place she never imagined as this powerful, persuasive.

She didn't care that she bore down on this stranger's hand with no shyness, didn't care that a stranger knew her body better than she knew her own. She only wanted to know what lay beyond the edge, wanted to experience the freefall into pure sensation.

"Say my name, Kate." The cowboy's warm velvet mouth dragged along her shoulder. "I want to hear you say it."

So simple a request. He didn't say he wouldn't bring her to fulfillment unless she did as he asked, but the implication was there. In the way he held the pressure of his hand steady, left her hovering on the brink. Such a simple request.

"Trey," she whispered, the taste of his name sweet on her tongue. "Trey, please."

And with his hand buried between her thighs, his finger deep in her heat, he lifted her back against him, the exquisite pressure just enough to send her over the edge, the tension unfurling in the most intense orgasm she'd ever had.

Blazin' New Trails

Kathryn must have dozed, because when she opened her eyes again, the bright sunlight in the suite had faded along with the nauseous soreness around the edges of her brain. She felt warm, relaxed, *sated* in a way that seemed impossible after a migraine that had made her faint.

The cowboy was exactly where she'd left him, except that the hands he'd so expertly stroked her with earlier now only cradled her close. She thought about playing possum, not wanting to disturb the languor of the moment or face the man responsible, but a sleepy yawn gave her away before she'd begun.

"Feeling better?" His voice was a gravelly murmur in the twilight-soaked quiet.

"Much."

She found his erection where she'd left it, too, snug up against her bottom, patiently waiting.

"How long have I been asleep?"

"A few hours."

"Did I spoil your plans?"

"Can't have much fun with a headache." His nose nudged her ear, a playful gesture that while not overtly sexual, brought to mind the intimacies they'd shared. "Too hard to concentrate. Besides, I've been entertaining myself."

His fingers grazed along her arms to emphasize his point, and a crazy little tingle sizzled through her in reply.

"Priming the well, have you?"

"The term is 'priming the pump,' city girl, and yes, I have."

He'd done a good job, Kathryn decided. She was aware of everything about him, from the possessive way he held her to the warm strength of his hands on her arms. When he transferred his touch to her hips and skimmed his fingers along the sensitive place that joined hips to thighs, her sex yielded up one slow throb that held the memory of his power over her.

She sighed. Her thighs parted without her consciously willing them. But instead of obliging her, the cowboy suddenly removed his hands and slid out from behind her, leaving her spread wide on the bed, cold and confused.

When his booted feet hit the carpeted floor, she rolled over, jerked the comforter over her and sat up in a hasty attempt at some dignity. "Was I supposed to resist?"

Pivoting around on a boot heel, he rose above her, tall and broad and masculine in a way that left her feeling as though she was no bigger than an ant crawling across Lady Liberty's feet.

"You did what you were supposed to do."

"So you're leaving?"

He reached out, his callused fingertips caressing her jaw, tilting her face upward to meet his gaze. "I've got to check in with my foreman and call Cody Wilson about his mare. I'll head back over for dinner after you've had a chance to settle in and make some calls. Take care of your business, Kate. I want your undivided attention."

He didn't *ask*, Kathryn noted, suspecting this was her first glimpse of the differences between a request and a command. His wishes. His timetable.

A half grin twitched at the corners of his mouth. "You're supposed to say 'yes, Trey.'"

"Oh," she said, not a little flustered. "Yes, Trey."

He smiled, a real smile now, one that drove the pencilpoint dimples deep into his cheeks and made him seem so attractive in that rugged sort of way. So male. So unfamiliar. So very potent with those challenging dark eyes asserting the sexual power he commanded.

Her body still echoed with the aftereffects of the intimacies he'd taken, a mass of vulnerable achy sensations that jabbed her with the reality that she was in over her head. The rules of his game were far beyond her comprehension.

"Joe should have dropped off your bags by now. I'll have them brought up and send one of the princesses to help you dress for dinner."

She nodded, though she needn't have bothered, since he obviously hadn't been waiting for her permission.

His hand slipped from her face, and he strode to the door, retrieving his hat from the telephone stand and planting it firmly on his head. "I'll be back soon." He paused, his broad shoulders filling the doorway as he turned back to her. "Get ready to become my princess."

His words hung in the distance between them, a challenge, a command, and surprisingly, his words made her eager . . . to please him? To run screaming? Kathryn couldn't say, but she knew what he was waiting for and said, "Yes, Trey."

His dark eyes flashed. He brought those skilled fingers to the brim of his hat in a polite goodbye before turning on his heel and departing. Kathryn watched him leave, heart pounding with a strange mixture of trepidation, excitement, and, yes, even embarrassment at the high-handed way he'd left her lying naked on the bed, *wanting*.

Leaping to her feet, she prowled the suite, barely noticing the tasteful mahogany furnishings or the attractive combination of greens and golds that adorned the rooms.

So this little scenario was all about what the cowboy wanted. Okay, she got that part. But how did she feel about serving his needs? Kathryn paused, considering, and realized she wasn't apprehensive at all, wasn't really offended by the idea either, just taken aback, out of her element.

She was used to being in control, of her actions, her emotions, her environment, and here the cowboy challenged her to give the control over to him.

Someone leads and someone follows, Kitty had once said while watching Fred Astaire and Ginger Rogers dancing across the screen. *It's the natural way of things.*

Then she'd pointed out that following could be harder than leading. Fred and Ginger danced the same dance, but Ginger danced every step backwards. He led; she followed and together they were awesome. There was a lesson in there somewhere, Kathryn was sure, but all she could find was a question: why had she never considered following before?

Veering out of the bedroom she pondered the answer in a tasteful sitting room decorated in pseudo-Victorian, formal, but not fussy or feminine. Had she been frightened? Of getting close? Of being hurt?

Glancing at a framed photo, Kathryn recognized the three white furballs in the picture, realized she stood in Kitty's suite. Of course the cowboy would bring the new madam to the former madam's suite.

She stared at the Maltese dogs, all impeccably groomed with bows in their white hair. Pink for the mother and blue for her two sons. Kathryn smiled. Kitty had loved her pooches to the point of obsession, a fact proven by their portraits of honor on her vanity.

Kathryn's own college graduation photo resided there as well but noticeably absent was the first photo she'd ever given Kitty—her high school graduation picture, which Kitty had admired from the full-size portrait.

I'm sorry I didn't know you then, Kathryn. You're a beautiful young woman with such fire in your eyes.

Kathryn had framed a smaller photo and presented it to Kitty as a gift, and she'd never again looked at her portrait without remembering Kitty's words—even after her broken engagement when she believed Kitty must have been mistaken.

Glancing around the room, she wondered what had happened to that photo, more sentimental, she believed, than the one currently residing on the vanity.

A knock brought Kathryn out of her thoughts. "Come in."

The door cracked warily and the blonde princess popped her head inside. "Lady Kate, it's me, Phoebe."

"Hi, Phoebe." Kathryn forced a welcoming smile and filed the name Phoebe away in long-term memory. "Please, call me . . . Kate." She might as well run with the dual identity thing. If she thought of herself as a different person, she just might get through whatever the cowboy had in store for her.

Phoebe kicked the door open with a sandaled foot and hauled in what Kathryn recognized as her garment bag.

"Oh, here, let me take that."

"No need." Phoebe walked straight through the sitting room to the bedroom. "It's not heavy. You weren't planning on staying long, were you?"

Kathryn followed, recognizing the accusation in Phoebe's voice. Not anger, she thought, but hurt.

"I wasn't," she answered honestly. "But as I'm sure you've heard, my plans have changed. I'll be extending my stay a bit."

"Trey told us." Stretching up on tiptoes, she fumbled to fasten the garment bag over the back of the closet door.

Kathryn came to her aid, lifting the bag to help the girl, who wasn't much taller than her own five feet, three inches.

"We've taken care of Kitty's things, so there's plenty of room in the closet for your stuff," Phoebe said. "Whatever's left in the room is what Kitty wanted us to leave for you."

"Oh," Kathryn said, surprised. "You mean like the furnishings?"

Phoebe laughed merrily. "Technically everything in the Palace is yours, Kate. But I meant clothes. Kitty wanted to leave you some things to get you started."

Peering into the closet, Kathryn glanced at the first item hanging there—a red beaded sheath dress hanging neatly in a clear plastic garment bag.

You should wear red, Kathryn, Kitty had once said. *It would look lovely with your vivid coloring.*

Kathryn could only stare, afraid to reply when her emotions skimmed so close to the surface.

"They're not hand-me-downs." Clearly misreading Kathryn's expression, Phoebe quickly pulled out another boutique garment bag, then another. "They're all brand new. She'd been shopping for a while. We all took turns driving her into the city on our off weeks." She smiled fondly. "Kitty knew she was nearing the end and wanted everything to be perfect after she'd gone."

Kathryn stared at the bright colored fabrics of the gowns in the closet, such a contrast to her own wardrobe of dark solids and neutrals at home, and again she could hear Kitty's voice through the years.

You're such a lovely girl, Kathryn. I'd love to see you celebrate your beauty and youth.

Kitty had seen so easily through her, and had cared—so much more than Kathryn had ever realized. Now she was gone. Leaving behind her brothel, her belongings and—Kathryn watched Phoebe rummage through the clothing—the people she'd cared about.

"What happened to her dogs?" she finally asked.

"They've been in such a sorry state since the funeral, Gwen's been letting them sleep on her bed."

The idea struck Kathryn as a bit inconsistent with her impression of the Amazonian princess with the riding crop, but she didn't comment.

"You should wear this tonight." Phoebe slipped a flesh-toned sequined sheath from its protective cover. The sequins shimmered when the light hit them, a striking rainbow of translucent color. "Trey'll be on his knees."

"I'm the only one who'll be on my knees tonight."

Phoebe gave a bright laugh. "Then all the more reason to wear this."

She seemed so earnest that Kathryn couldn't help but smile, reminded of days long ago in her school dormitory, when she and her schoolmates would spend hours deliberating the right clothing and cosmetics for their monthly co-ed dance with the boys from St. Peter's School.

"Trey said it'll be a bit before he gets back, so you've got some time to make yourself pretty." She backed out of the closet, then turned around before Kathryn had a chance to follow. "Don't let Trey take advantage of you. He's old hat and you're new to this game. If you have any questions about the menu or the prices, just ask. We'll all help you."

Kathryn appreciated the sentiment, yet her doubts must have shown clearly in her expression, because Phoebe added, "Trust me. The princesses stick together at the Palace. Always have, always will." With a decided shake of her pale blonde head, she swept through the door. "I know you may not have gotten that impression, but you threw us a curve. Bottom line is you're our madam as long as you're here."

Kathryn issued a very unladylike snort. "I'm not sure I'll make a very good . . . madam."

"Why ever not?" Phoebe looked genuinely puzzled. Then she rolled her eyes. "Oh, lord, don't tell me Gwen was right. You're not a virgin, at your age?"

"No, of course not."

Her denial hung in the air for long moment before Phoebe sniffed haughtily. "There's nothing wrong with being a virgin, Kate. Trust me. I lose my virginity at least twice a week."

This was the absolute last thing Kate expected to hear and for a moment she could only stare. Then a laugh burst unbidden from her lips. "Think the cowboy will have mercy on me if I pretend I'm losing mine, too?"

"You don't want Trey's mercy, Kate. You want every ounce of that man's lust. Trust me. Mmm-mmm." She paused in the bedroom doorway and gave a contented sigh. "The flesh-toned gown and no virginity. Trey'll be on his knees and that's exactly where you want him. Got it?"

"Got it," Kathryn said, in spite of her growing sense of amazement that she was making jokes about having sex with the same man Phoebe apparently knew very well. Twelve hours ago, jokes like this simply wouldn't have been possible.

Phoebe looked genuinely delighted and disappeared from the bedroom with a bouncy step. Kathryn watched her go with a smile. Life had certainly taken a turn since breakfast. All because of Kitty. Kitty, who'd done the outrageous and bequeathed her a brothel. Kitty, who'd cared enough to push her beyond the confining boundaries of her safe little world.

Plucking the flesh-toned gown from the closet, she hung it on the outside of the bathroom door. "There you go, Kitty. The least I can do is go along for the ride."

And when she picked up the phone to postpone her departure, Kathryn felt more relaxed than she had in a very long time.

Grinning Like a Jackass Eating Cactus

After arranging to have their meal sent up when he called, Trey made his way back to Kate's suite. When she didn't respond to his second knock, he let himself in and heard the shower. Grinning, he strode into the bedroom, wondering how Kate felt as she stood beneath the pulsing showerhead, water pouring over that sweet body of hers. Was she washing away the sickness? Or prettying herself up for him?

Trey hoped both, because just the thought of the night before them sent a downswell of blood south. He'd showered already, though he'd been mightily tempted to share that pleasure with her. And he would, as soon as they'd traveled farther down the trail to knowing each other.

He planned to get to know Kate very well. He wanted her. Leaving to check on Cody's mare and clear off his own plate at the ranch hadn't been as simple as putting on his John B. and walking out the door. Not with Kate rubbing her sex against his hand like a purring barncat.

When Trey saw a sparkly gown hanging on the outside of the bathroom door, the hangar keeping the door from closing properly, he decided right then and there not to deny himself some waterplay, even if he didn't think Kate was ready for him to get wet.

Setting his saddlebag on the floor by her dresser, he entered the bathroom. A double sink vanity claimed an entire wall beneath lighted mirrors, and he walked past, noting the array of toiletries efficiently arranged on top.

Efficiency and control. Kate sure did have her fill.

He stopped in the doorway of the adjoining room, the sight before him catching him by surprise like the onset of a Nevada sunset, a sight that still awed him, though he'd lived his whole life here.

Her face turned up to the shower spray, the water jetting over her delicate features, streaming down the curves and valleys of her naked body, glossing her in clouds of mist.

All sleek curves and creamy softness, she was the kind of woman a man claimed to quench his fires, a woman so sweet she raised his protective instincts, too. Her hair was a smudge of midnight behind the glass shower door, the fine points of her body all softly blurred, veiled as though he viewed her through a morning mist on the range.

Trey's pulse kettled in his veins like a bucking bronc, an adrenaline kick that made him dig his palm against his crotch to curb his response. No such luck.

Sinking onto the commode, he braced his legs apart to ease the vice of a troublesome seam, and sat back to enjoy the show.

Kitty had known he'd react to Kate like a virgin walking his first princess line-up. She'd been one talented madam, and her fine old hand had snared Kate into coming to the Palace and had backed him into making her stay.

She'd manipulated them both, and Trey couldn't say he was sorry. His needs were sparking like a brushfire in a drought season as he watched Kate lift her sleek arms to rinse her hair. He wanted to touch her, to explore every nook and cranny of that body God must have designed to tempt a man to eternal damnation with a smile on his face.

Though she was slightly built, she wasn't half-starved and frail like so many women. She was curvy and womanly, a woman created to touch. Even her motions were graceful, almost lyrical beneath the rush of water and the hiss of steam. With that water flowing over her in streaming ribbons, Trey could imagine her bathing in a sunlit pool under a mountain waterfall.

Awed, he watched as she bent slightly to soap a long leg, revealing the slim line of her back, the smooth turn of her pale backside, a quick flash of darkness between her thighs. His cock swelled painfully in response, and he squirmed on the commode lid to ease the pressure of that damned seam.

He was of half a mind to strip off his clothes and join her, but guessed he'd pushed his luck enough. Kate was a filly who needed a firm, but gentle wooing, and he aimed to take the reins and woo her proper.

Though he'd never been much for playing domination and submission games, filling his needs with more playful antics, he recognized Kate needed to let go of her almighty control. She was wound tighter than a twirl-twizzler roping his first calf and didn't look like she'd loosen up any time soon on her own.

He could help her with that, though it went against his grain to push her. He'd settled on using gentle force for the time being. Kate was an intelligent woman. She'd see the importance of what she meant to the Palace and what the Palace could mean to her soon enough. And once she did . . . well, then he could only hope for the best.

He'd have done his part and shown her the way, and, lord, was he eager to show her the way. *Too* eager, because when she spread her legs to the water in a seductive dance, the sooty splash of color between her thighs sprang words to his lips before he realized that talking would only end his private show.

"I want you to shave for me."

She reared around so quickly Trey thought for sure she'd slip and he'd wind up toting her back to bed unconscious again.

"Jeez, cowboy. You scared me half to death." Her hands were pressed to her chest, not to cover her pretty breasts, but as though she tried to keep her heart from galloping right out of her skin.

"I won't bite, pretty lady." He wrestled back a smile. "But I've got a hankering to taste your sex soft and smooth under my tongue."

Trey's heartbeat speeded up in time with the pulsing rush of the shower as he awaited Kate's response. She seemed frozen in place, the only change was the rapid rise and fall of her chest, and he wondered whether she was honestly mulling over her reply or simply shocked into silence.

Then, through the steamy glass, he detected a pink flush that started above those nice firm breasts. "Yes, Trey."

Those words shot through his body like a flash flood. "You can knock off a hundred dollars for the show."

"I thought there was a two-hundred dollar house minimum?"

He smiled. The lady learned quickly.

"I'll pay."

Slowly she lowered her hands from her breasts, and she reached toward the soap dish.

Trey's breath hitched as she rolled the bar of soap between her hands. Hiking a foot onto the edge of the tub, she bent slightly, making her breasts plump forward invitingly.

Her hair fell forward over her face, concealing her expression, but the rosy tinge creeping up her neck deepened, a soft focus blush prettier than any sunrise over the ridge.

Propping his elbows on his knees, Trey leaned forward, too, closing the distance between them, aroused by the way her breasts swelled when she took a heavy breath and rolled a soapy hand between her thighs, long, lingering caresses, designed to draw and hold his gaze.

They did. His blood pumped when she spread her thighs, leaving herself open to his gaze, reminding him of how she'd felt earlier, pressing that soft mound into his palm, urging him to stoke the fire inside her.

He wanted to touch her now. To thread his fingers through that soapy dark mass, feel the power of knowing it was his hand she responded to, he who made her purr silkily in his ear.

Shifting uncomfortably on the commode again, he watched as she parted the dark silk lips of her sex with pale fingers, thighs spread wide, torturing him with images of driving himself deep inside her. Feeling her sweet softness welcome him in that way had his cock straining in his jeans like a bronc in a chute.

The razor appeared in her hand, and she guided it over her skin, carving away the lush thickness in clean strokes. Water rinsed the remnants away, down her thighs in tufts of dark silk.

Trey had to anchor his hands on his knees to force himself not to slide open that glass door and join her. Watching her performance assaulted him with a lust he'd never felt before. Knowing she sought to please him excited him in a way he'd never explored before, a way he could become mighty used to.

The thought was new and startling. Trey liked being the center of Kate's thoughts, liked it with a dark sort of hunger he'd never felt before. Liked it enough that he fought a hard battle to sit still and just watch, when he wanted to feel her sleek moist body spread hot and willing beneath him.

"Come on out now, Kate. I want to watch you dry off."

"Yes, Trey."

Those words again, soft breathy bursts of sound that undermined his restraint, affected him with an intensity he had to wrestle to control. The steady pulse of the showerhead seemed to mock his best efforts, then the silence, as she flipped the water off. Awed by the sight, Trey watched as she rallied the courage to face him, a visible struggle that stiffened her spine, drew back her shoulders before she slid open the door and stepped out.

He wasn't a small man, and the quarters proved tight for her to maneuver around him, but he was too enamored by the sight of her dripping curves to leave his perch on the commode and give her more space.

Not when she was only inches away, so close he could smell the light flowery scent of her skin, see a bead of water roll over her hip and disappear into the curve of her inner thigh.

Dragging a towel off the rack, he held it out. "Here."

With a trembling hand, she took it, brought it up against her without ever meeting his gaze.

He sat back, fascinated by her struggle, waiting.

Her flush revealed she fought a war within, but he thought she might be winning, because she hiked her painted toes onto the rim of the commode seat between his legs, drew the thick towel up one shapely calf and launched a well-aimed attack on his senses, worthy of the two-hundred dollar house minimum.

Her hand trembled as she worked the towel lazily up her leg, each stroke buffing her creamy skin and directing his gaze a little higher toward the juncture between her thighs that flashed teasing glimpses of her freshly shaved sex, full pink lips slightly parted and pouting at his inattention.

Keeping her gaze lowered to her task, she dragged the corner of the bath towel into the valleys between each painted red toe, her full breasts jiggling with each stroke, kicking his heartbeat into a gallop.

Something about the smile tugging at the corners of Kate's pretty mouth suggested she was very aware of the effect she had on him, and very pleased. But still she avoided his gaze as she slipped one foot away, only to replace it with the other and begin the sexy show all over again.

Trey's breath came in arrested bursts, his every sense rushed with *her*. The sight of her sleek skin, feminine curves moving in a graceful swirl of motion that kicked off faint whiffs of her freshly-scrubbed skin, forced him to wedge his hands under his thighs to keep from gathering her into a naked wet bundle on his lap. Each breath of her slightly floral scent gnawed away at a little more of his restraint, until Trey was left asking the question: *what fool put him in charge?*

Ride for the Brand

Kathryn knew nothing at all about the cowboy except that he temporarily controlled her fate and was used to an entire brothel servicing his sexual needs. He knew so much about her. Kitty had shared not only the details of her life, but her deepest, darkest secret.

I need a woman with fire, Kathryn.

The cowboy knew, yet he'd told her to put on this sexy little show, knowing she wasn't any good at sexy shows. He'd told her to please him, and *she had*.

That hungry expression on his face and that bulge in his crotch were so reflective of his pleasure that Kathryn found herself not nearly so intimidated by her naked performance as she might have been. The effect left her feeling feminine and appealing in a way she'd never felt before.

Knowing the cowboy was in control, knowing she really had no choice in the matter was . . . well, *liberating*. Her task here was to keep that smile on his face and that bulge in his pants. Inhibitions and worries faded in the quest of her goal.

She wondered what a psychologist would say about finding such freedom in submission, then decided she really didn't want to know. She'd never approached anything before in her life with such an utter lack of control and, combined with that rapt hunger on the cowboy's face, Kathryn found herself spurred to a boldness she'd never imagined herself capable of.

Dragging the towel around her shoulders, she dried her back and neck with one swipe, then let the towel drop to the floor in a wet heap. "Would you hand me that lotion, please?"

The cowboy glanced askance at the vanity, zeroed right in on her favored sweet pea body cream and grabbed the tube with one sure shot. Blonde hair fell over his brow as he turned back to stare at her, his potent dark gaze demanding everything she had to give, and then some.

He was such a big man, those hard chiseled features and miles of rugged broad shoulder sucking up all the space and air between them. "I'll do the honors, pretty lady."

That gravelly whisper threaded through her, made her intensely aware of all her bare skin in contrast to his fully clothed self. He'd apparently showered and shaved while he'd been away and somehow his fresh shirt and knife-creased jeans made him seem primed for a night of sex as if he'd shown up on her doorstep with a bouquet of fresh flowers, a polite and very sweet gesture.

But there was nothing sweet about his stare. The heat in those dark eyes made her nipples gather tight and Kathryn suffered through another flush as he glanced right at the greedy peaks that had the temerity to tighten even more.

Judging by his smile, the man was clearly pleased he could affect her with no more than a glance. She wondered exactly what he'd do if she told him to keep his hands to himself, she'd lotion her own body, thank you very much, but found she wasn't willing to test that particular boundary yet. Not when the testing would mean denying herself his special brand of magic.

With a steady hand he squeezed the fragrant pink lotion into his palm, a sharp contrast to the way her insides trembled when she propped her foot between his thighs.

He glided his callused hands along her calves with strong, sure strokes, as though he'd performed the service on a thousand women before. Such innocuous attention shouldn't feel so . . . *possessive*, yet something about the way he worked his way steadily upward, as though he desired to touch her and needed no permission to do so, made her feel very possessed.

Kathryn savored the unfamiliar feeling. Gone was any uncertainty of consequences, any struggle of wondering if she was crazy to give herself to a stranger, even a stranger who could make her climax like he had. He'd simply take what he wanted and she found that thrilling in a dark sort of way.

With his gaze lowered to his task, he gave her a view of the top of his head, the wheat-blonde strands bleached pale from the sun, and she savored the simplicity of wondering what his hair would feel like, when she would get a chance to find out.

Not just yet, apparently, when he slid his work-rough hands along her thigh, kneading the lotion into her skin, tantalizing her as he edged closer and closer toward her newly bared sex.

She'd never realized how much that fine cover of pubic hair had protected her until the cowboy traced his tanned fingers over her, sweet pea lotion slicking callused fingertips against oh-so-sensitive skin and creating a friction that made her suck in a surprised breath.

The sound seemed to hang in the steamy air between them and the cowboy peered up from beneath his brow, his melting gaze raking every bare inch of skin along the way.

"This spot is definitely a winner." His lotion-slick fingers separated her sensitive folds, found that intimate knot of nerve endings and squeezed gently. "Can you feel my touch better freshly shaved, Kate?"

Kathryn felt his touch straight to her toes and grabbed his shoulders to hang on while she rode out the sensation.

"Yes, Trey," she managed on the edge of a breath.

Shaving had made a difference, even in contrast to the feel of his hands on her most intimate places only a few hours earlier. Her sex ached, that tiny core swelled with the need.

He rubbed his thumb in lazy circles, occasionally catching that responsive core between his thumb and forefinger and shooting another molten wave through her.

She grew woozy. Her breasts grew heavy, her nipples ripe for his touch. Her thighs began to vibrate with the intensity of her need and he must have noticed how he overwhelmed her because his free hand snaked around her waist and pulled her forward just before her legs gave way.

"Come here, pretty lady." He forced her to straddle his lap, spreading her sex wide. His hand unfurled beneath her, his rough palm rasping her tender skin with a breathtaking amount of friction before his thumb started up that dreamy rhythm again. "Tell me what you want, Kate?"

King Cowboy was actually asking? Kathryn glanced at him, surprised, but judging by that hooded expression, he was only interested in exercising some more control over her body. Not too difficult of a task. Her body had become slave to his touches and she barely recognized the sight of herself, naked and vulnerable, before this fully-dressed stranger. The clean scent of his freshly scrubbed hair filling her nostrils, his tanned face level with her breasts.

His hard mouth poised just inches before a beaded nipple.

"I want . . . Oh, Trey. I want to feel your mouth on me."

This was the scene from some erotic fantasy and when he dipped low to her breast, caught her nipple with a swirl of his tongue and a hot pull of his lips, Kathryn never wanted the fantasy to end.

She moaned, *loud*, and gave in to her desire to touch him. Threading her fingertips through the heavy strands, she anchored his mouth against her breast, shivered as he lavished hot attention on first one nipple then the other.

"Think we found another spot, pretty lady." He glanced up at her, dark eyes molten with a look of such hungry pleasure that she let out another sigh.

With his thumb tracing those crazy circles and his mouth sucking greedily on her nipple, Kathryn felt the tension inside her shooting into warp speed even faster than before. Her sex clenched in needy spasms and heat pooled low in her belly.

She wanted to experience that soaring ride to climax that she had earlier, wanted to know that her body's response hadn't been a one-shot deal. Only this time the cowboy kept the pressure steady, bringing her to each new peak, only to leave her there, waiting, aching, *wanting*.

She finally realized he had his own agenda this time around and it obviously wasn't about bringing her to fulfillment. Perhaps earlier had been a teaser, a means of convincing her to play this game. But now, now it was obvious the cowboy wanted to lift her to new heights and leave her hanging there to enjoy the view.

"That should do it," he whispered, withdrawing his mouth from a nipple.

She wanted to ask what he was talking about, but in the face of this urgent sense of loss, speech completely failed her. She could only stare, breathless, as he reached into his shirt pocket and withdrew a handful of gold jewelry.

"I brought you a present."

He captured her gaze and she saw pleasure in the dark depths, and something else entirely. He seemed almost . . . *eager*, she decided, and sensed that her response to his gift was somehow important to him.

He poured a golden chain into her palm. At first she thought he'd given her a necklace, but quickly realized this was like no necklace she'd ever worn before. The fine gold links made up a very long chain and three tweezer-like clamps were fastened at various intervals.

"What is it?" she asked.

"Hang on. I'll show you." He slipped his arm from around her waist and she braced herself steady on his lap as he lifted the chain and unfastened one of those shiny gold clamps.

"What is—" her jaw dropped open when he aimed for one of her nipples.

"Trust me," he said with a smile and latched that mean little clamp right onto a tender peak.

Kathryn gasped at the pinch, not quite pain, but not far from it. "Whoa, cowboy."

"Too tight?"

She breathed deeply, gave the sensation a chance. "Depends. What am I supposed to feel?"

He fastened the second clamp to her other nipple, then gave a tug that stretched her nipples tight. Kathryn gasped.

"I don't want you to hurt, but I want you to be very aware of how aroused you are. Are you?"

"Yes, Trey." But there was still a third clamp dangling from the chain and she eyed it skeptically. "And where, pray tell, does that go?"

He flashed a dimpled smile that flustered her by its sheer devilry. Patting her thigh, he motioned her to stand. "Hop up and I'll show you."

With a sort of morbid fascination, Kathryn did as he asked, then forced herself not to shy away when he slipped his hands between her thighs.

"Oh, no."

He coaxed that intimate knot that was distended and oh-so-sensitive from its fleshy hiding place. "Oh, yes."

He tightened the clamp gently and before she had a chance to even register the feel of that pain/pleasure pinch, he lowered his head and laved his rough-velvet tongue over her vulnerable bud.

Kathryn jumped away, knees shaking, breasts jingling, mouth emitting a sound that was a cross between a moan and a sob.

"I like the idea of you wearing my brand," the cowboy said earnestly. "You'll remember how I make you feel with every breath you take."

He wasn't kidding. Her breath came in tight ragged heaves, each one causing the chain to pull and the clamps to tug at her nipples, at her clitoris. The wild, urgent pounding deep inside left her hovering somewhere between *aching* and *desperate*.

She stared at the cowboy's satisfied grin and decided that she really had stepped into a new and strange land today. A land where Kathryn Roman, tireless junior partner to one of the country's top advertising firms became Kathryn Romanov, madam, branded by Trey Holliday, cowboy master.

Her sex gave one hard throb of pleasure.

Luck of the Draw

Trey retreated to the doorway to get a bird's eye view of Kate as she applied make-up. Leaning over the vanity, she peered into the mirror, her every move a study of creamy curves and liquid grace.

Gold chinked softly with her movements and he found himself riveted by the sound, by the sight of the chains swaying from her breasts, a narrow V that trailed over the smooth expanse of her belly. Her nipples had hardened to the size of small red grapes, ripe for his attention, and he found himself chomping at the bit to taste her again.

She aroused him in a way that tested his restraint—a first time in his memory. A princess named Sadie had taken his virginity long ago and she'd skilled him in the arts of self-control for many long steamy nights before declaring him ready to tackle loving. Kate was proving to be as apt a pupil as he'd once been and he was very pleased with the way the night progressed, the way she responded to him.

Something about her fierce independence challenged him to rein her in like a mustang, not to break her, but to test that strong will to see how far she could go. She'd come so far in such a short time already. Challenging him about her fees, and . . . he glanced at the gown hanging from the door, choosing clothes from her new wardrobe to please him.

He ran his fingers over the shimmery gown. "Nice choice, but you can save your pretty dress for later."

She gazed at his reflection in the mirror. "I thought we were having dinner."

"We are. We'll eat in your suite."

Those big blue eyes swept down over his own clothes and she frowned. "Oh, I see. I get to waltz around butt naked like your obedient little love slave."

"I like seeing you naked. You've got a fine body."

Though she pointed that dainty chin high in the air, Trey could tell by how hard she worked to look unmoved that she liked when he called her pretty. She needed to admit how much she liked it, too.

Moving toward her, he ignored the wary light that flared in her eyes when he caressed a finger along the cleft of her heart-shaped backside. "You've got a body made for admiring, and touching."

Goosebumps skimmed along her creamy skin like a breeze over the range and he ran his finger along her cleft again, just enough to separate those sweet cheeks and make her blush at the liberty he took. "No sense denying the obvious, Kate, you like when I touch you." He met her reflection in the mirror and smiled. "There's nothing wrong with that."

"Maybe not," she said saucily. "But it's going to cost you, cowboy."

He trailed his finger upwards along her spine, was rewarded this time when she shivered. "That's what makes this the perfect arrangement. I'm willing to pay."

Retreating, he sensed her staring after him as he grabbed his saddlebag from the bedroom. Withdrawing a leatherbound journal, he turned to head back into the bathroom to find that she'd followed him.

She stood in the doorway, natural and at ease, gold chains dangling, seeming to have overcome her nerves about displaying all her lovely bare skin.

"Another present," he said, presenting her the journal. "For keeping track."

"How much am I into you for?" She flipped through the pages, eyes growing wide. "Oh, no. I really had no idea the princesses made this kind of money. It'll take me forever to pay you off."

"That all depends."

"On what? Trust me, cowboy, nothing I know how to do is worth this much money."

He laughed, liking the bite of her humor. "Leave that for me to decide, since I'm the one paying."

"You're going to knock off two thousand bucks to spend the night with me?" she asked incredulously.

"For an in-party." He flipped back to the front of the journal and plucked out a house menu. "An in-party means I have your undivided attention for as long as I want you tonight. We can negotiate for the extras. Speaking of, you'll need to mark down that two hundred for the shower show."

She shot him a look that suggested he'd gone plum loco, but Trey saw her pleasure, too, in the slight straightening of her shoulders, the way she stood tall with pride. Unless he was way off the mark, Kate liked that he wanted her.

And there was something so inviting about knowing that, about her yielding her strong will to his that made her trust so much more worth the earning.

A love slave. Trey had never thought much about having one before, but then, he'd never met Kate in the flesh before.

"Are you hungry, pretty lady?" At her nod, he said, "I'll give a call then, because I'm starved."

He let his gaze trail over her, telling her without words that he was starved for a lot more than food.

The Cowboy's Lady

Kathryn discovered she wasn't hungry for food, after all. Her appetite seemed focused on the man who sat across the table, growing distinctly more ravenous with his every steamy glance. The perfect gentleman and dinner companion, the cowboy entertained her with tales of the Palace and Tex's Sweet, seemed intent on engaging her in conversations that compared life in Love to the life she knew in the city.

She found him a very intelligent man, which she supposed shouldn't come as a surprise given his various occupations. His wit had a dry edge that made her laugh often, and combined with his quicksilver smiles, she found their meal passing in a blur, the wine the only memorable course. Every sip chased away her inhibitions about sitting naked across from a fully dressed man, chased away nerves about what would come on her first in-date.

The cool air on her bare skin and the heat of the cowboy's glances combined to make her . . . *ready*. Her breasts had grown heavy and swollen, the clamps squeezing her nipples just enough to make them ache, yet not grow numb, the clamp between her legs making her squirm on the chair. She'd grown moist and achy and eager to find out what he had planned next.

"A tour of the Palace, I think," he said to her surprise. "You didn't officially re-open, but now that everyone knows you're here, they'll be lining up at the door. Place is probably full already. Do you feel up to an appearance? Has that headache gone?"

The last thing she wanted to do was play temporary madam. She didn't want to think about the responsibilities Kitty had saddled her with, didn't want to worry about how she was going resolve the problems. But to Kathryn's amazement, she found she didn't want to think about leaving the cowboy either. She'd much rather focus on easing this hungry ache he'd started with his skilled touches and possessive demands.

"Let's get it over with." The sooner they toured the place, the sooner they could be alone together again.

The cowboy stood, circled the table and extended his hand. "Then let's get you ready to meet your fans."

She slipped her hand into his, thrilled at the way he tightened his fingers around hers, a simple touch that shouldn't have amplified her awareness of him, but did.

"Fans?" she said. "I think Joe used the term 'posse.' "

The cowboy chuckled. "Now it's not that bad, Kate. Everyone's just disappointed you don't want to stay."

She wanted to ask if the cowboy would be as disappointed when she left, but couldn't bring herself to. Somehow his answer mattered, when it shouldn't, and she refused to fuel the flames of this absurd obsession by . . . well, obsessing.

Just because the cowboy made her feel sexier than she'd ever felt in her life implied no exclusivity on his part. The man was simply fulfilling his commitment to Kitty. That he was obviously enjoying himself in the process was only good fortune.

He led her into the bedroom, slipped the gown off its hanger. "Lift your arms."

"Cowboy," she said. "I have nothing on but your brand."

His dimples flashed. His dark gaze twinkled. "I know. I like knowing you're naked under all this finery."

His gaze held hers and arousal zipped through her at the pleasure she saw in those sparkling depths. "Yes, Trey."

His strong hands guided the gown over her head and down her body. The beaded fabric chafed her bare skin, a tantalizing friction that fired her sensitive nerve endings and increased that needy pulsing between her legs.

She'd only touched up her lipstick and fluffed her hair when the cowboy declared her perfect and with her hand in his, she went to greet her guests.

The cowboy hadn't been far off the mark when he'd said the Palace would already be filled with eager guests. And one glance into that busy dining room clued her in on why he'd had their meal sent to Kitty's suite. The princesses weren't the only employees the Palace's new madam would have to contend with. The place screamed *thriving business*.

The bar teemed with Stetsons, creased slacks and dress boots. Kate realized with surprise that, like the cowboy, these men had obviously dressed for their night out. Visits with the princesses were clearly taken seriously around Love.

One young man with a bouquet of roses left the bar to greet them. He inclined his head at the cowboy. "G'evening, Trey."

"This is Jess," the cowboy said, shaking the man's hand.

Jess handed her a bouquet of fresh roses with baby's breath, as Kathryn recognized the man who presented them as the town deputy. A peace offering, she suspected.

"I'm pleased to meet you, Lady Kate."

Lady Kate. Word sure got around quickly in Love.

"Thank you very much, Jess. They're lovely."

Two spots of red actually bloomed high on Jess's cheeks, and Kathryn realized he was actually blushing. With a head full of shiny black hair and bright blue eyes, he was a handsome young man, probably not much older than twenty.

Jess rocked back on his boot heels and smiled a shy grin. "Just wanted to say howdy and that I hope you decide to stay," he said, before beating a hasty retreat.

Kathryn watched him fade back in with a group of other young cowboys, lifted the roses to her nose and inhaled deeply. "He was very nice. Does he come here often?"

The cowboy frowned. "He's sort of connected to the place."

"Is he?"

"His full name's Jess Romanov."

Kathryn nearly dropped her roses.

The cowboy reached out to steady her bouquet, looking slightly uncomfortable. "Your cousin."

"I didn't know I had a cousin," she said dryly, wondering what else the man knew about her but had neglected to mention.

"Kitty's brother had four kids. Your mom was the oldest."

Burying her face in her bouquet under the pretense of enjoying the fragrant blooms, Kathryn schooled her expression, unwilling to let the cowboy know how much his news affected her.

Her mother had been a part of a family.

"My mother was supposed to run this place after Kitty, then," she finally asked. "Do you know what happened?"

He nodded. "Let's get through with your well wishers and we'll find a place to talk."

With a strong hand on her elbow, he steered her into the crowd, not allowing her time to wonder how many other family members she had floating around and knew nothing about. Within seconds, they were rushed by men of all ages and over the sea of heads, she could see Adoreé dancing on a raised platform, a seductive dance comprised of spangly scarves and bare skin.

Kathryn shook hands and smiled, quickly realizing that she may as well have worn the cowboy's brand outside her evening gown because every one of these men seemed to think they needed the cowboy's permission to talk to her. He dutifully introduced each and every one, as though their deference was his divine right. Kathryn supposed in this strange new land it was.

At one point she managed to scoot close to the cowboy and whisper, "You're just full of surprises tonight. I didn't realize the Palace had a stage, either."

He shrugged. "Some of the princesses enjoy dancing. Not all, but Adoreé spends her fair share of time up there."

And just where did the glamorous Adoreé rank on the cowboy's list of favored princesses, Kathryn wondered? She didn't ask, just followed him through the crowd, a smile plastered on her face, abandoning any attempt to place names with faces. As preoccupied as she was with the way her body ached, she didn't stand a prayer.

When they broke free of introductions and well wishes, the cowboy led her into the entrance room, which unlike most of the other rooms she'd seen so far was fairly empty.

Looping his arm through hers, he led her toward Katia's portrait, away from the doorman and the arriving guests.

"Glad to have you, Lady Kate," one man called out.

Kathryn waved absently. "These people were ready to lynch me this morning. Now I'm getting flowers. What's the deal?"

"You reopened," the cowboy said simply, plucking the bouquet from her grasp and handing it off to a passing waiter. "Take these to the kitchen and tell Jed to fix them up and send them to Lady Kate's room." When the waiter departed, the cowboy said, "Okay, Kate. What do you want to know?"

"How many other cousins I have roaming around would do for starters."

"Your mother had one sister and two brothers and they have fourteen children between them."

"I have *fourteen* cousins?" she asked incredulously. "I never had a clue."

All her life she'd yearned for a family. Now she'd found one in the unlikeliest place—a place overseen by a cowboy who was fast occupying too much time in her thoughts. The man hadn't been joking when he'd said he would surprise her. And judging by his expression, he wasn't exactly sure how she'd take his surprises, either. Worry creased his brow and his mouth had thinned to a tight line.

"Do you know why my mother left?"

"Kitty told me she fell in love and married very young and the man she married turned out to be more interested in her connection to the Palace than he was in raising his family. He behaved poorly and forced your mom into a messy divorce. Kitty thought your mom blamed her involvement with the Palace. She wanted a different life for you. She left Nevada and never looked back."

Kathryn didn't know what to say, had no grasp on the emotions rioting inside her, except that the scenario made sense. Her mother had been a very strong woman and if she'd made up her mind to put the Palace behind her . . . "Did they just let her go?"

The cowboy seemed to know she referred to the rest of the sizeable Romanov family and shook his head. "To my knowledge your aunt and uncles spent years trying to break the ice with her, but . . . well, she never warmed up and then she died." He slipped his hand over hers and squeezed reassuringly. "I know they went with Kitty to her funeral."

"Oh," was all Kathryn could say. On the day when she'd felt most alone in her whole life, she'd had family around her and had never even known. She peered up at the portrait of Katia, silently asked, "Was my mother right to protect me? Am I better off without them?"

Those bright blue eyes stared back, just as silent, but Kathryn's mind filled with memories of late nights with Kitty and how she'd always looked forward to the last week of the month when Kitty would arrive in the city with her pooches, how much less lonely her life had seemed during those weeks.

She also remembered a young man who shyly welcomed her with roses, a young man with striking blue eyes and black hair so similar to hers . . . so similar to the woman's in the portrait.

"Tell me about Katia, cowboy," she finally said. "How did a Russian princess wind up running a brothel and siring such a crazy family?"

My family.

He followed her gaze to the portrait, his smile seeming to approve her handling of such bittersweet revelations. He tightened his grip on her arm possessively and steered her away.

"Story starts when a lawman from Texas came to Nevada hunting a cattle rustler and winded up settling in White Pine County as sheriff.

Love wasn't much more than a miner's camp at the time, but he took a liking to it and set himself up here."

Kathryn didn't have the heart to point out that Love didn't strike her as much more than a mining camp now, but she said nothing, just ran a finger along the filigreed edge of a Tiffany wisteria lamp as they passed an antique buffet.

"The mines were booming in copper ore, and the miners were growing wealthy. But they played as hard as they worked, and Tex could barely control them. He decided they needed sex to vent their energies and the closest brothel was East in Ely, too far away to give them the sort of constant exposure to women he thought would civilize them."

With the gentlest pressure of their linked arms, the cowboy brought her to a halt in front of glass doors that opened onto the panoramic view of the ridge.

"Tex's first brothel was in town, above the saloon, but the idea took real good hold and the stable of ladies grew until the manager couldn't run the brothel and his business."

"He needed a madam to keep the ladies in line."

The cowboy nodded.

"So how did a Russian princess land the job?"

"Our princess was the Tsar's illegitimate niece, and given the trouble the royals were having at the time—" He fixed a doubtful gaze upon her. "I assume you learned about the Russian Revolution in all your fancy schools?"

"I did, indeed," Kathryn assured him. All her mother's money had gone for something, at least, and she bit back a smile because he seemed relieved that her "fancy schools" hadn't left out what he clearly considered a basic.

"The royal family couldn't openly acknowledge Katia and feared their enemies would find out about her. They set her up for a new life here in America."

"And she ended up as Tex Justice's madam?" Kathryn asked incredulously.

"Their enemies already knew about her and murdered the Cossacks who were charged with her protection at the same time the royal family was executed. Katia managed to escape and Tex got her purely by chance, when he came across her being sold as a slave. He bought her."

Kathryn stared at the night-draped spread of juniper and pinions that ascended the ridge both saddened and impressed by Katia's story.

"The Palace isn't what you expected, is it?" he asked, his voice a low whisper.

"Not at all," she admitted. "In my head I envisioned an Old West saloon. This really is a palace."

"Katia had a liking for Spanish Colonial and the Sears catalogue. Kitty added some, but it's pretty much the same."

"It's so open, so homey."

"It is a home. To quite a few people."

It seemed an intimate sort of admission, and she wondered if he was referring to himself as much as the princesses. When he guided her toward the magnificent antique organ and reached up to retrieve a small oval frame that sat on top, Kathryn could feel the heat of his body close to hers, and the clamps that dangled from her nipples seemed to suddenly grow heavier.

"The Princess used to play this organ." He held a faded picture up for her perusal. "Here she is entertaining at a party. If I'm remembering right, Tex brought it back from a trip East as a birthday gift."

Kathryn recognized the woman in the miniature as the woman in the portrait and realized the cowboy had been right. Katia had been a tiny woman, a fact not readily apparent in her portrait, yet obvious as she sat in front of the enormous organ. She was very beautiful. Though her image had been captured in profile, her easy smile and spirited expression shone clearly.

This woman had been her great-grandmother, a woman who, like Kathryn herself, had had a family that she hadn't been a part of. Had she been as lonely as Kathryn had always been? What had she endured before being purchased by Tex Justice's friend and brought to Nevada?

She appeared happy. What had she found at Katia's Palace that had made her seem so content? Kathryn peered around the elaborate room that had weathered close to a century with its sturdy wood floors and unmistakable attention to detail, and suspected she knew the answer.

"Did Tex build this place for her?"

"He did. Cut and carved each and every timber himself from the forest up the ridge."

Her great-grandmother had found love in Love, Nevada. And though Kathryn had never even known this woman had existed until six weeks ago, she felt a smile touch her own lips.

"Come on, Kate," the cowboy said. "I want to show you something."

He linked his body close and led her through another door that led to a dim hallway. She could hear the even threads of his breathing and the thud of his boots as they stepped from the thick carpet onto a polished wood staircase. At the top, a room opened before them and Kathryn found herself looking out over the bar through a wall of dark glass.

"What's this?"

"The madam's private showroom."

"Oh my." The room was lushly furnished for entertaining with cushioned sofas, a private bath and a small bar that occupied the opposite corner.

The cowboy must have sensed her uneasy curiosity because he said, "I don't know what else Kitty did in here, city girl, but she could get a bird's eye view of the action from this window without anyone knowing she was watching."

"I suppose that makes sense from a security angle."

"Mmm-hmm." Slipping his arms around her, he steered her in front of him, rested his chin on the top of her head and forced her to stare out over the crowd in the bar below. "Look at them, Kate. It's all about wanting. There's nothing shameful in a healthy need, nothing wrong with a healthy appetite. These boys want sex. The princesses want to give it to them. It's consensual. Respectful."

Judging by the happy crowd she saw socializing below, Kathryn would have to agree. She recognized several of the princesses in the crowd, chatting with various men, all dressed elegantly in evening formal wear. Adoreé entertained others with her sexy striptease, enjoying the lusty responses from her group of admirers.

As the cowboy had said, there appeared to be nothing shameful in a dose of healthy wanting. *Wanting.* That's what she was, and she remembered again what Kitty had said about some women just needing the right man to get them in the mood.

The cowboy felt like the right man.

Kathryn rested back against him, liking the feel of his strong arms around her. His brand had her entire body pulsing with a need to feel his hands on her. Adoreé's sultry dance was having an effect on her as well.

A beautiful woman, Adoreé was all long graceful lines and sleekly tanned skin. She danced with an easy rhythm that suggested sex in each rolling motion, in each well-timed graze of fingers along firm thighs, over the mound of her sex. The beaded halter top only covered enough of her breasts to hint at the hue of her nipples below. It had been tied loosely so her breast swayed as she shimmied around a pole, and revealed her toned bottom clad in nothing more than a matching g-string.

Cowboys crowded around her, their dazed glances and goofy smiles revealing just how much they were enjoying the show, and Kathryn remembered performing for her cowboy in the shower, how his appreciation and the desire in his eyes had made her feel cherished. She'd coaxed that same needy expression on his handsome face, wanted to again.

As though the cowboy sensed her restlessness and read her thoughts, he asked, "What do you want, Kate?"

His deep voice filtered through her, made her shiver. "I want to know why I respond when you touch me," she said softly. "I want to feel you inside me."

A low growl was his only reply before his hands rounded the curve of her shoulders and found the gown's zipper. Soon the fabric parted and the gown fell away, a beaded puddle at her feet, leaving her clad only in strappy high heels and the cowboy's brand.

Sweeping her into his arms, he waltzed her into motion, the only music the sounds of their breathing, their heels shuffing softly on the polished wood floor.

Her sensitive nipples brushed the cowboy's shirt, the fabric tugging on the clamps and sending firebolts of sensation through her. With one hand he held hers, but the other he cupped around her bottom, shaping the skin with his hot fingers, anchoring her against that bulge swelling in his jeans.

She'd never felt so free as when his hands were equally free to roam over her skin, to explore, and Kathryn sighed, a contented, purring sound just before the cowboy's mouth descended on hers, devouring hers, an intimacy, a pleasure, he'd not yet allowed her. His rough velvet tongue swept through her mouth, exploring every hollow with a bold thoroughness that spoke of a man who liked kissing. Hot hungry kisses. Slow leisurely kisses. Needy reckless kisses. Kisses that stole her breath with their wildness.

She'd never known a kiss like his before, a kiss that made her melt against him with a gasp. Her tongue tangled with his, yielded to the sparks raining through her, to the need to meet his tongue stroke for stroke, to make him gasp, too.

Suddenly their dance ended and he held her rooted to the spot, one hand snaking behind her to cup her head and draw her further into his kiss. Emboldened, Kathryn slid her hands along his broad back, felt the muscles gather beneath her fingers, realized that though he had much more skill at schooling his reactions, he was as affected by her as she was by him.

There was a certain intensity about him that reminded her of a summer storm, the moments between the blinding flash of lightning and the crash of thunder. The rigidity in his muscles, the way he braced his booted feet apart to lock himself into place and create a strong shelter for her naked body hinted of the power of his need.

She wanted to know, *needed* to know that his desire was as powerful as her own. Slipping a hand between them, she molded her fingers around the hard length of his erection safely restrained behind sturdy denim.

He didn't stop her when she fumbled with the button of his fly, just rocked back on his heels so she could slip her other hand between them and kissed her harder. Carefully Kathryn unzipped his pants, coaxed him from the parted denim and quickly discovered the mystery behind that absurdly large bulge.

"Sheesh, cowboy," she whispered against his lips as his erection sprang free, thick, perfectly shaped and proudly erect.

He chuckled. "I've never had any complaints."

"No doubt." She slipped her hand around him, filled her palm with his scorching heat, but the cowboy caught her lower lip between his teeth and nipped gently. "No touching me, Kate. I'm the one doing the touching right now."

She wondered why he denied her the pleasure of serving his needs, when he played master to her slave. But her role in this game wasn't to argue, so she slipped her hands around his waist and shimmied up to cradle that heat against her bare belly.

Suddenly his mouth blazed a trail of fiery kisses down her exposed throat and he forced her to arch backwards over his arm as he blazed that trail down . . . *down.*

Wrapping his fist in the chain that dangled from her breasts, he gave a slight tug that stretched her nipples and made her eyes flutter closed helplessly. Then his mouth was upon her, his tongue laving the sensitive tips, swirling and rolling, his jaw abrading her skin, a rough contrast that shot fresh showers of sparks through her.

All she could do was hang on and try to breathe through the intensity of her arousal, anchor her hand against his erection to prove she wasn't the only one about to erupt into flames.

He drew a swollen nipple into his mouth, one long hard pull that made her cry out.

"You respond to me because you're my woman, Kate." His words gusted hotly across her skin, his utter conviction, the possessiveness of his declaration jarring Kathryn from her daze. "I've been waiting for you a long time. Now you're mine."

The need in his voice made him sound as though he had indeed been waiting forever, but that couldn't be. They'd barely known each other a day.

Perhaps he sensed he'd distracted her, or maybe he was just so in tune with her physically he anticipated her reaction, but the cowboy drew upright to stare at her with an intensity in his dark eyes, an earnestness in his expression, that revealed he meant exactly what he'd said.

This man wanted to do more than play games with her.

Every inch of her naked skin seemed to blast out a warning. She was far too exposed, far too vulnerable. She pulled away, an instinctive reaction rather than a conscious one. Just as the cool air seared her wet breasts, his low growl told her she'd overstepped a boundary.

With a movement so sudden she jumped, the cowboy lashed those whipcord arms around her, twisted her around until she faced away from him before she'd even thought to resist. With his body, he crowded her against a winged chair, forced her to bend over until she lay draped across the arms, the muscles in her legs stretching, her bottom boldly exposed to his view.

Kathryn realized rather belatedly that she was playing games she knew nothing about with a stranger she barely knew. He'd been very respectful so far, but they hadn't discussed any parameters. She had no clue how far he would go. He'd said he wouldn't make love to her until she asked him to, but when he kneed her thighs apart, she half-expected to feel the heat of his erection prodding against her.

She should have recoiled at the thought of being taken forcibly, but to her utter mortification, Kathryn felt a dark thrill instead, a sense of profound disappointment when the cowboy only sank his fingers into her buttocks and hiked her bottom even higher into the air.

The lips of her sex separated, exposed to the cool air. The chain stretched taut, tugged on the clamps.

"Cowboy," she issued a warning that sounded more scared than warning as she pushed herself upright only to have him restrain her with a hand in the small of her back.

"The name's Trey, Kate. Use it and knock off another five hundred dollars for a half-and-half."

Kathryn couldn't remember exactly what a half-and-half was, but experienced a surge of pure rebellion at his high-handedness. Craning her neck, she caught him sinking to his knees behind her, his face level with her bottom and got a pretty good idea of what the first half involved.

"Trey," she croaked out, but the next sound out of her mouth was a gasp as he nipped the tender flesh inside her thigh.

She jumped. He spread her cheeks wide, his wicked tongue lashing out over her aroused sex, one bold wet stroke that traveled from her swollen clitoris back to where he had no business traveling.

"Trey!" his name rode out on the edge of a low moan as she shivered from head to toe.

He didn't reply. He didn't stop. He only began a well-aimed assault of his mouth on her most intimate places. His tongue tasted and teased her satin folds. His teeth tested the clamp, exploring her with a thoroughness that declared he had every right in the world to do so, as though he'd waited a lifetime for the privilege.

Some barely functioning part of her brain warned Kathryn she was in over her head here, that the cowboy was playing games with more far-reaching consequences than she knew. Though reason declared she should stop before getting in any deeper, she couldn't seem to murmur a single syllable that would distract the cowboy from his fiery attentions. Not when his attentions felt so delicious, so . . . *right*.

What she wanted didn't seem to matter anyway, because the cowboy had already decided he knew what was best for her. Right now *best* involved his tongue sinking into her heat, making her sex seize in hot wet spasms, making her abandon all thoughts of resistance. She arched her hips back with short thrusts.

The cowboy knew exactly what she needed. Sliding his hand between her thighs, he braced his palm beneath her, the heel of his hand riding against the clamp as he lifted her higher so his tongue penetrated deeper.

A liquid heat washed through her, and she had no choice but to abandon herself to it, though she found herself gasping and straining against him, combining her efforts with his to lift her even higher . . .

His tongue slid from her sex and trailed back to invade her nether parts. Kathryn cried out at the unfamiliar sensation, the insistent pressure that warred with her body's natural response to resist. But he didn't relent, just kept up that steady pressure, not quite intrusive, just *there*, until she writhed back against him, mindless to feel him inside her.

She exploded without warning, a huge engulfing burst that wrenched a moan from her lips. Clutching the arm of the chair, she hung on as fire poured through her. With his face buried between her cheeks and her bottom riding against his tongue, the cowboy rode out each clutching spasm until she caught her breath in broken sobs.

She tried to rally the energy to lift herself off the chair, needed to see his face, desperately needed to know that such a detonation of the senses was normal, but she hadn't moved before he was on his feet.

His powerful body was suddenly bending over hers, his rock-hard erection riding against her moist sex.

"Do you want me, Kate?" he asked in a throaty whisper.

"Yes, Trey."

With one deep thrust he sank into her heat. He slid his hands around her, grasping her breasts, using them to pull her up enough so her hips arched back and drove him even deeper.

His low growl resounded in her ear as he reared back, a gliding stroke that carried him almost out completely. Then he thrust back, stretching her, filling her, blinding her with a pleasure she'd never known existed, an intensity far beyond her comprehension, her control, that made her body begin to vibrate with such violence only his hands and the chair kept her from dissolving onto the floor in a heap.

She only knew that she didn't want him to stop, would have begged for his next silken stroke, and the next . . .

Then she came apart again.

Kathryn had no idea how long had passed before she felt the cowboy pull out. A sob caught in her throat, her sense of loss overwhelming when her body reacted so far beyond her control, her emotions pushed so close to the surface she didn't know whether she might laugh on the next ragged breath, or cry.

She was only vaguely aware of the cowboy's hands on her as he lifted her, rearranging her boneless body until she sat curled up in the comfortable chair. She couldn't find the strength to open her eyes, didn't care she must look like a pathetic heap, barely able to hold her head upright.

She heard the cowboy's heels rap across the floor, then a warm weight settled over her, enveloping her, coaxing her to snuggle within the soft folds of . . . a woolen throw, she decided.

She forced her heavy eyes open and found herself face-to-face with the cowboy's rock-hard erection. He was pulling his jeans back up, frowning as he shifted his hips to tuck that impressive equipment, still shiny from her body's juices, into his jeans.

Her warm yummy feeling drained away. She'd been so wrapped up in her own pleasure she hadn't realized the cowboy hadn't reached his own fulfillment. He'd annihilated her. She hadn't satisfied him.

His gaze flicked up, and he must have recognized her stricken look, because he abandoned his impossible task and knelt before her, turned his handsome face up to hers. His dark eyes were so earnest, her heart seemed to swell in her chest.

"I don't expect you to understand, Kate, but I can't make love to you until you're mine. Not just while you pay off your debt, but forever."

She gave a broken laugh, a ridiculous, hysterical sound that proved she was about to lose the fragile grasp she had on her emotions. "Forever? We haven't known each other a day."

"You haven't known *me* a day."

"I don't understand."

"I know." He stroked strands of hair from her cheek, such a tender gesture she didn't know what to make of him or his revelation. "Don't think about it now, Kate. Now is for enjoying how you feel." He gave her a goofy half-grin. "No fire? I don't think so."

It was the goofy half-grin that did it. The goofy half-grin that made a huge knot expand in her chest, forced tears to her eyes and pushed her emotions right over the edge.

One strangled gulp and she was crying, deep wrenching sobs that welled up from her soul in watery bursts, overwhelmed her with the knowledge that this stranger, a cowboy from a hick town called Love, had cared enough to help her find her fire.

She didn't know why, couldn't even rally enough energy to ask. But he did. She didn't know how she knew, but she did. And as if women dissolving into hysterics after multiple mind-blowing orgasms was the most natural thing in the world, he got to his feet and half sat on the arm of the chair, gathered her against him and let her weep her heart out on his broad chest.

As Crooked as a Snake in a Cactus Patch

Kathryn awoke the next morning to find herself alone in the madam's private showroom still curled up in the chair. Both the cowboy and his brand were gone, though she had no memory of him removing her clamps or leaving. All she had left was the memory of his hands and his mouth taking her to incredible heights and the glorious aches of a woman who'd been thoroughly and skillfully loved.

She decided that perhaps waking up alone was for the best. Her head was a muddle of thoughts she was best left alone with for the time being, but she couldn't help wondering if the cowboy would come back today, hoped he would.

Gazing through the wall of glass to the bar below, she found the Palace empty, the brass fixtures shining, the chairs neatly stacked on the tables and bar, as though a cleaning crew had made a late-night appearance.

After performing her morning ablutions in the private bath, she shimmied back into the beaded gown, which the cowboy had laid over the sofa, and prepared herself to face the new day as a changed woman from the city girl who'd arrived yesterday on the flight from hell with On-the-Wing Joe.

Though she had no clue what temporary madams did during the daytime, she decided not to try and puzzle it out without caffeine. An even bigger problem than her schedule loomed on her horizon—a phenomenon called a shadow migraine, which was a debilitating echo that typically followed a headache the size of the one she'd had yesterday.

After foolishly forgetting her medication in the frenzy to make this trip, Kathryn could only get her blood flowing to hopefully minimize the pain that would soon make an appearance. She didn't relish fainting again. Especially not when the cowboy wasn't around to catch her.

But she wasn't going to think about Trey Holliday right now. Not when just the thought of his smile, his strong arms and his twangy accent made her heart ache and her blood pound and her nipples tingle as though he'd awakened a hunger that was going to need constant feeding.

So, feeling as weak as a newborn—a feeling she couldn't entirely attribute to yesterday's ferocious migraine—she left the madam's showroom and made her way down the stairs.

The trail to the kitchen proved easy to find by following the scent of frying bacon. A wiry old man with a head full of grizzled hair stood over the stove, but no sight of the cowboy.

"Good morning," she said, glancing around the huge room, which resembled a food service prep area of a restaurant more than a kitchen. But there was a frilly curtain adorning the window over the sink and a table on the opposite wall, which lent the place a homey air.

The man turned around and sliced a beady black stare her way. "So you're the new boss. Care to tell me if we're keeping the doors open, ma'am, because everyone around here needs to get laid real bad." As an obvious afterthought, he wiped beefy hands on a white apron that was dingy from too many bleachings and extended one in greeting. "The name's Jedidiah. Most folks around here call me Jed."

Kathryn covered the distance between them. "Pleased to meet you, Jed. Most folks around here call me Kate. I'm afraid I can't answer your question just yet, but I hope you won't hold that against me. I seriously need a cup of coffee."

Jed's eyes sparked, his bushy brows drawing together like a hairy gray caterpillar, giving Kathryn the impression he wouldn't hold anything against her just yet.

Motioning to a sturdy wooden table in the corner of the big kitchen, he said, "Take a seat, Kate. I'm fixing up breakfast for myself. The folks around here won't start showing up for another hour yet. Want to join me?"

"Thank you. I'd like that. Just coffee for me, please." She wasn't awake enough to decide if she had an appetite and wasn't sure if food would set off another headache. So far she was holding her own.

After seeing Kathryn comfortably settled at the table with a mug of steaming coffee, Jed slid bacon and sunnyside eggs onto a plate and joined her.

"Are you the gourmand responsible for my delicious meal last night?" she asked in an attempt to make conversation that didn't involve an explanation about when she'd officially take on the job as madam. The truth was she barely remembered the meal, having been far too preoccupied with her own nakedness and wildfire responses to the sexy cowboy sitting across from her.

"I'll take that to mean you liked your supper," Jed said, tucking a napkin in his collar and reaching for a piece of bacon. "If you settle on staying, you'll have to tell me what a tiny thing like you eats. Can't be much more'n a rabbit does."

"I eat enough to keep me vertical." Kathryn shrugged and sipped her coffee.

Jed gave a bark of laughter that made her jump. "Well, I reckon you're right about that, Lady Kate." Cramming the bacon into his mouth, Jed stood and crossed the room. Pulling open a stainless steel door, which appeared to be a walk-in freezer from the icy steam blasting him, he disappeared for a moment only to reappear with a pint of ice cream, instantly recognizable as her favorite, Haagen Daz.

"Butter Pecan," he said. "Kitty told me what you liked, so I stocked up. Got Swiss Chocolate Almond and Macadamia Nut, too, for when you're in the mood for something different."

What was it about a pint of ice cream that made a lump stick in her throat, a lump not so different from the one she'd nearly choked on last night when the cowboy had held her in his arms and let her cry? It had nothing to do with this grizzled old man she'd never met before, welcoming her to the Palace with her favorite treat. Nothing at all.

But she found herself thanking Jed anyway, relaying the tale of the time she and Kitty had resorted to sucking out the last drips from a pint of Macadamia Nut with a cocktail straw.

His laughter told her he was very pleased with her response and for some reason Kathryn couldn't fathom, she was pleased to have put the smile on his face.

When barking erupted from somewhere beyond the kitchen, Kathryn spun around on her chair. "Kitty's pooches."

"Tell me you've got coffee, Jed," a raspy voice said as the Amazonian princess burst into the kitchen with three familiar white Malteses scampering around her ankles.

"Malted, Hambone, Lambchop." Kathryn sank to her knees, opened her arms to the hyper dogs who scrambled right up onto her lap as though no time had passed since their last visit.

That stupid lump in her throat started to choke her again.

"The brats are used to waking up at the crack of dawn with Kitty,"

Gwen said. "They haven't realized yet that the rest of us keep late nights."

"There's coffee in the pot, darlin'," Jed said, spearing an ample forkful of eggs into his mouth.

Gwen helped herself while Kathryn sat on the floor, petting and kissing the pooches, keeping her head lowered not to let the others see her blinking back tears. More than anything she'd seen since her arrival in Love, the pooches brought home to her just how much she missed Kitty.

Kitty had brought something to her life that Kathryn hadn't known had been missing. And only now realized how much she wanted someone in her life who cared.

Hambone curled in a tiny ball on her lap. She rubbed her nose on the top of Lambchop's head and scratched Malted behind the ears, absorbing the thought that there were other people in this town who might grow to care for her. People like the cowboy and Jed. And family like Jess, who'd welcomed her with a shy smile and fresh flowers. If she did nothing else today, she wanted to find out more about her family.

She listened absently as Gwen filled Jed in on the events of the past night. How Adoreé had had her heart broken yet again in her never-ending search for a rich husband. How two men had gotten into a fist fight over Phoebe and Jess Romanov had broken up the fight himself and then snatched Phoebe for the night from beneath both men's noses.

When she reached for her coffee mug from the table, she found Gwen getting up.

"Might as well work out," she said. "Got to keep this body the stuff that fantasies are made of." Grabbing her coffee mug, she glanced down at the pooches. "Come on, brats. Let's go."

But Kitty's pooches had obviously decided they'd found a comfortable place to stay and weren't following the direction. To Kathryn's surprise, Gwen didn't accuse them of conspiring with the enemy. She just rolled her eyes and asked, "Will you keep them with you for a spell, Lady Kate?"

"I'd love to."

"When you're over them, just bring them back to Jed. He'll know where to find me."

Kathryn nodded, and couldn't help but feeling she'd passed some sort of test for the Amazonian princess to trust her with her charges.

After Gwen had left, Jed refilled Kathryn's coffee mug and said,

"Don't let Gwen there put you off. She's got a heart of gold under her knife-sharp airs. The Palace here's the only home she's ever known. She gets overprotective."

It is a home. To quite a few people. Kathryn remembered the cowboy saying. Could the Palace be a home to her, too?

She was still mulling over the question an hour later after emerging from a hot shower to dress for the day. She chose a long floral skirt and cashmere sweater, the most casual of the outfits she'd brought. She hadn't given a thought to her attire when she'd packed for the trip, but now her suits seemed so out of place. She hadn't even packed a pair of slacks or flat shoes. In her mind this trip had been all about business.

It was turning out to be so much more.

The pooches were clearly at home in Kitty's suite and she left the closet to find them all sound asleep, each curled up in a tiny white ball on his and her own pillow under the large bay window that looked out over the ridge.

Kathryn didn't have the heart to wake them. Instead she pressed her nose to the bouquet of roses, which had been placed in a crystal vase on the dresser and inhaled deeply.

Orgasms, ice cream and roses. She could get used to this. Had Kitty known that when she'd bequeathed the place to her?

She thought you were too comfortable being alone, that you worked too much and didn't live enough. The cowboy had said. *She wasn't sure if you'd been taught how.*

Gazing down at the photos beside her college graduation photo, Kathryn knew beyond any doubt that if nothing else, Kitty had had her best interests at heart. Did the cowboy?

Where was he today? Had her hysterics last night turned him off? For a man used to having the princesses at his beck and call, her meltdown must have seemed tedious. The one time she'd tried to touch him, he hadn't been interested. Did he find her sexual inexperience just plain boring?

And why did that thought depress her so completely?

Retrieving the cowboy's journal from the dresser, she curled up on the bed, opened the book to take a closer look at exactly what expenses he'd been covering these past six weeks.

Salaries. Medical bills. Utilities. The usual stuff. Totals that seemed entirely uninteresting compared to her column—in-date, waterplay. . . .

The phone rang. Kathryn reached for it quickly, hoping not to disturb the dogs, felt a zing of disappointment when she heard Jed's voice on the line and not the cowboy's.

"What's up, Jed?"

"The mayor's here to see you, Lady Kate," he said. "I'm holding him and his cronies off at the door, but he's planted himself there like dry rot, says he won't leave until he talks to you."

"His cronies?"

"Don't wolves travel in packs in that big city of yours?"

Great. "I'm on my way. The dogs are sleeping, Jed. Will they be okay if I leave them?"

"In Kitty's suite?" He gave a sharp bark of laughter. "They're home. Just leave them and come on down."

Kathryn replaced the receiver in the cradle, took a deep breath and headed down to tackle her first official duty as temporary madam of the Palace.

Mayor Barclay was a slick looking cowboy dressed all in black with a string tie and an ornate silver belt buckle. He did indeed have cronies—two physically fit men dressed similarly in black, flanking him on both sides like bodyguards.

"Ms. Roman," he said, striding forward to greet her the minute she stepped through the door. "I'm glad to meet you in person. I'm sorry we're forced to conduct business on the doorstep, but the staff here has refused to invite me in."

The staff, indeed. Looked like everyone had turned out to line up along the porch like some bizarre sort of honor guard. Obviously some of the princesses had tumbled straight from bed to join the party and Gwen, who'd clearly been in the middle of her workout, glowered at the men, her formidable curves bathed in sweat, making her look like she was headed into battle more than ever.

Kathryn supposed she should feel better that so many people from the Palace had turned out, though she suspected their interest stemmed more from curiosity to find out if she'd sell the place out from under them rather than any interest in providing her back up against these men. Except for Jed, who'd sidled right up behind her, clutching a wooden rolling pin like he might have held a shotgun.

"There's no need, Mayor Barclay. I'm sure we can conduct our business quickly."

His smile never wavered as he motioned to one of his bodyguards, then accepted a clipboard holding papers she guessed were the contracts for the sale.

"I was expecting you at city hall yesterday to conduct our business."

She held the man's gaze steadily, wouldn't pull any punches. "As you may be aware, half the town met me at my plane yesterday, bringing several new concerns regarding the management change to my attention. I saw no point in meeting with you until I'd investigated their claims."

This clearly wasn't what Mayor Barclay wanted to hear but he managed to keep his smile in place. "Ms. Roman, I'm sure I can answer all your questions satisfactorily. I know you're pressed to return to New York."

While that had definitely been true, as Kathryn glanced back at the honor guard of sleep rumpled and sweaty employees, she realized that twenty-four hours had changed her priorities. Yesterday, she'd been thinking only of herself. Today . . . well, today she felt a need to think about a few others.

"I'm not prepared to ask my questions yet, nor to sign your papers," she said in her best boardroom tone, a tone the mayor apparently understood as his smile grew more strained. His bodyguards, too, as they moved a step closer.

Jed's burly chest was suddenly brushing her shoulder. Kathryn heard a sudden squeal of tires and absently glanced at the parking lot to see a shiny black and white sheriff's car jolt to a sudden halt. The mayor's reinforcements? Just what she needed.

"Now, Ms. Roman," the mayor said, not a little condescendingly. "We had all the details worked out before you ever stepped foot in Love. There's no need to go changing our agreement now."

She could see how Mayor Barclay might appeal to some people with his polished looks and slick smile, but Kathryn knew his type too well to buy into his reassurances.

"You misled me into believing that the town would preserve the Palace, not close it for business. Until I investigate my options, I won't sign any papers. I have nothing else to say."

The mayor snatched the hat from his head and his big-toothed smile faded. "I heard about how Trey had to carry you off the plane yesterday. Don't tell me he's already made you his whore. I thought you had more sense than that or I'd have met your plane myself."

"You didn't meet her plane because you knew that crowd would have lynched you, Barclay," Jed ground out. "You may have tricked folks into believing you were the right man to put in office on election day, but they've sobered up now."

Before the mayor got a chance to reply, he was jerked right off his feet by the scruff of his neatly pressed collar. He stumbled and landed in a cloud of dust on the sidewalk. His bodyguards went down with two muscled thuds beside him.

"I'd say you owe the lady an apology, Barclay." The sheriff, a brawny, rugged looking man with silver shot black hair, scowled down at him. "Best get it out of your mouth before my fist goes in it."

Kathryn glanced up at the men who stood over the mayor and his bodyguards with fists clenched and realized the sheriff and his posse weren't the mayor's reinforcements after all. She recognized Jess, noticed the similarities in appearance to the sheriff and their companion, and suspected what she hadn't yesterday—these men were more Romanov men.

Her family.

In a flash, the sheriff had hauled the mayor back up while Jess and his companion held the bodyguards down. Just as he'd promised, the sheriff planted his big fist square with a sickening crunch. The mayor's head snapped back and he staggered, would have gone down had the sheriff let him go. But he swung the mayor around, hauled him right up in front of her.

"Apologize, Barclay."

"My apologies, ma'am," the mayor said through a bloody lip.

Kathryn held his angry gaze with a stoic one of her own, not quite sure how to respond when faced with a scene straight from an old *Ponderosa* rerun. Noble cowboys protecting the lady from a black-hearted villain. If she wasn't so amazed, and yes, touched, she might have laughed.

"Now get on." The sheriff shoved the mayor toward the gate, threw his hat after him.

The mayor staggered, then shot to his feet like a bolt, grabbing his hat and shoving it back on his head. "You'll be hearing from my lawyer, sheriff, and you, too, Ms. Roman."

Jess and his companion escorted the men through the gate.

Kathryn didn't answer, was too busy staring at the sheriff, who was just as busy staring at her. "Thank you," she said and she meant it. Not only for tossing the mayor off the property, but for abandoning her to the cowboy yesterday.

"No need for thanks, little lady. I'm your Uncle Luke and I'm always glad to chase away any sidewinders who bother you."

His words hung in the air between them, a promise. She didn't know how to respond, only knew that she was touched in a way she'd never been touched before.

Kathryn may not have known what to do, but her uncle did. He opened those burly arms to her and said, "Haven't given you a hug since you were in diapers, little lady. Come 'ere."

His smile was so genuine that Kathryn didn't think twice. She stepped right into the big circle of his arms, rested her cheek against his broad chest. "Hi, Uncle Luke."

He stroked her hair with a beefy hand and said gruffly, "Glad you've come home, Kate."

The Round-up

Jed corralled everyone back inside for breakfast. Her uncle looped his arm through hers and escorted her back inside, saying, "We're having a dispute between the sheriff and mayor's offices this term and you've landed right in the middle."

"So I've heard," Kathryn said, gratefully accepting a mug of coffee from Jed as Jess and his companion filed through the crowd into the kitchen.

She greeted Jess with a smile. "My roses are opening beautifully this morning."

"I'm mighty glad you like them, ma'am."

"I understand I have you to thank for breaking up a fight last night."

"Just doing my job, ma'am."

She wondered if spending the night with Phoebe was part of his job description, too, but found that the thought of this red-cheeked cousin honing his skills with the lovely young Phoebe only made her smile.

"This here's my oldest son, Tanner." Uncle Luke wrapped an arm around Jess's companion's shoulder. "He used to pull your hair when you were a little 'un. Course, he wasn't much older himself at the time."

Tanner was a tall, strapping man, another cowboy like all the men in Love, with his boots and hat and polite smile.

She shook his hand in greeting. "I assume I don't have to protect my head from you anymore."

He gave a hearty laugh, patted her hand reassuringly. "No, you don't, Kate. In fact, I came to help your head today. I grew up to be the town doctor. Trey told me about your headache and asked me to drop by and see if you were feeling better this morning."

"Oh, that was . . . nice of him."

"So how're you feeling? Any aftereffects? Some people suffer from shadow migraines the following day."

"I know. I usually get them."

"Took your medication?"

"No. In my rush to make this trip, I forgot to pack it."

"What do you usually take? I can prescribe it for you."

She met the concern in his big blue eyes, not just doctor beside manner, but what seemed to be a real desire to help. "Thanks, Tanner, but I think I'm going to be just fine today. If I were going to have another headache, I'd have it already, which is really very odd, now that I think about it. My migraines are usually very predictable."

"Maybe it's just a side effect of small town living. We're pretty relaxed around here. Not much time for headaches and sickness. Keeps my schedule manageable."

Kathryn chuckled, but couldn't help remembering the cowboy's words about making more time to relax. After that off-the-Richter-scale migraine yesterday, she by all rights should be suffering today. She wasn't. In fact, she felt great.

"What are we going to do 'bout the mayor?" Jed joined them. "Can't do to have him strong arming Lady Kate here."

"Don't worry about Barclay, Jed," her uncle said. "I'll head over later and have a talk with him. He won't mess with Kate if he knows he'll have to take on the Romanovs, too. No walking through the door and fighting like a man for that one, not if he can sneak in through the back." Her uncle scowled. "We need to be worrying about how he's got the council and all those new folks who've moved into the new subdivisions on the outskirts of town sold on closing the Palace."

Kathryn glanced through the curtained window above the sink. The daylight revealed a silhouette of a ranch house up on the ridge. Was that the cowboy's place?

"The man's slicker than an oil spill," Tanner was saying. "It's hard to go up against someone who works like that. He's got folks panicked that the Palace is the root of all evil and that spending money at a supermall will keep their kids from becoming sex maniacs. He's won over those suburbanites, all the soccer mamas. They're plum fierce protecting their young 'uns."

"What's the Palace done to counter?" she asked curiously.

They all turned to gaze at her, clearly not understanding the question.

"The media," she explained. "Advertising, promotion to offset these negative views of the Palace."

They all stared blankly, which answered Kathryn's question. "For all its evils, the media can be put to constructive use on occasion, gentlemen. Sounds to me like you need a media blitz of the facts. Spell out how the Palace's zoning forces the town to stay within a certain population and how closing it to attract developers into the area will mean zoning changes that will not only skyrocket the population but invite other adult entertainment businesses to set up shop here. Let the people decide which is the lesser of the two evils. Then schedule a town meeting with an ad hoc committee to address everyone's concerns and come up with a—"

"Whoa, whoa, Kate," Uncle Luke said, his mug poised at his mouth. "You're right. *We* know the facts and anyone who hasn't been snowed by Barclay knows them, too. But not everyone else. We need to put all the cards on the table, sway some folks to our side. I'm thinking there's enough of us who see Barclay for the snake he is to convince a few more."

"It's a great idea," Jess said, his shy smile filling Kathryn with more satisfaction than she'd ever gotten from her work on the Simply Seductive campaign.

"I think it could work," Jed agreed. "Now the only thing we need is someone who knows how to run a media circus."

They all turned to look at her.

She ignored their looks. "What about the Palace's lawyer?" she asked brightly. "He was very helpful. I'm sure he can hook you up with a reputable firm."

"That lawyer is my nephew Sam," Uncle Luke said, looking as though he had no intention of letting her side skirt the issue at hand. "He's another cousin of yours. His mama's your Auntie Kay. She's chomping at the bit to see you, but we decided to honor Aunt Kitty's wishes. She wanted us to wait until you got to Love and Trey settled you in."

Kathryn buried her nose in her mug, stoically refusing to blush and let these men know why Kitty had been so determined for the cowboy to *settle* her.

"This is a family business, Kate," Tanner said, his bedside manner firmly in place.

A family business. She remembered wondering why Kitty had bequeathed a brothel to a New York ad exec and realized, as she gazed around at these men, that Kitty had left her the Palace to bring her home to her family.

Was she insane to think about returning to New York? In one visit to Love she'd found the family she'd always longed for, orgasms that she'd only dreamed about and a cowboy named Trey who wanted to possess her *forever*.

"I, uh, need to talk to the cowboy."

"Trey?" Uncle Luke asked.

She nodded.

"You got his cell phone number, Jed?"

"I'd rather go see him if that's possible." She wanted out of the Palace to clear her head and collect her thoughts.

"Where do you reckon he'd be about now?"

Jed glanced at his watch. "This time of day he'll be out riding the range."

Uncle Luke glanced at his sons. "We'll have to ride to find him then."

"Ride?" Kathryn asked. "You mean as in on the back of a horse?"

"No." Jess shook his head in horror, blue eyes growing wide. "Lady Kate, don't tell me you don't ride?"

Kathryn had no intention of disappointing her cousin. "Of course I ride, Jess," she said with a smile. "In Manhattan we ride in taxis. I can corral one from a block away."

Bucking Off a Man's Whiskers

Since Kathryn hadn't packed anything suitable for riding, Phoebe, who was close in size, provided a change of clothes. Dressed in a pair of jeans, boots and a flannel shirt, Kathryn felt like she'd stepped off the cover of a dude ranch promotional brochure.

The men in her family approved the change.

"Now you don't look nearly so much like a city girl," her uncle said as he hoisted her up behind Jess.

Though Jess wasn't a small man by any stretch of the imagination, he hadn't bulked up to his father or brother's dimensions yet, either. With her weight, they combined to make an acceptable burden for a horse.

They rode in the direction of the ridge with Uncle Luke picking her brain about ways to effectively use the media to present the facts about the mayor in a way that would portray the best side of the Palace and still have a G rating.

Kathryn tossed out ideas and charged her cousins with remembering them. Brainstorming sessions only happened once, and with everything cluttering her mind right now, she'd never recall a thing she'd said.

But then as they rode out on the cowboy's land, Kathryn found herself falling silent to admire the gorgeous spread of juniper and piñon trees along the lower ridge. Mountain streams cut down from the forest to slice through the range where cattle grazed. With the clear sunny sky, the land was as different from the close gray streets of New York City as though she had actually landed on another planet. How had Kitty left this open sky filled with sunshine for the slushy snow and leaden skies of New York as often as she had?

The answer was simple: Kitty had left because of *her*.

And before she had a chance to absorb yet more evidence of Kitty's love for her, the cowboy appeared over a grassy slope, silhouetted by the brilliant blue sky, just like out of a scene from a romantic Western movie. He sat astride a . . . brown horse. She had no idea of the different breeds, except to say that this one looked huge, even from this distance.

"Well, here's Trey now," Uncle Luke said.

Instead of riding out to meet him, her uncle just waved, then dismounted in a fluid leap for such a large man. Coming straight to her, he grabbed her around the waist and helped her slide from the back of Jess's horse.

"You're leaving?" she asked when her feet hit the ground.

"You don't need us anymore," Uncle Luke smiled. "You go hash things out with your cowboy, Kate. He's a good man."

Damn, and here she'd been thinking her secret was safe, but the smiles on her handsome cousins' faces convinced her they all knew why Kitty had wanted the cowboy to *settle* her.

"Thanks for the lift." She waved as they rode off.

Kathryn watched the cowboy ride toward her, stared agog as he drew near and two things became obvious—his horse was indeed huge and just the sight of him made awareness roar through her louder than car horns blaring in the Holland Tunnel during rush hour traffic.

A muscular display of man and beast, he rode naturally, as at home on that horse with the sun sparking on his blonde hair, sweat trickling down the corded muscles of his neck as he had sitting at the head of a table, trying to negotiate a compromise between a dozen angry princesses and one stubborn ad exec.

Kathryn forced herself not to shy away as he reined his horse to a stop close by, shoved the hat back from his brow and raked that warm gaze over her. "Howdy, Kate. How are you feeling today?"

"Fine, thank you."

He nodded appreciatively. "You're sure looking fine."

"Thanks." She smiled, so aware of the way his gaze caressed her, and the way her heart beat quicker in response.

"So what can I do for you today, pretty lady?"

"I want to make love with you, Trey."

He leaned back in the saddle, considered her with that small smile still playing around his mouth. "You do, do you? That's a big step."

She nodded, drawing a deep breath before she trusted herself to speak. "I think I've found everything I've ever wanted here. I need to understand where you fit in."

He didn't move. The breeze calmed on the air and the myriad sounds of the herd grazing lazily around them faded. Even his horse seemed unnaturally still, watching her with those big rolling eyes. Kathryn's lungs constricted around a breath as he waited, wondered. Would he take this chance on her?

Then she thought she noticed the faintest softening of his mouth and . . . "I want to make love with you, too."

And before she'd even caught her breath he swung off his horse and was lifting her onto the saddle.

"I'm taking you back to the ranch house." He swung up behind her, fixed his hard thighs around hers, took up the reins. "I want to make love to you in a real bed. My bed."

And they were off. The horse pounding over the range in a rumble of hammering hooves and churning muscle. She relaxed her body to move with the horse's rhythm, her back riding against the cowboy's chest, her bottom rocking steadily against his crotch, which responded to her presence with a gratifying increase in dimension.

He buried his face in her hair, nuzzled her neck with teasing kisses. She responded to his touch as though every nerve inside her had been tuned to his signal. Her breasts grew heavy and tight, her sex pulsed with achy little bursts that the seam of these jeans only whetted.

But he didn't touch her, only pressed on with his mouth, nibbling on all the tender places of her neck until she marveled that he could focus such lavish attention on her and still control his horse.

When they reached the crest of yet another gently rolling slope, the cowboy stopped his horse to let Kathryn take her first glimpse of Tex's Sweet ranch.

A variety of buildings bordered a corral, where several cowboys worked with horses in a scene straight off of a television rodeo. She recognized the main ranch house by its size, because like the Palace, the house sprawled over the landscape as bold in its southwestern simplicity as if it had sprang up from the earth.

Though the scene before her revealed a busy, working ranch, with the horses, a tractor hauling dirt and cowboys loading what appeared to be fencing into a pickup, Kathryn found the scene somehow tranquil, so different from the don't-look-up pace of the city.

Maybe it was all the fresh air and wide-open spaces. Or maybe the cowboy's look of pride as he identified the various outbuildings: the stables, the cookhouse, the bunkhouse and the blacksmith shop that made Kathryn fall in love on the spot. But fall in love she did. She had the absurd image of herself learning to ride in that corral, of kissing the cowboy goodbye on that porch before he rode off into a pastel-streaked sunrise to begin his workday.

The image was so incongruous with everything she'd ever known, everything she knew about herself that Kathryn might have laughed, if not for the wary expression on the cowboy's face.

"You like it." It wasn't a question.

"I do." She didn't even need to say the words because the cowboy's satisfied smile mirrored all the pleasure she felt.

With a snap of the reins, he plunged them down the slope into the thick of the Tex's Sweet ranch. He dismounted in a burst of masculine grace that made the pulsing little ache between her legs give an odd clench, then dragged her down into his arms. And held her there.

She blushed when whooping war cries and several variations of "All right, Trey!" greeted them from the cowboys milling around the place, but her cowboy only smiled, scooped her into his arms and carried her into his house as if she was a young bride on her wedding night.

He didn't give her a chance to admire his home or, indeed, even to notice the furnishings as he strode surefooted from one room to the next and up a flight of stairs, until he'd reached a bedroom. He kicked the door shut behind him.

A huge four-poster bed with what she suspected was a hand-sewn quilt occupied the center of the room. The rest of the furnishings were simple, only a dresser, a chair and a thickly-woven Native American rug, but there was a huge fireplace on one wall, while the other framed floor-to-ceiling glass doors that opened onto a balcony.

Once at the windows, the cowboy loosed his hold beneath her thighs and she slipped to her feet, shimmying full-bodied against him on her way down. She stood still, not willing to break the moment, wanting to savor the feel of her body against his, his warm breath gusting against her hair.

She pressed her cheek to his chest and gazed through the glass doors. She expected to see the cookhouse and the other outbuildings, but found herself staring at only a breathtaking vista of land, and . . . "Is that the Palace?"

"Tex added this room after bringing his princess home so he could see her, even when he couldn't be with her."

"That's so romantic."

"What would be even more romantic," he whispered against her ear, "would be for you to undress for me."

"Yes, Trey." She stepped out of his arms with a smile.

With no hint of shyness and only an amazing feeling of contentment, as though stripping for this man brought her more pleasure than anything she'd ever accomplished in her life, Kathryn unbuttoned the flannel shirt, shimmied the tight jeans down her legs and stood proudly for her cowboy to admire.

"God, you're beautiful." He reached out to cup his fingers along the satiny underside of a breast and she felt the heat of his touch sizzle straight to her toes.

She wanted to feel him naked against her, know how their bodies fitted together, knew an eagerness that made her reach for his vest. "May I, Trey?"

"Absolutely, pretty lady."

With her gaze lowered to her task, Kathryn shoved the vest over his shoulders and down his arms, unbuttoned his shirt with trembling fingers as she exposed his muscular chest.

He may have become intimately acquainted with her body during the past twenty-four hours, but she'd never seen much more of him than he'd showed her when he'd shoved his pants down his hips to take her in the showroom last night.

Now Kathryn savored each inch of his tanned skin, the dusky blond swirls of hair nestled into the cut ridges of his chest, the powerful arms that had held her so possessively.

He had to help her with his boots, though she promised herself that she'd be thoroughly versed in removing cowboy boots before long. Dragging his jeans down his trim hips forced her onto her knees and suddenly she was mouth level with that incredible erection.

"May I, Trey?"

"Nothing would please me more, pretty lady."

The pleasure in his voice inspired her. Leaning forward, she pressed her breasts against his knees and swirled her tongue along his hot length. She felt his muscles gather with that one stroke, knew a sense of heady satisfaction that had her running her hands along his hard thighs, cradling his heavy scrotum in her palm and drawing him into her mouth with a sigh.

The sight of his erection had stung her last night, as had the realization that he'd brought her to climax so thoroughly, while she'd left him to suffer the effects of unsatisfied arousal. Kathryn wanted him to lose control today. She wanted to know him completely, wanted to watch his handsome face sharpen with his pleasure, wanted to hear that throaty low growl as his body exploded inside hers.

And she seemed to be making headway toward fulfilling her wish. His muscles quivered, his erection swelled with her moist attentions and when she arched her throat to take him into her mouth even deeper, slipped her hands into his firm butt cheeks he emitted that throaty low growl, threaded his fingers into her hair and dragged her to her feet.

But she only remained upright for a second. Then she landed on the soft mattress and the cowboy was suddenly beside her, gathering her in his arms, pulling her against every hot hard inch of his body.

His mouth caught hers, all fire and need, and they were kissing, a bit desperately, as though they'd waited far too long to be together again, tongues tangling, breaths clashing. His hands raked the length of her body with such fierce tenderness that Kathryn longed to feel him inside her.

He didn't resist when she swung her leg over his, straddled him, using her hand to stroke that magnificent erection against her passion-wet folds. He growled again, a needy sound that did much to build confidence in her ability to drive him wild. He rocked against her, created friction against her hand, driving in just enough to prove that the feel of him inside her last night had been no figment of her imagination.

She wanted nothing more in that moment than to please him, to prove she could stoke as many fires in him as he stoked in her and with a boldness she hadn't known she'd possessed, she slipped her free hand between them, balanced herself with a hand on his chest and sat up. Right onto his erection.

He groaned. His hot gaze flew up to hers, surprised and so very, very pleased that she sighed and began to ride him with the same commanding mastery that he'd shown when riding his own horse in from the range.

He met her stroke for stroke, building tension inside her until all she could do was grab the headboard for leverage as she drove her hips down to meet his thrusts, gasping for air, because she could barely breathe past the building tide, each hard thrust carrying her higher.

When he sank his fingers into her bottom to step up her pace and ground out, "Oh, god, Kate," she felt the first hot rush of his climax, felt her own rushing up to meet it.

Kathryn wasn't exactly sure when she'd collapsed against him, didn't remember him tugging the quilt over their bare bodies, but she knew with a certainty she'd never felt before in her life that if she ever had to dream about how it would feel to be completely and thoroughly adored, cherished and *loved* by a man, she'd feel exactly the way she did right now with their hot bodies pressed together, hearts racing, breaths coming ragged in the stillness.

But she had to be mistaken, because she'd only known the cowboy for little more than a day.

You've only known me for a day, she recalled him saying last night in the showroom. *Don't think about it now, Kate. Now is for enjoying how you feel.*

The time had finally come to start thinking.

But before she could reason out about how best to broach the subject, a framed photo on the dresser caught her eye, a familiar frame that seemed out of place in this man's bedroom.

Without a word, she slipped out of the cowboy's arms, drawn to the photo, needing to know if by some fluke they'd owned two so similar. He let her go.

And Kathryn knew before she even reached out to take the unusual tri-gold frame in her hands, before she even dropped her gaze to the picture, that she'd find her own face staring back at her from her high school graduation photo.

She stared down at herself, a fresh-faced girl swathed in black velvet and pearls, a girl with so many dreams and such hope for her future. Had she come close to living up to her hopes? Or had she closed her heart like a fist, tried to cut emotion and people from her life just like her mother had?

One lonely beat of her heart told the truth.

Clutching the frame in suddenly shaky hands, she turned to the cowboy, to ask the only other question that needed asking, and found him propped up on an elbow, watching her intently.

She never even had to ask.

"I'm in love with you, Kate," he said simply. "I have been ever since Kitty came back from your mama's funeral and told me all about a beautiful little spitfire who faced the world with her head high and so much dignity that no one could get close."

Kathryn hadn't felt like that at all during her mother's funeral. She'd felt broken, needy and all alone in the world. Her mother may not have been much for overt affection, but she'd been Kathryn's only family and losing her to cancer so young had come as a huge blow.

"I don't know what it was about you . . ." His warm eyes reflected both amusement and amazement. "You were clear across the country, living a life I had no ken of, but you touched me somehow. Deeply. When Kitty showed me that photo, I just knew exactly what I wanted in my woman."

"But you didn't know me."

"Well . . ." He shot her that goofy half-grin, looked a bit sheepish. "I knew a lot about you. And I fantasized a good bit about the rest."

Fantasized? She shook her head, trying to clear it. *She* was this man's fantasy?

The very idea of no-fire Kate being any man's fantasy—let alone a man who had a stable of princesses vying for his attention—struck her as so ridiculous that she could only stare, and struggle to control her runaway heartbeat.

But she had to know. Good, bad or otherwise, she had to hear the truth from his mouth. He'd done things to her that she'd never dreamed of letting a man do. He'd brought her to pleasures that she'd never imagined existed. She had to know, because what he thought mattered.

The breath caught in her throat. Her heartbeat slowed to a crawl. She clutched the photo frame, needing something to cling to, an anchor against the uncertainty that raged through her. And then she forced the words past her suddenly dry lips. "How does the reality hold up to the fantasy?"

He swung his long legs over the edge of the bed, rose to his feet in a muscular burst of grace that took her breath away even though she wasn't actually breathing, because her breath had already locked tight in her chest, waiting, just waiting.

He strode to her, completely unfazed by his bold nakedness. He plucked the frame from her hands, set it carefully back on the dresser.

Slipping his hands over her jaw, he tilted her face up to his and the truth she saw in his expression brought tears to her eyes. "The reality beats anything I ever fantasized about, Kate, and trust me, I have a pretty vivid imagination."

She gave a watery chuckle. She just bet he did. After all, he'd been reared with a palace filled with princesses just clamoring for chances to help him explore that imagination.

And he wanted her.

"So . . . so what happens now?"

His molasses eyes softened and he stroked his thumbs along her jaw, so tenderly she felt her heart issue its very own sigh.

"I ask you to stay in Love with me."

"As the Palace's madam?"

"I think you're a very bright business woman. I have no doubt that you can get the Palace back on track and work out a situation that'll meet everyone's needs. I'll help you."

Kathryn had had a few thoughts along those lines already, inspired by discovering that the Palace was actually a family run business. And it just so happened that she had *lots* of family around town who might be persuaded to help her work up a new way to run the place. Kate would dearly love devoting her talents to the marketing end and living on this ranch and making babies with her very own cowboy.

"I don't know what the future will hold for us, Trey, but I'd like to take it on together."

He smiled that sexy grin that made her blood ignite, and said, "Nothing would please me more."

Slipping her arms around his waist, she melted against him. "Then we'd better get busy. I've got a lot of debt to work off because I plan on running up a whole lot more."

Jared's Wolf

by MaryJanice Davidson

To my reader:
When I wrote *Love's Prisoner* for **Secrets VI** and introduced Michael and Jeannie Wyndham, I was overwhelmed by your response. All your wonderful letters and phone calls boiled down to one request: more Wyndham werewolves! Your wish is my command. I hope you like Moira and Jared as much as you liked Jeannie and Michael.

Chapter One

Moira smelled him before she saw him.

She had been strolling through the rose garden, which sounded nice but was actually chilly and miserable, being mid-winter on Cape Cod. She shivered among bare branches, because she couldn't bear to watch her pack leader nuzzle his mate for another second. Which made her feel like a jealous cow. Which only contributed to her misery.

She was a werewolf. A good one, in fact, but that didn't mean she didn't get lonesome just like a regular person. It wasn't that she didn't adore Michael and Jeannie Wyndham. She would have killed for them. She *had* killed for them. They were her sun and moon and, like lovers, they established her world. She accorded her pack leaders the respect due an alpha male and female, but more than that, she loved them as friends.

But she was alone and likely always would be. Her mother had mated with a human and it had brought her nothing but pain. She had wanted more for her daughter. Moira had promised her mother she would settle only for absolute happiness in a mate. Fine and good, except it pretty much doomed Moira to a solitary life. Which, for a werewolf, was usually a disaster.

It was one thing when Michael had been a loner, too. Once Jeannie arrived (or, as Jeannie put it, "was kidnapped"), things were exciting for several months. Helping the new non-werewolf alpha female settle in had been one surprise after another. There had been no time to be lonesome.

Now Jeannie had given the pack a marvelous girl-child, had made her home with the werewolves, and never gave a thought to her old life. No conflict in that time, while good for the pack, meant there'd been nothing to distract Moira from her troubles.

Michael's utter happiness with his mate only made Moira more acutely aware of her own loneliness. She loved them, but could watch them snuggling, smell their lust, only so long before she needed to walk, or snivel in self-pity.

The pack, Moira thought grimly, was no place for loners. Werewolves were enormously social and tended to mate for life as soon as possible. Loners got into trouble, and a loner who got into too much trouble went rogue. Rogue was bad.

Very bad.

She shivered, remembering Gerald. He was the only rogue male she had ever run across and, by God, he was enough. Gerald was on her mind because his estranged eldest, Geraldine, had just left Wyndham manor after a brief visit.

After Gerald had been driven out, Geraldine had remained loyal to the worthless bundle of fur. Since no pack would welcome a rogue, the two had wandered the country for years. Admirable loyalty, but the price the poor girl had paid! Her father had been dead a year and Geraldine still roamed.

No, a werewolf alone did more harm than good, and she had no business begrudging Michael and Jeannie their happiness. Better to leave the house and take her poor attitude with her. Thus, the rose garden in February. Thus, she would probably catch a cold from skulking in the sparse snow—and serve her right! Thus, there was a stranger on the grounds.

Her thoughts derailed in sudden confusion as she sniffed and caught the scent again. Stranger, yes. Male. Not pack. Probably a reporter; Michael Wyndham was a charismatic, handsome billionaire frequently courted for interviews. Now that he'd married and had a daughter, "journalists" (her lip curled) constantly tried to get a picture of the baby for *People* magazine.

She would find the man and escort him off the grounds; the Wyndham estate was private property. Her woes aside, there was, as always, duty. She turned to search and saw the stranger about fifteen yards away.

She was suddenly furious with herself because he wouldn't have crept up on her, downwind or not, if she hadn't been busy drowning herself in an ocean of pity. And she was also amazed, because he looked . . . well, amazing.

The stranger, who was rapidly approaching, had dark blonde hair pulled back in a ponytail. He was quite tall, easily a head taller than she was, dressed in jeans so faded they were nearly white, and a black duster which swept past his knees. And his eyes . . . his eyes were the color of the ocean on the first day of winter, dark blue and filled with restrained fury. She caught his scent again: clean and crisp, like freshly ironed linen. Male linen. Incredibly gorgeous, highly masculine linen. Linen she could wrap herself in, sink her teeth into . . .

Her mouth popped open, both at the man's sudden appearance and his exceptional good looks. He was the handsomest non-pack member she'd ever seen. Too bad she had to kick him off their property.

He opened his mouth and she spoke, too; they said in unison, "You can't be here."

They reacted in unison, too: "*I* can't be here?"

Moira stared at him, almost afraid to speak, and heard him say, "I'm really sorry. It's incredibly dangerous here. I'll try not to hurt you."

His unbelievable speed so shocked her, she let him hit her. He struck her with the flat of his hand, just below her chin, hard enough to knock her back into the frozen ground, hard enough to render a human unconscious.

Instantly, he was lifting her into his arms, carrying her away like a demented bridegroom. Demented and blind—he hadn't noticed she hadn't been knocked out.

Outraged, she seized his nose and twisted. He howled and dropped her; her butt thudded into the dirt. He clapped both hands to his face, but not before she saw she had given him a nosebleed. Good.

"That hurt." She flipped to her feet and growled, literally growled. She could feel the fine hairs on the back of her neck come to stiff attention. If she'd been in her wolf form, her fur would have been standing out in bristly spikes. "You're an interloper, a trespasser, a creep, and this is private property."

"This is a derrible blace," he warned nasally, still clutching his nose. "You cad be here." He seized her elbow with a bloody hand and tugged. She set her feet and didn't move. He pulled harder. She kicked his ankle and heard the 'crack' and his groan at the same moment. "Lady, for Christ's sake, I'b drying do save your life here!"

"My life doesn't need saving, moron, idiot, twit. Get your degenerate hands off me or I'll snap your spine."

"Fuck it," he muttered. He let go of her so abruptly she staggered. Then he stepped back, pulled out a gun, and shot her in the throat.

Jared watched the gorgeous blonde topple over and had to fight a sigh of relief. Cripes, what a balls-up! He hadn't thought she'd ever go down. His own damned fault—he was so worried about really hurting her he'd gone too easy. Hadn't had the heart to give her a really firm slam. And he'd paid the price: his nose was still streaming blood. The tranquilizer had worked (thank goodness for the Boy Scout motto!), but now what?

After years of research, of greasing palms, of knocking skulls together, of doing anything to get the information he needed, finally, *finally*, he had the murdering bastards cornered. His reconnaissance trip had instantly been cut short when he'd run across the woman. He'd been watching the Wyndhams for weeks and had their routine memorized . . . this was the time of day when the grounds were usually deserted. But there she was—obviously she hadn't read his recon notes—right in the line of fire, looking at him with those big eyes, probably getting ready to inflate those pipes and screech like a banshee.

Who would have thought a five foot nothing girl with eyes the color of pale violets would be so hard to knock out? Who would have thought she'd pack such a wallop?

Who would have thought he wouldn't be able to stop staring at her?

He knelt, pulled the tranquilizer dart out of her throat, and checked her pulse. Nice and strong. Weirdly strong. It was as if she was in a light sleep, not a drugged unconsciousness. If he didn't know for a fact that werewolves were all men, he'd wonder . . .

He picked her up, surprised again at how light she was. His dirty laundry weighed more. Now what to do with her? He couldn't leave such a delectable morsel lying around for anyone to nibble. Besides, if she had the freedom to wander Wyndham's grounds, she was probably a source of information. Perhaps a slave to the werewolves.

Anger swelled at the thought of this little sweetie at the beck and call of those monsters. Well, he could help her, and she could certainly help him. When she woke up, he'd pump her for whatever info she could provide.

The thought of pumping the blonde brought a surge of heat to his groin, which annoyed the hell out of him. You've got a dirty mind, buddy, he told himself. Just because you haven't gotten laid in a while . . .

He started back toward his truck. Wyndham and his pack of murdering dogs weren't going anywhere. His sister had been waiting too long in her grave for vengeance. He'd get the information he needed, see blondie on her way, and come back to avenge his sister.

God help anyone who got in his way.

Chapter Two

Moira opened her eyes and said, "I'm going to rip off your skin for that."

Beside her, the idiot-twit-jerkoff who'd shot her jumped in surprise. She heard the 'thump' of his book hitting the floor, and sat up.

And nearly fell herself, as a wave of dizziness slammed into her. She quickly shut her eyes, and groped for the edge of the bed. "As soon as I get my hands on you. Death. Agony. Screaming. I foresee all of these happening to you. Perhaps several times."

He had picked up his book, and now she felt cool hands on her, easing her back. "Take it easy, cutie. The trank packs a punch."

"Believe me, schmuck, putz, moron," she said. "You don't know what a punch is."

"You shouldn't even be awake yet," he soothed.

She seized his wrist, twisted, ready to crush the bone into splinters, already hearing his screams . . .

"Cut that out, it tickles."

"Dammit! How long am I going to have the strength of a newborn?" She had meant to shout thunderously. Instead what came out was a pitiful wheeze.

"Probably for the rest of the day." And did the lout have the gall, the temerity, the *nerve* to sound apologetic? After punching her and shooting her and trespassing?

"Why were you trespassing?"

She opened her eyes and took in the room at a glance and a sniff: cream and white bedroom, south-facing window, double bed, wool blankets, hardwood floors in dire need of a waxing, mothballs in the closet, cedar lined wardrobe. And *him*, sitting on the lone chair, holding his book (*Vengeance for Dummies*) and looking at her with honest interest. His dark blue eyes were thoughtful, and bracketed with laugh lines. As if he ever laughed. His hair was down from the ponytail; the sandy strands brushed his shoulders.

"I'm glad you asked," he said. Unfortunately, she'd forgotten the question. "That's a bad place. Do you work there? Do they force you? It doesn't matter. You don't have to go back, sweetie."

"Thanks, *sweetie*." Ugh. Had this oaf been sent to warn the Wyndhams about something? Alarm pierced the fog produced by the drug. "Is Michael in danger? Or Jeannie?"

His face didn't change, but his lips went white. And his scent . . . it shifted so quickly it nearly burned her nostrils. Acrid smoke. The smell of danger, the smell of hate. "How long have you known him?" he asked slowly, pleasantly. "Wyndham?"

Be careful, Moira. "Forever," she said shortly. "He's my boss." *And a whole host of other things you'll never, never understand.* "And if he's in trouble, you've got to tell me. And if you're bringing trouble to him or his, I'll kill you."

"God, you're beautiful," he said softly, which was not the usual response to a death threat. "You should see how fierce you look. He's not worth that kind of loyalty. If you knew what he was . . ."

If you knew what I am . . . She was starting to get really, really angry. Oh, for a full moon right about now! It wasn't just the humiliation of being snatched practically from her front yard. It was that he was an ordinary man, nothing special at all, and he had made it look *easy*. "Who are you?" she practically snapped.

"The UPS guy. But we were talking about you, cutie."

"We were not." She felt like leaping from the bed and throttling the information out of him. "And you haven't answered my question."

"Well," he said with maddening reason, "you haven't, either."

Like that, is it? Think you can outsmart me, monkey boy? We'll see.

"My jaw," she said, "hurts like hell." She made her eyes go big; blinked pathetically. "Why'd you hit me? I wasn't doing anything."

Monkey boy had the grace to look embarrassed. "Sorry," he muttered. "I didn't want you to raise the alarm. Besides, you don't want to be there, anyway, hon. It's a bad place. It's going to get a lot worse, too."

Moira wasn't listening anymore. Her head was clearing, though her body still felt as limp as overcooked pasta. An alarming series of facts was ripping through her brain.

Fact: this man managed to get on the grounds without anyone spotting him until he was on top of her.

Fact: he knew how to fight.

Fact: he had come armed.

Fact: he had drugged her, taken her away, and no one knew, and no one had stopped him.

Fact: he didn't like Michael.

Fact: he seemed to like her.

Fact: she had to stop this man.

Fact: she couldn't do shit until she had her strength back.

Fact: she couldn't let him *leave* until she had her strength back. More, she wouldn't leave, not until she better understood exactly what he represented for her pack.

Conclusion? Nakedness was in her future. Possibly quite a lot of it. He was a man and she had, quite frankly, a nice rack. He'd take one look at her tits and forget everything except his name. She'd buy recovery time and pump him for all the information she could.

It was annoying: she could count on one hand how many times she'd gotten laid in the last two years; she was extremely selective. Or, as her friend Derik put it, "weirdly frigid." Now she had to expend precious energy to seduce this human.

Moira was not a promiscuous woman by any means . . . not, in fact, strictly a woman at all. A pack animal first and forever, everything she was, did, and said was shaped by that knowledge, that identity. When the leader was in danger, the pack was in danger.

When the pack was in danger, she'd do whatever it took.

"My head," she whispered, breath-soft.

"What?" the idiot said, bending closer.

Fighting the urge to shriek, "Gotcha!," she put her mouth right near the cup of his ear and murmured, "My head hurts sooooooo much . . . may I please have a glass of water?"

"Oh. Sure. I'm sorry, I should have . . ." Moron Boy moved away, and she couldn't help staring at the exceptional way his butt filled out the seat of his jeans. Yes indeedy, the world-class ass had a world-class ass. She wrenched her thoughts back on a more business-like track . . . then remembered his butt sort of *was* the business at hand, at least until her metabolism blasted the last of that hateful trank out of her system.

The idiot came back with a glass of water, which she promptly spilled all over her blouse. "Oh, it's cold!" she squealed, inwardly groaning—Derik would be laughing his head off if he could see this—and outwardly shuddering as her nipples came to stiff attention. What's-his-face had been helping her sit up, and nearly dropped her back into the pillows. "Do you have a shirt I can borrow?" She fumbled at the buttons of her soaked blouse.

Jared blinked, taking in Moira's smooth, pale skin as she stripped the wet fabric away. He wondered if she had a fever. He wondered if *he* had a fever. He knew who this little cookie was. He'd taken her prints while she'd been unconscious, scanned them into his laptop, and found out her name over an hour ago. Technology was swell.

Moira Wolfbauer, place of residence: Wyndham Manor. Place of business: Wyndham Manor. Employer: Michael Wyndham. But she'd tried her hand at social work just out of college, lucky for him, and thus her prints were on file. Mother deceased, father unknown. He'd pretended to know none of this, of course, and began a gentle interrogation, and hadn't been pleased to hear how protective she was toward the Wyndhams.

Obviously fond of the asshole, what was she up to? She'd threatened to kill him, had assaulted him, and was pulling off her blouse and—yep, there went the bra—a frothy, lilac-colored concoction that exactly matched her eyes.

All right.

It would take more than a wet blouse to distract him.

He was Jared Rocke and he would have his vengeance. He was Jared Rocke and she had the nicest rack he'd ever seen, all creamy white skin with nipples the color of wild roses. He was Jared . . . uh . . . Rocke . . . and . . .

"Aren't you cold?" he asked hoarsely.

"Extremely," she whispered, her hands on his shoulders, pulling him down, her mouth by his ear, her small white teeth sinking into his earlobe, and the sensation shot straight from his ear to his groin.

He groped, seeking a blanket to cover her, and instead his hands found the delicious firmness of her breasts. She arched against him, her tongue in his ear, and his mouth found her throat. She wriggled delightfully, tugged at him, and then his shirt was sliding off his shoulders and floating to the floor.

Her wriggling had been to good effect; she was nude, he was nude, their clothes a tumbled heap on the floor. Her soft skin made for an erotic contrast against the wool blankets, and for a moment all he could do was stare. Her violet eyes were huge, dominating her face, the arched golden brows above them making her look sweetly surprised. Her short hair was a delightful muss of tumbled blonde curls, curls so light they were almost silver, and her limbs were slim but strong-looking. Her nails were short, almost brutally so, and he had time for a quick, analytic thought: They're short because she bites them all the time. He wondered what a cookie this cute had to worry about. Men probably fell over themselves trying to take care of her.

Then she opened her arms and he fell into her embrace, and that was the end of his analysis. For the first time in years, thoughts of vengeance fled his mind as he buried himself in her creamy softness.

Moira braced herself for the oaf's full weight, but to her surprise he caught himself on his hands and came into her gently, almost carefully. His hand caressed her messy hair, and then his mouth came down on hers, his tongue skimming across her teeth and, when she obligingly parted her lips, probing her mouth. His taste overwhelmed her, all smoky masculine heat, and she gasped.

She'd never mated with someone who wasn't pack. This was partly out of self-imposed obligation to her mother and partly out of pure concern. She had always, in some part of her subconscious, worried about hurting an ordinary man. And really, wasn't that her problem? She had promised her mother she wouldn't mate into the pack . . . but couldn't bring herself to mate with an ordinary human. Now here she was, buying time, and he didn't seem so ordinary, this man, and his hands, what his hands were doing, that didn't seem all that ordinary eitherrrrrrrrrrr . . .

"Oh!" Her hips bucked. He moved, kneeling beside her, and his thumb settled back atop her clitoris, his fingers spread and resting against her thighs, barely touching, almost *not* touching, but moving so slowly and delicately that she could almost . . . feel it . . . and it was driving her crazy. Meanwhile, he had reached for her breast, was pinching her nipple between his thumb and forefinger, hard enough to almost hurt. Between the throbbing of her nipple and the light, delicate, feathery touch between her legs, she was halfway to a climax. Ridiculous! He'd been touching her for less than a minute. She wasn't a goddamned windup doll. She didn't even *like* him. She didn't even . . . she didn't . . . she . . . she felt a flood of heat between her legs and reached out.

She found him, hard and hot and long, and squeezed, and his eyes tipped up and he stared blindly at the ceiling, the muscles in his neck standing out in rigid relief. He turned his hand and his thumb was now wiggling inside her.

Moira reached for him again but he kept that maddening distance, almost as if he were afraid to be too close to her. She opened her eyes wide, and in the afternoon light had a postcard-perfect look at him, at the way the light bathed him, made him seem more tan than he was. She could see the muscles moving beneath his taut flesh and, reaching up, felt the tension in his abdomen. He was holding himself back, rigidly so, and she wondered why. She could smell his urgent lust and it kindled her own; she knew he wanted to shove her down and bury himself inside her until they were both screaming. So why did he hold back?

More, she wondered how she could have gotten caught up so quickly in what had started out as a stalling technique, an act she had been prepared to dislike, or at least find dull.

He smiled at her, reached for her, cupped her chin in his hand. They stared at each other and Moira forgot to breathe, so amazed that there could be such a tender, perfect moment between strangers.

Then he eased her over, onto her stomach, and nudged her thighs apart with his knee. She could feel his thumbs on either side of her spine, pressing, soothing, and instinctively arched into his touch. Then she felt a silky firmness, and realized he was dragging the tip of his cock down her spine, between the cleft of her buttocks, and pausing at the opening of her vagina. She waited expectantly, but he paused. Bent. Murmured.

"I'm Jared."

She said nothing, just surged toward him.

"And you're Moira."

The bare tip of him was teasing her nether mouth, almost easing inside but not quite, and she swallowed a groan. His fingers were on her, spreading her wide for him, but still he didn't enter, still he lingered.

"Say it, Moira."

"Jared." The word was nearly wrenched from her. "You're Jared."

He chuckled, deep in his throat, almost a purr. "Nice to meet you."

He pushed forward and was almost—almost!—inside her, but not quite. She began to shake. Had she imagined she'd have the upper hand in this seduction? Had she really?

"Please . . ."

"Moira, we're going to have a nice long talk when I'm finished." Coming inside her now, the full, engorged head pushing, pushing. "About you . . ." Another inch. "The company you keep . . ." Another. "And your boss." Abruptly he was gone from her, and she could have cried. His finger replaced his cock, dipping, teasing, feeling her slippery wetness, and then he was stroking the tight bloom of her anus, gently rubbing the rich core of nerve endings there. She made a surprised sound which escalated to a muffled shriek as he slowly pushed his finger past that tight muscular ring.

"Easy."

"Don't." She tried to scramble away—she had never, no one had *ever*—but he nudged her again and she couldn't get the leverage she needed. When he was up to the first knuckle she felt his cock at the mouth of her vagina, and there was no gentle easing this time, this time he was instantly inside her, while his finger slid around slowly, out just a touch and then back in, no big dramatic strokes, just an overall pressure and gentle wriggling. She could feel him everywhere, filling her up, taking everything . . .

"Yes, we'll have a nice long talk," he said, his voice so gritty she could scarcely understand him. He pulled out and his finger stilled; she was reasonably certain her heart would stop. "About your unfortunate choice of associates." He slammed all the way in.

She screamed.

She screamed into the pillow as he thrust, rocked, as he took her again and again, one hand on the small of her back, one hand . . . doing things inside her, doing things no man had ever . . . and always his cock, throbbing and huge and a terrible thing, doing his bidding, ignoring her pleas, her cries, just shoving and thrusting, and it was a terrible thing, a terrible *wonderful* thing, because somehow the tables had turned, she wasn't using him, he was using her.

She would kill him. She would kill him for making her scream. She would kill him if he stopped.

"Moira," he groaned. He wouldn't let her move, wouldn't listen to her cries, but his hands on her were gentle. "Moira, ah, *God.*" His tempo increased, he slammed into her, the bed moved, she braced herself and shoved back as hard as she could, because she could sense it, feel it, her orgasm was on the horizon, was almost there, and another finger joined the first inside her, stretching her, and that was enough, that tipped her over.

She tried to throw back her head and howl, but all that escaped was a wild groan as she bucked against him. She felt him clench behind her, felt his seed pour into her, could actually feel the temperature change as he heated her up from the inside, and came again, so quickly and fiercely that white spots danced on the edge of her vision.

He pulled out of her, away from her, and she collapsed, alone, on the bed. She lay on her stomach for long moments, shaking from the aftereffects of the most cataclysmic sex *(with a human! a human!)* she'd ever had, then finally rolled over and looked at him.

To her surprise, he'd pulled on his jeans, had sat down in the chair and was watching her with hungry interest, the way a wolf watches a limping fawn. She could still smell the musk they had made. Could smell herself, on him.

"Now," he said, smiling, and she didn't much care for that smile, not at all, "let's talk about your boss."

Chapter Three

Moira sucked in her breath in a startled, hurt gasp. "You . . . you were using me."

He blinked. "Well, you were using me first. In fact, you sort of gave me the idea."

She glared. She felt like a fool—where did she get off, accusing him of anything? She sounded like a brat. Well, she couldn't help it. Right now, she *felt* like a brat. He was right, but that didn't make accepting it easier . . . or lessen the hurt. However, she would eat her own eyeballs before letting him see how she felt. "Yes, that's true, I did start things," she said slowly. "It's just as well, since you apparently enjoy forcing women to get them to do what you want."

Score! Bright color jumped into his cheeks. Suddenly she felt a bit better. It was hard to feel triumphant, she thought, when her thighs were still throbbing from what he'd been doing to her. For a while—a teeny, tiny while—she'd forgotten all about the pack, about this man being a threat to her leaders. It just . . . just went completely out of her head. She could count how often this had happened on one finger. Yesterday, she would have been able to count it on no fingers.

Jared cleared his throat, obviously piqued to see her interest was elsewhere. "Now . . . where were we? Oh, right. Your scumsucking boss. You—"

"I'm not telling you spit about Michael Wyndham, you cretinous globulous fornicator, and you can just—stop laughing!"

He'd thrown his head back at "globulous" and was still chortling, despite her specific order to the contrary. He finally stopped and looked at her admiringly. "Has anyone ever told you how you insult people in threes? Cretinous-globulous-fornicator? Schmuck-putz-moron? Anybody mention this before?"

"Yes. Michael Wyndham, for one." That wiped the smirk off his face. "I don't know what you want with him or his, but he's—"

The brother I never had.

"—my dearest friend and not only am I *not* going to tell you things about him, I'm going to put you to the floor if you go near him with harmful intent."

Of course, now *Michael* would be laughing at the thought of her defense, because a pack leader who couldn't fight off intruders wouldn't be a pack leader very long. Still, her pride demanded some sort of action.

He shook his head at her. "You poor kid. You have no idea what he is, do you? I suppose you're fooled by a pretty face."

"I wasn't fooled by yours," she said coldly. He grinned. It made him look years younger. It made him look nice. When he most assuredly *was not.*

She sat up suddenly, testing herself, pleased to find she wasn't dizzy. In a bound she leaped out of the bed and stood on the floor, fists planted on her hips. Jared's gaze lowered to her breasts and she could practically hear his I.Q. dropping. Pretty soon his mouth would fall open and a silvery line of saliva would start tracking down his chin. "I'm *out* of here, schmuck, putz, idiot. I don't appreciate being kidnapped and drugged and—er—seduced—"

"Technically," he pointed out mildly, "you were the one to introduce sex into the equation. I was just—er—a willing pupil."

"Details. Anyway, stay away from the Wyndhams, or I'll pull off your ears and you can use them for cufflinks." With that, she whirled and marched toward the smell of Comet cleanser . . . presumably the bathroom.

It *was* the bathroom. Excellent. Shutting and locking the door behind her, she ignored the laughter coming from the bedroom. Moira had always been the shortest person in any room and was used to people—*men*—laughing at her fierceness. The laughter usually stopped when they had to spit out their back teeth to avoid choking.

It was time—past time—to get the hell out of Dodge. She didn't trust herself to remain around The Insufferable One. When he laughed he threw his head back and she thought about nibbling on his throat, licking until she tasted his sweat and—oh, yes, it was time to leave.

She spotted the window above the toilet and opened it. *Three stories up—hmmm. Big house.* She could easily get to the ground, but there was the small problem of being naked. Not that she cared—no werewolf cared—but she was supposed to pretend to care. A lot more humans lived in this town than werewolves, even here, the seat of Michael and Jeannie's power.

She snatched at the shower curtain—a silly thing with imprints of grinning ducks, and were the little bastards mocking her? They were!—and tugged it down. There was a paft-paft-paft! sound as the curtain hooks disengaged, but she didn't hear approaching footsteps. Good.

In a flash she wrapped it around herself, a sort of plastic, duck-laden toga. Wriggling through the window with a minimum of grunting, she dropped to the porch roof, about twenty-five feet straight down.

And fell through it.

That wasn't in the plan, she thought, dizzy with surprise. *Stupid old Cape Cod houses with shoddy porch roofs! And are those splinters in my . . . aarrgh! This day is never going to end.* She slowly climbed to her feet and heard Jared thundering down the stairs.

She ran.

Chapter Four

Moira limped into the combination dining hall/family room at Wyndham Manor (or, as Derik called it, Carnivore Central). For a moment she just watched them, drinking in the cozy domestic scene. She'd brought chaos and bad news (and splinters) with her, and was loath to disturb them.

Derik, her oldest friend, was deeply engrossed in a back issue of *Martha Stewart Living*. He was tall, broad, rippling, muscular, etc., etc., and made a quiche like nobody's business. His Chilean sea bass, served on a bed of sautéed spinach, could make grown men weep. Derik was convinced Ms. Stewart was a cleverly concealed werewolf, and read each magazine to tatters, looking for clues. When the article on steak *tartare* came out, he was sure she'd made a fatal slip.

Jeannie and Michael, her pack leaders, were stretched out on the carpet in front of a crackling fireplace. Baby Lara was lying between them. She would carefully extend a bare, pink foot (a foot that looked quite a bit like a pork chop with toes), giggle while her mother tickled it, then would withdraw, and slowly extend the other foot for her father.

Jeannie had settled in, if not seamlessly, at least with minimal trouble after that first hellish week. Moira often wondered if Jeannie thought of her old life. She'd never had friends to the manor, and never talked about her family. It was almost as if she hadn't really come alive until Michael had—almost literally!—swept her off her feet.

Moira felt the usual envy crawling up from the back of her throat, and fought it down. She was happy for Michael. She was. And she adored Jeannie. It was just . . . hard to take sometimes. That was all.

They were so happy, and she'd just had the best sex of her life with a man who was trying to pump her for information.

She delicately cleared her throat ("Ah-CHEM!"), gratified to hear the yells of dismay. After the bruising her pride (and bottom!) had endured today, she was grateful to be surrounded by family.

Jeannie, her best friend and the pack's alpha female, was yelling the loudest. The leggy blonde rushed over to her, holding baby Lara and raking Moira with her piercing, blue-eyed gaze.

"What the hell happened to you?"

"Glah!" Lara added, waving a chubby hand.

Moira caught the baby's hand, kissed it gently. Lara had her mother's lungs, and her father's charisma. With a headful of dark, glossy curls and eyes the color of good cognac, she was a striking infant.

Michael took her in at a glance—bumps, bruises, smelling of sweaty sex and plastic, tired and pissed off. "Who should I kill?" he asked calmly.

"Are you okay?" Derik asked, hurrying over to join their small group.

"Only my pride has been savaged." She felt the shower curtain start to slip and adjusted it. "But probably permanently." Directly to Michael and Jeannie: "Can we talk?"

"Don't pull that," Derik protested. A broad-shouldered blonde, he and Moira had often been mistaken for siblings. Except for the fact that he towered over her, they looked a great deal alike, although Derik's eyes were the green of wet leaves. "I want to hear what happened, too. Start with, 'I went for a walk,' and finish with 'then I walked in wearing a ducky shower curtain.' "

"Not now," she said, and hated it, because Derik really *was* like a brother to her, and she had no secrets from him. He'd informally adopted her as a littermate when she'd come to live at the mansion after her mother's death.

But the pack leader deserved to hear about the threat first—Jared had named Michael specifically. Michael would decide who to tell, after. "Come on, you guys. This shower curtain is itchy."

Jeannie unceremoniously handed Lara to Derik. The baby yelped in protest, then shrieked happily as Derik tossed her four feet in the air. "Later, Moira," he called after them. As in, *You'll be telling me the whole story, right?*

"Later, Dare." She used the nickname he'd had since they'd been small. The man would do anything if you triple-dog-dared him.

She marched into the soundproofed den and waited until Michael shut the door. Then she told them how she'd spent her afternoon. She left out nothing, save for how astounding and wonderful the sex had been. She was feeling very guilty about that.

Michael's eyes were thoughtful, distant. "Huh."

"'Huh,' he says." Jeannie shook her head in annoyance. "Let's go back to the house and find out what this Jared's problem is." Moira could see every one of the woman's protective instincts was aroused. "Or have him arrested."

"For?" Michael asked mildly.

"Trespassing." She was scowling, but leaned into him for comfort. The scowl eased as he gently rubbed her shoulders. "Being a flaming asshole. Rape."

Moira coughed. "Uh . . . it wasn't exactly . . ."

"Never mind semantics! He's out to get you, Mike. I won't have it, I tell you I *will not have it!*"

Moira didn't say anything. Jeannie had become one of the family, and was so utterly fearless, it was often hard to remember she wasn't a werewolf. This was hardly the first time someone had come gunning for Michael. He controlled an admirable fortune and had three hundred thousand werewolves at his back. He was a tempting target.

"I really think we need to go over there and fire a warning shot into his spine," Jeannie continued. Michael was still rubbing her shoulders, and she raised her hands and closed them over his, gripping tightly. "Fix him somehow. Neutralize his ass."

"What do you propose we do, dear one?"

"Um, hmm, I'm not sure, let me think, how about . . . *lock him up!*"

"Then he skips bail and he's out and about with a hidden agenda. No."

"You're insufferable. Must you always think of every stupid little thing?"

He smiled at her. There weren't many people who dared speak to Michael Wyndham in such a way. The pack had been deferring to him since he was in training pants. He loved his wife's sharp tongue. "Every stupid little thing? I thought of going after you, didn't I?"

"Har, har."

His smile faded and he looked right at Moira, who'd been watching their interaction with undeniable longing. "Moira, will you go back?"

"Of course." She had figured out the problem as quickly as Michael had. Obviously Jared was a dangerous man . . . but was he alone? What exactly did he want, and why? And how far was he going to go in order to achieve his goal? Did he want to bring down just

Michael, or Jeannie and baby Lara? The entire pack? For what purpose? When? She cursed herself for not having thought of this before
jumping out the window. But there was time to make up for it. "Let me
get changed and I'll leave right away."

"Leave?" Jeannie's fingers were twitching and Moira could tell,
just tell, her friend was wishing for her gun. "Why?"

Moira started sidling toward the door. When the Wyndhams
fought, chandeliers shook and foundations cracked. And Jeannie, a
good woman in all things, was still a human. She would never be pack,
and could never truly understand their motivations. She'd get it intel-
lectually. But she would never feel it.

"Moira is going to go back to that house, and stay with Jared, and
get all the information out of him she can, however she can." Michael
said this with admirable calm, then waited.

Jeannie's eyes widened and seemed to actually bulge. "Stay put!"
she snapped at Moira, who was tentatively reaching for the doorknob.
"Moira, you don't have to go."

"Really, I'd be more comfortable up in my room—"

"I meant back to *him*."

"Of course I have to. We need to know what he's up to. And I'm in
a unique position—he thinks I'm a cute bimbo twit. Also," she added,
ignoring the rush of heat to her cheeks, "he likes fucking me."

Jeannie gaped at her, then swung toward Michael. "Michael, don't
make her go! She doesn't have to—to whore for us."

Moira laughed, then clapped a hand over her mouth.

"Werewolves don't whore," he said, fighting a smile of his own,
"and I'm not making Moira do anything. She only came here as a
courtesy, you know. To—how d'you put it? Keep us in the loop." He
glanced at her over the top of his wife's head and they shared a moment of perfect understanding.

"It's not right," Jeannie said stubbornly.

"Protecting us? Your daughter? Our friends?"

"Well . . . okay . . ." She exhaled sharply, puffing blonde strands
out of her face. "I feel stupid having to say this out loud, but she
shouldn't have to sleep with him."

"It's a sacrifice I'm willing to make," Moira said, straight-faced,
but her cheeks felt very warm now. Michael looked at her sharply, and
arched a dark eyebrow.

"Moira," he said, "can take care of herself. It's not like you to mor-
alize, Jean."

Jeannie looked from her husband to her friend. She looked at them
the way one might look at a new form of life: with superstitious awe.

After a long moment, Jeannie shook her head. Usually the difference between their cultures and species didn't seem so great, but today the gap yawned. "You'll do as you please," she told him, "you always do. But expecting Moira to put herself in danger for you, to have sex with a bad guy for you . . . that's going too far. It's—" She glanced at Moira and stopped. Moira was staring at her with a total lack of comprehension. "Oh, forget it. I'm obviously the only one who's got a problem with this. Fine, knock yourself out, have a grand old time, don't forget to write."

She marched across the room, punctuating her exit by slamming the door. Michael turned and looked at the couch. "It's about as uncomfortable as it looks," he mournfully informed Moira. "What a pity I'll be sleeping there, probably for the rest of the week."

Who are you kidding? Try a month. Moira smiled wanly. "It's actually a little flattering—if she didn't think so highly of me, she wouldn't have such a problem with me going back. But I can't think of how to explain it to her . . . why it's *not* a problem. Why I have to do it . . . in fact, why I should be halfway back to the house already."

"Yes, but first this. You've got to be really careful. Not just for your own sake. If Jared gets too close . . ." He smiled, showing his teeth. They looked very white and very sharp and might have fooled someone slow to notice the smile didn't reach his eyes. "I'd hate for my wife to have to shoot another bad guy on my property. The noise might wake the baby."

"He won't get close to them. And even if he did," she said matter-of-factly, "it will be very hard for him to harm my lady and my future sovereign while I'm chewing on his spinal cord."

Now the smile did reach his eyes. "Oh, Moira. Have I told you how much I love you today?"

They laughed together, like littermates.

Chapter Five

Jared told himself to stop worrying about Moira.

Impossible.

Which was annoying, because he had far more important things to worry about. His sister's murder had been too long unavenged. He was in place at last, ready to strike, a blonde, blue jean wearing hammer of vengeance.

But instead of oiling his guns, practicing his sleeper hold and making sure his revenge T-shirt was clean—in general, fantasizing about blood and screaming and other good stuff like that—he was fretting about blondie.

He didn't dare go back out to the porch. Every time he saw the hole in the roof and the scattered debris on the floor, he cringed, an action frowned upon by the Marines and the varied underworld types who'd helped him prepare for this week. She had been so desperate to get away from him that she'd flung herself out the window! She had been so desperate to get away from him she had fled on foot—with nothing more than a duck-laden shower curtain covering that lovely bod! As each hour passed he felt more and more like a Grade A jerk . . . and more and more frantic with worry.

He'd canvassed the quiet neighborhood, with no luck. She'd probably holed up somewhere to nurse a thousand wounds (and a million splinters). Probably dying! All because of—

The doorbell rang.

Jared blinked. No one in town knew who he was, it was too early for Girl Scout cookies, and was there still such a thing as a Welcome Wagon?

Had *Wyndham* sent the Welcome Wagon?

As was his habit, Jared fretted while he cleaned his guns. So he actually held a freshly oiled Beretta. It was a moment's work to slap a full clip in and slide a load into the chamber. Still barefoot and shirtless from his earlier (incredible, wonderful, marvelous lovemaking) tryst with (beautiful, gorgeous Moira) blondie, he padded to the door. By the time he reached it, the delicate tapping became an insistent pounding. Jared flung the door open, his gun already leveled.

At Moira's forehead.

"You're a limited man," was all she said, walking past him. Carrying a suitcase, no less. He stared. He couldn't help himself. She looked as pretty as a spring daisy, wearing a yellow dress which made her eyes seem a darker lavender, almost purple. The hem of the dress stopped a modest inch below her knees, which did nothing to disguise the fact that she was walking around on a world-class pair of stems. The back of the dress plunged in a deep V, showing off creamy white skin.

"Well," she said, when it was obvious all he could do was gape at her, "I'm back."

"Huh?"

She rolled her eyes and muttered something under her breath. "I . . . said . . . I'm . . . back . . ." she enunciated loudly, as if he was feeble or deaf. Right now, he *felt* feeble. "I'm staying with you until we get this mess straightened out."

He had the dim feeling he was in the presence of a greater intellect. And awesome tits! He shook his head, hard. Focus, moron, he ordered himself. "Mess?"

"Yes. You're here to do something wretched, horrid, awful, to my friend and boss, Michael Wyndham. I'm here to talk you out of it."

Now he was focused, laser-sharp. "No chance."

"Why?"

"He—he's a monster. He killed someone I loved."

Not a blink from blondie. Not a twitch, not a fake show of sympathy. Just a cool, "No. He didn't."

Jared was surprised, both at her assurance and her inference. And frankly, not hearing her ooze sympathy was something of a relief. Women were either scared shitless of him, or felt sorry for him. Neither was conducive to horniness. And he didn't want Moira's pity. He especially didn't want her fear. It was very important she not be afraid. He couldn't bear it if she flinched back from him.

Jesus, why the hell did he care? Why should it matter if she was scared shitless of him? It would just make his job easier. And how could she defend the monsters so quickly, without knowing any of the details?

"Maybe not him," he said at last. "But one of his dogs."

At 'dogs' her upper lip curled, revealing lovely white teeth. He plunged ahead, unable to believe they were having this conversation. He was explaining things to the woman who worked for the man who **murdered his sister!** "Whatever or whoever, Wyndham is responsible. I don't give two fucks for the details. He's the boss dog. So he's going to tell me where I can find the dog responsible."

"I'll be glad to help you find out who hurt the person you cared for," she said quietly, hefting her suitcase and starting toward the stairs, "but you're wrong about Michael. Totally utterly completely wrong. I'll be around until I can convince you of that."

He watched her climb the stairs, silent. After a moment he wrenched his gaze from her legs and forced himself to think. His gut told him Moira was one of the good guys. His brain screamed exactly the opposite. But he was not the world's greatest thinker, as his father, training instructors, and commanding officers had pointed out on several occasions. He was alive today because he'd listened to his instincts and ignored his brain. He'd be a fool to ignore his gut now, when he was so close.

Moira was a veritable treasure trove of information. Not that she planned on telling him shit. His admiration, already high, went a notch higher. She was a safe, and if he cracked her with just the right tools, he'd get the gold.

After a while he unloaded the gun, put it away, and went up after her.

Chapter Six

"So . . . what? We're roomies?" Jared asked.

"Yes." Moira unpacked the suitcase, shoved her clothes into the empty bureau by the window. And tried very, very hard not to show how pleased she was to see him again. She wasn't the first woman in her family to feel like this, she remembered with excitement and despair. Her mother, too, had been torn between desire and duty. Except her mother had been human, and her father a beta werewolf who left to form his own pack. Left her mother, pregnant and alone in a city by the sea. If not for Michael's father taking them in . . .

There was a lesson there: love made you stupid. On her deathbed, her mother had praised her former lover, who'd planted his seed one night and then left to better himself. Moira loved her mother, but hated weakness.

"I appreciate what you're trying to do—I think," Jared was saying, sounding confused—as usual. "And I'm glad to see you're all right. In fact, I'm pretty interested in hearing the tale of your trip back to the mansion. And what you did with my shower curtain—I bought a new one, by the way, in case you need to—uh—freshen up. But I'm still a little confused."

"I'm not surprised."

He ignored the sarcasm. "What exactly do you do for Wyndham?"

"I'm his accountant."

"His accountant."

"Yes."

"Uh . . . you don't look like an accountant."

"Obviously I do, because I am one." 'Accountant' was understating it a bit. She had a Master's in Business Finance, another Master's in International Business Relations, and (this one had been for fun) a Master's in Japanese Literature. "What does your accountant look like?"

"I don't have an accountant," he admitted. "I made about eight grand last year."

Eight grand! She'd signed off on that much for the birthday celebration the week Lara had been born. Heck, her Christmas bonus had been almost twice that. "Hmm. The revenge business isn't terribly lucrative?"

He smiled, which, annoyingly, she felt down to her knees. "That's about right. You know, Moira, if you're going to stay here, we should probably set up some ground rules."

"Such as . . . ?" Here came the tiresome human stuff . . . he'd sleep on the couch, they'd draw up a bathroom schedule, they'd *talk* out their *feelings* in a really really *constructive* way. He'd explain about how difficult it was to be a modern man when all he really wanted to do was cry and share his enlightened consciousness with some poor bitch, and she'd pretend not to be semi-conscious with boredom.

She squared her shoulders. She would endure much for Michael and Jeannie and Lara. Torture. A physical beating. Sharing feelings in a constructive way. "I'm hearing what you are saying," she said, obediently quoting *Redbook*. "What rules?"

"Well," he said, and she noticed—how had this escaped her?—that he was unbuckling his belt. Now he was sliding his jeans down his long thighs and he wasn't wearing underwear. Now he was kicking the jeans in a pile, pulling his shirt over his head and yanking the band out of his hair. He grinned and then they were flying backward and landing on the bed, his cool nakedness pressed against her, warming her through the thin fabric of her dress. His hair tickled her chin and smelled like wild perfume. "The first rule, I think, is that we should be naked, pretty much all the time."

She laughed. She couldn't help it. Then she was laughing into his mouth as he kissed her. Her hands raced over him, greedy, and he was groping her with about as much finesse. She didn't care. Something about his scent drove her right out of her mind. She thought his first rule was a fine one.

Their thoughts:

He wants to hurt the pack.

She works for the monsters.

But in this moment of clean lust, logic had no force. The only thing that mattered was skin on skin, mouth on mouth. Preferably for hours.

There was a purring riiiiiiiip, and then her dress was in pieces. "I'll care about that," she said, panting, "later."

"I'll buy you a new one." He issued a low growl, and then his mouth was on one of her nipples, and then, even better, his teeth were.

"That dress was worth one tenth of your total earnings last year."

"God, I love it when you figure out percentages in your head," he moaned. She could feel his beard stubble between her breasts . . . on her stomach . . . between her thighs. "Now talk to me about IRA rollovers and 401(k)s."

She started laughing so hard she lost her breath entirely. Which was all right, because at that moment his tongue darted inside her, and she wouldn't have been able to breathe anyway.

Her hips bucked against his mouth and he reached up, seized her waist, and shoved her back firmly against the mattress. All the while his mouth busily explored between her legs, his lips sucking and kissing and his tongue was probing. Moira heard herself scream.

He pulled back abruptly, leaving her teetering on the edge, and she screamed again, this time in frustration. She scrambled toward him, but he caught her elbows and flipped her. Her face hit the pillows as she was forced down on her stomach.

"God, you have the *most* luscious ass," he groaned, and she felt his hands on her, his fingers kneading her skin, hard.

Hard enough to mark my flesh, she thought with black excitement. Her blood was up so high she literally saw red; the room before her was cloaked in a red haze. Her tongue felt thick in her mouth.

She flipped back over, and grabbed him, and he laughed at her. But he quit laughing when she locked her ankles behind his back and forced his pelvis toward hers. Women had superior lower body strength anyway, and besides, she was probably twice as strong as he was, possibly three times.

He let her do it. In fact, he helped—put his hands between her thighs and gently held her apart, so that when she levered her back up off the mattress to meet him, his cock slid inside her without pause. Right up to the hilt.

They stared at each other for a long moment, then started rocking together. Her legs were still wrapped around him but now he was holding her, too, holding her and kissing her deeply while they thrust against each other, while the bed squeaked out their rhythm.

Now his mouth was on her neck and he was gently biting her

throat, then greedily sucking her flesh. *His mark*, she thought again, and spun away into orgasm.

A moment later, so did he. Through a gaze slitted with pleasure, she watched his eyes roll back, felt him stiffen all over.

"Christ," he managed, right before collapsing on her.

"Yes, indeed," she replied. She started to push him off her, but he clung like a lamprey. "For heaven's sake, I need to get up and wash."

"No," he muttered sleepily. "Keep my smell on you. For a while."

A reasonable request. One she liked too much. She started to get up, but his arm tightened across her waist like a bar. She could have snapped it at the elbow, but didn't. Instead she nestled up next to him, and fell asleep.

Chapter Seven

Moira snapped awake in the dark. Where the hell was she?

"Don't. Don't. Don't."

Everything locked into place: she was in Jared's rented house. His stirring had awakened her. And what on earth was wrong with his voice? He sounded like a boy, not a man in his prime.

"Don't be dead. Oh, Jesus, don't . . . don't be. Dead. Dead. She's dead. My sister's dead! *Somebody help me!*"

She reached out a hand, too late. He sat up so abruptly the back of his head banged into the headboard, flung his arms out hard, belted her right below the eye. It didn't slow him down, or even bring him fully awake.

He lurched from the bed. She pressed a hand to her now-throbbing eye and forced her pupils to dilate. Suddenly what had been dark became light, and she got a good look.

The big, badass werewolf hunter stumbled around the room, hoarse sobs locked in his throat, compulsively rubbing at his hands. "Everywhere." His voice broke. "There's blood and it's just . . . oh, it's everywhere. Renee, my poor Renee."

He collapsed to his knees and scrubbed at the imaginary blood. Moira watched, horrified. In his recall of the night he found his sister's body, Jared had made the scene all too real for her. She could almost smell the blood.

What are you staring at him for, fool?

She was out of the bed in a bound and actually found herself stepping around the imaginary pool of blood. She bent to him. "Jared, love, it's a dream."

"Renee. Poor Renee. She fought and he . . . he . . . and I was too late. If I'd gotten home just half an hour earlier . . ."

You'd be dead, too. "Renee's out of her pain, dearest. Come back to bed."

"I can't—bed?"

"You're dreaming, Jared. It's just an awful, awful dream. Renee knows you tried. Renee knows you loved her—love her still. You've given your life up for vengeance, isn't that so?"

"It's . . . yes." Sounding stronger now; the boy's voice was leaving. The man was coming back.

"Lie down with me." She pulled him easily to his feet, although he had twelve inches and fifty pounds on her. She brought him back to bed as she would have led a child. "It's all right."

"No," he said, already slipping back into sleep. "It's never going to be all right."

About that, you may be right.

"Watch out, Moira. They're werewolves. I know it sounds incredible." He yawned, snuggled against her shoulder. "But they're the monsters from the fairy tales. Wyndham and his dogs."

"I know," she said softly. Thinking: *Oh, what will you do when I tell you I'm one of the monsters?*

And why did she care?

She was awakened by a delicious tickling between her breasts, and cracked one eye open to see Jared, nibbling her cleavage. It was still dark out—not even five o'clock in the morning.

"Did your mother wean you a bit too early, Jared?"

He snorted, the sound muffled against her flesh. "Very funny. Let's take a shower. My mouth tastes like a dead rat shat in it."

"Thanks for the visual. You should write for Hallmark—yee-ouch! Well, you should. And why are we getting up?"

He wouldn't look at her. "Can't sleep," he muttered. "Every time I fall all the way under, I—I wake back up. C'mon."

A few minutes later, morning ablutions completed, he was soaping her all over while the scalding shower beat down on them. Moira groaned aloud from the sheer pleasure of it. Her motto had always been, if it doesn't turn your skin bright red, it's not a shower.

They weren't talking about his dream. She wasn't sure he even remembered stumbling around the room, washing his dead sister's blood off his hands. She decided not to bring it up.

"You're probably the smartest woman I've ever met," he informed her out of nowhere, rinsing her breasts off again, then lathering his hands and running them over her slippery flesh. "And definitely the prettiest."

"Where'd *that* come from? And thank you. You're probably right. About the smart thing, I mean."

"And so modest!"

She shrugged under the water. "My whole childhood, I was my mother's doll. Little, blonde, cute. Something to be dressed up and fussed over. All she talked about was my looks. So it was all people talked to her about. I was a smart child, really smart. So *I* talk about *that*. My looks are boring."

"They're certainly not boring, cutie," he said, "but I can see how that would have been a major pain."

"Yes, it was. Sorry to digress into 'poor Moira's poor childhood' silliness." She shrugged, embarrassed. "Also, I think my breasts are clean enough."

"They're filthy," he solemnly informed her. "Really. Yech. I won't rest until I can eat off them."

She felt her lips twitch. "Indeed." His hands felt marvelous on her skin. She enjoyed the sensation for a moment, then went back to his earlier, most interesting comment. "The smartest, huh?" The pack took her brains for granted, and men who didn't know her didn't care that she was smart. She found it refreshing and marvelous to run into someone who noticed her brains, commented, and thought she was just fine. "Really? I mean, you must have known a lot of women." *Given your boudoir skills, I would guess thousands.*

"Mm-hmm," he said carelessly. "You've probably got twenty, thirty I.Q. points on me, easy." He sounded as threatened as if he was telling her she had two, three cup sizes on him, easy.

Opening her eyes wide, she ignored the stinging spray. "And that doesn't bother you?"

"Hell, no." He shrugged, water bouncing off his broad shoulders. "Everybody's good at something."

"Well." She chose her words carefully. This was one of the most interesting conversations she'd had in a while. "I'm definitely book smart. You're more . . . tricky, like. In a lot of ways, that's better than having a head for numbers."

"I know," he said casually.

"Now who's being modest?" She goosed him and he slapped her hand away.

"Careful, I almost maimed you with my incredible reflexes."

"Oh, sure."

His smile faded, and suddenly he looked through her, not at her. Just like that, he was somewhere else. "I was always good at fighting. Busting skulls, that stuff. I got in lots of fights as a kid—I mean, guys were *always* following my sister around, Renee, her name was . . ."

"I know."

He stopped talking. His hands stopped moving on her body. His eyes were narrow, blue slits. "How d'you know?"

"You dreamt about her last night. You were calling her name."

"Oh." She couldn't tell if it was the heat of the water or embarrassment at his vulnerability that made his face redden. "Okay. Say, I didn't hurt you, did I? Sometimes the nightmare . . . it makes me thrash about a bit. Sleepwalk, too."

"No," she lied. Of course she'd had a spectacular black eye during the night. And of course it had healed by morning.

"Oh. That's good." She pumped shampoo into her palm and started washing his hair, running her fingers through the long strands. He arched unconsciously beneath her touch for a moment, then continued. "Anyway, I'd get into fights to keep the boys respectful, you know? And my dad, before he died he signed me up for all these martial arts classes, and boxing, that kind of stuff. To keep me out of trouble—he figured if I was punching people in a class after school, I'd be too tired to get into fights. By the time I graduated high school I could pretty much kick anybody's ass. The Marines really liked having me around."

"I'll bet. That's why you took it upon yourself to find Renee's killer. It was your job to protect her. And when you couldn't, that last time, the least you could do . . ."

"Yeah."

They were silent, and then Jared rinsed his hair and started running his soapy hands down her back, started kneading her buttocks.

Moira thought, his *body* is his weapon. He's been using all those fighting skills to track down his sister's killer like a bloodhound. That's why he got the drop on me so easily. My whole life, I've taken my physical strength for granted. I couldn't do a karate chop if someone held a gun to my head. He's not an intellectual, and he doesn't have circus strongman strength. He's cunning, and quick, and can sneak up on people with no trouble.

He's more like a wolf, she realized with a bolt of excitement, than I am.

Could this man be the one? She would never worry about accidentally hurting Jared; he could take care of himself. Certainly it was no problem if he were to accidentally hurt her . . . she was a fast healer, and pain was, at times, almost a friend to her. Best of all, most wonderful of all, he absolutely didn't care that she was an adding machine on legs. That alone made it worth staying with him.

Her excitement derailed abruptly when she recalled one simple, devastating fact: he had no clue what she was. And once he found out, he would at least walk—run!—out of her life forever. Unless he considered her responsible for his sister's death, too.

How, she wondered forlornly, had the tables turned so quickly? Yesterday she would have seen him dead. Today tears sprang to her eyes at the thought of him leaving.

His hands were still stroking, still soaping, and she could feel his erection against her stomach. He pressed her close to him, holding her tightly.

"Moira, Moira," he whispered, his words almost lost under the thrumming of the shower, "a guy could fall in love. But if you're holding out on me . . ." He came into her, hard, a brutal shove, and she bit back a cry of mingled pain and pleasure. ". . . you'll live to regret it."

She didn't doubt it.

He picked her up, pulled her legs around him, and held her easily, pinning her against the slick tile like a butterfly to a board. He shoved, shoved, shoved, and it hurt, she wasn't ready for him, and she *loved* it, loved being used roughly. Had she really disdained coupling with a human because she thought they were weak? She had thrice his strength but, without leverage, could only take it. Take him. His length filled her up, took her over, he was deep, so deep. He was shoving angrily but his hands were gentle; she had a flash of intuition

(*he's angry because he wants me so badly . . . wants me but doesn't quite trust me*)

and then could only concentrate on what he was doing to her. She squirmed against the tile. "You're hurting me," she whispered.

"I know." He gently tongued her earlobe . . . then bit it.

Now his thrusts came easier because her body was easing his way, was flooding her with wetness. "Damn you," he whispered, his eyes gleaming, "I never wanted this to happen . . . ahhhhhhhhh . . ."

"I'm sorry," she gasped.

"You feel so slick, so sweet. I'm really close. I'm going to come and . . . you're . . . not."

"Don't you dare!" was as far as she got before she could feel him pulsing inside her. Abruptly, he pulled away, leaving her shaking with need.

"Jared . . ."

"What the hell are we going to do, bright eyes?"

"Jared . . ."

"It's a simple question, Moira," he said patiently, giving her nipple an impudent tweak. Oh, how she hated him. "A guy could fall in love, but I've got to keep my priorities straight."

His fingers. His fingers, between her legs, finding her throbbing clit. Stroking it, rubbing it. Even squeezing, very, very gently. Her legs trembled, threatened to spill her to the tile. Her head rolled back and forth against the shower wall. "You're smack in the middle of a mess, gorgeous, and I don't envy you at all. The question is, what are you going to do about it?"

"Please. Please. Please." The word was wrenched out of her, *shoved* out. "Please, Jared. Don't make me beg."

"But, sweetheart," his mouth very near her ear, "you *are* begging."

She moaned, lost. He took pity on her, knelt, gently spread her apart and lapped, lapped, lapped. She came at once, a shallow spasm that did nothing, that left her wanting him inside her, her need for him a bestial craving. "More," she gasped, demanded, urged. Begged.

He wordlessly led her from the shower, both of them dripping wet. Bent her over the tub. Took her again and again, until the room rang with her screams, until her legs wouldn't support her any longer and she collapsed to the floor, still feeling the spasms from her last orgasm.

Without a word, he lifted her to her feet, dried her with a big, fluffy towel, and tucked her into bed as if she were a precious treasure. Left her to nap.

Humans are weak, was her last thought before spinning into sleep. *In a pig's eye.*

Chapter Eight

When she woke, hours later, she was alone in the bed and utterly ravenous. The smell of frying bacon filled the room, filled her head, and she hurriedly pulled on some clothes and flew down the stairs.

She burst into the kitchen just as Jared slid three eggs onto a plate laden with bacon, toast, sliced tomatoes, home fries, and sausage links. "Morning, sunshine. Do you want some—" Snatching the plate away from him, she sat at the table, grabbed a fork, started shoveling. "—breakfast?"

"Nnnnf."

He grinned down at her. "God, you are the perfect woman. Super smart, awesome in bed, and you eat like a lumberjack." He ruffled her curls. "A sexy lumberjack."

"Mmmfff nnnggg mmmm," she said, or something like that. She swallowed. "This is good. Thanks very much. Being hungry does nothing for my manners." Human manners, she amended silently.

"I can't believe you're not throwing food at me." He turned back to the stove. "After this morning."

"Yes, yes, very non-PC, you beast, it's over between us, hate you forever . . . salt?"

He turned, blinked at her, then shook his head and nodded toward the salt shaker.

"What, I have to get up?" she complained. "You're standing right there."

"Cripes, you've got nerve!" He whipped around, exasperated. "You know, technically you're my prisoner. I mean, I *did* kidnap you."

"Yes, and then you lost me." At his scowl, she added, "Plus, you're standing *right there*. Besides, you and I both know you'd eat your own feet before hurting any woman. So spare me the 'you are my prisoner, fear me' crapola. And pass the damned salt! Please."

"I'll do it," he said, smirking, "if you'll show me your tits." He paused, obviously braced for shrieks of feminine dismay at his crude request . . . and nearly fell onto the frying pan as her T-shirt hit him in the face.

"Salt."

"Right." He fetched it for her, gave her left breast a friendly squeeze, and returned to his eggs.

"Thank you. Now there's bacon grease on my nipple."

"I'll take care of that for you," he said, scooping eggs onto another plate. He snapped a glance at her over his shoulder, and winked. "Later." He sat down across from her and fell to.

"Great. You could just pass me a napkin, you know."

"Spoilsport."

They ate in friendly silence, until Jared finally asked, "Do you remember last night?"

"Vividly."

"I mean . . . my dream."

"Yes." She stopped mopping egg yolk with her toast and looked up. "I'm very, very sorry about your sister."

He looked at her thoughtfully. She noticed he hadn't pulled his hair back in a ponytail, and had to keep brushing back the sandy blonde strands, keeping them out of his face. "And afterward. What I said afterward . . . I'm pretty sure I told you they're werewolves. Over at Wyndham's."

"Yes, you did." She answered his unspoken question. "I already knew."

Thunderstruck silence, followed by, "And you *work* for them?"

"They're my family." *Get it? My family? Don't make me say it, Jared. Figure it out.*

He shoved his plate back, stood, started pacing. She unobtrusively pulled his half empty plate toward her. Ah, two pieces of bacon left . . .

"Jesus, if I didn't know for a fact that all werewolves are male, I'd be really worried about—"

"*What?*"

"Don't try to deny it, pretty spy. You know, I had to take a long and very fucking strange road to get to this house, this town, and on the way I met some exceedingly weird people. And heard some strange shit."

"Werewolves are all men." She could barely get the sentence out without giggling. "Who told you that?"

"I paid good money for that information," he said proudly. "And I got it from an honest-to-God werewolf. I watched the beast change . . . into a bigger beast. And when the moon went down and the sun came up, he told me all about werewolves."

All about bullshit, more likely. "How'd you get him to talk?"

"I was resting the barrel of my shotgun against his testicles while we played Twenty Questions."

"Yes, that would do it." *So he'll never guess the truth about me. Not unless I tell him outright, or show him. So: good? Or bad?* Moira practically squirmed at the odd dilemma. Good for Moira-the-werewolf, because her main goal, always, was the pack's safety. Bad for Moira-the-woman, because this put more distance between her and Jared.

And why did she *care*?

He looked nonplussed at the way she hadn't been horrified to hear about the shotgun, and the testicles. That, in fact, she seemed to hardly be paying attention to his revelations. He resumed pacing. "Which is why you shouldn't be working there. What if one of them *bites* you, for Christ's sake? I didn't think to ask if a woman could get infected that way . . ."

"You're worried one of them will bite me?" She kept her voice calm, deliberately reasonable, unworried, in contrast to his violent emotions. His anger, coupled with fear for her, burned her nostrils. He was worried about her. She was annoyed and pleased at the same time.

"You might wind up . . . I don't know . . ."

"I do know. The biting thing is an old wives' tale. You're a werewolf or you're not. It's a whole different species, Jared, not the measles. Not something you catch."

He digested that, and she could practically hear the wheels turning in his mind. Could see the thought on his face: *Why would she lie? No reason, ergo it must be the truth.* She couldn't help but be warmed at this sign of trust between them. Never mind why would she lie . . . why should he believe her? And yet he did.

"A hundred years of bad movies are wrong?"

"Not to mention a thousand years of folklore." Moira suddenly remembered the time she and Derik were kids and had gone to see *An American Werewolf in London.* They had laughed so hard they were kicked out not forty-five minutes into the movie. "The truth is always much more boring than the fable it grew from."

"What if one of them kills you?"

"Never, ever happen."

"Bullshit. Put down that piece of toast, it's mine."

"You left your plate," she protested.

He threw up his hands. "Can we stay on track, please? One of them *has* killed, you don't deny that, right?"

"Right. But tell me why you think Michael knows who killed your sister."

Jared blinked, surprised at the abrupt question, but answered readily enough. "Everything traces back to Wyndham manor, to your boss. Ev-er-ee-thing. The police even had a suspect, but the guy got away clean. He worked there, lived there, probably even had a family there. Then I got close, and he was smoke. Wyndham told the cops he didn't know a thing about it, which was just about the biggest lie since 'this won't hurt a bit.' The suspect worked for Wyndham practically his whole life."

"Was this . . . about a year ago?"

"How'd you know?"

"I'm just trying to figure out the timeline."

"The name I had was Gerald somebody," Jared confirmed.

Oh shit, oh shit, oh shit. She strove to look thoughtful, rather than horrified. This was good news and bad. Good news because Gerald was dead, and thus unlikely to be murdering anyone else's sister now that he was so much meat in the ground. Bad because Jeannie, Michael's wife, had shot Gerald. Multiple times.

Of course Michael had denied knowledge of Gerald's whereabouts. He couldn't very well tell the police the truth: that Gerald was beneath the White Ivy rosebushes on the south lawn and, oh by the way, officers, would you like some tea before you haul my mate away in chains? She's pregnant, so make sure she takes her pre-natal vitamins in prison.

"I think I can help you," Moira said slowly. She had no idea what to do. Tell Jared everything and trust him to keep Wyndham secrets? Ha.

Tell him nothing and neutralize him? Hit him when his guard was down and bite the back of his neck until his strong heart stopped beating and his gorgeous eyes closed forever?

I've got a crush on the idiot.

Moira knew her limitations. She was intelligent—okay, *that* wasn't a limitation—but numbers were her game. She had no gift for leadership or strategy. That was Michael's job. She was a foot soldier, plain and simple.

Jared needed to hear about Gerald, but not from her. From

Michael and Jeannie, and no one else. Would Jared follow her to Wyndham Manor, unquestioning? Just trot right on over to what he assumed was the belly of the beast?

Ha.

"There's something on the back of your neck," she said sweetly.

"What?" He brought his hand up, brushed ineffectually. She put her hand on his shoulder, gently turned him around, and punched him at the base of his skull with her knuckle. Jared obligingly dropped without a sound, and she caught him on the way down.

I'm going to hear about this one for a while, she thought grimly, slinging him over her shoulder like a sack of toys.

Chapter Nine

He opened his eyes and saw he was surrounded by monsters, in a living room or den of some sort. Michael Wyndham, Moira, and Wyndham's hottie wife, Jeannie, were all bending over him, their faces like concerned moons. He was lying on a couch, and could hear the cheerful crackle of a fire nearby.

"You . . . bitch!" He sat bolt upright, then clutched the back of his neck, which was incredibly stiff. "Aarrgghh! What'd you hit me with, a piano?"

"I'm sorry, Jared." Moira-the-Judas had the nerve to look abashed. She blinked her big purple eyes at him and spread her hands helplessly. "I had to bring you here—we have things to tell you—but I didn't think you'd come if I asked."

"So you coshed me over the head with an iron and kidnapped me?" His hand slid down and around, but his holster was empty.

"Don't get too far up on that high horse of yours," Jeannie Wyndham said dryly. "You did the same thing to my friend yesterday." She waved his gun at him. Jared felt alternately nervous and aroused to see such a pretty woman handling his weapon so comfortably. "My *best* friend. And since you kidnapped my friend and are here in town solely to hurt my husband, you look stupid trying to sound outraged."

"Jeannie," Michael said quietly.

"Well, he does."

"Give him back his gun, please."

"Speaking of stupid." Despite her comment, she popped the clip, ratcheted a bullet out of the chamber, and gave him back all three, absently puffing a hank of blonde hair out of her eyes as she did so. He was so surprised he nearly dropped them on the floor.

"Will you listen?" Wyndham asked quietly. The guy had funny eyes—dark brown, ringed with yellow, dog's eyes, monster's eyes—but his voice was deep and soothing. Too soothing. Jared knew there were people in the world who could make you like them. It was a talent, like being able to raise only one eyebrow. Even knowing all he did about Wyndham, Jared still wanted to shake the guy's hand and hear what he had to say. Watch it, he warned himself. "Mister—ah—Moira?"

Moira cleared her throat. "Sorry. We should have done this right away. Jeannie and Michael Wyndham, this is Jared ... uh ..." She flushed. "I never did get your last name."

"And after all we shared," he said mockingly, and was gratified to see her blush deepen.

"Knock it off," Jeannie snapped. "You're still on my shit list, buddy-roo. I don't know *why* we're all tip-toeing around you. As far as I'm concerned, you're the bad guy." She smirked at him. "And you know what happens to the bad guy in books and movies, right, Jerked?"

"It's Jared," he said, and to his surprise he had to fight a smile. "Jared Rocke."

Jeannie's eyes widened. "Rocke? Your last name is Rocke? Oh my God, that's the silliest name ever."

Wyndham was looking heavenward, as if for divine intervention. "Jeannie . . ."

"Seriously. It's like a bad romance novel. 'Jared Rocke brooded darkly before sweeping Shanna Silverington into his strong, rugged embrace.' Barf. What's your nickname? Rocky? Rocco? Double barf."

Incredibly, Jared could feel himself relaxing. He sensed no menace from any of the three—of course, he hadn't sensed menace from Moira before she'd bashed him with a serving tray, either. Still, Moira was so contrite, and Wyndham so polite, and Mrs. Wyndham so refreshingly rude, it was hard to stay tense. And what the hell did *that* mean? That Moira was right? The monsters weren't all bad?

He coughed to cover his confusion. "My nickname in second grade was Jared Poopypants, for an incident I refuse to go into, no matter how long you and your husband torture me. Creditors call me Mr. Rocke. My friends call me Jared. I don't know what you guys are," he added truthfully.

"Let's find out," Michael said genially. "Something to drink, Mr. Rocke?"

"Barf," Jeannie said again, but went to the wet bar.

"Yeah, I'd love a beer," he admitted. "And a bottle of aspirin."

Wordlessly Moira stepped behind him, and then he felt her kneading his neck with her small, supple fingers. By the time Jeannie handed him an ice-cold, foamy beer, his neck felt much better. "I'm still pissed at you," he muttered.

She bent to whisper in his ear. "I know. You can take it out on me later. At the house. In your room." Her mouth was hovering outside the cup of his ear and his dick was paying close attention to the conversation. "Do you know any rope tricks?"

". . . your sister."

"Mr. Rocke?"

"Jared," he said automatically, trying to shake off the surge of excitement Moira's words had brought. Talk about the wrong place and time! "It's Jared."

"Thank you. I'm Michael, and you've met my wife, Jeannie. I was saying how sorry I was to hear about your sister."

"You'll be even sorrier when you hear the stuff I've been able to dig up."

Michael sat across from him holding a tumbler half full of Scotch. Moira declined a drink, staying behind Jared and gently rubbing his neck, and Jeannie sat next to her husband with a glass full of milk. At Jared's stare, she mumbled, "Still breastfeeding."

For some reason that made him laugh out loud. It seemed to emphasize the wholesome attributes of the room they were in, the pleasant people he was talking to. Death had no place here . . . not where women breastfed well-loved babies and potential girlfriends promised bondage games.

"I guess Moira can tell you what's been going on as well as I can," he said, because he wanted to hear what Moira had to say about the situation.

She ruffled his hair in response and started to speak. She spoke for quite a while, finishing with, ". . . and Jared's been tracking the killer. I think—I'm sure—it's Gerald."

Wyndham and his wife looked at each other. Jared was still trying to figure out why he hadn't loaded his gun and killed everyone. Except Moira. Probably except Moira—he still couldn't believe she'd gotten the drop on him so easily. He couldn't believe he was still thinking about the clothesline coiled neatly in the garage! 'Rope tricks,' she'd said. Jesus.

The woman—Jeannie—had thrown him off-guard, that was why he was off his stride. She was about as adorable as Moira, and what a temper! She hung around werewolves all day—was married to one!— and hadn't been killed or mutilated or anything like that.

It was sure something to think about.

Then there was his pretty, purple-eyed Moira. She was hiding stuff from him, but he was seeing it less as duplicity and more as loyalty. There was nothing he admired more than loyalty . . . hell, loyalty to his family had brought him here. It was all pretty damned confusing. He hadn't counted on it becoming confusing. It had seemed pretty fucking black and white just a few days ago.

"Gerald probably did kill your sister—and I'm very sorry," Michael said.

"Really really sorry, Rococo," Jeannie added. "I don't know what I'd do if something horrible happened to Michael or Lara."

Sympathy from the dogs—well, the dog and his wife—he hadn't expected. He had to look away from the genuine kindness on their faces. Liking the dogs was not in the plan. No, sir.

"I only met the man twice . . . and the second time I killed him," Jeannie added candidly. Jared looked back in a hurry.

"Jeannie . . ."

"Michael, we've got to tell him." She took a big slug of her drink, and went on passionately, unaware of her milk mustache. If I go to jail, I go to jail . . . but I don't think Jared's the type to rat out the killer of a killer."

"No, ma'am, I am not. Why don't you tell me what happened."

"Yes, why don't I? Okay. Gerald was this disgusting horrible werewolf—and no, that's not redundant, so don't say it. Although it's an opinion I had myself not too long ago," she added, giving her husband a formidable frown. "Anyway. This jerkoff was a wife beater, a puppy kicker, a daughter smacker. And he got the idea in his head that his wife was giving him too many girl babies . . . he really wanted a son. Never mind biology and X chromosomes and that any idiot knows that sperm dictates the baby's sex . . ."

"Honey . . ."

"Right, right, I'm staying focused. I *am*. Anyway. He kills his wife—nice, huh? And my husband decided the guy's ass was grass, except Gerald's daughters—he had three—intervened on their dad's behalf. Begged for his life. So Michael felt sorry for the girls and banished Gerald from the pack. So he went away and did whatever rogue werewolves do.

"Then, when I got pregnant and turned up here, Gerald snuck back to town and tried to kidnap me. He got onto the grounds during a full moon and hurt a lot of people, so I shot him. The end."

"And when was this?"

"Almost a year ago."

Jared shook his head. "That's not right. There have been six or seven murders since then. Same M.O. I've been researching every murder that matched my sister's."

Moira turned to him, surprised. "A serial killer? I thought you were focused on your sister."

"I started out focused on one death. Then, when I started digging, I realized there was a lot more going on."

"All the murders happening during a full moon," Michael said.

"Yes. That's how I knew it was one of you . . ." Freaks? Monsters? Degenerate killers? ". . . people."

Michael let that pass. "And do the victims all look alike?"

Wyndham, Jared realized with growing excitement, knew something. "Yes. They're all between five foot two and five foot four. They've all got long dark hair parted on the left, and blue eyes. Very pale skin." Jared watched Moira's eyes widen with understanding. "What is it, babe?"

"You've just described Gerald's late wife," she said, almost gasped. "That's exactly what she looked like!"

"But Gerald's dead," Jeannie protested. "Nobody's got any reason to kill women who look like his wife."

"Are you sure he's dead? I mean . . . he's a werewolf."

"Yeah, that's right," Jeannie replied, nodding. "A werewolf. Not a living god."

Michael coughed modestly. "Well . . ."

"Shut up, honey. Werewolves are perfectly mortal. I put multiple bullets in Gerald's head. He's deader than the dodo bird, trust me, Rocky."

"Well, his daughters aren't," Moira said quietly. "Maybe we should go have a talk with them. Don't they still live around here?" Then she froze. Everything within her locked for a long moment; shock had rendered her incapable of moving, even blinking.

"Moira . . . Moira!" Jared shook her arm lightly. "What is it? What's the matter?"

She gulped. Looked at Jared, then at Michael. "Geraldine," she said hoarsely. "Geraldine killed Jared's sister. Geraldine killed them all."

Uproar. But Jared said nothing. Just kept his gaze on Moira while she continued. "Remember, Michael? She was here early this week. Passing through town, she said. She's a loner, a drifter . . . Geraldine—"

"Geraldine, named for her father," Michael said with deadly quiet. "Geraldine, the eldest. The son Gerald wanted more than he wanted anything. How long did he pour poison in her ears, I wonder? How long has she been killing her mother over and over again, to appease her father, himself a year in his grave? If we can track her movements . . . match them to the deaths . . ."

"Oh, she can't!" Jeannie protested. "You guys are wrong. And it's *not* me being humanly naïve, it's not. You're wrong, is all . . . it's not Geraldine. She was *in this house*. She played with my daughter, for God's sake. She's the sweetest thing, even nicer than Moira."

Moira, who knew herself to be far from nice, just shook her head numbly. And Michael, who'd seen Moira tear apart two armed men once upon a time, simply said, "Gerald did not kill those women. Geraldine did. And you know it, Jeannie . . . just give it a minute."

"No," she said stubbornly, but a species of frightened doubt drifted across her face. "She didn't do this. I've had her in my home, and she didn't do this thing."

"That may be true, ma'am," Jared said politely, but he was standing up, "but appearances can be deceiving. As everyone in this room probably knows. I'm going to go check it out. Bye."

"Not by yourself, you're not," Moira said, and was on her feet and after him in an instant.

"Indeed," Michael said. *He* was on *his* feet.

Jared spun. "No way. This isn't yours."

Michael and Jared were now chest to chest, and Moira saw with dismay that her leader's shoulders were up and he was leaning far forward, almost looming over Jared, although the men were close in height. The classic stance of a werewolf defending his territory. "You're wrong about that, Jared. In fact, the plain truth is, this isn't *yours*."

"Tell that to my sister. Where were *you* when one of your damned out-of-control dogs was ripping my sister in two?"

Moira winced.

Michael's eyes—a weird gold color—went even more yellow. His mouth thinned and turned down in a sorrowful bow. "Exactly. That's why this—this ungodly mess is mine. For your sister. For all the other sisters. I was asleep at the switch. Now I have to fix it."

"Um, hello?" Jeannie tapped Michael on the shoulder. "Any reason you both can't go? I mean, don't get me wrong, all this chest-beating and me-boss batcrap is enthralling, really, but don't we have a murderer to catch?"

Michael unhunched. Jared turned to look at Mrs. Wyndham, who stared back with raised eyebrows. "She's right," he said after a long moment. Moira sighed with relief.

"She often is," Michael said fondly. "What a pity it appears to go straight to her head."

"What a pity you're going to bed with a fractured skull, pal." But Jeannie smiled as she said it, and the tension in the room ratcheted down several notches.

Chapter Ten

Who would go and who would stay turned out to be a moot point as Geraldine had a job. "Which I s'pose we should have thought of," Jeannie commented.

Interestingly, Geraldine was a cemetery caretaker. According to her supervisor, the job was seasonal and Geraldine attended to it when she was in town. "Sure I gave her the job," he replied to Michael's questions. "Felt sorry for her. Nasty business with her dad, eh?"

By necessity, Geraldine's hours were flexible. As she could be at work or at home, the two couples split up. Michael declined to let the rest of the family in on the problem, preferring instead to leave Lara in the pack's protection.

"If we can't handle this ourselves," he explained, "we deserve to get eaten. And if we *do* get eaten, I want to know Lara's safe."

"Yuck-o," was Jeannie's only comment.

Based on what the cemetery supervisor had said, the group felt sure Geraldine was most likely to be at work, so Michael and Jeannie took that address. On that issue, Michael would not budge.

"Arrogant asshole," Jared growled, jerking the car into reverse and squealing down the cemetery entrance—backward.

"Yes."

"Pushes people around all damn day."

"Yes."

"Wife seems nice, though. In a scary kind of way."

"She's beyond marvelous."

He grunted. "How come you didn't mention it?" He brought the car around. Tires squealed. Gravel flew.

Moira, nigh-invulnerable werewolf, tightened her seatbelt. "What?"

"No. I mean, how come you didn't tap me on *my* shoulder like Mrs. Wyndham tapped Mikie? And suggest we both go find Geraldine? I mean, you're super-smart. You must have figured it out. After all," he added with a grin, "you weren't suffering from testosterone overload like me and Michael."

Shocked, Moira replied, "That wouldn't have been my place." A beta female, thrusting herself between two alphas squaring off? Moira's mama didn't raise no fools. "Besides, I figured out who murdered your sister. What . . . did I not reach high enough for you? Are you implying I'm an underachiever?"

He had the grace to look abashed, and quickly changed the subject. "Listen, when we get there—"

"I am *not* staying in the car."

"Yes, you are. I'm not having anything happen to you, too."

Touched by his concern, it was a long moment before she could speak. When she did, she told him a bald truth: "I'm not having anything happen to you, either."

He smiled at her. "Guess we're fucked, then."

"Guess we are." As far as romantic declarations of love went, this one left much to be desired. *So how come you can't stop grinning, you twit?*

Jared pulled into Geraldine's driveway sedately enough, and Moira noticed he had a pleasant look on his face. "That's right, Geraldine, nothin' to worry about out here," he muttered, still smiling inanely as he shut off the engine. "Just a fella who wants to ask you a couple of questions . . . nothin' to get excited about . . ."

"Jared, really." Moira didn't try to hide her exasperation. "Now I'm definitely not staying in the car. You need me for this. You've got this silly idea in your head that because the full moon isn't until tomorrow night, Geraldine is harmless. I can assure you that's not the case. Soothing words and silly grins aren't going to put her at ease. She's going to know what you want the minute she gets close enough to smell you."

He had been nodding politely during her lecture, but now smirked. "And me without my Old Spice. C'mere, sugar."

What on earth was wrong with the man? she thought before he grabbed her and pulled her close. She would have imagined he'd be a bundle of nerves, this close to confronting his sister's killer—

Probable killer, her ever-logical mind interjected.

—but he practically whistled in contentment.

"Listen, weirdo," was as far as she got before his tongue plunged into her mouth. With anyone else this kiss would have been an alarming development. Since the tongue belonged to Jared, it was actually a quite enjoyable development. Yes, indeed. Most pleasant. Especially the way his lips were so soft, the way he kissed and licked and nibbled and—

CLICK.

—handcuffed her to the steering wheel.

Moira sat stock-still for a thunderstruck moment. Then, heedless of the lurking Geraldine and the quiet neighborhood, she shrieked. "What did you *do?*"

"Uh. Moira. Not so loud." He rubbed his ear. "I don't have to answer that question, do I? It's—what d'you call it—rhetorical."

She tugged experimentally. She couldn't get over the fact that he'd ruthlessly distracted her and then shackled her like a dog.

When she spoke, her voice was quite calm, but Jared looked at her warily anyway. "You carry handcuffs in your car?"

"Hey, I was a Boy Scout before I was a Marine."

"Boy Scouts carry handcuffs?"

"Okay, well, I'm out of here." And he was . . . he was opening the car, getting out, standing up. "Sorry, honey. But no way are you going anywhere near that killer. Not while I'm still breathing."

"Something which can be rectified!" she shouted. He winced and shut the car door. "And I'm a killer, too, you moron!"

He snorted, then turned and started for the house.

Moira fumed inside the car. Oh, it would serve him right if she stayed docilely put while Geraldine cuisinarted his entrails. For two cents, she'd do it.

Yeah, right.

"Lord, love has made me a fool," she mumbled aloud. Inwardly, she added, *I have fallen in love at last. With a man who has spent his entire adult life hunting my kind.* She normally got quite a kick out of irony. Not today.

She gave the handcuffs a hard yank. Metal groaned, but didn't break. She pulled again, and slipped her hand out of the now too-wide handcuff loop, then smacked it irritably, watching the cuffs swing from the steering wheel.

Well, that was that. No way would Jared be able to overlook that little feat of superhuman strength. One way or another, this would all be over tonight.

One way or another, this would all be over tonight. Jared expected to feel hot exultation, but instead only felt relief. Relief, and the hope that there could be a future with Moira after this was behind them. Assuming she would speak to him ever again.

Well, he didn't care if she gave him the silent treatment for a damn year, if she was safe. *Ten* years. He'd take furious over dead any day.

Jared paused on the porch, unsure what to do next. Ring the door-bell, he supposed, and look into the woman's—Geraldine's—eyes and see if he could find murder there. He hadn't counted on the dog being a woman. He hadn't counted on a lot of things when he started this strange journey.

He heard a light thump behind him and turned just in time to see Moira's sneakered foot slip up and out of sight as she pulled herself up on the porch roof.

He ground his teeth. Christ, the woman was a damn monkey! He should have known someone that smart would have learned how to pick a lock . . . probably kept the picks in her hair as barrettes or whatever. Now she was on the roof, probably finding an open window . . . aarrgh!

He raised a fist to pound on the front door when it suddenly jerked open, hard enough to blow strands of his hair back from his face.

An enormously tall woman stood before him, grinning. Her hair was the color of damp dirt, as were her eyes. She had incredibly white teeth, which made her smile hard to bear. Quite thin, her collarbones stood out clearly against the yellow T-shirt she wore, a color which accentuated her sallow complexion. She wore faded jeans with old stains on the thighs and knees—mud? Blood? She was barefoot and he saw her toenails were long enough to curl over the tops of her toes. He wondered in a distant part of his mind if she clicked when she walked on a wooden floor.

She looked cruel and hard, so he was unprepared for her soft, sweet, lilting voice: "Hello. Can I help you?"

He stared at her. His back itched where his gun was pressing against his flesh. "Uh . . . yeah. My name is Jared Rocke. Uh—" Why have you been killing women who look like your mama? How have you been able to fool the Wyndhams for so long? Are you aware you're the most frightening thing I've ever seen, and I used to live in Miami? "You're Geraldine Cassick, right?"

"Yes, of course." The woman's smile widened, if that was possible. Jared nearly shuddered. He had no idea how this woman had been passing herself off as human for so long. "Rocke. How's your dead sister? By the way, your cunt of a girlfriend isn't fooling anybody."

At "your dead" he reached for his gun. At "by the way" she slapped it out of his hand so quickly he didn't see her move, and didn't realize she'd cut him with her nails until later. At "isn't fooling" she seized his shirt collar and yanked him inside her house, shoving him hard enough to send him sliding across the hardwood floor, where he fetched up against the wall with a sickening thud. For a half second he thought the top of his head had fallen off. White stars exploded before his eyes.

"Now I'm *really* gonna kick your ass," he groaned, hoping his vision would clear soon.

"I'm terrified," she said in her weirdly cute, feminine voice. Her dad must have hated that voice, he thought dazedly, especially when he wanted a boy so bad. "Actually, I'm relieved. I can get rid of you and get back to business. I did *not* like having you sniffing up my backtrail, Roque."

"It's Rocke. You were waiting for me."

"Of course I was!" she said. She crossed the room with terrifying swiftness and squatted down to look at him. He could see two—no, three—of her heads, floating around him in a shaky semicircle. Her six eyes were gleaming, fanatical. "Where better than to hang out and wait for you than here, where Michael-king-shit-werewolf and his monkey bitch live? My home, where I know everyone and they know me and oh, isn't it terrible about my dad, but *you're* all right, Geraldine, you poor, poor thing."

Jared shook his head, desperate to clear it. Ten seconds ago he'd been standing on her porch. "Just in case I hadn't already figured you were off your fucking rocker," he informed her in a croak, "I think I've got it now."

She ignored him. "Except, Jared, you were *supposed* to kill *them*." Geraldine's tone became sweetly reproachful. "You were supposed to come to me *first*, because you figured my father had been doing the killings, and I would have told you the killer was *Michael*! But you—did—it—all—backwards." Each word was punctuated by a brisk, hard shake.

"It wouldn't have worked, nutjob," he managed, fighting to loose himself from her grip. Cripes, she was barely holding him, but her fingers felt like steel. He smashed his palm into the underside of her jaw, but her head barely moved. "You shouldn't have framed a dead man, Geraldine. That's where you took a wrong turn."

"I'm going to kill that half-breed cow you've been fucking," she informed him with conspirational tenderness. "I can smell her all over you. She actually let you touch her? Let a nasty, smelly, monkey *touch* her?"

He tried to bring a knee up, hard, into her belly, but she shifted easily. She started choking him, throttling him almost absent-mindedly while banging his head against the floor. "Mm—not—smelly—" was what he managed before things started to go dark around the edges.

Suddenly her grip relaxed, and he sucked in painful breaths. Geraldine's face was, as if by magic, slashed in four long streaks, bleeding. So much blood, it rained into his face, spattered his shirt.

"Half-breed is all right," Moira said, and he realized she was directly above them. Geraldine whined, clutched her face and scuttled back, blood pouring through her long-nailed fingers, pattering to the floor. "It's tactless, but accurate. Calling me a plump herbivore is not. Also," she added, glancing down at him, "I'm not speaking to you. But I *will* save your ass."

"—get—out—of—here—"

"Oh, shut up. And you," she said to Geraldine, stalking toward her, "are a nasty, smelly, wretched creature. Look at you. You look like you're going to Change any second. Feeling the stress of the coming full moon, Geraldine? How rude of you to show it."

"You're surprised by how I look," Geraldine hissed back, flipping to her feet. "That's because you never saw me. No one has ever! Seen! Me! Not your precious Michael or his bitch-dog or Derik or Mother or—my—my—"

"I don't care, Geraldine. It's too bad you had an unendurable childhood, but what gives you the right to kill? Worse, kill helpless humans? Nothing. Those women did nothing to you."

Jared watched the two women circle each other. They moved strangely—more like big cats than an accountant and a cemetery caretaker. He rubbed his eyes and looked again. Everything hurt, his throat was on fire and he was seeing two Moiras and two Geraldines, but he still couldn't look away. He noticed they were very careful about where they put their feet. It was almost like a dance or ritual—something very old, something stylized.

"No," Moira was saying, "those poor women did absolutely nothing to deserve their fate."

"They did! They—"

Moira went on, implacable. Her voice rang with truth and scorn. "You've shamed us all. You're crazy, but part of you knows. Part of you *knows* everything you are is wrong, and everything you've done.

Your father—Gerald—was the worst creature I've ever known. But that doesn't excuse *you*."

"Don't you talk about my father. You're not fit for him to piss on."

Moira shook her head. Her outrage had fled; now she just looked terribly tired. "You fooled us for a long time. But it's over now. You're not killing anyone tonight."

"Wrong, half-breed." Geraldine leapt. Moira dodged, pivoted quicker than thought, and sent her small foot into Geraldine's side. Jared's eyes widened; the 'crack' was very loud. Amazing! In between collecting college degrees for the hell of it and running the Wyndham finances, his Moira had apparently found time to get a black belt in karate.

Incredibly, Geraldine ignored the pain of broken ribs. He couldn't believe it, but she was still moving, and moving quickly—she spun and regained her center as rapidly as an adder. Too quickly for him to follow, both women were literally at each other's throats, locked in a brutal battle.

He tried to get up. He tried. And again. But . . . too hard, everything hurt, his head was spinning, everything was so fast, how did Moira adjust to things happening so fast? It was almost as if she, too, possessed that same inhuman speed and agility, as if his Moira was one of the . . .

Geraldine howled and all the hairs on the back of Jared's neck came to rigid attention. It was every bad or frightening sound he had ever heard, times ten. Everything that was in him wanted to run from the sound, get the hell out and never, never come back. The part of his brain devoted 100 percent to survival was wide awake and screaming at him to leave.

As if in response to the unearthly noise, Moira had made a final, desperate leap, and now she was—God, was she biting Geraldine? Her teeth were fastened at the juncture between Geraldine's neck and shoulder. The killer shrieked again and drove an elbow back into Moira's stomach. Moira grunted and held on. Geraldine's fist came up in a blur and then Moira was tumbling away. Geraldine pounced, quick as a cat.

Jared crawled toward them. He had no idea why. He sure as shit couldn't help Moira in his condition. But somehow he was on his knees and he crawled, crawled. He saw Moira's hand come up, try to shove Geraldine away. Saw her claw for Geraldine's eyes. He crawled faster.

He wouldn't let this bitch kill another woman he loved.

He groped for his pants leg, for the small pistol in the ankle holster. Geraldine hadn't known about it, or hadn't cared. It was practically a toy, anyway. A one-shot Derringer. His Marine buddies would laugh themselves into hernias if they saw him with it.

He stopped crawling. He heard another wet snap and didn't know whose bone had broken. Moira was kicking Geraldine away, turning, trying to get distance. Geraldine was giggling through a mouthful of blood. Jared found the pistol . . . and dropped it right out of his bloody grip.

"Geraldine," he croaked, "your daddy died screaming."

That got her attention; she snapped her head around so fast he practically heard it. Her eyes were huge; the irises looked like gold-flecked mud. "What? What did you say, monkey?"

"Which word didn't you understand, cow, goat, uh—mammal with extra stomachs?"

"Ruminator," Moira suggested faintly, trying to get to her feet and failing. He could see the bulge in her left leg, below her kneecap. He'd heard her bone break.

The monster would pay for that. "Ruminator, thanks, babe. Oh, Geraldine?" Groping, groping. Got it. Hang on. "After Moira and I settle your hash, we're gonna find your dad's grave and fuck right on top of it." Hang on. "That's not gonna be a problem, is—uurrggh!"

Geraldine had jumped high in the air—impossibly high, his rational mind had trouble believing this wasn't a fantastic illusion—and landed squarely on top of him. That was fine. That was perfect. "Bite me, dog," he growled. "Let's see those pearly whites."

Her head swooped toward his, ready to tear out his throat. *For my sister. For my love.* He could smell Geraldine's breath: rank, meaty. *This is the last thing my sister saw. Oh, God, help me now.* He brought the Derringer up, jammed it into her mouth so hard he felt teeth break. Had time to register the killer's almost comical look of surprise before he pulled the trigger and blew the back of her head off.

Geraldine fell forward, onto him. He screamed, in horror and despair and rage for the dead. "Moira!" he roared.

Somehow, Moira heaved the corpse off him. And that's about when everything went black.

Chapter Eleven

Jared opened his eyes, and Moira shrieked.

"Owwwww!"

"I'm sorry," she said at once. He could see she was quite pale. Her eyes dominated her face and their color was deep, nearly purple, startling and mesmerizing at once. "I'm just really, really happy you're awake."

"Amen, sister." He started to sit up, hardly able to take his eyes off her, then just as quickly gave up and flopped back onto the bed. "Argh, even my hair hurts. Is it dead?"

"Yes."

"Where am I?"

"Wyndham Manor. Also known as Dogs R Us."

"Funny girl." Jared glanced around the lush bedroom, which was roughly the size of his last apartment. Sunlight streamed through the west window. It was late, then. They'd gone to Geraldine's before lunch. "Geraldine. God, what a mess."

"That," Moira said tartly, "is an understatement. FYI, none of the others can face you right now. They're so embarrassed they didn't see this before. Years ago."

"They shouldn't be." Jared paused. Yes, he had really said that. Weirder, he'd meant it. Blaming the dogs—err, Moira's employers— had become habit. Bitter, but comforting in its familiarity.

But ten minutes with Geraldine had changed his mind about a lot of things. She'd been so fast, so ruthless. So inhuman and, at the same time, heartbreakingly victimized. "You guys thought you solved the problem when Gerald was killed. Who could blame you? You wanted the nightmare to be over. I don't think there's blame in that."

"Ha!" Moira's tone was bitter, and Jared could see she would be blaming herself for a long time. She, who prided herself on her fine intelligence, hadn't noticed the killer living four miles from her bedroom. A difficult pill to swallow. He doubted Moira would do so gracefully.

He almost smiled. Christ, he adored her. She could have been killed—they both could have—but she never quit. She looked as innocent and delicate as a Hummel figurine, but had the temper of a wolverine and the tenaciousness of a pit bull. With rabies.

His thoughts derailed in sudden confusion. Geraldine was dead. His sister was avenged. Now what? Settle down with Moira? His life had been about vengeance since . . . well, since forever. Would there now be room for other things? Was it possible? The idea was as wonderful as it was terrifying. Vengeance was a cold blanket, but he'd been able to wrap himself in it for years. Was there room now for more?

"I just don't understand how she held together so *long*," Moira muttered. She made a small fist and thumped her leg in agitation.

"I don't know how werewolves blend in with *any* humans," he said frankly.

Moira shook her head. "It's necessary. It's a skill learned early. What you saw—that wouldn't have fooled anyone. I think Geraldine was tired. She was tired, she wanted to be done. She quit holding herself together and stayed in her little house and waited for it to be over."

Jared thought back to the look on Geraldine's face when he shot her. Surprise, and . . . relief?

He would have bet his gun collection on it.

"By the way," the love of his life interrupted his thoughts with heavy sarcasm, "Mister-I-can-take-on-a-werewolf-in-her-prime-so-stay-in-the-car-Moira, you're not moving from that bed for a week. Among other things, you've got a nasty concussion and cracked ribs."

"I've got . . ." Memory returned; he lunged forward. "How's your leg?"

"Lie back down." She gently pushed him back against the pillows. "My leg?"

"It broke. I heard it break. Maybe we should take you to the hospital. Has Wyndham called a doctor?"

"Wyndham set it for me. You know, it wouldn't hurt you to call him Michael. Stop trying to get up." She sat down in the chair next to the bed, and propped her leg up on the mattress. The swelling was nasty, but Jared couldn't see the lump of broken bone any longer. Her leg was tightly wrapped in elastic. Not plaster.

"Huh. I guess it didn't break."

"Jared."

"Lucky for you, sugar, because that could have been nasty."

"Jared."

"And by the way, you must have had some kind of adrenaline rush in that hell house. You were tossing Geraldine around like she was made of paper. It was like watching the Hulk. A short blonde Hulk."

"*Jared.*"

"And I'm not staying here, cutie. Not even for you." He tossed the blankets back. "This place creeps me right the hell out. I'm heading back to my place, and I'd love it if you came with me. In fact, I insist on it. I need a sexy nurse to take care of me."

She was staring at him. Why was she looking at him so strangely? Part of him knew, part of him was pulling back the veil so he could see. He willed the understanding away. "Moira? Come on, let's book. What do you say, babe?"

"I can't do that."

"Sure, it's easy. We'll scoot down to the truck, hop in, make a quick stop at the Colonel's—I'd kill another werewolf just for some fried chicken—"

"*I'm* a werewolf."

He didn't blink. "No."

Her eyes widened. For a minute he thought she was going to fall out of the chair. She'd clearly been braced for any reaction except calm denial. "Yes, I *am*. I'm a werewolf. Tonight when the moon rises I'll be hairier than the drain in the locker room at the YMCA."

He calmly folded his arms across his chest. "No."

She leapt to her feet. Her cheeks were flushed, her forehead burning like a lamp. "Jared, stop it! You know I am, you *must* know. I'm a werewolf."

He shouted, although it hurt his head like hell. "I'm not having this discussion, no way, uh-uh, count me out, folks." Of course she wasn't. It was impossible. They were the monsters. She was Moira. *Ergo*, nuh-uh, not happening, no way.

She bellowed so loud he feared for the mirror across the room. **"I'm a werewolf!"**

No slouch in the vocals department, he roared back, "The hell you are!"

Moira's temper snapped. "Of course I am, you idiot! *Adrenaline rush?* Come on!"

"Science is on my side."

"Bullshit is on your side. You would have seen it before now, if you'd allowed yourself."

"You are *not*," he repeated stubbornly.

"I am, so, a werewolf."

"You're just saying that so I don't think they're all scum. Which, by the way, they are."

"They aren't, and I am one."

"No, you're not."

"*How can you say that*? You can only fool yourself for so long."

"Because I can't care about one!" he roared. "That's absolutely impossible and *not in the plan!* You're not you're not *YOU ARE NOT*! You leap around like a monkey because you've got a gymnastics background, you heal quickly because—I dunno, you've got a super immune system—you don't get tired but big deal, one of my buddies can go for three days without sleep, he does it all the time and it never bothers him except he gets really bad breath from drinking all that Mountain Dew . . . people are different."

She was holding her head in her hands. "Oh, my God. You're a moron."

"I mean, don't get me wrong." He could hear himself talking fast and faster, almost babbling, but it was impossible to stop. "You're definitely weird. I'll give you that. But the stuff you can do, it's all within the realms of good old *homo sapiens*."

"So I'm a liar? Or just crazy?"

He had no answer for that one. After a long pause, he said, "I don't know. Maybe after working for werewolves all this time you think you're . . . I don't know. I'm not the brains of this team."

"You got that right," she muttered.

"I just know you're not one of *them*. You're not. I won't believe it." And you can't make me, he added silently, stubbornly.

"Why?"

Because she had nothing, not one fucking thing, in common with Geraldine. Because he wanted to marry her and have kids with her and his kids weren't going to be fuzzy. Because his sister's killer was dead and he wanted to finally build a life without grief. Because.

"I just won't."

"You said you couldn't care about a werewolf," she said slowly, and now she stood, and walked to the door (*without a limp*, his mind pointed out treacherously) and turned. Her eyes shone with unshed tears. "I take that to mean you think you care about me."

"Yes." He paused. "I'm sorry. I had about a thousand nicer ways planned to tell you. I didn't mean to just blurt it out in mid-yell. I do care, Moira. From the minute you hightailed it down the road dressed in my shower curtain, I never wanted anything bad to happen to you, ever."

She winced away from him, as if his words hurt her. "You care about a lie then, Jared. There's no shame in not knowing things. But I won't be with someone who puts on blinders on purpose. And won't take them off, no matter what he hears and what he sees." She wrenched open the door and fled.

"Moira, don't go!" He slapped his hands over his eyes and writhed in agony. "Oh, God, my head . . . fuck."

The door slammed open, hard enough to crash against the wall and stick as the doorknob was imbedded in the wood.

A large, blonde man filled the doorway. *Filled.* His hair was the color of the sun, cut brutally short. His eyes were a deep, mesmerizing green. He was broad-shouldered and the T-shirt he wore did nothing to hide his excellent muscle definition. Given the man's ridiculously good looks and powerful build, Jared assumed he was dealing with a Wyndham werewolf.

"I'm going to shove your head so far up your ass," the man said with ominous calm, "that you'll be able to kiss your own colon."

"Go chase a mail truck," Jared snapped. "I've got bigger problems than whatever bit you on the ass today."

The man blinked. Held up one finger. Paused. Turned. Left. Jared heard a muffled sound from the hall—a snort? A chuckle? Then the stranger returned, looking stormier than ever. "You blew it, Monkey-boy."

"It's Rocke."

"Moira hasn't given a guy so much as a come-hither look in years, and you had her. She was yours, all you had to do was ask! She saves your life, helps you avenge your sister, then finally screws up her courage and tells your bigoted sorry ass the truth, and you rejected everything she is."

"Did you actually say come-hither?"

"Stop making me laugh. This is a serious thing, ape face."

"It's *Jared Rocke*, do I have to paint it on my forehead?"

"I'm going to throw you out the window." This in the same tone someone else might have said, "I'm going to fix you a cup of coffee." "The fall will probably kill you, but you'll be out of Moira's hair, and it'll make me feel better. Also, you deserve multiple broken bones for making my friend cry."

So saying, the man moved with that same terrifying quickness Geraldine had demonstrated. He seized the footboard of the bed and shoved. As if it was sliding across ice, the bed zipped across the carpet and slammed against the far wall . . . uncomfortably close to the window. But to Jared's human senses, the man had finished with ". . . making my friend cry." And suddenly his bed was against the window.

He supposed he should have been terrified.

"Bring it on, German Shepherd!" His head pounding, Jared thrashed feebly among the blankets. "As soon as I get out of this bed, we'll see who goes out the window!"

"Crud." The man blew out his breath in disgust. "I forgot your injuries wouldn't have healed yet. You guys are made of tissue paper, I swear."

"Derik!"

"What?" The man turned. Wyndham's wife stood in the doorway, hands on her hips. Jared inwardly groaned.

"Keep your hands off him," Jeannie warned, looking cutely threatening.

"I was only going to slap him around a little," Derik said defensively. "Wasn't even going to break the skin. Much."

"You and what army, Liver Snack breath?" Jared jeered.

"See? See? This guy's an asshole squared. *And* he made Moira cry." Derik kicked the footboard. Jared heard the 'crunch' of splintering wood. "For which he will bleed and puke and beg."

"Moira would jam your ass up to your shoulderblades—"

"Worth it," Derik said stubbornly.

"—and you know it. Besides, that's why *I'm* here. Ole Rockhead's got a concussion, so I figured I'd shriek at him for half an hour or so until he agreed to go after Moira."

At last the bickering couple had his attention. "Go after her? Where's she gone?"

"You think she was going to stay *here*? Tonight? She's out of here, pal. I doubt she'll be back until she gets word that you've moved on. Let me know," Derik added with a giant, toothy, terrifying smile, "if you need help packing."

Jared threw back the bedcovers again and stood. Instantly, the floor rushed up to his head. "What the—?"

Jeannie and Derik were bending over him. "You can't go anywhere," she informed him, while he tried to get up off the floor. "Geraldine really rattled your cage. You've got a bad concussion and about a zillion minor injuries."

"My knees work," he said through gritted teeth. Slowly, painfully, he rolled over onto all fours and started crawling for the door.

"Aw, nuts," Derik sighed.

"What?"

"I could get to like this puke."

Hand, hand, knee, knee. Hand, hand, knee, knee. What the hell had they done with his clothes? Oh, well . . . Derik could use a good mooning. Hand, hand, knee, knee.

"What if one of you guys gave him a transfusion?" Jeannie asked.

"It'd probably work," Derik replied indifferently. "Speed up his healing for a day or so. Enough to fix him up."

"Well, let's give him some blood, then."

"Forget it. He's too stupid to let you help."

"Hello?" Jared called irritably. He kept his gaze fixed on the bedroom door, which was now a mere eighteen miles away. "I can hear you two."

"I disagree," Jeannie said. "Not about him being stupid—"

"And me without my gun," Jared muttered.

"—but he'd probably do it if it meant he could get to Moira that much sooner. And Derik, it's really important he get to her before sundown. *Isn't it?*"

"Don't yell, I'm standing right in front of you. And I'm telling you, he won't do it. His tiny little mind can't get around the idea, and even if it did, he's a bigot. He's a—an anti-werewolfite!"

"Dammit, you two, am I even in the room?"

"Shut up," they said in unison. Then, from Jeannie, "No, wait. Derik, pick him up, would you?"

At once Jared felt himself effortlessly lifted and scooped into Derik's arms, as if he were a baby. A big, scowling, hairy baby. "I have to go," he nearly shouted, "and you two aren't helping." Moira was out there alone, thinking God knew what . . . because he was a jackass. He had to fix it right away. The thought of her unhappiness tormented him. He'd rather swallow a wasps' nest than be responsible for her pain.

Derik placed him on the bed, and Jeannie slapped her palms against his chest to keep him from rising. "Jared, if we give you a pint of werewolf blood, your injuries will be healed within the hour."

He stared at them.

"I told you," Derik said triumphantly. "Too dumb. He has no idea what you're talking about. Look, any minute he's going to start drooling."

There was a 'thud' as Jeannie's sneakered foot landed on Derik's instep. The smile on her face never wavered. "What do you say, Rocky?"

"I say you guys better not let word of this get out," he replied slowly. Thinking: *I'm going to pay a high price for my foolishness . . . but if it'll get Moira back, it's worth it.* "People will hunt you down just for the properties in your blood. You'd be werewolves and we'd be . . . vampires, I guess."

"Okay," Derik muttered, "*not* so dumb."

"Let's do it," he said firmly. "Right now. I gotta find Moira. She made me care and by God, she's stuck with me."

Jeannie pretended to wipe away a tear. "That's so beautiful."

"What are we standing around for? Make a fist, Lassie Boy. Somebody get a needle," Jared ordered.

Derik snorted. "A) I wouldn't piss down your throat if your heart was on fire . . ."

"Gross!" Jeannie cried.

". . . and b) I'm not giving you shit. Besides, we keep some blood on hand in case Jeannie gets hurt, or one of our other human friends."

"Derik," Jeannie said reprovingly, "you shouldn't—"

"Back off, blondie. I've known Moira my whole life. I'm not much interested in helping someone who makes her feel the way Fucko did today."

"Fucko is going to try to make things right," Jared said. "So get me that blood—"

"Don't say it," Derik warned.

"Fetch!"

Chapter Twelve

Jared ran. He ran past the rose garden, into the woods. His headache was gone. His pain was gone. He felt like he could jump over the mansion. He felt like he could defeat an army. All this, from a pint of werewolf blood.

He understood the pack's secrecy, the way they kept to themselves. And he respected their discipline in a way he never could have before. What was to stop werewolves from taking over the world? From slaughtering humans like cattle? Wyndham, of course. Wyndham kept them in line. And dealt with the rogues, when he had to.

He'd never love them, Jared thought, leaping over a felled tree trunk, nimble as a gazelle. Or a wolf. But he could sure learn to respect the hell out of them.

He turned his thoughts away from the pack, toward Moira. He could actually smell her . . . her light, flowery scent, like spring violets, called to him. He had thought finding her would be tricky in the woods, the dark. About as tricky as tying his shoes. Jeannie had warned him the effects of the blood—the heightened senses—would wear off by daybreak, but he didn't care. He only needed a little more—there!

He burst into a clearing and saw her. She was nude, kneeling on the grass. She was crying, he saw with dismay, and soothing herself by rocking back and forth.

They all have their favorite places, Jeannie had said. *Places they go when they don't want us to see them. Or hear them. Moira's is the clearing just past the orchard. She'll be there, Jared, and you'd better be nice to her when you find her.*

He had promised. He would have promised anything. And now

here was Moira, so upset she hadn't spotted him. Here was Moira, sobbing so hard her back shook with it. He had done this. Through stupidity or willfulness or plain Rocke stubbornness, he had wrought this.

He had no idea how to fix it.

He took a slow step forward just as Moira threw her head back.
"Oh!" she cried, almost screamed. "Oh! Ohhhh . . . ohhhhhhhhhh-
hhh . . . ouuuuuuuhhhhhhhh . . . ooooooooooooooo!"

One minute he was watching her cry, helpless. The next—and it
was that fast, that quick, if he'd blinked he'd have missed it—she was
standing on four paws. Her champagne-colored fur riffled in the brisk
wind. The moon came out from behind the clouds and still she cried up
at the moon, a wolf who dreamed she was a woman, or a woman who
dreamed she was a wolf.

He sat on the ground. He hadn't thought to, but really had no
choice . . . his knees unhinged and bam! He was on his ass in the
leaves. Suddenly, he was very glad—*very* glad—he didn't have his
gun. He didn't want his hands anywhere near a weapon right now
when he was so terrified. And fascinated.

He'd seen a werewolf change before, of course. Had been re-
volted, of course. But that had been a thug, someone he used for information. It hadn't been someone he cared about. Someone he'd held,
kissed, made love to in the dead of night. Showered with. Cooked
breakfast for. Oh, hell, it wasn't Moira.

And he'd denied her. Told her she couldn't be a werewolf.
Shrugged off her confession, turned his back on what she was. For
what? For vengeance? Renee *was* revenged. For his stupid, human
sense of the way things should be? Or simply because he didn't know
how to open to her?

"Moira," he said, but what came out was a whisper.

She turned and looked at him. In the moonlight, her eyes were
dark purple. She was as gorgeous a wolf as she was a woman.

She stepped away—no, *cringed* away, and he felt his face get hot
with shame. He had done that. Taken a fearless, gorgeous creature and
made her cower like a whipped hound. In a flash of understanding, he
realized Moira was all the things he cared about—good, intelligent,
strong, willful, charming—because of her heritage, not in spite of it.

Too bad he hadn't figured that out a little earlier.

"Moira," he said again, just as the wolf—just as *his* wolf spun and
ran out of the clearing.

He sprinted after her. "Wait! I get it now! You're a werewolf!
Great! Good! I figured it out!" And all she had to do was change right

before his eyes because he was so fucking stupid. But he wouldn't say that . . . not when she already knew . . .

"It's okay! The kids can be furry! I don't care, I swear!" Could she even understand English in her wolf form?

A tree branch swiped him across the cheek, hard enough to make his eyes water. He plunged ahead, ignoring the pain. "Moira, come back! I don't care that you've got more chest hair than I do!"

He was glad Jeannie had insisted he borrow a pair of Wyndham's sweatpants. They afforded his legs some protection, but the branches were scratching the shit out of his arms, chest, and face. It didn't matter. He had it coming, anyway.

Tripping over an exposed root, he went sprawling, sliding on his stomach across the forest floor. Gasping, he rolled to his feet and saw another wolf, one much bigger, with fur the color of sunlight and eyes so vividly green they were nearly hypnotic. The wolf's paws were as big as each of Jared's hands. Muscles flexed and bunched beneath the luxurious pelt as the wolf started toward him, laughing.

Laughing?

Yes. A wolf-laugh—Jared hadn't imagined such a thing was possible. The wolf made chuffing noises in its throat, and there was definitely an amused gleam in its eyes. Still, as it crossed in front of Jared, the wolf let out a warning growl and Jared realized that although the wolf didn't like him, it couldn't keep from laughing.

Derik.

And, on the heels of that thought, Jared realized he was in the middle of a forest filled with werewolves.

"I don't care," he said out loud, but of course he did care. He cared a shitload. "I'm not leaving without Moira."

He saw her, peeking at him from behind a tree. She had stopped running, then. Or . . . maybe heard him and came back? His heart pounded giddily at the thought.

"Moira, I'm sorry. I'm about ten thousand kinds of fool. Don't run anymore, and don't be afraid."

Slowly, the small, light-colored wolf came forward, staring at him. He couldn't read her expression as he could Derik's. In this moment, he had no idea if that was a good thing, or a bad thing.

She scratched at the dirt with her paw. Even her paws were small and delicate; the claws looked like mother-of-pearl. Scratching at the dirt . . . symbols?

Letters.

He went down on one knee to look. The moon was riding high, so bright it was hard to look at, lending more than enough light so he could see . . .

I-D-I-O-T.

He grinned down on her. "Oh, baby," he said, and gently reached out to touch her thick, glorious fur. "It must be love."

Chapter Thirteen

Moira moved silently through her room. Jared was asleep in her bed in the mansion, but she was too tired to be surprised. Sunrise after the moon had ridden her always left its mark; all she wanted was a quick shower and a ten-hour nap.

She remembered last night fairly clearly. Of course she didn't process information the same way as a human and a wolf. But she remembered seeing him in the clearing, knowing he had watched her Change. She remembered her hot shame, and running.

And then he'd come after her, Moira recalled.

She turned on the shower and stepped inside before the water had time to warm. He had come, had run after her yelling the silliest things, and making as much noise as a herd of rhinos on speed. Derik had actually rolled onto his back and waved all four paws in the air; it had been just too funny.

And despite his feelings on the subject of Jared—his loudly voiced feelings—Derik, a creature of irresistible curiosity, had gone *back*. He always liked a good show. Moira had followed, more concerned that Jared would trip and drive a branch through his eye than anything else.

And there he had been, scratched, bleeding from half a dozen places, and smelling strongly of the werewolf blood Jeannie had no doubt transfused into him. He hadn't flinched from her wolf form, hadn't pulled a gun on her.

Instead, he had told her the most amazing things. And touched her fur with a child's wonder. Even now, she could hardly believe he'd done that.

But now what? Happily ever after? Was it possible? More, was it what she wanted?

She finished showering, toweled herself dry, then slipped into bed. Beside her, Jared didn't even stir. She wasn't surprised; he was likely more tired than she was.

Time enough to worry about their future *(what future?)* later.

※ ～(ﾞﾟ)ﾉ ～※

She woke, practically purring. Flexed, hard. Gasped. And came, her orgasm a sweet surprise, like peeling an orange and finding a chocolate inside.

Jared's head was between her thighs, his fingers held her apart as he slowly and steadily licked, licked, licked. Given how wet she felt—how terrific she felt!—he'd obviously been at this for a few minutes at least.

"Jared . . ." A groan.

He laughed against her flesh. "Shut up, darling." His tongue, inside her. Now gone, and lightly stabbing her throbbing clit. His fingers, inside her, now gone. Rubbing, getting slick with her juice.

She could smell his arousal, violent and sharp, like cedar on fire. His need kindled her own; she realized she wasn't gasping, she was panting, heaving for breath, desperate to have him inside her.

And part of her, the fraction of the one percent of her concentration not focused on coming again, thought this was just fine. *He wouldn't be here with me, touching me, if he didn't still want to be with me.* She felt the sweet spasms of another orgasm ripple through her, and moaned.

"Jared," she said again, and reached for him.

"Moira, sweetie, I'm going to need a little help here." He was moving up her body, touching her everywhere with hands that smelled like sex. "Also, you're going to marry me."

"I—"

"But just so there's no doubt. I mean, I get that you're ten times stronger than me and twice as smart. No problem. But between us, sugar, there's never going to be any doubt about who wears the pants in the Rocke family."

"Can't you stop talking," she groaned, wild with impatience, "and fuck me?"

"Sure thing." He had crawled up far enough so that he was crouching over her chest, kneeling on her hands. The pressure was firm, but not painful. Her leverage, however, was for shit. "But first I need your mouth."

"Wha—" Then his hot, hard length was pushing past her lips, his musky scent was in her nostrils, her throat. He throbbed between her cheeks. She shifted her weight to take more of him, and realized she couldn't move.

Not that this was such a problem. But still. The idea. Jared had her pinned and despite her strength, there (was his cock, thick and rude) wasn't much to be done about it. Not that Jared (was rocking back and forth, pushing himself in and out of her mouth) would ever hurt her, but the fact was, she was giving him a blowjob whether she liked it or not. She (could feel her jaws forced wide, to accommodate him, could taste his saltiness) happened to like it. But wasn't that beside the point?

Then he was pulsing and her mouth was flooded with that bitter sweetness so peculiar to semen. He groaned as she swallowed, and his hands were in her hair, roughly caressing her curls.

He pulled out, and away, and collapsed beside her. "Definitely not the most PC moment of my life," he sighed, and pulled her into his arms.

"Do you even know what that stands for?" She tried to be irritated, but in truth, felt almost indecently satisfied. She could still taste him in her mouth.

"Perfect Cookies. You are, you know."

"What?" She cuddled against his side, ran her fingers gently over the scratches on his chest.

"Going to marry me."

"Gosh, Jared, are you *sure*? I mean, I'm *so* demented about being a werewolf and all . . ."

He squinched his eyes shut. "Okay, okay, I deserved that, have mercy. I suck, all right? Although, not as well as you do . . ."

She poked him in the ribs, hard. "Pig. And excuse me, but I can't help being astonished at how easy this is. I mean . . . Jared . . . I'm one of the monsters. The creature you sought for years."

"Nope. Geraldine . . . *she* was the creature. You're the woman I love."

She digested that in silence, absently toying with the hair on his chest.

"I mean, Geraldine was just one person in the . . . the group. Pack. Whatever. *One* person . . . she didn't define the pack. I can't paint all the other werewolves with the same brush." He paused expectantly.

"What do you want, applause?" She smiled and rolled her eyes at him. "You're not telling me anything I don't know."

"All I'm saying is, werewolves are like anybody else. They're some really fabulous ones—" He squeezed her. "—and some major assholes, but most of them are in between." Another expectant pause.

"Jared, I know all this. I've been trying to get this idea through your head for days."

"Well," he said tentatively, "what kind of werewolf do you think I'll be?"

She went up on one elbow; stared at him. "What?"

"Jeannie gave me a whole pint of werewolf blood . . ."

"I know; I smelled it on you last night."

". . . so I could get healed and go after you. I guess I'll get pretty hairy in a month or so." He contemplated his chest a little worriedly. "Hairier, I mean."

Astonishment left her wordless for a long moment. "You thought that the transfusion would make you pack . . . and you did it anyway. So you could find me." She could feel her face get hot; her eyes filled. "Oh, Jared . . ."

"Don't cry, babe. You can show me all the werewolf tricks. It'll be fine."

". . . you're such an idiot."

One golden eyebrow went up. "That's not very romantic."

"I told you before," she explained, laughing through her tears, "being a werewolf isn't something you can catch. You either are one, or you aren't. You could have a transfusion every day for a year, but you'd never howl at the moon." She kissed him on the mouth, a hearty smack. "But to think that you didn't know . . . and you did it anyway . . . I love you. For all sorts of reasons, but most of all for this."

"Hey, it was nothing," he bragged. "And I love you, too. And you *are* going to marry me."

"Yes, so you keep telling me."

He showed her his vulnerable side as he squeezed her again. "Yeah, but you haven't answered."

"Of course I'll marry you. I've been waiting for you . . ." She thought back over the vista of lonely years. ". . . for a long time."

He kissed her again, a hearty smack on the mouth. "I've got about a million questions. Like, if you shave your legs when you're in your human form, will your wolf form have bare legs? And how much Nair do you go through in a month, anyway?"

She closed her eyes. "I think I liked it better when you refused to see the truth."

"And what if we're making love and the moon comes up? I mean, I'm an open-minded guy, but—"

"Jared," she groaned, "you're killing me. And you'd better be teasing, because that's both ridiculous *and* disgusting. I can see I'm going to have to get you some books."

"So, how strong are you? Can you lift a car up over your head?"

"Jared . . ."

"Not a serious car, like a Cadillac . . . how about a Volkswagen, could you lift a Volkswagen?"

"Jared!"

"Quick! Let's arm wrestle. Winner has to do all the dishes for life."

She poked him in the shoulder, hard. "I can't believe I yearned for the day you'd accept the truth."

"Be careful what you wish for, bay-bee." His teasing grin faded and he looked at her anxiously.

"Can we have kids? I mean . . . can you . . . with a regular guy?"

"Yes." *And they'll be very special.* You never knew what you got when a human mated with a werewolf. You might get a werewolf. You might get a human. You might get a human with extraordinary strength and agility. You might get a werewolf who could control their Change. It was always a toss of the dice. It was always exciting.

"What will they be?" His gaze was curious, wondering. His fingers moved softly over her belly, as if already feeling for the life within. She could feel him against her thigh, already hard again, and hot. Wanting her as badly as she wanted him.

"They'll be whatever they want to be," she said, and kissed him again, pulled him to her, and opened herself to him. Body and soul.

My Champion,
My Love

※❦※

by Alice Gaines

To my reader:
Passion isn't only for the young, and good guys don't always finish last.

Chapter One

Upstate New York, 1888

The woman didn't strike Robert Albright as deranged. But the staff hadn't dressed her—or allowed her to dress herself—and now she was forced to greet him, a perfect stranger, in the middle of the afternoon wearing her dressing gown. If, indeed, she'd been sent to the Wainwright Asylum unjustly, he'd do what he could to have her released. If the patients here were mistreated, he'd look into that, too. Right now, his main concern was Mrs. Celeste Broder and her sanity.

She appeared more restless than insane. She'd paced from the window to Dr. Wainwright's desk and then back again as though measuring the dimensions of her prison in footsteps. Yards and yards of the best Belgian lace flowed and rustled behind her as she went. She stopped her meanderings at the window this time and turned to him, causing the sunlight to cast shadows from the iron bars onto her face and the length of her throat.

"Xenobia sent you?" she asked.

"She did."

One eyebrow rose as she studied him. "Do you know her well?"

"We met only once, when she asked me to check on you."

"Is she here? Now?"

"She went back to Manhattan," he answered. "She seemed to think that her friendship had gotten you into your present predicament somehow. She kept her visit to me a secret."

"Yes, of course. Dear Xenobia," she said, twisting her fingers together. "Still, I wish she could have come herself."

Mrs. Broder renewed her prowling. All long limbs and simmering impatience, she walked back and forth with her robe rustling around her ankles. But then, he'd no doubt act the same if he'd been locked away in this place for weeks.

He might have expected impatience from her, but he hadn't expected such beauty. Xenobia Stewart hadn't warned him that he'd be rescuing a tall, graceful woman with raven-black hair and limbs long and slender enough to belong to an angel.

Beauty or not, the woman needed his help, and he'd best remember that. Too many people in her life had taken advantage of her, if Mrs. Stewart's story was correct. He wouldn't add his own lust to those wrongs, no matter how deeply his own urges ran in those directions. But, damn, what a vision she made in all that lace. He couldn't have taken his eyes off her if his life had depended on it.

"What did Xenobia tell you about me?" she asked.

"That you'd been sent here unfairly. That you're perfectly sane, and that you needed someone to get you released."

"And why did she choose you, I wonder?" she said. "Do you regularly champion women you don't know, Mr. Albright?"

No, he didn't. In fact, he rarely spoke to women as beautiful as this one. He didn't find it entirely comfortable doing so now. "I imagine that Mrs. Stewart called on me because of my stature in the community."

"You're the mayor of that pretty town I passed on the way here," she said.

"Connogua Springs," he answered. "As the mayor, I'm concerned if anything improper goes on in this institution."

"This institution?" she repeated with a none-too-ladylike laugh. "Don't you mean this asylum? This haven where my tortured mind can find peace?"

"I'd be very interested in how you've been treated here," he answered.

"My mind's been treated well, I suppose. My body is quite another matter, but I don't suppose you want to hear about that, do you?"

His face heated to the roots of his hair. He didn't dare think about her body—tortured or not. He was already more aware than he should be of the curves under her gown that promised no corset but only more silk and lace. And skin—soft, warm skin.

The room felt hot suddenly, the air thickening until he had to think to breathe. He was having a very male reaction to Celeste Broder's presence, a reaction that would prove embarrassing in another moment. Curse his nature—he'd always been that way. Hot blooded. He needed to get away from her. Clear his head. He could work on her behalf from a distance. Investigate why she'd been imprisoned here and how she'd been treated. But from a distance, not so close that she overwhelmed his senses.

"I think I've heard all I need to for now," he said. He reached into his pocket and pulled out the note. Even after the days since Xenobia Stewart had given him the envelope, her perfume still wafted from the heavy vellum. Hideously expensive, if he was any judge, and too strong for a modest woman's taste. The scent hung all around him as he walked toward Mrs. Broder, his hand outstretched. "I'll deliver this to you and leave."

"No, please." She caught his hand, clutching both it and the envelope between her fingers. "Forgive me. I'm not at my best here. Kindness is so scarce. No one's very gracious within these walls, I'm afraid."

"I only want to help you, Mrs. Broder." But did he really? Or did he want something else entirely? Something sweet, but forbidden.

"Yes, of course. Please stay while I read the letter."

He shouldn't stay. If he had any sense, he'd leave. But the look of desperation in her eyes tore at him, so he nodded.

She went to the chair in front of Wainwright's desk and sank onto it, tearing open the envelope as she sat. She inhaled the perfume briefly and then read—her flush deepening over the patch of flesh revealed by the open throat of her robe. Her breath caught, so quietly he would have missed it if she hadn't held his attention so completely. She stopped reading for a moment and glanced up at him with the strangest expression in her eyes. Curiosity, definitely, but there was more, as well. Desire? Damn him for an idiot, but Robert could have sworn that look meant she wanted him.

She went back to reading the letter, and he did his best to control his imagination. He'd been without satisfaction too long. Since Millie's death. Hell, he'd been without complete satisfaction his entire life, despite Millie's good intentions. No wonder his mind wandered when he met a beautiful woman in her dressing gown. No wonder his member stiffened when she looked at him the way a woman looks at a lover.

She finished reading the letter, folded it carefully, and slipped it into the pocket of her robe. "Do you have any idea what this letter says?"

"I didn't read it, Mrs. Broder."

"That isn't what I asked. Did Xenobia tell you what her letter said?"

"No."

"Did you two discuss me?"

"Mrs. Stewart only said that you'd been put here against your will." He walked to the doorway and picked up his hat from its peg on the wall. "Now that you've read her note, I'll be on my way."

Mrs. Broder rose and reached out her hands toward him. "Please, don't go."

"I'll do what I can to have you released. You have my promise."

"But you don't know why I'm here. How can you release me if you don't even know why I'm here?"

"I won't tolerate sane people being locked away here, and it's clear to me that you're sane." He could hardly say the same thing about himself as he stood there, his hand hovering over the doorknob. He ought to leave. He ought to take his rapidly swelling erection and escape as quickly as possible. The woman held some sort of power over him—could seduce him with a mere look. If she continued to entreat him, her arms outstretched as though asking him for comfort, he'd surrender. He'd take her in an embrace, and then he'd be lost.

"I'll speak to the board of directors. I'll find you a lawyer," he said, finally clasping the doorknob in his hand. "I'll do whatever I have to to ensure your freedom."

"Please, Mr. Albright, stay. A few minutes longer. Please."

"Is that really necessary, Mrs. Broder?"

"Yes," she answered. "I want to tell you about myself before you hear about me from someone else. They'll make it all sound ugly." Her voice trailed off, and her chin trembled for a moment, but she took a few breaths and straightened her shoulders.

"They?" he asked. That seemed a safer question than what she meant by "hear about me."

"The doctors here. My husband's children—especially them." She walked toward the window and curled her fingers around the bars as she gazed out. "I have appetites, Mr. Albright. Appetites that might be tolerated in a man but not in a woman."

He removed his hand from the doorknob and dropped it to his side. "You needn't explain yourself to me."

"If I don't, someone else will, and then you'll think I'm unnatural just as the others do."

"No, I assure you . . ."

"This is perfectly humiliating," she muttered and resumed her pacing. She took angry steps, this way and that, as her fingers tangled with each other in front of her. "But, if I don't tell you, someone else will, and you'll think me disgusting."

He ought to do something to calm her, to comfort her. But what?

He'd always felt helpless where women were concerned, and this one bewildered him completely.

"I have no choice in this, no choice at all." She stopped walking and turned to face him. "I like sex."

His jaw dropped, and he stood, gaping at her while every word he might have said flew directly out of his head. Had she really said that she liked sex?

"Frigging, swiving, tumbling," she continued. "Whatever you call it, I like it." She paused for a moment, still twisting her hands together in front of her dressing gown. "At least, I think I do. I haven't really been given a chance to find out."

"Mrs. Broder . . ."

"I think about sexual congress constantly. I dream about it at night. What it would be like to be held in a lover's arms—not for simpering declarations of affection. And not for chaste, little kisses, either."

Her skin had taken on that flush again—the same livid rose she'd shown after reading Mrs. Stewart's letter. Could it be nervous distraction? Could the woman be mad, after all? If so, she had some contagious sort of hysteria—something that could reach right out to him and catch him up in the insanity. With his member fully erect and throbbing now, he needed to get the hell out of here before he disgraced himself.

"These are things you should discuss with a husband," he muttered.

"My husband is dead," she answered. "And it was pointless trying to talk to him when he was alive."

"You have my condolences, but still . . ."

"The idea that I might require more physical attention than he gave me repulsed him. The mere thought that I might want more than his late night gropings made him avoid me for weeks."

"Please," he said, "I don't want to hear any more of this."

"Until he could no longer control his 'animal nature,' as he put it and he had to satisfy himself inside me in the least amount of time possible."

Robert put his hand back on the doorknob and turned it. "I have to leave."

"Don't go." She rushed to him and placed both her hands on his arm. "I'm sorry. I am distraught. Anyone would be in my place."

The door moved open, pushed from the other side. The matron who'd been assigned to guard the doorway stuck her head inside. "Time to go back to your room, Mrs. Broder."

Mrs. Broder forced a smile that wouldn't fool a child. "But Mr. Albright and I haven't finished chatting, have we?"

The matron harumphed. "This wasn't a good idea. Dr. Wainwright and I told you as much, Mr. Albright."

"Please, just a few more minutes."

The matron crossed her arms over her chest and glared out of narrowed eyes. Mrs. Broder's chin began to tremble again, and her eyes turned liquid with the threat of tears.

"I remember well what you told me," Robert said, pushing the door closed again. "I'll call you when we're through."

"The very idea." The matron harumphed again. "I have other things to do besides stand in this hallway all day, Mr. Albright."

"I'm sure," he said as he guided her the rest of the way out of the room and closed the door behind her.

"Thank you." Mrs. Broder gave a sigh of relief. "I'm sorry to have been so crude with you, but I wanted you to understand why I'm here. How I feel."

Unfortunately, he knew too well how she felt. But, he'd never told anyone that. Never. And out of respect for Millie, he never would. "You have my sympathy, Mrs. Broder," he said. "I'll do whatever I can to get you released."

"You'll visit again, won't you?"

"I don't think that would be wise," he answered.

She held out her arms to him again in that gesture of vulnerability that tore at him. "Please."

"There's nothing I can do for you here that I can't do from the outside."

"But there is. Maybe they'll let me walk outdoors if you agree to take me."

That stopped him. "They won't let you go outside?"

"Not once since I've been here."

That shouldn't have surprised him. They wouldn't let her dress herself properly. How could they let her go outside? Curse Wainwright and his demand for utter control over his patients.

"I miss the sunshine," she continued. "I want to breathe fresh air again. Please say you'll come back and take me outdoors."

Damn, how could he refuse her? Even a beast of burden got to feel the sun on its face. He stood, staring at the doorknob for a moment. "All right," he said finally. "I'll be back."

"When?" she demanded.

"Soon," he answered. He'd pay a price for spending more time in her company, no doubt. The woman would drive him mad with long-ing. But, God help him, he couldn't let her stay caged up like an animal.

Celeste sat on her narrow bed and read Xenobia's note for the third time.

My dearest, it said.

Thank heaven I've found you. The moment I discovered where the children had you sent, I rushed to Connogua Springs myself to get you freed. Fate delivered me to the gentleman bearing this letter. Mr. Robert Albright is the mayor of Connogua Springs and of quite some upstanding reputation in the community. When I learned that he might be willing to investigate the practices of that den of vipers where you're imprisoned, I knew I had found the perfect champion for you.

By all accounts, Mr. Albright is discreet and unusually shy for a man in his position. In all, he's a wonderful fellow, and everyone who knows him adores him. But, there is one more bit of information you should have. Word has it that Mr. Albright is quite well endowed in the male drives and the machinery with which to set them into motion, if you catch my meaning. This news comes to me second hand, but Mr. A's late wife is said to have complained endlessly to her lady friends about his insatiable needs in their marriage bed. According to her, she could never satisfy him, and when she tried, she invariably found her-self severely weakened from having to accommodate the considerable bulk of his sex.

The story from some loose tongues in Connogua Springs—Mr. A being far too sensitive to breathe a word of such things himself—is that the demands of the marriage bed drove Mrs. A to an early grave. Pity. I'm sure that under such circumstances you or I would perish from an excess of bliss.

In any case, I'm certain that the man will not only manage to re-lease you from your captivity, but will make you an excellent lover as well. Take him to your bed at the first opportunity.

Forgive me for running away again to Manhattan, but I suspect that if your children were to discover my efforts to free you, they'd have you sent someplace farther away and even less appealing. I trust you'll be back with me soon, I want to hear all the details of how you get along with Mr. Albright and his considerable bulk.

As always, your devoted,

Xenobia.

Oh, thank heaven. Celeste raised the paper to her face and breathed in the scent of Xenobia's perfume. She didn't dare keep the letter with privacy so impossible in this damnable place. And yet, how could she destroy her first ray of hope, her lifeline to the outside world? She'd read it again later. She'd memorize every word and then tear it up. Truly, she would. Later. For now, she folded the letter and slipped it back into its envelope. She slid the envelope underneath her pillow and rested her palm on top as though she could feel the paper through the thickness of fabrics and goose down. Xenobia had found her, despite Young Horace and Violet—her "children"—packing her away in the middle of the night. Xenobia had not only found her, but she'd sent someone to rescue her.

Rescue. Finally, rescue. Not just from the asylum, but from all the restrictions and duties. All the obligations and fashions—corsets, teas, monogrammed thank-you notes to people she despised for gifts she couldn't bear to look at. Years of it all, first as a daughter and then as a wife. *Sit up straight, shoulders back. Speak when spoken to. Don't laugh, don't cry, don't breathe. Don't touch, don't touch, don't touch.*

Thirty-five years of living, and she still didn't dare touch anyone except herself, and that only in deepest secrecy. She wrapped her arms around her ribs and took a few deep breaths. How many times had she sat exactly like this, holding the anger inside? The frustration, the fear—no, the terror—that in the end life might have nothing more to offer. That the tiny triumphs of a new flower in her conservatory, a few moments of peace in her garden, a private dream of someplace better might be all the joy the world would ever hold for her.

She rose and walked to the window to gaze out across the long gravel drive where she'd just caught a glimpse of Mr. Robert Albright's modest gig leaving the grounds. Out of breath from having raced up the stairs to get one more look at him, she'd stood here—that dreadful Morton woman tsking her disapproval from behind—reassuring herself that he did exist. She hadn't imagined him.

Robert Albright didn't look like a rescuing knight. With his soft voice and thinning hair, he didn't even resemble the man of her fantasies. From the first day she'd become aware of the differences between men and women, she'd dreamed of one particularly handsome devil with strong arms and a wicked gleam in his eyes. Marriage had burned away the mysteries of what happened after ardent kisses and heated sighs, leaving a reality scarcely worth the grunting and sweating involved. If only marriage had satisfied a little of the hunger, too, she might have found some peace. Perhaps she wouldn't be standing here now, staring out a window and wishing that a perfect stranger would reappear on his charger to take her away.

Foolish woman. Was this what unsatisfied passions made of you? And yet . . .

She closed her eyes and did her best to recreate every detail of Robert Albright from memory. Had she imagined the breadth of his shoulders? The man hadn't spoken one unnecessary word, yet those he did he'd uttered in such a soft voice they might have whispered in on a breeze. As quiet as he'd been, he ought not to have dominated Wainwright's sterile office, but he had. He'd filled the room with those shoulders of his somehow. He'd brought in the smell of sunshine. And warmth, such heavenly warmth.

Saints above, such fancies. Celeste opened her eyes, turned, and stared at the blank walls around her.

Robert Albright had smiled at her, nothing more. But then, she wasn't used to people smiling at her. Certainly no one expressed any mirth in this place. Horace had only smiled when he'd bested some unfortunate soul at business. And the children . . . the children—best not to think of them and their insincere smiles or she'd start screaming.

Robert Albright had given her a smile that started in his eyes before it even got to his lips. A shy, uncomplicated smile she just knew she could trust, foolish woman that she was. Foolish, desperate woman.

Of course, none of those things had caused Xenobia to send Robert Albright to her. Xenobia didn't take flights of fancy when it came to men and their smiles. Mrs. Xenobia Stewart knew what went on between men and women, and she'd chosen Robert Albright for Celeste. What had the note said? *"Well endowed with the male drives and the machinery with which to set them in motion"?* *"You or I would expire from an excess of bliss"?* The mere idea that such a man might have been created for her sent a shock of pleasure through her.

Celeste turned back to the window. Gripping the rails and staring blankly outside did nothing to relieve the tension in her chest, just beneath her breasts, so she walked toward the center of the room and stared up at the ceiling, her hands in fists by her side. She'd almost learned something of her own nature before the children had her sent here. She'd read some books, finally. She'd come to realize that the lust that captivated the men in those stories burned just as fiercely in her. She'd finally understood the ache between her own legs and found the spot where she could rub to give herself some pleasure. She'd been on the threshold of more discoveries, so many more, when the children had found her books and brought all the discoveries to an end.

Now Xenobia had sent her Robert Albright, he of the endowments and drives. She shouldn't concentrate so wholly on his smile and his gentleness—as miraculous as they were—and neglect those other aspects of him. They were kindred spirits in matters of the flesh. Xenobia had said so.

What details did she have about her champion? He was an upstanding citizen—mayor of his little town. Did small town mayors indulge themselves with inmates of institutions like this one? Most likely not. Still, she'd spoken to him frankly enough about herself. She'd told him things no decent woman even told her husband. He'd flushed and stammered in response, but he hadn't run, bless him. Perhaps he'd pitied her—who knew?—but he hadn't run.

What else did she know about him? He'd been less than satisfied in his own marriage. If what the man's own wife had said served as Xenobia's source for that little bit of information, it could hardly be doubted.

What else? Nothing, really. Only his appearance—the long fingers that had played so seductively with the brim of his hat, the kind, amber light in his eyes. His lips. He had a beautiful mouth, or maybe she'd only imagined that. No, he had a very tempting mouth, with ample lips that curved in ways that would haunt her dreams. Men shouldn't have mouths like that if they didn't know how to use them to give a woman pleasure. Had Robert Albright tried to use that mouth to love his wife? Had the unfortunate woman denied him? Celeste wouldn't deny him, if only she could have the chance to know him so intimately.

Some women might find fault with his thinning hair, but honestly, what good could hair do in the heat of passion? If he made love to her, she'd cling to those shoulders as he rode her, not to his head.

Just the idea, the mental picture of him making love to her, sent her pulse to racing. He'd kiss her, shyly at first until she encouraged him. He'd touch her with his graceful fingers. She'd show him all the right places to touch her, and he'd smile as he did it. She'd touch him, too, and kiss him. Somewhere she'd find the knowledge of how to do that to drive him past any silly objections. Then, when neither of them could stand another moment of separation, she'd take that part of him deep inside her. His cock—that was what Xenobia called it—his rod, his member, all those other words for that glorious, hard, throbbing maleness she craved.

Oh, Lord, she'd begun to throb herself. Her poor sex—cunt, she needed to say the right word—her cunt ached, and moisture had pooled between her legs. Damn, now what was she to do?

She could spend the rest of the day in this state, pacing her room near climax. Ha, the pacing itself might make her come. As hot as she'd grown, the orgasm could double her over or send her crashing to the floor. Then, they'd all come running in to see what had set their most depraved inmate off this time. Thank you, but no.

Or, she could climb onto the bed and hope for a few minutes of privacy to put out the fire between her legs. No dignity was assured here, but maybe she'd be lucky.

She walked carefully to the bed, becoming more and more aroused with each step. Once there, she sat and listened for any sound from the hallway outside that might indicate Morton's presence. Nothing but silence answered, so she lay on her stomach and breathed deeply a few times. Slowly, she inched her gown up in front, taking the lace in fistfuls until it cleared the tops of her thighs. She closed her eyes and pictured Robert Albright and his broad shoulders and long fingers as she reached into her drawers and parted the lips of her sex. She imagined his touch as she found her already hardened pearl and began to stroke it.

Chapter Two

"How good of you to visit me again, Mr. Albright, and so soon."
Celeste knew very well that she was talking too much and far too fast,
but she couldn't help herself. Her heart hadn't stopped its fluttering
since the news that she had a visitor. She'd done her best not to hope
that her caller was Robert Albright as her fingers had fumbled with the
laces of her corset. But once her spirit had been set free, she hadn't
managed to bottle it up again. And then, she'd seen him—so tall and
handsome with his shy smiles and blushes—and her hopes had soared.

He'd come back to see her as he'd promised, and on the very
next day.

Could his haste in coming back mean he'd lain awake thinking of
her the night before, as she'd done thinking of him? He'd allowed her
to take his arm as soon as they'd left the main hospital building. But
then, he could hardly have refused that small gesture of intimacy without rejecting her outright. He wouldn't do that, would he? He might
have if he thought her a true degenerate after her confessions of the
day before. No, not even then. The man was far too kind to shun her so
obviously. Or was he?

If only she knew more about him. If only she knew more about
men in general.

"It's such a lovely day, and I've been inside for too long," she said
for lack of anything better. He'd scarcely spoken three words since
he'd escorted her onto the grounds. But he'd come back for her—that
spoke volumes, didn't it?

"Why didn't they allow you more freedom, Mrs. Broder?" he said
after a moment.

Celeste did her best to laugh lightly. "I'm sure I don't know why they do what they do here."

"I had quite some argument with Dr. Wainwright about your treatment," he said. "He claims you've been a very difficult patient."

"I suppose I haven't been completely agreeable with the staff," she answered.

He said nothing but glanced at her, raising an eyebrow.

"I suppose I've been rude to some of them," she admitted. "On occasion."

He smiled—just a slight crinkle to his eyes and a soft light of amusement. She took the opportunity to lean toward him to bask in the warmth of his body.

"Being locked away doesn't do good things for my temperament," she said.

He stopped walking and turned toward her. The action separated their arms, but Celeste let her fingers rest against the wool of his coat.

"How did you get here?" he asked softly.

"What have they told you?"

"I want to hear the story from you."

She gazed up into his face and found nothing to fear, at least not that she could read in his expression. He seemed only concerned, or perhaps, just receptive. Willing to listen. And his height, combined with the strength of his shoulders, seemed to offer comfort. Here she might find shelter, a safe haven for the battered ship she'd become since the children had stolen her freedom.

"Mrs. Broder?" he prompted.

"Yes, I'm sorry," she muttered. "I must seem quite distracted. It's just that you . . ."

"I?"

Dear heaven, she really had to stop dithering, or he would think her feeble-minded. Only, how could she stop imagining him as a champion and lover long enough to have a civil conversation with him?

"Might we sit down, do you think?" she said finally.

"Of course. There's a bench over here." He indicated a copse of yew trees with his arm.

She walked in front of him toward the bench, enjoying the crunch of gravel under her slippers. She hadn't lied when she'd told him that she hadn't been allowed outdoors since her arrival. The smell of lush grass and flowers, the sounds of birdsong, the feel of the sun on her shoulders—it was all so seductive. So delicious. And now she'd sit for as long as he'd accompany her in the shade of the yews, obscured from everyone. None of the staff—not Wainwright nor Morton—and none of the inmates could see them here. The mere thought of privacy, with this man, made her lightheaded. Her pulse beat at the base of her throat, and the skin at the back of her neck tingled. In another moment, she'd find herself swooning from all the stimulation if she didn't gather her wits.

She sat on the bench and patted the marble beside her. Albright gave her another smile—a shy one this time—and blushed, but didn't join her. A disappointment, but she would be patient if it killed her.

Resting her hands in her lap, she looked up at him. "My husband owned several newspapers and a publishing house," she began. "He was already quite wealthy when his first wife died."

"You were young when you married him," Mr. Albright said.

"Dr. Wainwright told you that?" she asked.

"Mrs. Stewart did."

"Ah yes, Xenobia," Celeste said. "I was past prime marriage age when Horace approached my father, but I was young enough to be stupid. Young, hopeful, and stupid."

"Insulting yourself won't accomplish anything."

"No, I suppose not." She sighed. "I don't know what I expected from marriage, really. I craved excitement, I know that much. I thought Horace's money would buy that for me."

Mr. Albright said nothing but just stood, his hands behind his back, regarding her. From his appearance and what she knew of him, he had to have passed his fortieth birthday. And yet, his physique measured favorably against a younger man's, even the pirate of her youthful dreams. The modest but flattering cut of his suit outlined the breadth of his shoulders and the length of his legs. If not for his shy manner, she could easily picture him lifting her in his arms and carrying her off to someplace sinful.

She sighed again. "Horace's children, Young Horace and Violet, were in school in Geneva. I pictured us joining them there, stopping in Vienna, and then continuing to the Orient. He quickly informed me that Europe was too full of 'damned Frenchmen' for his taste."

"He didn't like the French?"

"He thought even less of Italians," Celeste answered. "And the Orient was out of the question."

"Marriage wasn't what you'd expected."

"I don't suppose marriage is what anyone expects it to be, Mr. Albright. Weren't you surprised in your own marriage?"

"Yes . . . um . . . well . . ." His voice trailed off, and his cheeks flushed a lovely rose that crept up past his thinning hair line. His embarrassments were almost as endearing as his body was tempting.

"Must you really stand all the way over there?" she asked. "I have to twist my neck to look at you."

"Mrs. Broder . . ."

"Please call me Celeste."

"I shouldn't," he stammered. "That is, it isn't correct. We only met yesterday."

"And yet, I feel I know you." Such a silly cliché, and yet she meant it. She did feel as if she knew him, or would soon. If only he could allow himself to trust her. She smiled at him and patted the bench next to her again. "Please do sit down," she said. "You can always call for help if I try to molest you."

That got her a smile from him, a real one. "Are you that dangerous?"

"Absolutely. I'll steal your soul if you're not careful."

His smile grew broader. "I believe that."

He walked to the bench and sat beside her. She took the opportunity to wrap her arm around his again, and when he didn't pull away, she leaned against him. "Your marriage, Robert."

"We were talking about yours," he corrected.

"Oh, very well. My marriage." She let her fingertips travel the length of his sleeve, down to his wrist and back up. "When I learned that I wasn't to travel, I decided I'd have children and devote myself to them, but Horace didn't want any more. He had a very effective way for keeping me from getting in the family way. He avoided me."

Robert tried to pull away, but she held him fast. "I'd had urges for years—unmet cravings. I thought that at least marriage would bring me some relief from those. I thought men were slaves to their baser natures—perfect beasts. But it appeared that Horace had his own desires well under control, if he had desires at all."

"I don't think I should hear this."

"But you have to if you're to understand how I got here. Robert, please."

She reached down and intertwined her fingers with his. He seemed surprised at first, staring down at their hands as if no one had ever touched him that way before. Then his features softened, and he stroked her palm with his middle finger. The contact sent a tiny jolt of heat through her, from the underside of her wrist to the crook of her arm.

"Go on," he murmured.

Go on? When she could hardly catch her breath? And yet, it was so desperately important he hear her story and understand.

"Horace didn't want me that way," she continued, her voice unsteady. "From time to time his baser nature got the better of him, and he took his pleasure as quickly as he could in my bed. Even as rushed and unpleasant as those times were, I knew I wanted more. I needed it, Robert. Oh, how I needed it, and he denied me."

She stopped, and a little sob caught in her throat. She ought to hate herself for using tears to gain his sympathy, but she couldn't help herself. "You must think I'm unnatural. You must be thoroughly repulsed."

"Not at all, Mrs . . ." He squeezed her fingers. "Not at all, Celeste."

Dear heaven, could the man be any more dear? That soft rendering of her name would have won him a spot in her heart if his kindness hadn't already. Xenobia had sent her a fine champion, indeed. If she weren't careful, she'd find herself in love with the man after knowing him for less than a day.

Love? Maybe she belonged here, after all. Only a madwoman contemplated love with a man on their second meeting. And yet, the feel of his hand in hers, the scent of his shaving soap, the tempting curve of his lips, how could any sane woman resist such things?

He studied her face, his gaze wandering gently over her features in a manner that could only be called a caress. "If your husband didn't want you, why did he marry you?"

"I always wondered about that. I asked him more than once, but he wouldn't tell me. I finally learned that he had political ambitions and needed a wife. He died before he could realize his goals, and I ended up a very rich woman."

"That still doesn't tell me how you got here."

"The children disapproved of me," she answered. That was an understatement. "I'd tried to befriend them. Honestly. But I'm afraid they always resented my marrying Horace. So, as soon as their dear father was safely dead and buried, they hurried home from Europe to protect his interests."

"His interests?" Robert repeated, one eyebrow rising. "What interests could he have once he'd died?"

"His money, of course."

"Ah, yes."

"I was so naive. I had no idea how vicious people could become when a large inheritance was involved. And by the time they returned to New York, I'd already made a fatal mistake. I'd begun to enjoy myself."

Celeste sat in silence for a moment. If the next part of her story didn't frighten him off, she could hope for an end to her imprisonment. She might even dare hope for happiness.

"I'd met Xenobia Stewart before at some dinner party or other.

Alone among all the people in New York society, she seemed to see my restlessness. She alone seemed to understand that the trappings of wealth can't satisfy all of human hunger." Celeste took a breath. "She offered me friendship."

Robert looked into her eyes briefly. "Friendship."

"She offered more than friendship, actually." Celeste blushed and gripped his hand. "I turned that offer down. It's always been my blessing—or curse—to desire men exclusively."

He sighed—in surprise? relief?—if only she could tell. But, he still didn't pull away.

"So, when Horace died, I sought Xenobia out. She has . . . um . . . private evenings at her home. Soirées for intimate friends and intimate activities."

His cheeks turned a deep rose color. "I've heard of such things, although I've never met anyone who indulged in them."

"I didn't indulge," she added quickly. "I attended. I listened and learned, but I never . . . um . . . surrendered myself to . . . well . . . any of it. Not really, not in the flesh."

"It isn't my place to judge."

"I'd like your good opinion, Robert. I'm not without scruples. I'm not promiscuous. I'm only . . ." What? She was only what? Lonely? Craving human contact? How could she put a name to the ache inside her?

"Shhh," he whispered, quieting her.

"Xenobia gave me some books," she continued. "Voluptuous reading, things no decent woman should know about. Those I devoured as if I'd been starved for them all my life. They explained so much about how I felt. They felt like a lifeline to sanity. How ironic they'd prove my Achilles' heel."

"Your children found them," he said.

"My virtuous, upright children thought nothing of searching my room. Conventional morality doesn't extend to respecting privacy, it appears."

"I'm sorry."

"So," she said, gesturing around her, "those books and the fact that I'd attended several of Xenobia's parties were all Horace and Violet needed to prove I'd lost my reason. They had a judge friend of my husband's commit me here against my will. I suspect some money changed hands in the transaction."

"That's outrageous," he said. "Are you sure?"

"I had a great deal of their father's money. With me 'insane' and locked away, the children control my inheritance."

"Damn," he said. "That's unconscionable. I've never heard of such injustice."

Celeste took the first deep breath she'd managed since she'd begun her story. He was angry on her behalf, not repulsed by her history. The dear man, the precious, perfect man. She could dare to hope now, for freedom and more. With Robert Albright she might dare hope for so much more.

He rose from the bench, his hands clenched into his fists, and paced a few feet. "How could you be confined for mere reading when Mrs. Stewart is allowed to have her parties?"

"Xenobia's fabulously wealthy and answers to no one. I had to contend with the children and Horace's friend, the judge. Powerful enemies."

"And you had to face them alone." He straightened his shoulders. "Now you have an ally. Me."

She stood, walked to him, and took his hands in hers. "Then you will help me, Robert?"

He gave her fingers a gentle squeeze. "Of course."

"The accusations against me aren't entirely groundless. I did read those books. I did attend Xenobia's parties."

"You're as sane as I am," he declared.

"But I am a voluptuary. I do lust." *I lust for you, Robert. I want you.*

"All of us lust," he answered. "Only few of us will admit it."

She leaned toward him, tipping her face up. His breath caught, and a tiny tremor ran through him.

"Do you lust?" she whispered.

"All of us lust," he said.

She rested her palms against his chest and did her best to feel through all the layers of his clothing to sense his heartbeat. That didn't work, of course, and his expression gave nothing away. But a muscle near his mouth jumped, parting his lips no more than a feather's breadth.

Those lips had taken possession of her dreams, had occupied her thoughts until they'd nearly driven her frantic with wondering about the taste of them. Now, here they were, parted and only inches from her own. Did she dare to sample them?

Slowly, she rose toward him. When she wavered, he caught her elbows in his hands and steadied her. He was welcoming her, the dear man.

"May I kiss you, my precious Robert?" she heard her own voice ask. "May I touch my mouth to yours?"

"Celeste, I . . ." His voice came out unsteadily, but his hands held her firmly against his chest.

"Will you indulge me?" she breathed against his mouth. "Poor, sad sinner that I am?"

"Oh, yes." He said the words so softly they almost didn't register in her ears. But her heart heard them.

She moved the scant distance between them and pressed her lips to his. Neither of them moved for a long moment. They simply stood as before, Celeste leaning into the strength of his body while his hands supported her. She let her mouth rest against his softly, barely touching.

Such delicious textures, his lips. Soft, firm, sweet. She sampled the lower one, taking it between both of hers and nipping. He groaned deep in the back of his throat but didn't move. He held perfectly still and allowed her to explore him. She kissed him more fully, letting her mouth travel over his and then to his chin. She trailed kisses across the length of his jaw and rubbed her nose against the faint stubble on his cheek. She found his earlobe and nibbled on that until he trembled against her—his strong body shuddering.

She blew hot breath into his ear and followed that with the tip of her tongue, and something snapped inside him. With a growl, he pulled her against him, cupping her buttocks with his hands as his mouth sought hers and plundered it.

Over and over he kissed her, as if only her lips stood between him and hell. He devoured her upper lip and then the lower one. Thrusting his tongue between them, he probed her mouth until she couldn't breathe but could only gasp and return his passion with her own.

She'd lived for this her entire life. His kiss took her from dull non-being to brilliant, buzzing reality. She answered his fervor with passion she hadn't known she had. She slipped her arms around his neck and pulled herself fully against him until her breasts crushed against his chest—another set of sensations, almost painful in their erotic beauty.

On and on he went, merciless, generous, demanding. He trembled and moaned her name and held her against him with an almost frightening strength. She'd never felt the power of a man's body unleashed before. She'd never lived until this very moment. Her heart might burst with all the joy.

Then, suddenly, he stopped. He brought his hands up to her face and pressed her head to his chest, stroking her skin as though to comfort her.

"I'm sorry," he said in a rusty whisper.

"I'm not," she answered.

"I was taking advantage of your situation."

"It wasn't any advantage I didn't encourage."

"Still . . ." He held her gently, stroking her face. The tenderness of the gesture almost made her weep until she noticed something else. Something hard was pressing into her belly. His hardness, no doubt. His sex, his member, felt perfectly huge, impossibly long and thick. If only she had the courage to press her hand against the front of his pants, she'd get some better idea of his dimensions. But she'd spoil the moment if she did that. He'd given her so much this afternoon—his acceptance, his promise of support, the joy of his caress. So much. She'd have to be satisfied with all those gifts for now. Lovemaking would come later. One way or another, Robert Albright would be her lover, and she'd be the happiest woman in the world.

"I'm a gentleman, Celeste," he murmured after several heartbeats had passed between them. "I hope."

"I hope not," she answered. "My husband was a gentleman."

"Your husband was an ass."

She laughed. Oh, Lord, how long had it been since she'd really laughed? Robert laughed, too, and the sound echoed through his chest into her, such music.

She leaned back and gazed up into his face. She found him smiling at her, that expression of uncomplicated acceptance that had so endeared him to her on their first meeting. Dear Robert. Beloved Robert.

"So, will you help me?" she asked.

"Yes."

"And you'll come back to see me again?"

His smile broadened. "Certainly."

And will you be my lover? she added silently.

Of course, she heard him answer in her mind.

❧⟨ᗣᘐᗧ⟩❧

Robert drove home with a rock-hard erection that throbbed in his pants. Every jolt of the wheels traveled through his bones right to his cock, and no number of deep breaths brought him any relief. This was torture, pure torture. If he so much as touched himself, he'd spend, howling out his lust like a crazed animal. He might do that yet. He might have no choice. But right now, he'd torment himself with the image of Celeste Broder and what he'd almost done with her among the yews at the Wainwright Asylum.

Millie had never excited him like that. As much as he'd wanted his wife, as many hours as he'd spent lying next to her, aroused and aching, Millie had never sent him into such a frenzy. And to think, he'd only kissed Celeste. True, he'd brought her hips up hard against his rod and held her there, but truth be told, Long Tom had been ready for a coupling from the moment they'd entered that copse of yews. Just being alone with his raven-haired temptress was enough to make him as randy as a callow boy.

And he was going to do it again. God help him, he was going to get her someplace private and frig her until neither of them could stand.

Damn, when had his thoughts become so foul?

He pulled on the reins, bringing his horse to a halt. Sienna whinnied and shook his head, impatient to get back to the barn and some oats, no doubt. But much more jostling, and Robert's cock would spew copious amounts of sperm into his trousers.

He closed his eyes, counted to ten and then to twenty. Anything to get some control. But he'd never get control of his body if he couldn't control his mind. The images of Celeste wouldn't leave him—how her lips had felt under his, soft, pliant, and yet demanding. How her skin had flushed and her breasts had risen and fallen under her bodice as she'd worked to catch her breath. All that, and the shy way she'd asked permission to kiss him. *She'd* asked for *his* consent.

Why shouldn't he consent? Why shouldn't he consent to anything she asked of him? They were both grown and unencumbered with other attachments. He wouldn't be taking her innocence. Hell, he wouldn't be taking anything from her that she didn't freely offer. If she wanted him to take her to his bed, why shouldn't he? She did want him. He couldn't doubt that any longer. She wanted him. Mrs. Celeste Broder—wealthy, beautiful, passionate beyond any measure he'd ever hoped to find in a woman—wanted him.

He laughed out loud as the pure absurdity of it hit him. Robert Albright—a lad too shy to approach any girl he admired, a man too timid to propose marriage without sweating and stammering, a husband too frightened to speak to his own wife about his needs—that Robert Albright would soon enjoy the pleasures of the flesh with a voluptuous creature like Celeste Broder. He'd spend hours, longer if he could manage, in rapture, exploring every inch of her. He'd try every caress, every maneuver he could think of to satisfy her. And somewhere he'd find the courage to tell her what pleased him. If the words wouldn't come, he'd take her hand and show her. Damn, but he'd do it. All of it.

Millie's parents would never approve. The City Council would never approve. No one in town would approve. Fine, they'd never know, and if they did find out, they could keep their opinions to themselves.

Millie wouldn't approve. Dear Millie—his little love, his wife. But she'd died and left him. Would she expect him to remain celibate for the rest of his life? She'd never enjoyed sexual relations herself, but surely, even she would understand that a man needed that, needed to satisfy his sex between a woman's legs, as much as he needed to breathe. He'd kept a tight rein on his desires for all the years they'd been married, despite what it had cost him.

He was forty-five years old and had never had full satisfaction. He'd bed Celeste Broder and give her whatever else she needed—freedom, affection, his highest esteem—anything. He'd need some time to arrange all the details for their lovers' tryst, but arrange them, he would.

He'd approach the board of directors of the asylum and work for her release. But before he could gain her complete freedom, he'd beg for a few precious hours in his custody. He'd convince them that an afternoon at his home would help her mind to heal.

Ha, a glorious bit of irony there. Nothing in her mind needed healing, but her body did, and so did his. Eros would be their doctor and his bedroom their sanitarium. And if The Almighty had any sense of justice whatsoever, he'd make the encounter magnificent enough to make up for two lifetimes of deprivation.

Chapter Three

Celeste seemed calm enough as she crossed the threshold into Robert's house. God knew he was in enough turmoil for both of them. He'd never invited a woman to a tryst before, let alone in his own home. He'd done his damnedest to make everything perfect, but what if he'd failed? Celeste Broder was used to the finest of Manhattan society. When the time came for him to offer his hospitality—himself, his own person—would she find him lacking?

"May I take your wrap?" he asked, extending his hand toward her.

"It's lovely." She crossed the entryway into the sunlit foyer. Spinning in a near-circle, she took in the curving formal staircase, the rosewood center table with the bouquet he'd arranged himself, the antique clock against the wall. "Your home is utterly charming, Robert."

So much for his fears that she wouldn't like his house. For the first time that day, he managed to breathe deeply. "Thank you."

She handed him her shawl and scowled in a way that was more flirtatious than angry. "I should be furious with you for leaving me in that dreadful place for two full weeks with no word."

"I'm sorry you had to wait," he said, but didn't add that he'd also spent the past two weeks in an agony of anticipation and longing. "I had to go before the board of directors of the asylum to get you an afternoon free. They only meet once a month."

"But you did it, Robert," she answered. "Thank you."

He also didn't mention that he'd had to plead Celeste's case in full view and hearing of Wainwright and that matron, who'd glowered at him the whole time. He'd made enemies there, no doubt about it. He'd have to work through the board of directors in the future to win even the smallest concessions.

"Wainwright warned the board that you might try to manipulate the situation," he said.

"Did he?"

"Oh, yes." In fact, Wainwright had called her hysterical and devious.

"The pompous, old goat," she said.

"He especially advised me to keep clear of your machinations."

She laughed for a moment and then gave him a wickedly seductive smile. "And do you plan to heed his advice?"

"That depends on what your machinations are."

"My champion," she cried as she rushed to him, laughing, and threw her arms around his shoulders. "You've given me an afternoon of freedom, and I don't care what they said about me."

Still holding her shawl in one hand, he caught her in an embrace and held her against him. He'd probably regret that, having spent the entire day in a state of arousal in anticipation of her visit. Sensing that his satisfaction was near, Long Tom thickened and hardened at even this modest contact with her body. His poor cock would have to wait. He still had to get through checking that Francie had left and then tea before he found satisfaction.

Just then his two Afghan hounds burst into the room. Traveler and Georgette spotted Celeste and headed toward her, their paws slipping on the polished wood floor. Before Robert could stop the dogs' approach, Celeste squealed and dropped to her knees.

"Dogs!" she proclaimed, extending her arms to encircle the animals. "Your company, an afternoon free, and dogs, too. What a lucky woman I am."

"Get back, you two," he ordered the dogs.

"Don't you dare go." She buried her face into Traveler's fur. "I haven't played with a dog for years."

"I'm afraid their idea of play isn't ladylike."

"Good, because I don't want to be a lady this afternoon." Georgette licked Celeste's face as though they were old friends, and Celeste laughed with more abandon than he could remember since he'd met her. "I don't know if I should let you do that," she said to the dog. "Your master may not want to kiss me when you're done."

"Always," he said. "I always want to kiss you, Celeste."

She glanced up at him and smiled shyly. His member hardened further, almost jerking in his pants. Damn, but he wanted this woman.

A throat cleared at the threshold to the solarium.

"Ah, there you are, Francie," he said.

"Mr. Albright." His part-time maid nodded to him and then looked pointedly at Celeste, who rose and folded her hands together in front of her skirts.

"Mrs. Broder is my guest for tea," he said. That little bit of news would find its way all over town by morning, but he could do nothing about that now. "Would you see that it's set out, please?"

"Already done, sir."

"Good. Then thank Mrs. Kenny for me and head off for the day."

"She's gone, sir," Francie answered. "You told her to go home some time ago."

Celeste lowered her lashes, and one corner of her mouth lifted no more than a fraction of an inch. Just enough to express her approval.

"Thank you, Francie. I'd forgotten," he said. "Take the dogs with you and then run along."

Francie came just far enough into the foyer to grasp the dogs by their collars and take one more questioning look toward Celeste. With Traveler and Georgette under control, the maid turned and headed toward the back of the house.

Robert gestured toward the solarium. "Would you join me for tea, Mrs. Broder?"

"My pleasure, Mr. Albright." She went in the direction he'd indicated. He paused only to drape her shawl over the banister. As he did, the sound of the back door closing floated softly through the house. They were alone. Smiling, he followed Celeste.

She stood next to his prized white cattleya orchid, her nose no more than an inch from one of the flowers.

"That one isn't scented," he said.

"As beautiful as it is, it doesn't need perfume."

"The same's true of you," he said. He hadn't lied there. The mere sight of her—the soft flush to her skin, the length of her throat, the swell of her breasts bound deliciously by her corset—was enough to drive any man past the breaking point. He must have passed that point, though, because he thought he could make out the scent of her. Not rose water or some other pretense, but a hot, musky scent that invaded his nostrils and clouded his brain. The fertile aroma of his plants, combined with something else essentially hers.

She turned and smiled at him. "You enjoy horticulture?"

"It's one of my passions," he answered. His only passion until two weeks ago.

"I used to have a garden I loved," she said. "Horace didn't like my fingers dirty, but I insisted."

"I'll show you my garden in a bit."

"I'd like that."

"But first, let's have our tea." He gestured toward the white-washed, cast-iron table where Francie had set the teapot and the short-cake Mrs. Kenny had made that morning. Chilled bowls of strawberries and whipped cream stood nearby—only inches from her plate and the gift he'd wrapped that morning.

He pulled out her chair. After she sat, he let his fingers drift along the length of her throat. Her pulse beat rapidly just under her skin. Apprehension? Anticipation? Impossible to tell, but once she'd opened her present, she'd have no doubt what he intended for the rest of the afternoon.

She picked the parcel up and toyed with the ribbon. "For me?"

"A small gift to replace the one you lost."

She gave him a questioning look, but he just smiled and took his own seat while she unwrapped the package. When she saw the book, she let out a little gasp of surprise. "*The Pearl.* Wherever did you find this?"

"An obscure bookshop got it for me." A bookshop in a different town, three towns over, where no one knew him.

"You know what's in here, don't you?" she asked.

He did. In that book and four other erotic ones he'd bought and read himself in the past week. "I know."

"Are Lady Pokingham and her amorous adventures your standard reading?"

"They are now."

She put down the book and stared into his face for a long moment. "I don't think I want any tea, Robert."

Rejection. His heart stopped beating, and his chest suddenly felt empty. She was rejecting him, after all. "Do you want to go back to the asylum?"

"Of course not," she answered softly.

"Then, what?"

Under the table, she reached out a hand and pressed her palm against his erection. "This. This is what I want."

A jolt of pleasure shot through him—so powerful he jumped in his seat, nearly knocking the table and its contents into her lap. "Dear God, Celeste."

"Don't deny me, my darling. Please."

"Deny you?" he croaked. "Never."

She stretched out her fingers, as though measuring the length and width of him. If she was going to become frightened of his size, she'd do it now, because his member was fully engorged under her touch.

She showed no fear, though, but only smiled. "I've dreamed of you for two weeks now. Like this. Just like this. Does that shock you?"

"No." It did shock him, although he'd never tell her that. She might remove her hand if he did. "But I need to warn you that I won't last if you continue to do that."

She squeezed him, and his cock responded, growing longer and harder, although he would never have believed that possible.

"Mercy," he cried.

"None," she answered. "I want to look at you."

"We have all afternoon," he said. "I want to pleasure you first."

"Later. Please, Robert, show yourself to me."

He groaned and turned in his chair so that the front of his pants was exposed to her view. He couldn't have stood. He wouldn't have found the strength.

She gently spread his legs apart and dropped to her knees between them. In that position, she placed her mouth against the fabric of his pants, her hot, and moist breath seeping through to his flesh. His hips jerked, pressing his throbbing member against her lips. He reached out blindly with his hands, grasping for anything to use as an anchor, anything to distract him from her assault on his control. His fingers found the curving bars that held the seat of his chair, and he clung to them while his cock swelled and threatened to explode under her touch.

She stroked his length and then slowly unfastened the buttons of his fly to free him. When she had him fully exposed, she gasped. "She was right. Oh dear heaven, Xenobia told the truth."

"Xenobia?"

"Oh . . . yes. Xenobia told me that a man was beautiful when aroused. She didn't exaggerate."

Celeste closed her fingers around his shaft, and the sight of her white gloves against the livid purple of his cock sent him past any wonder of what Xenobia Stewart might have said. He was going to come, any moment now. Nothing on Earth could stop him.

Celeste stroked him, down to his sac and then back up. "How should I do this?"

"That's it . . . doing . . . fine," he managed between clenched teeth.

"What about the tip?" she murmured. "It's so large."

She flicked her thumb along the underside of the swollen head and then rubbed until a drop of fluid appeared. Gripping the rungs of the chair until his palms hurt, he fought the urge to surrender. *Going to come, going to come. Must . . . make . . . it . . . last.*

She squeezed again and stroked and stroked. Faster. Firmer. No hope. No hope to resist. He felt the climax starting and gave in to it. He watched his own cock jerk upwards—now, now, now—as his essence spurted out of him. He hung suspended in time while his semen sprayed all over her hand and her bosom. Finally, he collapsed against his seat and closed his eyes. In the peace that followed, even consciousness slipped away from him.

❦

Celeste watched Robert's face as he closed his eyes and drifted off into some private heaven. For now, she couldn't imagine anything more fascinating than the expression of joy on his features. Despite the urgency of her own arousal, she'd wait happily for Robert to recover. She sat up in her chair and basked in the sight of him.

Xenobia hadn't lied about his dimensions. Celeste had had no experience with men's members other than Horace's, which was to say almost no experience at all. She'd wondered often about how that part of a man was built, but she'd never imagined that one could be at once so large and so beautiful. Even in repose, it made her shiver with anticipation.

Robert opened his eyes finally, sighed, and smiled at her. She'd loved his smile since the first moment she'd seen it. Now it made her heart burst with happiness and pride.

His smile turned to an embarrassed grin, though, as he quickly picked up a linen napkin from the table and swiped at the white droplets that still adorned her bodice. "I am sorry."

"I'm not." The pressure of his hands against her breasts felt so blessedly good, she could hardly feel sorry about anything.

"I've never lost control like that," he said. "My lust may have ruined your dress."

"I don't care, as long as I pleased you," she said.

"Pleased me?" He laughed deep in his throat, a delicious, wicked sound. "Dear Celeste. You nearly killed me."

"I'll take that as a compliment."

He reached across the table and took her hand. "Oh, my darling."

"I've never done that to a man before. Reading about something is quite a different thing from doing it."

"My angel, I hope I do half as well for you."

Her heart thudded at that statement. What would he do for her? Would he touch her the same way, the way she'd imagined him stroking her while she pleasured herself? Would he drive her wild with his fingers and then let his enormous sex finish the job? When she next spent, would she do so all around his hardness? The mere thought stole her breath.

"Do you know what that does to me?" he asked.

"What?"

"The way your skin flushes. You did it the first day we met. I had to get away from you before the swelling in my pants became too obvious to miss."

She put her fingers over her mouth. "That day? In Wainwright's office? You were . . . that way?"

"I'm always 'that way' around you, sweetest. I'm getting 'that way' again right now."

She glanced quickly at him. He'd turned in his seat, but she could still make out the state of his member. It was swelling already and lengthening.

"Will you make love to me now?" she asked.

"Soon," he answered. "But first, I want to make you come the way you did me."

The throbbing accelerated between her legs, now so fast and hard she could feel it beating in rhythm with her heart. Moisture pooled there until her drawers were quite saturated. She had to work for breath, and the effort left her dizzy and weak.

He rose from his chair and helped her up. She watched his elegant fingers as he removed her gloves. For a moment, he stood and stared at the one that had stroked his member and still bore the evidence of his ejaculation. He slipped that into the pocket of his coat and smiled at her. "I'll treasure this always."

Such a sweet declaration almost brought tears to her eyes, but she fought them back and returned his gaze, putting every bit of her love into it. Gently, he turned her around and started undressing her. Her hat went first, landing on the tabletop, followed by the pins from her hair. While her curls fell all around her shoulders, his fingers worked on the fastenings of her dress. Layer by layer, the fabric fell away—first her bodice, then her skirts. Cool air washed over her as the warmth of his hands sank through her skin and into her bones. Petticoats came off and then her corset cover, and finally the corset itself, freeing her breasts from their confinement.

He reached around her and squeezed her breasts. She rested back against him and whimpered.

"My darling," he whispered against her throat. He kissed her there, nipping her skin to the edge of her shoulder as he eased her chemise down her arms. "My dear Celeste. My beautiful Celeste."

The cotton caught on her erect nipples, torturing the over-sensitive flesh. He pushed the chemise down and over her hips until it fell in a pool at her feet and then took her breasts in his hands again.

"Oh, Robert." She pressed back against him, against the renewed hardness of his member. If she didn't have him inside her soon, she'd die of frustration.

He touched her then. He slipped his hands over her belly and down into her drawers to stroke her sex. She shuddered and cried out as his fingers moved gently over the center of her arousal.

"Sweet," he murmured against her shoulder. "Hot, so hot. Wet and sweet."

"I can't bear it," she moaned. "Hurry. Please. Give me release."

But, instead of pushing her past the edge, he slid her drawers over her hips and helped her to turn and sit down. Breathing heavily, beyond mere torture now, she sat and watched as he dropped to his knees before her as she had done with him. He pulled the drawers over her feet and tossed them aside, leaving nothing on her body but her slippers and hose. Then he spread her legs.

Now, surely now he would touch her and end this agony. In another moment, she'd climax whether he touched her or not. But oh, how much more glorious it would be to feel his fingers on her as she came. She stretched forward, pushing her hips toward the edge of the seat. Toward him.

He still denied her, though. From under heavy eyelids, she watched as he reached to the table and dipped his finger into the whipped cream. That, then, he finally brought to her aching sex. With the other hand, he parted her lips, and he pressed the cream against her pearl. The coldness sent a jolt through her, shocking her out of her languor.

His touch gentled as he continued to rub the rapidly warming cream against her. Nothing had ever felt like this, even in her most heated dreams. Higher and higher she floated—so close to completion her whole body tensed and readied itself.

He reached for the cream again. This time she tried to steel herself for the cold, but nothing could save her from its icy burn. He rubbed it in again, at first slowly and then faster until she hovered right at the edge of sanity. Through a reddish haze of lust, she watched as he removed his finger and covered her throbbing sex with his mouth.

The instant he touched her with his tongue, she came. Throwing back her head, she cried out as the spasms raced through her. Over and over. Quicker. Harder. Each stronger and faster than the last until she lost all connection to reality and fell back against the chair. Spent.

Drained. And yet, as the drowsiness enveloped her, her inner muscles still clenched and unclenched, reluctant to surrender the last bit of sweetness.

She sat that way, absolutely motionless, for what seemed like forever. Slowly, consciousness of her own being returned and with it sounds. Birdsong—lovely and distant. A rustling of leaves. The beat of her own heart.

And breathing. Robert's breathing.

She opened her eyes and found him. His head rested, cheek down, on one of her thighs as he gazed up at her. The fingers of one hand were still splayed over her other thigh, making tiny indentations in her flesh.

The image of him looking at her that way—as if she were the most perfect woman in creation—made her chest hurt and her eyes burn. In just a scant hour—less—he'd taken something ugly and made it beautiful. He'd taken a gift that Horace had scorned and elevated it to a miracle.

She lifted an impossibly heavy arm and stroked the side of his face.

"Did I please you?" he asked.

She let out a sob. What other answer could she make to a question like that? Had he pleased her? Did the sun brighten the heavens? Did she love him with every bit of her heart and soul? Yes, yes, yes.

Love. She loved Robert Albright. First, her champion. Then, her lover. Now, her soul mate. He was her world. Whatever misery had driven her to this room at this moment, she blessed it now. She'd found love, finally—the only real reason to exist.

"Here," he said, as he rose on his knees and rubbed a tear away from her cheek with his thumb. "There's no reason to cry."

She laughed, even while the tears continued to come.

"I may not be much of a lover, but I don't think I'm that bad," he said.

That little bit of absurdity made her laugh even harder. "Not much of a lover?"

"Well, you're still sitting at the tea table, wearing nothing but shoes and hose." He cleared his throat. "And I . . . well, my pants are undone."

Glancing down, she discovered that his pants were, indeed, still open. He'd grown hard again, and his member stuck straight out from the opening in front. Her earlier teasing and caresses hadn't diminished him in the least. If anything, he looked thicker and harder and more beautiful than ever. Her pulse quickened to think how he would feel inside her.

She rested her arms around his neck and kissed him, for the first time that afternoon and all the sweeter after what they'd given each other since her arrival. Now, she wanted more.

"Mr. Albright," she murmured against his lips. "Are we going to have to sit through several cups of tea while trying to choke down that whipped cream? Or are you finally going to make love to me?"

He laughed and scrambled to his feet, scooping her up in his arms as he rose. "To hell with tea, and to hell with the whipped cream."

Chapter Four

Celeste covered her lover's face with caresses as Robert nudged a door open with his foot and carried her into a sun-drenched bedroom as lovely as any she'd ever seen. She stopped kissing him and clung to his neck. This was what she'd dreamed of when she pictured her wedding day and initiation into womanhood—to be swept up into the arms of the man she loved and to be carried to bed as though she were some delicate treasure. Instead, she'd lost her virginity, and her innocence, with Horace in a darkened hotel room after a long and tiring wedding reception. Nothing like this little piece of Paradise.

An open window let in a warm breeze along with the sunlight and the scent of roses and green earth. More flowers like the ones in the front hallway stood in an antique ewer on the bedside table. The bed itself had ornate wooden posts at each corner, topped by a canopy of eyelet lace. The comforter and coverlets had been turned down to expose dazzling white sheets.

Robert had planned their afternoon of lovemaking well. She'd suspected as much when he sent his servants home. The dear man. Could she possibly love him any more than she did right at this moment?

He walked to the bed and set her onto the crisp sheets as gently as if she were made of butterflies' wings. After sitting beside her, he took her hand and brought her fingers to his lips. She ought to have found the image strange—a large man kissing her palm and then the inside of her wrist, while his manhood projected from his pants, fully erect and perfectly enormous. Nothing seemed the least bit odd, though. This was Robert, her shy lover and champion of contradictions.

He leaned over and kissed her. First on the forehead and then the tip of her nose. Finally, he pressed his lips to hers and teased them apart. She took his face in her hands and answered with every bit of passion and love in her. His breath was sweet, his sighs even sweeter. She opened her mouth and grazed his lips with her tongue. He groaned, invading her mouth and sending a spiral of heat from her belly upward. As he ravished her mouth, the fabric of his vest rubbed against her nipples.

She grasped the lapels of his jacket and pushed the garment over his shoulders. "You're wearing entirely too many clothes."

He sat up and smiled at her. "So are you."

"I'm only wearing shoes and stockings," she answered.

"Far too many clothes." He lifted one of her feet, removed her slipper, and dropped it to the floor. He did the same for the other and then slid his fingers under the garter that held her stocking. The feel of his hand against her inner thigh brought back sensations of how he'd driven her mad earlier. She let him stroke her there, his gentle touch sending a flash of heat through her breasts. He slipped one stocking down her leg and then reached to the other garter. By the time he'd removed that stocking, too, her bosom rose and fell as she struggled for air.

This time, though, she'd take him with her into madness.

As much as she hated pushing his hands away, she managed to sit up and maneuver his jacket the rest of the way over his shoulders and then off his arms. After that, she started in on the buttons of his vest.

"I never saw my husband naked," she said. "It didn't matter with him, but I want to see all of you."

"I'm not young anymore," he answered. "I hope you're not disappointed."

She reached down and curled her fingers around his engorged sex. It thickened even further against her palm. "I won't be disappointed."

He gave her a devilish grin. He was getting good at those. The man who'd seemed almost frightened of her the first time they'd met now became the wicked pirate of her dreams. Now, this afternoon, in this bed with the smells of sunshine and roses wafting through the window and the pristine canopy overhead, she'd finally have her pirate.

She unbuttoned his vest and took that off him. Next went his shirt, so that he was naked from the waist up and she could finally gaze at his chest and the broad shoulders she'd admired since the first. Running her palms over him, she caressed his flat nipples with her thumbs. He trembled but kept his gaze evenly on her face.

"So beautiful," she whispered, as she traced his collar bone and dipped her fingertips into the hollows at the base of his throat.

"Hardly beautiful." He took her hands in his.

"More beautiful than beautiful."

He bent and removed his shoes and hose and then stood by the side of the bed. It took only an instant to slip his pants and drawers off, and finally he was naked.

Nature could scarcely have made a more perfect creature than Robert Albright. He might no longer have been young, but he stood straight and tall. Lofty brow, strong jaw, finely muscled neck leading to a broad chest with nothing to interrupt its classic lines. His belly looked firm for the stroking, and below lay the curling hairs that concealed the base of his sex—a base as thick as her wrist. The organ itself jutted a full nine inches from his torso, if she was any judge.

For the first time, the full impact of his size hit her. What would she do if she couldn't take all of him? She'd never had any man other than Horace, and he'd never presented this kind of problem.

"Frightened?" he asked.

She opened her mouth, but no sound came out. She moistened her lips and tried again. "A little."

"I'll be gentle with you," he answered. "I might not have been capable of gentleness before you . . . um . . . gave me some relief. But I can now."

"You'd never hurt me."

"No, I wouldn't."

She raised her arms. "Then, come to me, my lover."

He eased himself onto the bed and took her into his arms. Such joy to be with him this way—flesh to flesh, with not a scrap separating them. She rested back and welcomed his weight on top of her as he claimed her mouth in a kiss like none she'd ever experienced.

He held her under his solid length while his lips and tongue explored her on their own. He teased and cajoled her mouth while the heat of his body wrapped all around her. She answered with her own kisses, but no matter how she tried, she couldn't get enough of him. She let her hands travel over his back, testing his muscles as they bunched under her palms. He touched her as he kissed her. His fingers moved along her sides, now tracing her ribs and then sliding under her hips to pull her up and against his sex. She moved, parting her legs until the tip of him rested against the entrance to her core.

"Not yet," he gritted. "Ah, my love, not yet."

She shifted again, and the head of his member pressed against the throbbing nub between her legs. She couldn't stifle a cry as sheer pleasure knifed through her. Again, she moved against him, and again a shock of arousal followed, sending her close to oblivion.

He pulled back and gazed into her face while she whimpered in disappointment.

"Soon, my darling," he whispered. "First, let me worship you."

His body slid over hers as he nipped along the length of her throat. He didn't stop there, but moved his face into the cleft of her bosom while he gathered her breasts in his hands to nuzzle them with his nose. The fire in her belly burned hot in anticipation of what would come next, but nothing prepared her for the feeling of his lips on her nipple as he took the swollen flesh into his mouth and suckled.

When he'd finished teasing that nipple into a state of ecstasy almost too intense to bear, he switched to the other. She cradled his head, holding his face to her breast as she clasped her legs together and felt herself growing wet for him.

He placed a palm against her belly and stroked her there. Close to what she needed, but not close enough.

"Soon, my love," he whispered. "Soon."

"Robert," she gasped, breath all but impossible. "Please, Robert."

"First, I want to sip your nectar."

Oh, dear heaven. He meant to put his mouth between her legs again. "But, I want you inside me when I next spend."

He chuckled against the skin of her stomach. "Then, you'll have to resist coming while I feast on your cunny, won't you?"

"I can't," she cried. "You'll make me climax. I know it."

"Climax or not, as you want. But, I will have the taste of you again."

With no further warning, he moved lower and urged her knees apart. Too weak to resist, she parted her legs and allowed him to cover her sex with his mouth. Resist, he'd told her. Impossible. His tongue slid between the petals of her sex and found the exact spot to drive her mad. She squirmed to get free, but the action only brought her harder against his mouth and the flicking of his tongue.

"Please, Robert," she said. "I can't resist it."

He didn't stop, so she grabbed fistfuls of sheets and twisted them. She bit her lip until it hurt, but nothing could keep her from spending. She couldn't hold back, not another minute. He had to stop.

"Now," she shrieked, while she still had a tiny scrap of sanity. "Please, oh please. Take me now."

He rose above her, finally, and positioned himself between her legs. Reaching down, she grasped his sex to guide it to her. The tip of him slid inside her, bringing with it a set of sensations beyond description. Large, smooth, as hard as steel, it stretched her until she could take no more and she sobbed with frustration.

Too big. He was too big. An orgasm like none she'd ever had lay just out of her reach, and his cock was too big.

"Push, Robert," she said.

"I can't hurt you," he whispered into her ear.

"I don't care if you split me in two."

"Oh, God. Agony," he said.

"Please!"

"Wait." He took a few gasping breaths. "There's another way."

"Anything."

He rolled onto his back, his sex standing straight up and out from his body. She ran her fingers down it, measuring its incredible size. No wonder she hadn't been able to accept him all. What would they do now?

"Lower yourself onto me slowly," he said. "I'll help you."

She sat up and swung a leg over him, positioning her hips so that he could drive himself into her. If they couldn't do this easily, he'd have to use pressure. One way or the other, she would have all of him inside her.

Sinking his fingers into her hips, he guided her onto him. Once again, the head of his sex entered her, and the throbbing in her own sex almost sent her spinning out of control.

This time she stretched to take more of him, and she almost wept for joy as she watched that magnificent instrument begin to disappear inside her wetness.

"That's it," he said. His face contorted in pleasure. "Easy now. More. A little at a time."

"Yes," she crooned. "Yes. Yessssss."

She sank lower and lower onto him, slowly, loving every inch of his hardness as it entered her. She watched his face as she did. His total concentration went to the place of their joining, pure rapture on his face, and then his hips began to move. Gentle thrusts, up and into her. The movement helped her to accommodate him, as she grew wetter and hotter in response. Her own sex was on fire between her legs, and only a fierce struggle kept her from coming before he'd totally buried himself inside her. Biting her lip again, she pushed down and down onto him. Heaven. Hell. Bliss. Torture. She couldn't fight it any longer. Another moment. Just a little harder. Push.

He released her hips and placed his thumb over her pearl and rubbed. She gasped and held on. He stroked and rubbed and teased and rubbed some more, and she felt herself flying free from Earth. One last upward thrust of his hips buried him in to the hilt. Completion. She let herself come. She pushed herself forward, bringing her pearl against

his thumb as it feathered madness over her. She screamed in her pleasure, and the spasms started. Gripping his shaft with each contraction,
she shouted out her passion. When it was done, she fell against his
chest, his cock still buried deep against her womb.

Robert let Celeste rest for as long as he could, but in the end, he
couldn't wait for her to recover. He was too hard, too hot, and much
too aroused to put off his own orgasm. During his marriage, he'd managed—with a great deal of effort—to make Millie come a few times.
But she'd never done it with such abandon, and she'd never done it
with him inside her. The sensation was indescribable. Even now, moments after Celeste's release, her cunny still clutched at him in rhythmic spasms. She'd milk him dry in a moment, even if he just lay here
in total inaction. Inaction wasn't how he planned to end this interlude.

Her face lay against his chest, and he brushed the curls from her
forehead and pressed a kiss there. "Celeste, my darling?"

"Hmmmm," she answered.

There had to be gentle ways to rouse her, but Lord help him, he
couldn't wait for those. He raised his hips, moving himself inside her,
showing her that he was still rock hard.

"Oh!" She raised her head and looked into his eyes. "That is the
most extraordinary feeling."

"This?" he said, as he thrust again, harder and deeper this time.
The movement almost cost him what little control he still had.

"Oh, yes," she said, tipping her head back in what looked like pure
bliss. "I could happily let you do that all day."

"Not much chance of that, I'm afraid."

"You tire of me already?" The question sounded petulant, but she
smiled and began to move her hips so that her sex gripped his with a
sweetness he'd never dared to dream of.

"Tire of you?" He laughed, but the sound came out forced. "It's
only . . ." He moved again, starting a rhythm that would be the end of
him. "Long Tom's waited as long as he can. He needs his reward."

She rose up, placing her hands on either side of his waist, closed
her eyes, and answered his movements with her own. "I sympathize
completely."

She took him easily now. Her cunny still gripped him tightly, but
he slid in and out of her in fluid, maddening movements. He grasped

her hips and pushed up into her with all the passion inside him. "Then, you'll understand . . ."

"Understand what?" She rocked forward and back, squeezing him.

That was all it took. He could stand no more. He flipped her onto her back and buried himself so deeply in her he lost his very identity. He rested his face at the base of her throat and moved inside her with a mindless violence. Over and over—he couldn't help himself.

Instead of crying out in pain, she wrapped her legs around him and met his thrusts. Lusty, loud cries issued from her throat. Or maybe they were his. Or theirs. He didn't know. His passion claimed him—white-hot and undeniable. The pressure built at the base of his spine, and the orgasm was on him. Wild now, he thrust and thrust and thrust.

Just as he sent the first stream of sperm into her, she tensed all around him and then burst into her own climax. Her spasms sent him even higher, drawing him out into one explosion after another. Finally, his body could give no more, and he went limp, sobbing his rapture into her shoulder.

Until this moment, he'd never lived. Forty-five years of existence, and he'd never been truly alive. He ought to find that sad, but right now he couldn't manage to feel anything but utter peace. Repletion, fulfillment, peace. And love. Yes, love.

He loved this woman who now lay beneath him, her body a warm haven for his own. He'd loved her from the moment he first set his gaze on her radiant face. Now, he'd love her for the rest of eternity, because she completed him, made him whole in ways he'd never imagined. And he'd keep her with him, happy and safe from anything that could hurt her. If only she'd grant him that right.

He found the strength to sigh. That done, he reached deep into his reserves and commanded his muscles to roll off her.

⚜

Celeste whimpered at the separation from her lover's body. Her eyes still closed in bliss, she turned toward him and circled his neck with her arms.

"Did you really have to leave me?" she whispered into his chest.

"Only for now."

"Don't let now last too long."

He laughed. "You really will kill me."

He rolled onto his back, pulling her with him until her head rested on his shoulder. In that position, his fingers naturally fell onto the skin of her back, and he stroked her gently, sketching circles around and over her spine. She stretched like a cat and then settled her whole length against him, casting her leg over his.

"I've never experienced anything like that," she said. "Have you?"

"Never."

"Never with your wife?"

"Never," he repeated. "I wouldn't have thought it possible. Until now."

"What was she like?" Celeste asked. "Your wife."

"Millie was . . ." He sighed and stroked Celeste's shoulder. "She was delicate. Small. She died very young."

Ah, yes. She died having succumbed to Robert's demands in bed, according to Xenobia's note. The poor woman couldn't have appreciated what she had. She couldn't have realized what joy could be found in the arms of a lover like Robert. Celeste would certainly never make the same mistake, so she snuggled even closer to him.

He kissed her forehead and then moved briefly away from her to open the drawer of the bedside table. After a moment, he turned back and handed her a miniature portrait. "This was Millie shortly before we were married."

She glanced at the portrait briefly and then at Robert's face. The expression she found there tore at her heart. Sadness, love, longing, and something else—regret? Could he honestly feel that he'd contributed to his wife's death?

Life and love hadn't dealt with the darling man fairly. First, he'd had a wife who couldn't cherish the gift of passion he'd had to give her. Then, he'd been left alone by her death. Xenobia hadn't treated him fairly in writing that note and revealing his secrets. Celeste herself had taken advantage of his loneliness and all that wonderful passion inside him by not telling him honestly of Xenobia's plan for him to be her lover. She'd make that up to him somehow. She'd make him happy if it killed her.

"My father-in-law had this painted for me," he was saying. "The miniaturist is quite famous now."

"It's lovely," she murmured, although she could scarcely bring herself to look at the thing, she was that jealous of the woman who'd been lucky enough to call Robert husband.

He pulled her back against his chest and handed the painting to her. Millie had been blond and perfect, with a tiny, bow mouth and up-turned nose.

"She was very beautiful," Celeste said.

"No more beautiful than you," he answered. He took the painting from her and returned it to the drawer. Then he rolled over, squeezed her shoulders, and pressed a kiss to her forehead. "To me, you're the most beautiful woman in the world."

"That's because you're uncritical and generous with your feelings, Robert. I don't deserve you."

He pulled back and looked down into her face. "What an odd thing to say."

"It's true," she said. Oh, for heaven's sake, what was wrong with her? She hadn't done anything so terrible by not telling him the truth. But she had kept Xenobia's letter hidden in her room at the asylum. He'd not only be angry with her if that note came to light, he'd feel humiliated. First by his dead wife, then by Xenobia, now by her. She'd been stupid to keep the thing, of course. It could only cause the two of them misery. She'd destroy it the minute she got back to her room. And then, maybe some time in the future, she'd confess everything to him. Much later, after their love had had a chance to deepen and mature. Right now their new-found happiness was far too fragile to risk confession.

"You're not having regrets, are you?" he asked, his expression turning from one of puzzlement to outright concern. "I know this isn't the way these things are supposed to happen."

She grasped his face in her hands and stretched upward so that she could place a kiss on his lips. "I regret nothing. This has been the most wonderful afternoon of my life."

He smiled and blushed. "You flatter me."

"Not at all."

He took one of her hands in his and tangled their fingers together. "Good, because I know how I can make everything right."

"But it is right."

"I can make it even more right," he answered.

She laughed. "How could you possibly make this afternoon any better?"

"By making you my wife."

His wife? An audible gasp escaped her before she could stop it. She'd never dared to hope for anything so wonderful as a proposal from Robert. "You want to marry me?"

"If you'll have me," he answered. "I've earned a substantial amount of money of my own. I have a few good years left in me, and I'm an agreeable enough soul, or so I've been told."

"Agreeable?" She had to laugh at the inadequacy of the word. "Oh, Robert, you're wonderful. Perfect. Divine."

"And there is one extra benefit of marrying me," he said. "As your next of kin, I can have you signed out of the Wainwright Asylum, even over your children's objections."

"You can?"

"I consulted a lawyer. The children can try fighting me, but I'd win."

"Oh, Robert, I do love you so," she said. No other words would do. She threw her arms around his neck and covered his face with kisses. She'd be free. She'd have her lover, only he'd be her husband. If she'd known that her imprisonment would lead to such happiness, she would have thanked Horace and Violet for sending her away. She'd felt so desperate and trapped, and now Robert Albright was about to make her the luckiest woman alive.

He was laughing now, too, and nuzzling her neck with his nose. "I'll resign from the bank and turn Connogua Springs over to the town council. We'll travel, go anywhere you'd like."

"All I need to see with you is the inside of a bedroom," she answered.

"We'll have a harem all to ourselves in Baghdad. We'll share a tent on the Serengeti. We'll make love on the back of an elephant in India."

"That sounds bumpy," she said.

"We'll manage." He placed a hand over her breast and flicked at the nipple with his thumb.

"Mmmm," she crooned as she stretched, giving him easier access to her bosom, her belly, and anything else he cared to stroke.

"I love you, Celeste. I'll make you happy."

"You already have."

"Marry me," he said, as his fingers found their way between her thighs to start the fire inside her all over again.

"Yes," she whispered, as he touched the most intimate part of her. "Oh, yes. Yessss."

Chapter Five

Wainwright summoned them into his office the minute they returned to the asylum. Celeste could tell from the look of utter triumph on Morton's face that something unpleasant awaited them. The doctor's expression held more than a little smugness, too, badly disguised behind his normal air of arrogance and authority. The two of them appeared to think they'd caught Robert and Celeste at something. As if Wainwright and Morton knew how they'd spent their afternoon. The whole atmosphere in the room gave Celeste a sick feeling in the pit of her stomach. Nothing good was going to happen here.

Robert glanced at her out of the corner of his eye, concern plainly written on his face as if he felt the same foreboding she did. Please, Lord, let this be no more than one of Wainwright's lectures about her disordered state. Let her get through the interview and go upstairs to destroy that letter and plan her future life far away from here.

"Please sit down," Wainwright said, indicating two chairs that had been set in front of his desk.

"Is something wrong?" Robert asked. "I had the board's permission to take Mrs. Broder to visit my home."

"Very much against my clinical judgement," Wainwright said. "Boards of lay people shouldn't involve themselves in the care of patients. They have no expertise."

"No harm was done," Robert answered. "I've brought Mrs. Broder back, safe and sound."

"I'll be the judge of what's best for my patients," Wainwright said, his face positively livid with righteous indignation. "I can only imagine what went on during your 'harmless' visit."

What in heaven's name was the man talking about? He couldn't possibly know how she and Robert had spent the afternoon. She still glowed inside, despite some soreness, but she'd see these two in hell before she gave them any inkling of her joy. Pearls before swine.

"What's this all about?" she asked. "What do you want from us?"

"Sit down, Mrs. Broder," Wainwright ordered like the autocrat he was.

She glanced at Robert who gave her a tiny nod. To reassure her, no doubt. But how could he do that if they didn't know what they were facing? She sat and watched as he took the other chair. So near—near enough that she could reach out and take his hand if she dared. Instead, she twisted her fingers together and waited.

Wainwright cleared his throat—another one of his annoying habits. "While you were gone today, Mrs. Broder, an alarming discovery came to light."

"What discovery?"

The man opened a desk drawer and pulled out a piece of paper. No, not a piece of paper, but an envelope. He tapped it against the desk and studied Celeste. The scent of French perfume reached her. Xenobia's perfume. Dear God, he held Xenobia's note in his hand.

She shot out of her chair. "You searched my room."

"The maid found it when she was cleaning," Morton replied.

"That's a lie." No maid could have happened on that note where she'd buried it under her small clothes in a drawer. "You searched my room."

Morton didn't answer but only gave Celeste the same self-satisfied smile she'd worn when they first entered the office. Damn the woman, and damn that smile.

"You had no right," Celeste said, as she reached for the envelope in the doctor's hand.

He pulled back, yanking the envelope out of her reach. "Calm yourself, Mrs. Broder."

"Calm myself?" she repeated. "When you allowed that woman to search my room?"

"It's not *your* room," the doctor said. "It's part of this institution, and we're only trying to help you."

"Celeste, please," Robert said so softly the other two might not have heard him. But they did. At the use of her Christian name, the two of them looked knowingly at Robert and then back at each other.

Dear Lord in heaven, what if they meant to show him the note? Anything but that. If he read what Xenobia had written about him, he'd completely misunderstand. Everything would sound so contrived—as if she'd planned to use him for something ugly. Xenobia had even included intimate details of his body. If he read that, he'd realize that Xenobia had put it all down—even the dimensions of his sex—where people like Wainwright and Morton could find it and cluck their tongues. She couldn't let him know that. Above all, he must not read that note.

She took a deep breath and did the best she could to appear calm. Unfortunately, she'd begun to tremble. Badly. Her hand shook as she held it out to Wainwright. "Please, may I have that note? It's silly and embarrassing, really. Everyone knows how Mrs. Stewart is. No one takes anything she says seriously."

Wainwright's eyebrow came up. "Is that so?"

"Well, yes." Celeste did her best to laugh lightly. It came out desperately dishonest even to her own ears. "Xenobia gets such ideas into her head. She'll have forgotten them completely within a week."

Wainwright turned toward Robert. "I have to assume you delivered this note, Mr. Albright."

"Yes, I did."

"Do you have any idea what it says?" the doctor asked.

"No."

"I thought as much."

"I didn't see any harm in delivering a letter to one of your patients," Robert said.

"Mr. Albright," the doctor said in the tone he used to promise a scolding, "the layman can hardly imagine what goes on inside the brains of the insane."

"I'm not insane," Celeste shouted. The trembling grew even worse, until she shook with fear and rage. In another moment, she'd look like a madwoman. Robert knew better than to believe that, of course. But Lord only knew what he'd believe about her once he'd read that note.

"Our patients often appear rational, just as normal as you or me," Wainwright continued. "But underneath . . . ah, underneath . . . the perversions we have to contend with—it would shock you, sir."

"Don't listen to him, Robert," Celeste said. "It's a silly note, that's all. Not a word of it means anything."

"You're upset." Morton placed her hands on Celeste's shoulders. "Perhaps you'd like to go to your room."

Celeste shook off the woman's grip. "Of course, I'm upset. But, it isn't my room, and I don't want to go there."

Robert rose and looked into her eyes, silently offering his support and love. Love. She'd finally found love, and these two bastards were going to take it away from her.

"Please remain calm, Mrs. Broder," Robert said softly. "Whatever this is about we can settle it easily."

Morton put her hands on Celeste again, but Robert waved her away.

Celeste took a deep breath. Calm. She had to calm herself somehow, but the more she tried, the harder she trembled. "You must believe me, Robert," she said. "I didn't know you when I read that note. Everything's changed. I feel . . ."

Damn, but she couldn't get the words out, not in front of the doctor and his hired harpy. A sob rose in her chest before she could stop it. "This afternoon . . . oh heaven, this afternoon . . ."

"This afternoon?" Wainwright demanded. "What have you two been doing?"

"Nothing," she snapped. "We had tea. Strawberries. Whipped cream." This was coming out all wrong. She had to convince Robert that she loved him—deeply and truly. Instead, she sounded irrational.

"What happened this afternoon?" Wainwright asked again, this time addressing Robert.

Robert's skin turned a violent pink. "We had tea. As Mrs. Broder said."

"Tea." Wainwright practically snorted the word. "Then, perhaps you should see what sort of woman you took into your home, Mr. Albright."

"No." Celeste lunged for the envelope again, but Morton caught her from behind and held her back. She watched—oddly disconnected, as if from a distance—as Wainwright put the envelope into Robert's hand.

He opened the envelope, unfolded the paper, and began to read. After only a moment, he stopped reading and looked into her face. "What is this?"

"I'm sorry," she whispered. "Things aren't the way they sound in there. Please understand."

He didn't answer but went back to reading, his face falling with every new revelation. She could almost imagine each word hitting him like a blow. Such pain. She'd never meant to hurt him, but she'd caused him such pain.

After a moment, he fell back into his chair, elbows resting on his knees, head down. The note still rested in one hand. "Oh, God, Celeste . . ."

"Robert, listen to me, please."

"I regret having to show you that, Mr. Albright," Wainwright said. But he didn't regret it, not one tiny bit, the bastard. She'd happily scratch his eyes out, but Morton still held her firm.

Robert straightened in his chair, and his fingers crumpled the note into a mass in his palm. "I understand."

"You see now, finally, that I know what I'm doing with Mrs. Broder. You can have no more delusions about her character."

Delusions? Oh, God, it wasn't a delusion. Their lovemaking wasn't a delusion. The sweet way he looked at her—as if she were the most delicate, most treasured person on Earth—that wasn't a delusion. The way she loved him, with every part of her heart and soul—that wasn't a delusion.

"Patients like Mrs. Broder are the most deceptive," Wainwright continued. "They appear so earnest, they can often fool even the most highly trained professional."

"Stop talking about me as if I weren't here," she said.

Robert glanced up, his expression so full of hurt and anger she could hardly bear to look at him.

"I'm sorry," was all she could manage to say to him. Sadly inadequate, but the only words that came to mind. *I love you. I'm sorry. Forgive me.*

"Under the circumstances, there won't be any more afternoon visits," Dr. Wainwright said. "Mrs. Broder will remain here, where she belongs."

"I suppose so," Robert answered, his voice little more than a whisper.

No! "But you'll come back, won't you?" she said. "You have to come back."

"Mrs. Broder," Morton said, "don't make a spectacle of yourself."

"You don't understand." Celeste broke free of the woman and dropped onto her knees in front of Robert. "I can explain everything. Just give me a chance."

She reached for his hands, but he stiffened, pulling away from her. Then, slowly and carefully, he put the note into her hand and rose. "I have to go."

"You can't leave, not like this."

Morton caught her arms and pulled her to her feet and away from Robert.

He straightened his shoulders, brushed his coat, and looked around him as if seeing the room for the first time. "I apologize for any trouble I may have caused you or your staff, doctor."

"No need," Wainwright answered. "I think we understand each other now."

"Yes."

"Please." Celeste struggled in Morton's grip but couldn't get free.

The trembling returned and with it, tears. Hot and wet, blurring her vision until she couldn't even see her beloved clearly.

"Take care of her, will you?" Robert said.

"Rest assured, Mr. Albright," the doctor answered.

Then Robert was gone. He simply opened the door and left, taking her hope, her happiness with him.

✽❧☙❧✽

Nothing about Xenobia Stewart's manner nor her dress suggested she was anything other than a respectable widow approaching her middle age. Nor did the furnishings of her house—at least the ones Robert had seen so far—indicate what sort of parties she threw. Everything around him spoke of wealth, from the upholstered mahogany furniture to the statuary to the thick Oriental carpets. All in impeccable taste, all quite understated.

The woman herself made the perfect picture of petite, graying respectability as she indicated a chair in her drawing room overlooking Central Park and then took a seat nearby.

"So, you've seen Celeste?"

"Yes."

A wicked gleam entered her eyes. "More than once by now, I imagine."

He didn't answer. This woman and her meddling had brought him nothing but misery. She'd given him the illusion of love and then had torn that illusion from him. He had no obligation to supply her with information. He wanted only two things from her, and then he'd leave.

"How is Celeste?" Mrs. Stewart asked.

"I haven't seen her for several days." Several long days of missing her and wanting her with every fiber of his being. Several nights of lying in his empty bed, remembering the feel of her body next to his. And then remembering her face the last time he'd seen her in Wainwright's office. Her desperation, how she'd begged him to understand, to allow her to explain the unexplainable.

Mrs. Stewart cocked her head and studied him for a moment. "You haven't seen her for several days?"

"That's correct." Ten days, twenty-two hours, and some minutes, to be exact.

"What a pity," she said. "I thought the two of you would become great friends."

"So your letter to Celeste said."

The smile quickly disappeared from her face, as she paled. "You read that?"

"It was my misfortune."

"Celeste can't have shown it to you."

"Dr. Wainwright did."

"Wainright. The head of the asylum?" she exclaimed. She rose from her chair and paced across the carpet. "I never meant for . . . oh, dear Lord. The things I wrote in there, about you, about your . . ."

"Exactly."

She turned and looked at him, her hand at her breast, her eyes wide. "I'm so terribly sorry. I had no idea that would happen."

"One can hardly expect any other outcome in a place like that. Wainwright knows everything that goes into and out of there."

"Oh, dear." She walked back to her chair and dropped into it. "I'm sorry. I don't know what to say, Mr. Albright. I've wronged you terribly."

"I'd like to know how you got the information about my late wife." He took a breath. This whole issue disgusted him, but he had to know the truth. "I'd like to know how many people in Connogua Springs know about my private life."

"Oh, dear."

"How many people discuss my intimacies with my wife behind my back?" *How many discuss my sex drive, the size of my cock?*

"Hardly anyone. Truly," she answered. "The person who told me claimed it was a secret—not at all the subject of ordinary conversation. Dear Lord, I'm so sorry."

He'd accomplished his first objective in coming here, it appeared. She seemed to realize at least a small part of the harm she'd done. He'd keep to himself that, thanks to her, he'd fallen hopelessly in love only to discover that his happiness was founded on a sham. He wouldn't tell her how devastated Celeste had been the last time he'd seen her. Celeste, oh God, Celeste.

"I just thought I'd bring the two of you together," Mrs. Stewart said. "You seemed so perfect for each other."

His mind wandered back to exactly how perfect they'd been together. If only he could get those images out of his mind. How her body accepted him so completely, how she moved beneath him. He'd never find that sort of perfection again.

"You did enjoy each other, didn't you?" she said. "You did become involved."

He could hardly deny it, so he didn't answer, but he felt his skin heat. The color of his face would answer for him. Damn his tendency to blush.

"I knew it," she said. "I made a terrible mistake in writing that note, but I wasn't wrong about you and Celeste. You two were made for each other."

He most assuredly didn't intend discussing how he'd lost his heart to Celeste, so he'd best accomplish his second objective and go back to Connogua Spring.

"You'll have to get Celeste released on your own," he said. "I can't possibly fight Wainwright now. I'm sure you understand why not."

"He'd reveal your personal information," she said.

"I wouldn't put it past him."

"I've already taken steps to get Celeste free. I know more judges than her children do. I know a few judges rather intimately."

He blushed again, not at all interested in knowing what she meant by intimately. "Then, you can get her out of that place."

"It'll be tricky," she said. "I'm not a family member. But I think I can manage."

"Good. That's all I need to know." He rose. "I'll see myself out."

"Mr. Albright, wait." She got to her feet. "I know I've treated you badly, but you shouldn't punish Celeste for my mistakes."

"I don't care to discuss my personal life any further with you."

"I understand after the trouble I've caused you."

"Madame, you have no idea." He'd most likely never recover fully, not as long as his memories of making love to Celeste haunted him. He'd probably take those memories to his grave.

"You mustn't pass up a chance at happiness," she said. "When the Almighty creates that one, special love for you, it's a sin to toss that love aside."

"You don't know what you're asking."

"Don't I?" She reached out and placed a hand on his arm. "My Harold and I had our bad spots together, but he was the love of my life. I'd give up everything to have him back for one night."

"I really must go now."

He tried to pull away, but her grip on his arm tightened. "I mean it, Mr. Albright. I'd give up everything—absolutely everything—for one more night in Harold's arms."

"I'll bear that in mind," he answered.

"You do that. You'll see that I'm right. You and Celeste belong together."

The sun warmed Celeste's skin. Warmed it too much, actually. She should have brought a parasol. Last week, all the skin had peeled off the end of her nose from sunburn. When she got back to Manhattan— if she ever did get back to Manhattan—she'd be a very unfashionable shade of brown. She ought to care about that, really. But she'd earned her walks outdoors, and she'd take every bit of heat that the sun cared to give her. At least that way she felt something.

Oh Lord, what disgusting self-pity. She deserved all the misery she'd endured in the last two weeks. She might as well just wallow in it and get the job over and done. Then she could go back to convincing Wainwright that he'd "cured" her, get a lawyer, and get herself out of this institution—which was what she should have done in the first place. Not involve an innocent person like Robert.

Robert. Oh, my poor, darling Robert. She clenched her eyes shut, held her breath, and waited out the pain. There. In a minute it was gone again, and she could open her eyes.

That seemed shorter than the last time. And the interval between the stabs of longing and shame a bit longer. Maybe in another week she'd be able to go five minutes without picturing Robert's face as he finished reading that note. Maybe by the time she got back home she'd be able to go an hour without thinking of his smile, the warmth of his eyes, the feel of his hand stroking her breast.

"I'm sorry, my darling," she whispered. "I'm so sorry."

"So am I," a soft voice said from behind her.

She turned and raised a hand to shade her eyes. That was Robert's voice, and surely this must be Robert standing just behind her. But she couldn't make out his face, with the sun in her eyes. And the tears. She hadn't even known she was crying again.

"Tell me it's really you," she said. "I couldn't bear it if you were a mirage."

"You shouldn't be sitting in the sun like this," he answered.

His voice again. Did she dare to hope? "You came back, after all."

Robert, or the figment of Robert—her vision still wouldn't clear— held out a hand to her. "I know a more sheltered place to sit."

She rose and took his hand. That felt real enough—solid and warm. She swayed, leaning into him. He caught her elbow and stead- ied her, a slight smile curling his lips. Lord, but she'd never expected to see that smile again. Maybe she'd imagined it. Maybe she'd imag- ined this whole encounter.

Before she could say anything, he linked her arm through his and guided her toward the yews where they'd strolled on the first day he'd taken her out. Toward the spot where he'd first kissed her.

"They allow you out on the grounds now?" he said.

"Once I started obeying the rules," she answered. "There seemed no point in defying them any longer."

"That doesn't sound like the Celeste Broder I know."

"That woman was a fool."

He covered her fingers with his own as they continued walking. She ought to say or do something. Ask why he'd come. But she had the warmth of his body now and the gentle pressure of his fingers on hers. Selfish to the end, she'd allow herself to enjoy every minute of his presence and suffer the consequences later.

They came to the little copse of yews finally, and he gestured to the bench they'd shared on their first walk. She sat and waited for him to join her. He did but didn't touch her again. He only looked off into the distance. She let her gaze linger on his features. If this was all she'd have of him, she'd store away as many memories as she could.

"That letter," he said finally.

"I should have destroyed it," she said. "I should have known they'd find it. It was entirely my fault."

He didn't say anything—didn't berate her, although she deserved it. But still, he'd come back to see her. That spoke of forgiveness, even if he could never trust her enough to love her again.

"You mustn't blame Xenobia for this, either," she said. "Xenobia is what she is—an utter hedonist. I should have known better."

"Why talk of blame?" he asked. "Do you regret that afternoon we spent together?"

"No," she answered. "Oh, heaven, no. I'll always cherish those hours."

He studied her from the corner of his eye. "Then, what would you have done differently?"

How many times she'd asked herself the same question. "I don't know. I could have taken responsibility for getting myself out of here instead of acting like a spoiled child. I could have been honest with you."

"Honesty would have been nice."

"I could have given you the note to destroy. I've been looking inside myself quite a bit this past week, and I don't much like what I've found."

"Tell me, Celeste."

She looked down at her hands. "I shouldn't have married Horace if I didn't at least care for him. I could have found my own way in life. After he died, I could have used his money to do some good in the world instead of feeling sorry for myself."

"And give up your sensual nature?" he asked.

"A fine lot of good that nature did me," she replied. "Or you."

They sat in silence for a long time. She could have said so many things to him. That she was sorry, but that would sound hollow. That she loved him, but that would sound self-serving. That he was the finest person she'd ever known, but would he believe her?

Finally, after several moments, he sighed. "Let me ask you just one thing."

"Anything."

"And I want the truth."

"I'll never lie to you again, Robert."

He sat for a moment, his jaw clenched. "During our brief time together. Did you ever care for me? At least a little?"

"Care for you?" she repeated. "I loved you with all my heart. I still do. I always will."

He turned to her, his amber gaze staring into her eyes. "Truly?"

She put her palm against the side of his face and returned his gaze. "Truly, Robert Albright, and any woman who doesn't love you is a fool."

He placed his hand over hers as tears filled his eyes. "I've searched my own heart this week, and I discovered a few things, too."

"Yes, my darling."

"Mostly, that I was hurt at what Millie had said about me. I loved her so much. I thought she was happy with me."

"I'm sure she was. Don't trust those stories. Things get so distorted when they become gossip."

"I felt betrayed," he said. "First by Millie and then by you."

"I know, Robert. I'm so sorry."

"I've struggled with those feelings. I even went to visit Mrs. Stewart."

"Xenobia?" Celeste said. "What did she tell you?"

"She told me that love was more important than anything else. She told me I'd be a fool to lose you because of my hurt feelings." He brought her hand to his mouth and rubbed his lips over the knuckles. "She was right."

He looked at her with such adoration, her heartbeat jerked and stuttered in her chest. "Really?"

"I decided I won't let my pride make us both miserable. Not when we can share so much happiness," he said. "Marry me, Celeste. Forgive my stubbornness in running away from you and agree to be my wife."

"Are you sure you want me?"

"I only feel alive with you. Only you make me whole. Tell me you could learn to feel the same way."

"I do." She ran her arms around his neck and pressed her face against his. "Love me, Robert. Always."

He hugged her against him as if he'd never let her go. An unspoken promise she meant to hold him to. "We'll go to New York and spend all of Horace's money on making it a better place."

She laughed. "We'll stay here and be mayor and first lady of Connogua Springs."

"We'll explore the world and make love on the back of that elephant."

"The elephant. I'd forgotten the elephant."

"I haven't. I'm going to make love to you every way known to man."

She kissed him briefly. "And we'll make up a few new ways, too."

He smiled at her, that beloved and beautiful smile. "You'll marry me, then?"

"Take this for your answer, my champion, my love," she said, as she pressed her lips to his and gave herself up to his love.

About the author:

Alice Gaines lives in Oakland, California with her husband of 23 years, 100 or so orchids, and one Carolina corn snake named Sheikh Yerbouti. She also writes for Leisure Romance as Alice Chambers. Feel free to email Alice at **algaines@pacbell.net** or write to her at PMB 197; 5111 Telegraph Avenue; Oakland, CA 94609.

Kiss or Kill

by Liz Maverick

To my reader:
He's part man, part machine with his life on the line.
She's the woman who must decide his fate. How
would you try to figure out if a man . . . was man
enough?

Chapter One

Washington DC, 2043

Camille Kazinsky stood in the doorway of her apartment, shaking her head in disbelief. *"That's* the robo?"

"Yeah, and if you're Kazinsky, print here." The government rep handed her the sign-in machine, and then pushed a military-issue duffel bag toward her with his foot.

Camille absently supplied her fingerprint, staring up at the robo in fascination. He waited handcuffed and silent, towering over the man at his side. The only robos she'd seen before were the ones she'd shot at from a distance during live-fire training at the academy. Trainees were taught to think of robos as targets; objects. Now, Camille couldn't imagine thinking in terms of 'it' instead of 'he.' Of course, that was just the kind of sentiment she was supposed to avoid. The robo looked like a man, but he wasn't . . . was he?

'He' wore short black leather gloves that contrasted oddly with the tan fitted T-shirt and camouflage pants of his dingy summer fatigues. Above the gloves, red welts from the restraints covered his forearms. His gloved fingers moved slowly, restlessly, as if he felt pain although no discomfort showed on his face.

In fact, nothing showed on his face at all. His eyes were glazed over. Built like a tank, but nobody home. On the other hand, even if he did have the intelligence of a pea, he probably had a cock the size of what used to be Texas.

Camille suppressed a laugh and moved her gaze upward. He looked like he hadn't had the opportunity to get neat and clean in a while. Greasepaint and dirt from a former assignment still smeared his face and arms. His buzz cut had grown out, and dark dirty locks of hair curled slightly at the neck and fell in disarray over his forehead.

Suddenly, the robo clenched his gloved hands then released them, flexing the muscles in his arms. The obvious power in his body made Camille wonder what kind of mayhem he was capable of, what he'd done while in service, and why they thought he wasn't capable of doing his job anymore.

The robo turned his head a fraction and looked directly at her. He blinked a set of outrageously long lashes over crystalline green eyes before returning his glazed stare to the front. Camille swallowed and stepped backward, her heart pounding in her chest. For those few seconds they'd made eye contact, he'd pierced her with a look that spoke of intelligence and understanding. The government could simulate skin and cover mechanics with life-like prosthetics, but it was hard to fake the look in a man's eyes.

Curious, Camille reached out and pressed her fingers into the skin of the robo's forearm. The pads of her fingers skidded along his warm, slippery flesh. A wry smile twisted her lips; from what she could recall, he felt exactly the way she remembered a man's sweating body felt under her hands. Now *there* was an interesting way to try to tell the man from the . . . machine.

The government rep looked up from the sign-in machine. "What's so funny?"

"Nothing. It's just not what I expected." She slid her palm up to the vulnerable skin at the bend in the robo's elbow. Although his face remained expressionless, a muscle in his forearm pulsed to her touch, and Camille felt a hot prickle trail down her spine in response. "Shit," she murmured and pulled her hand back, flushing.

"Hey, sweetheart, you sure you can handle it?" the rep asked, giving her a long look up and down. "They can be unpredictable."

Camille killed her smile and turned cold eyes on him. Chauvinistic prick. Could she *handle* it? It wasn't the first time she'd heard that question, and she ought to be used to it by now.

She was tall enough, but her willowy frame, blue eyes and fine blonde hair never failed to give the impression that she was somehow unable to take care of business. The girls in her unit used to tease her that in any other occupation, her baby-doll looks would be an asset. Camille frowned, reminded that her friends weren't in the unit any more. Well, she might not be as strong as most of the men, but she was a hell of a lot smarter, and that's what's supposed to count in military intelligence.

She flipped the Class II automatic weapon slung down her back around to the front, then turned her ankle to reveal the knife clipped to the side of her combat boot. "It's no problem."

The rep shrugged and tossed her the restraint punch. "So, what'd you do wrong?"

Camille clenched her jaw. He obviously knew robo evaluation was the kind of assignment an academy trainee would get only if placed on disciplinary probation. Not that it was any of his business. She certainly wasn't looking for pity.

"I think we're done here," she said. Camille pointed her Class II at the robo. With her other hand she grabbed a handful of T-shirt and pulled, jerking him over the threshold. "Inside. Let's go."

The robo stepped forward into her living space and walked into the center of the room. It suddenly seemed a lot smaller than usual. Camille sighed as she heaved the duffel bag after the robo and closed the door. She spent so little time at home, there was no point in a bigger place. Her apartment was the low-end model, perfect for a single member of the military.

Not that she completely ignored the luxuries. She'd ponied up for a subscription to the region's hot water supply, plus two additional nozzles for total body coverage in the shower. After all, a girl had needs. Camille smiled to herself. Until returning home this morning with her probation papers in hand, she'd been in the field in close quarters with thirty antagonistic, hygienically-challenged male trainees for the last four months. It was good to be home. Unfortunately, this homecoming wasn't quite like being on holiday.

Camille turned back to the robo and chewed on the broken edge of her thumbnail as she tried to decide how to proceed. She'd skimmed the procedural manual, but it wasn't too helpful. She was expected to file either a termination or reclassification report on him, solely based on behavioral observation. Supposedly, the government would simply follow the recommendation in her report. Of course, she'd heard of people getting into serious trouble after a seemingly docile robo reclassified into civilian life later became violent. The last thing she needed now was more trouble.

Just how human did one of these things have to be, to be considered human enough? How much was too much? And how could you tell one way or the other if the damn thing refused to *do* anything?

"I'd appreciate your cooperation," Camille finally said to the robo. "We're stuck with each other until I make my decision about you, but I'd like to get back to my unit ASAP."

The robo blinked, his long eyelashes batting downward.

"Hello? This is about reclassification or termination. Life or death, here. That's what robo evaluation is . . . are you going to talk to me?"

Camille pressed her fingertips against the dull pain in her left temple. "This is like babysitting a piece of meat. What did I do to deserve this, huh, *Meat?*" But she already knew the answer: nothing. Her partner Danny had made the 'mistake,' killing a civilian during a training exercise, but she was paying for it.

Academy life was full of strange alliances and underhanded deals as the trainees jockeyed to climb the rankings and graduate. This was one tradeoff Camille could only sit back and hope would be worth it. She'd take the fall now, if it secured her future. Anyway, Danny hadn't really given her a choice.

The robo's fists clenched and released, reminding Camille she ought to check for injuries. She drew the restraint punch from her pocket, uncuffed the robo, then pulled off his T-shirt and tossed it toward her laundry. Then, she quickly recuffed his wrists and walked around him, trailing her hand over his warm skin. He was sleek, muscular, smelling of musk and gunpowder. Camille ducked her head a little closer as she circled and breathed him in, unnerved by her attraction to him but not wanting to move away.

The robo shifted his weight. He flexed his fingers again, this time with greater agitation. Camille unzipped the neck of her training suit to get a little more oxygen. She could feel the charge in the air, the increased tension in his stance, the impact of her touch on his body . . . and on her own. "Damn. Twice the cock, half the brain, and zero bullshit coming out of your mouth. I should be down on my knees thanking my lucky stars."

She came around to face him and shivered as the robo stared straight down into her training suit. She knew he could see her hard nipples rubbing against the inside of the thick fabric, and the thought made her instantly wet. It shocked her a little to think this robo could get to her so quickly. But then again, it had been a while. She'd made the mistake of hooking up with a fellow trainee only once.

Clenching the muscles of her thighs to ease the ache there, she swallowed hard and looked into the robo's eyes. Watching him closely, she moved one hand down, pausing over the cold metal of his belt buckle before turning her hand and sliding it down to the long, hot ridge straining at the tan fabric of his fatigues.

The robo sucked in a breath, a quiet, excited sound as she stroked her hand over his length. "This turns you on," Camille murmured. She licked her dry lips and unzipped the fly, taking him in her hand. Maybe

Old Texas had been an exaggeration, but he was beautiful; hot and sleek like titanium. As she ran her thumb over the moisture on the engorged head, the robo bucked slightly, but still never said a word. Suddenly, Camille felt strange about handling him and let go.

She stared at his throbbing cock, the wet tip thrusting upward. She wanted to take him in her mouth, run her tongue around his tip and taste him, make him admit she turned him on. But she just looked away and cleared her throat. "You follow me with your eyes but you don't really see anything. It's obvious you like it when I touch you, but you don't know what to do with feelings, do you?"

Still no answer. Frustrated, she walked toward the manual on the multi-purpose table, more to cool off than anything else. "It's going to be lonelier with you than—" On instinct, she swung around to face him.

He was watching her with the same sharp, piercing gaze she'd caught a glimpse of when she'd first taken custody of him. Of course, his expression faded the minute she walked back up to him.

"I saw that," Camille said, angry heat rushing into her face. "There's more going on in there than you want me to know, and I don't like being tricked. React to me. Right here, right now."

She searched his face for a crack in that blank expression, pissed that she'd doubted the initial signs and underestimated him. Snatching her knife off her boot clip, she launched into him, slammed one foot down on his boots and pressed the blade against his temple. Wrapping her free hand around his windpipe, she began to squeeze. "I'm going to terminate you," she growled, and waited for a reaction.

His restrained hands jerked up between them. Camille flinched but held her ground. She moistened her lips and looked into his eyes, mentally calming herself in preparation to kill him if necessary. His hands suddenly stopped short. Very slowly, he moved them toward his own throat and clamped down on Camille's wrist at his windpipe.

His eyes locked with hers, and she could see a very clear survival instinct in those green, green eyes.

"Man. Machine. Animal. Vegetable. What are you really?" Camille taunted him, testing him further. She gritted her teeth and cut the very tip of the blade into the flesh at his temple. A surge of adrenaline pumped through him. His body jerked with primal fury, his cock rock-hard against her.

Camille inhaled sharply, dizzy for a moment. Sweat slid down the side of her face, stinging her eyes. She watched the robo try to read her the way she was trying to read him. She struggled to control her response to him but knew he was taking it all in. Her breath coming out in harsh pants, the fresh sheen on her skin, the instinctive shift of her legs to get more of him against her before she caught herself. He read her well, and thrust his erection against the center of her spread legs. A wave of pleasure rocked her body as he pressed against her clit.

Her senses swamped by lust and fear, Camille shivered but refused to lose focus on the subtext, noting the subtle tightening of his grip around her wrist. Whether he was asking her not to kill him or suggesting that he might kill her if she tried, she couldn't say. Either way, Camille had to assume that he hadn't already tried to snap her wrist for a good reason.

She cut him deeper to remind him who was in control and a trickle of blood slid down the blade. The robo got the picture and released her wrist, never breaking eye contact.

"Damn," Camille breathed and pushed backwards off him, turning away. Her hands were shaking; she felt panicked, aroused and pissed all at once. "What the hell am I doing? This can't be normal. I'm getting hot for a fucking piece of machinery. Camille, you are totally self-destructing."

A low, intense voice spoke out from behind, the words breathed deeply into her left ear. "I think you need to relax."

Camille froze. *Holy shit.* Her sweating palm tightened around the knife in a death grip, and she slowly turned around. She found herself staring directly into green eyes that finally admitted to total comprehension. The robo's body language was non-threatening, but she backed up to a safe distance anyway, shifting her gaze down to the thick shaft still standing erect through the fly of his fatigues.

"Let me guess," the robo said quietly. "You're thinking, 'If I make him lie down and take him from the top, he's strong enough to roll me over and take the advantage.' And you lying down with me on top is obviously out of the question from a security point of view. If you go down on me, besides the fact that it's probably not what you had in mind, I could break your neck, even in handcuffs. That leaves only one option for you . . . am I close?"

Too close for comfort, but she wasn't about to admit it. Camille concentrated on breathing and sounding as normal and in control as possible. Coolly, she said, "How about a little more talk and a lot less action." She took her knife and threw it tip down into the tabletop. It hit the wood with a hollow sound, tiny red specks of his blood scattering out from the blade onto the surface.

The robo looked at the knife then turned back to Camille, running his gaze down the length of her body. "When was the last time someone did something nice for you?"

Camille eyed him suspiciously. He didn't know anything about her, so what was his game? "Well, *Meat*, I don't really know. Depends on what you mean by, 'nice.' Why don't you give me an example?" She pulled the knife back out of the wood and pretended to inspect it, watching him from the corner of her eye.

"Well . . . *Camille* is it? Why don't I just get down on my knees," he said pointedly, "and thank my lucky stars."

Camille stared at him in shock, realizing that on a fairly high level, he'd understood everything, from the moment she'd opened the door. She tried to remember everything she'd revealed while she was talking aloud, thinking *he* was the resident idiot.

"Lean against the table." The robo gestured behind her.

"What?"

"The edge of the table. Lean against it." He swiped a black-gloved thumb across his lower lip, the corner of his mouth quirking up in the hint of a smile. "You can leave your boots on."

Camille hesitated. "You're kidding." Suddenly, she laughed. "I think you're missing the big picture here. If you hurt me, I'll kill you myself, right now. Even if you don't hurt me, I might have you killed."

He took a step toward her, and Camille flashed the knife in his face. He eyed the knife and reached around the weapon with his bound hands to grasp the zipper tab of her training suit, slowly pulling it down, the zipper rasping and humming until he reached the bottom and brushed against her crotch with his knuckles.

She gasped, and he crowded her against the edge of the table, moving his thigh between her legs and pressing upward until Camille moaned.

"Take it off," he said.

Damn. He wasn't kidding. This rated right up there with some of the crazier things she'd ever gotten herself into . . . but she wanted this. She definitely wanted this. And why not? It wasn't every day you had a man going down on his knees for you. Volunteering, without even getting his first. A nice change.

The robo stepped back and moved his hands to the exposed skin where the two sides of her suit fell open. Camille swallowed hard as she watched the black leather massage her pale skin, his fingers tangling in the fine curls at the bottom of the gaping vee in her training suit. His erection brushed against her leg, and she squirmed at the thought of that gorgeous cock sliding between her thighs into her slick, aching heat.

Logic, Camille. Think. She was armed, she wouldn't have to let her guard down to get satisfaction . . . and didn't she deserve a little satisfaction after everything that'd happened?

Pulling her arms out of her suit, she pushed the material past her knees then looked back up at the robo with a challenging smirk. He hooked a black leather-clad forefinger into the string low on her hip and pulled her panties down so fast, it took her smirk along with them.

She could see in his eyes, gone dark liquid jade, that he wanted to fuck her badly. Too bad they both wanted that because that wasn't going to happen.

"Sit down," he said, his voice thick. He kneeled on the floor, and Camille sat on the edge of the table. She parted her legs until she was completely exposed to him, unbelievably wet, the aching throb at the center of her cunt matching her heartbeat in double-time. Vulnerable, were it not for the knife she held out at arm's length next to his face.

He lifted his cuffed hands above his head, used his elbows to keep her legs apart and licked her slick folds. Camille shuddered, straining to keep her eyes open and watch.

The greasepaint on his face smeared warm and thick across the inside of her thighs as he entered her with his tongue, gently drawing himself in and out. Camille gasped and arched up to him, spreading her legs wider, giving him total access.

He sucked her clit, and she nearly lost it. He licked her there again, once, twice, three times . . . it happened so fast. Camille cried out and threw her head back as she came, slamming backwards on the table. Unable to speak and unwilling to move as pleasure coursed through her body in tiny aftershocks, she just stared at him through a flurry of white as the scattered pages of the manual fell to the floor. *Damn. I think I just made a terrible mistake.*

Meat stood up and awkwardly thrust his erection back into his fatigues, then rolled his shoulders, whipped his head to one side and cracked his neck. He looked Camille straight in the eye, flashing a wicked smile with all the male arrogance of a job well done, and said, "*Now* we talk."

Chapter Two

The girl stared at him in shock for a moment, then burst into peals of laughter. "A guy who wants to talk after sex."

Meat blinked in confusion. He wiped the sweat off his forehead with his shoulder and turned away from the sight of her lithe body disappearing once more into the severe gray uniform.

"That was very impressive," she said. "I'm looking forward to seeing what other programming is available."

Meat's eyes narrowed. "I'm happy to oblige," he snapped. Nothing pissed him off faster than cheap shots about his non-human qualities. He strolled casually to the other end of the room, needing to cool off both his temper and his own unsatisfied needs.

The exhaustion built up over the last few weeks was catching up to him, dulling his wits and emphasizing his baser needs. Food, water, sleep, and something to calm the lust that burned low in his groin.

He glanced back at the girl. She sat on the table swinging her legs, tossing her knife from hand-to-hand, and watching him examine her living space.

She'd left the neck of her uniform half-zipped, showing off the smooth swells of her breasts, a hint of rosy nipple. He'd be willing to bet she'd done it on purpose, and had to admit it was a power play he was particularly susceptible to at the moment. He gazed at what she'd left open for him to see and chuckled softly. Point to Camille Kazinsky. Whatever he'd been expecting, it wasn't this.

"What's so funny," she asked, smiling back.

"Nothing. I'm merely enjoying the scenery."

Her smile vanished, and she stopped tossing the knife. "You sound like a Brit. Like an educated Brit. What's that all about? Is that part of the program?"

All business again. He'd thought he'd had her pegged in the few minutes it took to detect the undercurrent of desperation that ran through her. And he certainly thought he'd figured out his strategy. He might not be in the battlefield anymore, but seduction was a weapon he could definitely still wield . . . and one she definitely responded to.

But it wasn't as simple as that, was it? Her unpredictability had him way off-balance, making first one assumption and then another. "One of my trainers was a Brit. The other sounded like you."

"I'm surprised you even speak in complete sentences."

He snorted disdainfully and her eyebrows flew up, emphasizing the feline shape of her blue eyes. Truth be told, he'd never even seen anyone remotely like this Camille Kazinsky before. Her delicate kitten looks warred with everything else about her.

Sure, the legs, tits and blonde hair got his attention, but what kept it were those eyes, and a lush pair of full lips, burnt fuchsia from dehydration. She licked them constantly, her tongue flicking out like a cat lapping milk.

No, he'd certainly never seen a woman like Camille before; he'd certainly never touched one like her either. When he'd dipped his tongue between her legs and took in her taste and scent, he'd felt a desire so vicious it clouded any sense of manipulation or strategy.

He needed a better overall read. Maybe she got off on being ordered around. Maybe she'd like to take out some aggression on him. Maybe she needed a confidant. Maybe she just needed a daily fuck.

He circled the perimeter of the room, trying to keep his mind focused on the end goal. Not many additional clues to be gained from her living space.

Central living room, appearing to fan out in the standard layout to bathroom, kitchen, bedroom, and equipment room. Sparsely furnished with only the necessary furniture all color-coordinated in beige. A bookshelf next to the communications system, filled with academy manuals and a few random objects that seemed placed almost self-consciously, in a deliberate attempt to camouflage the general sterility of the place.

You had to play it safe at first, play dumb. Hang back and observe to determine what characteristics your evaluator liked about you . . . and then give them more of the same until the only option that makes sense to them at the end is reclassification.

"Meat? Hello? I thought you said you were ready to talk."

And if they wanted to call you Meat, you let them call you Meat.

He'd been called a lot worse, and his real name had never really mattered anyway.

She shrugged when he didn't answer, and tidied up the papers still on the table. He noted that her eyes flickered in his direction every now and again. She was always aware of where he was, always aware of the distance between them.

He was aware, too, by how the overwhelming desire that should have subsided by now gnawed at him even as he watched her from the other side of the room.

"What exactly would you like to know?" he asked woodenly, unwilling to let his voice reveal his growing excitement as she suddenly knelt down on her hands and knees, her body rocking as she reached out to collect scattered sheets of paper.

"Let's start with why you were deactivated. Did you . . . I don't know . . . 'break down'?"

Meat laughed, a hollow sound. He needed her to see his human qualities first, his robotics a distant second. "I'm not a toaster or a fastcook. I'm a man." He moved casually to the bookcase, watching her through his lashes as he pretended an interest in what she displayed there.

"A *man*, huh? I almost believe that you believe it. But what's important is whether I believe it." She looked over her shoulder at him, her sleek back arching slightly. "Why don't we go with that assumption for the moment. Tell me why you were deactivated."

Her back would be the same delicate pale color as her creamy white thighs; her ass would be as smooth and tight as the rest of her body. He glanced down as a sharp pain raced through his hand, drawing his attention to the rough piece of crystal he held tightly in one fist. Meat carefully released the jagged purple rock and put it back on the bookcase. "I don't know."

"They just one day up and said, okay, you there, your service is over?"

He swallowed hard, a little dizzy on his feet, suddenly, desperately thirsty. He looked down at Camille still on the floor, imagined kneeling down behind her and stripping the training suit off her body all over again, imagined himself without restraints running his palms delicately down her back, so delicately it didn't hurt him, it didn't burn her.

Releasing his rigid cock and sliding it along the narrow well of her satin-covered cheeks; taking himself to the edge by pressing his throbbing erection between two handfuls of that perfect ass and then slowly grazing over the smooth blue fabric of her panties down and under her body until they both moaned.

He'd keep those panties on, and pull the silky scrap of material aside just enough so he could watch as he sheathed himself inch-by-inch into the moist pink opening of her beautiful cunt, then bury himself to the hilt and thrust into her over and over again until they both cried out their release.

Suddenly, Camille stood up and brushed off her hands. "I'd appreciate an answer."

Meat shuddered as the image faded of his hands on her slim hips, his body crouched over her, impaling her from behind. "Sorry. Tired. Could you repeat the question?"

She gave him a funny look, and moved the stack of papers from the ground to the table. Then she walked to the recliner by the fireplace and plopped down into the chair, curling up with her head resting on the arm. "Why do you think they deactivated you?"

The human commanders became afraid because I was not so different from them. "They didn't say anything. As far as I can tell, nothing is different about my physical or mental capabilities now compared to my last campaign a month ago."

"Mmm," she said, looking him up and down. "So, what robotic parts do you have? I guess the obvious question is, what makes you different from a man?"

Meat walked up to the recliner and gazed down at her. "What do *you* think makes me different?"

She shifted back in the chair, putting more distance between them. "If you make me feel like a woman does that necessarily make you a man?" she asked with a smirk. "Maybe they programmed you especially well."

Meat stiffened at the insult but simply smiled as seductively as he could manage. "I don't think they could program what I'm thinking about right now. Would you like to find out?"

Camille tossed her hair back over her shoulder and laughed. "Evasion tactics. What's your game?"

He shrugged. "No game. I'm curious. I enjoyed giving you pleasure, and I'd like to get to know you better."

"That's lovely, but maybe flattery is part of a giant piece of software in your head. I have no idea just how human you really are. That's what I'm interested in finding out."

She flinched as he crouched down suddenly and moved his shackled hands toward her cheek, relaxing again in a moment when he simply brushed his knuckles against her skin. "I'd be willing to bet I'm at least as human as some of those men you work with. Maybe more." Her jaw tightened and he guessed he'd hit a sore spot.

"Believe me, I know how it is out there. You feel empty inside. It's like you against the world, sometimes." He spoke slowly, gauging her reaction. "It's . . . lonely, isn't it?"

She didn't speak at first, then suddenly cleared her throat. "Yes, well. Life's a bitch and then you die. Some of us sooner than others. Tell me what makes you a robo."

She was a tough one. Or at least that was what she wanted him to believe. He took his hands from her face and held them out to her, palms down. "Take off one of my gloves."

She hesitated, then climbed out of the chair and stood up, taking hold of his right wrist with one hand and slowly peeling the leather off with the other. Her touch was so gentle it tickled, a funny little feeling that charmed his senses in one instant and made him doubt his sanity in the next.

He quickly made a fist, then brought it up in front of her face. "Sorry to disappoint you, but this is all there is. Both hands."

Camille's eyes widened as he unclenched his fist and revealed the flexible metal plates implanted into his flesh from the tips of his fingers to the top of the palm of his hand. He waited for her expression to change to disgust or fear, but it never did. Instead, she simply examined him with an almost respectful curiosity.

"There's nothing robotic inside you?"

"No."

She looked at him suspiciously, but didn't say anything.

Meat could feel the metal in his hand heat up as she swept her fingertips against his palm, skin on skin, with a featherlight touch as erotic as the violent sexuality she'd displayed earlier.

She took his wrist and pulled his hands back up to her face, inhaling roughly as she placed his palm against her cheek and the metal made contact.

The rapid rise and fall of her breasts and the peaked nipples under the gray fabric of her training suit encouraged him, and he ignored the spiraling of his own desire to focus all of his attention on her.

"Whatever you like," he murmured. "I'll give it to you."

He ran his thumb across her mouth, and she tipped her head back slightly, parting her lips. He swallowed hard to control himself against the pleasure of her mouth gently closing around him, sucking at the hot, pulsing current.

She took him with half-closed eyes, like she'd probably suck his cock, running her tongue over and around the tip, encircling him with those lush lips and taking his entire length inside her down to the palm.

He snatched his thumb from her mouth and looked away, his mind confused, a jumble of unfocused images and thoughts clouding his mission.

She licked her bottom lip and watched him. "The metal's warm."

He nodded. "It tends to heat up when I'm experiencing extreme emotions."

A little breathlessly, she asked, "So you're experiencing extreme emotions, now?"

"Yes."

"Which ones? You don't look angry to me."

"Excitement. You excite me."

She looked surprised by his honesty. "What happens when you're angry?"

"At some point, the metal can burn."

"What happens when you're scared?"

"I don't get scared."

"Is that so?"

She likes vulnerability, Meat thought suddenly. And she responds well to the facts of my robotics. "Well, that's not true actually. Perhaps I'm scared that the more I tell you about robotics, the less you'll be inclined to recognize my human qualities."

"The more I know about you, the more I'll want to kill you?"

He nodded and she picked up his hand again, swirling her index finger delicately in his palm. "The less I know about you, the easier it will be to kill you without a qualm."

He took a chance. "Don't."

"Don't what? Touch you?" she teased.

"Kill me."

She inhaled quietly, like a whisper, but he heard the sound, and he could have sworn it was the sound of compassion.

※※(⁀◡⁀)☞※

Camille had cut her questioning short in favor of a meal, which Meat gratefully accepted although it took some skill to prevent himself from falling face first into the food tray with exhaustion.

She took the hint, and Meat thanked his good fortune when she grabbed one of her own pillows and tossed it to the floor onto the pallet she'd made up for him across the room from her bed.

Quickly, he held out his hands, thinking to take advantage of her mood.

"Nice try, Meat. I'm not stupid enough to try and sleep with you running around unchained. Lie down with your hands above your head."

Without a word, he did, and Camille clipped a second chain to the middle of his restraints and strung it to the metal pipe that ran from floor to ceiling. She obviously wanted him where she could see him and hear him. Smart. She'd wake up immediately if he tried anything.

She turned the lights off and changed before he could get accustomed to the darkness, but he could tell from the sound of the fabric against her bedcovers that she wore something silky.

He grinned into the darkness as she got into bed, biting his lip to keep from laughing at the sound of the safety latch clicking against her Class II weapon. She was sleeping with her gun when she could have been sleeping with him.

Interesting choice.

"Good night," he finally said. It seemed a little awkward, but hell, a little friendliness couldn't hurt matters.

She didn't answer, and then suddenly she got back out of bed. Meat tensed, instinctively preparing himself for an attack.

A shard of moonlight slipped through the drapes and illuminated her body as she walked across the room, the hem of her white silk nightgown swirling around her thighs, her blonde hair splayed down her back. She seemed fragile at first glance, but a second look revealed a covered field knife strapped to her bare leg, nearly camouflaged in the dim light.

His senses on the alert, Meat didn't move as she crouched down by his head and pulled the knife from its sheath, the fabric of her nightgown shifting to his advantage in every way.

Who's trying to seduce who? Meat wondered grimly. He waited with a guarded stare, unsure of her intent. If he had the use of his hands, he'd take the gorgeous breasts revealed by the dip of her neckline in his hands and suck on those tight peaks until she begged him for something even better.

"Kiss me," she said, simply. "I'm curious. I want to know what it's like with one of you."

Meat frowned, confused by her request. He adjusted his body, positioning his face on level with the blonde curls peeking out from between her legs as the hemline crept farther up her thighs.

She pressed her knees together and swung them to the side, looking at him strangely. "I just said, 'kiss.'"

Meat tried to think how he could fake his way through this.

She moved closer and put her hand on the back of his neck, lowering her mouth down to his level, her lips curved in a delicate smile. "It's just a kiss. Don't tell me I've found your Achilles' Heel."

"I don't have an Achilles' Heel," he said automatically, staring down the front of her nightgown. She smelled incredibly clean. That stuff he'd seen in the bathroom. A sweet scent . . . jasmine. Definitely a smell that never floated across any of the battlefields he'd ever fought on.

Pressing her lips against his, she swiped her tongue across his lower lip and finally pressed her moist warmth inside. Such a strange sensation. Meat suddenly had to suppress an inexplicable impulse to weep.

He followed her lead, copying her movements until instinct took over in a wave of lust. He plunged into her mouth with his tongue like he wanted to plunge between her thighs, imagining her urging him on, his free hands full of her curves.

He sucked on her tongue, and he could feel her lose herself a little, her hands skittering blindly across his overheated skin.

"You taste so sweet," he murmured, the metal chain above him clanking as the restraints hit their limit and he was left straining to reach her body with his cuffed hands.

She pulled away and stared at him, wrapping her arms against her body in a protective motion. "We could both use some sleep." She turned and climbed back into bed with her arsenal.

Meat touched his forearm to his lips and tried to get control of himself. Humans had brought him and his friends nothing but pain. He'd do well to remember that.

Camille manipulated him in a way he had no experience with. And he couldn't for the life of him see the point. She had nothing to lose in all this. All she had to do was decide whether or not he deserved to die. But if he couldn't understand, he couldn't defend himself . . . and he couldn't plan a proper counterattack.

He just needed sleep. Tomorrow he could reassert his dominance. He'd stay focused and detached, but encourage her attachment to him.

It would be a lot easier to stay focused and detached without aching balls and a rock-hard cock. Meat curled his knees up to his body in the dark and pressed his face down into the pillow to stifle his groan.

Chapter Three

Camille lay on her bed fully clothed, listening to Meat's breathing over the faint patter of rain outside.

He didn't look rested, and she guessed neither of them had slept much last night.

She remembered the look on his face after their goodnight kiss, and suspected she'd been closer to the truth than she realized. Meat definitely had feelings, but he just as surely didn't know what to do with them. Odd that he'd never kissed before. Of course, once he'd gotten the hang of it, it'd been like turning on the ignition.

She'd wanted him badly. She'd wanted to take those damn cuffs off and let him have at her. She dreamed about him ripping the pipe out of the wall just to get to her, pulling her on top of him with her nightgown sliding up around her waist and ordering her to ride him with that stormy, arrogant look on his face. Camille pressed her face into the comforter and giggled.

That was the problem. She understood her feelings exactly. A *big* problem considering this was an assignment that inherently required objectivity.

Meat's eyes flew open and he blinked a couple of times and then tried to stretch his arms. "Son of a bitch!" He looked at the restraints around his wrists and then turned and focused on Camille stretched out on the bed. "Camille Kazinsky."

She gazed at him. "Yeah?"

"I want to . . . I need to get cleaned up."

"Well, it's your lucky day. Water's finally back on." She got off the bed, then walked over to his pallet and unlocked the restraints from the pipe, her damp hair swinging around her shoulders. "Besides, it's important that you look nice for Danny. Ha-ha."

He quirked an eyebrow. "Who?"

"My partner. It's protocol to visit your partner when they're on probation, and I'm sure Danny wouldn't miss this opportunity to show a little sympathy."

Meat eyed her with a curious expression. Indicating with his chin the Class II lying on the bed next to her, he asked, "Is that for him or for me?"

She let out a short laugh. "I'm prepared to use it on either of you. In any case, before he gets here, you and I should have a talk about behavior."

"I'm an adult. An adult *man.*"

Camille looked at him sharply. "Watch the attitude. I'm totally serious. Danny's got connections."

"If your partner has connections, why didn't he get you out of probation?"

"It's not exactly in his best interest." She frowned. "Look, the bottom line is that when Danny gets here, if anything happens to make me look like I don't have everything completely under control . . . you get what I'm saying."

He didn't answer.

"Okay, let's go," Camille said, grabbing her weapon and urging him forward with a palm on his back. "I already put a change of clothes in the bathroom."

Meat looked over his shoulder at her. "You're coming with me?"

"Uh, yeah. Just like last night."

His shook his head slightly, eyes narrowed, but led the way to the bathroom.

She took his hands and unpunched the restraints, her gaze lingering on the raw welts revealed when she took the metal cuffs off. Snatching his hands away, he moaned in pleasure over his temporary freedom, the muscles in his back rippling as he stretched out and shook his cramped limbs.

She leaned against the door, thoroughly enjoying the scenery. "Go ahead, do what you gotta do."

"Are you going to watch everything I do? Are you going to watch me every time I take a piss? Would you like me to jerk off in front of you?"

Camille snorted, moving her hand subconsciously to the barrel of her Class II in reaction to his rising temper. Was he actually expecting her to blush? She didn't shock that easy. "I just took you out of restraints. You think I'm going to turn my back on you now?"

"I'm quite serious. I'd like some privacy."

Man, he was cocky. He'd never been anybody's property before, that was for sure. Everything he said, he said with that same voice. Quiet, urgent, deep, a little dangerous, meant to intimidate. Almost nothing he asked was really a question, what with that clipped speech at the ends of his sentences. Camille could tell he was used to giving orders, not so much taking them.

In truth, she wished he had a robotic monotone instead of that rich, seductive voice. She wished he had metal all over his body and that he moved in jerky fits and starts like the droids in those old-fashioned movies. It was starting to bother her that the only thing that seemed different about him from the full human guys back in the field was the way he made her feel inside.

"Sorry." She motioned in the direction of the toilet. "It's all yours."

"Suit yourself," he snarled. He turned the other way and stepped into the shower, very pointedly shifted his stance, and pissed into the drain.

Camille gaped and looked away, curling her lip in disgust. "This isn't the field."

He shut the door to the shower with a flourish. Camille rolled her eyes. The door was glass from top to bottom; completely transparent. He was just trying to get under her skin. Since he wasn't using it, she crossed over to the toilet and sat down. *Christ. Well, this was just great. A robo with attitude.*

Meat turned on the water and worked quickly to wash and rinse his hair.

From her morning shower, Camille knew just how cold the water was today. Meat muttered some obscenity or another but didn't say a word about the temperature. She didn't say a word either, she just pressed the button on the wall and turned on the hot water.

The hotpipe cables were always slow to kick in the first few times after restarting a subscription, but Meat still didn't complain about the goosebumps all over his body. When the heat finally hit, he looked at her suspiciously. Then, after a few more seconds, a smile bloomed across his face, and he put his hand out to the water, watching it collect in his palm like rain as the steam began to rise.

When was the last time someone did something nice for you, he'd asked. The real answer was that it seemed like forever. And equally as long since she'd gotten any pleasure out of the reverse.

He was chuckling now, obviously as thrilled with the heated water as Camille always was coming straight from the field. She opened the door of the shower to reach in and press the button for the surround spray. He just stood there in the middle, the hot water sluicing over his body from all sides. He tipped his head back, a look of ecstasy on his face that made Camille's nipples harden.

She'd seen him naked before bed last night, but here in the daytime, with the water streaming down his muscular body, well, he was spectacular. All this power and beauty in one man. She crossed her arms over her chest and looked away.

"Thanks."

She looked back up at Meat, and he was just standing there, staring at her, with a raging hard on and a look of such pure sexual frustration she almost had to laugh.

He must have seen the laughter in her look, because he answered with an intense stare and the hint of a smile. Then his lips parted, and he wrapped one hand around the head of his stiff cock. Camille dropped her arms to her sides, her pulse racing.

He swallowed hard and moved the circle of his fist down to the base of his cock, using his free hand to swipe the steam off a length of glass in one fierce motion.

She walked up to the clear streak to press her palms against the glass, grateful for how cool it felt under her hands, while the rest of her seemed to burn under his gaze.

Meat pumped his hand up and down more urgently now, and Camille slid her hands down the humid glass as if she were actually touching the body she only looked at.

With a gasp of pure pleasure, he tipped his head back, and his hand rammed down hard a few more times. Yelling out his relief like an animal, he looked directly into Camille's eyes, and came into the water at his feet.

Camille could hardly breathe by the time he closed his eyes and dropped his hand. She moved her shaking hands away from the glass and held them against her chest.

The door sensor sounded, jolting Camille back to reality. She had no clue how many times it had already rung.

Shit, Danny was here. Early.

She cleared her throat, wishing she could clear her head as easily, and said, "Remember, I'm armed and don't try anything while he's here."

Meat stepped out of the shower, naked and dripping wet. She

grabbed his bare hands, shut the restraints around his wrists, and tossed him his pants. "And put these on, will you?"

⁂〔♋〕⁂

Danny Dietrich stood on the threshold looking the same as usual; like he'd never sweat a day in his life.

While Meat had the powerful build and demeanor of a true fighter, Danny looked prettier, more like the politician he aspired to be. Even with a buzz cut and military uniform, he carried himself as if he wore an expensive business suit.

Posture really made a difference, thought Camille, standing up a little straighter. Not to mention, he probably would have looked even better to her if she didn't dislike him so much.

" 'Morning, Cami," he said cheerfully and stepped inside. "Protocol visit."

"I've been so hoping you'd come over today," she said in deadpan.

"I'm sure."

Still holding the door, she answered, "Well, it's been great. Thanks for stopping by."

Danny looked around the room. "So, how's it going?"

Camille rolled her eyes. "Look, I'm on assignment as we speak. So, if you don't mind . . ."

"Actually, I do. So, where is it? I'm dying to see one up close."

She went for the jugular. "Can't you just call Daddy and have him arrange a special tour of the robo training facilities for you?"

Anger flickered in Danny's eyes for just a moment. "I don't ask my father for favors like that. You know that."

Camille held up her hands in mock defense. "No, of course not. God forbid anyone should accuse you of moving up the ranks because of nepotism. Not to mention, you certainly wouldn't want a big government official like your dad to know you've had a few . . . difficulties, should I say, during training."

Danny eyed her as he rubbed the monogram on his signet ring, his expression equal parts charming and sinister. "You, of all people, should be glad I don't waste my connections on the small favors. That way, when it's do or die, I can get what I need."

He ran his hand along the smooth skin of his square jaw and added meaningfully, "Or what I need for someone else. Just remember, you keep your mouth shut, and I'll do my part to keep the other guys at bay until you graduate. You know you're on the edge as it is. And if it looks really bad for you, I might just call in a . . . Real. Big. Favor."

"I get it, Danny. Okay? My mouth didn't open when you were busy passing me the blame. I don't see what I gain by trying to convince anyone otherwise at this point. You know I want to graduate. That's what this is all about."

"Good, then."

"You'd just better keep your side of the bargain," she mumbled under her breath.

Danny looked at his watch. "Now as soon as you show me the robo, I'm out of here. Everyone's curious, and I want to tell 'em all what one's like up close."

Camille laughed and shook her head. "That will be nice for you. You'll be the center of attention."

"I'm glad you understand. Okay, show 'n' tell."

Camille was in no hurry to oblige. "You make him sound like an art project, or something."

Danny looked at her sharply. "Mmm. You make 'him' sound like you're one day into your assignment and already in danger of losing your elusive objectivity. Not exactly surprising."

He put his finger under Camille's chin and lifted her face to his. "My, my, Cami, your soft underbelly is showing again."

Camille knocked his hand away.

"Is he bothering you?"

Meat stood in the doorway, water from his hair dripping down his naked chest, his pants only partially buttoned. He looked big, strong, and threatening. And he was on her side.

Danny looked over his shoulder and then wheeled around, his jaw dropping. "Holy shit . . . This thing's built." A slow smile spread across his face. "I wish the others were here right now. Are the robotics inside?"

Meat ignored Danny's rude perusal and continued to look directly into Camille's eyes. "Because it seemed like he was bothering you."

Camille couldn't help but smile. "No, he's not bothering me. Danny wouldn't bother me, because Danny knows I know something that he wishes I didn't know."

Danny slowly approached Meat with his weapon at the ready, a look of awe on his face. "Check this thing *out*." He stretched his free arm out and snapped his fingers in front of Meat's face.

Camille swallowed nervously as Meat balled his hands into fists.

"Leave him alone, Danny."

Danny whipped his head around and then walked back up to

Camille. He tipped his head to one side and gave her a sympathetic smile. "Does Cami have a new best friend? Does Cami feel *sorry* for the robo?"

"Obviously not. I'm beginning to feel sorry for you because if anyone heard you talking like this, they'd have you committed. Feeling sorry is not the issue. Acting like an ass is the issue."

Meat snorted, and Camille shot him a warning look before continuing. "So, now you've stopped by, you can go back to the unit and tell them what a team player you are, standing by your shamed partner and all."

Danny shrugged. "Yeah, I plan to do that. But what's the rush? I've never seen a robo close-up." He walked around Meat, poking him and touching him as he moved. "This thing's pretty solid."

Camille tried to affect a confident nonchalance to distract Danny from taunting Meat. "Haven't you had enough? This isn't a social call."

"Isn't it? We were social once, weren't we?"

"For about five minutes in the back of a modified Humvee, I think. But the entire episode isn't particularly memorable."

"You slept with this guy?" Meat asked, looking Danny up and down with ill-concealed distaste.

Danny's eyebrow quirked up. "Oh, man, now it's jealous. This just gets better and better."

"Okay, you know what? Testosterone overload. Danny, you saw what you wanted, so why don't you leave."

Danny leered at Meat. "Yeah, sure. I ought to give you two a little privacy, eh, tough guy? You'd like that, wouldn't you? But Camille's hard to please, let me warn you." He moved his gaze to Camille. "Are you sure it understands all this?" He turned back to Meat, enunciating carefully, "Hard. To. Please."

Camille pressed at the headache throbbing just above her left eye as Danny walked around to Meat's back and ran his palm over the scars. "Jesus, look at these."

Meat stiffened, a look of revulsion on his face.

Time for this visit to end. "Danny, stop. I'm serious. Don't make me do something we'll both regret."

"You seem unusually on edge. Are you having trouble with the killing part of your assignment?"

Meat looked sharply at Camille, but held his tongue.

Danny caught the look. "Don't worry, robo. Nobody thinks Camille has what it takes. Of course, I could kill you for her, and no one would have to know." He swung his Class II into position, pointing it at Meat. "Now that would be a favor."

Camille pushed the barrel of Danny's gun away. "You and your favors," she said with disgust. "This situation is in *my* hands."

"Your hands," Danny said. "One little fingerprint to file that report. If the robo had any brains at all, it'd cut off your finger and take care of business. Funny. One little finger is all it takes to live . . ."

Danny raised the tip of his Class II up to the side of Meat's head. "And one little finger is all it takes to die." He slowly unclipped the safety.

Camille felt Meat tense beside her. She caught the way he stared at Danny with unveiled hostility, like a chained dog straining at its leash. She almost wished she hadn't made such a big issue of Meat controlling his behavior.

Danny fought hard and he had a strong bloodlust, but she could tell at a glance he didn't have Meat's strength, and she knew from experience he didn't have her agility.

Danny tilted his head and chuckled. "I think it's mad."

Camille could feel the heat coming off of Meat's body; she sensed he was about to jump out of his skin. If he made a move on Danny, two possible things could happen. Danny would report the incident, and she'd look like she was unable to control the robo. Or Danny would kill Meat, and she'd look like she was unable to control anybody.

Fact was, Danny looked like he'd truly relish blowing Meat's brains out all over Camille's living room, and his trigger happy ways were what got them both in this situation in the first place.

Camille shot a warning look at Meat, even as she struggled with her own temper. She gripped her Class II up at the shoulder pointedly and said, "Leave him alone. This is my assignment, and I'm prepared to defend my position."

"'Leave him alone.'" Danny laughed. "You *are* soft, aren't you, Camille? Just like all the other girls."

Camille gritted her teeth. "Get. Out. I've had enough."

"I'm going, I'm going . . ." Danny sighed loudly and backed up across the room and pressed the door release. ". . . but it's *so* tempting." He paused on the threshold, looking at them with a boyish lopsided smile, like a guilty schoolboy about to steal candy out of the teacher's drawer.

And in one smooth movement, he swung his weapon up, pointed it at Meat, and pulled the trigger.

Chapter Four

Meat hit the ground, the sound of Camille's scream ringing in his ears. She'd lunged toward him, knocking him down as she tried to shield him with her body.

Danny stared down at them incredulously. "It's not loaded, Cami. Man, you *are* soft. It's just a robo." In two strides he was out the door and gone.

Camille shifted her body to straddle Meat on her hands and knees while he lay face up beneath her on the floor. She looked down at him blankly through a tangled mass of gold hair.

Meat stared up at her in shock. "I think you would have just taken a bullet for me. Or at least shared one."

"God *damn* him." Camille sat back on his thighs and looked down at him, fists curled. She clearly wanted to punch something . . . or someone.

"He has something on you, doesn't he?" There was something strange going on here. The way she let him fawn and insult her. He knew that she had more of a spine than that, but she let him get away with it. "Does he have something on you?" Meat repeated.

Camille wasn't listening. "I let him get to me, every *god damn time*."

Meat searched her face, unsure what his tactics should be. Not entirely clear at the moment about the difference between his strategic tactics and his personal preference. "Even without a weapon, I'm more useful without the handcuffs."

"You think I trust you that much?" she spat out.

"Take them off, Camille," Meat said softly. "I'm not going to hurt you. By now you've got to know that I'm not some mindless robot with a kill reflex. And it's certainly not in my interest to hurt you." He hesitated. "I don't *want* to hurt you. I'd never hurt you. Take them off, and I'll prove that you can trust me. These hands will only give you pleasure."

She looked wild, a stormy expression on her face.

Meat replayed the scene in his mind. No wonder she was in trouble at the academy. There was obviously something wrong with her self-preservation instinct. He sure as hell wouldn't take a bullet for someone he didn't really know. They were all trained that way. Robos and humans alike. It's probably why she was so angry at herself now. He'd be smart to make her feel better about having done it.

He must be making Camille care about him, on some level, at least. How strange that her regard for him should feel so good, when it wasn't supposed to really matter at all.

"What you did there . . ." He hesitated, then stopped short of reminding her that she'd been kind to him. "Just take off the restraints, and I'll give you whatever you need."

She turned to look at him with eyes bright, almost feverish. "Go to hell, you manipulative shit."

Meat kept his mouth shut.

"You're trying to play me just like Danny. You're nothing more than a collection of metal parts and computer chips. And I'm messing up my situation just to save your ass. One small thing I asked of you. Don't do anything to make it look like I don't have total control. I wish Danny had blown your sorry head off."

It was irrational for her to blame him for this, and Meat guessed they both knew it. "So, hit me."

"What?"

"Hit me. You're pissed, go ahead and take it out on me. I can handle it."

"That's not what I want."

"What do you want, then?"

"I don't know."

"Don't you?" Meat locked his legs around her body and rolled her over, trapping her underneath him, his cuffed hands above her head.

She didn't struggle, which surprised Meat a little. She just eyed him angrily. "You're nothing but trouble for me."

"Nah. I don't think you mean that, Camille. I think you're just pissed as hell. I think you've been pissed as hell for a long time now, with no way to show it without getting yourself in trouble."

"What is that supposed to mean?" she ground out between her

teeth. "I knew what I was getting into when I sat for the academy entrance exam. I can take it."

"Sure, you can take it. But why bother?"

She stared at him in confusion and anger, almost as if this was the first time it had occurred to her that she really had a choice in the matter. "Excuse me?"

Meat shrugged. "You heard me."

"I *like* my job," she said, sounding like she was trying to convince herself as much as him.

"If Danny is a prime example of who you spend your time with on the job, I'm surprised you manage to use as much restraint as you do. As you said, you let him get to you every single time."

Her eyes narrowed, and she twisted her legs, trying to drag her body out from under him. "I like to think holding back is a positive. It's as difficult a skill to master as kicking ass. That's something Danny's never figured out."

"Then why does he always win?"

Camille stopped moving for a moment as she stared at him in shock, then just as abruptly pushed at his chest with fisted hands. "He doesn't. Get the hell off me."

Meat let more of his body weight press down against her. "If I get the hell off you, what are you going to do with all these 'feelings'?"

"You don't know anything about feelings, mine or yours. That's obvious."

Not nearly as obvious as the pounding of her heart against his body. "Mmm. I know a little, at least. I know you don't really want me to get the hell off you." He leaned down and licked her hard nipple through the fabric of her shirt. She arched underneath him in surprise and he immediately pulled his mouth away. "If you don't want to punch me in the face, I can think of other ways to ease your frustration . . . let me help you."

"Let you *help* me? Are you kidding? You just want me to set you free."

Meat winced internally at the well-aimed retort. "Obviously, in the big picture. I don't pretend otherwise. Right now I just want you to give me back my hands so I can fuck you properly like I know you want me to."

"You can fuck me from here to next Tuesday but it won't affect my decision about whether you live or die."

We'll see about that. He moved his hands from over her head down to her breasts, and massaged her nipple with the pulsing heat of his bare thumb.

Camille was panting now. "Who says you need your hands back?"

"Ripping our clothes off with my teeth will take too long."

"Figure something out. You're trained to solve tough problems under difficult conditions." She grabbed at his waistband, yanking the two sides of his fly apart. The zipper whizzed down, her mouth already pressed hot and wet to his chest, her hand moving inside to his balls.

His body instinctively jumped, giving Camille an in. She scrambled out from under him and flipped their positions, grabbing his bound hands and thrusting them above his head. She straddled him again, grinding his pulsing cock against the center of her thighs.

Meat thrashed his head to the side, and growled, "Give me my hands, or I swear to God . . ."

"What would you do? Huh? What?" Camille stripped off her shirt and bra and tossed them away. She bent down over his body, her breasts shifting down in front of his face and undid her fatigues. "What are you going to do? Huh, Meat? What are you going to do *now*?"

He took her breast in his mouth, sucking and pulling first at one nipple, then the other as she pressed his cock up to her clit and squirmed, building a frenzy inside him that made him crave even more.

She let go of him suddenly, and leaped up, thrusting one boot square on his chest while she pulled off the rest of her clothes and tossed them inside out across the room. When she was through, she took her foot off his chest, knocked the unlaced boot away and lowered herself back down, cunt to cock. "It's a real bitch not to be in control, I completely—"

He sat up, swinging the arc of his arms up and over her head, his bare hot cock brushing heavily against the moist center of her thighs.

"Oh, *god.*" She arched her back, running her palms over his back.

"What would you do if you were me? You let my arms go for this, and I swear you will not be sorry."

"I'm already not sorry," she gasped, biting her lips as she thrust back and forth, sliding the wet lips of her cunt along the surface of his cock.

Meat couldn't take it anymore. He was nearly out of his mind with the need to bury himself in her. He took the advantage as soon as he could get it, rolling them over, tackling her to the ground, pressing her naked body down into the carpet with his own. Desperate with lust, he plunged deep inside.

Tossing her head from side to side, Camille wrapped her arms tightly around his body, arching her body up to meet him and forcing him into her deeper and deeper until she screamed in climax.

"Go ahead and fuck me hard," she murmured into his ear, giving him free rein to let himself go.

And he did let himself go, slamming his bound fists into the floor above her head each time he rammed his cock deep inside her tight, slick passage, his frustration at not being free and his lust for her taking him to the boiling point.

She kissed him deeply as he came, swallowing his groan as his hot seed shot deep inside her body.

And then silence. Nothing but the faint smell of burning fiber from the singed carpet above her head where he'd grabbed fistfuls of the pile.

He rolled off her and they lay side-by-side on the carpet, staring up at the ceiling, Meat unwilling to break the spell.

Camille had no such reservations. "Do all robos have these hands?"

"What? Are you kidding me?"

"I need to ask you some more questions."

"Don't you ever give it a rest?"

"Why should I?" she asked curtly. "This is my assignment. If you're just fucking me so that I'll stop doing my job, you'd better think of a better strategy."

He gazed at her for a moment in silence, then answered in monotone. "Only a few of us have these hands. The DOD develops robos in small batches, to experiment for desirable combinations."

"What else is robotic in you?"

"Nothing. Other than my hands, I'm clean."

"What do your hands do?"

"If you're ready for another round, I'm happy to show you," he murmured suggestively.

"I'm waiting for a real answer."

He paused. "Not a whole lot anymore."

"Not a whole lot."

"They were created for special weaponry, and I don't have access to that equipment anymore."

"What do they do with weaponry?"

"They can act as a wireless device, transmitting third-party information to the weapon during the heat of battle. One man, one weapon, multiple forms of destruction on call."

"Very impressive."

"But as I said, I don't have access to that arsenal anymore, so my robotic abilities are irrelevant."

"They used you like a thinking remote control." She studied him. "And nothing's wrong inside you?"

"Nothing's wrong inside me," he said, somewhat testily. "I'm not saying all robos are this low-grade. But many are. I am."

She cocked her head and gazed at him, and Meat could almost see her wondering if this entire dialogue was part of some pre-written script. "Does it hurt?" she asked.

He shrugged. "They're mostly just ultra-sensitive."

"When did they do this to you?"

"After puberty."

"Do you have any family?"

"I was born in a government facility, educated, and trained there, then sent out to the field. There's no other family."

Camille stared at him. "Doesn't that bother you?"

"Not particularly."

She seemed concerned by that answer. Maybe he ought to have manufactured a past and a family to make his plight more sympathetic. It never occurred to him to bother. "Do you have a family?"

"They're dead now. Both were in government jobs." She smiled wistfully. "My mother wanted to be miltel, but they wouldn't let her in. Everything has to be so hard." She didn't speak for a long while, then yawned and said, "God, sometimes I feel like no matter how long I sleep, I'll always be tired."

"Camille."

She turned her head and looked at him.

"Whatever it is that . . ." He reached out his arms, hesitating for a moment, but she nodded just slightly and he pulled her on to his lap and put his arms around her, rocking her. "It's all going to be fine."

"Of course," she murmured, and leaned back, resting her full body weight against him. In another moment she was asleep.

She was naked, three feet from her nearest weapon, and now dozing off guard in the circle of his bound arms. And what bothered Meat most was that *he* felt vulnerable. His motives were confused, his mission clouded. It was hard to separate what he wanted to do from what he thought he was supposed to do.

Camille whimpered, and Meat held her closer. "Shh, kitten . . ."

She snuggled into his arms and smiled.

An hour later she sat up with a start and looked wildly around her. Meat watched her warily as she absorbed the fact that she'd left herself unguarded.

She shook her head in disbelief and reached out and slowly dragged her weapon toward her. She held it loosely in her hands and looked at Meat, deep in thought. Finally, she said a little too brightly as she stood up, "My back is killing me. Why don't we ever do this sort of thing in my bed?"

"You haven't invited me into your bed," he said simply.

She took him by the hand, running her fingers lightly over the metal pads. Then she slid her hand up to his wrist and pulled him up from the floor. "I'm inviting you now." She stood up and left the room, returning a moment later with the restraint punch. "Come on."

A funny look came over his face. "No," he said and stood stubbornly in place.

"No?"

"Sleeping with my arms chained to the bed would be more uncomfortable than the setup I've already got." He frowned. "Or did you just mean for one go-round?"

Camille looked ashamed. She held out her hand again.

Meat stepped backwards. "If it means you're going to start back at square one in terms of trusting me not to hurt you, I'd rather keep them on."

"I trust you," she blurted out.

He slowly held his hands out to her, half expecting her to laugh in his face at the last minute.

She punched the lock and the restraints fell open with a whizzing sound. Meat moved his hands apart. He took a deep breath, flexing his arms, and swinging them apart. "I feel like a new man."

She didn't answer. Just smiled and would have turned away, but he took her face in his hands and kissed her, the swirl of his tongue against hers making him want to start all over again. "Thank you. You have no idea how good this feels. I swear, I'm not going to give you trouble."

Chapter Five

For the next two weeks, trouble lurked in the back of Camille's mind.

Turned out Meat had a thing for the game of chess, and so Camille set up a board on a side table between the two recliners. Each night they played the game in front of the fire while it rained sheets of ice outside, and he waited for her to file the report that determined whether he would live or die.

Every time they sat down to play, the entire scenario struck Camille as perverse. She'd come to accept the fact that she cared about him a great deal. The reward of that unguarded smile that appeared whenever she did something nice for him that she didn't have to do, made her feel good.

Not that she'd said anything to him about her feelings.

The problem was that as she came closer to the filing deadline for his report, there was still a nagging detail, an unease that never went away, no matter how many times they made love.

"It's your move," Meat finally said in a grumpy tone.

Camille looked down at the board and grinned. "Checkmate! And it's about time." She looked up at him quickly. "You didn't just let me win, did you?"

Meat leaned back in his chair. "I don't 'just let people win.'"

The sharp tone caught her by surprise, and she looked up, but couldn't detect anything unusual about his expression.

But there it was. A comment, a tone, an expression, an odd movement. It was the possibility that everything he did and everything he said was carefully calculated to lead her to filing a reclassification report.

To think that after all this time, after everything she'd come to feel for him, that it could all be a lie was a concept that made her nearly sick to her stomach.

"I'd say best of three but I don't want to be here all night." He reached over and smoothed a hand along her thigh. "One more?"

"Sure."

Truth was, she'd taken this damn long making the decision because she'd never been happier. Odd in a way, because she'd always imagined graduation day would be the happiest time in her life. Or maybe that was just what she'd convinced herself to believe.

Camille put the last few chess pieces back in place and stared down at the board. No, she didn't want things to change, but there was some relief as the report-filing deadline loomed at the end of the week.

She knew she could only rest easy about how he honestly felt about her if his life wasn't at stake. When she did reclassify him as she planned, he wouldn't need her anymore. And she'd finally know the truth. Would he still want to be with her?

What they shared had to be real. It had to be. No man had ever held her in his arms and whispered in her ear that everything would be okay. No man could be programmed to know what the perfect thing to say would be, to know how each individual woman wanted to be touched. The way she felt had to be real. Didn't it?

Meat claimed the only thing he had were special implants in his hands. But he'd also admitted that most robos weren't as low-grade as that. Most had more robotics and some of them had internal components. And that was her dilemma. He could be lying about how human he really was, but if he was as human as he seemed, terminating him would be nothing less than murder.

"What did he do to you?"

"What?" Camille asked, startled.

"What did Danny do to you that put the wedge between you?"

The last person she wanted to talk about was Danny. "Danny's not unique. None of the guys are too friendly with me. Some are worse than others and because Danny's my partner, things with us are that much more complicated."

"What about the girls?"

"There aren't any girls in the unit anymore."

"They died?"

Camille choked in surprise. "No. They just didn't make it through training." She paused, unsure of how much to say. "I haven't seen any of them in months. I'm not supposed to be around those girls anymore. They say it reflects on me."

"What does?"

"Their weakness. The term used at the academy is 'soft.' We're not supposed to be soft."

"And that's why they failed out of the academy? Because they were soft?"

"That's right. Well, that's what they say. But it was pretty much fixed anyway."

Meat studied her face. "If you're the only woman in the unit who's made it this far, the other men should have a great deal of respect for your abilities."

"You'd think."

"With robos, no one cares if you're male or female. It's all about abilities and implants. But then again, our training might be a little different since we're assumed to have no emotions and you're assumed to have too many. If you're the only one left, you must be very good at what you do."

Camille shrugged. "I've worked really hard. This is what I've spent my whole life working toward. My mother wanted to be in miltel. They still weren't letting any women into the unit at that time, so it's a point of pride on her behalf as well as mine." She paused to make her next move, and then looked up at him. "By graduating I'll fulfill her dream."

"*Her* dream?"

"And mine. I meant mine, too. After all, I'm the only female left in my class, so I must want it pretty badly." Camille felt her face flush over the hesitation in her words. Obviously, she wanted it badly, or she wouldn't be doing this.

Quickly she added, "Maybe I just want to succeed more than some of the others that didn't make it through. But as you know, it ain't over 'til it's over, and they don't want me to graduate. Which is why this probation is particularly bad timing. There's just one more module in the training, and if I don't make it through that, it's over for me. So what's your story?"

"My story? There's not much to tell and you already know what that is."

"Well, you told me you've pretty much grown up in a military training environment. I can imagine what that's all about. But what about after?"

"That depends on you, doesn't it?"

Her heart pounded in her chest. "Let's forget that for a moment," she said quickly.

"I want what everybody wants. The ability to live my own life on my own terms. I want freedom."

"What would you do with freedom?"

"Play chess and fuck."

Camille burst out laughing. "The last couple of weeks must have been like heaven."

He stared at her, then looked down at the board.

Camille cleared her throat. "How would you make money?"

"I'd go freelance mercenary. I have some connections to help set me up."

"Reclassified robos, I'm guessing."

He nodded without looking up from the board.

"Freelance mercenary. Fair enough. A nice way to get people to leave you alone." She laughed and added, "Not to mention, no one tells you what to do . . . you have to be good to get enough contracts, though. And develop enough of a name to get passes into all the different territories." She watched him consider his next move. "I think you'd do very well going solo."

Meat moved his knight then looked up and said, "I can already tell that *you* are going to *lose*."

Camille gaped down at the board. "You take all the fun out of the game if you think that far ahead. This isn't the World Chess championship."

"But that's why I love playing. To be successful, I need to think long-term. Every move is deliberate, every move is planned. Keeps me sharp for the real world."

"Who'd've thought? Robos playing the cerebral game of chess between battles."

"All the time. Bullets versus rocks." He picked up his black knight and studied the piece, slowly turning it between his fingers. "The more plays you can anticipate, the more plays you can imagine in your head, the more successful your end result. A small move now may seem to be irrelevant or have no consequence, and only in the end can you see that the entire strategy depended on it."

Camille's smile faded.

"So . . . checkmate, it is," he said, as he knocked her white queen over with his knight. "Sorry about that."

He chucked her gently under the chin, and Camille grinned, her doubts fading away. "You're not sorry one bit."

"Uh-uh. Nevertheless, I still get the prize."

"Come and get it."

"You know I will." He stood up and scooped her out of her chair, carrying her into the bedroom.

I'm going to reclassify you, tomorrow, Meat, she said silently as he hovered over her and stripped off her clothing. And when I do that I'm going to have my proof. Because you won't need me any more after that, and I'll know the truth.

He laid her gently on the bed and slowly unbuttoned her shirt, leaving a trail of fire along her skin as he worked.

"You won the game, so why are you doing all the work?"

"This isn't work."

Camille smiled and stretched her legs out fully on the bed. Meat stripped everything else off her body except her panties, this time pink and lacy. He slipped his hand under the lace and Camille arched her back in pleasure as the warm metal and bare skin slid through the slickness.

"God, you're wet," he said, on a labored breath.

His words made her more so. She watched his face, his lips parting as he followed the movement of his hand underneath the pink fabric. He reflexively pressed his hips forward against the side of the bed as he made love to her swollen clit with his fingers, groaning at the contact.

When he took his hand away, Camille almost cried out in disappointment until she saw him remove his clothes. He lay down next to her, the muscles in his arms leaping as he moved over her in a push-up stance and then lowered his body over hers.

His erection grazed the sensitive skin between her thighs, and Camille arched up again to press up around him but he was too fast. He pushed himself back up, wearing an arrogant grin that didn't hide his obvious desire.

Once more he lowered his body down to hers, this time slipping the head of his cock just inside her. Camille writhed against him. "More. Give me more of you."

He leaned forward and swirled his tongue around her hard nipple, gently taking the tip between his teeth, until she shuddered.

"I want you *now*." Camille slipped her hands between them to push at his chest. Meat kissed her breast and moved back, once more finding her opening with his warm fingers, and running the faint current in his fingertips over her sensitive bud until she moaned for more. At last he pressed his thick shaft into her tight cunt, inch by slick inch until her moan became a scream of pure pleasure.

He looked into her eyes and there was no way Camille could believe this wasn't for real, his lips hovering a whisper away from her own as he slowly pumped his engorged cock between her thighs. He moved deliberately, pausing after pulling back to drive her desire as high as he could, forcing an anticipation that made them both crazy with want, and then sliding back inside and gently pressing on her clit with one hand.

He pulled back once more, and she reached down and took his balls in her hand, massaging them even as the tension built up inside her. He went a little wild, pumping into her faster, until the rhythm was in her blood, and the hot metal of his hands streaking over her body pushed her over the edge.

She came, a lightning bolt of pleasure rushing through her. Arching her back to milk the sensation for as long as she could, both hands at the base of his cock, holding his balls, and Meat bucking like a stallion as he worked to hold out for her.

"Camille!" He buried himself into her one last time and roughly pulled her body to his.

Camille could smell her jasmine scent all over his shuddering body, and she felt a sense of possession. "I'm falling in love with you," she whispered.

Meat stiffened, and she glided her hand down his back, slick with sweat, to smooth out the muscles that were already tensing up again.

She probably *was* in love with him, already, but that big question mark still stood between them. Well, she'd have her answer soon enough. And he'd have his. Smiling into his shoulder, she said, "It's okay if you don't understand yet. You will."

❈❈❈

Camille rose from bed, then slipped on her robe and padded out to the living room. In the quiet of the morning, she turned on her computer and called up her project file. Her heart raced as she entered the disk and pressed the button to file the report.

With trembling fingers she selected 'Reclassification,' and pressed her index finger into the touchscreen. With a shiver of excitement, she keyed in the security code upon request and waited for confirmation.

It took her five minutes to comprehend the significance of the return message flashing on the screen:

Request for Reclassification On Hold. Please Report to Headquarters Immediately.

On hold? Camille stared at the screen, then finally collected herself long enough to redo all the steps. Same result.

Either something was wrong with her system or the government wanted Meat to die.

She threw her robe to the floor and dashed into the equipment closet, pulling on a clean training uniform and fastening her body armor with sweating hands.

❦

Camille stood stiffly at attention in the center of the commander's office, amazed at how easily it all came back to her after so much time away. And at how the dread that lived with her here at the academy had disappeared over the past month.

"At ease, Kazinsky. We've been following your progress for some time now. You operate at an above-average level in many areas, but there is concern that you don't fit the profile of the elite unit we strive to develop."

The commander folded his hands on the desktop and smiled warmly at Camille. "Fit is extremely important. I think you know that."

"Sir, if this is your way of—"

"—I'm not finished."

"Yes, sir."

"We'd love to be proven wrong. You tried to file a reclassification report this morning, correct?"

"Yes, sir. It was rejected."

The commander pursed his lips. "The robo is to be terminated."

Camille swallowed hard, refusing to allow the panic in her heart to show. "Excuse me, sir. Robo evaluation involves an independent decision by the assigned evaluator. After deep consideration, I chose to reclassify the robo."

"Let's just say that you made the wrong choice."

Camille stared.

His tone hardened. "Terminate the robo, Kazinsky. Otherwise we'll have the answer we've been expecting. Are you soft or not?"

Camille looked down at the open file on the commander's desk; her file. "This was a setup."

The commander shrugged. "A test."

"You never meant for . . . the robo . . ." she tripped over her tongue on the term. "You never meant for the robo to be reclassified."

"It was never a relevant question. It was deactivated for the purpose of your assignment."

"You have no idea whether he really deserves to be terminated or not, do you?"

The commander's eyes narrowed. " 'He,' Kazinsky? Don't talk yourself into a corner."

Camille struggled with her temper. "This robo does not deserve to be terminated. This robo does not deserve to die simply to prove a point about me."

"That's its mission," the commander said simply. "And now its mission is over." He checked his watch and dug into his molars with his pinkie finger. "We've taken the hold off your report. You can go ahead and file. Kill it, or you don't graduate. You're dismissed."

The walls seemed to close in on her as she came to attention, saluted the commander and practically stumbled from the room in a daze.

Well done, Camille. You've finally found the physical and emotional connection you always craved in the man you must kill.

Chapter Six

Meat frowned as Danny opened the door to leave just as Camille came up the walkway. Nice timing.

Danny looked back over his shoulder at him and said, "Think about what I said. You know how to contact me." He turned back and saluted Camille cheerfully on the way out. "Been waiting awhile, Cami. Now I gotta run."

Camille watched Danny pass her on the walkway then turned to stare at Meat. She looked grim, with dark smudges under her eyes and a muscle straining at her jawline. "Why was he here?"

Meat shrugged. "He came to see you and had to settle for me."

She looked at him strangely. "I would have expected you two to try and kick the shit out of each other. I guess you made nice." She looked down at his hands. "And apparently the fact that you're not wearing restraints didn't bother him." She shot him a pointed look and stepped past him into the house, looking around curiously as if she expected evidence of a brawl. "So, what did you two talk about?"

Meat studied Camille's face. It looked like she was going to play innocent after all. "Where did you go this morning?" he asked.

"What?"

"I asked you where you went this morning."

"I asked you what you and Danny talked about." When Meat didn't answer, she crossed her arms over her chest. "You want to tell me what's going on here? I'm really not comfortable coming home to find Danny just leaving and you acting like *I'm* up to something."

He stared at the floor, his jaw clenched. "I kind of thought we were beyond the bullshit stage."

"That's what I thought, too." She wound a lock of hair around her finger then let it go, sighing. "Look, I've got a lot on my mind, and I . . . I'm going to lie down. I just need to lie down and think."

Meat's heart dropped. Danny said she'd walk in that door with intent to terminate. He said she'd gone to HQ and when she returned, she'd begin to emotionally disconnect herself from him. Danny had said a lot of things that made him wonder if he'd been a fool to ever hope that Camille would give him his freedom. "What is there to think about, Camille? Are you having trouble making up your mind about something?"

She turned slowly and cocked her head, studying his face. "Meat, Danny had no reason to come over and see me today. If you tell me what he told you, we can clear up any misunderstanding."

"Amongst other things, he mentioned that you have no choice but to kill me to stay at the academy. He said reclassification was not an option." The metal in his fingertips burned, and he had to struggle to hide his growing desperation. "Do you deny it?"

"He knew?" she blurted out.

Meat made a choking sound. "*You* knew, obviously."

"I just found out this morning."

"You expect me to believe that?"

"Yeah, I do. Danny would sell out his own mother if he could make it look good. He obviously told you a bunch of crap and now you need to figure out who to believe. I'm not lying to you, Meat. This assignment was a setup."

"Let's say I believe you. So you learn there's an ultimatum that means I die in less than forty-eight hours. And you come home and decide to go lie down and take a fucking nap so you can think about what to do?"

Her face paled.

"You hadn't decided, had you?" His hands fisted at his sides. "*Had* you?"

Camille swallowed. "Give me a break, you son of a bitch. I tried to reclassify you this morning, even knowing that once I did, you'd have what you wanted and you could stop acting like you cared about me, if that's what all this was. An act. But it was a chance I had to take because I cared about *you*. And now I'm starting to believe that I was right to walk in this door, hesitating to sacrifice my future for yours."

She tried to walk past him into the bedroom, but Meat grabbed her by the arm and swung her around. "Listen to what you're saying. You're hesitating to sacrifice a job I don't think you even like for my *life*." Meat nodded slowly. "I see how it is. This must have been a fun fantasy vacation for you, Camille."

Her voice trembling, she said, "I suggest you get your *head* out of your ass, because we have a serious problem."

"I'll say. One of us dies today."

She flung his hand away from her arm. "I tried to reclassify you."

"You get bonus points for that, all right? But it turns out what you did this morning when you claim the stakes weren't this high is irrelevant. All that matters is what you plan to do now."

"You don't care about me at all, do you? I was right to hesitate . . . You and Danny . . . oh, God. Let me guess, he promised you reclassification, didn't he?"

She must have seen the answer in his eyes, because she gasped and added, "I'm right! What the hell do you have that he wants? Don't tell me he offered to trade your freedom for my life . . . He has to know I'll keep my mouth shut. I can't believe . . ."

Meat wiped the sweat off his forehead with his sleeve. It wasn't her life Danny wanted, it was the videodisk showing Danny's part in the training accident. The only proof of his mistake. "Let me put it this way. Danny wants a sure thing. And he knows he can't control you absolutely."

The robos used in live-fire exercises were video-equipped. Danny realized that he couldn't go into a classified robo facility without raising suspicion. But another robo could, so he came to Meat to cut a deal. A deal Meat was willing to completely ignore if Camille hadn't still had doubts about reclassifying him when she'd walked through that door.

It was just as well she'd made it unnecessary for him to feel bad about choosing himself over her. All Meat wanted was reclassification. It really didn't matter how he got it. And he wasn't interested in wasting any more time.

He pulled Danny's pistol out from his back waistband and held it out in front of him at the ready.

Camille looked stunned. She gasped, her eyes tearing up. "Damn," she muttered. "And to think I almost missed the pleasure of seeing your true colors come out."

Meat heard the hint of panic in her voice. He could sympathize. He'd felt the same way when he realized she'd decided to terminate him. He didn't blame her. He'd do the same if the places were reversed.

He backed her up against the wall, and she put her hand up lightly against his chest. "You don't understand," she said softly.

"Yes, I do. You're going to have to terminate me to get what you want, and I'm not going to let that happen. Where's the report disk?"

Her expression hardened and her gaze moved to the knife on her bootclip. His pistol was up to her temple in an instant. "Don't even think about it."

He held the gun on her and carefully bent down and snapped off the knife.

Camille's eyes narrowed. "I thought you were something special."

"Now, there's a line. The report disk. Where is it?"

"You'd cut off my finger to file that report, wouldn't you?"

"Yeah, I would." He switched weapons and stuck the pistol back in his waistband, then grabbed her arm and bent it behind her back. He winced at her yelp of pain, pushing the thought to the back of his mind that he actually did have a problem with the idea of cutting off her finger. "I'm going to ask you for the last time. Where's the disk?" He applied more pressure to her arm, then eased up just as suddenly when he remembered that she was as much of a soldier as he was, and she'd never give him what he wanted for the cheap price of a broken arm.

He held her up against the wall, silently cursing that it had all come to this.

"You have no qualms betraying me to get what you want," she said, eyeing the knife nervously. "I'm just glad I didn't betray myself to give it to you. You're not worth it. You're just a fake, after all. Nothing about you is real or even remotely human."

"I *am* human," he ground out. He slammed her back against the wall and kissed her roughly, taking her mouth like a possession. She let him, her body unable to resist reacting to his. He pulled away, and wiped his mouth with the back of his hand. "Not that it matters anymore, but don't tell me that it isn't real on my side. You're the one who let me whore for you with your true intentions written out from the very beginning."

"You must be kidding me. Making an alliance with Danny makes you a fool *and* an asshole. You should have tried to work something out with me."

"There's nothing to work out. It's simple. Only one of us gets the prize we want."

"And you never let anyone win."

He held the knife between his teeth as he roughly patted her down, running his hands over the curves of her body and lingering more than necessary. Finally, he felt the disk and grabbed it from one of her inside pockets.

"So easy." Meat plugged the disk into the computer, called up Camille's file, then took a calming breath and turned back to her. "It's your turn." He grabbed her hand by the wrist and moved it to the touchscreen. "Do it."

"No." She was shaking, now.

"Do it, Camille."

She didn't answer, and he grabbed her hand and shoved it against the touchscreen. Her fingerprint triggered, and the computer requested the security code.

He held on to her with one hand and pressed his palm flat against the wall with the other, reveling in the pain of his implants, staring at the screen.

"This requires more than a fingerprint to file. You have to give me a code." He laughed in disbelief.

Camille didn't say a word.

"Fuck! Fuck, Camille!" The desperation he heard in his own voice shamed him. "What do you want from me? I don't want to die, can't you understand that?"

Tears slipped down her face, but she didn't make a sound.

He struggled to regain his self-control. "Can't you understand?"

"I understand everything," she said, her mouth a grim slash. "You screw me blind, and I'm supposed to do whatever the hell you want."

"Are you trying to turn me on?" he said sarcastically.

"Are you turned on? Does the idea of hurting me turn you on?"

"No, it doesn't," he said, his voice like ice. "But some other things do." He whipped her around and shoved her face first against the wall, forcing her hands up against the wall in an imitation of a de-arming procedure.

He could hear her breathing start to come in pants. "Are you excited or scared?"

At first she didn't answer, but then she looked over her shoulder. "I can't believe you could fake it that well. Last night was . . . last night I saw the look in your eyes. There's no way you don't care about me."

"You make the mistake of equating sex with caring. I don't think it makes a difference. You're excited, and so am I. You're excited," Meat repeated, wanting her to admit it.

"So. What," she spat out. "Apparently, it doesn't mean anything."

He placed the palm of his hand over the tops of hers against the wall and ran his other hand down her arm. He moved his hands down in front and placed them over her breasts, squeezing them and running his hands over her nipples until there was no question of her arousal.

"Do you want me to stop?" he asked.

"I want you to . . . I want it like it was."

He just grabbed the two sides of her shirt and ripped it off her body. She was panting now, and he moved to her waistband, running the edge of the knife down the seams and cutting the fabric away from her body.

She pulled her hands off the wall and tried to turn around, but he caught her hands. She struggled like a wildcat, her eyes revealing all the same confusion and anger he felt in the second before he turned her back around and pressed her against the wall with his body.

He moved her arms back up above her head, then took his knife and snapped the strings of her bra and panties until she was naked in front of him, save for her boots. So beautiful. So, so beautiful. Why did it have to end like this? Why did it have to end at all?

He ran his thumb down that well, running it down over the tight pink opening of her beautiful ass, underneath, where it skidded across the creamy wet truth of how badly she wanted him. Camille made a sound, obviously angry that her desire should be obvious to him at a time like this.

"You still want me," he whispered into her ear, as he unzipped his pants and let his rigid cock rest against the pale skin of her ass.

She slammed her forehead against the wall. "Damn you."

"Tell me you still want me." He had no idea why he would beg her to say this, he just knew he wanted to hear the words.

Her voice thick with tears, she said, "*I'm* no liar. I still want you."

He lifted her right leg up under the knee, folding it against the wall, opening her to him. He knelt down and flicked his tongue over her sweet little asshole and then swept it to her wet cunt.

"Oh, God," she moaned. "This is how we started, and I guess it's how we'll end."

He didn't like thinking about the end. He stood up and thrust his cock deep inside her.

She gasped, pressing back against his groin, and he fucked her hard and fast, almost daring her not to come.

When she cried out, he himself released. He let go of her, his heart pounding against her back, unsure of what he wanted to do.

She stayed up against the wall while he zipped up and sat down in the chair to watch her put her ripped shirt back on.

Meat put his head in his hands. "I'm supposed to hurt you now, do you get that? That's what makes sense here. That's what a smart soldier would do to get the code. I know what all the training guides say *you're* supposed to do in this situation, so I know how to trick you. I know all the psychology. Do you get what's supposed to happen here, now?"

He was definitely losing it. He could barely speak above a hoarse whisper. He didn't even want to look at her.

"Supposed to?" she asked, her voice choked with tears.

"That's what a smart soldier with a good sense of strategy would do," he said woodenly. "A soldier who hadn't lost objectivity."

He sat there, harsh breathing the only sound in the room. Suddenly, he stood up and took her hand, dragging her to the pallet he'd slept on in those first few nights. He took the restraints and bound her hands together, then chained her to the same metal bar. "Goodbye, kitten."

She stared at him, her eyes huge in her pale face.

He tossed the restraint punch across the room and walked out.

Moving quickly to her equipment room, he stuffed a handful of dry rations, a blanket, the knife, and Danny's pistol into his duffel bag before heading for the door.

He hit the door release, and a pain deep inside took root as he paused on the threshold of Camille's apartment without really knowing why.

She didn't call out to him, and he stepped out into the cold.

Tears streamed down Camille's face as she reviewed her options. The son of a bitch. "You're bigger than me and stronger than me and you've clearly got more field experience than me, but I'm not going down without a fight."

Chapter Seven

Meat couldn't have hurt Camille any more than he had. What he'd done made him feel sick enough. He cared too much to do what he should have done, and the only option left was to run as fast and as far as he could before someone let her loose and she sent the marshals after him.

The rain hit the streets in slushy waves. Meat looked around him, the acrid odor of the wet cement almost comforting, the urban battlefield solid and familiar under his feet.

He only had Danny's pistol and the knife, and he felt strangely unarmed in this familiar setting without the normal accoutrements of battle. He looked down at the metal in his hands; useless, without the right equipment.

He felt unprepared, unsure for the first time since he'd dreamed about freedom, what it might mean for a renegade robo flagged in all the systems as an escapee marked for termination.

Meat's eyes had grown accustomed to the dark now. He stepped out from the overhang into the mist of his breath and took up at a jog toward the city gates.

The way the cold seeped into his skin disoriented him. He'd been in worse conditions during weeks of fighting for oil rights in the Siberian Territory, but he couldn't remember the cold ever cutting into him so mercilessly.

He was getting soft. Too much time around Camille had changed him. He could only hope the change would prove to be for the good, because right now this was pretty miserable, slogging through the deserted streets.

He needed to keep his mind off Camille, that was—

The image of Camille in his mind shattered as the broad side of a Class II smashed into his shoulder and arm. He lost his footing on the frozen street and went down, letting go of the duffel bag to concentrate on absorbing the fall by curling his body. He took it on a roll with his arms curled around his head as he hit the street corner, the concrete curb taking his breath away.

"Do you think I'm stupid?" Camille's voice hit him along with a wave of jasmine perfume.

"I realize I have shortcomings. I never said I was perfect. I'm too *nice* to be a good miltel soldier, for one thing. They've been trying to tell me that for months. Years, really. 'You're too likely to empathize with the enemy,' they said. Well that's all too true, isn't it? But one thing in my favor is that I'm not stupid."

Breathing better now, he tried to roll into a sitting position, but she slammed her boot on his chest. He groaned as the side of his head fell backwards into the cold water pooling at the side of the gutter, a cold stream seeping into his ear.

"I know how to track down one *super-size* guy running through the streets toward the border during *curfew*, wearing a *T-shirt* in freezing weather. It's really not that hard." She paused. "What's the matter, Meat, cat got your dick? You should be trying to seduce me about now to get out of this mess."

"Why delay the inevitable," he said grimly. "Are you going to do it yourself? Right here? Now?"

His betrayal sparked in her eyes as bright and clear as the raindrops on her lashes. "I can't believe you think I'd let you get away." Her mouth twisted. "Losing a robo in my custody would kill my career forever." She looked directly at him for just a moment, enveloping him in the ice-blue stare of her eyes, then shifted her gaze just slightly to the side as if she couldn't bear to look at him.

The frigid water slapped against his cheek as he lay on his side in the street with Camille standing over him, and he welcomed it; reminded him of how she'd made him feel, and he'd almost lost his freedom because of it.

He knew that time was running out. His mind switched back into battle mode with so little resistance it was almost frightening.

"Toss out the pistol," she said.

"What?"

"I know you have it." She crushed down on his bent knee with her boot. Meat grunted, quickly working through the pain and rolled off the pistol he was concealing underneath his body.

Camille moved off his knee and took the pistol, the look in her eyes one of resigned and unflinching duty.

And as she straightened up, their eyes met, hers revealing a searching look that asked him to prove her wrong, to prove he hadn't betrayed her, worked her over, played her for a fool.

He didn't beg; he just watched. She lifted the pistol and moved her finger to the trigger in what seemed like slow motion.

The curve of her delicate forefinger against the black metal. The last second of indecision where she seemed to change her mind, and he leapt toward her as the clip unloaded, her body jerking at the recoil. The tang of gunpowder in his nostrils and the terrible pain that spread like an ocean tide across his body. The sound of the gun clattering down on the pavement.

He pulled Camille down with him as he fell forward, both weapons falling to the pavement, her scream bouncing off the empty alleys in the silent streets.

She struggled to recover her weapons as he held her around the legs.

The killer instinct, they called it. Ah, Camille, your so-called friends are right. You really don't have it, do you? But I still do. In spades. I can almost taste the metal in my blood. And the gunpowder . . . these are my triggers.

She thrashed in his grip as he dragged himself up her body, blood running down his arm over his hand as he moved above her.

"The patrol will be by here any minute," she gasped out. "Let me go. You know I could have killed you." She struggled for another moment, then let her upper body rest back on the ground, leaving her white throat exposed as she looked left and right, scrabbling around helplessly in the dim light with her hands for one of the weapons. She looked terrified.

"You should have shot me through the head, but you couldn't do it. I made you care about me and you couldn't do it."

She just stopped moving entirely, the futility of her efforts seeming to crash down around her. She lay on the pavement, his weight binding her to the cold stone, her eyelashes fluttering as the rain picked up again.

She was waiting for him to kill her, gasping in tight intermittent breaths like a fish running out of oxygen.

Brave Camille. He knew she wouldn't beg for her life either.

"I can't believe I thought I could love you," she said suddenly, between gulps of air. And then she reared up, and backhanded him across the face.

Without a second thought, Meat knocked her back onto the pavement, watching her beautiful face as she lost consciousness.

He stared at her, half-wishing she'd wake up and fight back. He wiped a streak of grit from her cheek and held her face in his hands. She was so pale, her lips turning a faint blue around the edges from the cold, and even though he knew what he'd done couldn't possibly have killed her, his heart nearly jumped out of his throat.

He dragged himself off her and slid a hand behind her head to check for blood, nearly insane with relief to pull back his fingers wet only with rain.

As he kneeled down with his head bowed over her to protect her face from the hail that began to pelt from the sky, he cried for the first time.

He cried thinking that he could still save himself if he ran, but now realizing that he'd never leave her like this, hurt, alone and cold in the dirty streets.

She said he'd understand and he did. He loved her. More than the dream of freedom.

Sirens sounded in the distance, reminding Meat of reality. The metal in his hands was beginning to freeze, but he ignored the pain, awkwardly searching the duffel bag for a blanket.

He wrapped Camille in the blanket and looked around carefully as the sirens drew closer. Then, he picked her limp body up in his arms and turned for home.

Chapter Eight

In five hours he would be a dead man.

Meat had given Camille a mild sedative before leaving the house again. It hadn't taken him long to track down what Danny wanted, but he didn't like the idea of her waking up while he was gone and needing something for the concussion.

When he returned, he wrote a quick note and tucked it along with the small black videodisk containing Danny's training accident under the chunk of crystal on the bookcase, then nearly jumped out of his skin to find Camille standing in the door of the bathroom.

"Whatever you gave me, I feel like crap. We need to talk."

Meat frowned. "I want you back in bed." He turned her around, put his hand on her back and pushed her back into the bedroom.

"I've been out of bed since you've been gone." She rubbed the back of her head, frowning.

"Back in bed. Now."

"But—"

He shushed her with a finger to her lips. "There will be time later." He didn't like lying, but it was better than saying goodbye.

"I need to talk to you. It's about your status. Hey, don't you walk away from me!" From behind the bedroom door, Camille yelled, "Fine! I'll just go back to bed, then."

He smiled in spite of himself and checked the time as he went back into the bathroom to get cleaned up. He changed out of his wet uniform, lingering in the shower, ignoring the sting of the hot water in the bullet wound in his arm.

Once out, he pulled on fresh fatigue pants and boots, shaved, then gave himself the best buzz cut he could manage, lowering his razor just as Danny Dietrich's reflection appeared in the mirror.

"The door was open," Danny said.

Meat nodded, and carefully wound a fresh bandage around his upper arm.

"Did you get it?" Danny asked.

Meat could see the strain in his face. He reached around Danny to pull his clean shirt off the hook. He put the T-shirt on and turned back to the mirror, carefully smoothing the fabric over his chest. "Let's move into the living room. I don't want to bother Camille."

Danny nodded and disappeared.

Meat pulled Danny's pistol from under the bathmat piled up on the floor, and checked to make sure it still had clips. He pulled one of the black leather gloves from his pocket and slid his right hand into it, then wiped the gun all over with a towel and stuck it behind him in his waistband. He was as ready as he'd ever be.

He joined Danny in the living room.

Danny stood up immediately. "Did you get the videodisk?"

Meat folded his arms over his chest. "How's my reclassification coming along?"

Danny glanced nervously in the direction of Camille's bedroom. "Fine, fine. It's looking good."

"But it's not settled, is it?"

"It will be. Give me the videodisk, and I'll make it happen."

"If I believed that, I wouldn't have run. You're a liar, Danny," Meat said softly.

Danny rubbed his fingers together at his sides. He must be sweating.

"I'm the only chance you've got if Camille doesn't come through. And if she hasn't done it by now, buddy, it's not looking good, is it?"

"No, it's not looking good at all. For either of us." Meat pulled the pistol out of the back of his waistband and pointed it at Danny.

Danny swallowed but didn't lose his cool. "You're making a big mistake."

"I don't think so." He cut through the distance between them in an instant, grabbing Danny's throat with his bare hand. "It's only going to get worse; I get angrier than this."

Danny struggled, panicking in Meat's grip as the implants heated up. It wouldn't be too long before the metal could burn.

"Take the gun," Meat said.

"Wha?"

"Take the gun. It's yours."

Danny took the gun from Meat's gloved hand, and Meat released Danny's neck to avoid making burn marks, but he left his palm hovering close to his skin.

Danny looked down at the gun, wobbling in his hand. "I get it. You want my fingerprints on this thing."

"That's right. And now I want you to shoot me. Aim true on the first shot if you're feeling generous."

"Jesus! Are you crazy?"

"Shoot me, or I'll kill you."

"Fine," Danny said. A single bead of sweat trickled down his temple, and he wiped it away with his uniform sleeve. "With you this close I'll be able to claim self-defense."

"It will look curious given what's on the videodisk. Either way, you'll still have the scandal."

"You *do* have the video. Shit!" He looked helplessly around the room. "Where is it?"

Meat shrugged. "It's safe for now. Could we get on with this?"

"You *are* crazy. You're willing to die for Camille's career?"

Meat was quickly losing his patience. "Yes. Let's get this over with."

Danny just stared at him, so he pressed the hot metal in his hands against Danny's skin.

Danny swallowed and raised the gun; his hand was shaking so hard, Meat figured he'd better not count on a quick and painless death.

And then, just like that, a shot rang out. Easy. Too easy.

Meat waited for the pain to hit, but there wasn't any pain. Just Danny standing there staring off beyond Meat's shoulder with a glazed look on his face and a tiny trickle of blood running down the thumb of his empty hand.

Meat could hardly think over the pounding of his heart. He looked down at his body; couldn't see anything but the bandage wrapped around his arm and Danny's gun lying on the carpet.

"Camille," Danny said in a voice so tiny it was hardly there at all. Meat turned and looked behind his shoulder where Camille stood in the doorway, wiping her pistol off on her white silk robe.

Camille stopped cleaning the pistol and took a couple of slow, deep breaths to calm her rapid breathing. That had been uncomfortably close.

"Camille?"

She looked up, fixing Danny with blazing eyes. "Are *you* still here? Get the fuck out."

Danny picked up his gun and backed up, looking like he wanted to puke. His heel struck the door, and he stumbled, then turned and ran without another word.

She turned to Meat, undone by the sight of the bandage around his arm. Leaning her shaky weight on the doorjamb, she swallowed hard and stared at the carpet under her feet. "I really shot you. I can't believe it. I mean, I can believe I *shot* you, because I'm obviously capable . . . but I shot *you* . . . I . . ."

Meat walked up to Camille and took the gun out of her hands, his chest heaving from the adrenaline in his system. He tossed the gun on the nearest recliner, then grabbed her by the shoulders. "Are you crazy? Are you fucking insane? You could have had everything! What were you thinking?"

He was undone; his eyes burning into hers, fierce and wild. He couldn't get any more words out so he just shook her, his fingers digging into her shoulders.

Camille raised her chin, her trembling voice giving her false bravado away. "Now wait just one minute. I didn't think you even cared about me. Technically, you deserved to be shot, when it gets right down to it."

He let one of his hands drop, the fist clenching and unclenching as he worked to come down from the intensity of his emotions. "I'm not talking about then. I'm talking about now. I left the videodisk for you. You'd have him under your thumb, with no more problems at the academy. You'd have graduation and your career. You should have let Danny kill me."

Camille pushed angrily against his chest, gaining a little space as she caught him off balance and he stepped back. "You big idiot. I mean, I realize I shot you, but tell me you never really believed I could let you die." She shook her head in disbelief. "I reclassified you when you were out this morning. My career's over."

Meat's mouth opened in shock, but no sound came out. Finally, he managed one word: "Why?"

"Why do you think?" Camille asked, near tears, inexplicably angry. "I can't believe you. You almost went and got yourself ki—"

"—Camille?"

"Yeah?"

"Shut up." Meat placed his bare hand behind her neck and kissed her hard, pressing roughly into her mouth, his tongue sweeping against hers as if he'd been kissing her his whole life. He pulled her body up against him, as close to him as he could get her, his hands strong and possessive.

He kissed her as if he needed her heat, her touch to burn off the raw emotion that threatened to overwhelm him, and when he finally broke away, he rested his hot, wet mouth to her cheek and quietly exhaled. And just before he released her, Camille could feel his lips curve against her in a smile.

She swallowed, her heart racing. "I think I get what you're trying to say."

He held her out at arm's length and said, "I knew you were something special from the moment you stuck your knife into the side of my head. A real sense of style. That's my girl."

It was a relief to hear his cavalier tone once more. Camille stroked her fingers over his palm and said, "That job wasn't really my dream, you know. I don't need it anymore. I have you."

"Yeah, you do. So, quit thinking there's a problem somewhere." His hands slipped beneath the white silk, sliding it off her shoulders to pool at her arms.

"What are you doing?" Camille asked innocently.

Meat put his hand on her thigh, sliding his palm slowly up the curve of her body, leaving a trail of warmth in his wake. "First aid. I'm making sure that concussion didn't have any lasting effects. I'm sorry I hurt you." He stroked the side of her neck with his warm fingertips, his mouth pressed hot and greedy to her collarbone.

"You think you can accomplish anything with a little seduction, don't you?" she accused, not minding one bit.

He gave her an unintelligible response, then pressed a kiss between her breasts. Camille smiled as her knees went weak. She leaned back against the wall again, running her fingers through his newly-cropped hair. A girl could get used to this sort of treatment. "Meat?" she said softly. "I really am sorry about the bullet in your arm."

"A nice clean hole. Stop thinking about it. I already picked the bullet out and dumped some antiseptic in. I'm fine."

He swirled his tongue around the tight pink tip of one breast, then the next, gently biting her nipples until Camille shivered from the sensation. "In fact, I think I told you earlier everything was going to be fine."

"Yeah." She took his hand and threaded her fingers through his. "You were right."

He bent down and trailed his tongue down the middle of her body, the robe falling to the ground in a whisper as his tongue found the soft skin of her stomach.

"You're right about something else," she said. "I should really be in bed right now."

He smirked and scooped her up in his arms, carrying her into the bedroom. He laid her down on the bed and kneeled above her on his hands and knees, trying to pick up where he'd left off, but Camille wasn't having it.

She scooted down underneath him, between his legs until she could practically feel the heat at his groin on her face. She unfastened his fatigues. The muscles in Meat's abdomen contracted as she pulled his fatigues down his lean hips, teasing the hot shaft that jutted out to her with tiny licks of her tongue.

"Camille, you need to rest," he ground out. "Let me . . . oh, *man* . . . you don't have to do this. Don't want to get too rough."

"Oh, but I want to. And I like it rough. Don't you start thinking I'm too delicate."

She played with him, sucking the head of his cock, flicking over the moisture at the tip. Running her hand up the length of him, and then moving down to stroke his balls with her tongue, his unbridled reaction building up tension in her own body.

She took him deep in her throat and he growled, arching his back, his muscles jerking as she sucked on him harder.

"Stop!" He pulled away from her, panting and wide-eyed for a moment. "Come here," he said, his voice low and silky with want. Camille lowered herself down, his cock sliding thick and slow up between her drenched cleft. She rode him, the hot metal in his fingers caressing the insides of her thighs.

He swore under his breath, lifting his hips up from the bed to press himself even farther inside her. She tilted her head back, and he grasped a handful of her hair, wrapping it around his fingers, and pulling her head back gently as she moved faster and faster.

He moved his free hand to her clit, letting his fingers play against the wetness there. Looking into his eyes she gasped, and leaned forward with a wild toss of her head. Her hair whipped out of his grasp in a wave of gold as she came, calling out to him. Then she lifted up from his body and plunged back down on his cock, and he followed her over the edge, roaring out his climax.

Camille held him inside her for a while, with her head resting over his heart. Finally, she slid off him onto her side and ran her hand over his chest, tracing a long scar with her finger. "Why did you . . . I mean, when did you . . ."

Meat rolled over onto his side to face her, his head leaning on his hand. "When you love someone, you give up total self-preservation."

Camille chuckled. "Who'd have thought you'd turn out to be the romantic in this relationship."

※ℒℭ⅁ℰ✦

Meat watched Camille barrel through the tinted glass doors of the academy. She stood at the top of the long set of stone steps and looked down toward the transport where he waited.

She still wore her body armor, but the insignia was missing from the arms of her training suit and she wasn't carrying any weapons.

He stuck his head out of the window of the transport. "Hey, kitten, look sharp! The road awaits. I have this whole wide world to see."

She cocked her hip and looked up, holding her hand out for signs of rain.

Suddenly she let out a little shriek of joy and ran down the steps to the transport. She opened the driver's side door. "Move over," she said. "You don't have your license yet."

"Fine with me, the steering wheel bothers my hands. So, we're all done?"

Camille nodded. "I gave Danny his video—or a copy of it anyway—he finally sucked it up and called Daddy to make it so I wasn't going to be kicked out . . . and then I quit."

"You sure that's what you want?"

"Are you kidding? Let's go." She slid into the driver's seat, then turned once more to Meat with a grin. "One more thing. If I'm going to be your girl, maybe I should use your regular name instead of 'Meat'?"

Meat frowned. "I like it."

"Excuse me?"

"You gave it to me. It means I belong to you."

"That's absurd. It was an insult."

"Not anymore."

"Tell me your real name."

"Mattheson."

"What? That's your last name, right?"

"Yeah."

"What's your first name?"

He paused. "My first name?" He had to smile. "No one's ever asked me my first name before. It's Peter."

Camille started to laugh.

"What the hell is so funny about 'Peter'?"

"I don't know. It just doesn't suit you. Now that I've been calling you Meat since I've known you."

"My point exactly. Kitten, you can call me whatever you want."

She covered her lips with her fingertips, choking back giggles. He'd never seen her look so happy. He never thought he'd feel this way either.

"Do we have enough supplies?" she asked as she punched the ignition. "It might be a while before we get our first contract."

"Don't you trust me?" he asked. "Your clothes, my clothes, a small arsenal, and two months' worth of frozen meals. What more could a girl want?"

Camille gave him a seductive little grin as she eased the transport away from the curb and turned toward the Northern horizon. "I'll fill you in when we get to our first overnight."

About the Author:

Unfortunately, Liz Maverick is not one of those lucky authors who could spell five-syllable words as a young babe and write fully plotted stories before she could walk. However, what she lost in time, she made up in enthusiasm.

After exhausting her left-brain in pursuit of an MBA degree, this former dot-commer chucked it all and found her true calling (and luckily rediscovered all that dormant right-brain matter in the process) as a writer. Kiss or Kill *is her first published work. You can visit her at* **www.lizmaverick.com**.